John Murray

Report on the scientific results of the voyage of H.M.S. Challenger

During the years 1873-76

John Murray

Report on the scientific results of the voyage of H.M.S. Challenger
During the years 1873-76

ISBN/EAN: 9783742833808

Manufactured in Europe, USA, Canada, Australia, Japa

Cover: Foto ©Andreas Hilbeck / pixelio.de

Manufactured and distributed by brebook publishing software
(www.brebook.com)

John Murray

Report on the scientific results of the voyage of H.M.S. Challenger

THE

VOYAGE OF H.M.S. CHALLENGER.

ZOOLOGY—VOL. XXIII.

REPORT

ON THE

SCIENTIFIC RESULTS

OF THE

VOYAGE OF H.M.S. CHALLENGER

DURING THE YEARS 1873-76

UNDER THE COMMAND OF

Captain GEORGE S. NARES, R.N., F.R.S.

AND THE LATE

Captain FRANK TOURLE THOMSON, R.N.

PREPARED UNDER THE SUPERINTENDENCE OF

THE LATE

Sir C. WYVILLE THOMSON, Knt., F.R.S., &c.

REGIUS PROFESSOR OF NATURAL HISTORY IN THE UNIVERSITY OF EDINBURGH
DIRECTOR OF THE CIVILIAN SCIENTIFIC STAFF ON BOARD

AND NOW OF

JOHN MURRAY

ONE OF THE NATURALISTS OF THE EXPEDITION

ZOOLOGY—VOL. XXIII.

Published by Order of Her Majesty's Government

PRINTED FOR HER MAJESTY'S STATIONERY OFFICE

AND SOLD BY

LONDON:—EYRE & SPOTTISWOODE, EAST HARDING STREET, FETTER LANE
EDINBURGH:—ADAM & CHARLES BLACK
DUBLIN:—HODGES, FIGGIS, & CO.

1888

Price Forty Shillings

CONTENTS.

Page 107, line 9, for "*globulosa*" read "*gibbosa*."
Page 112, line 18, add "*Cuvierina columella*."

ERRATUM IN PART LXVI.

EDITORIAL NOTES.

This Volume contains Parts LXV., LXVI., LXX., LXXI., and LXXII. of the Zoological Series of Reports.

Part LXV.—The First Part of the Report on the PTEROPODA, by Dr. Paul Pelseneer, treating of the GYMNOSOMATA, was published in 1887 in Volume XIX., and forms Part LVIII. of the Zoological Series of Reports.

This Second Part of the Report, by the same author, deals with the THECOSOMATA, and contains 132 pages of letterpress and 2 plates, in addition to woodcuts.

Part LXVI.—In this Third and concluding Part of the Report on the PTEROPODA, Dr. Pelseneer treats of the Anatomy of the whole group and discusses the relations of the PTEROPODA to the other Mollusca. The Part consists of 97 pages of letterpress and 5 lithographic plates, in addition to other illustrations in the text.

Part LXX.—The First Part of the Report on the HYDROIDA collected during the Expedition, by Professor S. J. Allman, F.R.S., was published in 1883 in Volume VII., forming Part XX. of the Zoological Series of Reports; it treated of the PLUMULARIDÆ (Plumularinæ).

The present Memoir is the Second and concluding Part of Professor Allman's Report, and treats of the remaining families of the order.

In consequence of the extent and representative character of the collections Professor Allman has been able to give, in addition to the zoological descriptions, a very valuable and comprehensive sketch of the morphology and life-history of these animals. This Part consists of 160 pages of letterpress, 39 plates and a map.

Part LXXI.—Had any special attention been paid to collecting ENTOZOA during the Expedition, a much larger number of species would probably have been obtained than are described in this short but valuable Report by Dr. O. von Linstow of Göttingen, one of the first authorities on this group of animals. The Report consists of 18 pages of letterpress, 2 lithographic plates and a woodcut.

Part LXXII.—In this Report Mr. Edgar A. Smith has brought together systematic lists showing the present state of our knowledge of the HETERO-PODA, founded on the collections made during the Expedition. The Report, which consists of 56 pages and 5 woodcuts, will be most useful to future investigators.

JOHN MURRAY.

CHALLENGER OFFICE, 32 QUEEN STREET,

VOYAGE OF H.M.S. CHALLENGER.

ZOOLOGY.

REPORT on the PTEROPODA collected by H.M.S. Challenger during the Years 1873-76. By PAUL PELSENEER, D.Sc. (Brussels).

PART II.—The THECOSOMATA.

INTRODUCTION.

ABOUT the end of the year 1885 I was entrusted with the task of making a systematic and descriptive Report on the Gymnosomatous Pteropods and an anatomical one on the entire order, and in the beginning of the present year (1887) the entire Report on the Pteropods was entrusted to me for completion.

The Report is thus divided into three portions as follows :—

1. The systematic survey of the Gymnosomata, which has been already published.[1]

2. The present Report on the Thecosomata, which along with the former includes the entire systematic survey of the Pteropods collected on the Challenger Expedition.

3. The anatomy of the Thecosomata and Gymnosomata.

As with the Gymnosomata, so in regard to the Thecosomata, I have been forced to make a monographic study of the entire subgroup. But I have not here described all the species actually known, partly because they are on the whole more familiar than the Gymnosomata, and partly because the delay which has been involved in the completion of the entire Report made such a survey impossible. I shall therefore restrict myself to an enumeration of the indubitably genuine species among the entire list of those hitherto described, and to synoptic tables in which these are distinguished from one another.

[1] Zool. Chall. Exp., part lviii.

And as to the species collected on the Challenger Expedition, I shall not describe those which are already sufficiently well known, and in regard to which there is no manner of doubt or dispute. I shall restrict my descriptions to the doubtful or imperfectly known species, attempting at the same time to make their systematic arrangement more lucid and less complex.

It is a noticeable fact that in general works on the systematic relations of Molluscs, the diagnoses of the families and genera of Pteropods are always the same, and that from a comparatively ancient date, just as if they had been verbally copied by successive authors. And since they have not been modified with the progress of research, the result is that they are often incorrect. I have therefore taken particular care with the diagnoses of families and genera, and have based these on specimens which I have myself studied. The diagnoses I have framed as simply and methodically as possible.

My monographic study of the subgroup Thecosomata has been based upon the following collections :—

1. The dry and preserved specimens in the British Museum.

2. The dry shells of Thecosomata in the Brussels Museum.

3. The Thecosomata collected on the "Triton" expedition.

4. The Thecosomata collected by Mr. John Rattray, F.R.S.E., during the cruise of the steamship "Buccaneer" on the western coast of Tropical Africa (1885–86).

5. The Thecosomata collected by the Italian vessel "Vettor Pisani" during the scientific expedition round the world (1882–85).

6. The Pteropods captured by Surgeon David Bruce, M.B., near Malta (1886).

7. The Thecosomata collected at the Zoological Station at Naples during my stay there (from February to July 1887).

I must also gratefully acknowledge my indebtedness to Mr. Edgar A. Smith, of the Zoological Department of the British Museum, from whom I have received much assistance, to Professor Ch. Vélain, of Paris, and to Mr. W. H. Dall, of the U.S. National Museum.

After enumerating the species I shall discuss the geographical distribution of the group. The phylogenetic relations of the different genera can only be satisfactorily discussed after some treatment of the anatomy, and will therefore be discussed in the anatomical Report.

THE HABITS OF THE THECOSOMATOUS PTEROPODS.

I have nothing to add here either in regard to the history of the group or the differences between the two subdivisions. The subject has been sufficiently discussed in the Introduction to my Report on the Gymnosomatous Pteropoda.[1]

---

[1] Zool. Chall. Exp., part lviii. pp. 1–6.

So too in regard to the habits of the Thecosomata. Like the Gymnosomata they are pelagic Molluscs, which descend to a certain depth to avoid bright light, and reascend when the light is feeble or absent, and when the sea is calm. They feed mainly on Protozoa (Radiolaria, Foraminifera, Infusoria) or on lower Algæ, while the Gymnosomata prey upon decidedly higher animals. This difference of diet is the condition effecting the notable diversity in the structure of the alimentary system, and especially of the buccal and stomachic armature.

THE THECOSOMATA OF THE CHALLENGER EXPEDITION.

The Thecosomatous Pteropods collected on the Challenger Expedition, which form the material bases of the present Report, comprise two distinct series:—

1. The Thecosomata captured alive in the tow-nets, and preserved in alcohol or in microscopic preparations mounted in Canada balsam or in glycerine. These were entrusted to me towards the end of 1885 for use in my Report on the anatomy of the group.

2. The dry shells from deep-sea deposits, the importance of which will be discussed in the special report on the sea-bottom. This collection was selected from the deposits in the Challenger Office and also by Mr. Alfred E. Craven, who at one time proposed to write the Conchological Report on this group. It passed into my hands in the beginning of 1887, when a large number of the specimens had been already assorted.

I. The Thecosomata taken alive were gathered from seventy stations, and include twenty-eight species representing all the known genera. Among these species there is no new form, though a certain number have been hitherto insufficiently known or only once recorded.

The following table indicates the distribution of these species among the different genera.

Limacina,	6
Peraclis,	1
Clio, .	10
Cuvierina,	1
Cavolinia,	8
Cymbulia,	1
Gleba,	1
that is, among 7 genera,	28 species.

II. The Thecosomata dredged from the deposits of the deep sea occur in all those known by the title " Pteropod ooze," and also in others. I have received the shells from the sediments of twenty-one stations most rich in Thecosomata. The results of the study of these shells are detailed in this Report under the title of "Deposit-shells."

In the different shell-containing sediments which I have examined, I have found twenty-four species of Thecosomata, of which a dozen occur in considerable abundance at many of the stations. One of these forms is quite new. The various forms are distributed as follows in the different genera—

Genera.	Species previously known.	New Species.
Limacina, ...	6	...
Peraclis, ...	1	1
Clio, ...	8	...
Cuvierina, ...	1	...
Cavolinia, ...	7	...

Besides these twenty-four species there are five which do not occur in the Challenger collection of preserved Thecosomata. The total number of Pteropoda Thecosomata thus amounts to thirty-three, of which one is new, and a number either insufficiently known or not previously figured.

Limacina, .	8
Peraclis, .	2
Clio, .	12
Cuvierina, .	1
Cavolinia, .	8
Cymbulia, .	1
Gleba, .	1

that is, in 7 genera,   33 species.

DESCRIPTION OF GENERA AND SPECIES.

PTEROPODA, Cuvier.

THECOSOMATA, de Blainville.

Pterocephala, Wagner, 1885.[1]
Eupteropoda, Boas, 1886.[2]

THE GENERA AND FAMILIES OF THECOSOMATA.

In the Systematic Report on the Gymnosomatous Pteropoda, I have noted a number of genera formerly included in the group Pteropoda, but which ought long ago to have been relegated elsewhere.

Among the Thecosomata too, a number of forms have been rather recently included which do not belong to the group of Pteropods. Such are, for instance, *Cheletropis* and *Sinusigera*, which are really larvæ of Streptoneural Gastropods, whose velum has been mistaken for a fin;[3] and as to *Halopsyche* (*Euribia* and *Psyche*), it is one of the Gymnosomata, as I have noted in my previous Report.

But even after abstracting the names of genera which ought without hesitation to be removed from the systematic nomenclature of Thecosomata, there remains a long list of titles, which have been invented for living forms really belonging to the Thecosomata, but of which the majority cannot be retained. Such titles are proportionately more numerous than the generic names established for the Gymnosomata, and this because the generic diagnoses of the Thecosomata have been almost always based upon the shell. To this, which is nothing more than a simple ectodermic secretion, conchologists have attached too much systematic importance. There are indeed certain subgroups of Thecosomata, including a number of generic titles, greater than that of the genuine species.

[1] Die Wirbellosen des weissen Meeres, Bd. i. p. 119.
[2] Spolia atlantica, p. 179.
[3] Gastropods of the family of Cæcidæ also have long been considered as Thecosomatous Pteropods, under the title Odontidium.

Against such a tendency it is necessary to protest and to revert to a less rigid conception of what constitutes a genus, and though one does attach considerable systematic importance to the shell, this must not be exaggerated so as to lead to the erection of a separate genus for species which differ in some minute feature in the shell, but agree with one another in the rest of their characters. In addition to several differences of some importance in regard to the shells, it will be necessary to justify the establishment of a genus by at least one characteristic difference either in the soft structure of the animal, or in certain hard parts like the operculum or the buccal armature, which are generally of real importance in generic and specific diagnoses.

From this it follows that a large number of the generic titles discussed below must either be abandoned or regarded as synonyms. Some of them again may be considered as designating generic subdivisions, though these are not in any way indispensable in so comparatively small a group as the Thecosomata.

I shall append, from the literature of the group, an alphabetical list of the various generic names given to living Thecosomata :—

Agadina, Gould.	*Heterofusus*, Fleming.
Archonta, Montfort.	*Hyalæa*, Lamarck.
Balantium, Leach.	*Hyalocylis*, Fol.
Campylonaus, Gray.	*Limacina*, Cuvier.
Cavolinia, Abildgaard.	*Orbignyia*, A. Adams.
Cleodora, Péron and Lesueur.	*Peracle*, Forbes.
Clio, Linné.	*Pleuropus*, Eschscholtz.
Corolla, Dall.	*Protomedea*, O. G. Costa.
Creseis, Rang.	*Rheda*, Humphreys.
Cuvieria, Rang, *non* Péron.	*Scæa*, Philippi.
Cuvierina, Boas.	*Spiratella*, de Blainville.
Cymbulia, Péron and Lesueur.	*Spirialis*, Eydoux and Souleyet.
Diacria, Gray.	*Styliola*, Lesueur.
Embolus, Jeffreys.	*Tiedemannia*, delle Chiaje.
Euromus, H. and A. Adams.	*Tricla*, Oken, *non* Retzius.
Gleba, Forskål.	*Triptera*, Auctorum, *non* Quoy and
Heliconoides, d'Orbigny.	Gaimard.
Helicophora, Gray.	

Of these thirty-four titles

I. Two ought to be provisionally set aside as doubtful, for reasons which I shall afterwards submit :—

Agadina, Gould.	*Triptera*, Quoy and Gaimard.

II. Twenty-five are duplicates, and ought therefore to be retained simply as synonyms of Thecosomatous genera:—

Archonta, Montfort, . .	= *Cavolina*, Abildgaard.
Balantium, Leach, . .	= *Clio*, Linné.
Campylonans, Gray, . .	= *Peraclis*, Forbes.
Cleodora, Péron and Lesueur, .	= *Clio*, Linné.
Carolla, Dall, . .	= *Gleba*, Forskål.
Creseis, Rang, .	= *Clio*, Linné.
Cuvieria, Rang, .	= *Cuvierina*, Boas.
Diacria, Gray, .	= *Cavolinia*, Abildgaard.
Embolus, Jeffreys, .	= *Limacina*, Cuvier.
Euranus, Adams, . .	= *Peraclis*, Forbes.
Heliconoides, d'Orbigny, .	= *Limacina*, Cuvier.
Helicophora, Gray, . .	= *Limacina*, Cuvier.
Heterofusus, Fleming, .	= *Limacina*, Cuvier.
Hyalea, Lamarck, . .	= *Cavolinia*, Abildgaard.
Hyalocylix, Fol, . .	= *Clio*, Linné.
Orbignyia, A. Adams, .	= *Cavolinia*, Abildgaard.
Pleuropus, Eschscholtz, .	= *Cavolinia*, Abildgaard.
Protomedea, O. G. Costa, .	= *Limacina*, Cuvier.
Rheda, Humphreys, . .	= *Cavolinia*, Abildgaard.
Scæa, Philippi, . .	= *Limacina*, Cuvier.
Spiratella, de Blainville, .	= *Limacina*, Cuvier.
Spirialis, Eydoux and Souleyet,	= *Limacina*, Cuvier.
Styliola, Lesueur, . .	= *Clio*, Linné.
Tiedemannia, delle Chiaje, .	= *Gleba*, Forskål.
Tricla, Oken, . . .	= *Cavolinia*, Abildgaard.

As to the genus *Valcatina*, Bornemann,[1] Fischer[2] is evidently in error in stating that it includes living Pteropods, for all the forms which he describes are fossils. It is likewise probable that most of the latter are not even Pteropods.

The genera *Euchilotheca*, Fischer; *Flabellulum*, Bellardi; *Gamopleura*, Bellardi; *Poculina*, Bellardi; *Tibiella*, Meyer, and the genus *Valcatina* mentioned above are only known as Tertiary fossils; and they are further very closely allied to various extant genera.

I completely abstract certain primary fossils usually referred to the Pteropoda. I

[1] Die microscopische Fauna des Septarienthones von Hermsdorf bei Berlin, Zeitshr. d. deutsch. geol. Gesellsch., Bd. vii. p. 18.
[2] Manuel de Conchyliologie, p. 430.

have a deep conviction that these organisms do not really belong to the group in question, and am firmly of opinion that Pteropods do not occur as fossils till the end of the Lower Tertiary. I shall afterwards revert more explicitly to this point in the anatomical part of the Report, in connection with the origin and phylogeny of the group.

Among the living Thecosomata really known there are, then, strictly speaking, only eight genera, including one new genus established in this Report.

These genera are :—

Limacina, Cuvier.	*Cavolinia*, Abildgaard.
Peracle, Forbes.	*Cymbulia*, Péron and Lesueur.
Clio, Linné.	*Cymbuliopsis*, n. gen.
Cuvierina, Boas.	*Gleba*, Forskål.

The following table indicates the chief diagnostic characters :—

KEY TO THE GENERA.

I. Calcareous shell quite outside the mantle.
  1. Shell twisted into a spiral.
    A. Shell with somewhat gentle whorls, a moderately wide opening, and a columella not prolonged into a recurved rostrum, ... *Limacina*.
    B. Shell with rapidly ascending whorls, with a very wide opening and a columella prolonged into a recurved rostrum, ... *Peracle*.
  2. Shell straight and bilaterally symmetrical.
    A. Shell larger at the aperture than just behind.
      a. Shell without constriction behind the aperture, . . *Clio*.
      b. Shell with a constriction immediately behind the aperture, . *Cuvierina*.
    B. Shell narrower at the aperture than just behind, . . . *Cavolinia*.
II. Cartilaginous shell covered by the pallial epithelium.
  1. Voluminous shell with a marked cavity.
    A. Thick shell, with the cavity not extending dorsally to the very end, . *Cymbulia*.
    B. Shell with thin walls, cavity extending dorsally to the very end, . *Cymbuliopsis*.
  2. Flattened shell with almost no cavity, ... *Gleba*.

As to the relations of these eight genera with the other Pteropods, we have already noted in the Systematic Report on the Gymnosomata,[1] that Fol doubts whether *Cymbulia* has not more affinity with the Gymnosomata than with the Thecosomata. Wagner also separates the genus *Cymbulia* from the Thecosomata, and in order to get over the difficulty without solving it, creates for these animals a third division among the Pteropods, viz., Alata.[2]

In reality the members of the genus *Cymbulia* do not differ from the typical Thecosomata which Souleyet included in his family "Hyalea" except in external appearance.

---

[1] Zool. Chall. Exp., part lviii. p. 6.   [2] Die Wirbellosen des weissen Meeres, Bd. i. p. 119.

In their entire organisation (existence of a pallial cavity ; number of tentacles ; position of the penis, fins, cerebral ganglia, &c.) they agree with the Thecosomata, as we shall see in our anatomical Report. On the other hand, their special characters make it convenient to erect for them a special family, which appears to be a far preferable course to uniting them, as Woodward[1] has done, with the Cavoliniidæ, in which he has also included the Gymnosomatous *Halopsyche*.

As to the other Thecosomata, they form a more uniform group, within which one may pass from one form to another without remarking any very considerable modification. It is true, however, that in this group some forms differ from the majority in having the shell twisted into a spiral, as also in the position of the anus and of the pallial cavity. The existence of these last two differences in forms otherwise closely allied will be explained in the anatomical part of the Report. The differences just mentioned make it possible to separate the forms in question, and to erect them into the family Limacinidæ, which, however, Souleyet unites with the typical Thecosomata.[2]

As to all the rest, they form a most natural family—Cavoliniidæ, from which there is no reason to separate the genus *Cuvierina*, under the name of Tripteridæ, as Gray[3] and the brothers Adams[1] have done. The last mentioned genus in fact differs but very slightly from certain types of Cavoliniidæ, such as the species of *Clio* of the section *Creseis*, from which indeed they are distinguishable only by the presence of a partition towards the middle of the shell, and by the constriction behind the aperture.

Among the Thecosomatous Pteropods, we thus recognise only three families :—

1. Limacinidæ, including the genera *Limacina* and *Peraclis*.
2. Cavoliniidæ, ., ., *Clio, Cuvierina,* and *Cavolinia.*
3. Cymbuliidæ, ., ., *Cymbulia, Cymbuliopsis,* and *Gleba.*

Family I. LIMACINIDÆ.

1847. *Limacinidæ*, Gray, A List of the Genera of Recent Mollusca, their synonyms and types, Proc. Zool. Soc. Lond., p. 203.
1852. *Spirialidæ*, Chenu, Manuel de Conchyliologie, t. i. p. 113.

Characters.—Shell external, twisted into a left-handed spiral, with a spiral operculum. Animal with a dorsal pallial cavity, and a ventral columellar muscle ; anus situated on the right side.

Description.—The shell, which is always delicate as in other pelagic animals, is of small size, and is translucent with slight colouring. The spire and the operculum differ considerably in form in the various species.

[1] A Manual of the Mollusca, p. 304, 1856.   [2] Histoire naturelle des Mollusques Ptéropodes, p. 32.
[3] Catalogue of the Mollusca in the Collection of the British Museum, pt. ii., Pteropoda, p. 23.
[4] The Genera of Recent Mollusca, vol. i. p. 54.

The operculum is very delicate, glassy, and transparent. It is fixed by a portion of its surface to the posterior face of the ventral lobe of the foot.

The animal is twisted like the shell which it completely fills, and into which it may be completely retracted. The margin of the mantle bears, on the right-hand side, and somewhat ventrally, a long extensile appendage. The posterior lobe of the foot, which bears the operculum and is topographically ventral, is hollowed out on the middle of its free margin. The fins do not exhibit, towards their distal extremity, the area without muscular fibres which is usually to be observed in the genus *Clio*.[1]

As regards the systematic relations of the genera and species, the family Limacinidæ is still but imperfectly understood. This is in part doubtless due to the small size of the animals which form the family. They have hitherto been but rarely studied, and even in special works on Pteropods are often slurred over, as for instance in the memoirs of Quoy and Gaimard and of Rang. In the same way Troschel and Gegenbaur in their studies on the Pteropods of the Mediterranean have not discussed a single member of this family, and we may also note that Pfeffer, who has published an important description of the Thecosomata in the Hamburg Museum, has quite overlooked the Limacinidæ.

The investigation of the numerous specimens of this family which were collected on the Challenger Expedition has enabled me to make an almost complete study of the entire family. The results of my investigation I therefore proceed to submit.

If one considers the living species alone, one finds in the literature of the subject that there are no less than thirty-six different specific names applied to forms referred to this family. In this number I do not include, be it understood, the manuscript species, or those which have been simply recorded without description or figure—*Limacina carinata*, Jeffreys,[2] *Spirialis diversa*, Monterosato,[3] *Spirialis contorta*, Monterosato.[4] These I evidently could not take into account.

Since the work of Souleyet,[5] Boas is the only naturalist who has attempted to make a synthetic study of this group.[6]

From the researches of these authors it may be concluded that there are now seven species adequately enough known by their shell, operculum, and anatomy to leave no doubt as their systematic position. These species are the following, and in citing them I shall retain the original generic titles, omitting for the present the discussion of their proper generic distribution.

[1] Boas considers this space as corresponding to the hollow which separates the small tentacle-like lobe of the fin of some species of *Limacina* and *Clio* of the subgenus *Cresis*, from the margin of this fin (Spolia atlantica, p. 182, pl. v. figs. 70-79).

[2] The French Deep-Sea Exploration in the Bay of Biscay, Rep. Brit. Assoc., 1880, p. 387.

[3] Nuova rivista delle conchiglie Mediterranee, p. 50.

[4] *Ibid.*, p. 50.

[5] Histoire naturelle des Mollusques Ptéropodes.

[6] Spolia atlantica, pp. 38-50.

1. *Atlanta inflata*, d'Orbigny.
2. *Atlanta lesueurii*, d'Orbigny.
3. *Clio helicina*, Phipps.
4. *Spirialis australis*, Eydoux and Souleyet.
5. *Limacina balea*, Müller.
6. *Atlanta trochiformis*, d'Orbigny.
7. *Atlanta bulimoides*, d'Orbigny.

The considerable number (twenty-nine) of other forms described (often very imperfectly, and without examination of the animals) includes the following forms. I should rather say did include the following when I undertook this Report, for as the result of the investigation about to be recounted, certain changes in the grouping become necessary. Thus one species in Group III. must be referred to Group I., while two species of Group II. must be placed at the end of the seven species chronicled above.

I. One, which I cannot regard as a Pteropod : *Limacina turritelloides*, Boas.

II. Four, which appear to me to belong quite clearly to the Thecosomatous Limacinidae :—

Embolus triacanthus, Fischer.
Limacina antarctica, Woodward.
Limacina helicoides, Jeffreys.
Atlanta reticulata, d'Orbigny.

III. Four, which seem to me much less certain, but in regard to which the reports of those who have studied them are not sufficient to admit of a positive conclusion as in the case of the two preceding groups. Until further information is forthcoming they must be regarded as doubtful :—

Limacina (?) *cucullata*, Gould.
Agadina gouldi, A. Adams.
Agadina stimpsoni, A. Adams.
Atlanta rotunda, d'Orbigny.

IV. Finally, all the other specific titles are synonyms either of some of the seven well-known species, or of the four included in the second group :—

Argonauta artica, Fabricius,	
Limacina helicialis, Lamarck,	
Spiratella limacina, de Blainville,	} = *Clio helicina*, Phipps.
Limacina pacifica, Dall,	
Peracle flemingii, Forbes,	
Limacina balea, Müller,	
Scæa stenogyra, Philippi,	
Spirialis gouldii, Stimpson,	} = *Heterofusus retroversus*, Fleming.
Spirialis jeffreysii, Forbes and Hanley,	
Spirialis macandrei, Forbes and Hanley,	
Heterofusus alexandri, Verrill,	
Limacina naticoides, Rang,	= *Atlanta trochiformis*, d'Orbigny.

Atlanta rangii, d'Orbigny (?), . . ⎫
Spiralis ventricosa, Eydoux and Souleyet, ⎬ = *Atlanta lesueurii*, d'Orbigny.
Spiralis rostralis, Eydoux and Souleyet, ⎭

Protomedea elata, O. G. Costa, . ⎫ = *Atlanta inflata*, d'Orbigny.
Limacina scaphoidea, Gould, . . ⎭

Peracle physoides, Forbes, . . ⎫
Spiralis clathrata, Eydoux and Souleyet, ⎬ = *Atlanta reticulata*, d'Orbigny.
Spiralis recurvirostra, A. Costa, . ⎭

To these known species I can also add a new form included in the Challenger collection, which may without hesitation be referred to Group II. of undoubted Limacinidæ. Another form, which cannot be identified with any of those hitherto known, seemed at first to be referable to Group III. above, but subsequent examination has shown that it must rather be placed in Group I. along with another species of the same nature.

How are these different species to be distributed throughout the family? Or, in other words, how many distinct genera can be distinguished.

The question is indeed a most difficult one, and there are almost as many opinions on the subject as there are investigators of the group. Very few of the expressed opinions, however, claim much serious attention, for there has hardly been any previous attempt to make a systematic synthesis of the family Limacinidæ.

If we turn to the table of genera (p. 8) we see that twelve generic titles have been invented for living Thecosomata with spiral twisting, that is to say, just the same number of genera as there are certainly admissible species. I append the titles in chronological order :—

1. *Limacina*, Cuvier, 1817.
2. *Heterofusus*, Fleming, 1823.
3. *Spiratella*, de Blainville, 1824.
4. *Heliconoides*, d'Orbigny, 1836.
5. *Spirialis*, Eydoux and Souleyet, 1840.
6. *Helicophora*, Gray, 1842.
7. *Peracle*, Forbes, 1844.
8. *Scæa*, Philippi, 1844.
9. *Campylonaus*, Gray, 1847.
10. *Euromus*, A. and H. Adams, 1858.
11. *Protomedea*, O. G. Costa, 1861.
12. *Embolus*, Jeffreys, 1869.

What increases the confusion resulting from this superfluity of generic nomenclature in a group with so few forms, is the fact that several of these names have been used in different ways by different authors. Hence a complex and contradictory set of synonyms.

Gray (1850),[1] Gould (1852),[2] and Boas (1886)[3] have tried to simplify the matter by uniting all the known species in a single genus with the oldest title, *Limacina*, Cuvier. But it must be noted that Gould knew but few species of Limacinidæ, and that for one form which he regarded as new he even thought that it might be well to create a new genus. Jeffreys[4] also unites in a single genus, *Limacina*, all the species which he discusses except *Atlanta inflata*, d'Orbigny, for which he establishes a genus *Embolus*, although a certain species which he calls *Limacina* differs more from the typical *Limacina* than does *Atlanta inflata*. And besides, as we shall afterwards see, that solution of the difficulty which seeks to unite in a single genus all the living Limacinidæ is not in conformity with the differences of organisation exhibited by the various types.

There is only one way of restoring order to the confused nomenclature, and that is to find for each generic title the connotation given to it by its inventor, and the type to which it was originally applied. In this way alone can one recognise with any certainty what are the synonymous titles, and eliminate the more recent tautologies.

Let us then see what titles ought to be expelled from the nomenclature.

I. It is necessary first of all to abstract the genus *Agadina*, Gould, which, as we shall immediately see, has been too inadequately and imperfectly diagnosed to admit of any accurate conception being framed in regard to the organisms to which it ought to be applied.

II. The genus *Spiratella* was founded in 1824 by de Blainville for *Clio helicina*, Phipps. But for the same species the genus *Limacina* was erected by Cuvier in 1817. The name *Spiratella* need not therefore be retained.

III. The genera *Heliconoides*, d'Orbigny (1836), *Spirialis*, Eydoux and Souleyet (1840), and *Helicophora*, Gray (1842), are all based upon the same series of small forms, but without reference to any particular type. This series includes among its species three forms of shell, and to this it is due that the above titles have been used with different connotations by different authors (the brothers Adams, Bronn, Carus, Fol, Sars, &c.).

These forms of shell are—(1) a more or less elevated spiral with a simple lip ; (2) a depressed spiral with a rostrated lip ; and (3) with a very large aperture and a columella prolonged into the rostrum ; and they have all received different names. The adoption of these new names evidently involves the abandonment of the titles noted above in the original sense of their authors. The new names corresponding to the three forms of shell are as follows :—

---

[1] Catalogue of the Mollusca in the Collection of the British Museum, pt. ii., Pteropoda.
[2] The Mollusca and Shells of the U.S. Exploring Expedition.
[3] Spolia atlantica.
[4] New and peculiar Mollusca, &c., procured in the "Valorous" Expedition, Ann. and Mag. Nat. Hist., ser. 4, vol. xix. p. 337.

1. *Heterofusus*, Fleming (1823), and *Scæa*, Philippi (1844); the former based on *Heterofusus retroversus*, Fleming, the latter on *Scæa stenogyra*, Philippi. But as these two species are identical, the two generic titles are absolutely synonymous, and the more recent ought to disappear.

2. *Protomedea*, O. G. Costa (1861), and *Embolus*, Jeffreys (1859); the former based on *Protomedea elata*, O. G. Costa, and the latter on *Atlanta inflata*, d'Orbigny. But as the two species are synonymous, the two generic titles are equally so; and since the name *Protomedea* was applied in 1834, by de Blainville, to a Cœlenterate, it ought to disappear.

3. *Peracle*, Forbes (1844), *Campylonaus*, Gray (1847), and *Euromus*, A. and H. Adams (1858); the two last based on *Atlanta reticulata*, d'Orbigny (= *Spirialis clathrata*, Eydoux and Souleyet), and the first on *Peracle physoides*, Forbes. But as these two specific types are now recognised to be identical, the three generic titles are obviously so too, and the two more recent ought to be disused.

Having reached this stage of our critical review, we see that the maximum number of generic titles which can be adopted for the Limacinidæ does not exceed those four— *Limacina*, *Heterofusus*, *Embolus*, and *Peracle*—since we may abstract *Heliconoides* (= *Spirialis* = *Helicophora*), this genus being succeeded by the three generic titles referring to the three forms of shell which it includes.

But are *Heterofusus* and *Embolus* really distinct, with this simple difference, that in the second the spire is depressed and the lip rostrate? This can hardly be, for in almost all the genera of Gastropods there are species with short and others with elongated spirals, and the same is true of the rostrate lip. Thus in a group adjacent to the Limacinidæ, the important genus *Clio* (= *Cleodora*) exhibits nearly related species, some with a rostrum on the dorsal surface and others without. Nevertheless these forms are much too closely allied to be generically separated, and ought not the same to apply to *Heterofusus* and *Embolus?* Both exhibit in fact an umbilicate shell, with whorls increasing somewhat gently, and a semilunar operculum, with a right-handed spiral of few turns; nor do the animals exhibit any difference in their structure.

But besides having these characters in common, they share them with *Limacina*, from which they do not differ in any character sufficient to establish a generic distinction, although, as I have already noted, the reverse has been maintained by Gray, Gould, Boas, and to a certain extent by Jeffreys. It must be remarked on the other hand that Souleyet, who created the genus *Spirialis* (including *Heterofusus* and *Embolus*), recognised that it ought to be united with *Limacina* if there were an operculum in the latter.[1] But it is now sufficiently demonstrated that in *Limacina* an operculum does exist.

It is true that Sars maintains the generic distinction of *Limacina* and *Spirialis* (in

[1] Voyage de la Bonite, Zoologie, t. ii. p. 211.

the restricted sense of *Heterofusus*), principally on the ground of the transverse striæ (at right angles to the axis), which are found in *Limacina helicina*. But this character cannot be regarded as of the value of a generic distinction. If we turn for instance to a group but slightly removed from the Limacinidæ, the species of *Clio* of the subgenus *Creseis*, we see that *Clio chierchiæ*, Boas, also possesses these transverse striæ which are wholly absent in the other three species of the same subgenus. Yet one would not on that account dream of establishing a generic distinction on that simple fact, and *a fortiori* one cannot separate *Limacina* (*s. str.*) from "*Spirialis.*"

As to the genus *Peraclis*, Forbes it is so distinct that it must be retained, although d'Orbigny has referred its typical species to *Heliconoides*, Souleyet and A. Costa to *Spirialis*, and Gray, Jeffreys, and Boas to *Limacina*,

Peraclis differs indeed from the genus *Limacina* (as this has been defined above) in having a shell which is not umbilicate, has a few whorls ascending very rapidly, a larger aperture, a columella prolonged into a rostrum twisted into a spiral, and, further, in possessing a subcircular operculum, with a multispiral, left-handed coil. To this operculum neither d'Orbigny, Souleyet, nor Boas have attached the degree of importance demanded by its peculiar structure. But even if we do not take account of these differences, the structure of certain portions of the animal of *Peraclis* separates it markedly from all other Limacinidæ, as we shall afterward see, and necessitates the formation of a distinct group, opposed to all the rest of the family.

From the foregoing it results that there are among the living Limacinidæ only two different genera, *Limacina* and *Peraclis*, which may be readily distinguished by turning to the synoptic table of genera (p. 8).

Limacina,[1] Cuvier.

1817. *Limacina*, Cuvier, Le Règne animal, t. ii. p. 380.
1823. *Heterofusus*, Fleming, On a reversed species of Fusus, Mem. Wern. Soc., p. 498.
1824. *Spiratella*, de Blainville, Mollusques, Dict. d. Sci. Nat., t. xxxii. p. 284, iv. p.
1836. *Heliconoides*, d'Orbigny (*pars*), Voyage dans l'Amérique méridionale, t. v. p. 174.
1840. *Spirialis*, Eydoux et Souleyet (*pars*), Description sommaire de plusieurs Ptéropodes nouveaux ou imparfaitement connus, Rev. Zool., t. iii. p. 235.
1842. *Heliocphora*, Gray, Synopsis of the contents of the British Museum, p. 59.
1844. *Scæa*, Philippi, Fauna Molluscorum utriusque Siciliæ, p. 164.
1861. *Protomedea*, G. O. Costa (*pars*), Microdoride Maliterranea, p. 73.
1869. *Embolus*, Jeffreys, British Conchology, vol. v. p. 114.

Shell umbilicate, with turns gradually increasing; with a fairly large aperture; and with a columella not prolonged into a rostrum; surface smooth or striated. The height of the spire, the form of the surface and that of the aperture, and the size of the

[1] Diminutive of *Limax*.

umbilicus vary according to the species. *Operculum* semilunar, with a right-handed spiral of a few whorls.

Animal with an indistinctly defined head, which is only marked externally (1) by the lips on the border of the mouth and (2) by the tentacles.

1. *Lips:* two dorso-ventral folds on the cephalic surface of the fins, united dorsally, diverging ventrally, where they are continued by a fold of the cephalic surface of the fins, and extend laterally to the edge of the fins. They thus enclose a ciliated area which plays an important part in alimentation.[1] The mouth, split dorso-ventrally, is situated between these lips, in the angle formed by their union.

2. *Tentacles*, asymmetrical, the left always less developed and further back than the right. The latter is very long and retractile into a sheath. The tentacles thus exhibit absolutely the same form as those of the Cavoliniidæ. Souleyet[2] noted that in *Limacina helicina* the right tentacle *seemed* to be situated in a sheath, and[3] that in his "*Spirialis*" the minuteness of the organs did not permit him to observe whether this was again true. I have been able to convince myself that this sheath exists, not only in *Limacina helicina*, but in all the small species in which I have been able to study the animal, viz., *Limacina inflata, Limacina lesueuri, Limacina australis, Limacina trochiformis.*

Fins elongated, enlarged, truncated at their free end. In certain species—*Limacina helicina* (where the structure has been noted by P. J. van Beneden under the name of tentacles), *Limacina antarctica* and *Limacina australis* (where it was equally distinct)— the fins exhibit, towards the middle of their dorsal margin, a small narrow projecting lobe of a special structure. A similar structure exists in *Clio* in the subgenus *Creseis*. I have assured myself that in *Limacina inflata, Limacina lesueuri,* and *Limacina trochiformis* this small lobe is not present, and Boas vouches for its absence in *Limacina bulimoides*. In the other species the animal has not yet been examined.

I cannot attach any great systematic importance to the presence or absence of this minute lobe, or regard it as furnishing basis for generic or subgeneric distinction, for otherwise the entire organisation is so absolutely analogous in all the species of *Limacina*, and the lobe is present in *Limacina australis*, and absent in *Limacina retroversa*, species so closely allied that some authorities have doubted whether they were really distinct.

On turning to the table of species of Limacinidæ, it will be seen that there are only ten species which belong to the genus *Limacina* properly so called. Of these, seven are well known by their shell, their animal, and their operculum, while the other three are sufficiently well known to enable one to judge with some certainty in regard to their systematic position.

---

[1] See Boas, Spolia atlantica, p. 191.—An identical disposition is found in the Cavoliniidæ.
[2] Histoire naturelle des Mollusques Ptéropodes, p. 60.
[3] Voyage de la Bonite, Zoologie, t. ii. p. 209.

These ten species may be thus distinguished :—

KEY TO THE SPECIES.

I. Shell with a toothed lip.
  1. A single tooth on the lip, ... *Limacina inflata.*
  2. Three teeth on the lip, ... *Limacina trinacantha.*
II. Shell without teeth on the lip.
  1. Spire very short.
    A. Shell with transverse striæ (at right angles to the axis).
      a. Mouth higher than broad, ... *Limacina helicina.*
      b. Mouth broader than high, ... *Limacina antarctica.*
    B. Shell without transverse striæ.
      a. Whorls hardly separated by a suture, *Limacina helicoides.*
      b. Whorls separated by a deep suture, . *Limacina lesueuri.*
  2. Spire high.
    A. Mouth quadrangular, columella arched to the right.
      a. Umbilicus widely open, ... *Limacina australis.*
      b. Umbilicus constricted, ... *Limacina retroversa.*
    B. Mouth oval, columella arched to the left.
      a. Umbilicus constricted, spire somewhat short, . *Limacina trochiformis.*
      b. Umbilicus very narrow, spire elongated, . *Limacina balimoides.*

* [1]. *Limacina inflata* (d'Orbigny).

  1836. *Atlanta inflata,* d'Orbigny, Voyage dans l'Amérique méridionale, t. v. p. 174, pl. xii. figs. 16–19.
  1840. *Spirialis rostralis,* Eydoux et Souleyet, Description sommaire de plusieurs Ptéropodes nouveaux ou imparfaitement connus, Revue Zoologique, t. iii. p. 236.
  1850. *Limacina inflata,* Gray, Catalogue of the Mollusca in the Collection of the British Museum, pt. ii., Pteropoda, p. 31.
  1852. *Limacina scaphoidea,* Gould, The Mollusca and Shells of the U.S. Exploring Expedition, p. 485, pl. li. fig. 602.
  1861. *Protomedea data,* O. G. Costa, Microdoride mediterranea, p. 74, pl. xi. fig. 5.
  1870. *Embolus rostralis,* Jeffreys, Mediterranean Mollusca, Ann. and Mag. Nat. Hist., ser. 4, vol. vi. p. 86.
  1882. *Protomedea rostralis,* Fischer, Sur la faune Malacologique abyssale de la Méditerranée, Comptes rendus, t. 94, p. 129.

Shell, animal, and operculum : for description and figures see Souleyet, Voyage de la Bonite, Zoologie, t. ii. p. 216, pl. xiii. figs. 1–10.

Habitat.—This *Limacina* is distributed in all the warm seas. It has been recorded from the following localities :—

Atlantic Ocean, from 42° N. to 40° S.; Mediterranean, frequently collected at Naples, where I have often observed it; found also, as represented by empty shells, in a large number of deep dredgings in the Mediterranean, *e.g.*, off Crete (Jeffreys);[2] Ægean Sea (Jeffreys);[3] and on different parts of the Mediterranean coast (Sicily, Piedmont, &c.).

[1] The species collected by the Challenger are marked by an asterisk.
[2] *Ann. and Mag. Nat. Hist.,* ser. 4, vol. vi. p. 401.   [3] *Ann. and Mag. Nat. Hist.,* ser. 4, vol. vi. p. 86.

Indian Ocean; to the south-east of Arabia ("Vettor Pisani" Expedition, March 8, 1883); Gulf of Bengal and Ceylon (Kiel Museum); St. Paul and Amsterdam Islands (38° 42′ S. lat., 77° 34′ E.) (Professor Vélain, under the MS. title *Spirialis appendiculatus*).

Pacific Ocean; China Sea ("Galathea" Expedition); Corea Strait (Jeffreys);[1] Honolulu in the Philippines ("Vettor Pisani," August 28, 1884); North-West Pacific to 48° N. ("Galathea"); East Pacific, Panama, &c. ("Vettor Pisani," March 7, 1884); South-East Pacific to 40° S. (Knocker).[2]

Challenger Specimens.—I. Living specimens.

Station 142, December 18, 1873; Cape of Good Hope to 46° S.; lat. 35° 4′ S., long. 18° 37′ E.

Between Stations 162 and 163, April 3, 1874; Melbourne to Sydney; lat. 39° 7′ S., long. 149° 18′ E.

Station 175, August 12, 1874; Fiji to Raine Island; lat. 19° 2′ S., long. 177° 10′ E.

Station 181, August 25, 1874; Fiji to Raine Island; lat. 13° 50′ S., long. 151° 49′ E.

Station 201, October 26, 1874; Amboina to Samboangan; lat. 7° 3′ N., long. 121° 48′ E.

Station 216A, February 16, 1875; Samboangan to New Guinea; lat. 2° 56′ N., long. 134° 11′ E.

Between Stations 264 and 265, August 24, 1875; Sandwich Islands to Tahiti; lat. 13° 15′ N., long. 152° 2′ W.

Station 337, March 19, 1876; Tristan da Cunha to Ascension Island; lat. 24° 38′ S., long. 13° 36′ W.

On April 26, 1876; off St. Vincent (Cape Verde Islands); lat. 16° 49′ N., long. 25° 14′ W.

II. Deposit shells.

Station VIII., February 12, 1873; off Canary Islands; lat. 28° 3′ 15″ N., long. 17° 27′ 0″ W.; depth, 620 fathoms; bottom, volcanic mud.

Station 3, February 18, 1873; Tenerife to Sombrero Island; lat. 25° 45′ N., long. 20° 14′ W.; depth, 1525 fathoms; bottom, hard ground.

Station 23, March 15, 1873; off Sombrero Island; lat. 18° 24′ N., long. 63° 28′ W.; depth, 450 fathoms; bottom, Pteropod ooze.

Station 24, March 25, 1873; off Culebra Island; lat. 18° 38′ 30″ N., long. 65° 5′ 30″ W.; depth, 390 fathoms; bottom, Pteropod ooze.

Station 32B, April 3, 1873; St. Thomas to Bermuda; lat. 32° 10′ N., long. 64° 52′ W.; depth, 950 fathoms; bottom, coral mud.

---

[1] Notice of some Shells dredged by Captain St. John, R.N., in Corea Strait, *Journ. Linn. Soc. Lond.* (Zool.), vol. xiv. p. 422, 1870.

[2] On Pelagic Shells collected during a Voyage from Vancouver Island to this Country, *Proc. Zool. Soc. Lond.*, p. 616, 1868.

Station 33, April 4, 1873 ; off Bermuda ; lat. 32° 21′ 30″ N., long. 64° 35′ 55″ W.; depth, 435 fathoms ; bottom, coral mud.

Station 75, July 2, 1873 ; off Fayal (Azores); lat. 38° 38′ 0″ N., long. 28° 28′ 30″ W.; depth, 450 fathoms ; bottom, volcanic mud.

Station 76, July 3, 1873 ; off the Azores; lat. 38° 11′ N., long. 27° 9′ W.; depth, 900 fathoms ; bottom, Pteropod ooze.

Station 78, July 10, 1873 ; off the Azores; lat. 37° 26′ N., long. 25° 13′ W.; depth, 1000 fathoms ; bottom, volcanic mud.

Station 85, July 19, 1873 ; off Palma Island ; lat. 28° 42′ N., long. 18° 6′ W.; depth, 1125 fathoms ; bottom, volcanic mud.

Station 120, September 9, 1873 ; off the coast of South America, between Pernambuco and Bahia ; lat. 8° 37′ S., long. 34° 28′ W.; depth, 675 fathoms ; bottom, red mud.

Station 122, September 10, 1873 ; off the coast of South America, between Pernambuco and Bahia ; lat. 9° 5′ S., long. 34° 50′ W.; depth, 350 fathoms ; bottom, red mud.

Station 174, August 3, 1874 ; off Kandavu Island; lat. 19° 6′ 0″ S., long. 178° 14′ 20″ E.; depth, 140 fathoms ; bottom, coral mud.

Station 185, August 31, 1874 ; off Raine Island ; lat. 11° 35′ 25″ S., long. 144° 2′ 0″ E.; depth, 155 fathoms ; bottom, coral sand.

Station 219, March 10, 1875 ; Admiralty Islands to Yokohama ; lat. 1° 54′ 0″ S., long. 146° 39′ 40″ E.; depth, 150 fathoms ; bottom, coral mud.

Station 335, March 16, 1876 ; Tristan da Cunha to Ascension Island; lat. 32° 24′ S., long. 13° 5′ W.; depth, 1425 fathoms ; bottom, Pteropod ooze.

Observations.—I regard the specimens brought by Mr. Ch. Vélain from the Islands of St. Paul and Amsterdam (French Transit of Venus Expedition, 1874) as identical with the above species. They were described under the MS. title *Spirialis appendiculatus*, and are characterised by the fact that "the last whorl exhibits on its dorsal region a narrow, flattened surface, corresponding to the rostrum of the free margin" (M. Vélain's MS.).

In almost cosmopolitan animals like *Limacina inflata* and other Thecosomata, it must be noted that there is a greater expression of variability than in species of less extensive distribution. For this reason the creation of new species must not be accepted without full consideration. Many of the so-called "species" are at most local varieties, and in the case just noticed, the difference emphasised by M. Vélain is of minimum importance, and may be observed on specimens from other sources.

It must have been by a slip of the pen that Jeffreys[1] has associated this form with "*Spirialis macandrei*," Forbes and Hanley (= *Limacina retroversa*). With some

[1] On the Marine Testacea of the Piedmontese Coast, *Ann. and Mag. Nat. Hist.*, ser. 2, vol. xvii. p. 180.

hesitation the same author[1] also unites *Bellerophon minuta*, Forbes,[2] with the present species. But the perfect bilateral symmetry of this very minute shell makes it more probable that it is only a young *Oxygyrus keraudreni* (Heteropod).

*2. Limacina triacantha (Fischer) (Pl. I. figs. 1, 2).

1882. *Embolus triacanthus*, Fischer, Diagnoses d'espèces nouvelles de Mollusques recueillis dans le cours de l'Expédition scientifique de l'aviso le Travailleur (1880, 1881), Journ. de Conchyl., t. xxx. p. 49.

Characters and Description.—Smooth globular shell, flattened above. Spire very short. Three whorls, expanded and overlapping, lying almost in the same plane as in the preceding species. Suture well marked. Mouth large and widened; lip with three teeth, one above almost on the suture, one inferior, and the third on the lower half on the face of the longer portion of the curve. The two last teeth are the largest, and with each tooth there corresponds a longitudinal rib, somewhat narrow and projecting, parallel to the axis of the shell. The two superior ribs do not extend over the whole of the last coil. Straight columella. Narrow umbilicus. Colour whitish, the three ribs brown.

Dimensions.—The maximum diameter and height of the shell are almost equal, and measure 4½ mm. in the larger specimens.

The animal and the operculum are unknown.

Habitat.—Atlantic Ocean, to the south of Spain, at a depth of 1205 metres.

Challenger Specimens.—Deposit shells.

Station 23, March 15, 1873; off Sombrero Island; lat. 18° 24' N., long. 63° 28' W.; depth, 450 fathoms; bottom, Pteropod ooze.

Station 24, March 25, 1873; off Culebra Island; lat 18° 38' 30" N., long. 65° 5' 30" W.; depth, 390 fathoms; bottom, Pteropod ooze.

Station 33, April 4, 1873; off Bermuda; lat. 32° 21' 30" N., long. 64° 35' 55" W.; depth, 435 fathoms; bottom, coral mud.

Station 76, July 3, 1873; off the Azores; lat. 38° 11' N., long. 27° 9' W.; depth, 900 fathoms; bottom, Pteropod ooze.

Station 85, July 19, 1873; off Palma Island; lat. 28° 42' N., long. 18° 6' W.; depth, 1125 fathoms; bottom, volcanic mud.

Observations.—It is quite likely that *Embolus elatus*, Seguenza[3] (not *Protomedea elata*, Costa), from the Sicilian Pliocene is identical with the above species. The diagnosis,[4]

[1] On Mediterranean Mollusca, Ann. and Mag. Nat. Hist., ser. 4, vol. vi. p. 86.
[2] Report on the Mollusca and Radiata of the Ægean Sea, &c., Rep. Brit. Assoc., p. 186, 1843.
[3] Studii stratigraphici sulla formazione pliocenica, Bull. del R. Comit. geol., fasc. 5, 6, p. 148, 1875.
[4] Studii paleontologici sulla fauna malacologica dei sedimenti pliocenici depositati a grandi profondità, p. 31.

unaccompanied by any figure, does not, however, admit of certain decision on this point.

The fact that this species has only been found in the deep-sea deposits, and that over a wide area, but has never been collected alive at the surface, raises the question whether it be not really extinct. The remains of fossil Elasmobranchs and Cetaceans found at the bottom of modern seas make this hypothesis more plausible.

Although neither the animal nor the operculum of *Limacina triacantha* have been as yet observed, there cannot be any doubt that the form in question is a Pteropod. It is indeed difficult to decide, in the absence of the animal, that an empty shell, twisted in a left-handed spiral, really belongs to the Thecosomatous Pteropods and the group Limacinidæ, and not to some Gastropodous group, but in the present case there can hardly be any hesitation, as is shown by the following characters :—

1. The constancy of the left-handed spiral of the shell, which is observed in all the specimens, shows that we have not to deal with an abnormal left-handed example of a right-handed Gastropod.

2. The great breadth of the transverse diameter is not what is normally found in left-handed Gastropods, which usually exhibit an elongated spiral.

3. The thinness of the test is also suggestive.

4. The predominance of Thecosomatous Pteropod shells in the sediments from which the present species was dredged is in itself an argument.

5. The numerous resemblances between the species and *Limacina inflata* suggest a close affinity.

3. *Limacina helicina* (Phipps).

1774. *Clio helicina*, Phipps, A voyage towards the North Pole, p. 195.
1774. *Clione helicina*, Pallas, Spicilegia zoologica, fasc. x. p. 38.
1780. *Argonauta arctica*, Fabricius, Fauna grœnlandica, p. 386.
1819. *Limacina helicialis*, Lamarck, Histoire naturelle des animaux sans vertèbres, t. vi. p. 291.
1824. *Spiratella limacina*, de Blainville, Dict. d. Sci. Nat., t. xxxii. p. 284.
1832. *Spiratella arctica*, Deshayes, Encyclopédie méthodique, Vers, t. iii. p. 138.
1841. *Limacina arctica*, Möller, Bemærkninger til slægten Limacina, Kroyer, Nat. Hist. Tidsskr.,
 1 Række, Bd. iii. p. 488.
1852. *Limacina helicina*, Souleyet, Histoire naturelle des Mollusques Ptéropodes, p. 61.
1872. *Limacina pacifica*, Dall, Description of sixty new forms of Molluscs from the West Coasts
 of North America and the North Pacific Ocean, Amer. Journ. of
 Conch., vol. vii. p. 138.

For description and figures, I refer to Sars, Mollusca regionis arcticæ Norvegiæ (1878), p. 328, pl. 29, fig. 1.

Habitat.—The area of distribution is similar to that of *Clione limacina.*—Davis Strait ; Hudson Strait ; Greenland ; Iceland ; Jan Meyen Island ; Southern Norway ; White Sea (Wagner) ; Spitzbergen ; Nova Zembla ; Sea of Okhotsk ; North Pacific : Monterey,

South Alaska (35° 50′ N.) (Dall); Arctic Ocean: Point Barrow (surface temperature, 40°·2 F. to 42°) (Dall);[1] Aleutian Islands (Krause).

Observations.—I. As in all other species of *Limacina* there is an operculum, but it is caducous in the older specimens. I emphasise the presence of this operculum, because recent works, such for instance as Claus's Textbook, still characterise *Limacina* (s. str. type *Limacina helicina*) by the absence of this structure. In 1878 Sars definitely demonstrated its existence.

The caducous character of the structure is no isolated fact, for we know not only genera (*Pleurotoma*, *Voluta*, &c.) in which certain species have, and others have not, an operculum, but also species in which it is sometimes present, sometimes absent, according to the individual (*Volutharpa ampullacea*, Middendorf).

II. I consider *Limacina pacifica*, Dall, as identical with *Limacina helicina*. In fact, according to Dall and Krause, this form differs from *Limacina helicina* only in having more whorls on its spire, and in the absence of an operculum. But these are precisely the characters of the adult *Limacina helicina*, with which *Limacina pacifica* is therefore identical.

*4. *Limacina antarctica*, Woodward (Pl. I. figs. 3, 4).

1856. *Limacina antarctica*, Woodward, A Manual of the Mollusca, p. 207, *nomen tantum*, pl. xiv. fig. 4.

Characters and Description.—Subdiscoidal, flattened shell, with a spire very slightly elevated, rather depressed. Six whorls, ribbed superiorly like those of *Limacina helicina*, and, in spite of the slight elevation of the spire, quite distinct, and separated by a well-defined suture. The whorls are rounded externally and inferiorly, the last is much expanded. Large mouth, broader than high, rounded off externally, and not prolonged into an angle. Arched columella. Large umbilicus, not surrounded by a keel as in *Limacina helicina*. Transverse striæ, perpendicular to the axis, arched, regular, and equidistant.

Dimensions.—Maximum diameter 4 to 5 mm.; the height equal to about half the diameter.

Operculum unknown, probably like that of *Limacina helicina*, and caducous in the adult specimens, which alone have been examined.

Animal very like that of the preceding species. The anterior (dorsal) marginal lobe of the fin is very small, though perhaps somewhat contracted in the only specimen in which I was able to examine it. The posterior lobe of the foot is markedly hollowed out on its free margin. Tentacles like those of *Limacina helicina*; the left rudimentary, the right very long, situated in a sheath, and further forward than the left.

[1] Report on the International North Polar Expedition to Point Barrow, 1885, Report on the Mollusks, p.

Habitat.—Antarctic Ocean, where it seems to replace *Limacina helicina*, between 63° and 64° S. lat. (Ross, under the title "*Argonauta arctica*").

Challenger Specimen.—Living. Station 153, February 14, 1874; in vicinity of Antarctic ice; lat. 65° 42′ S., long. 79° 49′ E.

Observation.—The single specimen in the Challenger collection had its shell quite broken into small fragments. The description of the shell has been based on the unpublished figures of Hooker (1840). Two of these are reproduced on Pl. I. figs. 3, 4, entirely on the responsibility of Hooker.

*3. *Limacina helicoides*, Jeffreys (Pl. I. fig. 5).

> 1877. *Limacina helicoides*, Jeffreys, New and peculiar Mollusca of the Family Eulimidæ and other Families of Gastropoda as well as of the Pteropoda, procured on the "Valorous" Expedition, Ann. and Mag. Nat. Hist., ser. 4, vol. xix. p. 338.

Characters and Description.—Shell smooth and shining, with a depressed, but not flattened spire, of three or four whorls, rounded but not expanded, with a continuous surface, that is to say, only separated by a slightly marked, though distinct suture. Aperture somewhat elongated, and angular anteriorly. Columella twisted in a spiral.

Colour.—Horny brown.

Dimensions.—Height and transverse diameter almost equal, measuring 3·75 mm.

Operculum and animal unknown. This species is perhaps in the same position as *Limacina trispinosa*.

Habitat.—Atlantic Ocean to the north of the Equator, always at the bottom, with the shell empty :—"Valorous" Expedition, Station 12; lat. 56° 11′ N., long. 37° 41′ W.; at a depth of 1450 fathoms. "Porcupine" Expedition (1869), west of Ireland, Station 28; lat. 56° 44′ N., long. 12° 52′ W.; at a depth of 1215 fathoms. "Porcupine" Expedition (1870), Station 17, Bay of Vigo (not Bay of Biscay as Jeffreys says[1]); lat. 39° 42′ N., long. 9° 43′ W.; at a depth of 750 to 1095 fathoms. "Travailleur" Expedition (1880), Bay of Biscay.[2]

Challenger Specimen.—Deposit shell.

Station 78, July 10, 1873; off the Azores; lat. 37° 26′ N., long. 25° 13′ W.; depth, 1000 fathoms; bottom, volcanic mud.

---

[1] Ann. and Mag. Nat. Hist., ser. 4, vol. xix. p. 338.
[2] Jeffreys, The French Deep-Sea Exploration in the Bay of Biscay, Rep. Brit. Assoc., 1880, p. 387.

*6. *Limacina lesueuri* (d'Orbigny).

1836. *Atlanta lesueurii*, d'Orbigny, Voyage dans l'Amérique méridionale, t. v. p. 177, pl. xx. figs. 12-15.

1836. *Atlanta rangii*, d'Orbigny, Voyage dans l'Amérique méridionale, t. v. p. 176, pl. xii. figs 25-28.

1840. *Spirialis ventricosa*, Eydoux et Souleyet, Description sommaire de plusieurs Ptéropodes nouveaux ou imparfaitement connus, Revue Zoologique, t. iii. p. 236.

1850. *Limacina ventricosa*, Gray, Catalogue of the Molluscs in the Collection of the British Museum, pt. ii., Pteropoda, p. 32.

1886. *Limacina lesueurii*, Boas, Spolia atlantica, K. dansk. Vidensk. Selsk. Skriv., 6 Raekke, Bd. iv. p. 46, pl. iii. figs. 33, 34.

For description and figures I refer to Souleyet.[1] I shall restrict myself to noting that in the form of its aperture, columella, and umbilicus, this species is closely allied to *Limacina australis* and *Limacina retroversa*, with which it forms a very natural subgroup. Though the spire is depressed, it preserves none the less the distinctness of its whorls, which are separated by a very well defined suture.

Animal without a small lobe on the anterior dorsal margin of the fin.

Habitat.—The following localities have been recorded :—Atlantic Ocean, from 36° S. (d'Orbigny) to the Bay of Biscay (Pfeffer).[2] Indian Ocean, Islands of St. Paul and Amsterdam (Vélain, under MS. title *Limacina crossei*). West Pacific Ocean, 30° N. lat., 170° W. long. ("Galathea" Expedition), towards Batavia (Boas);[3] East Pacific Ocean (d'Orbigny), to 42° S. lat. (Knocker).

Challenger Specimens.—I. Living specimens.

Between Stations 162 and 163, April 3, 1874 ; on the route from Melbourne to Sydney ; lat. 38° 7′ S., long. 149° 18′ E.

Station 175, August 12, 1874 ; Fiji to Raine Island ; lat. 19° 2′ S., long. 177° 10′ E.

Station 216A, February 16, 1875 ; north of New Guinea ; lat. 2° 56′ N., long. 134° 11′ E.

Between Stations 246 and 247, July 4, 1875 ; Yokohama to Sandwich Islands ; lat. 36° 42′ N., long. 171° 46′ E.

Between Stations 264 and 265, August 24, 1875 ; Sandwich Islands to Tahiti ; lat. 13° 15′ N., long. 152° 2′ W.

Station 337, March 19, 1876 ; Tristan da Cunha to Ascension Island ; lat. 24° 38′ S., long. 13° 36′ W.

On April 26, 1876 ; off St. Vincent (Cape Verde) ; lat. 16° 49′ N., long. 25° 14′ W.

On May 7, 1876 ; off the Azores ; lat. 34° 22′ N., long. 34° 23′ W.

[1] Voyage de la Bonite, Zoologie, t. ii. p. 210, pl. xiii. figs. 11-16.

[2] Uebersicht der auf S.M. Schiff Gazelle und von Dr. Jagor gesammelten Pteropoden, *Monatsber. d. k. preuss. Akad. d. Wiss. Berlin*, p. 245, 1879.

[3] Spolia atlantica, p. 47.

11. Deposit shells.

Station VIII., February 12, 1873; off Canary Islands; lat. 28° 3′ 15″ N., long. 17° 27′ 0″ W.; depth, 620 fathoms; bottom, volcanic mud.

Station 3, February 18, 1873; Tenerife to Sombrero Island; lat. 25° 45′ N., long. 20° 14′ W.; depth, 1525 fathoms; bottom, hard ground.

Station 23, March 15, 1873; off Sombrero Island; lat. 18° 24′ N., long. 63° 28′ W.; depth, 450 fathoms; bottom, Pteropod ooze.

Station 24, March 25, 1873; off Culebra Island; lat. 18° 38′ 30″ N., long. 65° 5′ 30″ W.; depth, 390 fathoms; bottom, Pteropod ooze.

Station 33, April 4, 1873; off Bermuda; lat. 32° 21′ 30″ N., long. 64° 35′ 55″ W.; depth, 435 fathoms; bottom, coral mud.

Station 85, July 19, 1873; off Palma Island; lat. 28° 42′ N., long. 18° 6′ W.; depth, 1125 fathoms; bottom, volcanic mud.

Station 120, September 9, 1873; off the coast of South America, between Pernambuco and Bahia; lat. 8° 37′ S., long. 34° 28′ W.; depth, 675 fathoms; bottom, red mud.

Station 122, September 10, 1873; off the coast of South America, between Pernambuco and Bahia; lat. 9° 5′ S., long. 34° 50′ W.; depth, 350 fathoms; bottom, red mud.

Station 185, August 31, 1874; off Raine Island; lat. 11° 35′ 25″ S., long. 144° 2′ 0″ E.; depth, 155 fathoms; bottom, coral sand.

Observations.—1. It is very probable that *Atlanta rangii*, d'Orbigny, which Souleyet[1] has hesitatingly referred to his *Spirialis ventricosa*, is identical with the above species. But since the somewhat imperfect description and figure of d'Orbigny exclude the possibility of absolute certainty, it is better to adopt, as we have done, the specific title *lesueuri*, although this species does not occur in d'Orbigny's work till several pages after *Atlanta rangii*.

11. *Atlanta rotundata* of the same authority,[2] which Souleyet[3] regards as a variety of his *Spirialis ventricosa*, appears to us very different indeed. In our opinion it is not even a Pteropod, as we shall explain further on in our appendix to the Limacinidæ.

*7. *Limacina australis* (Eydoux and Souleyet) (Pl. I. fig. 6).

1840. *Spirialis australis*, Eydoux et Souleyet, Description sommaire de quelques Ptéropodes nouveaux ou imparfaitement connus, Revue Zoologique, t. iii. p. 237.

Characters and Description.—Smooth shell, with spire somewhat elevated, with a blunted or obtuse apex, with six or seven bulging whorls, separated by a very deep suture,

---

[1] Histoire naturelle des Mollusques Ptéropodes, p. 63.
[2] Voyage dans l'Amérique méridionale, t. v. p. 175, pl. xii. figs. 20-24.
[3] Histoire naturelle des Mollusques Ptéropodes, p. 63.

with the last whorl much expanded and convex, and projecting more in proportion than all the foregoing. Aperture quadrangular, somewhat angled in front; columella straight, reflected to the right; umbilicus broad.

Colour.—Milky.

Dimensions.—2 to 2·5 mm. in height, about 1·5 mm. in maximum diameter.

Operculum approximately oval, with an almost straight columellar margin, and with a spiral portion measuring barely two-fifths of the entire length.

The animal exhibits a small lobe on the dorsal margin of each fin.

Habitat.—Cape Horn (Souleyet).

From its discovery by Souleyet this species was not reobserved until the Challenger Expedition. Jeffreys[1] follows Vérany in noting the coast of Piedmont as a locality of *Spirialis australis*, and this has been repeated without question by various authors.[2] The statement is, however, entirely erroneous, and has in all probability reference to *Limacina trochiformis*.

The specimens collected by the Challenger show that this species has a somewhat wide distribution round the South Pole, where it occupies, along with *Limacina antarctica*, a position analogous to that of *Limacina retroversa* and *Limacina helicina* in the north.

Challenger Specimens.—Living.

Station 146, December 29, 1873; Marion Island to Crozets; lat. 46° 46' S., long. 45° 31' E.

Station 149, January 9, 1874; at Kerguelen Island; lat. 49° 8' S., long. 70° 12' E.

Station 150, February 2, 1874; Heard Island; lat. 52° 4' S., long. 71° 22' E.

Between Stations 154 and 155, February 21, 1874; in vicinity of Antarctic Ice; lat. 63° 30' S., long. 89° 8' E.

Observations.—Boas[3] has expressed hesitation in regard to the possible specific identity of *Limacina australis*, *Limacina retroversa*, and *Limacina trochiformis*. They are, however, as we shall see, three very distinct forms.

In the first place, as regards *Limacina trochiformis*, it belongs along with *Limacina bulimoides* to a special group of *Limacinæ* quite different from that to which *Limacina australis* and *Limacina retroversa* are to be referred. It is characterised by the presence of a shell with oval, rounded aperture, with the columellar margin reflected to the left, and with a very narrow umbilicus. In *Limacina bulimoides* and *Limacina trochiformis* also the animal is without any lobe on the fin. In *Limacina australis*, on the other hand, the opening of the shell is quadrangular, with the columellar margin reflected to the right, with a very broad umbilicus, and a tentacle-like lobe on the dorsal margin of the

[1] On the Marine Testacea of the Piedmontese Coast, Ann. and Mag. Nat. Hist., ser. 2, vol. xvii. p. 160.
[2] For instance Weinkauff, Die Conchylien des Mittelmeeres, t. ii. p. 428.
[3] Spolia atlantica, p. 46.

tin. Furthermore, the spire is proportionally much shorter in *Limacina trochiformis*, and the operculum has a form differing from that of all the other species in the large extent of its spiral portion (three-sevenths) and in the convexity of its columellar margin.[1] In *Limacina australis*[2] the columellar margin of this operculum is almost rectilinear, and the spiral portion hardly attains to more than a third of the total length. *Limacina trochiformis* has certainly less affinity with *Limacina australis* than *Limacina lesueuri*, in spite of the depressed spiral of the latter.

As to *Limacina retroversa*, it is certainly more nearly allied to *Limacina australis* than *Limacina trochiformis*, but the characters which distinguish it from that form are quite distinct enough to be recognised as specific. Thus the umbilicus of *Limacina retroversa*, while quite distinct, is very narrow,[3] in contrast to that of *Limacina australis*, which as we have seen is very broad.[4] The spire is pointed in *Limacina retroversa*, but obtuse in *Limacina australis*, where the whorls are besides more convex, less numerous, and separated by a shallower suture. Even at first sight *Limacina australis* is distinguished from *Limacina retroversa* by the expansion of the last coil and by its projection beyond those in front. Finally, in *Limacina retroversa* the spiral portion of the operculum is much more reduced than that of *Limacina australis*.[5]

8. *Limacina retroversa* (Fleming).

1788. (?) *Turbo lunaris*, Gmelin, Systema naturæ, i. p. 3587.

1823. *Heterofusus retroversus*, Fleming, On a reversed species of Fusus, Mem. Wern. Nat. Hist. Soc., vol. iv. p. 498, pl. xv. fig. 2.

1841. *Limacina lobra*, Möller, Bemaerkninger til slægten Limacina, Kröyer, Nat. Hist. Tidsskr., 1 Rakke, Bd. iii. p. 489.

1844. *Psyche flemingii*, Forbes, in Thompson, Report on the Fauna of Ireland, Rep. Brit. Assoc., 1843, p. 249.

1844. *Sxæa dewogyra*, Philippi, Fauna Molluscorum utriusque Siciliæ, p. 164, pl. xxv. fig. 20.

1846. *Spirialis dewogyra*, Lovén, Index Molluscorum litora Scandinaviæ occidentalia habitantium, Oversigt k. Vetensk.-Akad. Förhandl., 1846, p. 4.

1849. *Spirialis flemingii* and *Spirialis retroversa*, Forbes and Hanley, History of the British Mollusca and their Shells, vol. ii. pp. 384, 385, pl. lvii. figs. 4, 5, 6, 7.

1849. (?) *Spirialis jeffreysii*, Forbes and Hanley, Ibid., vol. ii. p. 386, pl. lvii. fig. 8.

1850. *Limacina retroversa*, Gray, Catalogue of the Mollusca in the collection of the British Museum, pt. 2, Pteropoda, p. 33.

[1] Souleyet, Voyage de la Bonite, Zoologie, Mollusques, pl. xiii. fig. 33.
[2] Souleyet, Ibid., pl. xiii. fig. 24.
[3] Sars, Mollusca regionis arcticæ Norvegiæ, pl. 29, figs. 2c, 3b.
[4] Souleyet, Voyage de la Bonite, Zoologie, Mollusques, pl. xiii. fig. 23.
[5] Sars, Mollusca regionis arcticæ Norvegiæ, pl. 29, figs. 2d, 3d.

1851. *Spirialis gouldii*, Stimpson, Description of two new species of shells of Massachusetts, Proc. Boston Soc. Nat. Hist., vol. iv. p. 8; and Shells of New England, p. 27, pl. i. fig. 4.

1857. *Heterofusus balea*, Mörch, in Rink, Grønland geographisk, statistisk og naturhistorisk beskrevet, p. 86.

1872. *Heterofusus alexandri*, Verrill, Recent Additions to the Molluscan Fauna of New England, &c., Amer. Journ. Sci. and Arts, ser. 3, vol. iii. p. 284.

1878. *Spirialis balea* and *Spirialis retroversa*, Sars, Mollusca regionis arcticæ Norvegiæ, pp. 329, 330, pl. 29, figs. 2, 3.

For description and figures see Sars, *loc. cit.*

Habitat.—North Atlantic, on the coast of America, from 63° N. (Davis Strait) to 39° 53′ N. (Massachusetts Bay, Verrill); Iceland; coasts of Europe, from Lofoden Island to 50° N., though not yet recorded from Behring Straits.

All records which mention this species as having been found in more southerly localities, and notably in the Mediterranean, are erroneous, and ought to apply to *Limacina trochiformis*, with which *Limacina retroversa* has been confused by Jeffreys,[1] Weinkauff,[2] Costa,[3] and other conchologists. *Limacina retroversa* is no longer found in the Mediterranean, though it occurs in circa-Mediterranean Pliocene and Quaternary deposits (" *Scæa stenogyra* ").

In the deep-sea deposits this species is found in the North Atlantic over an area extending somewhat further south, and it has thus been dredged in the Bay of Biscay by the French " Travailleur " Expedition (1880).[4]

Observations.—I. Some authorities (Jeffreys, Gould, Sars, Verrill, &c.) regard *Heterofusus retroversa* and *Limacina balea* as two distinct forms.

Sars supports this in his descriptions and figures. According to him, the two forms differ, apart from size which cannot be regarded as distinctive, especially in the fact that in *Limacina balea* the surface is longitudinally striated (parallel to the axis of the shell) and that its spire is proportionally longer.

To the first of these two points, it may be answered that in *Limacina retroversa* the surface also exhibits longitudinal striæ, less marked, it is true, but distinctly recognisable,[5] and that in *Scæa stenogyra*, Philippi,[6] which Sars identifies with *Limacina balea*, the surface is on the contrary " lævissima." This point of distinction does not, therefore, appear conclusive.

[1] British Conchology, vol. v. p. 116.
[2] Die Conchylien des Mittelmeeres, Bd. ii. p. 466.
[3] Pteropodi della fauna del Regno di Napoli, p. 19.
[4] Jeffreys, The French Deep-sea Exploration in the Bay of Biscay, Rep. Brit. Assoc., 1880, p. 387.
[5] Sars, Mollusca regionis arcticæ Norvegiæ, pl. 29, fig. 2*; Gould, Report on the Invertebrata of Massachusetts, ed. 2, pl. xxvii. figs. 345–348.
[6] Philippi, Fauna Molluscorum utriusque Siciliæ, pl. xxv. fig. 20.

As to the argument based on the relative height of the spire, the average proportion of height to maximum diameter is $\frac{40}{27}$ in *Limacina balea*, and $\frac{32}{27}$ in *Heterofusus retroversus*. But in *Spirialis gouldii*, Stimpson, identified by Sars with *Limacina balea*, and with very well marked transverse striation, the apparently very exact figure given by Stimpson[1] exhibits the above ratio as $\frac{31}{27}$, less, that is to say, than that of *Heterofusus retroversus*, while in *Scæa stenogyra*, with smooth surface, the ratio according to Philippi's figure is $\frac{37}{27}$.

It is thus seen that the relative height of the spire varies as well as the striation of the surface, and that the variations of these two features are independent. We are, therefore, led to conclude that *Limacina balea* and *Heterofusus retroversus* are not two specifically distinct forms, but belong to a single species which exhibits a certain number of varieties.

*9. *Limacina trochiformis* (d'Orbigny).

> 1836. *Atlanta trochiformis*, d'Orbigny, Voyage dans l'Amérique méridionale, t. v. p. 177, pl. xii. figs. 29–31.
> 1840. *Spirialis trochiformis*, Eydoux et Souleyet, Description sommaire de quelques Ptéropodes nouveaux ou imparfaitement connus, Revue Zoologique, t. iii. p. 237.
> 1850. *Limacina trochiformis*, Gray, Catalogue of the Mollusca in the Collection of the British Museum, pt. ii., Pteropoda, p. 33.
> 1852. *Limacina naticoides*, Rang, Histoire naturelle des Mollusques Ptéropodes, pl. x. figs. 1, 2.

For description and figures see Souleyet.[2]

The umbilicus of the shell is very small in this species. The dorsal (anterior) margin of the fin does not exhibit any tentacle-like lobe.

Habitat.—Atlantic Ocean, from 41° N. to 28° S.; Mediterranean, Naples (where I have often observed it alive), Malta (David Bruce); the shell has been dredged at a great number of localities in the Mediterranean—Crete (Jeffreys), &c.; Indian Ocean, south-east of Arabia (Blanford); Pacific Ocean, China Sea (Gray), Malay Archipelago (Copenhagen Museum); Equatorial Pacific to 132° W.; South-east Pacific to 30° S. (d'Orbigny).

Challenger Specimens.—I. Living specimens.

Between Stations 162 and 163, April 3, 1874; Melbourne to Sydney; lat. 38° 7′ S., long. 149° 18′ E.

Station 216A, February 16, 1875; north of New Guinea; lat. 2° 56′ N., long. 134° 11′ E.

[1] Shells of New England, pl. i. fig. 4.   [2] Voyage de la Bonite, Zoologie, t. ii. p. 223, pl. xiii. figs. 27–34.

Between Stations 264 and 265, August 24, 1875; Sandwich Islands to Tahiti; lat. 13° 15′ N., long. 152° 2′ W.

Station 337, March 19, 1876; Tristan da Cunha to Ascension Island; lat. 24° 38′ S., long. 13° 36′ W.

II. Deposit shells.

Station 120, September 9, 1873; off the coast of South America, between Pernambuco and Bahia; lat. 8° 37′ S., long. 34° 28′ W.; depth, 675 fathoms; bottom, red mud.

Station 219, March 10, 1875; Admiralty Islands to Yokohama; lat. 1° 54′ 0″ S., long. 146° 39′ 40″ E.; depth, 150 fathoms; bottom, coral mud.

Observations.—I have already stated that Boas has expressed doubts as to the specific distinctness of *Limacina australis*, *Limacina retroversa*, and *Limacina trochiformis*, and I have shown that *Limacina australis* could not be identified with either of the other two species.

As concerns the latter, they have been deplorably confused by a great many authors, Jeffreys,[1] MacAndrew, Weinkauff,[2] A. Costa,[3] Monterosato, &c., who have attributed to *Limacina retroversa* a geographical distribution much more extensive than it really possesses, by crediting it with localities such as the Mediterranean, the Canaries, &c., which ought to refer to *Limacina trochiformis* alone. *Limacina trochiformis* differs however from *Limacina retroversa* (as also from *Limacina australis*, which belongs to same group), (1) in the oval form of the mouth, which is rounded anteriorly, and has the columellar margin recurved to the left, in contrast to *Limacina retroversa* where the mouth is quadrangular, pointed anteriorly, and with a rectilinear columellar margin; (2) in the constant shortness of the spiral in proportion to its last whorl, and (3) in the formation of the operculum, in which the spiral portion is large in *Limacina trochiformis*, and very small in *Limacina retroversa*.

10. Limacina bulimoides (d'Orbigny).

> 1836. *Atlanta bulimoides*, d'Orbigny, Voyage dans l'Amérique méridionale, t. v. p. 179, pl. xii. figs. 36–38.
>
> 1840. *Spirialis bulimoides*, Eydoux et Souleyet, Description sommaire de quelques Ptéropodes nouveaux ou imparfaitement connus, Revue Zoologique, t. iii. p. 238.
>
> 1850. *Limacina bulimoides*, Gray, Catalogue of the Mollusca in the Collection of the British Museum, pt. ii., Pteropoda, p. 34.

For description and figures see Souleyet, Voyage de la Bonite, Zoologie, t. ii. p. 224, pl. xiii. figs. 35–42.

[1] British Conchology, vol. v. p. 116.
[2] Die Conchylien des Mittelmeeres, t. ii. p. 428.
[3] Pteropodi della fauna del Regno di Napoli, p. 19.

The umbilicus of the shell is almost imperceptible. There is no tentacular lobe to the fin, as Boas has already noted.

Habitat.—Atlantic Ocean, from 40° S. to 30° N.; Indian Ocean, south-east of Arabia ("Vettor Pisani" Expedition, March 8, 1885); Pacific Ocean, Botany Bay (Angas);[1] China Sea and West Pacific to 40° N. ("Galathea" Expedition); Equatorial Pacific, South Pacific to 37° S. (Knocker); South-east Pacific (d'Orbigny).[4]

The empty shells of this species have been gathered from the deep-sea deposits in the Mediterranean, where the species is no longer found alive, in the Ægean Sea (Jeffreys), and in the Mediterranean dredgings of the "Travailleur" (Fischer);[2] in the North Atlantic (by the "Valorous" Expedition,[4] and by the first "Porcupine" Expedition, 1869).

Challenger Specimens.—I. Living specimens.

Between Stations 162 and 163, April 3, 1874; Melbourne to Sydney; lat. 38° 7′ S., long. 149° 18′ E.

Station 175, August 12, 1874; Fiji to Raine Island; lat. 19° 2′ S., long. 177° 10′ E.

Station 181, August 25, 1874; Fiji to Raine Island; lat. 13° 50′ S., long. 151° 49′ E.

Station 201, October 26, 1874; Amboina to Samboangan; lat. 7° 3′ N., long. 121° 48′ E.

Station 243, June 26, 1875; Yokohama to Sandwich Islands; lat. 35° 24′ N., long. 166° 35′ E.

Between Stations 247 and 248, July 4, 1875; Yokohama to Sandwich Islands; lat. 36° 42′ N., long. 179° 50′ W.

Station 337, March 19, 1876; Tristan da Cunha to Ascension Island; lat. 24° 38′ S., long. 13° 36′ W.

On April 26, 1876; off St. Vincent (Cape Verde); lat. 16° 49′ N., long. 25° 14′ W.

Near Station 354, May 7, 1876; off Azores; lat. 34° 22′ N., long. 34° 23′ W.

II. Deposit shells.

Station VIII., February 12, 1873; off Canary Islands; lat. 28° 3′ 15″ N., long. 17° 27′ 0″ W.; depth, 620 fathoms; bottom, volcanic mud.

Station 3, February 10, 1873; Tenerife to Sombrero Island; lat. 25° 45′ N., long. 20° 14′ W.; depth, 1525 fathoms; bottom, hard ground.

Station 23, March 15, 1873; off Sombrero Island; lat. 18° 24′ N., long. 63° 28′ W.; depth, 450 fathoms; bottom, Pteropod ooze.

Station 24, March 25, 1873; off Culebra Island; lat. 18° 38′ 30″ N., long. 65° 5′ 30″ W.; depth, 390 fathoms; bottom, Pteropod ooze.

Station 32a, April 3, 1873; St. Thomas to Bermuda; lat. 32° 10′ N., long. 64° 52′ W.; depth, 950 fathoms; bottom, coral mud.

[1] Angas, *Proc. Zool. Soc. Lond.*, 1871, p. 99.
[2] It is cited from Sicily after Allery by Tiberi, *Ann. Soc. Malacol. Belg.*, t. xiii. p. 76.
[3] *Comptes rendus*, t. xciv. p. 1201.   [4] *Ann. and Mag. Nat. Hist.*, ser. 4, vol. xix. p. 337.

Station 33, April 4, 1873; off Bermuda; lat. 32° 21′ 30″ N., long. 64° 35′ 55″ W.; depth, 435 fathoms; bottom, coral mud.

Station 85, July 19, 1873; off Palma Island; lat. 28° 42′ N., long. 18° 6′ W.; depth, 1125 fathoms; bottom, volcanic mud.

Station 120, September 9, 1873; off the coast of South America, between Pernambuco and Bahia; lat. 8° 37′ S., long. 34° 28′ W.; depth, 675 fathoms; bottom, red mud.

Station 122, September 10, 1873; off the coast of South America, between Pernambuco and Bahia; lat. 9° 5′ S., long. 34° 50′ W.; depth, 350 fathoms; bottom, red mud.

Station 185, August 31, 1874; off Raine Island; lat. 11° 35′ 25″ S., long. 144° 2′ 0″ E.; depth, 135 fathoms; bottom, coral sand.

Station 219, March 10, 1875; Admiralty Islands to Yokohama; lat. 1° 54′ 0″ S., long. 146° 39′ 40″ E.; depth, 150 fathoms; bottom, coral mud.

Peraclis,[1] Forbes (*emend.*).

1836. *Heliconoides*, d'Orbigny (*pars*), Voyage dans l'Amérique Méridionale, t. v. p. 174.
1840. *Spirialis*, Eydoux et Souleyet (*pars*), Description sommaire de quelques Ptéropodes nouveaux ou imparfaitement connus, Revue Zoologique, t. iii. p. 235.
1844. *Peracle*, Forbes, Report on the Mollusca and Radiata of the Ægean Sea, and on their distribution, considered as bearing on Geology, Rep. Brit. Assoc., 1843, p. 186.
1847. *Campylonaus*, Gray (*non* Benson), A List of the Genera of Recent Mollusca, their synonyms and types, Proc. Zool. Soc. Lond., 1847, p. 149.
1858. *Euromus*, A. and H. Adams, The Genera of Recent Mollusca, vol. ii. p. 613.
1876. *Limacina*, Jeffreys (*pars*), New and Peculiar Mollusca of the Family Eulimidæ and other Families of Gastropoda, as well as of the Pteropoda procured in the "Valorous" Expedition, Ann. and Mag. Nat. Hist., ser. 4, vol. xix. p. 337.

Characters and Description.—Shell with spire short but projecting, with bulging whorls rapidly increasing towards the very large and elongated aperture, which ends anteriorly in a very sharp angle. Spiral columella, prolonged into an elongated rostrum. No umbilicus. Surface smooth or finely reticulate.

Operculum subcircular, multispiral, left-handed.

Animal previously unknown, or supposed to be identical with that of the other Limacinidæ. Krohn[2] and Costa[3] have observed the living animal, but have not perceived the differences between it and the true *Limacina* type. The differences are as follows :—

1. Head distinct, prolonged into a proboscis analogous to that of the Cymbuliidæ (for example the old larvæ of *Gleba*).

---

[1] *Per*, meaning exaggeration, and *aclis*, a small javelin, in allusion to the long rostrum of the shell.
[2] Beiträge zur Entwickelungsgeschichte der Pteropoden und Heteropoden, p. 43, under the name of *Spirialis clathrata*.
[3] At Naples, under the name of *Spirialis recurvirostra*.

2. Lips with lateral angles, and united ventrally.

3. Tentacles symmetrical, of the same size and without sheath.

4. Posterior or opercular lobe of the foot broad at the base, instead of being slightly constricted as in *Limacina*, and less developed in proportion to the fins, which are large, long, truncated at their distal extremity, and without the small tentacle-like lobe.

5. Visceral ganglia forming three distinct masses, as in the Cymbuliidæ.

Observations.—I. Boas has made a mistake in figuring the operculum as twisted in a right-handed spiral.[1] The coil is left-handed, as d'Orbigny has represented it.[2] This arrangement is quite unique, for in all the operculate Mollusca the twisting of the operculum is in the opposite direction to that of the shell. *Atlanta* is the only right-handed Mollusc in which the operculum is coiled to the right. In all the left-handed operculate Molluscs the operculum is coiled to the right—*Limacina*,[3] *Triforis*,[4] *Lacoochlis*.[5] *Peraclis* thus forms a remarkable exception.

II. The initial portion of the spire does not project, so that the apex is always obtuse.

III. Boas[6] notes in "*Limacina*" *reticulata* (= *Peraclis*) a small tentacle-like lobe on the fin as in *Limacina helicina*; this observation was made on an insufficiently preserved specimen, and has not been figured. I have examined not only the preserved specimen of the Challenger Expedition, but living specimens from the Mediterranean, and am able to state that the fin does not bear any lobe. Costa's figures[7] are perfectly correct in this respect. Boas must have mistaken a fold of the fin margin for the lobe.

D'Orbigny, the discoverer of the only species as yet known, considered it, as well as all the small forms of *Limacina* (the *Spirialis* of Souleyet), as Heteropods of the genus *Atlanta*. Forbes, who gave a second specific title to the form in question, and created for it the generic title *Peracle*, also regarded it as a Heteropod. Gray also regarded it as such, under the title *Campylonœus*.[8]

Souleyet was the first to place this form, with a third specific title, among the Pteropods, but was unable to investigate the animal. Subsequently Costa figured the paired fins of the animal, to which he gave a fourth specific title, and made its position as a Pteropod indisputable.

The structure of the genus has, however, remained quite unknown till now. I have been able to investigate it to some extent, and to show that it is of the highest interest

---

[1] Spolia atlantica, pl. iii. fig. 30.
[2] Voyage dans l'Amérique méridionale, t. v. pl. xiii. fig. 30.
[3] Souleyet, Voyage de la Bonite, Zoologie, Mollusques, pl. xiii.; Sars, Mollusca regionis arcticæ Norvegiæ, pl. 29.
[4] Sars, Ibid., pl. xviii. fig. 31.
[5] Sars, Ibid., pl. xviii. fig. 29.
[6] Spolia atlantica, p. 50, note 2.
[7] Annuario del Museo Zoologico della R. Univ. Napoli, t. iv. pl. iv. fig. 12.
[8] Proc. Zool. Soc. Lond., p. 143, 1847.

and importance in connection with the phylogenetic relations of the different families of Thecosomata. This I shall show in the anatomical portion of this Report.

KEY TO THE SPECIES.

A. Shell with simple lip, ... *Peraclis reticulata.*
B. Shell with lip exhibiting a tooth towards the suture, . *Peraclis bispinosa.*

*1. *Peraclis reticulata* (d'Orbigny) (Pl. I. figs. 7, 8).

> 1836. *Atlanta reticulata*, d'Orbigny, Voyage dans l'Amérique méridionale, t. v. p. 178, pl. xii. figs. 32–35, 39,
>
> 1840. *Spirialis clathrata*, Eydoux et Souleyet, Description sommaire de quelques Ptéropodes nouveaux ou imparfaitement connus, Revue Zoologique, t. iii. p. 138.
>
> 1844. *Peracle physoides*, Forbes, Report on the Molluscs and Radiata of the Ægean Sea, considered as bearing on geology, Rep. Brit. Assoc., 1843, p. 186.
>
> 1865. *Spirialis recurvirostra*, A. Costa, Di una nuova specie mediterranea di Molluschi "Pteropodi" del gen. Spirialis, Rendiconto d. real. Acad. d. Sci. Napoli, Anno iv. p. 125 (1867); Illustrazione della Spirialis recurvirostra, Annuario del Museo Zoologico della R. Univ. Napoli, t. iv. p. 56, pl. iv. fig. 12.
>
> 1870. *Spirialis physoides*, Jeffreys, in Carpenter and Jeffreys, Report on Deep-Sea Researches, Proc. Roy. Soc., vol. xix. p. 173.
>
> 1876. *Limacina physoides*, Jeffreys, New and Peculiar Molluscs of the Eulimidæ and other families of Gastropoda, as well as of the Pteropoda procured in the "Valorous" Expedition, Ann. and Mag. Nat. Hist., ser. 4, vol. xix. p. 337.

Characters and Description.—Shell elongated, formed of four bulging whorls, separated by a deep suture, and exhibiting a very slight keel on the side of the spire. The latter is somewhat short, obtuse at its apex, owing to the absence of projection of its initial portion ; the last turn is very large. The opening is very large, elongated, and angled anteriorly. The columella is spiral with a prolonged pointed rostrum, which follows in its curvature the spiral of the columella. The surface exhibits a raised hexagonal reticulation, the sides of the hexagons bearing a regular row of minute teeth.

Colour.—Brownish-yellow.

Dimensions.—Maximum length 4 mm.; diameter 2·3 mm.

Operculum.—Glassy, with about four whorls ; the surface of insertion small.

Animal.—Corresponding with the generic description.

Observations.—I. The reticulation of the surface becomes less marked from the apex of the spire towards the aperture. On the first whorls it projects markedly, while towards the mouth it almost disappears, and the colour of the shell becomes clearer. On the empty shells, obtained from deep-sea deposits, the surface is perfectly smooth, and the shell is then clear and translucent, with a brownish-grey colour. This makes me think that the reticulation of the surface is confined to the epidermis.

II. The reason for the numerous titles applied to the present species is that the specimens have been studied in very different conditions.

Hitherto only one author has studied the living Pteropod in its adult state, namely Costa, who described it as *Spirialis recurvirostra*.

The two oldest descriptions of this species, that of d'Orbigny (under the title *Atlanta reticulata*) and that of Souleyet (under the title *Spirialis clathrata*), refer to young individuals. This is clearly shown from their smaller size (2½ mm.), the fewer turns in the spiral (three), the incompletely developed columellar rostrum, and the well-developed reticulation towards the aperture.

As to this reticulation, I have noticed that in the single specimen obtained on the Challenger Expedition, which was at the same stage as that observed by d'Orbigny and Souleyet, the markings are hexagonal, and not tetragonal as one might suppose with low-power examination.

Finally, the empty shells from deep-sea deposits, which have lost their superficial reticulation and brown colour, have been described by Forbes, Jeffreys (1871), and Fischer (1882)[1] under the specific title *physoides*.

Habitat.—Pacific Ocean, 20° S., 87° W. (d'Orbigny); perhaps in the Atlantic, at the Canaries (Krohn);[2] Mediterranean, Naples, during the day, at a depth of 100 metres or more.

The empty shells of this species have been dredged at various points in the Mediterranean; in the deep-sea dredgings of the "Travailleur" (Fischer); on the coast of Algiers ("Porcupine" Expedition, 1870, Station 51, 36° 55′ N., 1° 10′ E.); off Crete (Jeffreys)[3] in the Ægean Sea (Forbes), and finally in the North Atlantic ("Valorous" Expedition).[4]

Challenger Specimens.—I. Living.

Between Stations 264 and 265, August 24, 1875; on the route from the Sandwich Islands to Tahiti; lat. 13° 15′ N., long. 152° 2′ W.

This single specimen was stained and mounted in balsam. In order to examine the reticulation of the shell and the form of the fins, I had to extract the specimen from the balsam, and in this operation the shell was broken.

II. Deposit shells.

Station 23, March 15, 1873; off Sombrero Island; lat. 18° 24′ N., long. 63° 28′ W.; depth, 450 fathoms; bottom, Pteropod ooze.

---

[1] *Comptes rendus*, vol. xciv. p. 1201.
[2] *Beiträge zur Entwickelungsgeschichte der Pteropoden und Heteropoden*, p. 43.
[3] *Ann. and Mag. Nat. Hist.*, ser. 5, vol. xi. p. 401.   [4] *Ann. and Mag. Nat. Hist.*, ser. 4, vol. xix. p. 337.

Station 24, March 25, 1873; off Culebra Island; lat. 18° 38′ 30″ N., long. 65° 5′ 30″ W.; depth, 390 fathoms; bottom, Pteropod ooze.

Station 33, April 4, 1873; off Bermuda; lat. 32° 21′ 30″ N., long. 64° 35′ 55″ W.; depth, 435 fathoms; bottom, coral mud.

Station 85, July 19, 1873; off Palma Island (Canaries); lat. 28° 42′ N., long. 18° 6′ W.; depth, 1125 fathoms; bottom, volcanic mud.

Station 122, September 10, 1873; off the coast of South America, between Pernambuco and Bahia; lat. 9° 5′ S., long. 34° 50′ W.; depth, 350 fathoms; bottom, red mud.

*2. *Peraclis bispinosa*, n. sp. (Pl. I. figs. 9, 10).

Characters and Description.—Shell elongated, smooth on the surface, with three or four bulging whorls on the spiral. The suture is milled, that is to say, the face of the whorls turned towards the spiral, which is somewhat depressed and slightly keeled, exhibits transverse ridges. In consequence of the twisting these ridges come to be disposed radially. The aperture is very large and long; the lip is hollowed out towards the suture, and bears in front of this hollowing a tooth directed outwards and towards the apex of the shell. Between this tooth and the excavation the margin of the aperture is slightly reflected inwards. The columella is prolonged into a very long rostrum which is straight throughout its entire length.

Colour.—Milky-white.

Operculum and animal unknown.

Dimensions.—Length 7·5 mm.; maximum diameter about 6 mm.

Observations.—I. In the specimens from deep-sea deposits (the only specimens known) the surface is smooth. Perhaps in the living specimens the surface may be reticulated as in *Peraclis reticulata*.

II. It is possible that the *Spirialis diversa* of Monterosato[1] was based on young specimens of *Peraclis bispinosa*. The above species has not yet been described, but Seguenza[2] notes in regard to fossil specimens that "*Spirialis diversa*" resembles "*Spirialis recurvirostra*" (*Peraclis reticulata*), and that it exhibits a toothed suture.

Challenger Specimens.—Deposit shells.

Station VIII., February 12, 1873; off Canary Islands; lat. 28° 3′ 15″ N., long. 17° 27′ 0″ W.; depth, 620 fathoms; bottom, volcanic mud.

Station 33, April 4, 1873; off Bermuda; lat. 32° 21′ 30″ N., long. 64° 35′ 55″ W.; depth, 435 fathoms; bottom, coral mud.

Station 75, July 2, 1873; off Fayal (Azores); lat. 38° 38′ 0″ N., long. 28° 28′ 30″ W.; depth, 450 fathoms; bottom, volcanic mud.

---

[1] Nuova rivista delle Conchiglie mediterranee, p. 50.

[2] Studii paleontologici sulla fauna malacologica dei sedimenti pliocenici depositati a grandi profondità, p. 30.

Station 76, July 3, 1873; off the Azores; lat. 38° 11′ N., long. 27° 9′ W.; depth, 900 fathoms; bottom, Pteropod ooze.

Station 78, July 10, 1873; off the Azores; lat. 37° 26′ N., long. 25° 13′ W.; depth, 1000 fathoms; bottom, volcanic mud.

Station 85, July 19, 1873; off Palma Island (Canaries); lat. 28° 42′ N., long. 18° 6′ W.; depth, 1125 fathoms; bottom, volcanic mud.

APPENDIX TO THE LIMACINIDÆ.

I. Gould has described,[1] under the name of "*Limacina* (?) *cucullata*," a Mollusc which he found to be different from the forms of *Limacina* previously described. For this he eventually proposed to erect the new genus *Agadina*.

The species and genus are, however, described and figured in a fashion so incomplete, and in addition characterised so insufficiently, that it is impossible to decide with any certainty as to their systematic position. One may, however, notice that according to Gould's figures the shell, which measures 6 mm. in diameter, exhibits a right-handed spiral which is not the case with any member of the Limacinidæ.

One must therefore entertain very grave doubts as to the position of this species. It seems to me most probable that it is a *Limacina antarctica* ill-drawn (*cf.* Gould's figure with fig. 4, Pl. II., after Hooker).

The specimen in question was obtained from the Antarctic Ocean (60° 0′ S., 106° 20′ E.). I have carefully sought among the Pteropods of the Challenger collection from that region, but have not been able to find anything corresponding to Gould's description.

A. and H. Adams have nevertheless retained[2] among the Limacinidæ the title *Agadina*; and in 1867 A. Adams described under this generic title two new species, but without any information as to the organisms.

In these, however, in contrast to the *Agadina* of Gould, the shell is perfectly left-handed, and the mouth does not in any way recall the bell-like form of *Limacina cucullata*. And furthermore the operculum of one of the forms is described (though without any notice of the direction of the coils) as multispiral. In this there is a resemblance to *Peraclis*, and there seems some reason therefore to regard the above types as true Limacinidæ.

I have found among the preparations of surface animals collected on the Challenger Expedition, which have been stained and mounted in balsam, one of the species described by A. Adams (*Agadina stimpsoni*), and another form of the same group, which is, however, quite distinct from either of the species above noted.

Having found several specimens of *Agadina stimpsoni* and of *Agadina*, n. sp., I have

---

[1] The Mollusca and Shells of the U.S. Exploring Expedition, p. 486, pl. ii. fig. 603.

[2] *Proc. Zool. Soc. Lond.*, 1867, p. 309.

sacrificed one of each in order to examine the animals. To do this the specimens had to be removed from the balsam, and the shell destroyed by acetic acid.

I was then able to recognise that the so-called Limacinidæ were only Gastropod larvæ.

If it be useful to communicate new truths, it is not less necessary to destroy old errors. I have for this reason devoted a few sentences to show that the types of *Agadina* (in the sense in which A. and H. Adams use the term) are not really Pteropods.

*1. *Agadina stimpsoni*, A. Adams (Pl. I. figs. 11–14).

> 1867. *Agadina stimpsoni*, A. Adams, Description of New Species of Shells from Japan, Proc. Zool. Soc. Lond., 1867, p. 309, pl. xix. fig. 23.

Shell smooth, discoidal, without spire; three and a half whorls gradually increasing, rolled up in the same plane; rounded oblique aperture, with slightly bell-shaped margins; deep umbilicus, with slightly marked rays.

Colour.—Yellowish-white.

Dimensions.—1 mm. in diameter.

Operculum.—Horny, circular, externally concave, multispiral, with four and a half whorls gradually increasing, left-handed, surface of insertion very large.

Animal bearing on its head a four-lobed velum; dorsal pallial aperture; thick columellar muscle; foot large and strong, bifid in front, with a long broad creeping surface, and bearing the operculum at the posterior end; no fins.

The small size of this species, and the manipulations which the specimen had to undergo (the action of chloroform to remove the balsam, and of acetic acid to dissolve the shell), after having been stained and mounted in balsam for twelve years, did not allow me to study its structure in any detail. But what has been elucidated is sufficient to enable one to decide the group of Mollusca to which this form belongs, and the stage of development arrived at.

Habitat.—Kino Osima (Japan), A. Adams.

Challenger Specimens.—Living.

Station 175, August 12, 1874; Fiji to Raine Island; lat. 19° 2' S., long. 177° 10' E.

Near Station 206, January 9, 1875; China Sea; about lat. 17° 54' N.; long. 117° 14' E.

Station 216A, February 16, 1875; North of New Guinea; lat. 2° 56' N., long. 134° 11' E.

2. *Agadina gouldi*, A. Adams.

> 1867. *Agadina gouldi*, A. Adams, Description of New Species of Shells from Japan, Proc. Zool. Soc. Lond., 1867, p. 309, pl. xix. fig. 22.

Shell smooth, helicoid, formed of three and a half bulging and rapidly ascending whorls; spire not projecting above the last turn; oblique aperture with margins slightly expanded; umbilicus very narrow.

Dimensions.—1·5 mm. in diameter.

Operculum and animal unknown, but almost certainly like those of the two other species here enumerated.

Habitat.—Kino Osima (Japan), A. Adams.

*3. *Agadina*, n. sp. (Pl. I. figs. 15, 16).

Shell smooth, globular; spire short, but projecting beyond the last whorl; three bulging whorls, overlapping, and somewhat obliquely twisted; aperture rounded, oblique, with margins slightly expanded; umbilicus almost suppressed, covered by the last turn, which exhibits a keeled projection over this spot.

Operculum horny, circular, multispiral, with four and a half whorls, gradually increasing in a left-handed spiral; the surface of insertion very large.

Animal.—Without fins, resembling that of *Agadina stimpsoni*, but with the lobes of the velum more pointed, and the foot more elongated anteriorly.

Challenger Specimens.—I. Living.

Station 175, August 12, 1874; Fiji to Raine Island; lat. 19° 2′ S., long. 177° 10′ E.

Station 216A, February 16, 1875; north of New Guinea; lat. 2° 56′ N., long. 134° 11′ E.

II. Deposit shells.

Station 120, September 9, 1873; off the coast of South America, between Pernambuco and Bahia; lat. 8° 37′ S., long. 34° 28′ W.; depth, 675 fathoms; bottom, red mud.

Since this form, like the two before it, is only the larval form of some Gastropod, there is no occasion to give it a specific title.

It is evident that these species cannot be ranked among the Pteropods. The absence of fins, the presence of a four-lobed velum when the shell has already three whorls on its spire, the presence of a foot with a creeping surface, are facts sufficient to demonstrate that we have here to deal with pelagic larvæ of streptoneural Gastropods.

This shows very distinctly the dangers of elaborating a zoological system without due regard to comparative anatomy.

Woodward's[1] statement that the true Limacinidæ may be distinguished by their left-handed twisting "from the fry of *Atlanta, Carinaria* and most other Gastropods" is thus quite inexact.

What enables one always to distinguish the Limacinidæ from the larvæ of Gastro-

[1] Manual of the Mollusca, 1856, p. 207.

pods, known by the title *Agadina*, even when the animals themselves are not known, is the horny, perfectly circular operculum of the latter (glassy in the Limacinidæ). In the operculum of *Agadina*, furthermore, the coils of the spire have a left-handed twist, and increase slowly, so that the nucleus of the spiral is much larger than in the Limacinidæ. The external surface is also concave; the aperture is obliquely rounded, with margins somewhat expanded, slightly thickened, and united, i.e., the lip and the columellar margin are continuous by means of a small callus on the latter, which is absent in the Limacinidæ.

But to what streptoneural Gastropods do these larval "*Agadina*" forms belong? The marine left-handed Gastropods are not, indeed, very numerous. But it must be remembered that some Gastropods, with right-handed spirals, have their initial portion or nucleus twisted to the left. This is not improbably the case with the larval forms in question, for there the left-handed twisting of the operculum in all likelihood corresponds to a right-handed twisting of the shell.

I. To the group "*Agadina*" I also refer *Atlanta rotundata*, d'Orbigny,[1] which Souleyet regarded as a variety of *Limacina lesueuri* (his *Spirialis ventricosa*). The shell is discoidal and flattened; the spire in no way projects beyond the last coil; the mouth is rounded, and broader than high, with slightly thickened margins. The operculum figured by d'Orbigny appears concentric, but as the objects are small and difficult to define, it seems to me more likely that the operculum is multispiral, as in the other forms of "*Agadina*."

D'Orbigny's specimens were obtained in the Pacific Ocean, 36° S., 38° W. This form has only been chronicled on one other occasion, by Marrat,[2] on a voyage from South America to Liverpool. His specimens are deposited in the Liverpool Museum.

II. In closing this appendix to the family Limacinidæ it is necessary to note that the "*Agadina*" forms are not the only left-handed larvæ of Gastropods which have been taken for Pteropods. The same is true of *Limacina turritelloides*, Boas,[3] the empty shells of which I found in the Challenger collection (Station 216A, north of New Guinea). By every one familiar with the classification of Gastropods, this form would be at once recognised as a young left-handed *Cerithium* (*Triforis*), nor have I any doubt that this *Limacina turritelloides* is identical with the form which Craven has described under the title *Sinusigera perversa*.[4] Like *Triforis*, this exhibited a multispiral operculum, with right-handed twisting. Craven has, in fact, subsequently acknowledged[5] that his *Sinusigera perversa* (from the Indian Ocean) is only a pullus of *Triforis*.

[1] *Voyage dans l'Amérique méridionale*, t. v. p. 175, pl. xii. figs. 20-24.
[2] On a collection of Pteropods and Heteropods, *Ann. and Mag. Nat. Hist.*, ser. 4, vol. ii. p. 229.
[3] *Spolia atlantica*, p. 49, pl. iii. fig. 35.
[4] *Monographie du genre Sinusigera*, *Ann. Soc. Malacol. Belg.*, t. xii. p. 112, pl. iii. fig. 4.
[5] *Note sur le genre Sinusigera*, *Ann. Soc. Malacol. Belg.*, t. xviii. p. xxvi.

Family II. CAVOLINIIDÆ.

1841. *Hyalidæ*, d'Orbigny, Mollusques de Cuba, t. i. p. 70.
1842. *Cavoliniidæ*, d'Orbigny, Paléontologie française, Terrains crétacés, t. ii. p. 4.
1842. *Cleodoridæ*, Gray, Synopsis of the Contents of the British Museum, p. 92.
1869. *Cliidæ*, Jeffreys, British Conchology, vol. v. p. 118 (non Woodward, 1856).
1875. *Orthocouques*, Fol, Sur le développement des Ptéropodes, Archives d. Zool. Expér., sér. 1,
      t. iv. p. 177.
   incl. *Cuvieridæ*, Gray, 1842 = *Tripteridæ*, Gray, 1850.

Characters.—Shell external, calcareous, inoperculated, bilaterally symmetrical, not rolled up in a spiral, but at its apex often dorsally recurved. Animal with its pallial cavity ventral, and its columellar muscle dorsal; the anus situated on the left.

Description.—The shell has a variable form, which may always be referred to a hollow cone, more or less modified, flattened dorso-ventrally or circular in section. The apex is quite straight, recurved or truncated; the mouth broad or narrow; with longitudinal or transverse ribs, &c. The initial portion of the shell is generally distinct from the rest, and represents the embryonic shell.

The animal may be entirely retracted within the shell. The form of the fins and of the posterior lobe of the foot varies considerably. The mouth, the lips, and the tentacles resemble those of the Limacinidæ (except *Peraclis*).

In regard to the classification, as in the Limacinidæ, we find a large number of genera established by too zealous conchologists for the reception of the species belonging to this family. Abstracting genera based on Tertiary fossils, we find seventeen different generic titles applied to living Cavoliniidæ. These are enumerated in alphabetical order:—

Archonta, Montfort, 1810.	*Hyalæa*, Lamarck, 1801.
Balantium, Benson, 1837.	*Hyalocylis*, Fol, 1875.
Carolina, Abildgaard, 1791 (non Bruguière, 1792).	*Orbignyia*, Adams, 1859.
	Pleuropus, Eschscholtz, 1825.
Cleodora, Péron and Lesueur, 1810.	*Rhoda*, Humphreys, 1797.
Clio, Linné, 1767 (non Müller, 1776).	*Styliola*, Lesueur, 1825.
Creseis, Rang, 1828.	*Tricla*, Oken, 1815 (non Retzius, 1788).
Cuvieria, Rang, 1827 (non Péron, 1807).	*Triptera*, Auctorum (non Quoy and Guimard, 1824).
Cuvierina, Bosc, 1886.	
Dinevia, Gray, 1842.	

Of these seventeen titles:—

1. Three alone ought to be preserved as applicable to well-established genera—

    (1) *Clio*; (2) *Cuvierina*; (3) *Cavolinia*.

2. Three designate well-marked subgeneric divisions of the genus *Clio*—

(1) *Creseis;* (2) *Hyalocylix;* (3) *Styliola.*

3. One represents the young state of some *Cavolinia: Pleuropus.*

4. Finally, the ten remaining titles may be preserved as synonyms of the three genera—

Balantium, *Cleodora,* } = *Clio.*		*Archonta,* *Diacria,* *Hyalæa,* *Orbignyia,* *Rheda,* *Tricla,* } = *Cavolinia.*
Cuvieria, *Triptera,* } = *Cuvierina.*		

For the distinctive characters of the three genera *Clio, Cuvierina,* and *Cavolinia,* I refer to the synoptic table of genera (p. 8).

Clio,[1] Linné.

1756. *Clio,* Browne, The Civil and Natural History of Jamaica, p. 386.
1767. *Clio,* Linné, Systema naturæ, ed. 12, t. 1, pt. 2, p. 1094 (non O. F. Müller, 1776).
1810. *Cleodora,* Péron and Lesueur, Histoire de la famille des Mollusques Ptéropodes, Ann. Mus. Hist. Nat. Paris, t. xv. p. 66.
1825. *Styliola,* Lesueur, MS., in de Blainville, Manuel de Malacologie, p. 655.
1828. *Creseis,* Rang, Notice sur quelques Mollusques nouveaux appartenant au genre Cleodora, et établissement et monographie du sous-genre Creseis, Ann. d. Sci. Nat., sér. 1, t. xiii, p. 302.
1837. *Balantium,* Benson, Notice on Balantium, a Genus of the Pteropodous Mollusca, Journ. Asiat. Soc. Bengal, vol. vi. p. 151.
1875. *Hyalocylix,* Fol, Sur le développement de Ptéropodes, Archives d. Zool. Expér., t. iv. p. 177.

To the Thecosomata which I have united in this genus several generic titles have been applied, as may be seen from the synonyms.

Besides these generic titles, we have to note a considerable number of specific designations, of which only a very small fraction can be retained as applicable to really existing species of the genus *Clio.*

After abstracting all the so-called forms of *Clio* which are really Gymnosomata (see the first part of this Report),[2] there remains the following formidable list of specific titles attributed to living species. A certain number of extant species are also

---

[1] Mythological name.
[2] Zool. Chall. Exped., part lviii. pp. 44, 45.

found in the most recent Tertiary deposits, and have received other titles in that connection.

Creseis acicula, Rang.	Cleodora lessonii, Rang.
Creseis acus, Eschscholtz.	Cleodora lobata, Sowerby.
Cleodora andreæ, Boas.	Cleodora martensii, Pfeffer.
Hyalæa australis, d'Orbigny.	Creseis monotis, Troschel.
Cleodora balantium, Rang.	Cleodora munda, Gould.
Balantium bicarinatum, Benson.	Cleodora obtusa, Quoy and Gaimard.
Cleodora brownii, de Blainville.	Cleodora occidentalis, Dall.
Creseis caligula, Eschscholtz.	Clio pellucidum, Gray.
Clio caudata, Linné.	Creseis phæostoma, Troschel.
Cleodora chaptalii, Souleyet.	Cleodora placida, Gould.
Cleodora chierchiæ, Boas.	Balantium politum, Craven, MS.
Creseis clava, Rang.	Cleodora pygmæa, Boas.
Creseis compressa, Eschscholtz.	Clio pyramidata, Linné.
Cleodora compressa, Souleyet.	Cleodora quadrispinosa, Rang.
Creseis conica, Eschscholtz.	Styliola recta, Lesueur.
Creseis conoidea, A. Costa.	Balantium recurrum, Benson.
Hyalæa corniformis, d'Orbigny.	Clio rugosum, Gray.
Creseis cornucopiæ, Eschscholtz.	Creseis rugulosa, Cantraine.
Cleodora curvata, Souleyet.	Creseis spinifera, Rang.
Hyalæa cuspidata, Bosc.	Creseis striata, Rang.
Clio depressa, Gray.	Creseis striata, Delle Chiaje.
Cleodora exacuta, Gould.	Cleodora subula, Quoy and Gaimard.
Cleodora falcata, Gould.	Cleodora sulcata, Pfeffer.
Cleodora falcata, Pfeffer.	Hyalæa tricuspidata, Bowdich.
Cleodora flexa, Pfeffer.	Cleodora trifilis, Troschel.
Cleodora inflata, Souleyet.	Creseis unguis, Eschscholtz.
Cleodora lamartinieri, Rang.	Creseis virgula, Rang.
Hyalæa lanceolata, Lesueur.	Styliola vitrea, Verrill.

Creseis zonata, Delle Chiaje.

These fifty-seven names may be classified as follows :—

1. One may be discarded as not referring to a Pteropod, viz., Creseis rugulosa, Cantraine,[1] which is really a Gastropod of the genus Cæcum.

2. One refers to the adult stage of another genus of Thecosomatous Pteropods, viz., Cleodora obtusa, Quoy and Gaimard, which is probably the same as Cuvierina columnella.

[1] Malacologie Méditerranéenne et littorale, Mém. Acad. d. Sci. Bruxelles, t. xiii. p. 32.

3. Seven names refer to young stages of the Thecosomata of the genus *Cavolinia*, viz. :—

Cleodora compressa, Souleyet = *Cavolinia trispinosa*.
Cleodora curvata, Souleyet = *Cavolinia uncinata*.
Clio depressa, Gray = *Cleodora compressa*, Souleyet = *Cavolinia trispinosa*.
Clio pellucidum, Gray = *Pleuropus pellucidus*, Eschscholtz = *Cavolinia inflexa*.
Balantium rugosum, Gray = *Hyalæa rugosa*, d'Orbigny = *Cavolinia gibbosa*.
Cleodora pygmæa, Boas = *Cavolinia quadridentata*.
Cleodora trifilis, Troschel = *Cavolinia*, sp.

The attentive study of the forms designated by the remaining specific titles shows that thirty-three of these ought to be discarded, and considered only as synonyms of the fourteen remaining species.

Creseis acus, Eschscholtz,	= *Creseis acicula*, Rang.
Balantium bicarinatum, Benson,	= *Cleodora balantium*, Rang.
Cleodora brownii, de Blainville,	= *Clio pyramidata*, Linné.
Creseis caligula, Eschscholtz,	= *Creseis virgula*, Rang.
Clio caudata, Linné,	= ? *Clio pyramidata*, Linné.
Creseis clava, Rang,	= *Creseis acicula*, Rang.
Creseis compressa, Eschscholtz,	= *Creseis striata*, Rang.
Creseis conoidea, O. Costa,	= *Creseis conica*, Eschscholtz.
Hyalæa corniformis, d'Orbigny,	= *Creseis virgula*, Rang.
Creseis cornucopiæ, Eschscholtz,	= *Creseis virgula*, Rang.
Cleodora exacuta, Gould,	= *Clio pyramidata*, Linné.
Cleodora falcata, Gould,	= *Creseis virgula*, Rang.
Cleodora falcata, Pfeffer,	= *Balantium politum*, Craven, MS.
Cleodora flexa, Pfeffer,	= *Creseis virgula*, Rang.
Cleodora inflata, Souleyet,	= *Cleodora balantium*, Rang (young).
Cleodora lamartinieri, Rang,	= *Clio pyramidata*, Linné.
Hyalæa lanceolata, Lesueur,	= *Clio pyramidata*, Linné.
Cleodora lessoni, Rang,	= *Hyalæa cuspidata*, Bosc.
Cleodora lobata, Sowerby,	= *Clio pyramidata*, Linné.
Cleodora martensii, Pfeffer,	= *Clio pyramidata*, Linné.
Creseis monotis, Troschel,	= *Creseis striata*, Rang.
Cleodora munda, Gould,	= *Creseis virgula*, Rang.
Creseis phærostoma, Troschel,	= *Creseis striata*, Rang.
Creseis placida, Gould,	= *Creseis virgula*, Rang.
Cleodora quadrispinosa, Rang,	= *Hyalæa cuspidata*, Bosc.
Styliola recta, Lesueur,	= *Cleodora subula*, Quoy and Gaimard.

Balantium recurvum, Benson, .	= *Cleodora balantium*, Rang.
Creseis spinifera, Rang, .	= *Cleodora subula*, Quoy and Gaimard.
Cleodora striata, Delle Chiaje, .	= *Creseis conica*, Eschscholtz.
Hyalæa tricuspidata, Bowdich,	= *Hyalæa cuspidata*, Bosc.
Creseis unguis, Eschscholtz, .	= *Creseis virgula*, Rang.
Styliola vitrea, Verrill, .	= *Creseis conica*, Eschscholtz.
Creseis zonata, Delle Chiaje, .	= *Creseis striata*, Rang.

The genus *Clio* thus includes fourteen real species, of which eleven are included among the spoils of the Challenger.

Creseis virgula, Rang.	*Cleodora sulcata*, Pfeffer.
Creseis acicula, Rang.	*Cleodora chaptalii*, Souleyet.
Creseis conica, Eschscholtz.	*Cleodora balantium*, Rang.
Cleodora chierchiæ, Boas.	*Balantium politum*, Craven, MS.
Creseis striata, Rang.	*Cleodora andreæ*, Boas.
Cleodora subula, Quoy and Gaimard.	*Clio pyramidata*, Linné.[1]
Hyalæa australis, d'Orbigny.	*Hyalæa cuspidata*, Bosc.

This genus is thus the richest of the Thecosomata, and indeed of the entire group of Pteropods. It is also that which exhibits the greatest variety of forms. It may well be asked whether all the species should be ranged in uniform succession in a homogeneous series, or whether further classification is not possible.

Rang, Philippi, Souleyet, Gould, Pfeffer, Boas, &c., are of opinion that all the species ought to bear the same generic title, and the anatomical researches of Souleyet have shown that the structure is nearly the same in the different forms examined.

On the other hand, the conchologists who are never afraid of a multiplicity of names generally divide into three or four genera the series of forms which we comprise under the title *Clio*.

But the attempt towards classification most worthy of attention is certainly that of Fol,[2] who bases his arrangement on the ontogenetic development of Mediterranean forms.

Fol divides the living species of *Clio* into the four following genera :—

Hyalocylis, Fol ; type *Creseis striata*, Rang.
Styliola, Lesueur ; type *Cleodora subula*, Quoy and Gaimard.
Cleodora, Péron and Lesueur ; type *Clio pyramidata*, Linné.
Creseis, Rang ; type *Creseis acicula*, Rang.

[1] *Cleodora occidentalis*, Dall, appears to be nearly related to *Clio pyramidata*. From an unpublished figure which Mr. Dall has been good enough to send me, it possesses between each fin and the posterior lobe of the foot a conical tentacle, which is not found in *Clio pyramidata* ; but as I have not been able to examine specimens of "*Cleodora occidentalis*" I cannot give a decided opinion on this question.

[2] Sur le développement des Mollusques Ptéropodes, *Archives d. Zool. Expér.*, sér. 1, t. iv. pp. 177, 178.

This classification has been adopted in Fischer's[1] Manual of Conchology, and in part also in that of Tryon.[2]

It is however necessary to remark that Fol distributes these four genera in a manner altogether peculiar, separating most of the species from the group at present under discussion. Thus in our family of Cavoliniidæ (his Orthoconques) he distinguishes, abstracting the genus *Cuvierina*, three subgroups,—Hyaléacées, Styliolacées, and Creseidées. *Hyalocylix* is referred to the first, along with the *Cavolinia* forms. *Styliola* and *Cleodora* are included in the Styliolacées. *Creseis* is placed among the Creseidées.

I cannot admit that these different forms are separated in this way, or in any way equally deep and trenchant.

Fol's distinctions, which are based exclusively on embryonic characters, form an insufficient foundation for the classification of the adults. For it must be noted that the forms in question are pelagic larvæ in which, as Fritz Müller long ago remarked,[3] true genetic characters are mingled with those which are merely adaptive, and provisionally acquired for the free, independent, pelagic larval life.

On the other hand, the different forms of *Clio* exhibit a type of structure which unites them in one and distinguishes them from the other Thecosomata, and especially from the "Hyaléacées" of Fol (among which the "*Cleodora*" forms are certainly more nearly allied than the *Hyalocylix*).

Nevertheless, it cannot be denied that among the species which I have united within the genus *Clio* there are several distinct types, separated not only by the embryonic differences on which Fol's classification is based, but also by certain structural features, which will be discussed in the anatomical portion of this Report. Yet, at the same time, I maintain that these distinctions are not of sufficient import to justify the establishment of separate genera.

I therefore propose to consider the different types above referred to as subgenera of *Clio*, and since these subgeneric divisions correspond approximately to the genera recognised by Fol, I shall preserve as designations of these subgeneric sections the four titles which Fol has used, viz., *Creseis*, *Hyalocylix*, *Styliola*, *Clio* (= *Cleodora*). As to *Balantium*, I do not find that it exhibits any characters which would warrant its being separated from the subgenus *Clio* (= *Cleodora*), s. str.

Within these four sections, the species known to be genuine are distributed in the following fashion :—

1. Subgenus *Creseis*.

Creseis virgula, Rang.	*Creseis acicula*, Rang.
Creseis conica, Eschscholtz.	*Cleodora chierchiæ*, Boas.

[1] Manuel de Conchyliologie, pp. 435–437.
[2] Facts and Arguments for Darwin, p. 114.
[3] Structural and Systematic Conchology, vol. ii. pp. 90, 91.

2. Subgenus *Hyalocylix.*

Creseis striata, Rang.

3. Subgenus *Styliola.*

Cleodora subula, Quoy and Gaimard.

4. Subgenus *Clio, s. str.*

Balantium politum, Craven, MS.	*Hylæa australis*, d'Orbigny.
Cleodora andreæ, Boas.	*Cleodora sulcata*, Pfeffer.
Cleodora balantium, Rang.	*Clio pyramidata*, Linné.

Hyalæa cuspidata, Boas.

The four sections may be distinguished as follows :—

    I. Shell without lateral keels.
        1. Shell without dorsal longitudinal groove.
            A. Shell with a circular section,   1. *Creseis.*
            B. Shell flattened dorso-ventrally, with transverse grooves over
                its entire length,   2. *Hyalocylix.*
        2. Shell with a dorsal longitudinal groove,   3. *Styliola.*
    II. Shell with lateral keels,   4. *Clio*, including *Balantium.*

Subgenus *Creseis*,[1] Rang (*s. str.*).

1828. *Creseis*, Rang, Notice sur quelques Mollusques nouveaux appartenant au genre Cleodora, &c., Ann. d. Sci. Nat., sér. 1, t. xiii. p. 302.
Styliola, Auctorum, *non* Lesueur.

Characters and Description.—Shell elongated, of conical form, with a circular transverse section, with a smooth surface on its initial portion at least, with the embryonic portion not marked off by a deep constriction, with a rounded apex.

Animal with the left tentacle very rudimentary, the fin exhibiting a small narrow projecting lobe on the proximal half of the dorsal (anterior) margin, the opening of the mantle as broad as that of the shell.

[1] Mythological name.

KEY TO THE SPECIES.

I. Shell entirely destitute of transverse grooves.
  1. Shell at its initial portion of a dark brown colour.
    A. Shell with a very marked and somewhat abrupt dorsal curve, and with
        the transverse diameter increasing rapidly at the point of curvature, 1. *Clio virgula.*
    B. Shell with a slight curvature, and with the transverse diameter
        increasing uniformly, ... 2. *Clio conica.*
  2. Shell straight, much elongated, with the initial extremity of a whitish
    colour, ... 3. *Clio acicula.*
II. Shell with transverse grooves all over its broader portion, . . . 4. *Clio chierchiæ.*

*1. *Clio* (*Creseis*) *virgula* (Rang).

    1828. *Creseis virgula*, Rang, Notice sur quelques Mollusques nouveaux du genre Cleodora, &c.,
        Ann. d. Sci. Nat., sér. 1, t. xiii. p. 316, pl. xvii. fig. 2.
    1829. *Creseis unguis*, Eschscholtz, Zoologischer Atlas, Heft iii. p. 17, pl. xv. fig. 4.
    1829. *Creseis cornucopiæ*, Eschscholtz, *Ibid.*, p. 17, pl. xv. fig. 5.
    1829. *Creseis caligula*, Eschscholtz, *Ibid.*, p. 18, pl. xv. fig. 6.
    1836. *Hyalæa corniformis*, d'Orbigny, Voyage dans l'Amérique méridionale, t. v. p. 120, pl. viii.
        figs. 20–23.
    1850. *Styliola virgula*, Gray, Catalogue of the Mollusca in the Collection of the British
        Museum, pt. ii., Pteropoda, p. 17.
    1850. *Styliola corniformis*, Gray, *Ibid.*, p. 18.
    1852. *Cleodora virgula*, Souleyet, Voyage de la Bonite, Zoologie, t. ii. p. 196, pl. viii.
        figs. 16–25.
    1852. *Cleodora munda*, Gould, The Mollusca and Shells of the U.S. Exploring Expedition,
        p. 489, pl. li. fig. 607.
    1852. *Cleodora placida*, Gould, *Ibid.*, p. 489, pl. li. fig. 606.
    1852. *Cleodora falcata*, Gould, *Ibid.*, p. 490, pl. li. fig. 608.
    1879. *Cleodora fæxa*, Pfeffer, Bericht über die von S. M. Schiff "Gazelle" und Dr. Jagor
        gesammelten Pteropoden, Monatsber. d. k. preuss. Akad. d. Wiss. Berlin,
        1879, p. 241, figs. 15, 16.

For description and figures I refer to Souleyet, *loc. cit.* (see the synonymy above).

Habitat.—Atlantic Ocean, from 41° 25′ N. (Verrill) to 35° 10′ S. (Boas), both towards the new and the old world.

Indian Ocean; from the Gulf of Bengal to 29° S., especially towards the west (south-east of Arabia, Blanford) to 65° E.

Pacific Ocean: eastern portion, from 35° N., about the Bay of Yedo ("Galathea" Expedition), to 32° S., New South Wales (British Museum), China Sea ("Galathea" Expedition), Coral Sea (Pfeffer); central portion, from 24° N. ("Vettor Pisani" Expedition) to 30° S. (Knocker); North-east Pacific (Gould as "*Cleodora falcata*"); South-east Pacific, Juan Fernandez Island (d'Orbigny).

Challenger Specimens.—I. Living specimens.

Station 106, August 25, 1873; St. Vincent (Cape Verde) to St. Paul's Rock; lat. 1° 47′ N., long. 24° 26′ W.

Between Stations 162 and 163, April 3, 1874; Melbourne to Sydney, lat. 38° 7′ S., long. 149° 18′ E.

Station 164A, June 13, 1874; off Sydney; lat. 34° 9′ S., long. 151° 55′ E.

Station 181, August 25, 1874; Fiji to Raine Island; lat. 13° 50′ S., long. 151° 49′ E.

Station 209, January 22, 1875; Manila to Samboangan; lat. 10° 14′ N., long. 123° 54′ E.

On February 6, 1875; at Samboangan; lat. 6° 40′ N., long. 122° 57′ E.

Station 216A, February 16, 1875; north of New Guinea; lat. 2° 56′ N., long. 134° 11′ E.

Between Stations 229 and 230, April 3, 1875; Admiralty Islands to Yokohama; lat. 24° 49′ N., long. 138° 34′ E.

Station 230, April 5, 1875; Admiralty Islands to Yokohama; lat. 26° 29′ N., long. 137° 57′ E.

Between Stations 264 and 265, August 24, 1875; Sandwich Islands to Tahiti; lat. 13° 15′ N., long. 152° 2′ W.

Station 299, December 14, 1875; Valparaiso to Gulf of Penas; lat. 33° 31′ S., long. 74° 43′ W.

Station 348, April 9, 1876; Ascension Island to St. Vincent (Cape Verde); lat. 3° 10′ N., long. 14° 51′ W.

On April 26, 1876; off St. Vincent; lat. 16° 49′ N., long. 25° 14′ W.

On April 29, 1876; off St. Vincent; lat. 18° 8′ N., long. 30° 5′ W.

II. Deposit shells.

Station 23, March 15, 1873; off Sombrero Island; lat. 18° 24′ N., long. 63° 28′ W.; depth, 450 fathoms; bottom, Pteropod ooze.

Station 24, March 25, 1873; off Culebra Island; lat. 18° 38′ 30″ N., long. 65° 5′ 30″ W.; depth, 390 fathoms; bottom, Pteropod ooze.

Station 33, April 4, 1873; off Bermuda; lat. 32° 21′ 30″ N., long. 64° 35′ 55″ W.; depth, 435 fathoms; bottom, coral mud.

Station 120, September 9, 1873; off the coast of South America, between Pernambuco and Bahia; lat. 8° 37′ S., long. 34° 28′ W.; depth, 675 fathoms; bottom, red mud.

Station 185, August 31, 1874; off Raine Island; lat. 11° 35′ 25″ S., long. 144° 2′ 0″ E.; depth, 135 fathoms; bottom, coral sand.

Station 219, March 10, 1875; Admiralty Islands to Yokohama; lat. 1° 54′ 0″ S., long. 146° 39′ 40″ E.; depth, 150 fathoms; bottom, coral mud.

*2. *Clio (Creseis) conica* (Eschscholtz) (Pl. II. figs. 1, 2).

1829. *Creseis conica*, Eschscholtz, Zoologischer Atlas, Heft iii. p. 17, pl. xv. fig. 3.

1830. *Creseis striata*, Delle Chiaje, Memorie sulla storia e notomia degli animali senza vertebre, pl. lxxxii. fig. 12.

1869. *Creseis conica*, A. Costa, Pteropodi del golfo di Napoli, Rendiconto d. reale Accad. d. Sci. Napoli, 1869, p. 58.

1872. (?) *Styliola vitrea*, Verrill, Recent Additions to the Molluscan Fauna of New England and the adjacent waters, &c., Amer. Journ. Sci. and Arts, vol. iii. p. 284, pl. vi. fig. 7.

1873. *Creseis conoidea*, A. Costa, Pteropodi della Fauna del Regno di Napoli, p. 17, pl. iv. fig. 6.

Characters and Description.—*Shell* conical, moderately elongated; smooth over its entire surface; a very slight and regular dorsal curvature; the transverse diameter increasing gently and uniformly; the posterior extremity of a dark brown colour; the embryonic portion separated by a well-marked constriction, and thinning off towards the somewhat slender apex (Pl. II. fig. 2).

Animal like that of *Clio (Creseis) virgula*, but distinguished at first sight by this marked feature that the mass formed by the stomach and liver is situated much further forward than in the above species. For while in *Clio virgula* the broad œsophagus is very long, and the mass in question removed from the posterior extremity of the shield (pallial gland) by more than the length of the latter, in *Clio conica* it is situated immediately behind the shield. With this difference there is obviously correlated the abrupt and precocious enlargement of the shell in *Clio virgula*, and the gentle uniform increase in *Clio conica*.

Observations.—I. There can be no doubt in regard to the species figured by Eschscholtz. It is not *Clio (Creseis) acicula*, since it is much too short in proportion, and has its posterior extremity of a dark brown colour. It is not *Clio (Creseis) virgula*, since it exhibits neither the abrupt curvature nor the precocious enlargement of diameter exhibited by that form, and since the visceral mass is situated anteriorly. Neither is it *Clio (Styliola) subula*, although Gray[1] and Souleyet[2] so regard it. The absence of a dorsal groove, the colour of the posterior extremity, and the shortness of the posterior lobe of the foot are enough to show that it is not.

The "*Creseis conica*" of Eschscholtz is in fact the species which one finds at Naples, and in all probability that which Delle Chiaje noted under the name of "*Creseis striata*."

A. Costa, thinking he had discovered a new species, described this form as *Creseis conica*, ignoring the fact that this title had been already used by Eschscholtz. Becoming aware of this, but failing to recognise the identity of the two forms, he changed the name *conica* to *conoidea*.

[1] Catalogue of the Mollusca in the Collection of the British Museum, pt. ii., Pteropoda, p. 17.

[2] Histoire naturelle des Mollusques Ptéropodes, p. 56.

II. The figure given by Eschscholtz has been referred by Gray and by Souleyet (not without hesitation) to *Clio subula*; I have indicated above that this identification is impossible.

On the other hand Boas, who is of opinion [1] that *Clio virgula* and *Clio acicula* should be united, figures [2] under the title "*Cleodora acicula*" a specimen which undoubtedly belongs to the species under discussion. At the same time he designates as "*Cleodora acicula*" [3] the specimens of the "Vettor Pisani" Expedition, which also resemble *Clio conica*. The latter is distinguished from *Clio acicula* not only in the characters of the shell noted above, but also in the conformation of the liver, which agrees with what is found in *Clio virgula*. *Clio conica* is beyond dispute more nearly allied to *Clio virgula* than to *Clio acicula*.

Dimensions.—Besides being distinguished by certain characters of the shell and of the animal, *Clio conica* is also marked by its size, which never exceeds 7 mm.

Habitat.—Atlantic Ocean : coast of Brazil (Eschscholtz) ; coasts of North America (if, as I believe, *Styliola vitrea* = *Clio conica*).

Mediterranean : Naples.

Pacific Ocean : eastern portion, 0° N., 84° 40′ W. ("Vettor Pisani" Expedition).

Challenger Specimens.—Deposit shells.

Station 219, March 10, 1875 ; Admiralty Islands to Yokohama ; lat. 1° 54′ 0″ S., long. 146° 39′ 40″ E. ; depth, 150 fathoms ; bottom, coral mud.

*3. *Clio (Creseis) acicula* (Rang).

1828. *Creseis acicula*, Rang, Notice sur quelques Mollusques nouveaux du genre Cleodora, &c., Ann. d. Sci. Nat., sér. 1, t. xiii. p. 318, pl. xvii. fig. 6.

1828. *Creseis clava*, Rang, *Ibid.*, p. 317, pl. xvii. fig. 5.

1829. *Creseis acus*, Eschscholtz, Zoologischer Atlas, Heft iii. p. 17, pl. xv. fig. 2.

1836. *Hyalea aciculata*, d'Orbigny, Voyage dans l'Amérique méridionale, t. v. p. 123, pl. viii. figs. 29–31.

1850. *Styliola recta*, Gray, Catalogue of the Mollusca in the Collection of the British Museum, pt. ii., Pteropoda, p. 18.

1852. *Cleodora acicula*, Souleyet, Voyage de la Bonite, Zoologie, t. ii. p. 194, pl. viii. figs. 10–17.

For description and figures, see Souleyet, *loc. cit.* (in the above list of synonyms).

Habitat.—Atlantic Ocean, from 48° N. to the Cape of Good Hope (Pfeffer), and to 40° S. (Knocker). Mediterranean : Naples, &c. Indian Ocean : from the Gulf of Bengal to 29° S. (Boas) ; from Zanzibar (Pfeffer) to near Australia (95° E.).

Pacific Ocean : West, China Sea (Boas) ; Central Pacific, from 10° N. (Knocker) to 23° S. (Pfeffer), and towards 153° W. ; Eastern Pacific towards the equator, 88° W. ("Vettor Pisani" Expedition).

[1] Spolia atlantica, p. 202.　　　[2] *Ibid.*, pl. vi. fig. 94.　　　[3] *Ibid.*, p. 61.

Challenger Specimens.—I. Living specimens.

Station VIIF., February 2, 1873; off Madeira; lat. 32° 27' 0" N., long. 16° 40' 30" W.

Station 62, June 18, 1873; Bermuda to Azores; lat. 35° 7' N., long. 52° 32' W.

Station 63, June 19, 1873; Bermuda to Azores; lat. 35° 29' N., long. 50° 53' W.

Station 81, July 13, 1873; Azores to Madeira; lat. 34° 11' N., long. 19° 52' W.

Station 164A, June 13, 1874; off Sydney; lat. 34° 9' S., long. 151° 55' E.

Station 175, August 12, 1874; Fiji to Raine Island; lat. 19° 2' S., long. 177° 10' E.

Station 181, August 25, 1874; Fiji to Raine Island; lat. 13° 50' S., long. 151° 49' E.

Near Station 190, September 13, 1874; south of the Arrou Islands; lat. 8° 18' S., long. 135° 7' E.

Station 200, October 23, 1874; Amboina to Samboangan; lat. 6° 47' N., long. 122° 28' E.

Station 201, October 26, 1874; Samboangan to Manila; lat. 7° 3' N., long. 121° 48' E.

Station 209, January 22, 1875; Manila to Samboangan; lat. 10° 14' N., long. 123° 54' E.

On February 5, 1875; at Samboangan.

On February 6, 1875; at Samboangan; lat. 6° 40' N., long. 122° 57' E.

Station 216A, February 16, 1875; north of New Guinea; lat. 2° 56' N., long. 134° 11' E.

Station 237, June 17, 1875; Yokohama to Sandwich Islands; lat. 34° 37' N., long. 140° 32' E.

Station 256, July 21, 1875; Yokohama to Sandwich Islands; lat. 30° 22' N., long. 154° 56' W.

August—September, 1875; Sandwich to Tahiti.

Between Stations 292 and 293, October 31, 1875; Tahiti to Valparaiso, lat. 38° 50' S., long. 108° 6' W.

Station 323, February 28, 1876; Falkland Islands to Rio de la Plata; lat. 35° 39' S., long. 50° 47' W.

Station 326, March 3, 1876; Rio de Janeiro to Tristan da Cunha; lat. 37° 3' S., long. 44° 17' W.

Station 327, March 4, 1876; Rio de Janeiro to Tristan da Cunha; lat. 36° 48' S., long. 42° 45' W.

Station 339, March 23, 1876; Tristan da Cunha to Ascension Island; lat. 17° 26' S., long. 13° 52' W.

Station 349, April 10, 1876; Ascension Island to St. Vincent (Cape Verde); lat. 5° 28' N., long. 14° 38' W.

On April 26, 1876; off St. Vincent; lat. 16° 49' N., long. 25° 14' W.

On April 29, 1876; off St. Vincent; lat. 18° 9' N., long. 30° 5' W.

Station 353, May 3, 1876; St. Vincent to Azores; lat. 26° 21' N., long. 33° 37' W.

II. Deposit shells.

Station 23, March 15, 1873 ; off Sombrero Island ; lat. 18° 24′ N., long. 63° 28′ W.; depth, 450 fathoms ; bottom, Pteropod ooze.

Station 24, March 25, 1873 ; off Culebra Island ; lat. 18° 38′ 30″ N., long. 65° 5′ 30″ W.; depth, 390 fathoms ; bottom, Pteropod ooze.

Station 33, April 4, 1873 ; off Bermuda ; lat. 32° 21′ 30″ N., long. 64° 35′ 55″ W.; depth, 435 fathoms ; bottom, coral mud.

Station 33c, April 22, 1873 ; off Bermuda ; lat. 32° 15′ N., long. 65° 8′ W.; depth, 1950 fathoms ; bottom, Globigerina ooze.

Station 85, July 19, 1873 ; off Palma Island (Canaries); lat. 28° 42′ N., long. 18° 6′ W.; depth, 1125 fathoms ; bottom, volcanic mud.

Station 120, September 9, 1873 ; off the coast of South America, between Pernambuco and Bahia ; lat. 8° 37′ S., long. 34° 28′ W.; depth, 675 fathoms ; bottom, red mud.

Station 122, September 10, 1873 ; off the coast of South America, between Pernambuco and Bahia ; lat. 9° 5′ S., long. 34° 50′ W.; depth, 350 fathoms ; bottom, red mud.

Station 185, August 31, 1874 ; off Raine Island ; lat. 11° 35′ 25″ S., long. 144° 2′ 0″ E.; depth, 135 fathoms ; bottom, coral sand.

Station 219, March 10, 1875 ; Admiralty Islands to Yokohama ; lat. 1° 54′ 0″ S., long. 146° 39′ 40″ E.; depth, 150 fathoms ; bottom, coral mud.

NOTE.

According to Boas, the three preceding species are really identical. Little desirous as I am to multiply the number of species, I cannot admit the accuracy of this identification.

Clio acicula is distinguished from the two other species, not only by some characters of the shell (posterior portion whitish, opaque, instead of being transparent and dark brown), but also by some structural features, and especially by the nature of the liver, which is represented by a much reduced mass of acini, while the pyloric cæcum attains very conspicuous development.

It must be allowed that the other two species (*Clio virgula* and *Clio acicula*) are nearer neighbours, but the diagnostic characters which have been noted above make a union of the two species impossible.

4. *Clio (Creseis) chierchiæ* (Boas).

1886. *Cleodora chierchiæ*, Boas, Spolia atlantica, p. 62, pl. iii. fig. 39***.

Characters and Description.—This minute species (2·5 mm. in length) is very distinctly characterised and is readily distinguished from all the other members of the group by the fact that the shell, over about two-thirds of its length, is covered with transverse grooves, which are closely approximated and equidistant like those of *Clio striata*. This cannot be regarded as teratological, for this species has been collected in different localities and in great abundance. Nor is it a young stage, for none of the observed specimens exceeded the size indicated. *Clio chierchiæ* differs notably from *Clio striata* in the absence of curvature on the shell, by the form of the embryonic shell, and by the form of the fins.

Habitat.—Different localities near Panama ("Vettor Pisani" Expedition).

Subgenus *Hyalocylix*,[1] Fol.

1875. *Hyalocylix*, Fol, Sur le développement des Ptéropodes, Archives d. Zool Expér., sér. 1, t. iv. p. 177.
   Creseis (*pars*), Rang.
   Styliola (*pars*) auctorum (non Lesueur).
   Cleodora (*pars*), Souleyet, Boas, &c.

Characters and Description.—Shell conical, slightly compressed dorso-ventrally (oval transverse section); the apex recurved dorsally; the surface marked with transverse grooves from the well-marked constriction defining the embryonic shell on to the aperture.

The animal has a conspicuous left tentacle; the fin has a marginal non-muscular area, situated towards the dorso-lateral corner; the posterior lobe of the foot is extremely short; the aperture of the mantle as large as that of the shell.

This "subgenus" includes only a single species.

*5. *Clio* (*Hyalocylix*) *striata* (Rang) (Pl. II. fig. 3).

1828. *Creseis striata*, Rang, Notice sur quelques Mollusques appartenant au genre Cleodora, &c., Ann. d. Sci. Nat., sér. 1, t. xiii. p. 315, pl. xv. fig. 7.
1829. *Creseis compressa*, Eschscholtz, Zoologischer Atlas, Heft iii. p. 17, pl. xv. fig. 7.
1830. *Creseis sonata*, Delle Chiaje, Memorie sulla storia e notomia degli animali senza vertebre, pl. lxxxii. fig. 9.
1850. *Styliola striata*, Gray, Catalogue of the Mollusca in the Collection of the British Museum, pt. ii., Pteropoda, p. 18.
1854. *Creseis phantoma*, Troschel, Beiträge zur Kenntniss der Pteropoden, Archiv f. Naturgesch., 1854, p. 206, pl. viii. figs. 5–7.

For description and figures, I refer to Souleyet, Voyage de la Bonite, Zoologie, t. ii. p. 191, pl. viii. figs. 1–4.

Observations.—I. In the preserved specimens the embryonic shell is almost always deciduous, so that this portion is hardly known. Fol alone[2] has figured it from young specimens. Having observed it on the living adults, I am able to give a more definite

---

[1] From ὕαλος, glassy, αὐλός, cup.
[2] Sur le développement des Ptéropodes, Archives d. Zool. Expér., sér. 1, t. iv. figs. 2, 4.

representation (Pl. II. fig. 3). This embryonic portion has a rounded apex, it is distinctly expanded, and separated by a well-marked constriction from the rest of the shell. It seems most closely to resemble that of *Clio australis*.

II. Troschel has figured,[1] under the name of *Creseis monotis*, a small Thecosomatous form "without shell." This seems to me to be only a bad representation of a *Clio striata*. I have often observed living specimens of this species which had lost their shell.

III. The name "*Creseis fasciata*," Delle Chiaje, which is cited by several authors, is the Italian title given to this form by Delle Chiaje. The Latin designation, which the same authority uses, is *Creseis zonata* (see the synonyms above).

Habitat.—Atlantic Ocean: from 36° 30′ N. to 40° S., especially towards the Old World. Mediterranean, on the coasts of Europe and Africa.

Indian Ocean: from the Gulf of Bengal to 25° S. (Boas). Red Sea (Issel).

Pacific Ocean: China Sea (Boas); New South Wales (British Museum); Equatorial Pacific, 147° 48′ W. (Knocker); Chili ("Vettor Pisani" Expedition).

Challenger Specimens.—I. Living specimens.

Station 175, August 12, 1874; Fiji to Raine Island; lat. 19° 2′ S., long. 177° 10′ E.

Station 181, August 25, 1874; Fiji to Raine Island; lat. 13° 50′ S., long. 151° 49′ E.

Station 200, October 23, 1874; Amboina to Samboangan; lat. 6° 47′ N., long. 122° 28′ E.

Station 201, October 26, 1874; Samboangan to Manila; lat. 7° 3′ N., long. 121° 48′ E.

Station 230, April 5, 1875; Admiralty Islands to Yokohama; lat. 26° 29′ N., long. 137° 57′ E.

Between Stations 247 and 248, July 4, 1875; Yokohama to Sandwich Islands; lat. 36° 42′ N., long. 179° 50′ W.

Station 254, July 17, 1875; Yokohama to Sandwich Islands; lat. 35° 13′ N., long. 154° 43′ W.

Station 282, October 7, 1875; Tahiti to Valparaiso; lat. 23° 46′ S., long. 149° 59′ W.

Station 337, March 19, 1876; Tristan da Cunha to Ascension Island; lat. 24° 38′ S., long. 13° 36′ W.

On May 12, 1876; off the Azores; lat. 42° 52′ N., long. 28° 54′ W.

II. Deposit shells.

Station 24, March 25, 1873: off Culebra Island; lat. 18° 38′ 30″ N., long. 65° 5′ 30″ W.; depth, 390 fathoms; bottom, Pteropod ooze.

Station 33, April 4, 1873; off Bermuda; lat. 32° 21′ 30″ N., long. 64° 35′ 55″ W.; depth, 435 fathoms; bottom, coral mud.

---

[1] Beiträge zur Kenntniss der Pteropoden, *Archiv f. Naturgesch.*, 1854, Bd. i. p. 288, pl. viii. figs. 8, 9.

Station 85, July 19, 1873 ; off Palma Island (Canaries); lat. 28° 42′ N., long. 18° 6′ W.; depth, 1125 fathoms; bottom, volcanic mud.

Station 120, September 9, 1873 ; off the coast of South America, between Pernambuco and Bahia; lat. 8° 37′ S., long. 34° 28′ W.; depth, 675 fathoms; bottom, red mud.

Station 185, August 31, 1874 ; off Raine Island ; lat. 11° 35′ 25″ S., long. 144° 2′ 0″ E.; depth, 135 fathoms; bottom, coral sand.

Station 219, March 10, 1875 ; Admiralty Islands to Yokohama ; lat. 1° 54′ 0″ S., long. 146° 39′ 40″ E.; depth, 150 fathoms ; bottom, coral mud.

Subgenus *Styliola*,[1] Lesueur.

1825. *Styliola*, Lesueur, in de Blainville, Manuel de Malacologie, p. 655.

Characters and Description.—*Shell* conical, straight, considerably elongated ; the surface smooth, with a dorsal groove not parallel to the axis of the shell, but slightly oblique, turning from left to right, with only the anterior extremity (which ends in a rostrum) in the median line ; the embryonic portion only vaguely separated from the rest of the shell, and ending in a pointed apex.

The animal with the two tentacles distinctly visible ; the transparent, non-muscular, marginal area of the fin situated towards the middle of the lateral margin ; the posterior lobe of the foot is long.

Observation.—The name *Styliola*, first used in 1825 by Lesueur in the Manuel de Malacologie of de Blainville, has been regarded by English and American conchologists as synonymous with the later title, *Creseis*, Rang. This opinion is based, however, on a misinterpretation of the typical species, *Styliola recta*, Lesueur (*sine descriptione*), which has been taken by these authors for *Clio acicula*. But the descriptions given of the genus *Styliola* enable one to infer that *Styliola recta* is really *Clio subula*, and not *Clio acicula*.

The difference between *Styliola* (in the usage of Lesueur) and *Creseis* (s. str.) may be gathered from a comparison of the two descriptions given above. The structural features, as will be shown in the Anatomical Report, go to show that *Styliola* is much more nearly related to *Clio* (s. str.) than to *Creseis*, and on the contrary that the forms included under the latter designation have retained some more archaic characters of the Limacinidæ.

This subgeneric section includes only a single species.

[1] Diminutive of στύλος, column.

*6. *Clio (Styliola) subula* (Quoy and Gaimard).

1825. *Styliola recta*, Lesueur, in de Blainville, Manuel de Malacologie, p. 655 (*nomen tantum*).

1827. *Cleodora subula*, Quoy et Gaimard, Observations zoologiques faites à bord de l'Astrolabe, &c., Ann. d. Sci. Nat., sér. 1, t. x. p. 233, pl. viii. figs. 1–3.

1825. *Cuvieria acicula*, Rang, Notice sur quelques Mollusques nouveaux du genre Cleodora, &c., Ann. d. Sci. Nat., sér. 1, t. xiii. p. 313, pl. xvii. fig. 1.

1828. *Creseis subula*, Rang, *Ibid.*, pl. xviii. fig. 1.

1836. *Hyalea subula*, d'Orbigny, Voyage dans l'Amérique méridionale, t. v. p. 119, pl. viii. figs. 15–19.

1850. *Styliola subula*, Gray, Catalogue of the Mollusca in the Collection of the British Museum, pt. ii., Pteropoda, p. 17.

1852. *Cleodora subulata*, Souleyet, Voyage de la Bonite, Zoologie, t. ii. p. 191, pl. viii. figs. 5–9.

For description and figures, see Souleyet (*loc. cit. supra*).

Habitat.—Atlantic Ocean ; from 41° N. to 25° S. (Pfeffer), towards the coasts both of the Old World and of America (Antilles, &c.); Mediterranean, Naples, &c. The empty shells have been dredged at numerous localities in the Mediterranean (Tunis, &c.).

Indian Ocean ; southern portion, from 17° 20′ S. to 38° 28′ S. (Boas); on the coasts of Africa (Zanzibar, Port Natal), and towards Australia.

Pacific Ocean ; eastern portion, Malay Archipelago (Amboina, New Guinea), east coast of Australia to 32° S. (Pfeffer, Angas); western portion, from 23° N. to 35° S.

Boas has remarked[1] the absence of this species below the equator, and notes the same in regard to *Cuvolinia gibbosa*. This has been noticed in regard to other Molluscs, as I have remarked for instance in regard to *Lesueuria rubra*.[2] It is, however, less explicable in the case of Molluscs which can shift their ground so readily as the Pteropods. But as a matter of fact, *Clio subula* is found in the Pacific Ocean both to the south and to the north of the equator.

Challenger Specimens.—I. Living specimens.

Near Station 160, March 15, 1874; off Melbourne ; lat. 39° 45′ S., long. 140° 40′ E.

Near Station 160, March 16, 1874; off Melbourne ; lat. 39° 22′ S., long. 142° 27′ E.

Station 164A, June 13, 1874 ; off Sydney ; lat. 34° 9′ S., long. 151° 55′ E.

Station 175, August 12, 1874 ; Fiji to Raine Island ; lat. 19° 2′ S., long. 177° 10′ E.

Station 181, August 25, 1874 ; Fiji to Raine Island ; lat. 13° 50′ S., long. 151° 49′ E.

Near Station 230, April 3, 1875 ; Admiralty Islands to Yokohama; lat. 26° 29′ N., long. 138° 34′ E.

On April 4, 1875 ; Admiralty Island to Yokohama ; lat. 25° 33′ N., long. 137° 57′ E.

Station 231, July 10, 1875 ; Yokohama to Sandwich Islands ; lat. 37° 37′ N., long. 163° 26′ W.

Station 254, July 17, 1875 ; Yokohama to Sandwich Islands ; lat. 35° 13′ N., long. 154° 43′ W.

[1] Spolia atlantica, p. 66.　　[2] Sur l'aire de dispersion de Lesueuria rubra, *Bull. Scient. Nord*, 1886, p. 235.

Station 256, July 21, 1875 ; Yokohama to Sandwich Islands ; lat. 30° 22′ N., long. 154° 56′ W.

Station 294, November 3, 1875 ; Tahiti to Valparaiso ; lat. 39° 22′ S., long. 98° 46′ W.

Station 332, March 10, 1876 ; Rio de Janeiro to Tristan da Cunha ; lat. 37° 29′ S., long. 27° 31′ W.

On April 28, 1876 ; off St. Vincent ; lat. 17° 47′ N., long. 28° 28′ W.

On May 12, 1876 ; off the Azores ; lat. 42° 52′ N., long. 28° 54′ W.

II. Deposit shells.

Station VIII., February 12, 1873 ; off the Canary Islands ; lat. 28° 3′ 15″ N., long. 17° 27′ 0″ W.; depth, 620 fathoms ; bottom, volcanic mud.

Station 3, February 18, 1873 ; Tenerife to Sombrero Island ; lat. 25° 45′ N., long. 20° 14′ W.; depth, 1525 fathoms ; bottom, hard ground.

Station 23, March 15, 1873 ; off Sombrero Island ; lat. 18° 24′ N., long. 63° 28′ W.; depth, 450 fathoms ; bottom, Pteropod ooze.

Station 24, March 25, 1873 ; off Culebra Island ; lat. 18° 38′ 30″ N., long. 65° 5′ 30″ W.; depth, 390 fathoms ; bottom, Pteropod ooze.

Station 33, April 4, 1873 ; off Bermuda ; lat. 32° 21′ 30″ N., long. 64° 35′ 55″ W.; depth, 435 fathoms ; bottom, coral mud.

Station 35c, April 22, 1873 ; off Bermuda ; lat. 32° 15′ N., long. 65° 8′ W.; depth, 1950 fathoms ; bottom, Globigerina ooze.

Station 75, July 2, 1873 ; off Fayal (Azores) ; lat. 38° 38′ 0″ N., long. 28° 28′ 30″ W.; depth, 450 fathoms ; bottom, volcanic mud.

Station 78, July 10, 1873 ; off the Azores ; lat. 37° 26′ N., long. 25° 13′ W.; depth, 1000 fathoms ; bottom, volcanic mud.

Station 85, July 19, 1873 ; off Palma Island (Canaries) ; lat. 28° 42′ N., long. 18° 6′ W.; depth, 1125 fathoms ; bottom, volcanic mud.

Station 120, September 9, 1873 ; off the coast of South America, between Pernambuco and Bahia ; lat. 8° 37′ S., long. 34° 28′ W.; depth, 675 fathoms ; bottom, red mud.

Station 122, September 10, 1873 ; off the coast of South America, between Pernambuco and Bahia ; lat. 9° 5′ S., long. 34° 50′ W.; depth, 350 fathoms ; bottom, red mud.

Station 164, June 12, 1874 ; off Sydney ; lat. 34° 8′ S., long. 152° 0′ E.; depth, 950 fathoms ; bottom, green mud.

Station 185, August 31, 1874 ; off Raine Island ; lat. 11° 35′ 25″ S., long. 144° 2′ 0″ E.; depth, 135 fathoms ; bottom, coral sand.

Station 219, March 10, 1875 ; Admiralty Islands to Yokohama ; lat. 1° 54′ 0″ S., long. 146° 39′ 40″ E.; depth, 150 fathoms ; bottom, coral mud.

Station 335, March 16, 1876 ; Tristan da Cunha to Ascension Island ; lat. 32° 24′ S., long. 13° 5′ W.; depth, 1425 fathoms ; bottom, Pteropod ooze.

Subgenus *Clio*, Linné.

1767. *Clio*, Linné, Systema Naturæ, ed. 12, p. 1094 (non Müller, 1776).
1810. *Cleodora*, Péron et Lesueur, Histoire de la Famille des Mollusques Ptéropodes, Ann. Mus. Hist. Nat. Paris, t. xv. p. 66.
1829. *Balantium*, Anonymous (Children, *fide* Gray), Journ. Roy. Inst., vol. xv. p. 220.

Characters and Description.—*Shell*, of a somewhat angular form, colourless, compressed dorso-ventrally, with lateral keels. An anterior transverse section is thus always angular laterally. There is generally a crest or rib extending longitudinally along the back, and usually projecting. The embryonic shell varies in form, but is always definitely separate from the rest.

Animal.—The aperture of the mantle is smaller than the aperture of the shell; the margins are laterally united for a certain distance, as in *Cavolinia*; the simple lateral prolongations of the mantle corresponding to the lateral keels hardly extend beyond the margin of the shell; the fin has a non-muscular space situated towards the middle of the distal margin; the left tentacle is always distinctly visible; there is a triangular dorsal lobe between the two fins, and formed by the union of the two lips; the anus is situated far in front, near the aperture of the mantle.

KEY TO THE SPECIES.

I. Shell with lateral keels over its entire length.
  1. Shell with dorsal ribs very slightly projecting.
    A. Shell with a broad posterior portion,   *Clio andreæ.*
    B. Shell with a narrow posterior portion,   *Clio polita.*
  2. Shell with dorsal ribs markedly projecting.
    A. Shell with three dorsal ribs,   *Clio balantium.*
    B. Shell with five dorsal ribs,   *Clio chaptali.*
II. Shell with no lateral keels on the posterior portion.
  1. Shell without lateral spines.
    A. Shell with the lateral margins almost parallel,   *Clio australis.*
    B. Shell with the lateral margins very divergent.
      a. Transverse grooves on the posterior portion, dorsal ribs multiple,   *Clio sulcata.*
      b. No posterior transverse grooves, the dorsal ribs undivided,   *Clio pyramidata.*
  2. Shell with lateral spines,   *Clio cuspidata.*

7. *Clio andreæ* (Boas).

1885. *Cleodora andreæ*, Boas, Spolia atlantica, p. 80, pl. i. fig. 1, pl. ii. fig. 12.

This species, which closely resembles *Clio polita* (see below), is distinguished by its greater breadth, especially in the posterior portion, by its two equally bulging faces, by its more marked flattening, by its curvature, especially localised on the posterior portion, and contrasting with the straight anterior region. This curvature is dorsal over the greater portion of its length, but is slightly ventral towards the apex. The embryonic portion is not separated by a projecting ring from the rest of the shell. The length is also considerable, 20 mm.

Habitat.—South Atlantic Ocean, 33° 30' S., 1° 0' W.

*8. *Clio polita* (Craven, MS.) (Pl. II. figs. 4–6).

> 1880. *Cleodora falcata*, Pfeffer, Die Pteropoden des Hamburger Museums, Abhandl. Naturwiss.
> Ver. Hamburg, Bd. vii. p. 96, pl. vii. fig. 19 (not Gould, 1852).
> *Balantium politum*, Craven, MS. (British Museum).

Characters and Description.—Shell, slender, narrow posteriorly, smooth over its entire surface, more bulging ventrally than dorsally, exhibiting on the former surface four slight longitudinal grooves, but none on the latter. The lateral keels are well-marked, sharp, projecting, parallel to the axis of the shell, more delicate than those of *Clio balantium*, and not hollow-edged. The dorsal curvature is uniform and continuous. Pfeffer has indeed figured two specimens of this species, one of which exhibits a regular curvature (fig. 19b), while the other is much recurved posteriorly (fig. 19a), and has based his description on the latter. But all the specimens which I have seen from the collections of the "Valorous" and the Challenger also resemble fig. 19b, which I am therefore warranted in regarding as the normal type. The middle of the lips does not project anteriorly. The embryonic shell has a bulging oval form, rounded on its posterior portion, and separated from the rest of the shell by a well-marked constriction, limited by a small projecting ring.

The animal I have not observed. The soft parts are "dunkel-schwarz-violett" according to Pfeffer.

Dimensions, 10 to 11 mm.

Habitat.—North Atlantic Ocean, Davis Strait ("Valorous" Expedition), 44° N., 31° W. (Hamburg Museum).

Challenger Specimens.—Deposit shells.

Station 78, July 10, 1873; off the Azores; lat. 37° 26' N., long. 25° 13' W.; depth, 1000 fathoms; bottom, volcanic mud.

Station 85, July 19, 1873; off Palma Island (Canaries); lat. 26° 42' N., long. 18° 6' W.; depth, 1125 fathoms; bottom, volcanic mud.

Station 120, September 9, 1873; off the coast of South America, between Pernambuco and Bahia; lat. 8° 37' S., long. 34° 28' W.; depth, 675 fathoms; bottom, red mud.

*9. *Clio balantium* (Rang).

1829. *Balantium recurvum*, Anonymous (Children, *fide* Gray), Journ. Roy. Inst., vol. xv. p. 220, pl. vii. fig. 107.

1834. *Cleodora balantium*, Rang, Magasin de Zoologie, 1834, pl. xliv.

1836. *Hyalæa balantium*, d'Orbigny, Voyage dans l'Amérique méridionale, t. v. p. 116, pl. viii. figs. 1–4.

1837. *Balantium licarimatum*, Benson, Notice on Balantium, a Genus of the Pteropodous Mollusca, Journ. Asiat. Soc. Bengal, vol. vi. p. 151.

1852. *Cleodora inflata*, Souleyet, Voyage de la Bonite, Zoologie, t. ii. p. 188, pl. vii. figs. 17–19 (young).

For description and figures, I refer to Souleyet, Voyage de la Bonite, Zoologie, t. ii. p. 186, pl. vii. figs. 11–16.

Habitat.—Atlantic Ocean; intertropical (21° 30′ N. to 19° 30′ S., Boas); 44° N. (Atlantic?) (Pfeffer); toward 40° N., coast of America (Verrill, fragments).[1]

Indian Ocean; exclusively in the southern portion, 33° S. towards Africa (Boas), towards Australia (Pfeffer), Islands of St. Paul and Amsterdam (Benson).

Challenger Specimens.—Living.

Station 216A, February 16, 1875; north of New Guinea; lat. 2° 56′ N., long. 134° 11′ E. (young).

*10. *Clio chaptali* (Souleyet) (Pl. II. fig. 7).

1852. *Cleodora chaptali*, Souleyet, Voyage de la Bonite, Zoologie, p. 183, pl. vii. figs. 1–5.

The above form appears to be a distinct species, but very strictly localised, for it has not been reobserved since its discovery by Souleyet. I only know a single adult specimen (dry shell), which is deposited in the British Museum.

Characters and Description.—Shell somewhat bulging, with its apex recurved dorsally, with its lateral edges uniformly and markedly diverging, in contrast to *Clio balantium*, where they describe a sigmoid curve. The lateral keels are sharp and not hollow-edged, as they are in *Clio balantium*; they run parallel to the axis of the body, and are not at all turned ventrally; this admits of the ventral surface being as bulging as the dorsal. The latter bears five longitudinal ribs, instead of three as in *Clio balantium*. The middle of the lips hardly projects anteriorly. The embryonic shell is separated from the rest by a well-marked constriction, in front of which the shell broadens out again. The embryonic portion, however, in contrast to that of *Clio balantium*, does not enlarge behind the constriction, and is terminated posteriorly by a much-pointed apex (Pl. II. fig. 7).

The animal, according to Souleyet, very closely resembles *Clio balantium*.

[1] Catalogue of the Marine Mollusca added to the fauna of New England during the past ten years, Trans. Connect. Acad., vol. v. p. 557.

Habitat.—Atlantic Ocean ; near the Cape of Good Hope (Souleyet).

Challenger Specimen.—Living, young.

Station 181, August 25, 1874 ; Fiji to Raine Island ; lat. 13° 50′ S., long. 151° 49′ E.

11. Clio australis (d'Orbigny) (not Bruguière) (Pl. II. fig. 8).

    1834. *Hyalæa australis,*[1] d'Orbigny, Voyage dans l'Amérique méridionale, t. v. p. 117, pl. viii. figs. 9–11.

    1850. *Balantium australe,* Gray, Catalogue of the Mollusca in the Collection of the British Museum, pt. ii., Pteropoda, p. 15.

    1852. *Cleodora australis,* Souleyet, Voyage de la Bonite, Zoologie, t. ii. p. 189, pl. viii. figs. 20–23.

For figures and description, see Souleyet (*loc. cit.*).

Habitat.—This species appears to have a geographical distribution like that of *Spongiobranchæa australis* and *Limacina australis,* that is to say, localised in the southern regions of the three great oceans around the South Pole.

Cape Horn (d'Orbigny); South-east Pacific (48° S., 86° W., Souleyet); (?) south-east of the Cape of Good Hope, 38° 50′ S. (Boas).

Challenger Specimens.—Living.

Station 159, March 10, 1874 ; Termination Land to Melbourne ; lat. 47° 25′ S., long. 130° 22′ E.

Observations.—Boas[2] has united with the present species *Clio sulcata,* Pfeffer. But the latter is certainly a distinct species, also collected towards the South Pole by the Challenger Expedition, and the embryonic shell[3] which Boas has figured as that of "*Cleodora australis*" is precisely similar to *Clio sulcata,* and very different from that of *Clio australis* (Pl. II. fig. 8). For in the latter the embryonic shell is separated from the other portion by a much broader and deeper constriction, and is terminated posteriorly by a rounded extremity.

12. Clio sulcata (Pfeffer) (Pl. II. figs. 9–11).

    1879. *Cleodora sulcata,* Pfeffer, Uebersicht der auf S. M. Schiff Gazelle, und von Dr. Jagor gesammelten Pteropoden, Monatsber. d. k. preuss. Akad. d. Wiss. Berlin, 1879, p. 240, figs. 11, 12.

Characters and Description.—Shell slender, with a very slight curvature, with the ventral surface only slightly projecting, but not re-entrant. The surface adorned with transverse ridges ; nine longitudinal ridges occur in close proximity on the anterior portion of the dorsal surface. The margins of the aperture, as Pfeffer has noted, are very fragile,

---

[1] The name *Hyalæa australis* was already used in 1816 by Péron (Voyage de découvertes aux terres australes, pl. xxxi. fig. 5), but it only occurs on the plate, and no description is given. As the figure refers to *Cuvierina tridentata,* I think the specific title *australis* may be fitly retained for the above species of *Clio.*

[2] Spolia atlantica, p. 68.   [3] *Ibid,* pl. iv. fig. 46.

so that it is difficult to describe the exact form of the lips, though this is probably intermediate between that of *Clio australis* and that of *Clio pyramidata*. The embryonic shell is almost directly continuous with the other portion, from which it is separated only by a narrow groove. The posterior extremity is pointed.

The figure 17c of Pfeffer (pl. vii., *loc. cit.*) represents the curvature of the shell as if it were ventral. The specimen figured must then have been abnormal, for in all the specimens of *Clio sulcata* which I have seen the curvature was dorsal, as it is indeed in all the curved Cavoliniidæ.

The animal resembles that of neighbouring species (*Clio australis* and *Clio pyramidata*). The left tentacle is readily visible; the posterior lobe of the foot is of considerable length, and the other external characters are those of the genus *Clio* in the strict sense. There are no lateral prolongations of the margins of the mantle.

This form is undoubtedly a distinct species which cannot be referred either to *Clio australis* (as by Boas) or to *Clio pyramidata*. It differs from both in the fact that the ventral surface of the shell is not at all re-entrant. And further it differs from *Clio australis* (with which it has a closely analogous geographical distribution) in its much more divergent lateral margins and in its embryonic shell, as may be seen by comparing the figures of the two species. This form was the *Clio* observed on the last expedition of the "Astrolabe," to which I have referred in my Report on the Gymnosomata.[1]

Dimensions.—The shell measures 2 cm. in length.

Habitat.—Like *Clio australis*, this form was found in the southern region of the Pacific Ocean, lat. 50° 34′ S., long. 83° 44′ W., and lat. 45° 35′ S., long. 122° 1′ W. (Pfeffer); also in the Southern Ocean, near Kerguelen Island; and in the Antarctic Ocean (see the following Challenger localities).

Challenger Specimens.—Living specimens.

Station 150, February 2, 1874; Heard Island; lat. 52° 4′ S., long. 71° 22′ E.

Between Stations 154 and 155, February 21, 1874; in vicinity of Antarctic ice; lat. 63° 30′ S., long. 89° 8′ E.

Station 156, February 26, 1874; in vicinity of Antarctic ice; lat. 62° 26′ S., long. 95° 44′ E.

*13. *Clio pyramidata*, Linné.

1767. *Clio pyramidata*, Linné, Systema Naturæ, ed. 12, p. 1094.
1813. *Hyalea lanceolata*, Lesueur, Mémoire sur quelques espèces d'animaux mollusques et radiaires recueillis dans la Méditerranée près de Nice, Nouv. Bull. Soc. Philom. Paris, t. iii. p. 284, pl. v. fig. 3.
1825. *Cleodora brownii*, De Blainville, Manuel de Malacologie, pl. xlvi. fig. 1.
1836. *Hyalea pyramidata*, d'Orbigny, Voyage dans l'Amérique méridionale, t. v. p. 113, pl. vii. figs. 25–29.
1841. *Cleodora lamartinieri*, Rang, in d'Orbigny, Mollusques de Cuba, p. 83.

[1] Zool. Chall. Exped., pt. lviii. p. 62.

1852. *Cleodora lanceolata*, Souleyet, Voyage de la Bonite, Zoologie, t. ii. p. 179, pl. vi. figs. 17-25.

1852. *Cleodora exacuta*, Gould, The Mollusca and Shells of the U.S. Exploring Expedition, p. 488, pl. li. fig. 605.

1877. *Cleodora labiata*, Sowerby, in Reeve, Conchologia iconica, t. xx., Pteropoda, fig. 26.

1880. *Cleodora martensii*, Pfeffer, Die Pteropoden des Hamburger Museums, Abhandl. d. Naturw. Ver. Hamburg, Bd. vii. p. 95, pl. vii. fig. 16.

For figures and description, see Souleyet (*loc. cit.*).

Habitat.—This species has a cosmopolitan distribution, and exhibits noteworthy variations in form.

The most northerly locality is Spitzbergen (British Museum), then Bergen, Iceland, Davis Strait, the whole of the Atlantic towards both continents and down to 40° S., and all the Mediterranean.

Indian Ocean; from the Gulf of Bengal to 40° S. (Boas), off the coasts of Africa, Natal, Zanzibar (Pfeffer), and as far as Australia, Swan River (British Museum).

Pacific Ocean; western portion, Japan, Gulf of Yedo ("Galathea" Expedition), Yellow Sea (British Museum), China Sea (Boas), Malay Archipelago, Eastern Australia to 40° S. (Pfeffer); North-east Pacific, 44° N., 154° W. (Gould, as "*Cleodora exacuta*"); South-east Pacific, 27° 11' S., 88° 52' W. ("Galathea" Expedition).

Challenger Specimens.—I. Living.

Station 62, June, 18, 1873; Bermuda to Azores; lat. 35° 7' N., long. 52° 32' W.

Station 63, June 19, 1873; Bermuda to Azores; lat. 35° 29' N., long. 50° 53' W.

Station 142, December 18, 1873; Cape of Good Hope to parallel of 46° S.; lat. 35° 4' S., long. 18° 37' E.

Near Station 160, March 15, 1874; off Melbourne; lat. 39° 45' S., long. 140° 40' E.

Station 175, August 12, 1874; Fiji to Raine Island; lat. 19° 2' S., long. 177° 10' E.

Station 230, April 5, 1875; Admiralty Islands to Yokohama; lat. 26° 29' N., long. 137° 57' E.

Station 251, July 10, 1875; Yokohama to Sandwich Islands; lat. 37° 37' N., long. 163° 26' W.

Station 254, July 17, 1875; Yokohama to Sandwich Islands; lat. 35° 13' N., long. 154° 43' W.

Station 256, July 21, 1875; Yokohama to Sandwich Islands; lat. 30° 22' N., long. 154° 56' W.

Station 293, November 1, 1875; Tahiti to Valparaiso; lat. 39° 4' S., long. 105° 5' W.

Station 332, March 10, 1876; Rio de Janeiro to Tristan da Cunha; lat. 37° 29' S., long. 27° 31' W.

Between Stations 332 and 333, April 28, 1876; off St. Vincent (Cape Verde); lat. 17° 47' N., long. 25° 28' W.

On May 12, 1876; off the Azores; lat. 42° 52' N., long. 28° 54' W.

II. Deposit shells.

Station VIII., February 12, 1873; off Canary Islands; lat. 28° 3' 15" N., long. 17° 27' 0" W.; depth, 620 fathoms; bottom, volcanic mud.

Station 3, February 18, 1873; Tenerife to Sombrero Island; lat. 25° 45' N., long. 20° 14' W.; depth, 1525 fathoms; bottom, hard ground.

Station 23, March 15, 1873; off Sombrero Island; lat. 18° 24' N., long. 63° 28' W.; depth, 450 fathoms; bottom, Pteropod ooze.

Station 24, March 25, 1873; off Culebra Island; lat. 18° 38' 30" N., long. 65° 5' 30" W.; depth, 390 fathoms; bottom, Pteropod ooze.

Station 33, April 4, 1873; off Bermuda; lat. 32° 21' 30" N., long. 64° 35' 55" W.; depth, 435 fathoms; bottom, coral mud.

Station 35c, April 22, 1873; off Bermuda; lat. 32° 15' N., long. 65° 8' W.; depth, 1950 fathoms; bottom, Globigerina ooze.

Station 75, July 2, 1873; off Fayal (Azores); lat. 38° 38' 0" N., long. 28° 28' 30" W.; depth, 450 fathoms; bottom, volcanic mud.

Station 76, July 3, 1873; off the Azores; lat. 38° 11' N., long. 27° 9' W.; depth, 900 fathoms; bottom, Pteropod ooze.

Station 78, July 10, 1873; off the Azores; lat. 37° 26' N., long. 25° 13' W.; depth, 1000 fathoms; bottom, volcanic mud.

Station 85, July 19, 1873; off Palma Island (Canaries); lat. 28° 42' N., long. 18° 6' W.; depth, 1125 fathoms; bottom, volcanic mud.

Station 120, September 9, 1873; off the coast of South America, between Pernambuco and Bahia; lat. 8° 37' S., long. 34° 28' W.; depth, 675 fathoms; bottom, red mud.

Station 122, September 10, 1873; off the coast of South America, between Pernambuco and Bahia; lat. 9° 5' S., long. 34° 50' W.; depth, 350 fathoms; bottom, red mud.

Station 164, June 12, 1874; off Sydney; lat. 34° 8' S., long. 152° 0' E.; depth, 950 fathoms; bottom, green mud.

Station 185, August 31, 1874; off Raine Island; lat. 11° 35' 25" S., long. 144° 2' 0" E.; depth, 135 fathoms; bottom, coral sand.

Station 219, March 10, 1875; Admiralty Islands to Yokohama; lat. 1° 54' 0" S., long. 146° 39' 40" E.; depth, 150 fathoms; bottom, coral mud.

Station 246, July 2, 1875; Yokohama to Sandwich Islands; lat. 36° 10' N., long. 178° 0' E.; depth, 2050 fathoms; bottom, Globigerina ooze.

Station 323, February 28, 1876; Falkland Islands to Rio de la Plata; lat. 35° 39' S., long. 50° 47' W.; depth, 1900 fathoms; bottom, blue mud.

Station 335, March 16, 1876; Tristan da Cunha to Ascension Island; lat. 32° 24' S long. 13° 5' W.; depth 1425 fathoms; bottom, Pteropod ooze.

(ZOOL. CHALL. EXP.—PART LXV.—1887.)　　　　　　　　　　Tli 9

*14. *Clio cuspidata* (Bosc).

1802. *Hyalæa cuspidata*, Bosc, Histoire naturelle des Coquilles, t. ii. p. 241, pl. ix. figs. 5–7.

1820. *Hyalæa tricuspidata*, Bowdich, Elements of Conchology, pl. vi. fig. 1.

1830. *Cleodora lessonii*, Rang, MS., in Lesson, Voyage autour du Monde de la Coquille, t. ii. pt. i. p. 247, pl. x. fig. 1.

1833. *Cleodora cuspidata*, Quoy et Gaimard, Voyage de l'Astrolabe, Zoologie, t. ii. p. 384, pl. xxvii. figs. 1–5.

1852. ? *Cleodora quadrispinosa*, Rang, Histoire naturelle des Mollusques Ptéropodes, pl. v. fig. 6.

For figures and description see Souleyet, Voyage de la Bonite, Zoologie, t. ii. p. 176, pl. vi. figs. 11–16.

Habitat.—Atlantic Ocean, from 60° N. to 37° S.; Mediterranean; Indian Ocean, from Ceylon to 42° S., from Africa to Australia.

It has not been recorded from the Pacific previously to the Challenger Expedition.

Challenger Specimens.—I. Living specimens.

Near Station 230, April 4, 1875; Admiralty Islands to Yokohama; lat. 25° 33′ N., long. 137° 57′ E.

Station 254, July 17, 1875; Yokohama to Sandwich Islands; lat. 35° 13′ N., long. 154° 43′ W.

II. Deposit shells.

Station 23, March 15, 1873; off Sombrero Island; lat. 18° 24′ N., long. 63° 28′ W.; depth, 450 fathoms; bottom, Pteropod ooze.

Station 78, July 10, 1873; off the Azores; lat. 37° 26′ N., long. 25° 13′ W.; depth, 1000 fathoms; bottom, volcanic mud.

Station 85, July 19, 1873; off Palma Island (Canaries); lat. 28° 42′ N., long. 18° 6′ W.; depth, 1125 fathoms; bottom, volcanic mud.

Cuvierina,[1] Boas.

1825. *Cuvieria*, Rang, Description de deux genres nouveaux appartenant à la classe des Ptéropodes, Ann. d. Sci. Nat., sér. 1, t. xii. p. 322 (not Péron, 1807).

Triptera, auctorum, not Quoy and Gaimard.

1886. *Cuvierina*, Boas, Spolia atlantica, p. 131.

Characters and Description.—*Shell* straight, elongated, with a smooth surface, with the posterior half conical and pointed, generally caducous in the adult. The anterior half is swollen medially, but constricted behind the aperture. A partition, concave in front, is found towards the middle of the entire length of the shell, and close beside this the truncation is formed. The transverse section is circular, except towards the aperture, where it is a little compressed, and appears somewhat reniform. Behind

[1] Named after Cuvier.

the aperture the shell is contracted, but bulges out again towards the partition. The embryonic portion is separated from the rest of the shell by a shallow constriction.

Animal with the aperture of the mantle as large as that of the shell, with fins as in *Clio* (*Styliola*) *subula* and other species of *Clio* in the strict sense. The posterior portion of the foot is slightly hollowed out in its middle region.

Adult specimens with the posterior portion intact are very rare. Benson[1] and d'Orbigny[2] were the first independently to describe the form of the entire shell, which was not known to Rang when he established the genus "*Cuvieria*."

Cuvierina is nearly allied to *Clio*, so much so indeed that Souleyet[3] was inclined to unite "*Cuvieria*" with "*Cleodora*" as a single division or subgenus. Similarly, according to Lesson,[4] Rang proposed in his unpublished Monograph to unite the above forms in a subgenus of "*Cleodora*."

Among all the species of the genus *Clio*, *Clio* (*Styliola*) *subula* exhibits the closest affinity with *Cuvierina*. Nevertheless, the constriction of the shell behind the mouth, the median partition, and the constant truncation, definitely distinguish *Cuvierina* from all the forms of *Clio*, and warrant its position as a distinct genus.

But, on the other hand, there is no sufficient reason to establish a distinct family, as Gray[5] and the brothers Adams[6] have done.

It is an entire abuse of nomenclature to apply to this genus the title *Triptera*, Quoy and Gaimard. Nothing could be more uncertain than what *Triptera rosea*[7] really is, as the title is applied to a Pteropod without a shell.

The genus *Cuvierina* includes only a single living species.

* *Cuvierina columnella* (Rang).

> 1824. ? *Cleodora obtusa*, Quoy et Gaimard, Voyage de l'Uranie, Zoologie, p. 415, pl. lxvi. fig. 5.
>
> 1827. *Cuvieria columnella*, Rang, Description de deux nouveaux genres appartenant à la classe des Ptéropodes, Ann. d. Sci. Nat., sér. 1, t. xiii. p. 323, pl. xlv. figs. 1–8.
>
> 1835. *Cuvieria oryza*, Benson, Corrected characters of the genus Cuvieria and Notice of a second species inhabiting the tropical Indian Ocean, Journ. Asiat. Soc. Bengal, vol. iv. p. 698.
>
> 1850. *Triptera columnella*, Gray, Catalogue of the Mollusca in the Collection of the British Museum, pt. ii., Pteropoda, p. 23.

[1] Corrected characters of the genus Cuvieria of Rang, &c., Journ. Asiat. Soc. Bengal, vol. iv. p. 698, 1835.
[2] Voyage dans l'Amérique méridionale, t. v. pp. 124, 125, pl. viii. fig. 36.
[3] Voyage de la Bonite, Zoologie, t. ii. p. 203.
[4] Voyage autour du Monde de la Coquille.
[5] Catalogue of the Mollusca in the Collection of the British Museum, pt. ii., Pteropoda, p. 23.
[6] The Genera of Recent Mollusca, vol. i. p. 54.
[7] Description de cinq genres de Mollusques, &c., Ann. d. Sci. Nat., sér. 1, t. vi. p. 76, pl. ii. fig. 5, 1825.

1850. *Cuvieria urceolaris*, March, Catalogus conchyliorum quae reliquit C. P. Kjærulf, p. 32.

1879. *Triptera columella (sic)*, Pfeffer, Uebersicht der auf S.M. Schiff "Gazelle" und von Dr. Jager gesammelten Pteropoden, Monatsber. d. k. preuss. Akad. d. Wiss. Berlin, 1879, p. 243, fig. 18.

1879. *Triptera cancellata*, Pfeffer, Ibid., p. 243, fig. 19.

For description and figures I refer to Souleyet, Voyage de la Bonite, Zoologie, t. ii. p. 205, pl. xii. The best figure of the complete shell is to be found in the Spolia atlantica of Boas, pl. iii. fig. 39.

Habitat.—Atlantic Ocean; from 43° 23′ N. (Boas) to 40° S., both towards the New and Old Worlds. According to Souleyet, this species has been found towards Cape Horn, but this appears to me to require confirmation. The locality Spitzbergen, noted in the British Museum, is certainly erroneous.

Indian Ocean; from the Gulf of Bengal (British Museum) to 35° 30′ S., from Africa (Zanzibar, the Cape, &c.) to Australia.

Pacific Ocean; western portion, China Sea (Boas), Malay Archipelago, east coast of Australia (Pfeffer and Angas); eastern portion, from 23° N. to 42° S. (Knocker).

Challenger Specimens.—I. Living specimens.

Station 53, May 26, 1873; Halifax to Bermuda; lat. 36° 30′ N., long. 63° 40′ W.

Station 62, June 18, 1873; Bermuda to Azores; lat. 35° 7′ N., long. 52° 32′ W.

Station 63, June 19, 1873; Bermuda to Azores; lat. 35° 29′ N., long. 50° 53′ W.

Station 175, August 12, 1874; Fiji to Raine Island; lat. 19° 2′ S., long. 177° 10′ E.

Station 181, August 25, 1874; Fiji to Raine Island; lat. 13° 50′ S., long. 151° 49′ E.

Station 216A, February 16, 1875; north of New Guinea; lat. 2° 56′ N., long. 134° 11′ E.

Station 230, April 5, 1875; Admiralty Islands to Yokohama; lat. 26° 29′ N., long. 137° 57′ E.

Station 254, July 17, 1875; Yokohama to Sandwich Islands; lat. 35° 13′ N., long. 154° 43′ W.

Station 280, October 4, 1875; Tahiti to Valparaiso; lat. 18° 40′ S., long. 149° 52′ W.

Station 288, October 21, 1875; Tahiti to Valparaiso; lat. 40° 3′ S., long. 132° 58′ W.

Near Station 288, October 22, 1875; Tahiti to Valparaiso; lat. 40° 0′ S., long. 131° 36′ W.

Station 294, November 3, 1875; Tahiti to Valparaiso; lat. 39° 22′ S., long. 98° 46′ W.

Near Station 354, May 7, 1876; St. Vincent towards Azores; lat. 34° 22′ S., long. 34° 23′ W.

II. Deposit shells.

Station 23, March 15, 1873; off Sombrero Island; lat. 18° 24′ N., long. 63° 28′ W.; depth, 450 fathoms; bottom, Pteropod ooze.

Station 24, March 25, 1873; off Culebra Island; lat. 18° 38' 30" N., long. 65° 5' 30" W.; depth, 390 fathoms; bottom, Pteropod ooze.

Station 33, April 4, 1873; off Bermuda; lat. 32° 21' 30" N., long. 64° 35' 55" W.; depth, 435 fathoms; bottom, coral mud.

Station 78, July 10, 1873; off the Azores; lat. 37° 26' N., long. 25° 13' W.; depth, 1000 fathoms; bottom, volcanic mud.

Station 85, July 19, 1873; off Palma Island (Canaries); lat. 28° 42' N., long. 18° 6' W.; depth, 1125 fathoms; bottom, volcanic mud.

Station 120, September 9, 1873; off the coast of South America, between Pernambuco and Bahia; lat. 8° 37' S., long. 34° 28' W.; depth, 675 fathoms; bottom, red mud.

Station 122, September 10, 1873; off the coast of South America, between Pernambuco and Bahia; lat. 9° 5' S., long. 34° 50' W.; depth, 350 fathoms; bottom, red mud.

Station 185, August 31, 1874; off Raine Island; lat. 11° 35' 25" S., long. 144° 2' 0" E.; depth, 155 fathoms; bottom, coral sand.

Station 335, March 16, 1876; Tristan da Cunha to Ascension Island; lat. 32° 24' S., long. 13° 5' W.; depth 1425 fathoms; bottom, Pteropod ooze.

Carolinia,[1] Abildgaard.

1791. *Carolina*, Abildgaard, Om Carolina natans, Anomia tridentata Forskalri, Skriv. Naturhist. Selsk., 132. i. Heft. ii. p. 173 (now Bruguière, 1792).
1797. *Rhoda*, Humphreys, Museum Calonnianum.
1801. *Hyalea*, Lamarck, Système des animaux sans vertèbres, p. 139.
1810. *Atolanta*, Montfort, Conchyliologie systématique, t. ii. p. 50.
1815. *Tracta*, Oken, Lehrbuch der Zoologie, t. i. p. 327 (*err. typ.* 273).
1825. *Pleuropus*, Eschscholtz, Bericht über die Zoologische Ausbeute während der Reise von Cronstadt bis St. Peter und Paul, Oken, Isis, 1825, Bd. i. p. 735.
1842. *Diacria*, Gray, Synopsis of the Contents of the British Museum.
1859. *Orbignya*, A. Adams, On synonyms and habitats of Carolinia, Diacria, and Pleuropus, Ann. and Mag. Nat. Hist., ser. 3, vol. iii. p. 45.

Characters and Description.—The shell, which is generally of a horny brown colour, is especially characterised (in the adult state, of course) by its much-contracted aperture, which is, however, very broad transversely. The lateral portions of this aperture, which are narrower than the middle part, are almost separated from it by a more or less developed tooth rising from the ventral lip and fitting into a dorsal depression. The dorsal lip, which is longer than the ventral, is always more or less ventrally recurved; the ventral lip, much recurved dorsally, is constricted a little in front of the aperture, and then reflected ventrally. The ventral surface is always bulging. The special form of *Carolinia* depends on the fact that the sides of the shell

[1] Named after Carolini or Caslini.

diverge abruptly outwards so that the lips appear much prolonged anteriorly. The sides of the shell are often prolonged into a more or less projecting point. The embryonic shell is not separated by a distinct constriction, except in *Cavolinia trispinosa* and *Cavolinia quadridentata.*

The animal somewhat resembles in its external characters the species of *Clio* strictly so called. Its special characters chiefly consist in the breadth of the posterior lobe of the foot and in the presence of lateral prolongations of the mantle, which project from the lateral portions of the aperture (side clefts of the adult) and may cover a considerable portion of the shell.

Many authors (A. Adams, Gray, Fischer, Boas, &c.) call this genus "*Cavolinia*, Gioeni," and do so on the authority of Abildgaard, according to whom Gioeni first used this title in his work entitled "Descrizione di una nuova Famiglia e di un nuovo Genere di Testacei trovati nel littorali di Catania." This small memoir (8vo and not 4to as is always noted) is somewhat rare, and does not appear to have been actually seen by the authors who cite it from Abildgaard. For in the memoir itself it may be seen that while Gioeni has indeed represented *Cavolinia tridentata* in his figures xiv.–xvi., he does not give it its title. Caulini is referred to on p. xxvii, note *a*, as the first to observe the animal of this species, but there is no question of naming in his honour the "nuovo Genere di Testacei."

The name "*Cavolina*" (em. *Cavolinia*) only dates from 1791, and its author was Abildgaard. It has, nevertheless, the priority over *Cavolinia*, Bruguière, which was not published till 1792,[1] and ought to be employed in preference to the title *Hyalæa*, Lamarck, 1801.

Although the shells of *Cavolinia* have a much constricted aperture, different individuals within the same species may exhibit very noteworthy divergences in regard to size. The difference is sometimes very striking, so that in some species the diameter of certain individuals may be four times that of others (*Cavolinia longirostris*, after Boas).[2]

From this fact it has been inferred (Pfeffer)[3] that, in order to grow, the shells of *Cavolinia* must first of all lose all the contracted portion by absorption, since growth can only take place by the apposition of fresh material at the margin of the aperture.

But this hypothesis of partial absorption is altogether imaginary. As Boas has already pointed out,[4] there is no trace of a line of reabsorption on the shells of large size, and it is further a very strong argument against the theory that the posterior (oldest) portion of the small individuals does not correspond exactly to the homologous portion

[1] Encyclopédie Méthodique; Histoire naturelle des Vers, t. i.
[2] Spolia atlantica, p. 206.
[3] Die Pteropoden des Hamburger Museums, Abhandl. Naturw. Ver. Hamburg, t. vii. p. 75.
[4] Spolia atlantica, p. 207.

of the large specimens, which, however, it is bound to do, if in the latter the contracted portion is absorbed and the posterior portion alone left. This residue ought obviously to be identical and superposable in individuals of any size whatever.

The small-sized specimens, like the large, are individuals which will not increase further, which have attained their limit of growth, as is otherwise indicated by the complete development of the reproductive system. The smaller size of the shell depends on its surface being developed along a curve with smaller radius than in the large-sized individuals.

On the other hand, there are several forms of Cavoliniidæ, to which distinct specific titles are given, notably those which Boas calls "Hyalea plates," where the union of the two lips of the shell by the so-called "appareil de fermeture" has not been developed. All these forms, as we shall immediately show, are individuals which have not yet attained sexual maturity, and belong to species already known, as Cantraine first suspected.

But this condition of immaturity, associated as it undoubtedly is with reduced development of the reproductive organs,[1] may be prolonged to a very late stage, and the shell may be very large before the formation of the "appareil de fermeture." This can be easily demonstrated by examining a large number of specimens, as for instance of *Cavolinia tridentata* at Naples. In this form, to which our attention was first directed by Dr. Paul Schiemenz, one finds, even at the same stage of development, considerable difference in size.

It is certain that there are notable differences in the size of adult specimens (with completely developed reproductive organs, and with perfected closing apparatus); and the theory of the partial absorption of the shell must be dismissed.

But as I have already pointed out, those young stages which we have discussed have been regarded as distinct species, and have been referred either to the genus *Cavolinia* (*Hyalæa*) or to the genus *Clio* (*Cleodora*), or to a special genus, *Pleuropus*.

And besides these entirely superfluous terms, we also find for the forms which properly belong to this genus a profuse superabundance of specific titles, just as in the cases of *Clio* and the Limacinidæ.

As these Thecosomata are pelagic animals with a very wide geographical distribution, there is no inconsiderable exhibition of variation in the form of the shell. Thus have arisen numerous variations, distinguished by very slight divergences. But on the basis of minimal distinctions, conchologists have not hesitated to establish a large number of "new" species.

If we abstract the titles which ought to be referred to other genera altogether[2]

---

[1] See Gegenbaur (*Hyalea complanata*), Untersuchungen über Pteropoden und Heteropoden, pl. i. fig. 1; Souleyet (*Hyalea lævigata*), Voyage de la Bonite, Zoologie, pl. v. fig. 14; Huxley (*Cleodora curvata*), On the Morphology of the Cephalous Mollusca, *Phil. Trans.*, 1853, pl. iv. figs. 4, 5.

[2] Also Nudibranchs, designated *Cavolina* (Bruguière).

(d'Orbigny placed in the genus *Hyalæa* = *Cavolinia* all the members of the family Cavoliniidæ), or even to other groups, and confine our attention to the forms really belonging to this genus, we shall find, for extant species, fifty-four specific titles, of which three are used with several connotations, which increases the mischief still further.

Hyalæa affinis, d'Orbigny.	*Hyalæa limbata*, d'Orbigny.
Hyalæa angulata, Souleyet.	*Pleuropus longifilis*, Troschel.
Hyalæa australis, Péron.	*Hyalæa longirostris*, Lesueur.
Hyalæa chemnitziana, Péron and	*Hyalæa minuta*, Sowerby.
Lesueur.	*Hyalæa mucronata*, Quoy and
Hyalæa complanata, Gegenbaur.	Gaimard.
Cleodora compressa, Souleyet.	*Cavolina natans*, Abildgaard.
Hyalæa cornea, Lamarck.	*Hyalæa obtusa*, Sowerby.
Hyalæa costata, Pfeffer.	*Hyalæa papilionacea*, Quoy and
Hyalæa cumingii, Sowerby.	Gaimard.
Cleodora curvata, Souleyet.	*Pleuropus pellucidus*, Eschscholtz.
Hyalæa cuspidata, Delle Chiaje	*Hyalæa peroni*, Lesueur.
(non Bosc).	*Cavolina pisum*, Mørch.
Hyalæa depressa, Bivona (non	*Cleodora pygmæa*, Boas.
d'Orbigny).	*Hyalæa quadridentata*, Lesueur.
Hyalæa depressa, d'Orbigny.	*Hyalæa quadrispinosa*, d'Orbigny.
Hyalæa ecaudata, Lesueur.	*Hyalæa reeviana*, Dunker.
Hyalæa elongata, Lesueur.	*Hyalæa rotundata*, Boas.
Hyalæa femorata, Gould.	*Hyalæa rugosa*, d'Orbigny.
Hyalæa fissirostris, Benson.	*Hyalæa teniobranchea*, Péron and
Hyalæa flava, d'Orbigny.	Lesueur.
Hyalæa forskahlii, Lesueur.	*Hyalæa triacantha*, Bronn.
Hyalæa gegenbauri, Pfeffer.	*Anomia tridentata*, Forskål.
Hyalæa gibbosa, Rang.	*Cleodora trifilis*, Troschel.
Hyalæa globulosa, Rang.	*Hyalæa trispinosa*, Lesueur.
Pleuropus hargeri, Verrill.	*Hyalæa truncata*, Krauss (non
Hyalæa imitans, Pfeffer.	Lesueur).
Hyalæa inermis, Gould.	*Hyalæa truncata*, Lesueur.
Hyalæa inflexa, Lesueur.	*Hyalæa uncinata*, Hoeninghaus (non
Hyalæa intermedia, Sowerby.	Rang).
Hyalæa labiata, d'Orbigny.	*Hyalæa uncinata*, Rang.
Hyalæa lævigata, d'Orbigny.	*Hyalæa uncinatiformis*, Pfeffer.

Hyalæa vaginellina, Cantraine.

An attentive examination of this superfluity of titles shows that there are amongst them only eight genuine species, all obtained on the Challenger Expedition.

All the other titles are synonyms of these eight species. It is necessary, however, to distinguish :—

1. Thirteen titles referring to the young stages of several of these eight forms :—

Hyalæa complanata, Gegenbaur,	.	= *Cavolinia tridentata*, Forskål.
Hyalæa depressa, d'Orbigny,	.	= *Cavolinia inflexa*, Lesueur.
Hyalæa lævigata, d'Orbigny,	.	= *Cavolinia longirostris*, Lesueur.
Hyalæa rotundata, Boas,	.	= *Cavolinia globulosa*, Rang.
Hyalæa rugosa, d'Orbigny,	.	= *Cavolinia gibbosa*, Rang.
Hyalæa truncata, Lesueur,	.	= *Cavolinia* sp.
Cleodora compressa, Souleyet,	.	= *Cavolinia trispinosa*, Lesueur.
Cleodora curvata, Souleyet,	.	= ? *Cavolinia uncinata*, Rang.
Cleodora pygmæa, Boas,	.	= *Cavolinia quadridentata*, Lesueur.
Cleodora trifilis, Troschel,	.	= *Cavolinia* sp.
Pleuropus harpeci, Verrill,	.	= *Cavolinia gibbosa*, Rang.
Pleuropus longifilis, Troschel,	.	= *Cavolinia tridentata*, Forskål.
Pleuropus pellucidus, Eschscholtz,		= *Cavolinia inflexa*, Lesueur.

2. Four titles which may be applied to local varieties of some species :—

Hyalæa affinis, d'Orbigny,	= var. of *Cavolinia tridentata*.
Hyalæa costata, Pfeffer,	= var. of *Cavolinia quadridentata*.
Hyalæa labiata, d'Orbigny,	= var. of *Cavolinia inflexa*.
Hyalæa truncata, Krauss,	= var. of *Cavolinia tridentata*.

3. All the other titles are absolutely synonymous with those of the eight genuine species :—

Hyalæa angulata, Souleyet,	= *Cavolinia longirostris*.
Hyalæa australis, Péron,	
Hyalæa chemnitziana, Péron and Lesueur,	= *Cavolinia tridentata*.
Hyalæa cornea, Lamarck,	
Hyalæa cumingii, Sowerby,	
Hyalæa cuspidata, Delle Chiaje,	= *Cavolinia trispinosa*.
Hyalæa depressa, Bivona,	
Hyalæa ecaudata, Lesueur,	= *Cavolinia longirostris*.
Hyalæa elongata, Lesueur,	= *Cavolinia inflexa*.
Hyalæa femorata, Gould,	= *Cavolinia longirostris*.
Hyalæa fissirostris, Benson,	

Hyalæa flava, d'Orbigny,	. .	= *Cavolinia gibbosa.*
Hyalæa forskahlii, Lesueur,	. .	= *Cavolinia tridentata.*
Hyalæa gegenbauri, Pfeffer,	. .	= *Cavolinia gibbosa.*
Hyalæa imitans, Pfeffer,	. .	= *Cavolinia inflexa.*
Hyalæa inermis, Gould,	⎫	
Hyalæa intermedia, Sowerby, .	⎬ = *Cavolinia quadridentata.*	
Hyalæa limbata, d'Orbigny, .	. .	= *Cavolinia longirostris.*
Hyalæa minuta, Sowerby,	. .	= *Cavolinia quadridentata.*
Hyalæa mucronata, Quoy and Gaimard,	.	= *Cavolinia trispinosa.*
Cavolina natans, Abildgaard, .	.	= *Cavolinia tridentata.*
Hyalæa obtusa, Sowerby,	.	= *Cavolinia longirostris.*
Hyalæa papilionacea, Quoy and Gaimard,	⎫	
Hyalæa peroni, Lesueur,	. ⎬ = *Cavolinia tridentata.*	
Cavolina pisum, Mörch,	.	= *Cavolinia globulosa.*
Hyalæa quadrispinosa, d'Orbigny,	.	= *Cavolinia quadridentata.*
Hyalæa reeviana, Dunker,	.	= *Cavolinia trispinosa.*
Hyalæa teniobranchea, Péron and Lesueur,		= *Cavolinia tridentata.*
Hyalæa triacantha, Bronn, .	.	= *Cavolinia trispinosa.*
Hyalæa uncinata, Hoeninghaus,	.	= *Cavolinia inflexa.*
Hyalæa uncinatiformis, Pfeffer,	.	= *Cavolinia uncinata.*
Hyalæa vaginellina, Cantraine,	.	*Cavolinia inflexa.*

There remain the following eight titles, which represent genuine and distinct species :—

Hyalæa trispinosa, Lesueur.	*Hyalæa gibbosa*, Rang.
Hyalæa quadridentata, Lesueur.	*Anomia tridentata*, Forskål.
Hyalæa longirostris, Lesueur.	*Hyalæa uncinata*, Rang.
Hyalæa globulosa, Rang.	*Hyalæa inflexa*, Lesueur.

From the above list of synonyms of *Cavolinia*, it appears that a number of generic titles have been applied to the present group of Thecosomata.

One may well ask if all these names should be rejected and none retained, or, in other words, if the genus *Cavolinia* is indeed homogeneous and indivisible. It appears to me so to be beyond dispute.

I. *Rheda*, *Hyalæa*, *Archonta*, and *Tricla* are absolutely synonymous with *Cavolinia*, for the simple reason that they refer to the same type, *Anomia tridentata* of Forskål.

II. *Pleuropus* is a designation based on young stages of typical *Cavolinia*, which Boas names " *Hyalæa*, B."[1] They refer to specimens in which the closing apparatus was not yet developed—*Pleuropus pellucidus*, *Pleuropus longifilis*, *Pleuropus kargeri*. Gray

[1] Spolia atlantica, p. 92.

was the first [1] to note the affinities of "*Cleodora curvata*," Souleyet, to this group, but he did not detect what these four forms really represented, and regarded "*Pleuropus*" as a group within the genus *Clio*.

The adults of most of the species of *Pleuropus* are known. As to the others, it is possible to predict, from some of their features, what forms they will probably turn out to be when arrived at sexual maturity. The designation *Pleuropus* is therefore to be abandoned.

III. *Diacria* is a characteristic conchological genus. Gray erected it for the reception of *Carolinia trispinosa* and two young stages of typical *Carolinia* forms (group B of Boas), viz., *Hyalæa depressa*, d'Orbigny, and *Hyalæa lævigata*, d'Orbigny, which it would have been more natural to place beside *Pleuropus*. He leaves in the genus *Carolinia*, *Carolinia quadridentata*, though it is in all respects the neighbour of *Carolinia trispinosa*. And, further, he places the same species (*Carolinia orbignyi*, Rang, fossil) both in the genus *Diacria* and in the genus *Carolinia*.[1]

On the other hand, the brothers Adams,[2] and others after them, take this title *Diacria* as synonymous with *Pleuropus*,[3] and therefore add to *Carolinia trispinosa* and to the two forms *Hyalæa depressa* and *Hyalæa lævigata* all the other young forms regarded as independent species. At the same time they agree with Gray in leaving *Carolinia quadridentata*, separated from *Carolinia trispinosa*, beside the typical *Carolinia* forms.[5]

Now, it is certain that if *Carolinia trispinosa* is to be separated from the other species of *Carolinia*, *Carolinia quadridentata* must go with it. The two species are in their structure most closely allied, and form a well-defined subgroup contrasting with the six other species.

And if, in their embryonic shell, in the form of their fins, and in the posterior portion of the foot, they present resemblances to *Clio* (*Cleodora*), they at the same time exhibit the characteristic features of *Carolinia* in a way that makes separation impossible. They are certainly the most archaic living forms of the genus, but not sufficiently distinct to warrant a separate genus. One may, however, follow Boas in establishing a subsection (*Hyalæa*, A), within the genus *Carolinia*.

IV. *Orbignya*, which was only regarded as a subgenus by A. Adams, is based on *Carolinia inflexa*, which is usually considered as allied to *Clio* (*Cleodora*). There is,

---

[1] Catalogue of the Mollusca in the Collection of the British Museum, pt. ii., Pteropoda, p. 14.

[2] This Catalogue is in other respects full of inaccuracies and carelessness. It would be desirable to re-edit it, especially since the collection of Pteropods in the British Museum is many times richer to-day than it was in 1850.

[3] The Genera of Recent Mollusca, vol. ii. p. 611.

[4] Similarly Pfeffer, Uebersicht der auf S.M. Schiff Gazelle und von Dr. Jager gesammelten Pteropoden, *Monatsber. d. k. preuss. Akad. d. Wiss. Berlin*, 1879, p. 236.

[5] Pfeffer (Die Pteropoden des Hamburger Museums, *Abhandl. d. Nature. Ver. Hamburg*, t. vii.) places *Carolinia trispinosa* in the subfamily Cleodorina, and *Carolinia quadridentata* in the subfamily Hyaleina.

however, no warrant for this opinion. *Cavolinia inflexa* certainly belongs to the second subgeneric section of *Cavolinia*, including the more typical or more highly specialised forms, all, in fact, except *Cavolinia trispinosa* and *Cavolinia quadridentata*. Its elongation and its flattening are not a whit more extraordinary than the expansion and shortening of *Cavolinia globulosa*.

From the above observations this results, that the huge list of species is reduced by analysis to eight, and that, without going to an extreme like d'Orbigny, who united all the Thecosomata of the family Cavoliniidæ into a single genus *Hyalæa*, it may be said that at least the eight species above mentioned form a tolerably homogeneous unit within a single genus.

The eight species thus allowed to exist may be distinguished in the following fashion :—

KEY TO THE SPECIES.

I. Dorsal lip thickened into a pad.
  1. Shell with lateral points,   *Cavolinia trispinosa.*
  2. Shell without lateral points,   *Cavolinia quadridentata.*
II. Dorsal lip with a thin margin.
  1. Posterior portion of the ventral lip markedly projecting laterally,   *Cavolinia longirostris.*
  2. Ventral lip not more developed than the dorsal.
    A. Shell without appreciable lateral points.
      a. Shell narrows at the end of the lips than anteriorly.
        α. Ventral surface rounded,   *Cavolinia globulosa.*
        β. Ventral surface with an anterior transverse keel,   *Cavolinia gibbosa.*
      b. Shell as broad at the end of the lips as anteriorly,   *Cavolinia tridentata.*
    B. Shell with distinct lateral points.
      a. Upper lip flattened posteriorly,   *Cavolinia uncinata.*
      b. Upper lip directed straight forwards,   *Cavolinia inflexa.*

The best series of figures of these eight species is undoubtedly that given by Boas.[1] We shall, therefore, refer to these figures, since it is useless to figure afresh species already sufficiently well known, and hopeless to expect better figures than those of Boas.

*1. *Cavolinia trispinosa* (Lesueur).

    1821. *Hyalea trispinosa*, Lesueur, MS. in de Blainville, Hyale, Dict. d. Sci. Nat., t. xxii. p. 82.
    1827. *Hyalea mucronata*, Quoy et Gaimard, Observations Zoologiques faites à bord de l'Astrolabe, &c., Ann. d. Sci. Nat., sér. 1, t. x. p. 231, pl. viiia, figs. 1, 2.
    1832. *Hyalea depressa*, Bivona, Descrizione di una nuova specie di Jale, &c., Efemeridi scientifiche e litterarie per la Sicilia, p. 57, pl. i. figs. 4, 5.
    1841. *Hyalea cuspidata*, Delle Chiaje, Descrizione e notomia degli animali senza vertebre del Regno di Napoli, pl. clxxx. figs. 1, 2 (non d'Orbigny).

[1] Spolia atlantica, pl. i. figs. 3–11 ; pl. ii. figs. 14–21.

1850. *Diacria trispinosa*, Gray, Catalogue of the Molluscs in the Collection of the British Museum, pt. ii., Pteropoda, p. 10.

1850. *Diacria mucronata*, Gray, *Ibid.*, p. 11.

1853. *Hyalea recurva*, Dunker, Index Molluscorum, &c., p. 2, pl. i. figs. 17–20.

1858. *Pleuropus trispinosus*, A. and H. Adams, The Genera of Recent Mollusca, vol. ii. p. 611.

1858. *Pleuropus mucronatus*, A. and H. Adams, *Ibid.*, vol. ii. p. 611.

For description and figures, see Boas, Spolia atlantica, p. 94, pl. i. fig. 3; pl. ii. fig. 14.

Habitat.—Atlantic Ocean; from 60° 15′ N. ("Triton" Expedition) to 40° S. (Knocker), both towards the New World and towards the Old; Mediterranean (Delle Chiaje, Cantraine, Costa, Macdonald, &c.).

Indian Ocean; from the Gulf of Bengal (Pfeffer) to 41° S. (Boas), and from Africa (Natal, Madagascar, &c.) to Australia.

Pacific Ocean; western portion, Yellow Sea (British Museum), China Sea (Boas), 13° N., 156° E. ("Vettor Pisani" Expedition); South-west Pacific (Pfeffer), Port Jackson (Angas); North-east Pacific to 30° N. (Knocker).

Challenger Specimens.—I. Living specimens.

Station VIIr., February 2, 1873; off Madeira; lat. 32° 27′ 0″ N., long. 16° 40′ 30″ W.

Station 62, June 18, 1873; Bermuda to Azores; lat. 35° 7′ N., long. 52° 32′ W.

Station 63, June 19, 1873; Bermuda to Azores; lat. 35° 29′ N., long. 50° 53′ W.

Station 181, August 25, 1874; Fiji to Raine Island; lat. 13° 50′ S., long. 151° 49′ E.

Station 230, April 5, 1875; Admiralty Islands to Yokohama; lat. 26° 29′ N., long. 137° 57′ E.

II. Deposit shells.

Station 23, March 15, 1873; off Sombrero Island; lat. 18° 24′ N., long. 63° 28′ W.; depth, 450 fathoms; bottom, Pteropod ooze.

Station 24, March 25, 1873; off Culebra Island; lat. 18° 38′ 30″ N., long. 65° 5′ 30″ W.; depth, 390 fathoms; bottom, Pteropod ooze.

Station 33, April 4, 1873; off Bermuda; lat. 32° 21′ 30″ N., long. 64° 35′ 55″ W.; depth, 435 fathoms; bottom, coral mud.

Station 35c, April 22, 1873; off Bermuda; lat. 32° 15′ N., long. 65° 8′ W.; depth, 1950 fathoms; bottom, Globigerina ooze.

Station 70, June 26, 1873; Bermuda to Azores; lat. 38° 25′ N., long. 35° 50′ W.; depth, 1675 fathoms; bottom, Globigerina ooze.

Station 75, July 2, 1873; off Fayal (Azores); lat. 38° 38′ 0″ N., long. 28° 28′ 30″ W.; depth, 450 fathoms; bottom, volcanic mud.

Station 76, July 3, 1873; off the Azores; lat. 38° 11′ N., long. 27° 9′ W.; depth, 900 fathoms; bottom, Pteropod ooze.

Station 78, July 10, 1873 ; off the Azores ; lat. 37° 26′ N., long. 25° 13′ W.; depth, 1000 fathoms ; bottom, volcanic mud.

Station 85, July 19, 1873 ; off Palma Island (Canaries); lat. 28° 42′ N., long. 18° 6′ W.; depth, 1125 fathoms ; bottom, volcanic mud.

Station 120, September 9, 1873 ; off the coast of South America, between Pernambuco and Bahia ; lat. 8° 37′ S., long. 34° 28′ W.; depth, 675 fathoms ; bottom, red mud.

Station 122, September 10, 1873 ; off the coast of South America, between Pernambuco and Bahia ; lat. 9° 5′ S., long. 34° 50′ W.; depth, 350 fathoms ; bottom, red mud.

Station 164 ; June 12, 1874 ; off Sydney ; lat. 34° 8′ S., long. 152° 0′ E.; depth, 950 fathoms ; bottom, green mud.

Station 185, August 31, 1874 ; off Raine Island ; lat. 11° 35′ 25″ S., long. 144° 2′ 0″ E.; depth, 135 fathoms ; bottom, coral sand.

Station 335, March 16, 1876 ; Tristan da Cunha to Ascension Island ; lat. 32° 24′ S., long. 13° 5′ W.; depth, 1425 fathoms ; bottom, Pteropod ooze.

*2. *Cavolinia quadridentata* (Lesueur).

> 1821. *Hyalæa quadridentata*, Lesueur, MS., in Blainville, Hyale, Dict. d. Sci. Nat., t. xxii. p. 81.
> 1836. *Hyalæa quadrispinosa*, d'Orbigny, Voyage dans l'Amérique méridionale, t. v. p. 85.
> 1850. *Cavolina quadridentata*, Gray, Catalogue of the Mollusca in the Collection of the British Museum, pt. ii., Pteropoda, p. 8.
> 1852. *Hyalæa inermis*, Gould, The Mollusca and Shells of the U.S. Exploring Expedition, pl. li. fig. 604.
> 1877. *Hyalæa minuta*, Sowerby, in Reeve, Conchologia iconica, t. xx., Pteropoda, fig. 9.
> 1877. *Hyalæa intermedia*, Sowerby, Ibid., fig. 10.
> 1879. *Hyalæa costata*, Pfeffer, Uebersicht der auf S.M. Schiff Gazelle und von Dr. Jagor gesammelten Pteropoden, Monatsber. d. k. preuss. Akad. d. Wiss. Berlin, 1879, p. 234.

For description and figures, see Boas, Spolia atlantica, p. 99, pl. i. fig. 4 ; pl. ii. fig. 15.

Habitat.—Atlantic Ocean ; from 34° 30′ N. to 17° 0′ S. (Knocker).

Indian Ocean ; from the Gulf of Bengal to the Cape (Pfeffer), from the coasts of Africa (Red Sea, Madagascar, Natal) to Australia. The specimens from the Indian Ocean all belong to the form *costata*.[1]

Pacific Ocean ; western portion, Yellow Sea (British Museum), China Sea (Boas), Port Jackson (Angas) ; eastern portion from 36° N. to 28° S. (Knocker).

Challenger Specimens.—I. Living specimens.

Station 175, August 12, 1874 ; Fiji to Raine Island ; lat. 19° 2′ S., long. 177° 10′ E.

Station 181, August 25, 1874 ; Fiji to Raine Island ; lat. 13° 50′ S., long. 151° 49′ E.

Station 216A, February 16, 1875 ; north of New Guinea ; lat. 2° 56′ N., long. 134° 11′ E.

---

[1] Pfeffer (Die Pteropoden des Hamburger Museums, *Abhandl. Naturw. Ver. Hamburg*, t. vii. p. 91) also records the form *costata* from the Atlantic.

August—September 1875, Sandwich Islands to Tahiti.

Station 337, March 19, 1876; Tristan da Cunha to Ascension Island; lat. 24° 38′ S., long. 13° 36′ W.

On April 29, 1876; off St. Vincent (Cape Verde); lat. 18° 8′ N., long. 30° 5′ W.

Station 353, May 3, 1876; St. Vincent to Azores; lat. 26° 21′ N., long. 33° 37′ W.

II. Deposit shells.

Station VIII., February 12, 1873; off Canary Islands; lat. 28° 3′ 15″ N., long. 17° 27′ 0″ W., depth, 620 fathoms; bottom, volcanic mud.

Station 3, February 18, 1873; Tenerife to Sombrero Island; lat. 25° 45′ N., long. 20° 14′ W.; depth, 1525 fathoms; bottom, hard ground.

Station 23, March 15, 1873; off Sombrero Island; lat. 18° 24′ N., long. 63° 28′ W.; depth, 450 fathoms; bottom, Pteropod ooze.

Station 24, March 25, 1873; off Culebra Island; lat. 18° 38′ 30″ N., long. 65° 5′ 30″ W.; depth, 390 fathoms; bottom, Pteropod ooze.

Station 33, April 4, 1873; off Bermuda; lat. 32° 21′ 30″ N., long. 64° 35′ 55″ W.; depth, 435 fathoms; bottom, coral mud.

Station 85, July 19, 1873; off Palma Island (Canaries); lat. 28° 42′ N., long. 18° 6′ W.; depth, 1125 fathoms; bottom, volcanic mud.

Station 120, September 9, 1873; off the coast of South America, between Pernambuco and Bahia; lat. 8° 37′ S., long. 34° 28′ W.; depth, 675 fathoms; bottom, red mud.

Station 122, September 10, 1873; off the coast of South America, between Pernambuco and Bahia; lat. 9° 5′ S., long. 34° 50′ W.; depth, 350 fathoms; bottom, red mud.

Station 185, August 31, 1874; off Raine Island; lat. 11° 35′ 25″ S., long. 144° 2′ 0″ E.; depth, 155 fathoms; bottom, coral sand.

Station 219, March 10, 1875; Admiralty Islands to Yokohama; lat. 1° 54′ 0″ S., long. 146° 39′ 40″ E.; depth, 150 fathoms; bottom, coral mud.

*3. *Cavolinia longirostris* (Lesueur).

1821. *Hyalæa longirostris*, Lesueur, MS., in de Blainville, Hyale, Dict. d. Sci. Nat., t. xxii. p. 81.

1821. *Hyalæa crassata*, Lesueur, *Ibid.*, p. 82.

1836. *Hyalæa limbata*, d'Orbigny, Voyage dans l'Amérique méridionale, t. v. p. 101, pl. vi. figs. 11–13.

1852. *Hyalæa angulata*, Souleyet, Voyage de la Bonite, Zoologie, t. ii. p. 152, pl. v. figs. 1–6.

1852. *Hyalæa femorata*, Gould, The Mollusca and Shells of the U.S. Exploring Expedition, pl. li. fig. 663.

1861. *Hyalæa sinirostris*, Benson, Notes on the Pteropodous genus Hyalæa and description of a new species, Ann. and Mag. Nat. Hist., ser. 3, vol. vii. p. 26.

1877. *Hyalæa obtusa*, Sowerby, in Reeve, Conchologia iconica, t. xx., Pteropoda, fig. 8.

For description and figures, see Boas, Spolia atlantica, p. 102, pl. i. fig. 5; pl. ii. fig. 16.

Habitat.—Atlantic Ocean; from 47° N. (Boas) to 40° S. (Knocker), towards both New and Old World.

Indian Ocean; from the Gulf of Bengal to 36° S. (Boas), from the coast of Africa (Red Sea, Arabia, Zanzibar) to Australia.

Pacific Ocean; western portion, Yellow Sea (British Museum), China Sea (Boas), Malay Archipelago, Australia, Tasmania; eastern portion, from 30° N. to 12° S. (Knocker).

Challenger Specimens.—I. Living.

On April 14, 1873; off Bermuda; lat. 32° 10′ N., long. 64° 53′ W.

Station 106, August 25, 1873; St. Vincent to St. Paul's Rocks; lat. 1° 47′ N., long. 24° 26′ W.

Between Stations 162 and 163, April 3, 1874; Melbourne to Sydney; lat. 38° 7′ S., long. 149° 18′ E.

Station 175, August 12, 1874; Fiji to Raine Island; lat. 19° 2′ S., long. 177° 10′ E.

Station 181, August 25, 1874; Fiji to Raine Island; lat. 13° 50′ S., long. 151° 49′ E.

Station 209, January 22, 1875; Manila to Samboangan; lat. 10° 14′ N., long. 123° 54′ E.

Station 213, February 8, 1875; Samboangan to New Guinea; lat. 5° 47′ N., long. 124° 1′ E.

Station 230, April 5, 1875; Admiralty Islands to Yokohama; lat. 26° 29′ N., long. 137° 57′ E.

August—September 1875; Sandwich Islands to Tahiti.

Station 269, September 2, 1875; Sandwich Islands to Tahiti; lat. 5° 54′ N., long. 147° 2′ W.

Between Stations 292 and 293, October 31, 1875; Tahiti to Valparaiso; lat. 38° 50′ S., long. 108° 6′ W.

Station 338, March 21, 1876; Tristan da Cunha to Ascension Island; lat. 21° 15′ S., long. 14° 2′ W.

Station 345, April 4, 1876; Ascension Island to St. Vincent; lat. 5° 45′ S., long. 14° 25′ W.

Station 349, April 10, 1876; Ascension Island to St. Vincent; lat. 5° 28′ N., long. 14° 38′ W.

Station 352, April 13, 1876; Ascension Island to St. Vincent; lat. 10° 55′ N., long. 17° 46′ W.

Station 353, May 3, 1876; St. Vincent to Azores; lat. 26° 21′ N., long. 33° 37′ W.

II. Deposit shells.

Station 23, March 15, 1873; off Sombrero Island; lat. 18° 24′ N., long. 63° 28′ W.; depth, 450 fathoms; bottom, Pteropod ooze.

Station 24, March 25, 1873; off Culebra Island; lat. 18° 38′ 30″ N., long. 65° 5′ 30″ W.; depth, 390 fathoms; bottom, Pteropod ooze.

Station 33, April 4, 1873 ; off Bermuda ; lat. 32° 21' 30" N., long. 64° 35' 55" W.; depth, 435 fathoms ; bottom, coral mud.

Station 78, July 10, 1873 ; off the Azores ; lat. 37° 26' N., long. 25° 13' W.; depth, 1000 fathoms ; bottom, volcanic mud.

Station 120, September 9, 1873 ; off the coast of South America, between Pernambuco and Bahia ; lat. 8° 37' S., long. 34° 28' W.; depth, 675 fathoms ; bottom, red mud.

Station 122, September 10, 1873 ; off the coast of South America, between Pernambuco and Bahia ; lat. 9° 5' S., long. 34° 30' W.; depth, 350 fathoms ; bottom, red mud.

Station 185, August 31, 1874 ; off Raine Island ; lat. 11° 35' 25" S., long. 144° 2' 0" E.; depth, 155 fathoms ; bottom, coral sand.

*4. *Cavolinia globulosa* (Rang).

> 1850. *Cavolina globulosa*, Rang, MS., in Gray, Catalogue of the Mollusca in the Collection of the British Museum, pt. ii., Pteropoda, p. 8 (without description).
>
> 1850. *Cavolina pisum*, Mörch, Catalogus conchyliorum quae reliquit C. P. Kjerulf, p. 32, pl. i. fig. 7.
>
> 1852. *Hyalea globulosa*, Rang, MS., in Souleyet, Voyage de la Bonite, Zoologie, t. ii. p. 142, pl. iv. figs. 20–24.

For description and figures, see Boas, Spolia atlantica, p. 107, pl. i. fig. 7 ; pl. ii. fig. 18.

I retain for this form the specific title *Cavolinia globulosa*, since the figure to which Gray refers in his Catalogue is that of Souleyet's Atlas (Voyage de la Bonite), which appeared (without text) before the catalogue of Mörch, and designates the species in question as "Hyale globuleuse, Rang."

Habitat.—Indian Ocean ; from 40° 0' N. to 34° 30' S. (Boas), from the coast of Africa, Red Sea (Issel), Zanzibar, Natal (Pfeffer), to Australia.

Pacific Ocean ; western portion, from 13° N. ("Vettor Pisani" Expedition), China Sea (Boas), Malay Archipelago ; eastern portion, from 2° N. to 12° S. (Knocker).

Souleyet[1] and A. Adams[2] have cited this species as from the Atlantic, but without any precise information. Pfeffer[3] alone notes a single definite locality, lat. 1° S., long. 25° W. I am inclined to suppose that this was some error in labelling, and that *Cavolinia globulosa* does not occur in the Atlantic. It is not recorded either by d'Orbigny, Benson, or Knocker ; and Boas, who has examined so much material from the Atlantic, does not note a single specimen as occurring there. And, finally, although the Challenger explored so much of the intertropical Atlantic, and traversed it several

---

Histoire naturelle des Mollusques Ptéropodes, p. 38.

[1] On the Synonyms and Habitats of Cavolinia, Diacria and Pleuropus, Ann. and Mag. Nat. Hist., ser. 3, vol. iii. p. 55.

[2] Die Pteropoden des Hamburger Museums, Abhandl. Naturw. Ver. Hamburg, t. vii. p. 84.

times going and returning, I have not found in the Challenger collection a single
Atlantic specimen of *Cavolinia globulosa*.

Challenger Specimens.—Living specimens.

Near Station 213, February 7, 1875; at Samboangan; lat. 5° 59′ N., long. 123° 38′ E.

Station 216A, February 16, 1875; north of New Guinea; lat. 2° 56′ N., long. 134° 11′ E.

*5. *Cavolinia gibbosa* (Rang).

1836. *Hyalea gibbosa*, Rang, MS., in d'Orbigny, Voyage dans l'Amérique méridionale, t. v.
p. 95, pl. v. figs. 16–20.

1836. *Hyalea flava*, d'Orbigny, *Ibid.*, p. 97, pl. v. figs. 21–25.

1880. *Hyalea papenbauri*, Pfeffer, Die Pteropoden der Hamburger Museums, Abhandl. Naturw.
Ver. Hamburg, Bd. vii. p. 86, figs. 5, 7.

For description and figures, see Boas, Spolia atlantica, p. 109, pl. i. fig. 6; pl. ii.
fig. 17.

Habitat.—Atlantic Ocean; from 43° 10′ N. to 38° 16′ S., from the coasts of America
to those of the Old World; Mediterranean, Messina, &c.

Indian Ocean; southern portions, 22° S. (Boas) to 41° S. (Pfeffer), from Africa
(Madagascar, Natal) to Australia.

Pacific Ocean; western portion, Yellow Sea (British Museum), China Sea (Boas),
16° N., 165° E. ("Vettor Pisani" Expedition), Port Jackson (Angas), off Tahiti (Knocker);
South-east Pacific ("Galathea" Expedition).

Challenger Specimens.—I. Living specimens.

Station VIIF., February 2, 1873; off Madeira; lat. 32° 27′ 0″ N., long. 16° 40′ 30″ W.

Between Stations 162 and 163, April 3, 1873; Melbourne to Sydney; lat. 38° 7′ S.,
long. 149° 18′ E.

Station 230, April 5, 1875; Admiralty Island to Yokohama; lat. 26° 29′ N.,
long. 137° 57′ E.

Station 249, July 7, 1875; Yokohama to Sandwich Islands; lat. 37° 59′ N.,
long. 171° 48′ W.

August—September 1875; Sandwich Islands to Tahiti.

II. Deposit shells.

Station 23, March 15, 1873; off Sombrero Island; lat. 18° 24′ N., long. 63° 28′ W.;
depth, 450 fathoms; bottom, Pteropod ooze.

Station 24, March 25, 1873; off Culebra Island; lat. 18° 38′ 30″ N., long. 65° 5′ 30″
W.; depth, 390 fathoms; bottom, Pteropod ooze.

Station 70, June 26, 1873; Bermuda to Azores; lat. 38° 25′ N., long. 35° 50′ W.;
depth, 1675 fathoms; bottom, Globigerina ooze.

Station 78, July 10, 1873; off the Azores; lat. 37° 26′ N., long. 25° 13′ W.; depth,
1000 fathoms; bottom, volcanic mud.

Station 85, July 19, 1873 ; off Palma Island (Canaries); lat. 28° 42′ N., long. 18° 6′ W.; depth, 1125 fathoms ; bottom, volcanic mud.

Station 185, August 31, 1874; off Raine Island; lat. 11° 35′ 25″ S., long. 144° 2′ 0″ E.; depth, 135 fathoms ; bottom, coral sand.

*6. *Cavolinia tridentata* (Forskål).

1773. *Anomia tridentata*, Forskål, Descriptiones animalium quæ in itinere orientali observavit, p. 124.

1791. *Carolina natans*, Abildgaard, Nyere Efterretning om det Skahlyr som Forskål har beskrevet under Navnet Anomia tridentata, Skriv. naturhist. Selsk., Bd. i., Heft 2, pl. x.

1801. *Hyalæa cornea*, Lamarck, Système des animaux sans vertèbres, p. 140.

1804. *Hyalæa papilionacea*, Bory de St. Vincent, Voyage dans les quatre principales îles des mers d'Afrique, t. i. p. 137, pl. v. fig. 1.

1810. *Hyale teniobranche*, Péron et Lesueur, Histoire de la famille des Mollusques Ptéropodes, Ann. Mus. Hist. Nat. Paris, t. xv., pl. ii. fig. 13.

1813. *Hyalæa peroni*, Lesueur, Mémoire sur quelques animaux mollusques, &c., Nouv. Bull. Soc. Philom., t. iii. p. 284.

1813. *Hyalæa elæomitziana*, Lesueur, Ibid., p. 284.

1816. *Hyalæa australis*, Péron, Voyage de découvertes aux terres australes, t. i., pl. xxxi. fig. 5 (*sine descriptione*).

1821. *Hyalæa forskahlii*, Lesueur, MS., in de Blainville, Hyale, Dict. d. Sci. Nat., t. xxii. p. 79.

1836. *Hyalæa affinis*, d'Orbigny, Voyage dans l'Amérique méridionale, t. v. p. 91, pl. v. figs. 6–10.

1848. *Hyalæa truncata*, Krauss, Südafricanische Mollusken, p. 34, pl. ii. fig. 12 (non Lesueur).

1850. *Cavolinia blainei*, A. Adams, On the Synonyms and Habitats of Cavolinia, Diacria and Pleuropus, Ann. and Mag. Nat. Hist., ser. 3, t. iii. p. 44.

1877. *Hyalæa cumingii*, Sowerby, in Reeve, Conchologia iconica, t. xx., Pteropoda, fig. 5.

For description and figures see Boas, Spolia atlantica, p. 115, pl. i. fig. 8 ; pl. ii. fig. 19.

It is not possible to maintain the specific distinctness of " *Hyalæa affinis*," d'Orbigny, and *Cavolinia tridentata* ; the two forms merge into one another (Boas, Spolia atlantica, pl. vi. fig. 100).

Habitat.—Atlantic Ocean ; from 39° 53′ N. (Verrill) to the latitude of the Cape of Good Hope, towards both Old and New Worlds ; Mediterranean.

Indian Ocean ; from 5° N. to about 40° S., from the coast of Africa (Zanzibar) to Australia.

Pacific Ocean ; western portion, Yellow Sea (British Museum), China Sea (Boas), Malay Archipelago (Borneo, &c.) (Gray), lat. 13° N., long. 156° E. ("Vettor Pisani" Expedition); South-east Pacific to 37° S. (Knocker).

Challenger Specimens.—1. Living specimens.

Station 241, June 23, 1875 ; Yokohama to Sandwich Islands ; lat. 35° 41′ N., long. 157° 42′ E.

Station 254, July 17, 1875; Yokohama to Sandwich Islands; lat. 35° 13′ N., long. 154° 43′ W.

II. Deposit shells.

Station 78, July 10, 1873; off the Azores; lat. 37° 26′ N., long. 25° 13′ W.; depth, 1000 fathoms; bottom, volcanic mud.

Station 120, September 9, 1873; off the coast of South America, between Pernambuco and Bahia; lat. 8° 37′ S., long. 34° 28′ W.; depth, 675 fathoms; bottom, red mud.

*7. *Cavolinia uncinata* (Rang).

> 1836. *Hyalea uncinata*, Rang, MS., in d'Orbigny, Voyage dans l'Amérique méridionale, t. v. p. 93, pl. v. figs. 11–15.
>
> 1850. *Cavolina uncinata*, Gray, Catalogue of the Mollusca in the Collection of the British Museum, pt. ii., Pteropoda, p. 7.
>
> 1880. *Hyalea uncinatiformis*, Pfeffer, Die Pteropoden des Hamburger Museums, Abhandl. Naturw. Ver. Hamburg, Bd. vii. p. 85.

For description and figures, see Boas, Spolia atlantica, p. 119, pl. i. fig. 10; pl. ii. fig. 20.

The position of a distinct species cannot be allowed to the form *Hyalæa uncinatiformis*, which Pfeffer only distinguishes by certain features of colour and size.

Habitat.—Atlantic Ocean; from 40° 5′ N. (Verrill) to the Cape of Good Hope (British Museum), towards both Old and New Worlds.

Indian Ocean; from the Gulf of Bengal (15° 30′ N.) to 40° S., from Africa, Red Sea (British Museum), south-east of Arabia (Blanford) to near Australia, 111° 40′ E. (Boas).

Pacific Ocean; western portion, Yedo, Yellow Sea (British Museum), China Sea (Boas); eastern portion from 2° 0′ N. to 8° 8′ S. ("Vettor Pisani" Expedition).

Challenger Specimens.—I. Living specimens.

Station 100, August 16, 1873; St. Vincent to St. Paul's Rocks; lat. 7° 1′ N., long. 15° 55′ W.

August—September 1875; Sandwich Islands to Tahiti.

II. Deposit shells.

Station 23, March 15, 1873; off Sombrero Island; lat. 18° 24′ N., long. 63° 28′ W.; depth, 450 fathoms; bottom, Pteropod ooze.

Station 24, March 25, 1873; off Culebra Island; lat. 18° 38′ 30″ N., long. 65° 5′ 30″ W.; depth, 390 fathoms; bottom, Pteropod ooze.

Station 85, July 19, 1873; off Palma Island (Canaries); lat. 28° 42′ N., long. 18° 6′ W.; depth, 1125 fathoms; bottom, volcanic mud.

Station 120, September 9, 1873; off the coast of South America, between Pernambuco and Bahia; lat. 8° 37′ S., long. 34° 28′ W.; depth, 675 fathoms; bottom, red mud.

Station 122, September 10, 1873; off the coast of South America, between Pernambuco and Bahia; lat. 9° 5′ S., long. 34° 50′ W.; depth, 350 fathoms; bottom, red mud.

Station 185, August 31, 1874; off Raine Island; lat. 11° 35′ 25″ S., long. 144° 2′ 0″ E.; depth, 135 fathoms; bottom, coral sand.

*8. *Cavolinia inflexa* (Lesueur).

> 1813. *Hyalea inflexa*, Lesueur, Mémoire sur quelques animaux mollusques, &c., Nouv. Bull. Soc. Philom., t. iii. p. 285, pl. v. fig. 3.
> 1821. *Hyalea elongata*, Lesueur, MS., in de Blainville, Hyale, Dict. d. Sci. Nat., t. xxii. p. 82.
> 1835. *Hyalea caudellina*, Cantraine, Bull. Acad. d. Sci. Bruxelles, t. ii. p. 380.
> 1836. *Hyalea labiata*, d'Orbigny, Voyage dans l'Amérique méridionale, t. v. p. 104, pl. vi. figs. 21-25.
> 1836. *Hyalea recurva*, Hoeninghaus, MS., in Philippi, Enumeratio Molluscorum utriusque Siciliæ, p. 101, pl. vi. fig. 18 (non Rang).
> 1880. *Hyalea imitans*, Pfeffer, Die Pteropoden des Hamburger Museums, Abhandl. Naturw. Ver. Hamburg, Bd. vii. p. 90, pl. vii. fig. 9a.

For description and figures, see Boas, Spolia atlantica, p. 123, pl. i. fig. 11; pl. ii. fig. 21.

It is not possible to admit the specific separation of the forms *labiata* and *inflexa*, which are linked to one another by gradual transitional forms (Boas, *loc. cit.*, pl. vi. fig. 98). It is more natural to regard them simply as local varieties, though it must be noted that they are not always respectively confined to distinct localities, but may occur together, as for instance in the Indian Ocean.

Habitat.—Atlantic Ocean; from 41° 35′ N. (Boas) to 40° S. (Knocker), towards both Old and New Worlds; Mediterranean.

Indian Ocean; from the Gulf of Bengal (Pfeffer) to 42° S. (Benson), from the coast of Africa (Zanzibar) to Australia.

Pacific Ocean; western portion, Strait of Corea, China Sea (Boas), Port Jackson (Angas); eastern portion from 13° N. to 42° S.

Challenger Specimens.—I. Living.

Station 142, December 18, 1873; Cape of Good Hope to 46° S.; lat. 35° 4′ S., long. 18° 37′ E.

Station 143, December 19, 1873; Cape of Good Hope to 46° S.; lat. 36° 48′ S., long. 19° 24′ E.

Station 175, August 12, 1874; off the Fiji Islands; lat. 19° 2′ S., long. 177° 10′ E.

Station 181, August 25, 1874; Fiji to Raine Island; lat. 13° 50′ S., long. 151° 49′ E.

Near Station 230, April 4, 1875; Admiralty Islands to Yokohama; lat. 25° 33′ N., long. 137° 57′ E.

Station 230, April 5, 1875 ; Admiralty Islands to Yokohama; lat. 26° 29' N., long. 137° 57' E.

Station 256, July 21, 1875 ; Yokohama to Sandwich Islands ; lat. 30° 22' N., long. 154° 56' W.

Station 295, November 5, 1875 ; Tahiti to Valparaiso ; lat. 38° 7' S., long. 94° 4' W.

Station 327, March 4, 1876 ; Rio de Janeiro to Tristan da Cunha ; lat. 36° 48' S., long. 42° 45' W.

II. Deposit shells.

Station 24, March 25, 1873 ; off Culebra Island ; lat. 18° 38' 30" N., long. 65° 5' 30" W.; depth, 390 fathoms ; bottom, Pteropod ooze.

Station 33, April 4, 1873 ; off Bermuda ; lat. 32° 21' 30" N., long. 64° 35' 55" W.; depth, 435 fathoms ; bottom, coral mud.

Station 78, July 10, 1873 ; off the Azores ; lat. 37° 26' N., long. 25° 13' W.; depth, 1000 fathoms ; bottom, volcanic mud.

Station 85, July 19, 1873 ; off Palma Island (Canaries); lat. 28° 42' N., long. 18° 6' W.; depth, 1125 fathoms ; bottom, volcanic mud.

Station 120, September 9, 1873 ; off the coast of South America, between Pernambuco and Bahia ; lat. 8° 37' S., long. 34° 28' W.; depth, 675 fathoms ; bottom, red mud.

Station 122, September 10, 1873 ; off the coast of South America, between Pernambuco and Bahia ; lat. 9° 5' S., long. 34° 50' W.; depth, 350 fathoms ; bottom, red mud.

Station 185, August 31, 1874 ; off Raine Island ; lat. 11° 35' 25" S., long. 144° 2' 0" E.; depth, 135 fathoms ; bottom, coral sand.

Station 323, February 28, 1876 ; Falkland Islands to Rio de la Plata ; lat. 35° 39' S., long. 50° 47' W.; depth, 1900 fathoms ; bottom, blue mud.

Station 335, March 16, 1876 ; Tristan da Cunha to Ascension Island ; lat. 32° 24' S., long. 13° 5' W.; depth, 1425 fathoms ; bottom, Pteropod ooze.

As we have seen above, there are thirteen specific titles with various generic designations (*Hyalæa, Cleodora, Pleuropus*) applied to forms which we regard as young stages of some species of *Cavolinia*.

Of these thirteen names it is necessary in the first instance to eliminate (1) *Hyalæa complanata*, Gegenbaur, 1855 (= *Hyalæa longifilis*, Troschel, 1855), and (2) *Pleuropus pellucidus*, Eschscholtz (mistakenly identified by Gray as *Cleodora curvata*, Souleyet), which, in spite of the inadequacy of the figure and description given by Eschscholtz, appears to correspond to *Hyalæa depressa*, d'Orbigny. Since the figures and description given by the latter are more satisfactory, his designation *Hyalæa depressa* is the one adopted.

As to the remaining eleven titles, the last author who has given a systematic account of Pteropods, namely Boas, mentions seven of them which he regards as representing adult forms and distinct species. These are :—

1. *Cleodora compressa*, Souleyet.	4. *Pleuropus longifilis*, Troschel.
2. *Cleodora pygmæa*, Boas.	5. *Hyalæa rotundata*, Boas.
3. *Cleodora curvata*, Souleyet.	6. *Hyalæa lævigata*, d'Orbigny.

7. *Hyalæa depressa*, d'Orbigny.

It is necessary to examine these forms individually.

*1. *Cleodora compressa*, Souleyet.

> 1850. *Clio depressa*, Gray, Catalogue of the Mollusca in the Collection of the British Museum, pt. ii., Pteropods, p. 14 (*sine descriptione*).
> 1852. *Cleodora compressa*, Souleyet, Voyage de la Bonite, Zoologie, t. ii. p. 181, pl. vi. figs. 26–32.

From Souleyet's figure it may be inferred that this Pteropod did not exhibit fully developed reproductive organs, and was not therefore an adult.

The form in question ought to be referred to *Cavolinia trispinosa*. To this view, formerly suggested by Pfeffer,[1] Boas objects that in *Cleodora compressa* the mouth is narrower, and that in proportion to the height *Cavolinia trispinosa* is thicker than *Cleodora compressa*. But these comparisons only hold true with a *Cleodora compressa* which is much flattened and a swollen *Cavolinia trispinosa*, and are not sufficient to disprove our opinion, which is based on the following facts :—

1. The embryonic portion, the general form of the shell, and the curvature of the sides are identical in *Cleodora compressa* and *Cavolinia trispinosa*.

2. The fins and the posterior lobe of the foot in *Cleodora compressa* have absolutely the same form as in *Cavolinia trispinosa*.

3. The dorsal surface of the shell of *Cleodora compressa* exhibits three ridges disposed in exactly the same way as in *Cavolinia trispinosa*, and not as in the genus *Clio* (*Cleodora*).

4. As concerns geographical distribution, the two forms are equally cosmopolitan.

Like Souleyet and Boas, the palæontologist Searles Wood[2] has regarded the young fossil *Cavolinia trispinosa* as a distinct species which he has named *Cleodora infundibulum*.

Habitat.—" *Cleodora compressa* " has been noted in the Atlantic Ocean (Souleyet, Rattray) and also in the Pacific Ocean (" Vettor Pisani " Expedition).

[1] Uebersicht der auf S.M. Schiff Gazelle und von Dr. Jagor gesammelten Pteropoden, *Monatsber. d. k. preuss. Akad. d. Wiss. Berlin*, 1879, p. 237.
[2] Catalogue of Shells found in the Crag, *Ann. and Mag. Nat. Hist.*, ser. 1, vol. ix. p. 459, pl. v. fig. 15, 1842.

Challenger Specimens.—1. Living specimens.

Between Stations 162 and 163, April 3, 1874; Melbourne to Sydney; lat. 38° 7' S., long. 149° 18' E.

Station 181, August 25, 1874; Sydney to Raine Island; lat. 13° 50' S., long. 151° 49' E.

Between Stations 247 and 248, July 4, 1875; Yokohama to Sandwich Islands; lat. 36° 42' N., long. 179° 50' W.

II. Deposit shells.

Station 219, March 10, 1875; Admiralty Islands to Yokohama; lat. 1° 54' 0" S., long. 146° 39' 40" E.; depth, 150 fathoms; bottom, coral mud.

2. *Cleodora pygmæa*, Boas.

1886. *Cleodora pygmæa*, Boas, Spolia atlantica, p. 84, pl. iv. fig. 57.

The close resemblance which this form presents to *Cleodora compressa* shows that it must be the young stage of a species nearly allied to *Cavolinia trispinosa*. But the only species very nearly related to the latter is *Cavolinia quadridentata*.

In the last mentioned, as in *Cavolinia longirostris*, the initial portion of the adult shell is caducous, and is as yet quite unknown, so that *Cleodora pygmæa* fills up a blank.

The three dorsal ribs of *Cleodora pygmæa* correspond absolutely to those of *Cavolinia quadridentata*. The latter is more globular than *Cavolinia trispinosa*; *Cleodora pygmæa* is also less flattened than *Cleodora compressa*. Finally, the geographical distribution of the two forms is virtually the same; *Cleodora pygmæa* has only been found in localities where *Cavolinia quadridentata* also occurred, in the Indian and Pacific Oceans.

3. *Cleodora curvata*, Souleyet.

1850. *Clio pellucida*, Gray (*pars*), Catalogue of the Mollusca in the Collection of the British Museum, pt. ii., Pteropoda, p. 14.

1852. *Cleodora curvata*, Souleyet, Voyage de la Bonite, Zoologie, t. ii. p. 185, pl. vii. figs. 6–10.

Boas, following Souleyet, regards this form as a species of *Clio* (*Cleodora*), and denies that it is only a young stage.[1] Nevertheless it must be noted (1) that the figure of Souleyet shows that the genital organs are scarcely developed, a good proof that the form is not adult, and (2) that the absence of a marked constriction limiting the embryonic shell shows that the form in question is a *Cavolinia* and not a *Clio*. Krohn[2] has already identified it as a young *Cavolinia*.

[1] Spolia atlantica, p. 81.
[2] Beiträge zur Entwickelungsgeschichte der Pteropoden und Heteropoden, p. 43.

As to the species to which this young form should be referred, the slight curvature of the lateral margins leads me to believe that it belongs to a species in which the posterior portion is relatively much developed; and the great breadth of this region in proportion to its length, as well as the absence of dorsal ribs, lead me to regard *Cleodora curvata* as simply a young stage of *Carolinia uncinata*. It may be further noted that *Cleodora curvata* has only been found in the Atlantic where *Carolinia uncinata* is most abundant.

To his *Cleodora curvata* Souleyet[1] referred *Hyalæa rugosa*, d'Orbigny. But the latter appears to me to differ considerably in being less thick, in having a proportionately greater length, and in exhibiting a less marked curvature.

Finally, the form described by Huxley under the title *Cleodora curvata* is not a *Clio* at all, since Huxley himself speaks[2] of the "shell fissured laterally," and of the "filiform appendages of the mantle." It is also a *Carolinia*, but differs from the *Cleodora curvata* of Souleyet, and corresponds to *Hyalæa depressa*, d'Orbigny (see below).

4. *Pleuropus longifilis*, Troschel.

> 1854. *Pleuropus longifilis*, Troschel, Beiträge zur Kenntniss der Pteropoden, Archiv f. Naturgesch., Jahrg. xx. Bd. i. p. 208, pl. viii. figs. 1, 3.
> 1855. *Hyalæa complanata*, Gegenbaur, Untersuchungen über Pteropoden und Heteropoden, pp. 40, 211, pl. i. fig. 1.
> 1886. *Hyalæa longifilis*, Boas, Spolia atlantica, p. 128, pl. iv. figs. 64, 65.

Cantraine has already recognised in this form (which he identified with *Hyalæa lævigata*, d'Orbigny) the young stage of *Carolinia tridentata*. It is to this species that one must refer the forms described by Troschel and Gegenbaur.

At the suggestion of Dr. Paul Schiemenz, I took occasion at Naples to examine numerous specimens of *Hyalæa tridentata*, among which I could note all the transitions, in size and thickness, between *Pleuropus longifilis* and the typical adult *Carolinia tridentata*. I also observed that the stage *longifilis* might be abnormally prolonged to a late period, and then developed into specimens of large size and flattened form, with the closing apparatus not yet developed, and with the reproductive system still immature.

5. *Hyalæa rotundata*, Boas.

> 1886. *Hyalæa rotundata*, Boas, Spolia atlantica, p. 129, pl. iv. figs. 59–61.

This form is certainly the young stage of *Carolinia globulosa*. That this is so is sufficiently demonstrated by the following characters common to the two forms:—

1. Dorso-ventral dilation of the shell;

---

[1] Histoire naturelle des Mollusques Ptéropodes, p. 52.
[2] On the Morphology of the Cephalous Mollusca, Phil. Trans., 1853, p. 42.

2. The inconsiderable breadth of the posterior portion ;

3. The similar disposition of dorsal ribs ;

4. The shortness of the rostrum or posterior point.

6. Hyalæa lævigata, d'Orbigny.

1836. *Hyalæa lævigata*, d'Orbigny, Voyage dans l'Amérique méridionale, t. v. p. 110, pl. vii. figs. 15, 19.

1850. *Diacria lævigata*, Gray, Catalogue of the Mollusca in the Collection of the British Museum, pt. ii., Pteropoda, p. 11.

1858. *Pleuropus lævigatus*, A. and H. Adams, The Genera of Recent Mollusca, vol. ii. p. 611.

I refer this form to *Cavolinia longirostris*, with which it appears to have most affinity :—

1. In the horizontal direction of the posterior margins ;

2. In the way the ventral lip extends posteriorly beyond the dorsal ;

3. In the two inconspicuous dorsal grooves ;

4. In the curvature of the posterior portion (in *Cavolinia longirostris* the initial portion of the shell is always broken off, but even the direction of the truncature shows that the portion which has disappeared would have been much recurved dorsally). It is of course not to be imagined that "*Hyalæa lævigata*" is the caducous portion of *Cavolinia longirostris*, to which only its posterior recurved portion corresponds.

The geographical distribution of the two forms is the same. *Cavolinia longirostris* is abundant in localities where *Hyalæa lævigata* has been found.

*7. Hyalæa depressa, d'Orbigny.

1825. *Pleuropus pellucidus*, Eschscholtz, Bericht über die zoologische Ausbeute während der Reise von Cronstadt bis St. Peter und Paul, Oken, Isis, 1825, p. 735, pl. v. fig. 2 (*male*).

1836. *Hyalæa depressa*, d'Orbigny, Voyage dans l'Amérique méridionale, t. v. p. 110, pl. vii. figs. 11–14.

1850. *Clio pellucida*, Gray, Catalogue of the Mollusca in the Collection of the British Museum, pt. ii., Pteropoda, p. 14.

1850. *Diacria depressa*, Gray, Ibid., p. 11.

1853. *Cleodora curvata*, Huxley, On the Morphology of the Cephalous Mollusca, &c., Phil. Trans., 1853, p. 42, pl. iv. figs. 4, 5.

1858. *Pleuropus depressus*, A. and H. Adams, The Genera of Recent Mollusca, vol. ii. p. 611.

Souleyet[1] has referred *Pleuropus pellucidus* to *Clio cuspidata*, and Gray to "*Cleodora curvata*," Souleyet. These identifications appear to me erroneous, as in my opinion *Pleuropus pellucidus* corresponds to *Hyalæa depressa*. But as the description and figure given by Eschscholtz are equally bad, it is better to ignore entirely the title which he has bestowed.

[1] Histoire naturelle des Mollusques Ptéropodes, p. 48.

On the other hand, Souleyet[1] expresses his belief that *Hyalæa depressa* is only a young state of *Carolinia inflexa*. This opinion[2] seems to me correct. In fact my examination of a specimen of *Hyalæa depressa* showed me that this form was sexually immature, with incompletely developed accessory genital glands, while on the other hand the slight thickness of the shell, the length, the comparative narrowness, and the curvature of the posterior portion, are in favour of Souleyet's theory; and besides, *Hyalæa depressa* has been found almost always where *Carolinia inflexa* occurred in abundance, namely, in the Pacific Ocean, 20° S., 87° W. (d'Orbigny), 5° N., 115° W.; Callao to Honolulu ("Vettor Pisani" Expedition, June 9, 1884); in the Indian Ocean, Colombo to Aden ("Vettor Pisani" Expedition, March 10, 1885); and, finally, in the Atlantic (Challenger Expedition).

Challenger Specimens.—I. Living specimens.

Station 216a, February 16, 1875; Samboangan to New Guinea; lat. 2° 46′ N., long. 134° 11′ E.

On May 4, 1875; at Yokohama.

Station 350, April 11, 1876; Ascension Island to St. Vincent; lat. 10° 55′ N., long. 17° 46′ W.

II. Deposit shells.

Station 219, March 10, 1875; Admiralty Islands to Yokohama; lat. 1° 54′ 0″ S., long. 146° 39′ 40″ E.; depth, 150 fathoms; bottom, coral mud.

There remain four other names, which are not mentioned by Boas, viz.,

Hyalæa truncata, Lesueur.[3]	*Cleodora trifilis*, Troschel.[5]
Hyalæa rugosa, d'Orbigny[4] (*Balantium rugosum*, Gray).	*Pleuropus kargeri*, Verrill.[6]

Souleyet[7] refers the two former to his "*Cleodora curvata*." This appears to me inaccurate. *Hyalæa rugosa* (which has been found in the South-east Pacific) differs from "*Cleodora curvata*" in being less thick, in being longer in proportion to breadth, and in having a less marked curvature.

I regard this form and *Pleuropus kargeri* (North-west Atlantic) as two successive stages of *Carolinia gibbosa*. The length, the slight thickness, the moderate curvature of the initial point in both forms, as well as the slight divergence of the lateral margins, support this opinion.

[1] Histoire naturelle des Mollusques Ptéropodes, p. 44.

[2] Shared by Weinkauff (Die Conchylien des Mittelmeeres, t. ii. p. 424).

[3] In de Blainville, Hyale, Dict. d. Sci. Nat., t. xxii. p. 82.

[4] Voyage dans l'Amérique méridionale, t. v. p. 118, pl. viii. figs. 12–14.

[5] Beiträge zur Kenntniss der Pteropoden, Archiv f. Naturgesch., 1854, Bd. i. p. 205, pl. viii. fig. 4.

[6] Catalogue of the Mollusca added to the Fauna of New England during the past ten years, Trans. Connect. Acad., vol. v. p. 555.

[7] Histoire naturelle des Mollusques Ptéropodes, p. 52.

As to "*Cleodora trifilis*," it is difficult to determine to what adult form this young stage should be referred. But the absence of any well-marked constriction separating the embryonic shell, and the presence of three lateral appendages on each side of the mantle, show clearly that we have here to do with a *Cavolinia* and not with a *Clio* (*Cleodora*). But according to Troschel the posterior portion of the shell is not curved, while all the species of *Cavolinia* (except the group *Cavolinia trispinosa* and *Cavolinia quadridentata*, where the embryonic shell is markedly separate) exhibit a dorsal curvature of the initial portion. The position of "*Cleodora trifilis*" must therefore remain uncertain.

Family III. CYMBULIIDÆ.

1841. *Cymbulida*, Cantraine, Malacologie méditerranéens et littorale, Mém. Acad. Sci. Bruxelles, t. xiii. p. 33.
Hyalaida, pars, Auctorum.
1885. *Alata*, Wagner, Die Wirbellosen des weissen Meeres, Bd. i. p. 119.

Characters.—" Shell " straight, bilaterally symmetrical, so-called cartilaginous, quite enveloped in the mantle. The animal cannot completely retire within it. The animal has a ventral pallial cavity, and the fins form a broad disc, on the dorsal margin of which the cephalic portion is laid back.

Description.—The " shell " of the adult Cymbuliidæ is considerably elongated in a dorso-ventral direction. It is somewhat hollowed out in the form of a boot or slipper, and is more or less broadly open ventrally. It is not homologous with the calcareous shell of other Thecosomata. In the Cymbuliidæ the homologue of the latter falls off at the close of the larval life. As to the cartilaginous "deutoconch" or "pseudoconch," it is the result of thickening of the integument. Nor is it the only illustration of such a structure among the Thecosomata, for in *Cavolinia tridentata*, on the anterior portion of the dorsal lip of the shell, there is a small covering portion with the same structure as the " shell " of the Cymbuliidæ, and similarly produced by the mantle, the prolongations of which may cover a considerable portion of the shell.

The deutoconch of the Cymbuliidæ, which is only covered by a delicate epithelial layer, is very readily lost,[1] as the result of which the members of this family have often been described as naked.

The animal has its visceral portion relatively little developed, and the foot, modified as a fin, greatly predominates. The cephalic portion is distinct; it extends beyond the dorsal margin of the fin, and is reflected on the anterior portion of the latter, forming a sort of proboscis, more or less elongated, sometimes remaining free (*Gleba* and *Cymbuliopsis*) or fixed to the surface of the fin. The lips do not consist as in the typical Thecosomata (Cavoliniidæ) of two dorso-ventral folds, united dorsally above the mouth, and continued on divergently to the ventral margin of the fins without re-uniting

[1] By "*Cymbulia*" ovata, Quoy and Gaimard, *Gleba cordata*, Forskål, &c.

ventrally below the mouth; on the contrary they completely surround the mouth, dorsally and ventrally, without being in any way continued on to the fin. Their disposition recalls, especially in the young specimens, that of *Peraclis*.

The two tentacles are absolutely symmetrical, and the right one is not enclosed in a sheath. The penis is situated on the dorsal surface of the head, in the median line in the adult.

The orientation of these animals is given but unsatisfactorily in malacological descriptive works. This is especially true, as we shall see, of *Cymbulia*, and is due to the marked external difference between the Cymbuliidæ and the other Thecosomata.

From a systematic point of view the family is yet more unsatisfactorily known than even the Limacinidæ. For the shell of the adult Cymbuliidæ not only has a morphological import different from that of the other Thecosomata, but is also different structurally, and does not admit of being preserved in the dry state. In consequence of which it has received but little attention from the "dry-skin philosophers"; and as in the general systematic treatment of Mollusca, at least as regards genera and species, the conchologists have the upper hand, the result is that our knowledge of the systematic relations of this group is in a rudimentary state, and that the information we possess of the animals is of a most restricted and incomplete character.

It is very unfortunate that the materials as yet at command have not enabled me to make any great progress. I can only interpret more clearly the known facts, correct certain errors, and complete or elucidate certain observations.

The generic names hitherto applied to the forms in this family are four in number :— *Corolla*, *Cymbulia*, *Gleba*, and *Tiedemannia*. Of these four names, two, namely *Corolla* and *Tiedemannia*, are, as we shall afterwards see, synonymous with *Gleba*. There only remain *Cymbulia* and *Gleba* to take account of.

But to distribute the different species of Cymbuliidæ between these two genera, and to determine their respective boundaries, is no easy task, especially with the slight utilisable material at command. This difficulty is increased by the fact that we have shells without animals and animals without shells, and that the latter have been described as naked, while in reality all the adult members of this family possess the so-called "cartilaginous" pseudoconch.

If we survey the different specific titles given to forms referred to the Cymbuliidæ, we find, in addition to the four names of genera, the following seventeen names of species :—

Cymbulia calceola, Verrill.
Cymbulia cirroptera, Gegenbaur.
Cymbulia norfolkensis, Quoy and Gaimard.

Cymbulia ovata, Quoy and Gaimard.
Cymbulia peroni, de Blainville.
Cymbulia proboscidea, Gray.
Cymbulia punctata, Quoy and Gaimard.

Cymbulia quadripunctata, Gegen-
baur.
Cymbulia radiata, Quoy and Gaimard.
Tiedemannia charybdis, Troschel.
Tiedemannia chrysosticta, Krohn.

Tiedemannia creniptera, Krohn.
Tiedemannia napolitana, Delle
Chiaje.
Tiedemannia scyllæ, Troschel.
Corolla spectabilis, Dall.

Gleba cordata, Forskål.

But it is necessary to note that among the above there are :—

1. One title applied to a Gymnosomatous form, Cymbulia norfolkensis, Quoy and Gaimard, which is a Halopsyche (see Report on Gymnosomata).[1]

2. Numerous titles applied to young stages, which have been regarded as distinct forms (after the embryonic development there are yet notable external differences between the very young Cymbuliidæ and the adult forms) :—

Cymbulia punctata, Quoy and Gaimard,
Cymbulia radiata, Quoy and Gaimard,

Tiedemannia scylla, Troschel,
Tiedemannia charybdis, Troschel,

are certainly young forms of Gleba. So too the Cymbulia cirroptera of Gegenbaur is in all probability only the young form of this genus Gleba, nor can I regard Cymbulia quadripunctata, Gegenbaur, as an adult individual.

3. Three titles are synonyms for other species :—

Cymbulia proboscidea, Gray = Cymbulia peroni, de Blainville.
Tiedemannia napolitana, Delle Chiaje, }
Tiedemannia creniptera, Krohn, } = Gleba cordata, Forskål.

There thus remain six titles :—

Cymbulia calceola, Verrill.
Cymbulia peroni, de Blainville.
Cymbulia ovata, Quoy and Gaimard.

Tiedemannia chrysosticta, Krohn.
Corolla spectabilis, Dall.
Gleba cordata, Forskål.

It is necessary now to note that of these six species there are only two which are really well known. These are Cymbulia peroni and Gleba cordata, both from the Mediterranean. The others are very imperfectly known, as for instance Cymbulia ovata and Gleba spectabilis. The latter and Tiedemannia chrysosticta have not yet been figured ; of Cymbulia ovata and Gleba spectabilis I have been able to examine specimens, but these were unfortunately in an insufficient state of preservation.

In utilising the information which we possess in regard to these six forms, we have to face the difficulty which I have mentioned above, the difficulty namely of distributing the different forms between the two genera Gleba and Cymbulia, or, in other words, of establishing the exact limits and differential characteristics of the two genera.

[1] Zool. Chall. Exp., pt. lviii. p. 85.

If we restrict our attention to *Cymbulia peroni* and *Gleba cordata*, the question is indeed simplified. We see then, in *Gleba*, a free elongated proboscis, a fin with continuous margin, without ventral lobe, and a "shell" of considerable delicacy, almost without cavity, and with a nearly smooth surface; while in *Cymbulia*, on the contrary, we find a fin with a ventral lobe, a short proboscis, not at all free, and a thick "shell" with a marked cavity and with a spiny surface. Thus we understand how the differentiating characters of the two genera are given with so much definiteness by the authors[1] who establish their generic diagnosis according to these two forms.

But these two forms (*Cymbulia peroni* and *Gleba cordata*) are precisely the two extremes of the series of Cymbuliidæ, and if we turn from these to the four other forms already enumerated, we find :—

1. In *Tiedemannia chrysosticta* and in *Corolla spectabilis*, which belong to the genus *Gleba*, the proboscis is very short, as is also the case in a form from the Atlantic, figured by Boas (pl. iii. fig. 31, Spolia atlantica).

2. In "*Cymbulia*" *ovata* and in "*Cymbulia*" *calceola*, the fin presents a continuous margin and no ventral lobe. In these respects they thus resemble *Gleba*, while the proboscis, which is indeed short, is free, and resembles that of *Tiedemannia chrysosticta* and *Corolla spectabilis*. The "shell," on the other hand, is altogether different, both from that of *Cymbulia* and that of *Gleba*, for it is rather thin, with a tuberculated surface, and with a very large cavity.

J. D. Macdonald also figures[2] a *Cymbulia* from the Indian Ocean without a ventral lobe to the fin. I have unfortunately been unable to see his specimens, but I entertain much doubt as to the form of this fin, since the "shell" of this form is very like that of *Cymbulia peroni* from the Mediterranean, and the latter, like one of the Challenger forms from the Western Pacific, exhibits a well-developed ventral lobe on the fin.

On the other hand, "*Cymbulia*" *calceola* and "*Cymbulia*" *ovata*, which are entirely destitute of the above lobe, agreeing in this particular with the *Cymbulia* of Macdonald, possess a shell quite different from *Cymbulia peroni*, the *Cymbulia* figured by Macdonald, and *Cymbulia parridentata*, n. sp., from New Zealand. This shell is not pointed dorsally, and does not exhibit ventrally the special truncation seen in the three forms above mentioned. It has a distinct slipper-like form, with thin walls, with a deep cavity, and without spines along its aperture.

From the above it must be evident that the genera *Cymbulia* and *Gleba* are nearer one another than might be inferred from the contrast between *Cymbulia peroni* and *Gleba cordata*. It also becomes obvious that it is impossible to refer to these two genera alone all the forms which have been referred to the family Cymbuliidæ. "*Cymbulia*" *ovata* and "*Cymbulia*" *calceola* cannot be placed within either genus,

[1] See Gegenbaur, Untersuchungen über Pteropoden und Heteropoden, p. 40, note 1.
[2] On the General Characters of the genus Cymbulia, *Proc. Roy. Soc.*, vol. xxxviii. p. 252.

and demand the establishment of a new division which I propose to call *Cymbuliopsis*.

The only way of distributing the different species of Cymbuliidæ seems to me to be as follows :—

1. *Gleba;* proboscis free, fin with a continuous margin, shell flattened, with almost no cavity.
2. *Cymbuliopsis;* proboscis free, fin with a continuous margin, shell in form of a slipper, with a very large cavity.
3. *Cymbulia;* proboscis fixed throughout its entire length, fin with a ventral lobe, shell thick, with a reduced cavity.

The genus *Cymbulia* will include (1) *Cymbulia peroni*, de Blainville, (2) *Cymbulia parvidentata*, n. sp., (3) a form of which a specimen without shell was collected by the Challenger in the Western Pacific Ocean, and very probably also the *Cymbulia* of the Indian Ocean figured by Macdonald.

The genus *Cymbuliopsis* will include (1) *Cymbulia ovata*, Quoy and Gaimard, and (2) *Cymbulia calceola*, Verrill.

Finally, the genus *Gleba* will include (1) *Gleba cordata*, Forskål, (2) *Tiedemannia chrysosticta*, Krohn, and (3) *Corolla spectabilis*, Dall.

Cymbulia,[1] Péron and Lesueur.

1810. *Cymbulia*, Péron et Lesueur, Histoire de la famille des Mollusques Ptéropodes, Ann. Mus. Hist. Nat. Paris, t. xv. p. 66.

Characters and Description.—The "*shell*" or deutoconch, described as cartilaginous or gelatinous, is elongated in a dorso-ventral direction, and has a moderately elongated cavity and a pointed dorsal extremity. The external surface is covered with tubercles arranged in rows parallel to the main axis, the dorsal extremity is always dilated and projects more or less markedly.

The animal has a natatory disc of considerable breadth, and a ventral lobe on the foot. The cephalic portion is reflected on the dorsal margin of the fin, but is fixed throughout its length, and constricted towards its distal extremity. A radula and jaws.[2]

The orientation of *Cymbulia*, and indeed of all the species of Cymbuliidæ, has been generally misunderstood, especially in general works on Mollusca. First of all, in regard to the position of the animal within the shell there has been a difference of opinion somewhat analogous to that ancient discussion in regard to *Nautilus*.

---

[1] Corruption of *Cymbula*, slipper.

[2] Woodward, in his Manual of the Mollusca (1856), notes two stomachal plates, while in 1839 van Beneden recognised four, and this any one might verify. Nevertheless the manuals of conchology have continued to copy from Woodward, and mention only two plates, as for example in the Structural and Systematic Conchology of Tryon—a compilation destitute of scientific value.

De Blainville criticises the figure of Péron and Lesueur,[1] and affirms that the animal is turned in the wrong direction in relation to the shell. He figures *Cymbulia* with the animal turned in the opposite direction.[2] But his characteristic love of criticism is in this instance at fault, for it is in his figure that the animal is inverted. The uncertainty as to the orientation of the animal in relation to the shell is doubtless due to the readiness with which shell and animal are separated, and the difficulty of preserving the specimens in their natural position. The same reason has led some authors to assert in regard to *Cymbulia* what has been affirmed of the female *Argonauta*, that the shell was not produced by the animal at all.[3]

In regard to the position of anterior and posterior extremities of the shell and of the animal, Woodward's Manual of the Mollusca, which has been followed by all subsequent treatises, represents the pointed extremity of the shell of *Cymbulia peroni* as anterior, and the truncated end as posterior. Macdonald,[4] however, does not accept this statement, but gives a diametrically opposite interpretation. According to him the truncated extremity is anterior. Both these conclusions are inaccurate.

The source of error lies in the external differences between the shell of Cymbuliidæ and those of Cavoliniidæ, and in the great elongation of the dorso-ventral axis, which has led to its being regarded as antero-posterior.

To elucidate the true orientation of the shell, it is necessary to make an examination of the animal itself. An investigation of the latter shows that the pallial cavity, which in all the Thecosomata (except the Limacinidæ) opens ventrally, in consequence of a secondary process to be explained in the Anatomical Report, opens in *Cymbulia peroni* in the direction of the truncated extremity of the shell. This extremity ought therefore to be considered as ventral. On the other hand, the dorsal portion of the animal, as determined by the position of the tentacles, is situated on the side of the pointed end. This extremity is therefore to be regarded

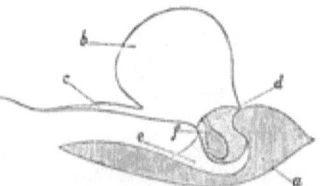

Fig. 1.—Sagittal section of a *Cymbulia*; *a*, shell; *b*, fin; *c*, ventral lobe of the foot and its whip-like process; *d*, visceral mass; *e*, pallial cavity; *f*, alimentary canal.

as dorsal, and the antero-posterior axis of the shell is the short axis at right angles to the surface of the fins.

Among the forms referred to this genus only one is well known. There is also a second new form of which unfortunately only the shell is known.

[1] Histoire de la famille des Mollusques Ptéropodes, *Ann. Mus. Hist. Nat. Paris*, t. xv. pl. iii. fig. 10.
[2] Manuel de Malacologie, pl. xliii. fig. 3.
[3] Cantraine, Malacologie méditerranéenne et littorale, *Mém. Acad. Sci. Bruxelles*, t. xiii. p. 35.
[4] On the General Characters of the Genus Cymbulia, *Proc. Roy. Soc.*, vol. xxxviii. p. 251.

I have already mentioned that I have much doubt in regard to the form of the fin in the "Cymbulia" from the Indian Ocean, as figured by Macdonald. I am of opinion that this species (if distinct from the Mediterranean Cymbulia peroni) belongs to the above genus and bears a ventral lobe on the fin. This seems the more likely since Cymbulia peroni, in which the ventral lobe is indubitably present, has also been figured by Deshayes[1] as if it were really absent.

Finally, a fourth form of this genus is represented by a specimen without a shell, collected by the Challenger in the Pacific Ocean. It is possible that this form corresponds to Cymbulia parvidentata, n. sp., from New Zealand, of which only the shell is known. This cannot, however, be affirmed as fact. The single specimen of the above-mentioned form is stained and mounted in balsam; it is therefore impossible to give any satisfactory description.

The above facts comprise all we know about the Cymbuliidæ, from a systematic point of view. Abstracting the two forms last mentioned, we may distinguish the other two as follows :—

KEY TO THE SPECIES.

1. Shell with a somewhat broad cavity, with strong spines, chiefly along the aperture, ... *Cymbulia peroni.*
2. Shell with a very narrow cavity, with small and uniform spines, . . *Cymbulia parvidentata.*

1. *Cymbulia peroni*, de Blainville.

> 1818. *Cymbulia peroni*, de Blainville, Dict. d. Sci. Nat., t. xii. p. 333, pl. lix. fig. a.
> 1850. *Cymbulia proboscidea*, Gray, Catalogue of the Mollusca in the Collection of the British Museum, pt. ii., Pteropoda, p. 25 (non Krohn, 1844).

This form is sufficiently well known to dispense with a fresh description. I shall restrict myself to distinguishing it from the next species. The dorsal portion of the shell is swollen and short; the extremity is markedly obtuse; the shell does not exhibit any constriction at the middle of its length; the two lines of tubercles, which end in the two ventral points, are distinctly parallel, and the spines which bound the aperture are larger on the right than on the left.

Among the numerous figures of this species, many are poor, and few satisfactory. That of Boas[2] has been based on a small specimen, preserved in alcohol. The best idea of the living animal is obtained from the figure given by Delle Chiaje.[3]

Habitat.—Mediterranean ; Nice, Villefranche, Civita Vecchia, Naples, Messina.

---

[1] Traité élémentaire de Conchyliologie, pl. cii. fig. 3.
[2] Spolia atlantica, pl. iv. fig. 30.
[3] Descrizione et notomia degli animali senza vertebre del Regno di Napoli, pl. xxxii. fig. 1.

Kroha [1] collected in the Atlantic, off Tenerife, some larval forms of *Cymbulia*, but as the adults were not observed, it is not known whether they belong to the present species or not.

Observations.—I. *Cymbulia quadripunctata*, Gegenbaur, is not an adult form. I have no hesitation in describing it as a young *Cymbulia peroni*, for I have observed at Naples, among young forms of *Cymbulia* entirely like one another, an individual with purple spots on the fins as in Gegenbaur's species; but the presence of these spots is no specific distinction.

II. It is uncertain whether the *Cymbulia* of the Indian Ocean figured by Macdonald is identical with *Cymbulia peroni*. It is distinguished especially by the much longer dorsal portion and by the straight contours.

2. *Cymbulia parcidentata*, n. sp. (Pl. II. figs. 12, 13).

Characters and Description.—*Shell* slender, proportionally narrower and more elongated than the above, and exhibiting a constriction towards the middle of its length, the dorsal portion long and pointed, the spines on the surface of small size and very uniform even on the borders of the aperture, where they are very large and distinct in *Cymbulia peroni*. The two rows of spines which end in the ventral points exhibit at their middle a re-entrant angle corresponding to the constriction of the shell. The cavity of the latter is very narrow and of little depth.

Animal unknown.

Dimensions.—Smaller than the preceding species, the shell 3·5 cm. in length.

Habitat.—Cook Strait, New Zealand (the type specimen is in the British Museum).

*3. *Cymbulia* sp. (?).

A specimen of a *Cymbulia*, without its shell, with the fin as in *Cymbulia peroni*, that is to say, bearing a ventral lobe ending in a whip. As the specimen was stained and mounted in balsam, it is difficult to give any detailed description. I shall not bestow on it any specific title. It is possible that it belongs to the above species, in which the animal is still unknown, both forms occurring in the Pacific Ocean.

Challenger Specimen.—Station 254, July 17, 1875; Yokohama to Sandwich Islands; lat. 35° 13′ N., long. 154° 43′ W.

Embryonic shells of *Cymbulia* (Pl. II. fig. 14) have been collected at the following locality :—

Station 216A, February 16, 1875; north of New Guinea; lat. 2° 56′ N., long. 34° 11′ E.

[1] Beiträge zur Entwickelungsgeschichte der Pteropoden und Heteropoden, p. 10.

Cymbuliopsis,[1] n. gen.

Characters and Description.—"Shell" in form of a slipper, with thin walls, and a very large cavity extending to the dorsal extremity. The latter is rounded, while the ventral extremity, which is very delicate, ends in a level margin. The whole external surface is covered with small, uniform tubercles; the aperture is of considerable size; its margins do not bear spines.

The animal has a fin without ventral lobe, that is to say, with a continuous ventral margin. The proboscis is free throughout its entire length, but is short and broad. No radula or jaws.

FIG. 2.—Sagittal section of the shell of *Cymbuliopsis*, in which the dotted line indicates the aperture.

Two species described as *Cymbulia* ought to be referred to this genus—*Cymbulia ovata*, Quoy and Gaimard, and *Cymbulia calceola*, Verrill.

KEY TO THE SPECIES.

1. Shell somewhat constricted at the two ends, aperture shorter than the half-length of the shell, ... *Cymbuliopsis ovata.*
2. Shell rather broad at the two ends, aperture longer than the half-length of the shell, ... *Cymbuliopsis calceola.*

1. *Cymbuliopsis ovata* (Quoy and Gaimard) (Pl. II. figs. 15, 16).

> 1832. *Cymbulia ovata*, Quoy et Gaimard, Voyage de découvertes de l'Astrolabe, Zoologie, t. ii. p. 373, pl. xxvii. figs. 25–30.
> 1852. *Cymbulia ovularis*, Rang, Histoire naturelle des Mollusques Ptéropodes, pl. xi. figs. 1–6.

Characters and Description.—Shell ovoid, very broad in the middle region, constricted towards the ends, and especially at the ventral extremity, where it is very little thickened. The external surface is covered with small uniform tubercles, regularly distributed, but somewhat distant. The aperture is very nearly as long as the half-length of the shell.

The animal exhibits all the characters of the genus. The proboscis is somewhat broad towards the extremity. Quoy and Gaimard have mistaken the proboscis for the ventral lobe of the fin of *Cymbulia*. The fins which they note as being separated by a hollow, have a continuous margin like *Cymbuliopsis calceola* and *Gleba*.

Dimensions.—The shell measures from 2 to 3 cm. in length.

Habitat.—Amboina (Quoy and Gaimard). The British Museum collection includes several specimens, but without note of locality.

[1] *Cymbulia*, and ὄψις, appearance.

2. *Cymbuliopsis calceola* (Verrill).

> 1880. *Cymbulia calceola*, Verrill, Notice of the remarkable Marine Fauna occupying the outer banks off the southern coasts of New England, Amer. Journ. Sci. and Arts, ser. 3, vol. xx. p. 394.
>
> 1882. *Cymbulia calceola*, Verrill, Catalogue of the Marine Mollusca added to the fauna of New England during the past ten years, Trans. Connect. Acad., vol. v. p. 553, pl. lviii. fig. 33.

Characters and Description (after Verrill).—*Shell* ovoid, rounded, but of considerable breadth at the two extremities. The external surface is covered with numerous rounded tubercles; the aperture is larger than the half-length of the shell; the ventral margin is almost straight.

Animal of a pale yellow colour, with a very large fin, exhibiting an entire and continuous margin.

Dimensions.—Maximum length of shell 4 cm., transverse diameter of the fin 67 mm.

Habitat.—Eastern coast of North America, about lat. 40° N., long. 70° W. (Verrill).

Observations.—This species has been somewhat better described than the preceding *Cymbuliopsis ovata*, with which it seems to have close affinities. Verrill does not mention whether the proboscis is free along its entire length, but this seems to me very probable since it is so in the preceding species. I cannot, however, admit the suggestion of Boas,[1] who regards this species as a *Gleba* (*Tiedemannia*). To this view the form of the shell is altogether opposed. On the other hand, it is possible that the "*Tiedemannia*" with short proboscis, from the equatorial Atlantic (lat. 2° N., long. 26° W.), which Boas has figured,[2] may be identical with Verrill's species of *Cymbuliopsis*. In spite of certain points of resemblance, the suggestion cannot, however, be made with any confidence, since the shell was absent in the specimen described by Boas. It is equally difficult to interpret other forms of Cymbuliidæ which have been found without their shells. Thus we have *Argivora parva*, Lesueur,[3] from la Martinique (Antilles), described as a naked *Cymbulia*, but admitting of no certain decision.

Gleba,[4] Forskål.

> 1774. *Gleba*, Forskål, Icones rerum naturalium, pl. xliii. fig. D.
>
> 1830. *Tiedemannia*, Delle Chiaje, in van Beneden's Exercices Zootomiques, Mém. Acad. Sci. Bruxelles, t. xxv. p. 23.

Characters and Description.—*Shell* somewhat short, broad, much flattened, rounded at the dorsal extremity, slightly truncated at the ventral. The cavity is almost absent, so

---

[1] Spolia atlantica, p. 142.
[2] Ibid., pl. iii. figs. 31, 32.
[3] In de Blainville, Manuel de Conchyliologie, p. 655.
[4] *Gleba*, earth-clod.

that the aperture occupies the entire length of the shell. There is a second nuchal portion of the same nature (at least in *Gleba cordata* = *Tiedemannia neapolitana*).

Animal with a cephalic portion ("trompe") more or less elongated, free over its entire length, situated in front of the fin, and enlarged towards its distal extremity.

Fig. 3.—Sagittal section of the shell of *Gleba*; the dotted line indicates the aperture.

Near this the fin forms a disc, with continuous margin, and without ventral lobe. No radula or jaws.

The shell of this genus was observed for the first time by Krohn[1] in *Gleba cordata*. It falls off so readily that specimens without their shells are very frequent, and it is difficult to preserve a specimen intact, with the shell in its natural position. This fact explains how the older authorities (Forskål, van Beneden, Delle Chiaje, &c.) did not observe the shell of *Gleba cordata*, and have even described other species as naked.

There is certain evidence of the presence of this genus in almost all the seas. Unfortunately, a large proportion of the available material consists of incomplete or ill-preserved specimens, while many of the forms noted are only known in their young and immature stages.

The number of species known in their adult state is really only three:—*Gleba cordata*, Forskål, "*Tiedemannia*" *chrysosticta*, Gegenbaur, "*Corolla*" *spectabilis*, Dall, and of these the last two have not yet been figured.

KEY TO THE SPECIES.

I. Proboscis long, .	*Gleba cordata.*
II. Proboscis short.	
1. Gibbed spots on the fin, .	*Gleba chrysosticta.*
2. Fins of an uniform colour, .	*Gleba spectabilis.*

1. *Gleba cordata*, Forskål.

1774. *Gleba cordata*, Forskål, Icones rerum naturalium, pl. xliii. fig. D.
1839. *Tiedemannia neapolitana*, Delle Chiaje, in van Beneden, Exercices zoolomiques, Mém. Acad. Sci. Bruxelles, t. xii. p. 22, pl. ii. fig. 1.
1844. *Cymbulia proboscidea*, Krohn, Ueber eine neue Pteropoden Art, Archiv f. Naturgesch., 1844, Bd. i. p. 327.
1844. *Tiedemannia creniptera*, Krohn, *Ibid.*, pl. ix. fig. A.
1847. *Tiedemannia neapolitana*, Krohn, Nachträge zu den Aufsätzen über Tiedemannia, &c., Archiv f. Naturgesch., 1837, Bd. i. pl. ii. figs. a, c.

This species has been generally but poorly figured. The best drawings are those given by Krohn (*loc. cit.*) and by Gegenbaur,[2] which supplement each other,

---

[1] Nachträge zu den Aufsätzen über Tiedemannia, &c., *Archiv f. Naturgesch.*, 1847, Bd. i. pl. ii. figs. B, c.
[2] Untersuchungen über Pteropoden und Heteropoden, pl. v. fig. 1.

though the tentacles are not shown in the latter. On the margin of the fins the animal has five very characteristic indentations, which escaped the notice of van Beneden but are shown in the drawing of Forskål. Krohn regarded these as characteristic of a particular species, *Tiedemannia creniptera*, distinct from the *Tiedemannia* "*napolitana*" of Delle Chiaje and van Beneden; but he has subsequently acknowledged the identity of the two forms. The shell appears smooth in small specimens, but bears in the large forms regular tubercles, which are, however, less developed than those of *Gleba spectabilis*.

Habitat.—Mediterranean; Nice, Naples, Messina.

Some remains of a species of *Gleba* with a long proboscis were found in the Atlantic, lat. 24° to 25° N., long. 32° to 33° W. (*fide* Boas),[1] and previously to this Krohn observed at Tenerife larvæ of *Tiedemannia* which he named *neapolitana*.[2] Possibly this was the Mediterranean species, or one very nearly related to it.

2. *Gleba chrysosticta* (Krohn).

Tiedemannia chrysosticta, Krohn, MS., in Troschel, Beiträge zur Kenntniss der Pteropoda, Archiv f. Naturgesch., 1854, Bd. i. p. 218.

According to Krohn, Troschel, and Gegenbaur, this species differs from the preceding, which it resembles in size, in having a shorter proboscis and golden spots on the integument. But there are no drawings of this species, and the descriptions do not say whether the proboscis is very broad, nor whether there are indentations on the distal edge of the fins. Notwithstanding the courteous search made by Dr. Jules Barrois at Villefranche and by Professor Nicholas Kleinenberg at Messina, I have unfortunately been unable to procure specimens which would have enabled me to complete the diagnosis of this form.

Habitat.—Mediterranean; Messina (Krohn, Troschel, Gegenbaur), Villefranche (Paneth).[3]

*3. *Gleba spectabilis* (Dall).

1872. *Corolla spectabilis*, Dall, Description of sixty new forms of Mollusca from the West Coast of North America and the North Pacific Ocean, Amer. Journ. of Conch., vol. vii. p. 137.

Characters and Description.—The animal has a short proboscis, which is very broad, especially towards its free extremity; the fin is subtriangular, with no indentations on the distal edge.

Dall has established for this form the new genus *Corolla* on account of the following characteristics:—the pendent visceral mass and absence of shell. Now in *Gleba* ("*Tiedemannia napolitana*" for example), when the shell has fallen off, the

---

[1] Spolia atlantica, p. 141.
[2] Beiträge zur Entwickelungsgeschichte der Pteropoden und Heteropoden, p. 19.
[3] Beiträge zur Histiologie der Pteropoden und Heteropoden, Archiv f. mikrosk. Anat., Bd. xxiv. p. 231, 1885.

visceral mass is pendent and then presents the aspect[1] which is seen in an unpublished drawing of *Corolla spectabilis*, kindly sent me by Mr. Wm. H. Dall. In regard to the other parts, fin, proboscis, &c., this drawing shows a structure quite analogous to the *Gleba*. *Corolla* is then simply a *Gleba* that has lost its shell. The specimen, unfortunately in a bad condition, obtained by the Challenger in the North Pacific, shows this clearly. The specimen includes not only the animal but several bits of the shell. When put together the latter corresponds to the general form of the shell of *Gleba cordata*, somewhat thicker dorsally, very thin on the ventral edge, and bearing on its surface regular and very clearly marked tubercles. Unfortunately, the damaged condition of this shell does not permit me to give a satisfactory drawing.

Mr. Wm. H. Dall has, however, abandoned the idea of his *Corolla* being entirely destitute of shell. In sending me the drawing of the animal he wrote to me that he thought *Corolla* possessed "some sort of a shell like *Cymbulia*," adding that in the region where he had captured *Corolla* he had found in his tow-net "some oval thin crystalline gelatinous slipper-shaped shells," "covered with little points." This entirely agrees with the description I have given of the debris collected by the Challenger.

Dimensions (of Challenger specimen).—Diametrical breadth of the fin a little more than 5 cm., approximate length of the shell 4 cm.

Habitat.—North-east Pacific Ocean ; lat. 42° 50′ N., long. 147° 25′ W. (Dall).

Challenger Specimens.—Living specimen.

On June 29, 1875 ; Yokohama to Sandwich Islands ; lat. 35° 49′ N., long. 171° 46′ E.

The presence of the genus *Gleba* has been recorded at other localities in the Pacific Ocean :—China Sea (Boas),[2] a form with a short proboscis ; New Ireland, about 4° S., 152° W. (Quoy and Gaimard),[3]—*Cymbulia punctata*, also with a short proboscis, and recognised as *Gleba (Tiedemannia)* by most subsequent authors. Unfortunately these forms are too imperfectly known to be entered in the catalogue of the species.

Lastly, the Challenger Expedition has collected larval shells of *Gleba* (Pl. II. fig. 17) in the following place :—

Station 216A, February 16, 1875 ; north of New Guinea ; lat. 20° 56′ N., long. 134° 11′ E.

Several of the young forms of Cymbuliidæ, which have lost their shells, are described as distinct species, under different generic names, and some of these probably belong to the genus *Gleba*.

[1] Van Beneden, Exercices Zootomiques, *Mém. Acad. Sci. Bruxelles*, t. xli. pl. ii. fig. 1.

[2] Spolia atlantica, p. 141.

[3] Voyage de découvertes de l'Astrolabe, Zoologie, t. ii. p. 377, pl. xxvii. figs. 35, 36.

Cymbulia radiata (Quoy and Gaimard,[1] from Amboina). Figure 33 represents a somewhat advanced stage. Gegenbaur and Adams have recognised it as a *Gleba*.

Cymbulia cirroptera, Gegenbaur,[2] from Messina. Lastly, *Tiedemannia scyllæ*, Troschel,[3] and *Tiedemannia charybdis*, Troschel,[4] are also certainly young stages of *Gleba*, as indeed Troschel himself suspected. But in regard to all these young stages, observations are as yet too insufficient to enable one to determine with certainty the adult forms to which they belong.

SUMMARY.

As the result of the preceding survey of the system of the Thecosomata, forty-two species may be recognised, and these are distributed in the following manner :—

Genera.	Species.
Limacina, .	10
Peraclis, .	2
Clio, subgenus *Creseis*, .	4
,, *Hyalocylis*,	1
,, *Styliola*,	1
,, *Clio, s. str.*,	8
Cuvierina, .	1
Cavolinia, .	8
Cymbulia, .	2
Cymbuliopsis, .	2
Gleba, .	3
8	42

Of these forty-two species, there are only five which I have not been able to study myself, and only nine which have not been collected by the Challenger.

[1] Voyage de découvertes de l'Astrolabe, Zoologie, t. ii. p. 375, pl. xxvii. figs. 33, 34.
[2] Untersuchungen über Pteropoden und Heteropoden, p. 53, pl. iii. fig. 21.
[3] Beiträge zur Kenntniss der Pteropoden, Archiv f. Naturgesch., 1854, Bd. i. p. 219, pl. ix. figs. 12, 13.
[4] Ibid., p. 220, pl. ix. figs. 14, 15.

The expedition has thus collected about 75 per cent. of known species, and if in this group it has only discovered a single new species, it has furnished numerous particulars relating to the geographical distribution both at the surface and in the deposits of the deep sea.

From a systematic point of view the most complete results are those which refer to the family Limacinidæ, the species of which are now clearly defined. The genus *Peraclis*, hitherto mistaken, has been studied and definitely re-established, an important fact in view of the light which the knowledge of this genus sheds on the relations of the Thecosomata to one another and to other Molluscs. In short, the classification of the family Cymbuliidæ has been defined as far as is meanwhile possible.

The anatomical results of the study of the Thecosomata are as important as those which were obtained from the study of the Gymnosomata, and, along with the latter, render it possible to determine the real affinities of the Pteropods, as will be shown in the third part of this Report.

GEOGRAPHICAL DISTRIBUTION.

A STATION LIST OF THE THECOSOMATOUS PTEROPODA OF THE CHALLENGER EXPEDITION.

I. Stations where Living Specimens were collected by Trawling or Dredging.

STATION VIIF. February 2, 1873 ; off Madeira ; lat. 32° 27′ 0″ N., long. 16° 40′ 30″ W.; surface temperature, 63° F.

Clio (Creseis) acicula. | *Cavolinia trispinosa.*

Cavolinia globulosa.

On April 14, 1873 ; off Bermuda ; lat. 32° 18′ N., long. 64° 53′ W.

Cavolinia longirostris.

STATION 53. May 26, 1873 ; Halifax to Bermuda ; lat. 36° 30′ N., long. 63° 40′ W.; surface temperature, 73° F.

Cuvierina columnella.

STATION 63. June 19, 1873 ; Bermuda to Azores ; lat. 35° 29′ N., long. 50° 53′ W.; surface temperature, 71° F.

Clio (Creseis) acicula. | *Cuvierina columnella.*

Clio pyramidata. | *Cavolinia trispinosa.*

STATION 81. July 13, 1873 ; Azores to Madeira ; lat. 34° 11′ N., long. 19° 52′ W.; surface temperature, 71° F.

Clio (Creseis) acicula.

STATION 100. August 16, 1873 ; St. Vincent to St. Paul's Rocks ; lat. 7° 1′ N., long. 15° 55′ W.; surface temperature, 79° F.

Cavolinia uncinata.

STATION 106.   August 25, 1873 ; St. Vincent to St. Paul's Rocks; lat. 1° 47′ N., long. 24° 26′ W.; surface temperature, 78°·8 F.

Clio (Creseis) virgula. | Cavolinia longirostris.

Near Station 129.   September 19, 1873 ; off Bahia ; lat. 19° 6′ S., long. 35° 40′ W.; surface temperature, 74° F.

Cavolinia uncinata. | Cavolinia inflexa.

STATION 142.   December 18, 1873 ; Cape of Good Hope to parallel of 46° S.; lat. 35° 4′ S., long. 18° 37′ E.; surface temperature, 65°·5 F.

Limacina inflata. | Clio pyramidata.

Cavolinia inflexa.

STATION 143.   December 19, 1873 ; Cape of Good Hope to parallel of 46° S.; lat. 36° 48′ S., long. 19° 24′ E.; surface temperature, 73° F.

Cavolinia inflexa.

STATION 146.   December 28, 1873 ; Marion Island to the Crozets ; lat. 46° 46′ S., long. 45° 31′ E.; surface temperature, 43° F.

Limacina australis.

STATION 149.   January 9, 1874 ; at Kerguelen Island; lat. 49° 8′ S., long. 70° 12′ E.; surface temperature, 40° F. (?).

Limacina australis.

STATION 150.   February 2, 1874 ; Heard Island ; lat. 52° 4′ S., long. 71° 22′ E.; surface temperature, 37°·5 F.

Limacina australis. | Clio sulcata.

STATION 153.   February 14, 1874 ; in vicinity of Antarctic ice ; lat. 65° 42′ S., long. 79° 49′ E.; surface temperature, 29°·5 F.

Limacina antarctica.

Between Stations 154 and 155.   February 21, 1874 ; in vicinity of Antarctic ice ; lat. 63° 30′ S., long. 89° 8′ E.; surface temperature, 32° F.

Limacina australis. | Clio sulcata.

STATION 156.   February 26, 1874 ; in vicinity of Antarctic ice ; lat. 62° 26′ S., long. 95° 44′ E.; surface temperature, 33° F.

Clio sulcata.

STATION 139. March 10, 1874 ; Termination land to Melbourne ; lat. 47° 25′ S., long. 130° 22′ E.; surface temperature, 51°·5 F.

Clio australis.

On March 15, 1874 ; off Melbourne ; lat. 39° 45′ S., long. 40° 40′ E.; surface temperature, 59° F.

Clio (Styliola) subula. | *Clio pyramidata.*

On March 16, 1874 ; off Melbourne ; lat. 39° 22′ S., long. 142° 22′ E.; surface temperature, 62° F.

Clio (Styliola) subula.

Between Stations 162 and 163. April 3, 1874 ; Melbourne to Sydney ; lat. 38° 7′ S., long. 149° 18′ E.; surface temperature, 65° F.

Limacina inflata.	*Clio (Creseis) virgula.*
Limacina lesueuri.	*Cavolinia trispinosa* (young, as
Limacina trochiformis.	" *Cleodora compressa* ").
Limacina bulimoides.	*Cavolinia longirostris.*

STATION 163. April 4, 1874 ; Melbourne to Sydney ; lat. 36° 57′ S., long. 150° 34′ E.; surface temperature, 72° F.

Limacina bulimoides.

STATION 164A. June 13, 1874 ; off Sydney ; lat. 34° 9′ S., long. 151° 55′ E.; surface temperature, 70°·2 F.

Clio (Creseis) virgula.	*Cavolinia inflexa* (young, as
Clio (Creseis) acicula.	" *Hyalæa depressa* ").
Clio (Styliola) subula.	

STATION 175. August 12, 1874 ; Fiji to Raine Island ; lat. 19° 2′ S., long. 177° 10′ E.; surface temperature, 77°·5 F.

Limacina inflata.	*Clio (Styliola) subula.*
Limacina lesueuri.	*Clio pyramidata.*
Limacina bulimoides.	*Cuvierina columnella.*
Clio (Creseis) acicula.	*Cavolinia quadridentata.*
Clio (Hyalocylix) striata.	*Cavolinia longirostris.*

Cavolinia inflexa.

STATION 181.   August 25, 1874 ; Fiji to Raine Island ; lat. 13° 50′ S., long. 151° 49′
E.; surface temperature, 80° F.

Limacina inflata.	*Clio chaptali.*
Limacina bulimoides.	*Cuvierina columnella.*
Clio (Creseis) virgula.	*Cavolinia trispinosa* (and young, as
Clio (Creseis) acicula.	" *Cleodora compressa* ").
Clio (Hyalocylix) striata.	*Cavolinia quadridentata.*
Clio (Styliola) subula.	*Cavolinia longirostris.*

Cavolinia inflexa.

Near Station 190.   September 12, 1874 ; south of Arrou Islands ; lat. 8° 56′ S., long.
135° 7′ E.; surface temperature, 79° F.

Clio (Creseis) acicula.

STATION 200.   October 23, 1874 ; Amboina to Samboangan ; lat. 6° 47′ N., long.
122° 28′ E.; surface temperature, 84° F.

Clio (Creseis) acicula.	*Clio (Hyalocylix) striata.*

STATION 201.   October 26, 1874 ; Samboangan to Manila ; lat. 7° 3′ N., long.
121° 48′ E.; surface temperature, 83° F.

Limacina inflata.	*Clio (Creseis) acicula.*
Limacina bulimoides.	*Clio (Hyalocylix) striata.*

STATION 209.   January 22, 1875 ; Manila to Samboangan ; lat. 10° 14′ N., long.
123° 54′ E.; surface temperature, 81° F.

Clio (Creseis) virgula.	*Clio (Creseis) acicula.*

Cavolinia longirostris.

On February 5, 1875 ; at Samboangan ; surface temperature, 82° F.

Clio (Creseis) virgula.	*Clio (Creseis) acicula.*

On February 6, 1875 ; at Samboangan ; lat. 6° 40′ N., long. 122° 57′ E.; surface temperature, 81° F.

Clio (Creseis) virgula.	*Clio (Creseis) acicula.*

Cavolinia globulosa.

STATION 213.   February 8, 1875 ; Samboangan to New Guinea ; lat. 5° 47′ N., long.
124° 1′ E.; surface temperature, 81° F.

Cavolinia longirostris.

STATION 216A. February 16, 1875; north of New Guinea; lat. 2° 56′ N., long.
134 11′ E.; surface temperature, 82° F.

Limacina inflata.	*Cuvierina columnella.*
Limacina lesueuri.	*Cavolinia quadridentata.*
Limacina trochiformis.	*Cavolinia longirostris* (young, as
Clio (Creseis) virgula.	*Hyalæa lævigata*).
Clio (Creseis) acicula.	*Cavolinia globulosa.*
Clio balantium.	Fry of *Cymbulia* and *Gleba.*

Between Stations 229 and 230. April 3, 1875; Admiralty Islands to Yokohama;
lat. 24° 49′ N., long. 138° 34′ E.; surface temperature, 71° F.

Clio (Creseis) virgula.	*Clio (Styliola) subula.*
Cavolinia gibbosa.	

Near Station 230. April 4, 1875; Admiralty Islands to Yokohama; lat. 25° 33′ N.,
long. 137° 57′ E.; surface temperature, 69° F.

Clio (Styliola) subula.	*Cavolinia gibbosa.*
Clio cuspidata.	*Cavolinia inflexa.*

STATION 230. April 5, 1875; Admiralty Islands to Yokohama; lat. 26° 29′ N., long.
137° 57′ E.; surface temperature, 69° F.

Clio (Creseis) virgula.	*Cavolinia trispinosa.*
Clio (Hyalocylix) striata.	*Cavolinia longirostris.*
Clio pyramidata.	*Cavolinia gibbosa.*
Cuvierina columnella.	*Cavolinia inflexa.*

On May 4, 1875; at Yokohama; surface temperature, 60° F.

Cavolinia inflexa (young, as " *Pleuropus pellucidus*"; *fide* Willemoes Suhm).

STATION 237. June 17, 1875; off Japan; lat. 34° 37′ N., long. 140° 32′ E.; surface
temperature, 73° F.

Clio (Creseis) acicula.

STATION 241. June 23, 1875; off Japan; lat. 35° 41′ N., long. 157° 42′ E.; surface
temperature, 69°·2 F.

Cavolinia tridentata.

STATION 243. June 26, 1875; Yokohama to Sandwich Islands; lat. 35° 24′ N., long.
166° 35′ E.; surface temperature, 71° F.

Limacina bulimoides.

On June 29, 1875 ; Yokohama to Sandwich Islands ; lat. 35° 49′ N., long. 171° 46′ E.; surface temperature, 69° F.

Gleba spectabilis.

Between Stations 247 and 248.   July 4, 1875 ; Yokohama to Sandwich Islands ; lat. 36° 42′ N., long. 179° 50′ W.; surface temperature, 70° F.

Limacina lesueuri.   *Cavolinia trispinosa* (young, as
Limacina bulimoides.   " *Cleodora compressa* ").
Clio (Hyalocyliz) striata.

Cavolinia inflexa (young, as " *Hyalæa depressa* ").

STATION 249.   July 7, 1875 ; Yokohama to Sandwich Islands ; lat. 37° 59′ N., long. 171° 48′ W.; surface temperature, 65°·2 F.

Cavolinia gibbosa.

STATION 251.   July 10, 1875 ; Yokohama to Sandwich Islands ; lat. 37° 37′ N., long. 163° 26′ W.; surface temperature, 65° F.

Clio pyramidata.

STATION 254.   July 17, 1875 ; Yokohama to Sandwich Islands ; lat. 35° 13′ N., long. 154° 43′ W.; surface temperature, 72° F.

Clio (Hyalocyliz) striata.   *Clio cuspidata.*
Clio pyramidata.   *Cavolinia tridentata.*

Cymbulia sp.

STATION 256.   July 21, 1875 ; Yokohama to Sandwich Islands ; lat. 30° 22′ N., long. 154° 56′ W.; surface temperature, 74° F.

Clio (Creseis) acicula.   *Clio pyramidata.*
Clio (Styliola) subula.   *Cavolinia inflexa.*

Between Stations 264 and 265.   August 24, 1875 ; Sandwich Islands to Tahiti ; lat. 13° 15′ N., long. 152° 2′ W.; surface temperature, 78° F.

Limacina inflata.   *Peraclis reticulata.*
Limacina lesueuri.   *Clio (Creseis) virgula.*
Limacina trochiformis.   *Clio (Hyalocyliz) striata.*

STATION 269.   September 2, 1875 ; Sandwich Islands to Tahiti ; lat. 5° 54′ N., long. 147° 2′ W.; surface temperature, 81°·2 F.

Cavolinia longirostris.

STATION 272. September 8, 1875; Sandwich Islands to Tahiti; lat. 3° 48′ S., long. 152° 56′ W.; surface temperature, 79° F.

Limacina lesueuri.

"August—September 1875," without indication of Station, in the trip from Sandwich Islands to Tahiti.

Clio (Creseis) acicula.	*Cavolinia longirostris.*
Cavolinia quadridentata.	*Cavolinia gibbosa.*

Cavolinia uncinata.

STATION 280. October 4, 1875; Tahiti to Valparaiso; lat. 18° 40′ S., long. 149° 52′ W.; surface temperature, 77°·2 F.

Cuvierina columnella.

STATION 282. October 7, 1875; Tahiti to Valparaiso; lat. 23° 46′ S., long. 149° 59′ W.; surface temperature, 73°·2 F.

Clio (Hyalocylix) striata.

STATION 288. October 21, 1875; Tahiti to Valparaiso; lat. 40° 3′ S., long. 132° 58′ W.; surface temperature, 54°·5 F.

Cuvierina columnella.

Near Station 288. October 22, 1875; Tahiti to Valparaiso; lat. 40° 0′ S., long. 131° 36′ W.; surface temperature, 54° F.

Cuvierina columnella.

Between Stations 292 and 293. October 31, 1875; Tahiti to Valparaiso; lat. 38° 50′ S., long. 108° 6′ W.; surface temperature, 54° F.

Clio (Creseis) acicula.	*Cavolinia longirostris.*

STATION 293. November 1, 1875; Tahiti to Valparaiso; lat. 39° 4′ S., long. 105° 5′ W.; surface temperature, 53°·7 F.

Clio (Styliola) subula.	*Clio pyramidata.*

STATION 294. November 3, 1875; Tahiti to Valparaiso; lat. 39° 22′ S., long. 98° 46′ W.; surface temperature, 57°·5 F.

Cuvierina columnella.

(ZOOL. CHALL. EXP.—PART LXV.—1887.) Tu 15

STATION 295.   November 5, 1875 ; Tahiti to Valparaiso ; lat. 38° 7′ S., long. 94° 4′ W.; surface temperature, 58°·5 F.

Cavolinia inflexa.

STATION 299.   December 14, 1875 ; Valparaiso to Gulf of Penas ; lat. 33° 31′ S., long. 74° 43′ W.; surface temperature, 62° F.

Clio (Creseis) virgula.

STATION 323.   February 28, 1876 ; Rio de la Plata to Tristan da Cunha ; lat. 35° 39′ S., long. 50° 47′ W.; surface temperature, 73°·5 F.

Clio (Creseis) acicula.

STATION 326.   March 3, 1876 ; Rio de la Plata to Tristan da Cunha ; lat. 37° 3′ S., long. 44° 17′ W.; surface temperature, 67°·8 F.

Clio (Creseis) acicula.

STATION 327.   March 4, 1876 ; Rio de la Plata to Tristan da Cunha ; lat. 36° 48′ S., long. 42° 45′ W.; surface temperature, 70°·2 F.

Clio (Creseis) acicula. | *Cavolinia inflexa.*

STATION 332.   March 10, 1876 ; Rio de la Plata to Tristan da Cunha ; lat. 37° 29′ S., long. 27° 31′ W.; surface temperature, 64° F.

Clio pyramidata.

STATION 337.   March 19, 1876 ; Tristan da Cunha to Ascension Island ; lat. 24° 38′ N., long. 13° 36′ W.; surface temperature, 77° F.

Limacina inflata.   *Limacina bulimoides.*
Limacina lesueuri.   *Clio (Hyalocylix) striata.*
Limacina trochiformis.   *Clio (Styliola) subula.*
                      Cavolinia quadridentata.

STATION 338.   March 21, 1876 ; Tristan da Cunha to Ascension Island ; lat. 21° 15′ S., long. 14° 2′ W.; surface temperature, 76°·5 F.

Cavolinia longirostris.

STATION 339.   March 23, 1876 ; Tristan da Cunha to Ascension Island ; lat. 17° 26′ S., long. 13° 52′ W.; surface temperature, 76° F.

Clio (Creseis) acicula.

STATION 345. April 4, 1876; Ascension Island to St. Vincent; lat. 5° 45′ S., long. 14° 25′ W.; surface temperature, 82°·8 F.

Cavolinia longirostris.

STATION 348. April 9, 1876; Ascension Island to St. Vincent; lat. 3° 10′ N., long. 14° 51′ W.; surface temperature, 84° F.

Clio (Creseis) virgula.

STATION 349. April 10, 1876; Ascension Island to St. Vincent; lat. 5° 28′ N., long. 14° 38′ W.; surface temperature, 83°·5 F.

Clio (Creseis) acicula. | *Cavolinia longirostris.*

STATION 350. April 11, 1876; Ascension Island to St. Vincent; lat. 7° 33′ N., long. 15° 16′ W.; surface temperature, 84° F.

Cavolinia inflexa (young, as "*Hyalæa depressa*").

STATION 352. April 13, 1876; Ascension Island to St. Vincent; lat. 10° 55′ N., long. 17° 46′ W.; surface temperature, 77°·7 F.

Cavolinia longirostris.

On April 26, 1876; off St. Vincent; lat. 16° 49′ N., long. 25° 14′ W.; surface temperature, 74° F.

Limacina inflata. | *Limacina bulimoides.*
Limacina lesueuri. | *Clio (Creseis) virgula.*
Clio (Creseis) acicula.

On April 28, 1876; off St. Vincent; lat. 17° 47′ N., long. 28° 28′ W.; surface temperature, 73° F.

Clio pyramidata.

On April 29, 1876; off St. Vincent; lat. 18° 8′ N., long. 30° 5′ W.; surface temperature, 73° F.

Clio (Creseis) virgula. | *Clio (Styliola) subula.*
Clio (Creseis) acicula. | *Cavolinia quadridentata.*

STATION 353. May 3, 1876; St. Vincent towards Azores; lat. 26° 21′ N., long. 33° 37′ W.; surface temperature, 70°·7 F.

Clio (Creseis) acicula. | *Cavolinia quadridentata.*
Cavolinia longirostris.

Near Station 354.   May 7, 1876 ; St. Vincent towards Azores ; lat. 34° 22′ N., long.
   34° 23′ W.; surface temperature, 68° F.

Limacina lesueuri.	*Clio (Styliola) subula.*
Limacina bulimoides.	*Cuvierina columnella.*

On May 12, 1876 ; off the Azores ; lat. 42° 52′ N., long. 28° 54′ W.; surface temperature,
   59° F.

Clio (Hyalocylix) striata.	*Clio pyramidata.*

II. PRINCIPAL STATIONS AT WHICH SHELLS OF THECOSOMATA WERE FOUND IN THE DEPOSITS.

Shells of Thecosomata are never found in sediments from a depth greater than 2000
fathoms.   The greatest depth from which they have been procured, as far as I am
aware, is 1950 fathoms (Station 35c).

This absence of the calcareous shells of Thecosomata from the greater depths is due,
according to Mr. John Murray, to the greater proportion of carbonic acid gas in the
water at those depths and to the more rapid solution of these shells in sea water under
great pressure.   This results in the solution of the delicate Pteropod shells at lesser
depths than many other more massive pelagic shells.

The Stations cited below are the principal sources of the deposits which I have
examined.   The list of Pteropoda Thecosomata (as well as of other organisms) found in
the other deposits will be found in the Report on the Deep-Sea Deposits by Mr. John
Murray and Mr. A. Renard.

It is of importance to inquire whether the distribution of the shells of different
species found in the bottom-deposits corresponds to the actual distribution of the living
specimens, or in other words whether the superficial distribution has or has not altered
since the time when the shells began to be deposited on the bottom, and whether any
species represented by empty shells in a given deposit are also found in actual life
at the surface of the same locality.

This inquiry has hitherto yielded but little positive result.   The most striking fact
concerns the distribution of *Limacina bulimoides*, which is not now known as a living
form in the Mediterranean or in the North Atlantic north of 39° N. lat., but is found
in the deep bottom-deposits of both these seas.   In the North Atlantic *Peraclis
reticulata* seemed also to occur further to the north in the deposits than at the surface.
It must be noted that these two forms are species frequenting the warmer waters.   On
the other hand *Limacina retroversa*, which frequents the colder waters, extends somewhat further south in the deposits than at the surface.

The investigation of a larger number of deposits will probably reveal other facts of
a like nature.

STATION VIII. February 12, 1873; off the Canary Islands; lat. 28° 3′ 15″ N., long. 17° 27′ 0″ W.; depth, 620 fathoms; bottom, volcanic mud.

Limacina inflata.
Limacina lesueuri.
Limacina bulimoides.
Peraclis bispinosa.

Clio (Styliola) subula.
Clio pyramidata.
Cavolinia quadridentata.
Cavolinia inflexa.

STATION 3. February 18, 1873; Tenerife to Sombrero Island; lat. 25° 45′ N., long. 20° 14′ W.; depth, 1529 fathoms; bottom, hard ground.

Limacina inflata.
Limacina lesueuri.
Limacina bulimoides.

Clio (Styliola) subula.
Clio pyramidata.
Cavolinia quadridentata.

Cavolinia inflexa.

STATION 23. March 15, 1873; off Sombrero Island; lat. 18° 24′ N., long. 63° 28′ W.; depth, 450 fathoms; bottom, Pteropod ooze.

Limacina inflata.
Limacina triacantha.
Limacina lesueuri.
Limacina bulimoides.
Peraclis reticulata.
Clio (Creseis) virgula.
Clio (Creseis) acicula.
Clio (Styliola) subula.

Clio pyramidata.
Clio cuspidata.
Cuvierina columnella.
Cavolinia trispinosa.
Cavolinia quadridentata.
Cavolinia longirostris.
Cavolinia gibbosa.
Cavolinia uncinata.

Cavolinia inflexa.

STATION 24. March 25, 1873; off Culebra Island; lat. 18° 38′ 30″ N., long. 65° 5′ 30″ W.; depth, 390 fathoms; bottom, Pteropod ooze.

Limacina inflata.
Limacina triacantha.
Limacina lesueuri.
Limacina bulimoides.
Peraclis reticulata.
Clio (Creseis) virgula.
Clio (Creseis) acicula.
Clio (Hyalocylix) striata.

Clio (Styliola) subula.
Clio pyramidata.
Cuvierina columnella.
Cavolinia trispinosa.
Cavolinia quadridentata.
Cavolinia longirostris.
Cavolinia gibbosa.
Cavolinia uncinata.

Cavolinia inflexa.

STATION 32B.   April 3, 1873 ; St. Thomas to Bermuda ; lat. 32° 10′ N., long. 64° 52′
W.; depth, 950 fathoms ; bottom, coral mud.

Limacina inflata.   *Limacina bulimoides.*

STATION 33.   April 4, 1873 ; off Bermuda ; lat. 32° 21′ 30″ N., long. 64° 35′ 55″ W.;
depth, 435 fathoms ; bottom, coral mud.

Limacina inflata.   *Clio (Hyalocylix) striata.*
Limacina triacantha.   *Clio (Styliola) subula.*
Limacina lesueuri.   *Clio pyramidata.*
Limacina bulimoides.   *Cuvierina columnella.*
Peraclis reticulata.   *Cavolinia trispinosa.*
Peraclis bispinosa.   *Cavolinia quadridentata.*
Clio (Creseis) virgula.   *Cavolinia longirostris.*
Clio (Creseis) acicula.   *Cavolinia inflexa.*

STATION 35C.   April 22, 1873 ; off Bermuda ; lat. 32° 15′ N., long. 65° 8′ W.; depth,
1950 fathoms ; bottom, Globigerina ooze.

Clio (Creseis) acicula.   *Clio pyramidata.*
Clio (Styliola) subula.   *Cavolinia trispinosa.*

STATION 70.   June 26, 1873 ; Bermuda to Azores ; lat. 38° 25′ N., long. 35° 50′ W.;
depth, 1675 fathoms ; bottom, Globigerina ooze.

Cavolinia trispinosa.   *Cavolinia gibbosa.*

STATION 75.   July 2, 1873 ; off Fayal (Azores) ; lat. 38° 38′ 0″ N., long. 28° 28′ 30″
W.; depth, 450 fathoms ; bottom, volcanic mud.

Limacina inflata.   *Clio (Styliola) subula.*
Peraclis bispinosa.   *Clio pyramidata.*
                        Cavolinia trispinosa.

STATION 76.   July 3, 1873 ; off the Azores ; lat. 38° 11′ N., long. 27° 9′ W.; depth,
900 fathoms ; bottom, Pteropod ooze.

Limacina inflata.   *Clio pyramidata.*
Peraclis bispinosa.   *Cavolinia trispinosa.*

STATION 78. July 10, 1873 ; off the Azores ; lat. 37° 26′ N., long. 25° 13′ W.; depth, 1000 fathoms ; bottom, volcanic mud.

Limacina inflata.
Limacina triacantha.
Limacina helicoides.
Peraclis reticulata.
Peraclis bispinosa.
Clio (Creseis) acicula.
Clio (Hyalocylix) striata.
Clio (Styliola) subula.
Clio polita.

Clio pyramidata.
Clio cuspidata.
Cuvierina columnella.
Cavolinia trispinosa.
Cavolinia quadridentata.
Cavolinia longirostris.
Cavolinia gibbosa.
Cavolinia tridentata.
Cavolinia inflexa.

STATION 85. July 19, 1873 ; off Palma Island (Canaries); lat. 28° 42′ N., long. 18° 6′ W.; depth, 1125 fathoms ; bottom, volcanic mud.

Limacina inflata.
Limacina triacantha.
Limacina lesueuri.
Limacina bulimoides.
Peraclis reticulata.
Peraclis bispinosa.
Clio (Creseis) acicula.
Clio (Hyalocylix) striata.
Clio (Styliola) subula.

Clio polita.
Clio pyramidata.
Clio cuspidata.
Cuvierina columnella.
Cavolinia trispinosa.
Cavolinia quadridentata.
Cavolinia gibbosa.
Cavolinia uncinata.
Cavolinia inflexa.

STATION 120. September 9, 1873 ; off the coast of South America, between Pernambuco and Bahia ; lat. 8° 37′ S., long. 34° 28′ W.; depth, 675 fathoms ; bottom, red mud.

Limacina inflata.
Limacina lesueuri.
Limacina trochiformis.
Limacina bulimoides.
Clio (Creseis) virgula.
Clio (Creseis) acicula.
Clio (Hyalocylix) striata.
Clio (Styliola) subula.

Clio polita.
Clio pyramidata.
Cuvierina columnella.
Cavolinia trispinosa.
Cavolinia quadridentata.
Cavolinia longirostris.
Cavolinia tridentata.
Cavolinia uncinata.

Cavolinia inflexa.

STATION 122.   September 10, 1873 ; off the coast of South America, between Pernambuco and Bahia ; lat. 9° 5′ S., long. 34° 50′ W.; depth, 350 fathoms ; bottom,
red mud.

Limacina inflata.

Limacina lesueuri.

Limacina bulimoides.

Peraclis reticulata.

Peraclis bispinosa.

Clio (Creseis) acicula.

Clio (Styliola) subula.

Clio pyramidata.

Cuvierina columnella.

Cavolinia trispinosa.

Cavolinia quadridentata.

Cavolinia longirostris.

Cavolinia uncinata.

Cavolinia inflexa.

STATION 164.   June 12, 1874 ; off Sydney ; lat. 34° 8′ S., long. 152° 0′ E.; depth, 950
fathoms ; bottom, green mud.

Clio (Styliola) subula.   Clio pyramidata.

Cavolinia trispinosa.

STATION 174.   August 3, 1874 ; off Kandavu Island ; lat. 19° 6′ 0″ S., long.
178° 14′ 20″ E.; depth, 140 fathoms ; bottom, coral mud.

Limacina inflata.

STATION 185.   August 31, 1874 ; off Raine Island ; lat. 11° 35′ 25″ S., long. 144° 2′ 0″
E.; depth, 135 fathoms ; bottom, coral sand.

Limacina inflata.

Limacina lesueuri.

Limacina bulimoides.

Clio (Creseis) virgula.

Clio (Creseis) acicula.

Clio (Hyalocylix) striata.

Clio (Styliola) subula.

Clio pyramidata.

Cuvierina columnella.

Cavolinia trispinosa.

Cavolinia quadridentata.

Cavolinia longirostris.

Cavolinia gibbosa.

Cavolinia uncinata.

Cavolinia inflexa.

STATION 219.   March 10, 1875 ; Admiralty Islands to Yokohama ; lat. 1° 54′ 0′ S.,
long. 146° 39′ 40″ E.; depth, 150 fathoms ; bottom, coral mud.

Limacina inflata.

Limacina trochiformis.

Limacina bulimoides.

Clio (Creseis) virgula.

Clio (Creseis) acicula.

Clio (Creseis) conica.

Clio (Hyalocylix) striata.

Clio (Styliola) subula.

Clio pyramidata.

Cavolinia trispinosa (young, as
" Cleodora compressa ").

Cavolinia quadridentata.

Cavolinia longirostris (young, as
" Hyalæa lævigata ").

Station 246.   July 2, 1875 ; Yokohama to Sandwich Islands ; lat. 36° 10′ N., long.
178° 0′ E.; depth, 2050 fathoms ; bottom, Globigerina ooze.

Clio pyramidata.

Station 323.   February 28, 1876 ; Falkland Islands to Rio de la Plata ; lat. 35° 39′ S.,
long. 50° 47′ W.; depth, 1900 fathoms ; bottom, blue mud.

Clio pyramidata. | *Cavolinia inflexa.*

Station 335.   March 16, 1876 ; Tristan da Cunha to Ascension Island ; lat. 32° 24′ S.,
long. 13° 5′ W.; depth, 1425 fathoms ; bottom, Pteropod ooze.

Limacina inflata. | *Cavolinia trispinosa.*
Clio (Styliola) subula. | *Cavolinia inflexa.*
Clio pyramidata. | *Cuvierina columnella.*

B. GEOGRAPHICAL DISTRIBUTION OF THE GENERA.

When I indicated the geographical divisions (pelagic provinces) which might be
adopted for the geographical distribution of the Gymnosomatous Pteropoda,[1] I had not
been entrusted with the Systematic Report on the Thecosomata, which was still in the
hands of Mr. Alfred E. Craven.   Consequently these divisions were based, not on the
study of all the Pteropoda, but only on the very limited group of the Gymnosomata,
and therefore in circumstances very unfavourable to generalisation, and apt to lead to
multiplied subdivisions.

For the sake of uniformity, however, I have here used the same subdivisions as in
the case of the Gymnosomata, and it will be seen that they apply tolerably well to the
Thecosomata also.

It is to be observed, in the first place, that the Thecosomata are in general more
cosmopolitan than the Gymnosomata.   But it is possible that, after a more complete
study of the latter, certain forms may be found to be less localised.

In the Report on the Gymnosomata, the absence of materials made me wonder
whether there did not exist, for the western part of the southern Atlantic, a special
pelagic province (the Brazilian).   The study of the Thecosomatous Pteropoda has con-
vinced me that there is none, and that this " province " is identical in character with the
South-west African.   It seems advisable therefore to unite it to the latter to form a
South Atlantic province, in contrast to the North Atlantic one, from which it distinctly
differs in the presence of some particular species.   This South Atlantic province includes
the region situated to the south of the great equatorial current and to the north of 39° S.;
and is traversed by the South Atlantic and by the Brazilian currents.   In the diagrams

[1] Zool. Chall. Exp., pt. lviii. pp. 61, 62.

of geographical distribution the name South-west African province will therefore be replaced by that of South Atlantic.

Genera of Thecosomata have been observed in all the warm and temperate seas, that is to say, in eight out of ten pelagic provinces. In the case of several of these provinces the first mention of certain genera is due to the results of the Challenger Expedition ; for example in the case of the South Atlantic, Australasian, North Pacific, and South-east Pacific.

The maximum geographical extension is found in the genus *Limacina*, as comprehended in this Report. In fact *Limacina* is not absent from any of the ten provinces which have been adopted in the Systematic Report on the Gymnosomata.

Peraclis is more local ; at least it has not hitherto been observed except in the North Atlantic (including the Mediterranean), West Pacific, and South-east Pacific provinces. But it seems to me probable that it will afterwards be found in the other warm seas, at least in the South Atlantic, Indian Ocean, and Australasian provinces. (Empty shells of *Peraclis reticulata* and *Peraclis bispinosa* have already been got in sediments from the bottom of the sea, at lat. 9° 5′ S., Station 122.)

In the group of Cavoliniidæ the genera and even the subgeneric sections are almost all cosmopolitan, not being absent even in the cold provinces (Arctic and Antarctic). Thus forms of *Clio* belonging to the subgenera *Creseis, Hyalocylix,* and *Styliola* have been found in all the eight warm and temperate provinces.

The subgenus *Clio, s. str.,* although with a geographical distribution not quite so extensive as the genus *Limacina*, has been found in the eight warm and temperate, and in the two Arctic (*Clio pyramidata*) and Antarctic provinces (*Clio australis* and *Clio sulcata*).

Lastly, the geographical distribution of the genera *Cavolinia* and *Cuvierina* also extends throughout the eight warm and temperate provinces.

Leaving the calcareous-shelled Thecosomata, and passing to the Cymbuliidæ, we find that like *Peraclis* and the different genera of the Gymnosomata they have as yet been insufficiently studied. The presence of the genus *Cymbulia* has been proved in the following provinces—the North Atlantic, Indian Ocean, and Australasian ; that of the genus *Cymbuliopsis* in the North Atlantic and Australasian ; and that of the genus *Glebа* in the North Atlantic and Australasian.

As with the genera of Gymnosomata, I here collect the data respecting the geographical distribution of the genera of Thecosomata in a table which sums up the subject in an intelligible way. This table has been made exclusively from the study of specimens taken alive, as one cannot take into account the empty shells of the deposits in establishing the geographical distribution of pelagic animals like the Pteropoda.[1]

---

[1] With reference to this statement, as well as those made by Dr. Pelseneer on p. 116, as to the correspondence between the distribution of pelagic organisms on the surface and their dead remains on the bottom, I may state that in almost all instances when these remains have been found on the bottom of the ocean, further researches have shown the presence of the living animals in the surface waters at all events at some period of the year.—J. M.

	Arctic.	North Atlantic.	South Atlantic.	Indian Ocean.	Austral- asia.	West Pacific.	East Aus- tralian.	North Pacific.	South- East Pacific.	Ant- arctic.
Peraclis, ...		×				×			×	
Limacina, ...	×	×	×	×	×	×	×	×	×	×
Clio (Creseis), . .		×	×	×	×	×	×	×	×	
„ *(Hyalocylix)*, .		×	×	×	×	×	×	×	×	
„ *(Styliola)*, .		×	×	×	×	×	×	×	×	
„ s. str., . .	×	×	×	×	×	×	×	×	×	×
Cuvierina, . . .		×	×	×	×	×	×	×	×	
Carolinia, . . .		×	×	×	×	×	×	×	×	
Cymbulia, . . .		×		×[1]	×[2]		×	×[3]		
Cymbuliopsis, . .		×			×					
Gleba, . . .		×			×[4]	×[5]		×		

C. THE SPECIES OF THECOSOMATA ARRANGED IN PROVINCES.

I. Arctic Province.

    Limacina helicina. | *Limacina retroversa.*

                Clio pyramidata.

II. North Atlantic Province.

    Limacina inflata.   *Clio (Creseis) virgula.*

    Limacina triacantha.   *Clio (Creseis) conica.*

    Limacina helicoides.   *Clio (Creseis) acicula.*

    Limacina lesueuri.   *Clio (Hyalocylix) striata.*

    Limacina retroversa.   *Clio (Styliola) subula.*

    Limacina trochiformis.   *Clio polita.*

    Limacina bulimoides.   *Clio balantium.*

    Peraclis reticulata.   *Clio pyramidata.*

    Peraclis bispinosa.   *Clio cuspidata.*

[1] The *Cymbulia* from the Indian Ocean, figured by Macdonald, see p. 95.

[2] The larva of *Cymbulia* collected by the Challenger, see p. 99.

[3] The *Cymbulia* sp., collected by the Challenger, see p. 99.

[4] The larva of *Gleba* collected by the Challenger, see p. 104.

[5] The *Gleba* mentioned by Boas, see p. 104.

Cuvierina columnella.
Cavolinia trispinosa.
Cavolinia quadridentata.
Cavolinia longirostris.
Cavolinia gibbosa.
Cavolinia tridentata.

Cavolinia uncinata.
Cavolinia inflexa.
Cymbulia peroni.
Cymbuliopsis calceola.
Gleba cordata.
Gleba chrysosticta.

III. South Atlantic Province.

Limacina inflata.
Limacina lesueuri.
Limacina trochiformis.
Limacina bulimoides.
Clio (Creseis) virgula.
Clio (Creseis) conica.
Clio (Creseis) acicula.
Clio (Hyalocylix) striata.
Clio (Styliola) subula.
Clio andreæ.
Clio balantium.

Clio chaptali.
Clio pyramidata.
Clio cuspidata.
Cuvierina columnella.
Cavolinia trispinosa.
Cavolinia quadridentata.
Cavolinia longirostris.
Cavolinia gibbosa.
Cavolinia tridentata.
Cavolinia uncinata.
Cavolinia inflexa.

IV. Indian Ocean Province.

Limacina inflata.
Limacina lesueuri.
Limacina trochiformis.
Limacina bulimoides.
Clio (Creseis) virgula.
Clio (Creseis) acicula.
Clio (Hyalocylix) striata.
Clio (Styliola) subula.
Clio balantium.
Clio pyramidata.

Clio cuspidata.
Cuvierina columnella.
Cavolinia trispinosa.
Cavolinia quadridentata.
Cavolinia longirostris.
Cavolinia globulosa.
Cavolinia gibbosa.
Cavolinia tridentata.
Cavolinia uncinata.
Cavolinia inflexa.

V. Australasian Province.

Limacina inflata.
Limacina lesueuri.
Limacina trochiformis.
Limacina bulimoides.
Clio (Creseis) virgula.
Clio (Creseis) acicula.

Clio (Hyalocylix) striata.
Clio (Styliola) subula.
Clio balantium.
Clio chaptali.
Clio pyramidata.
Cuvierina columnella.

Cavolinia trispinosa.
Cavolinia quadridentata.
Cavolinia longirostris.
Cavolinia globulosa.

Cavolinia gibbosa.
Cavolinia tridentata.
Cavolinia uncinata.
Cavolinia inflexa.

Cymbuliopsis ovata.

VI. West Pacific Province.

Limacina inflata.
Limacina lesueuri.
Limacina trochiformis.
Limacina bulimoides.
Peraclis reticulata.
Clio (Creseis) virgula.
Clio (Creseis) conica.
Clio (Creseis) acicula.
Clio (Hyalocylix) striata.
Clio (Styliola) subula.

Clio pyramidata.
Clio cuspidata.
Cuvierina columnella.
Cavolinia trispinosa.
Cavolinia quadridentata.
Cavolinia longirostris.
Cavolinia globulosa.
Cavolinia gibbosa.
Cavolinia tridentata.
Cavolinia uncinata.

Cavolinia inflexa.

VII. East Australian Province.

Limacina inflata.
Limacina lesueuri.
Limacina trochiformis.
Limacina bulimoides.
Clio (Creseis) virgula.
Clio (Creseis) acicula.
Clio (Hyalocylix) striata.
Clio (Styliola) subula.

Clio pyramidata.
Cuvierina columnella.
Cavolinia trispinosa.
Cavolinia quadridentata.
Cavolinia longirostris.
Cavolinia gibbosa.
Cavolinia inflexa.
Cymbulia parvidentata.

VIII. North Pacific Province.

Limacina inflata.
Limacina lesueuri.
Limacina bulimoides.
Clio (Creseis) virgula.
Clio (Creseis) acicula.
Clio (Hyalocylix) striata.
Clio (Styliola) subula.
Clio pyramidata.

Clio cuspidata.
Cuvierina columnella.
Cavolinia trispinosa.
Cavolinia quadridentata.
Cavolinia gibbosa.
Cavolinia tridentata.
Cavolinia uncinata.
Cavolinia inflexa.

Tiedemannia spectabilis.

IX. South-East Pacific Province.

Limacina inflata.
Limacina lesueuri.
Limacina trochiformis.
Limacina bulimoides.
Peraclis reticulata.
Clio (Creseis) virgula.
Clio (Creseis) conica.
Clio (Creseis) acicula.
Clio (Creseis) chierchiæ.

Clio (Hyalocylix) striata.
Clio (Styliola) subula.
Clio pyramidata.
Cuvierina columnella.
Cavolinia longirostris.
Cavolinia gibbosa.
Cavolinia tridentata.
Cavolinia uncinata.
Cavolinia inflexa.

X. Antarctic Province.

Limacina antarctica.
Limacina australis.

Clio australis.
Clio sulcata.

CONTENTS.

INDEX.

PLATE I.

PLATE 1.

Figs. 1, 2. *Limacina triacantha* (Fischer).

      Fig. 1. Shell, from the aperture; magnified fourteen diameters.
      Fig. 2. Shell, from the apex; magnified fourteen diameters.

Figs. 3, 4. *Limacina antarctica*, Woodward. (After Hooker's unpublished figures.)

      Fig. 3. Shell, from the aperture; magnified ten diameters.
      Fig. 4. Shell, from the apex; magnified five diameters.

Fig. 5. *Limacina helicoides*, Jeffreys. Shell, from the aperture; magnified eight diameters.

Fig. 6. *Limacina australis* (Eydoux and Souleyet). Shell, from the aperture; magnified eight diameters.

Figs. 7, 8. *Peraclis reticulata* (d'Orbigny).

      Fig. 7. Shell (from deep-sea deposit), from the aperture; magnified twelve diameters.
      Fig. 8. Operculum, from the outside. *a*, Surface of insertion.

Figs. 9, 10. *Peraclis bispinosa*, n. sp.

      Fig. 9. Shell, from aperture; magnified six diameters.
      Fig. 10. Shell, from apex; magnified seven diameters.

Figs. 11–14. "*Agadina*" *stimpsoni*, A. Adams.

      Fig. 11. Shell, from aperture, with operculum *in situ*; magnified eighteen diameters.
      Fig. 12. Shell, from apex; magnified twenty-two diameters.
      Fig. 13. Animal, from left side; magnified twenty diameters. *a*, velum; *b*, visceral mass; *c*, aperture of pallial cavity; *d*, operculum; *e*, foot.
      Fig. 14. Lower surface of the foot; magnified twenty diameters. *a*, operculum.

Figs. 15, 16. "*Agadina*" sp.

      Fig. 15. Shell, from aperture; magnified twenty-two diameters.
      Fig. 16. Shell, from umbilicus; magnified twenty-two diameters.

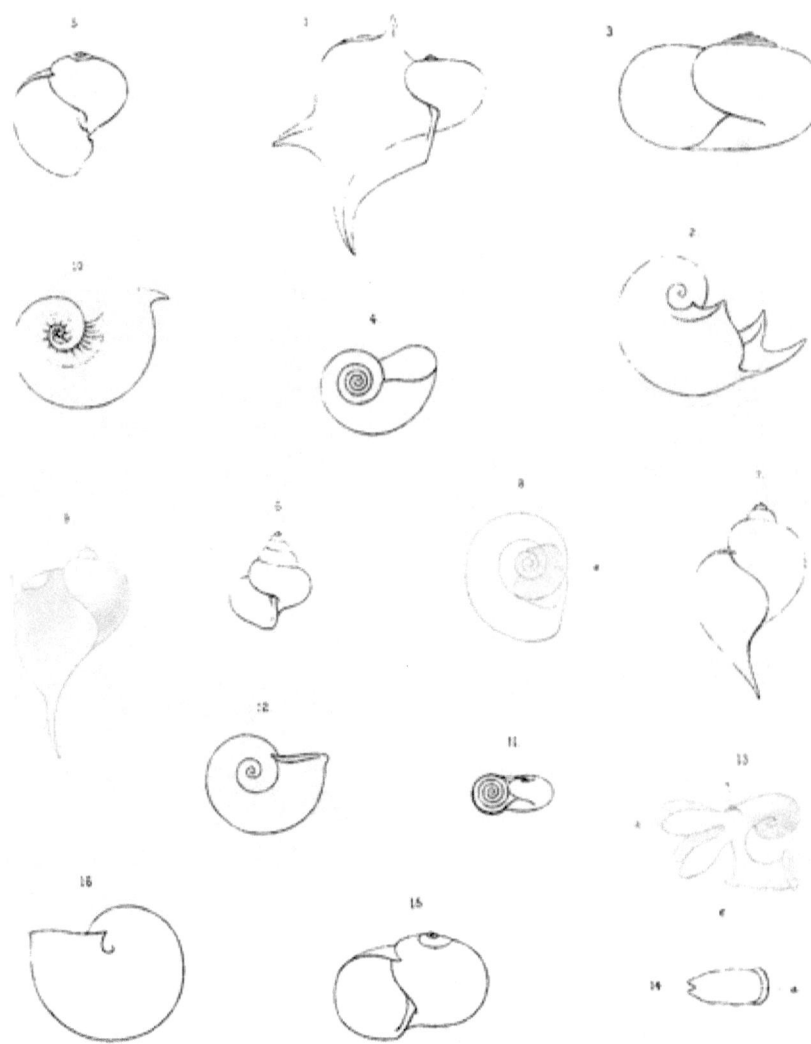

PLATE II.

PLATE II.

Figs. 1, 2. *Clio (Creseis) conica* (Eschscholtz).

      Fig. 1. Shell, from left side; magnified ten diameters.
      Fig. 2. Embryonic shell, from left side.

Fig. 3. *Clio (Hyalocylix) striata* (Rang).   Embryonic shell, from ventral surface.

Figs. 4–6. *Clio polita* (Craven, MS.).

      Fig. 4. Shell, from right side; magnified six diameters.
      Fig. 5. Shell, from dorsal surface; magnified six diameters.
      Fig. 6. Embryonic shell, from ventral surface.

Fig. 7. *Clio chaptali* (Souleyet).   Embryonic shell, from ventral surface.

Fig. 8. *Clio australis* (d'Orbigny).   Embryonic shell, from ventral surface.

Figs. 9–11. *Clio sulcata* (Pfeffer).

      Fig. 9. Shell, from right side; magnified four diameters.
      Fig. 10. Shell, from dorsal surface; magnified four diameters.
      Fig. 11. Embryonic shell, from ventral surface.

Figs. 12, 13. *Cymbulia parvidentata*, n. sp.

      Fig. 12. Shell, from anterior side; magnified two diameters.
      Fig. 13. Shell, from posterior side; magnified two diameters.

Fig. 14. Larval shell of *Cymbulia*, from aperture, with operculum *in situ*.

Figs. 15, 16. *Cymbuliopsis ovata* (Quoy and Gaimard).

      Fig. 15. Shell, from anterior side; magnified two diameters.
      Fig. 16. Shell, from left side; magnified two diameters.

Fig. 17. Larval shell of *Gleba*, from aperture.

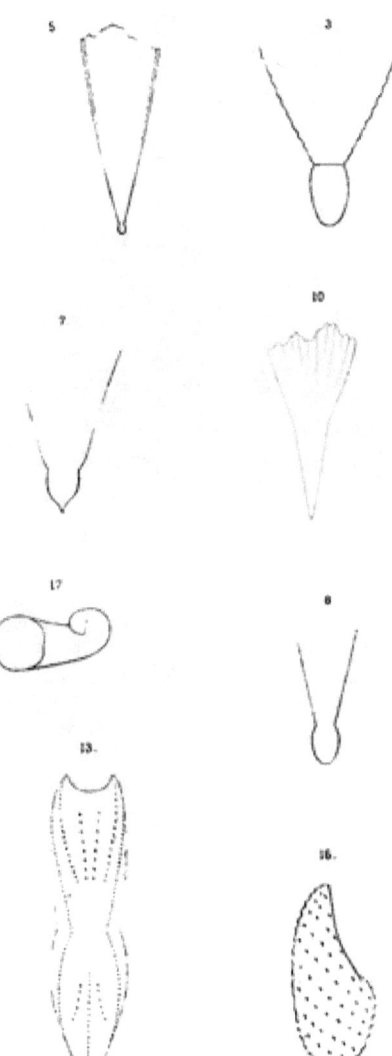

VOYAGE OF H.M.S. CHALLENGER.

ZOOLOGY.

REPORT on the Pteropoda collected by H.M.S. Challenger during the
Years 1873-76. By Paul Pelseneer, D.Sc. (Brussels).

PART III.—ANATOMY.

INTRODUCTION.

The collection of Pteropoda, preserved in alcohol, brought home by the Challenger,
includes specimens of all the known genera except *Cymbuliopsis* and *Clione*.

This collection having been placed in my hands for purposes of systematic study, I
was, when this part of the work was concluded, in an exceptionally favourable position
for undertaking a monographic examination of the organisation of this group of animals.
Since the publication of Souleyet's memorable work, the anatomy of the Pteropoda has
been studied almost exclusively by means of European species, and this is the first time
since that epoch that such an important collection as the present one has been made,
including, as it does, forty-four species out of the sixty-three actually known, and
specimens of nearly all the genera.

Hence although the time at my disposal was very limited. I could not allow an opportunity to escape which would probably not soon occur again.

By adding to the Challenger collection some specimens of *Clione limacina* which
Mr. John Murray placed at my disposal, and a specimen of *Cymbuliopsis* of my own, I
was able to investigate all the known genera of Pteropods, so that the conclusions at
which I have arrived have not been drawn from the organisation of a few species only,

but from that of the entire group, each genus, and usually several species of each genus, having been studied.

As the conclusion of these researches an analytical exposition of the whole organisation of each genus might be expected, but this would have extended the present Report beyond reasonable dimensions, and would have occasioned much repetition, since several of the genera of Pteropoda are very closely related, and the number of distinct types is far from large. Besides, as I have already remarked, the limited time at my disposal did not permit me to enter upon an anatomical monograph, and indeed, even if a longer period had been available, the following considerations would have deterred me from such a course :—

1. We already possess a very considerable acquaintance with numerous points in the organisation of the Pteropoda, thanks to the general works, based upon several different genera, of van Beneden,[1] Souleyet,[2] and Gegenbaur,[3] and to the special memoirs, treating only of a single form, of Eschricht[4] and Wagner.[5] In many respects an anatomical monograph would simply be a reprint of what has been published by these authors.

2. The systematic position of the Pteropods is the subject of much discussion, and their phylogenetic relationships have been very variously interpreted.

For several years[6] I have followed Spengel,[7] along with Grobben[8] and Boas,[9] in the opinion, not shared by most zoologists, that the Pteropoda do not constitute a distinct class among the Mollusca, comparable with the Cephalopoda, Gastropoda, Scaphopoda, and Pelecypoda. Further, I am, like Boas, of opinion that even within the Gastropoda they do not constitute a primary division, but only a group of much lower rank among the Opisthobranchiate division of the Tectibranchiate Euthyneura.

This opinion, it must be added, is not new ; it was expressed during the first half of this century by de Blainville.[10] Souleyet[11] was the first, and indeed the only, investigator who has attempted to give any proof of it, and he was not very successful,

[1] Exercices Zootomiques, Mém. Acad. Sci. Bruxelles, t. xii., 1839 ; Mémoire sur la Limacina arctica, op. cit., t. xiv., 1841.

[2] Voyage de la Bonite, Zoologie, t. ii. pp. 37–288, 1852.

[3] Untersuchungen über Pteropoden und Heteropoden, 1855.

[4] Anatomische untersuchungen über die Clione borealis, 1838 ; in Danish, Anatomiske Undersøgelser over Clione borealis, K. dansk. Vidensk. Selsk. Afhandl., 7 Deel, p. 327.

[5] Die Wirbellosen des weissen Meeres, Bd. i. pp. 89–120, 1885.

[6] Die Geruchsorgane und das Nervensystem der Mollusken, Zeitschr. f. wiss. Zool., Bd. xxxv. p. 373, 1880.

[7] The cephalic appendages of the Gymnosomatous Pteropoda, Quart. Journ. Mic. Sci., N.S., vol. xxv. p. 506, 1885. Description d'un Nouveau genre de Ptéropode Gymnosoma, Bull. Soc. Dép. Nord, p. 226, 1886. Recherches sur le Système Nerveux des Ptéropodes, Arch. de Biol., t. vii. p. 127, 1886.

[8] Morphologische Studien über den Harn- und Geschlechtsapparaten sowie die Leibeshöhle der Cephalopoden, Arb. Zool. Inst. Wien, Bd. v. p. 245, 1884.

[9] Spolia atlantica, Bidrag til Pteropodernes Morfologi og Systematik, &c., K. dansk. Vidensk. Selsk. Skrie., Raekke 6, Bd. iv. p. 12.

[10] Manuel de Malacologie, p. 480.

[11] Voyage de la Bonite, Zoologie, t. ii.

because he had opposed to him the dogmatic views of Cuvier, which were then all-powerful. Recently, however, the authors above mentioned have returned to an opinion closely resembling that of de Blainville; but in order to place this upon a firm basis, further demonstration is still necessary.

On these grounds I have proposed to make the present Report a comparative anatomical study of these animals rather than a descriptive anatomical monograph, and shall attempt mainly to throw light upon their systematic position; and by the permission of Mr. John Murray to conclude this third part of my Report upon the Pteropoda by an exposition of my views regarding their relations to the other groups of Mollusca.

Having thus defined the object of the present work and the spirit in which it is conceived, I may say a few words regarding the method which has been followed in its elaboration and the manner in which I have divided it.

The first portion of this Report bears upon the descriptive anatomy of the Pteropoda, taken genus by genus, treating first of the Thecosomata, then of the Gymnosomata. As I have indicated above, no attempt will here be made to discuss the whole organisation of each genus, but I shall study especially—

1. The points neglected or misinterpreted by previous authors, in order, if possible, to elucidate them.

2. The points which seem to me to have an important bearing upon the relations and systematic position of the Pteropoda.

In this portion I shall not attack the question of the embryonic development of the Pteropoda. Too few embryos were collected by the Challenger to furnish any new facts which might serve as a basis for a discussion of this special subject. The histology of the Pteropoda, too, will only occupy an unimportant place in our discussion, for the specimens collected by the Challenger were not preserved with a view to histological examination. Hence, in order to fill up the numerous lacunae which will occur in the present work, I hope to publish hereafter the results of my examination of fresh specimens at the Naples Zoological Station.

In the second part it is proposed to study the relations and affinities of the group of Mollusca called Pteropoda by a comparison of their organisation (as ascertained by the investigation described in the first part) with that of other Mollusca.

CONTENTS.

I. ORGANISATION OF THE PTEROPODA.

I propose to study the Thecosomata and the Gymnosomata separately, and as I have enumerated the differential characters of these two divisions in the Systematic Report on Gymnosomata,[1] there is no need to repeat them here. The phylogenetic origin of the two groups will be examined in the sequel.

I. THECOSOMATA.

We shall now proceed to examine in succession each of the genera recognised in the Systematic Report on the Thecosomata.[2]

Family I. LIMACINIDÆ.

The knowledge of the organisation of the Limacinidæ is of the utmost consequence in the morphological study of the Pteropoda, because the true phylogenetic relations of the typical Thecosomata (Cavoliniidæ) are entirely concealed by an adventitious modification upon which we shall enlarge hereafter. This masks their true relationship, and if the Limacinidæ did not exist at the present time it would probably be impossible to explain this modification, and consequently very difficult to establish the real affinities of the Thecosomata.

The only information we possess regarding the organisation of the Limacinidæ is to be found in the memoir of van Beneden on *Limacina arctica* (=*helicina*),[3] and in the rather brief anatomical study of the "genus" *Spirialis*, published by Souleyet in the Voyage of the "Bonite."[4] These two works, however, in addition to being brief, include numerous gaps and several inaccuracies, which defects I shall endeavour to remedy.

Limacina helicina (*Limacina arctica*), the species studied by van Beneden, is of large

[1] *Zool. Chall. Exp.*, part lviii. pp. 4–6.
[2] *Mém. Acad. Sci. Bruxelles*, t. xiv.
[3] *Zool. Chall. Exp.*, part lxv.
[4] *Voyage de la Bonite, Zoologie*, t. ii. pp. 206–215.

dimensions, whilst *Limacina australis*, which was the subject of Souleyet's investigations, is one of those small forms classed by him under the generic name *Spirialis*. He recognised, however, their close relationship to the larger *Limacinæ*, the only difference which he stated to exist between them—the absence of the operculum in *Limacina*—has been found to have no foundation, for it is only that the adults in the large forms have lost the operculum. In consequence of the small size of his specimens a number of points in their organisation have escaped him.

In the Challenger collection there was only one specimen of a large *Limacina* (*Limacina antarctica*) which I have therefore been compelled to preserve intact ; but since Mr. John Murray has placed in my hands a number of specimens of *Limacina helicina* from Hudson's Strait, I have been able to study a great part of the organisation of the genus, upon a large species and upon small forms (*Limacina lesueuri* and *Limacina australis*), which latter have served more especially for special points and for purposes of comparison.

Lastly, as regards the genus *Peraclis*, the form studied is *Peraclis reticulata ;* but as specimens of this genus are very rare, I have only been able to make use of two, and hence have not been able to push my researches so far as I could have wished.

In all the Limacinidæ the shell is sinistral, and hence the animal is coiled in a left-handed direction ; but although twisted in this manner, in all its organisation the animal is dextrorsal, that is to say, that in the asymmetrical disposition the right side predominates ; it is here that are found the anus, the genital aperture, and the copulatory organ.

This is a fact opposed to the usual condition in the sinistrorsal Gastropods. In *Physa*, for example, the spiral (and hence the shell) is sinistral ; the anus, the genital aperture, and the copulatory organ are all placed on the left side, and hence it is this side which predominates in the asymmetry of the animal. Thus the direction of the spiral corresponds with the kind of asymmetry observed in this Mollusc.

The difference between these two cases shows, however, that the mode of asymmetry in a Mollusc is in no way dependent upon the direction of its coil. In *Physa* there is a complete *situs inversus;* and it is this which has brought about the left-handed twisting of the animal and the sinistral character of its shell, for we are acquainted with no Gastropod which has acquired a left-handed asymmetry of organisation, and had at the same time preserved a dextral shell. In this case, then, the sinistral coiling appears to be only one of the consequences of the *situs inversus*.

On the contrary, as we see in the Limacinidæ, an animal with dextral organisation may be coiled sinistrally. The case of the Limacinidæ, too, does not seem to be unique, since, according to Bouvier,[1] the genus *Lanistes* (*Ampullaria* with left-handed spiral) also has a dextral organisation.

The direction of the spiral, then, does not permit us to determine the mode of the

[1] Sur le système nerveux typique des Proebranches dextres ou sénestres, *Comptes rendus*, t. ciii. p. 1276, 1886.

asymmetry of the Mollusc, any more than this latter enables us to determine the direction of the spiral (in contradistinction to the opinion of Lacaze Duthiers[2]); hence an animal with dextral asymmetry may be twisted directly or inversely, or may not be twisted at all (Patelloid Gastropoda).

Besides, the direction of the spiral must be of very slight morphological importance, since in the same genus (*Neptunea, Pyrula, Vertigo*, &c.) there are some species which are dextral, and others which are normally sinistral.

1. *Limacina.*

The Head is distinct, surrounded on each side by the fins, which reach to the dorsal aspect, where is found a pair of tentacles.

These latter are asymmetrical, the left being much less developed than the right; in *Limacina helicina* and *Limacina antarctica* it is almost completely atrophied, and is situated rather posteriorly to the right. In *Limacina inflata* and *Limacina lesueuri* it is somewhat larger. In all the Limacinæ the right tentacle is very long when fully developed (Pl. I. fig. 1, *a*), and is surrounded at the base by a short everted sheath, such as is found in certain Nudibranchs. This sheath also occurs in the smaller forms ("*Spirialis*"), where Souleyet[3] did not succeed in finding it.

The Foot.—The fins form at the anterior extremity of the body a natatory surface, oblique with respect to the transverse plane of the body, the ventral margin being lower than the dorsal. On this surface the mouth opens, and at the right, near the dorsal margin outside the lip, is the orifice of the copulatory organ, to which the seminal groove leads, passing from the right side of the cervical region over the dorsal border of the fin.

On the dorsal margin of the fin, near the middle, is a little tentaculiform lobe, which differs in structure from the remainder of the fin, and contains the termination of a slender nerve; probably it is a tactile organ. This lobe or papilla does not exist in all species. I have only demonstrated its presence in *Limacina helicina, Limacina antarctica,* and *Limacina australis;* it is wanting on the other hand in *Limacina bulimoides, Limacina trochiformis, Limacina lesueuri,* and *Limacina inflata.*

This little lobe corresponds to an analogous organ found in the subgenus *Creseis,* of the genus *Clio.* Van Beneden[3] regarded it as a tentacle, and Huxley[4] identified it with the long cephalic appendage of *Halopsyche.* These two opinions are both erroneous.

The fins are continuous and united ventrally by the posterior lobe of the foot, which is slightly notched in the middle of its ventral border, and carries the operculum. I have

---

[1] Du système nerveux des Gastéropodes pulmonés aquatiques, *Arch. de Zool. Expér.*, viz. 1, t. i. p. 462.

[2] Voyage de la Bonite, Zoologie, t. ii. p. 209.

[3] Mémoire sur la Limacina arctica, p. 3, *Mém. Acad. Sci. Bruxelles,* t. xiv.

[4] On the Morphology of the Cephalous Mollusca, *Phil. Trans.,* 1853, p. 41.

already said that in *Limacina helicina* and *Limacina antarctica* the operculum is caducous in fully-grown specimens, a fact which explains how it is that these species have often been regarded as lacking this organ.

The Mantle is open dorsally, and united to the body behind the foot (on the ventral surface of a spread out *Limacina*). Its margin is simple; it presents, on the right side, a little ventrally, a rather narrow lobe, terminating in a point, and called the "balancer," the considerable development of which perhaps enables it to play the part of a counterpoise during swimming, the coiled Pteropods not being symmetrical like the straight forms. Possibly this lobe is also sensory, as its whole surface is ciliated.

The dorsal portion of the mantle which covers the pallial cavity presents a rather thick glandular area, corresponding to the "shield" of the Cavoliniidæ. The structure of this organ is already known and is practically the same in *Limacina* as in the Cavoliniidæ; but in the present case it is asymmetrical (Pl. I. fig. 5, *a*) and uniform in structure throughout its extent.

The Digestive Tract.—The mouth opens in the natatory plane formed by the two fins enveloping the cephalic region; it is situated towards the dorsal border of this plane and bounded by two lips, united dorsally and separating towards the other side.

The mouth is succeeded by a buccal mass, the cavity of which encloses two lateral jaws, such as have already been described by Sars.[1] The number of folds presented by these jaws varies in different species. The disposition of the radula agrees with that of all the odontophorous Mollusca, but the ribbon is very short, the number of transverse rows being but small. The number of longitudinal series is three, as in all the Thecosomata.

On either side of the radula opens a salivary gland. These organs have escaped the attention of the different naturalists who have studied *Limacina* (van Beneden,[2] Souleyet[3]). According to Gegenbaur[4] they are wanting in all Thecosomata, nevertheless all these are provided with them. In *Limacina* these glands are small, short, oval, and without a differentiated duct.

The œsophagus, rather long and longitudinally plicated within, leads into an enlargement of the digestive tube called the stomach, which here, as in all Thecosomata, is in reality a masticatory gizzard. Its walls have about the centre a large muscular transverse band, which actuates a number of horny plates situated within it.

These masticatory plates are four in number and are placed symmetrically (two ventral and two dorsal); a fifth has not been observed by the anatomists, although the embryologists have recorded its existence (Krohn,[5] Fol[6]). The four symmetrical plates

[1] Mollusca regionis arcticæ Norvegiæ, pl. xvi. fig. 17.   [2] Mémoire sur la Limacina arctica, loc. cit.
[3] Voyage de la Bonite, Zoologie, t. ii. p. 210.
[4] Untersuchungen über Pteropoden und Heteropoden, p. 10.
[5] Beiträge zur Entwickelungsgeschichte der Pteropoden und Heteropoden, p. 42.
[6] Sur le développement des Ptéropodes, *Arch. de Zool. Expér.*, sér. 1, t. iv. p. 162.

are of a rectangular outline, elongated in the direction of the axis of the digestive tube, the dorsal pair being a little shorter than the ventral. Their free surface bears a rather sharp prominent crest. The fifth plate is situated behind the other four, between the two dorsal ones; its form is almost triangular, one of the angles being directed forwards. These masticatory plates have a structure resembling that of the "shell" of the Cymbuliidæ, but are rather more dense; striæ of growth may be observed in them, and they are covered by the gastric epithelium.

Behind the muscular band the stomach gradually narrows to pass into the intestine, and into this hinder portion of the organ on the left side opens the bile-duct.

Huxley[1] asks with respect to the Limacinidæ "whether the first flexure of the intestine is also dorsal" (like the pallial cavity) "or whether, as in all other Pteropods, it is ventral." In *Limacina* from its origin the intestine bends towards the right and dorsally, and eventually opens at the right side of the pallial cavity. Its flexure is thus the same as that called "dorsal" or "hæmal" among the Gastropods (Pl. I. fig. 3).

The Circulatory and Excretory Organs.—The heart is situated at the posterior end of the pallial cavity, and is even visible, owing to the transparency of the mantle, behind the shield. It presents an auricle directed towards the left and a ventricle lying posteriorly, both contained in a pericardium, which is quite excluded from the circulation. In front of the heart is the elongated, thin-walled kidney, arising from the pericardium, with the cavity of which it communicates. It enlarges anteriorly in such a way as to form an elongated triangle whose base is forwards, and opens into the pallial cavity by a small narrow aperture.

The Generative Organs.—The gonad, which in this case is a hermaphrodite gland, occupies all the initial portion of the visceral mass. The efferent duct arises anteriorly at the ventral aspect of the gland, and then passes forwards across the intestine and to the right of the œsophagus. This duct (Pl. I. fig. 3, *j*) is very thin at its origin but expands about its middle, where its walls become glandular; it then contracts again and reaches the accessory glands (albuminiparous and muciparous glands) and the receptaculum seminis.

The genital aperture is situated at the right side of the cephalic region, and is protected by a kind of little operculum. At this opening commences the spermatic groove (Pl. I. fig. 3, *l*), formed by a fold of skin, which is directed towards the dorsal surface of the head, passes to the right side of the right tentacle, and reaches the anterior surface of the fins, where it terminates at the opening of the copulatory organ. This is the same disposition as that already known to exist in the Cavoliniidæ. When protruded the copulatory organ divides into two branches, for instance in *Limacina lesueuri* (Pl. I. fig. 2, *c*).

Nervous System.—The nervous centres are united around the œsophagus behind the buccal mass. The cerebral ganglia (Pl. I. fig. 7, *c*) are situated at the sides of the œsophagus, and connected by a long supra-œsophageal or dorsal commissure.

[1] On the Morphology of the Cephalous Mollusca, loc. cit., p. 43.

The infraœsophageal portion of the nervous centres (Pl. I. fig. 8) consists of two portions : an anterior, pedal, and a posterior, visceral. The pedal group (b) is composed of two large symmetrical ganglia, pressed one against the other and in juxtaposition with the corresponding cerebral ganglion. On the posterior margin of each is an otocyst (e).

The visceral group consists of two ganglia, each of which is also approximated to the cerebral ganglion of its own side ; they are, however, asymmetrical, inasmuch as the right ganglion (c) is much larger than the left (d), and the groove which separates them does not lie in the middle line of the body, but is displaced towards the left. The rule of Lacaze Duthiers,[1] according to which, in sinistrorsal Gastropods, the left half of the visceral commissure is the more developed, does not therefore hold good in the present case.

This asymmetry was unobserved by van Beneden and Souleyet, and has not since been recorded, although it is very striking ; van Beneden[2] figures two symmetrical ganglia, and Souleyet[3] a single symmetrical ganglionic mass as in Cavolinia.

> (1) *Cerebral Ganglia.*—From the anterior portion of these ganglia proceed the nerves which supply the head and tentacles (Pl. I. fig. 7, i). They probably also give origin to the auditory nerves which proceed to the octocysts, as is observed in all other Mollusca, and as I have also seen in certain Thecosomatous and Gymnosomatous Pteropods, as I shall show further on ; I have not, however, been able to make out this nerve in *Limacina*.
>
> (2) *Pedal Ganglia.*—These give origin at their anterior aspect to large nerves passing to the foot and the fins (Pl. I. fig. 8, f) ; a branch of the nerve to each fin goes to the little lobe which is found on its anterior border in certain *Limacinæ*.
>
> (3) *Visceral Ganglia.*—These ganglia are asymmetrical not only in point of size but also in the nerves which proceed from them ; from the large ganglion on the right proceed three nerves, only one from that on the left.
>
>> (i.) *Right Ganglion.*—The outer nerve (1) passes to the right side of the mantle and to the osphradium, and is probably homologous with the branchial nerve of Gastropods ; the two median nerves (2, 3) supply the viscera (heart, kidney, and generative organs).
>>
>> (ii.) *Left Ganglion.*—The single nerve (4) goes to the left side of the mantle.

The preceding description relates to *Limacina helicina*. In the small forms ("*Spirialis*" of Souleyet) the disposition of the nerve centres is the same. Souleyet[4]

[1] Du système nerveux des Gastéropodes pulmonés aquatiques, *Arch. de Zool. Expér.*, sér. 1, t. i. p. 494, No. 13.

[2] Mémoire sur la Limacina arctica, *Mém. Acad. Sci. Bruxelles*, t. xiv. pl. v. figs. 7, 13.

[3] Voyage de la Bonite, Zoologie, Mollusques, pl. xi. fig. 21.

[4] Ibid., t. ii. p. 213.

describes the visceral ganglia in "*Spirialis*" *australis* as like those of *Cavolinia*, that is as forming a single mass. I have had the opportunity of studying this form as well as *Limacina helicina*, and can state that in it, as well as in *Limacina lesueuri*, *Limacina trochiformis*, and *Limacina inflata*, the ganglia of the visceral commissure are disposed in the same asymmetrical fashion. The distribution of the nerves is also certainly identical, but it is difficult to distinguish this in the case of such small animals.

The enteric or stomato-gastric nervous system includes a pair of buccal ganglia, united by a thick and rather long commissure. These ganglia are placed in contact with the œsophagus below the pedal ganglia; each of them is joined to the corresponding cerebral ganglion by a thin connective. They give off anteriorly the nerves to the buccal mass, and posteriorly two filaments which pass along the œsophagus to the stomach, where they ramify and anastomose, so as to form a plexus whose appearance varies a little in different individuals. Some ganglionic thickenings are observed in the plexus.

2. *Peraclis.*

The *Head* is quite differently shaped from that of *Limacina*; it is quite distinct, as I have already had occasion to point out in the systematic part of this Report; it has the form of a short proboscis issuing from the dorsal margin of the fin (Pl. I. fig. 9, a), the two lips uniting dorsally and ventrally; the two tentacles are symmetrical, and have no sheath. It is this proboscis which in Costa's figure [1] might easily be taken for the ventral lobe of the foot, which would be notched in the middle of its free margin.

The *Foot*.—The fins have no tentaculiform lobe; the ventral lobe of the foot is not notched in the middle of its free margin, but is broader at the base than at this margin.

The *Mantle* has on its right margin, a little ventrally, an appendage in the form of a triangular lobe, analogous to the balancer of *Limacina*. The dorsal pallial gland (shield) is shorter than in *Limacina*. It is not homogeneous, as in the case of this latter, which resembles that of *Clio* (subgenus *Creseis*), but presents alternating transverse bands (Pl. I. fig. 10). It is asymmetrical like that of *Limacina*.

The *Digestive Tract* agrees with that of *Limacina*, both in the relative position of its constituent parts and in their shape. As in *Limacina* there are two lateral jaws, two little salivary glands, and five large masticatory gastric plates, of which four are symmetrical, and the fifth triangular, posterior, and dorsal. Furthermore, as in *Limacina*, the bile-duct opens into the left of the digestive tract, and the flexure of the intestine is dorsal and to the right.

The visceral anatomy of *Peraclis* is otherwise very similar to that of *Limacina*, and

[1] Illustrazione della Spirialis recurvirostra, *Ann. Mus. Zool. R. Univ. di Napoli*, anno iv. pl. iv. fig. 12.

I have scarcely been able to establish any noteworthy differences either in the principal parts of the circulatory and excretory apparatus, or in the organs of generation. As in *Limacina*, there are at the end of the hermaphrodite duct a large muciparous gland, an albuminiparous gland, and a receptaculum seminis (Pl. I. fig. 11).

Nervous System.—The cerebral and pedal ganglia are disposed as in the case of *Limacina* and all Thecosomata; that is to say, the former, united by a long cerebral commissure, give origin to the nerves of the head and tentacles, and the latter to the nerves of the fins and posterior lobe of the foot.

But that which distinguishes the central nervous system of *Peraclis* from that of *Limacina* is the arrangement of the visceral commissure. Instead of the two asymmetrical ganglia we have here three ganglia, the two lateral of which are symmetrical, and a little smaller than the central one (Pl. I. fig. 12, c, d, e).

This disposition is identical with that which I have already indicated as occurring in *Cymbulia*,[1] and which, as will appear in the sequel, is characteristic of the whole family Cymbuliidæ.

In an animal so small as *Peraclis* it is very difficult to distinguish clearly the nerves issuing from the ganglia. I have seen, nevertheless, the nerve (*1*) proceeding from the right visceral ganglion, and a larger (genital) nerve (*3*) proceeding from the median ganglion, comparable with the corresponding nerves in *Cymbulia*. Further, I cannot doubt that the visceral nerves in *Peraclis* have a disposition identical with that found in all the Cymbuliidæ; that is to say, each lateral ganglion gives off a pallial nerve, of which I have made out that on the right, and the large median ganglion gives off from its right side a slender visceral nerve in addition to the large genital one.

The buccal or stomato-gastric ganglia are similar in form and arrangement to the corresponding parts in *Limacina*.

Family II. CAVOLINIIDÆ.

These are the typical Thecosomata, the forms which have been most frequently studied, and which are consequently the best known. Their visceral anatomy being tolerably well known, there are certain points over which I may pass rapidly.

It has already been shown[2] that this family contains three genera, namely, *Clio*, *Cuvierina*, and *Cavolinia*, and furthermore, that the first of these includes divisions of subgeneric value, *Creseis*, *Hyalocylix*, and *Styliola*, which differ from each other in certain points of their organisation. We shall examine the three genera of this family in succession, and during the discussion of the genus *Clio* we shall have occasion to demonstrate some characters which distinguish its different sections.

---

[1] *Recherches sur le système nerveux des Ptéropodes*, *Arch. de Biol.*, t. vii. p. 117, pl. iv. fig. 12.
[2] *Zool. Chall. Exp.*, part lxv. p. 41.

1. *Clio.*

The Head in *Clio* resembles that of *Limacina*, but *Creseis* has the left tentacle very little developed, as in *Limacina*, whilst in the others (*Hyalocylix, Styliola,* and *Clio, s. str.*) it is almost as large as the right.

It has also been shown above, as a distinctive character, that in *Creseis* the fins are provided with a little tentacular lobe on the dorsal margin, as in *Limacina*. In *Hyalocylix* the area on the margin of the fin devoid of muscular fibres is situated towards the dorso-lateral angle. In *Styliola* and *Clio* (*s. str.*) this area is found towards the middle of the lateral margin.

The Foot has the posterior lobe rather short in *Creseis*, short in *Hyalocylix*, and long in *Styliola* and *Clio* (*s. str.*).

The Mantle is quite open in front in *Creseis, Hyalocylix,* and *Styliola*, whilst in *Clio* (*s. str.*) its margins are slightly united at the sides, so that the aperture of the mantle is narrower than that of the shell. In all four subgenera the lateral lobe of the mantle (balancer) is less developed than in the Limacinidæ, and is situated on the left side.

The pallial gland (shield) is bilaterally symmetrical in all cases, but presents a different appearance in the different subgenera. In *Creseis* it is homogeneous, like that of *Limacina*. In *Hyalocylix* (Pl. II. fig. 4) a transparent transverse band divides it into an anterior and a posterior portion, the former of which further exhibits on each side a small distinct triangular patch. In *Clio* (*s. str.*) (*e.g., Clio pyramidata,* Pl. II. fig. 2), in the anterior portion, in the centre of a more transparent space, is a median rhomboidal tract, on each side of which are two rather narrow bands.

The pallial cavity, which is ventral in contradistinction to the Limacinidæ, extends rather far backwards, owing to the generally elongated form of the genus *Clio*.

The Digestive Tract.—The mouth, lips, and the whole buccal mass are disposed as in *Limacina*. The jaws are firmer; they and the radula have been described and figured so often that it is not necessary to dwell upon them further.

All forms of the genus *Clio* possess very appreciable salivary glands, which are rather short, ovoid, and without any differentiated duct.

The œsophagus varies in length, being rather short in *Clio* (*s. str.*) and *Styliola*, long in *Hyalocylix* and *Creseis*, and of inordinate length in *Clio* (*Creseis*) *virgula*; it is strongly folded in the direction of its length.

The stomach possesses, as in the Limacinidæ, five large masticatory plates, four quadrangular and symmetrical (Pl. II. fig. 1, *g*), like the corresponding plates of *Limacina*, and a fifth triangular, situated on the ventral aspect, posterior to the preceding (Pl. II. fig. 1, *h*). The two ventral quadrangular plates are shorter than the two dorsal (Pl. II. fig. 5).

But, in addition to the five large plates, several species have in front of them double the number of small plates (Pl. II. fig. 5, *b*) ; these latter[1] are triangular, and are situated in front of the four large symmetrical plates and of the intervals between them. They alternate in size, the four which are situated in front of the large plates being smaller than the others.

In most species of *Clio* a narrow cæcum of varying length opens into the posterior portion of the stomach.

The liver agrees in form and situation with that of *Limacina*, but its duct opens into the posterior part of the stomach on the *right* side (Pl. II. fig. 1). *Clio (Creseis) acicula* retains in this respect a primitive disposition, the part corresponding to the liver in the adults of other species being but slightly developed.

The intestine is bent to the left and ventrally ;[2] its termination is at a greater or less distance forward, according to the subgenus in question ; in *Creseis* and *Hyalocylix* (Pl. II. fig. 1) the anus is placed very far back in consequence of the great length of the œsophagus ; in *Styliola* the œsophagus is not so long, and the intestine terminates further forwards ; lastly, in *Clio* (*s. str.*) the anus is situated far forwards, not far from the aperture of the mantle (Pl. II. fig. 7, *e*).

In the pallial cavity, close to the anus, between the mantle and the intestine, is a flattened gland, somewhat triangular in form and somewhat similar in structure to the shield (pallial gland). This organ (Pl. II. fig. 7, *f*), which I propose to call the "anal gland," does not appear to have been mentioned by any previous author.

The Circulatory and Excretory Organs.—The disposition of the central circulatory organ is well known (Pl. II. fig. 8) ; it is situated on the ventral surface in front of the genital gland ; the auricle (*b*) is behind and the ventricle (*a*) in front. Both are rather elongated, and situated in a very long pericardium (*c*).

The kidney is placed close to the latter (Pl. II. fig. 8, *d*) ; it is flattened, with thin almost transparent walls, and has the form of an elongated more or less recurved triangle, the apex being directed backwards. It communicates (through *f*) with the pericardium and opens into the pallial cavity by a narrow orifice (*e*), situated towards the left angle at the base of the triangle. This orifice escaped the notice of Souleyet,[3] so that he was unable to interpret the kidney correctly.

As to the gills, they are entirely absent in *Clio* as well as in *Limacina*. The organs which have been regarded by previous writers (van Beneden,[4] Souleyet,[5] &c.) as gills are merely folds of the mantle in specimens preserved in spirit.

---

[1] They are visible even in the larva ; compare Fol, Sur le développement des Ptéropodes, *Arch. d. Zool. Expér.*, sér. 1, t. iv. pl. vi. fig. 6, *qs*.

[2] Gegenbaur is mistaken when he depicts (Untersuchungen über Pteropoden und Heteropoden, pl. ii. fig. 1, *g*) the intestine as curved dorsally in *Clio (Creseis) acicula*.

[3] Voyage de la Bonite, Zoologie, t. ii. pp. 168, 169.   [4] Exercices zootomiques, part ii. p. 42.

[5] Voyage de la Bonite, Zoologie, t. ii. p. 170.

The Generative Organs.—The genital gland (Pl. II. fig. 1, k) occupies the posterior part of the visceral mass. The duct (l) issues from it dorsally, passes to the left side of the alimentary canal and then to its ventral surface, and terminates by opening at the right side of the cephalic mass (o).

At the distal extremity of the genital duct are situated the accessory genital glands (Pl. II. fig. 1, m). In *Clio* (*Creseis*) *acicula* I have sought in vain for the receptaculum seminis with a long duct, figured by Gegenbaur.[1] In *Styliola* only the receptaculum seminis is a little elongated. Generally (*Creseis*, *Hyalocylix*) there is a swelling (probably glandular) near the origin of the genital duct.

The genital aperture is connected by a ciliated spermatic groove with the orifice of the penis (Pl. II. fig. 1, q), which is placed as in *Limacina*.

The Nervous System.—In all species of *Clio* the cerebral and pedal ganglia agree in structure and position with those of *Limacina*.

If the nervous system of *Clio* be examined by a series of transverse sections, it is found (Pl. II. fig. 9) that though each cerebral ganglion is outwardly single, yet it contains two distinct centres; the pleural ganglion (b) is fused with the cerebral ganglion proper (a), and is not recognisable on superficial examination. The same is the case in all Thecosomata, except as we shall see in *Cuvierina*, in which the pleural ganglion is just noticeable externally.

In *Clio*, as in all the other Cavoliniidæ, the ganglionic elements of the visceral commissure do not form a bilaterally symmetrical mass as has been usually represented, and as indeed I myself have previously figured in a somewhat diagrammatic sketch of the central nervous system of *Cavolinia*.[2]

The left half of the visceral ganglionic mass is always larger than the right; and in the case of *Clio* this is particularly prominent in the subgenus *Creseis*. This shows clearly that, as in *Limacina*, the ganglion called "abdominal" is fused with one of the anterior visceral ganglia (in all the Cavoliniidæ this is the subintestinal), for the visceral nerves (that is to say, those of the abdominal ganglion, viz., the visceral nerve supplying the heart and the kidney, and the genital nerve) and the left pallial nerve issue from the left portion of the visceral ganglionic mass, whilst from the right half of this mass there issues only the right pallial nerve, which supplies the right half of the mantle and the osphradium.

The description given by Stuart[3] of the nervous system of *Clio* (*Creseis*) *acicula* is so strange and inaccurate that it would require too long to attempt to correct it here.

The enteric or stomato-gastric nervous system is composed of the same elements as that of *Limacina*, and only differs from it in the fact that the two buccal ganglia are approximated to each other instead of being separated and joined by a commissure.

[1] Untersuchungen über Pteropoden und Heteropoden, pl. ii. fig. 3, c, d.
[2] Recherches sur le système nerveux des Ptéropodes, Arch. de Biol., t. vii. pl. iv. fig. 11.
[3] Ueber das Nervensystem von *Creseis acicula*, Zeitschr. f. wiss. Zool., Bd. xxi. pl. xxiv. A.

The otocysts are situated on the ventral face of the central nervous system, between the pedal and visceral ganglia; each of them encloses a number of otoliths (Pl. II. fig. 9, *d*).

Osphradium.—The right pallial nerve (*l*, in the figures of the central nervous system) bifurcates shortly after its origin. Its posterior branch leads to a ciliated pad, situated on the inner face of the mantle. This pad, nervous in its nature, is the osphradium, which has the same position and structure in *Clio* as has been represented by Gegenbaur in *Cavolinia*. Its deeper portion is a ganglionic band with numerous cells, whilst the superficial portion consists of an epithelium with ciliated columnar cells.

2. *Cuvierina.*

The Head and Foot.—In this genus the head and tentacles agree with those of *Styliola* and *Hyalocylix*, and the fins with those of *Styliola* and *Clio* (*s. str.*). The posterior lobe of the foot resembles that in the two latter subgenera, but is somewhat notched in the centre of its free border (Pl. II. fig. 6, *b*).

The Mantle.—The mantle-opening, like that of *Clio* (subgenus *Clio*, *s. str.*) is as large as the opening of the shell, the margins of the mantle being entirely separated.

The shield (pallial gland) is long, and is divided into two halves by a transparent transverse band, like that of *Hyalocylix*, but it does not exhibit the two small latero-anterior portions of this latter. As for the lateral lobe of the mantle (balancer), situated here, as in all Cavoliniidæ, on the right side, it is somewhat reduced, and does not arise from the very border of the mantle but a little within it; on the other side, in an almost symmetrical position, is another appendage somewhat similar to it and of almost the same size. The columellar muscle is very large.

The Digestive Tract.—An examination of this part of the body shows that the jaws, closely resembling those of other Cavoliniidæ, are well developed, and that the radula is proportionally longer than in other Thecosomata. The salivary glands resemble in shape those of other Cavoliniidæ, but are much larger.

The œsophagus, at a little distance from the buccal mass, traverses a partition (Pl. II. fig. 6, *f*) which exists indeed in all Pteropoda. The stomach and liver are like those of *Styliola* and *Clio* (*s. str.*), but I have seen no gastric cæcum.

The flexure of the intestine is lateral in *Cuvierina*, as in all Thecosomata, and to such an extent that the œsophagus and intestine are here almost in the same longitudinal plane, and not at all in the same sagittal plane.

The anus is situated far forward, near the mantle-opening, as in *Clio* (*s. str.*). It presents an anal gland as in other Cavoliniidæ.

The Circulatory and Excretory Organs.—*Cuvierina* has no gill any more than *Clio*, and further, there do not exist between *Clio* and *Cuvierina* any differences in the form and disposition of the heart and kidney.

The Generative Organs.—The genital duct has no vesicula seminalis in its course. The accessory genital glands resemble those of *Clio*, but the genital aperture is characterised by the frequent presence of a long flattened appendage, situated on its ventral aspect. This organ is narrow at its base, and divides further on into two branches, of which the right terminates in a point, whilst the left enlarges as it proceeds, expands into the form of a fan, and is truncated at its extremity where it ends in a pad. This appendage, like the whole cervical region, is innervated by the pedal ganglion. Its function is not hitherto known with certainty. Several naturalists have erroneously taken it for the penis (the penis of *Cuvierina* is situated in the same position as that of other Cavoliniidæ, and is of the same form); but it seems probable that it is an accessory copulatory organ, and assists the two individuals *in coitu* in maintaining their attachment to each other. The somewhat frequent absence of this appendage and its variable degree of development lead me to think that it is a temporary organ.

The Nervous System of *Cuvierina* is on the whole constituted like that of other Cavoliniidæ. The cerebral and pedal ganglia resemble those of *Clio*, and give origin to the same nerves.

The pedal ganglia show clearly a small second commissure in front of the first (Pl. III. fig. 1, *e*).

The pleural ganglia, which were discovered in *Clio* by transverse sections of the nervous system, are here recognisable externally, as distinct from the three other ganglia of the same side (Pl. II. fig. 10, *c*).

The visceral ganglia, which in *Clio* were seen to form a mass, composed of two asymmetrical but not separate halves, form here two ganglionic masses, closely approximated but still distinct, as in *Limacina*, with this difference, that the larger ganglion is on the left and the smaller on the right.

The large ganglion corresponds to the larger half of the visceral ganglionic mass of *Clio*; in fact the same nerves issue from it: the left pallial nerve (Pl. III. figs. 1, *4*), and the nerves of the "abdominal" ganglion (genital, *3*, and visceral, *2*); whilst from the right ganglion issues only the right pallial nerve (*1*) which also supplies the osphradium.

There are no differences in the form and position of the otocysts and the osphradium between *Cavolinia* and *Clio*.

3. *Cavolinia.*

It has already been pointed out that this genus consists of two groups :—(A) formed by *Cavolinia trispinosa* and *Cavolinia quadridentata*; (B) including the other six species admitted in the systematic portion of this Report. These two groups, although agreeing in their essential characters, differ in certain points to which allusion will afterwards be made.

The Head, in all species of *Cavolinia*, resembles that of *Clio* (*s. str.*). Both tentacles are well developed, the right especially attaining large dimensions.

The Foot is of different form in the two groups. In group A (*Cavolinia trispinosa* and *Cavolinia quadridentata*) the fins are like those of *Clio* (*s. str.*), as also the posterior lobe of the foot, which is long.

In group B (typical *Cavoliniæ*) the fins are not so narrow dorso-ventrally, and they form a muscular surface, almost undivided, with the posterior lobe of the foot. This latter is very short and almost as broad as the united fins, from which it is scarcely separated.

The Mantle in *Cavolinia* has a form quite peculiar to the genus, which gives it its most striking character, and is reflected in the disposition of the shell.

The mantle-opening is narrow dorso-ventrally; morphologically indeed it extends as far as the posterior extremity of the lateral slits of the shell, for it is up to this point that the opening of the latter extends. The margins of the mantle, however, are united together by a narrow transverse membrane, as far as in front of the closing apparatus of the shell. These margins are prolonged beyond this united membrane, and may extend outwards by the lateral slits in the shell, just as the separate margins extend through the anterior aperture of the shell, in such a way as to cover during the life of the animal almost the whole external surface of the shell (in the typical *Cavoliniæ, e.g., Cavolinia tridentata*).

Besides this in the *Cavoliniæ*, in a restricted sense (that is, excluding *Cavolinia trispinosa* and *Cavolinia quadridentata*), there arises between the margins of the mantle thus prolonged beyond the uniting membrane, on either side posteriorly, a very extensile appendage, which may be double or triple according to the species and according to the state of development, and may float out behind. These appendages possibly correspond to the two symmetrical appendages on the margins of the mantle of *Cuvierina*.

Cavolinia trispinosa and *Cavolinia quadridentata*, which do not possess these symmetrical appendages, are provided on the left side with a lateral lobe (balancer) like that of *Clio*.

The pallial gland, symmetrical as in all the Cavoliniidæ, presents transverse opaque and transparent bands of unlike histological nature. The columellar muscle, which is rather broad, is situated dorsally as in all the Cavoliniidæ, and only directed ventrally at the anterior portion where it bifurcates, passing on either side of the œsophagus to be distributed to the fins and posterior lobe of the foot. This muscle, however, is not really symmetrical, that is to say, situated exactly in the median line; it is oblique, and this is especially visible in *Cavolinia longirostris* (Pl. III. fig. 2), where the insertion of the muscle into the shell, instead of being in the centre of the posterior truncation, is in its right hand angle.

The Digestive Tract.—The anterior portion (buccal mass, œsophagus) resembles that of the other Cavoliniidæ already examined. The stomach, like that of *Clio*, possesses a fifth large triangular masticatory plate, situated behind the four others, and on the ventral side.

All the species of *Carolinia* have a posterior gastric cæcum, such as has already been described in some species of *Clio*.

The liver in the typical *Carolinia* is like that of the preceding genus in shape, and its duct opens at the right side of the hinder portion of the stomach. In the group A (*Carolina trispinosa* and *Carolinia quadridentata*, Pl. III. fig. 3) this organ has an arrangement unique among the Thecosomata: it is composed of two lobes, quite separated, and having each its own duct. These two lobes of the liver are placed to the right and left of the stomach, and their ducts open separately on either side of the gastric cæcum, the duct of the right lobe being much longer than that of the left.

In all *Carolinia* the anus opens almost dorsally, quite behind the liver. Close to the anus is a flattened anal gland, as in other members of the family.

The Circulatory and Excretory Organs.—The heart is situated on the right beside the genital gland. The kidney is towards the ventral aspect of the latter and behind it, disposed almost transversely. In *Carolinia* the kidney is not at all spongy; its structure is the same as that found in other Cavoliniidæ.

In all the typical *Carolinia* (*i.e.*, the six species included in group B) there is a gill, as Boas[1] has already pointed out. In *Carolinia inflexa* it is smaller than in the other forms.

The form and structure of this organ are well known, since Souleyet described and figured it in *Carolinia tridentata*. I will only remark that the gill of *Carolinia* is not symmetrical, as might be imagined. The right hand portion is more developed than the left, for it extends farther forwards, besides which it is more dorsal in position. It corresponds to the anterior part of the gill in the Gastropoda.

The Generative Organs.—A consideration of the generative organs as a whole shows that some differences exist between the typical Cavoliniidæ and the two species included in group A.

In the latter the genital gland is quite ventral in position, and it is developed equally on the right and left sides. In the typical *Carolinia*, on the other hand, the gland is quite asymmetrical, and largely developed on the left side.

The genital duct in group A presents an elongated swelling on its course, which is lacking in the typical forms; these, however, are provided with a vesicula seminalis which has the form of a long cæcum, without any dilatation at its extremity, and coiled several times upon itself (Pl. III. fig. 2, A). *Carolinia inflexa* has an ovoid vesicula

[1] Spolia atlantica, p. 207.

seminalis, with a very short duct (Pl. III. fig. 4, c). *Cavolinia longirostris* appears to form a transition between this arrangement and that observed in the other typical *Cavoliniæ*, for in this species the vesicula seminalis has the form of a long cæcum, towards the extremity of which is a swelling, which is wanting in the other species of *Cavolinia* (*s. str.*).

On the other hand, there are in all *Cavoliniæ*, at the distal extremity of the genital duct, the same accessory glands as in other Thecosomata; a large muciparous gland and smaller albumen-gland close together. In group A, however, there is a pyriform receptaculum seminis at the end of a long duct, a little in front of these glands.

The genital aperture (Pl. III. fig. 4, e), the ciliated seminal groove (f), and the orifice of the penis, are situated as are the corresponding parts of other Cavoliniidæ. The penis encloses a horny stylet (*e.g.*, in *Cavolinia trispinosa*, Pl. III. fig. 5), which Souleyet[1] did not notice in the genus.

The Nervous System.—In *Cavolinia*, as in all other Thecosomata, the cerebral ganglia are situated at the sides of the œsophagus, and connected by a long supracœsophageal commissure. They are in reality cerebro-pleural ganglia, for each encloses a pleural centre within it.

The pedal ganglia, as in *Cuvierina*, and probably all other Thecosomata, have a second small anterior commissure, which is readily visible in a series of transverse sections of the central nervous system.

As in the case of *Clio* the visceral mass is formed of two asymmetrical halves, the right being the smaller of the two. All the figures, therefore, which represent this mass as symmetrical are incorrect.

Thus in the typical *Cavoliniæ* the visceral ganglia are disposed as in *Clio*, and the nerves take origin in the same manner. The two pallial nerves (*1* and *4* in the figures of the nervous system) are very strong in this species, in correlation with the presence of the pallial appendages and of the extensible margins of the mantle. In *Cavolinia inflexa* the two halves of the visceral ganglionic mass are rather further separated, but still asymmetrical.

In the forms included in group A (*Cavolinia trispinosa* and *Cavolinia quadridentata*) the ganglionic elements of the visceral commissure are clearly separated, as in *Cuvierina*, into two asymmetrical ganglionic masses (the right being the smaller), but to a less extent than in *Cuvierina*. The nerves take origin in a manner similar to that described in the latter genus.

This clear separation of the ganglia in group A shows beyond doubt that these species are the most archaic of the living forms of this genus—a view which is supported by the presence of the balancer, as in *Clio*, and the less specialised character of the foot.

On the other hand, the absence of a gill, the characters of the mantle, of the genital

[1] Voyage de la Bonite, Zoologie, t. ii. p. 125.

organs, and of the embryonic shell, show also that these two species are most nearly allied to *Clio*, which is a more ancient genus than *Carolinia*. Finally, the presence of a liver divided into two separate lobes distinguishes them from the other typical species of *Carolinia*.

These differences, upon which I did not lay sufficient stress in my systematic Report on the Thecosomata, lead me to regard the group A as a subgenus of *Carolinia*, and the name *Diacria*, Gray, 1842, created for the species *Carolinia trispinosa*, appears to me suitable for it.

Family III. Cymbuliidæ.

The animals of this family differ greatly, in appearance at least, from those contained in the two preceding families. The disposition of the various parts of the body, as compared with other Thecosomata, has already been explained.[1]

When a member of the Family Cymbuliidæ and another form, one of the Cavoliniidæ for example, are placed in corresponding positions, it is easy to see that their organisation is similar in all essential respects.

The three genera of this family will now be examined in succession.

1. *Cymbulia*.

The Head, as we have had occasion to indicate when speaking of *Peraclis*, differs from that of the above-mentioned Thecosomata, in the fact that it is distinct, situated at the dorsal side of the fin, and flattened down upon this latter without being free, as in *Gleba*.

It is further characterised by its two symmetrical tentacles, of equal size and with no sheath at their base, as well as by the position of the orifice of the copulatory organ, which is in the middle line of the dorsal surface of the head, a little behind the tentacles.

As regards the latter, Gegenbaur[2] throws doubt upon the existence of a nerve in the interior of these sensory organs. As we shall see, however, a nerve is distributed there, and terminates in a little ganglionic enlargement.

The Foot is in the form of a large undivided natatory disc, extending ventrally as far as the head, which is bent backwards.

The ventral lash-like appendage is not homologous with the posterior pedal lobe of the Cavoliniidæ and Limacinidæ. This latter, which also bears the operculum in the Limacinidæ, corresponds to the posterior operculigerous part of the foot of the Gastropoda. On the contrary, the filiform appendage of *Cymbulia* and of the larva of *Gleba* is

[1] Zool. Chall. Exp., part lxvi. pp. 96, 97.
[2] Untersuchungen über Pteropoden und Heteropoden, p. 45.

situated *in front* of the lobe which bears the operculum.[1]   (It has already been remarked that the larval *Cymbuliæ* have an operculum.[2])

So far as I can judge, this appendage seems to be most properly comparable with the middle part of the foot of the Heteropoda which carries the sucker, and is called by Grobben[3] "rudimentär Sohle des Protopodiums." These two portions occupy strictly corresponding situations.

I do not, however, agree with Fol[4] that this appendage of the Cymbuliidæ corresponds with the posterior lobe of the foot of the Gymnosomata. I think rather that this last is homologous with the central and posterior parts of the foot of the Aplysioidea.

The Mantle extends ventrally, and also a little dorsally, much further than in the Cavoliniidæ, in order to form the cartilaginous "shell," which is in fact nothing more nor less than an induration of the subepithelial dermic layer of the mantle.

The pallial gland (Pl. III. fig. 8, *a*; Pl. IV. fig. 7), which is a modification of the internal epithelial layer of the mantle, differs from that of the Cavoliniidæ in being obviously asymmetrical, the right portion being the larger. It is divided into anterior and posterior parts by a transparent band, which is itself asymmetrical (see Pl. III. fig. 8).

Since *Cymbulia* does not possess a true shell, the columellar muscle, corresponding to that of the Limacinidæ and Cavoliniidæ is entirely wanting.

The space between the fin and the "shell" (Pl. IV. fig. 1, *d*) is freely open and leads into the pallial cavity. On removing or cutting through the fin (Pl. III. fig. 7, *e*) the opening of the mantle-cavity is seen to be asymmetrical, thus differing from that of the Cavoliniidæ; this opening is in fact decidedly turned to the right.

In consequence of the reduction of the dorsal surface of the animal the pallial cavity appears to extend along the dorsal side to just below the heart (Pl. IV. fig. 1, *n*) between the kidney and the visceral mass (*h*) (digestive and generative organs),[5] which appears to hang freely into the mantle-cavity. It must be noticed that the aboral extremity of this visceral mass almost corresponds to the ventral prominence of the same mass in *Cavolinia gibbosa*, for example, where there is a tendency to the dorso-ventral elongation so pronounced in *Cymbulia*.

Thus the ventral surface of *Cymbulia* reaches a little further than this aboral extremity of the visceral mass.

On either side of the visceral mass there may be seen on the inner wall of the mantle rather large muscular bundles, arising where the fin joins with the visceral mass and

---

[1] Krohn, Beiträge zur Entwickelungsgeschichte der Pteropoden und Heteropoden, pl. i. fig. 13, d.
[2] Zool. Chall. Exp., part lxv. pl. ii. fig. 14.
[3] Zur Morphologie des Fusses der Heteropoden, Arb. Zool. Inst. Wien, t. vii. p. 224.
[4] Sur le développement des Ptéropodes, Arch. d. Zool. Expér., sér. 1, t. iv. p. 193.
[5] This is clearly shown in fig. 1 of my systematic Report on the Thecosomata (Zool. Chall. Exp., part lxv. p. 97).

extending into the mantle. These muscles are probably constrictors of the pallial cavity ; and they have perhaps an influence on the successive dilatations of the kidney. It was these muscles which van Beneden[1] took for gills ; but, as will subsequently appear, *Cymbulia*, like *Clio*, is destitute of these organs.

The Digestive Tract.—The mouth is not as in the Cavoliniidæ and Limacinidæ (except *Peraclis*) bordered by lateral lips ; here the lips are dorsal and ventral, and are produced along the sides of the proboscis to unite and become continuous with the dorsal margin of the fin.

The horny portions of the buccal mass have already been described, notably by Troschel ; it is only necessary to note that the two jaws are situated more ventrally than in the Cavoliniidæ.

Into the buccal cavity open the two salivary glands (Pl. IV. fig. 2, c) which, though readily visible, have not been noticed by any previous author.

The œsophagus is very large (Pl. IV. fig. 2, d), and scarcely distinctly separable from the stomach (e). This latter contains within it the same large masticatory plates as in the Cavoliniidæ ; the fifth posterior plate, though still triangular, differs a little in form, being very elongated.

The stomach does not present at its posterior extremity a true cæcum like that of *Cavolinia* and some species of *Clio*, but only a large and not very deep *cul de sac*. The intestine does not arise at the posterior extremity of the stomach but a little anterior to it.

The liver is constituted like that of the typical *Cavoliniæ;* according to Gegenbaur[2] it opens into the stomach by from three to six canals. I have only been able to see, however, two of these hepatic ducts. This multiplicity of ducts among the Thecosomata is an archaic character, which the Cymbuliidæ have retained.

The intestine is longer and more coiled than in the preceding forms of Thecosomata, but morphologically the curvature is the same as in the Cavoliniidæ. The intestine is entirely enveloped in the liver, only the extreme portion of the rectum being free. The anus is not situated so far to the left as in the Cavoliniidæ, scarcely passing the median line, but the terminal part of the intestine is directed distinctly towards the left side.

The Excretory and Circulatory Organs.—The kidney is situated on the dorsal aspect of the visceral mass, at the bottom of the pallial cavity. It is almost symmetrical in form and extends along the mantle, across both sides of the visceral cavity, in such a manner that when looked at in profile by reason of its transparency the lumen appears almost circular (Pl. IV. fig. 1, h). The walls of this organ are exceedingly thin and transparent as in *Clio*. It opens into the pallial cavity by an oval aperture (m) surrounded

[1] Exercices Zootomiques, pl. i. fig. xii. b.
[2] Untersuchungen über Pteropoden und Heteropoden, p. 48.

by a sphincter, on the right side.   On the other hand it opens into the pericardium
as in all Mollusca.

The heart (Pl. IV. fig. 1, *n*), within its large pericardium, lies at the base of the pallial
cavity under the penis, above the kidney, and on the dorsal surface of the visceral mass.

As was remarked above, gills are entirely wanting.   Very probably in the Cymbuliidæ, as in all the abranchiate Thecosomata (*Clio, Cuvierina*, &c.), respiration is
carried on by some parts of the integument.

The Generative Organs.—The genital gland (Pl. III. fig. 9, *a*) is slightly asymmetrical, its left side being more developed than the right; it is somewhat excavated in
front to receive the accessory glands and the genital duct.   This latter (*b*), very thin at
its origin, enlarges rapidly throughout its middle portion, and then narrows again till it
reaches the accessory glands.   It is not very long and surrounds these latter.

They form a large mass situated anteriorly and a little to the right, and include a
large muciparous gland (*d*) and a small albuminiparous gland (*e*) on the right side of the
duct.   These two glands, along with an ovoid receptaculum seminis (*c*) with a short
duct, open into the distal enlarged portion of the genital duct.

The genital aperture (*f*) is situated in front on the right of the visceral mass (Pl. IV.
fig. 1, *j*).   A spermatic groove, ciliated, proceeds from it towards the dorsal surface on
the right side; a little posterior to the genital opening, this groove becomes transformed
into a canal by the fusion of its margins (Pl. IV. fig. 1).   This canal opens into the
cavity occupied by the copulatory organ.

This latter, as I have already had occasion to remark, is situated on the dorsal
surface of the head.   It has the same structure as in other Thecosomata; but the position of its orifice is different, being situated in the middle line of the dorsal surface of
the head (*k*), a little behind the tentacles.

The Nervous System.—The central nervous system (Pl. IV. fig. 1, *o*) is placed a little
farther back than in the preceding forms.

As regards the cerebral and pedal ganglia the central nervous system of *Cymbulia*
resembles that of other Thecosomata (compare figs. 1 and 10, Pl. III.), as was recognised
by van Beneden, Gegenbaur, and Souleyet. · That is to say—

1. The cerebral ganglia are situated at the sides of the œsophagus (Pl. III. fig. 11, *a*),
and united by a long supraœsophageal cerebral commissure (*e*).

2. The pedal ganglia (*b*) are situated below the œsophagus, approximated to each
other and to the cerebral ganglia; they are not fused with the visceral ganglia, however,
as is represented in the figure of von Jhering.[1]

These latter have been the subject of great disagreement among the four anatomists
who have studied the genus *Cymbulia*, and especially between the figures and description of one of them.

[1] Vergleichende Anatomie des Nervensystemes und Phylogenie der Mollusken, pl. v. fig. 19.

The figure of the nervous system of *Cymbulia* given by Souleyet[1] shows three ganglionic enlargements on the visceral commissure, whilst the text states only that " la disposition du système nerveux est la même que chez les autres Ptéropodes testacés."[2] Now it has been shown that in these latter the ganglia of the visceral commissure form a mass composed of two asymmetrical halves, more or less clearly separated.

On the other hand, van Beneden[3] describes the elements of the visceral commissure as " une paire de ganglions," whilst Gegenbaur[4] agrees with Souleyet in saying that the nervous system of *Cymbulia* resembles that of typical Thecosomata. Finally, von Jhering, the last who has studied these organs, describes and figures[5] the elements of the visceral commissure as fused with the pedal ganglia in such a way as to form two large symmetrical infræsophageal ganglionic masses, upon which the otocysts are placed.

The investigation which I have made of the nervous system of *Cymbulia*[6] has shown that Souleyet's figure is by no means complete with respect to the nerves which proceed from the visceral ganglia, but it is *absolutely accurate* as regards the number and disposition of the ganglionic enlargements, that is to say, that there are three closely placed visceral ganglia, separated only by constrictions, and of which the outer are approximated to the cerebral ganglia (Pl. III. fig. 10, *c*, *d*, *e*).

The two outer ganglia are symmetrical, the median is the largest (fig. 10, *d*). It may further be seen (figs. 10 and 11) that the visceral ganglia are quite distinct from the pedal ganglia (*b*), in contradiction to what is stated by von Jhering. The central nervous system of *Cymbulia*, seen from the ventral surface, can only present the appearance attributed to it by the last-named author, before the surrounding connective-tissue has been removed from it.

The nerves which arise from the visceral ganglia are four in number, as follows,—one springs from each lateral ganglion (*1* and *4*), and two (not one only as depicted by Souleyet) which issue from the unpaired median ganglion (*2* and *3*). The stronger of these latter proceeds from the left of the ganglion, the more slender on the right side.

The nerves of the lateral ganglia (*1* and *4*) supply the mantle; the nerves from the median ganglion proceed to the genital (*6*) and to the circulatory and excretory organs (*2*).

The nerves from the other ganglia are distributed in the following manner :—

From each cerebral ganglion arise three nerves (and not two as I stated formerly[7]); an incipient transverse segmentation, which recurs more clearly expressed in *Gleba*, may be observed in the cerebral ganglia (Pl. III. fig. 11). From the dorsal segment proceeds

[1] Voyage de la Bonite, Zoologie, Mollusques, pl. xv. bis, fig. 38.
[2] Ibid., t. ii. p. 239.
[3] Exercices Zootomiques, p. 11.
[4] Untersuchungen über Pteropoden und Heteropoden, p. 44.
[6] Loc. cit., pl. v. fig. 19.
[5] Recherches sur le système nerveux des Ptéropodes, Arch. de Biol., t. vii. p. 117.
[7] Ibid., pl. iv. fig. 13.

the tentacular nerve (the existence of which was doubted by Gegenbaur); the two nerves from the ventral segment supply the cephalic region (proboscis, lips, &c.).

From each pedal ganglion two large cords proceed laterally to innervate the fin, within which they are very widely ramified.

The enteric or stomato-gastric system is constituted as follows:—The buccal ganglia (Pl. IV. fig. 2, g) are connected to the cerebral ganglia by very short cords, in contradiction to the condition figured by von Jhering.[1] These ganglia are closely approximated, and not separated by a long commissure as is indicated by the figure of this author.

The buccal ganglia give off in front and at the sides threads which innervate the buccal mass and the salivary glands. Posteriorly, a strong nervous cord (" nerf stomacal " of Lacaze Duthiers) extends over the œsophagus as far as the stomach (Pl. IV. fig. 2, h), where these two nerves form a gastric plexus (i).

This exhibits considerable regularity, and is composed of two nervous rings, one on the anterior and one on the posterior portion of the stomach; these are united by four threads passing between the four masticatory plates. At the points of junction between these threads and the rings there are small ganglionic enlargements.

This regular gastric plexus probably exists in all the Thecosomata, but the small size of the stomach in other species renders its demonstration difficult, whilst in *Cymbulia*, where the stomach is larger and the nerves thicker, it is much more easily seen.

An identical arrangement has recently been recorded in the Tectibranchiate Opisthobranchs by Lacaze Duthiers.[2] In these animals (e.g., *Philine*) the two "nerfs stomacaux" lead to the regular gastric plexus formed by an anterior and a posterior gastric nervous ring, which are united by threads passing between the masticatory plates.

The otocysts are situated posteriorly on the ventral surface of the pedal ganglia. Formerly I stated[3] that von Jhering was in error in representing an auditory nerve leading from the otocyst to the cerebral ganglion. I now recognise that I was mistaken; since that time I have had an opportunity of studying the same species as von Jhering, *Cymbulia peroni*, in which the otocysts are deeply coloured with dark brown pigment, which extends along the auditory nerve, and thus renders it very easy of detection.

2. *Cymbuliopsis*.

In the sum total of its external characters (form of the fin, proboscis, &c.) this genus resembles *Gleba* rather than *Cymbulia*, but the shape of the hardened portion of the mantle differs widely from the corresponding part of *Gleba*.[4]

[1] Vergleichende Anatomie des Nervensystemes und Phylogenie der Mollusken, pl. v. fig. 19.
[2] Considérations sur le système nerveux des Gastéropodes, Comptes rendus, t. ciii. p. 585.
[3] Recherches sur le système nerveux des Ptéropodes, Arch. de Biol., t. vii. p. 116, note 5.
[4] Compare the systematic Report on the Thecosomata, Zool. Chall. Exp., part lxv. fig. 2, p. 100 (Cymbuliopsis), and fig. 3, p. 102 (Gleba).

The Mantle.—The pallial gland, so far as I was able to observe on the badly preserved specimen at my disposal, presents the same appearance as that of *Gleba*. It is clearly asymmetrical, and is divided by a transverse band, also asymmetrical, as in the other Cymbuliidæ.

The aperture of the pallial cavity also exhibits the asymmetrical disposition already noticed in *Cymbulia*, and the pallial cavity has the same extent as in this latter genus.

The Digestive and Generative Organs.—As in *Gleba*, neither a buccal mass nor horny structures in the mouth are to be found. The digestive and generative organs are similar on the whole to those of *Gleba*, and consequently to those of *Cymbulia*. The terminal portion of the intestine is clearly directed towards the left side of the median line.

The visceral mass, which as in these two genera is suspended freely in the pallial cavity, presents at its aboral aspect a rather thin prominent ring. It resembles a sucker in form, and I am unable to give any adequate explanation of its function.

The Circulatory and Excretory Organs.—The heart and the kidney have the same situation and mutual relations as in the other genera of the family.

The Nervous System also is disposed as in *Cymbulia* and *Gleba*, that is to say, the visceral commissure is composed of three closely-placed ganglia. This special conformation of the visceral commissure, then, is a very definite character of the family Cymbuliidæ, and is only shared by the genus *Peraclis*.

The cerebral ganglia are slightly segmented as in *Cymbulia*, and the pedal ganglia do not differ from those of this genus. The otocysts too are disposed in the same manner, and the innervation of the various organs is quite similar.

3. *Gleba.*

The Head differs from that of *Cymbulia* in being free, and projecting in the form of a more or less elongated proboscis in front of the fin. The tentacles are quite similar to those of *Cymbulia*, and are situated in the same position, so that in those forms which have an elongated proboscis they are a long way behind the mouth.

As in the preceding genera, the opening of the copulatory organ is situated a little posterior to the tentacles and in the middle line in the adult, whilst in very young individuals it is placed a little towards the right side (Pl. III. fig. 12, *b*).

The Foot forms a very large natatory disc with even margins, and having neither a space devoid of muscular fibres at the lateral extremity of the dorsal margin, as in *Cymbulia*, nor a ventral appendage. During development this appendage exists and is very long, but it becomes much reduced in the older larvæ (Pl. III. fig. 12, *c*), and disappears entirely in the adult.

The Mantle has on the whole the same disposition as in *Cymbulia*, except that the hardened portion, commonly known as the "cartilaginous shell," is neither so much developed nor so thick.[1]

The pallial gland is asymmetrical (Pl. IV. fig. 3, a) and divided into an anterior and a posterior portion by an asymmetrical transparent band, which presents near its middle a narrow more opaque band.

Neither buccal mass, jaws, radula, nor salivary glands are to be found; the œsophagus is very extensile. As regards the rest of the visceral anatomy, all that has been noticed in *Cymbulia* holds good here also, and I have nothing to add to what has been published by previous authors (van Beneden, delle Chiaje, and chiefly Gegenbaur).

The Central Nervous System (Pl. IV. fig. 4) is constructed on the same plan as that of *Cymbulia*, but it may be noted that the segmentation of the cerebral ganglia (a) is more marked than in this latter genus. Besides this, each of the two segments has on its posterior aspect a little globular swelling, of the same structure as the superficial layer of the ganglia, that is to say, composed of large nervous cells. No nerves arise from these swellings.

The ganglionic elements of the visceral commissure (c, d) are disposed in the same manner as in the typical genus of the family, there being three closely approximated ganglia.

The innervation is quite similar to that of *Cymbulia*. From each cerebral ganglion a nerve (i) passes to the tentacle, where it expands into an olfactory or rhinophoral ganglion. From each pedal ganglion are given off laterally the two large nerves which ramify in the fin, and anteriorly a more slender nerve (h) which innervates the retractor muscle of the proboscis.

Finally, the nerves from the visceral ganglia are disposed as in *Cymbulia* (3, 4).

PHYLOGENETIC RELATIONS OF THE THECOSOMATA TO EACH OTHER.

From a comparative study of the organisation of the different Thecosomata we ought to be able to ascertain which form has preserved the most traces of the primitive structure of the group, that is, which of the recent species is the most nearly related to the ancestral form from which all the other Mollusca of the group Thecosomata have been derived.

It is our ignorance of this actual primitive form which has led to false conclusions regarding the affinities of the Pteropoda. The knowledge of this form will permit us to attempt the solution of the problem (which we shall do in the second part of this Report)—which of the recent Mollusca are the most nearly related to those forms which have given origin to the group Thecosomata.

[1] Compare the systematic Report, Zool. Chall. Exp., part lxv. fig. 1, p. 97 (*Cymbulia*), and fig. 3, p. 102 (*Globa*).

The most primitive form among the living Thecosomata has scarcely been sought for in any special manner, and opinions differ very greatly on this subject; some think that it is to be found among the Cavoliniidæ (*Clio*, subgenus *Creseis*), others are of opinion that it belongs to the family Limacinidæ.

In order to arrive at a positive result on this question we shall study the mutual relations of the three groups of Thecosomata (Limacinidæ, Cavoliniidæ, Cymbuliidæ), comparing their organisation.

These relations are not very easy to explain, taking into consideration the great apparent differences presented by the three above-named families—differences which have not been sufficiently considered hitherto in the relationships which the three groups bear to each other.

1. If in the first place we consider the Cymbuliidæ, we find that their affinities are very obscure. Boas[1] seems to regard them as specialised Cavoliniidæ, and for my own part, before I had had the opportunity of studying the organisation of the genus *Peraclis*, I was in a state of the most complete uncertainty regarding their relationships. The knowledge of this genus, however, has thrown some light upon their affinities.

Apart from the presence of the "cartilaginous shell," which has no homology with the calcareous shells of other Thecosomata, we may see that the Cymbuliidæ differ from the Cavoliniidæ by very definite characters, particularly in the shape of the head, which, in the former, is very distinct and quite symmetrical as regards the tentacles, which have no sheath, and in the arrangement of the central nervous system, which has three visceral ganglia instead of two closely placed as in the Cavoliniidæ.

On the other hand, we have seen that among the Limacinidæ, *Peraclis*, which, in all other respects resembles the Cymbuliidæ quite as much as does any of the Cavoliniidæ, has a distinct head agreeing with that of the older larvæ of the Cymbuliidæ in its general form and also in the symmetry of its tentacles, which are further devoid of a sheath; besides this the nervous system is constructed on the same type and has three visceral ganglionic masses arranged in the same manner.

Of all other Thecosomata, then, *Peraclis* is the one which most closely resembles the Cymbuliidæ, and with which this family has the closest affinity.

2. On the other hand, the Cavoliniidæ, as well as the Cymbuliidæ, have undoubted affinities to the Limacinidæ, but these are with the genus *Limacina*, which presents numerous resemblances to the subgenus *Creseis* of *Clio*. The head is indistinct and has the same asymmetrical arrangement as regards the tentacles and penis; besides which the fins in *Creseis* present the small tentacular lobe which is found in many *Limacinæ*.

If, however, the Cavoliniidæ and Cymbuliidæ, which are not directly connected with each other, have each of them close affinities with the Limacinidæ (*Limacina* or *Peraclis*), these relations between the straight Thecosomata (Cavoliniidæ and Cymbuliidæ),

---

[1] Spolia atlantica, p. 188.

and the coiled Thecosomata (Limacinidæ) are not rendered any the less easy of explanation, in consequence of the fundamental difference existing between the two groups: namely, that the pallial cavity is dorsal in the coiled and ventral in the straight forms, and that the anus is on the right side in the former and on the left side in the latter.

Souleyet[1] and Grobben[2] have endeavoured to explain these differences by the coiling of the Limacinidæ, but this explanation is insufficient, for if one imagine a *Clio* of the subgenus *Creseis* coiled in the same manner as a *Limacina*, the relative position of the dorsal surface of the head and the pallial cavity cannot change.

Huxley[3] foresaw that the difference is not so great as it appears, when he said, " I cannot think that any real variation will be found to occur among closely allied forms, in a matter so fundamentally connected with their whole structure and mode of development." He had not, however, quite grasped the real cause, for he thought that the displacement of the pallial cavity to the dorsal surface in the Limacinidæ is only a continuation of the process which carries the anus to the left in the Cavoliniidæ.

Boas[4] was the first to give a clear and simple explanation of this apparently deep-seated difference. His explanation may be summarised as follows :—

The anterior or cephalic part (including the buccal mass, central nervous system, genital aperture, and copulatory organ) is so disposed to the other part in one of these great groups that it would require to be twisted through 180 degrees in order to assume the position found in the other.

By this means all the differences which exist between the straight and the coiled Thecosomata are readily explicable, and the two groups themselves may be referred to a common type.

In favour of this hypothesis of "partial rotation" several arguments have been adduced by Boas, and I am able to add others which render the explanation still more satisfactory. Indeed, the sum total of these arguments allows us to demonstrate with almost mathematical certainty the above-mentioned rotation.

In fact we may see (Pl. III. fig. 6) that—

1. The pallial cavity, which is dorsal in the Limacinidæ, is on the opposite aspect, that is to say, is exactly ventral, in the straight Thecosomata.

2. The lobe of the mantle-margin, which is at the right side in the Limacinidæ, is on the left in those straight Thecosomata which possess it.

3. The osphradium (olfactory organ of Spengel) is situated on the right in the straight Thecosomata and on the left in the Limacinidæ.

4. The retractor (columellar) muscle, which is dorsal in the straight Thecosomata,

[1] Voyage de la Bonite, Zoologie, t. ii. pp. 208-210.
[2] Morphologische Studien über den Harn- und Geschlechtsapparat sowie die Leibeshöhle der Cephalopoden, *Arb. Zool. Inst. Wien*, t. v. p. 62.
[3] On the Morphology of the Cephalous Mollusca, *Phil. Trans.*, 1853, p. 43.   [4] Spolia atlantica, p. 164.

is ventral in the Limacinidæ (the Cymbuliidæ. in which the calcareous shell falls off at the end of embryonic development, have of course no retractor muscle.)

5. The fifth large gastric plate, which is dorsal in the Limacinidæ, is ventral in all the straight forms.

6. The aperture of the bile-duct, which is at the right in all the straight Thecosomata, is at the left in the Limacinidæ.

7. The intestine, which ends at the right of the pallial cavity in the Limacinidæ, ends at the left of the same cavity in the straight forms.

8. The genital duct, which arises from the dorsal edge of the gland in the straight Thecosomata, springs from the ventral side in the Limacinidæ.

9. The shell, in those straight forms which have any curvature, is bent towards the dorsal surface, whilst in the Limacinidæ the shell is twisted ventrally.

Thus on comparing these two groups it appears that, taking one of them as a standard, the anterior part of the other has rotated upon the posterior part through a half revolution (180 degrees) upon the longitudinal axis or *vice versâ*.

Now since we have seen that each of the two families of straight Thecosomata has clear affinities with the Limacinidæ, without their exhibiting any relationship to each other, we have still to show which of the three families is the most primitive, and what has been the line of their descent.

I. As regards the Cymbuliidæ and Limacinidæ, there can be no doubt that the Limacinidæ are the more primitive and have given origin to the Cymbuliidæ. The development of the latter furnishes in support of this view excellent arguments which have not hitherto been sufficiently appreciated:—

1. The embryonic shell of the Cymbuliidæ is a coiled one, whence these forms are classed by Fol[1] among his "Campyloconques" in opposition to the Cavoliniidæ, which he terms "Orthoconques"; but neither Krohn[2] nor Fol[3] state whether the shell is dextral or sinistral, and it is impossible to ascertain this from the figures given by Krohn.[4] I have seen many embryonic shells both of *Cymbulia* and *Gleba*,[5] and all were sinistral like the shells of the Limacinidæ.

2. In the older embryos, which yet bear shells, the pallial cavity is dorsal[6] and the anus to the right,[7] just as in the coiled Pteropods.

3. These same embryos then carry an operculum on the foot, which is multispiral as has already been pointed out by Krohn,[8] who, however, did not notice the direction of the spire. The examination of numerous specimens with the operculum *in situ* enables me to affirm that its spire is always sinistral. Now this

[1] Sur le développement des Ptéropodes, *Arch. d. Zool. Expér.*, sér. 1, t. iv. p. 178.
[2] Beiträge zur Entwickelungsgeschichte der Pteropoden und Heteropoden.
[3] *Loc. cit.*
[4] *Loc. cit.*, pl. i. figs. 12, 14.
[5] Zool. Chall. Exp., part lxv. pl. ii. figs. 14, 17.
[6] Krohn, *loc. cit.*, p. 15.
[7] Krohn, *loc. cit.*, p. 20.
[8] Krohn, *loc. cit.*, pl. i. fig. 15.

is precisely what is observed in *Peraclis*, whose operculum closely resembles that of the young Cymbuliidæ.

4. Besides this it has been pointed out that the older larvæ of the Cymbuliidæ, in which the proboscis is not yet reflexed in front of the fin, have the head shaped exactly like that of *Peraclis* (compare for example *Gleba*, Pl. III. fig. 12); it is quite symmetrical as regards the tentacles, with the same small prominent proboscis, the penis even being also situated on the right side. Further, in *Peraclis*, as in all the Cymbuliidæ, the central nervous system has three visceral ganglia.

We may say then that the Cymbuliidæ have descended from "Limacinoid" ancestors, and that among the recent Limacinidæ *Peraclis* is the form which most closely resembles those ancestors.

II. It now remains, then, for us to ascertain which of the two families, Limacinidæ and Cavoliniidæ, is the more primitive; that is to say, are the Cavoliniidæ descended from the Limacinidæ or have they given origin to them? Very numerous arguments speak in favour of the former hypothesis, and show that the rotation of 180 degrees, which has been alluded to above, has taken place from right to left in a Limacinoid type to give rise to the Cavoliniidæ, whilst the converse is impossible.

1. Let us consider first the relations of the digestive tract and genital duct. We see (Pl. I. fig. 3) that in the Limacinidæ the duct arises on the ventral side of the gland and passes directly to the right side of the body, making a quarter of a revolution (90 degrees) round the digestive tract (see Pl. III. fig. 6). In the Cavoliniidæ (Pl. II. fig. 1) the duct arises on the dorsal edge of the genital gland, and instead of proceeding directly to the right side of the body where the genital aperture is situated, it passes by the left side, then ventrally, and finally reaches the right side, having thus made three-quarters of a revolution (270 degrees) around the digestive tract (see Pl. III. fig. 6). It is clear that of these two routes the shorter (that is, 90 degrees) is the more primitive. It follows then that in the Cavoliniidæ, considering the genital aperture which is in the head as fixed, the visceral portion where the genital gland is situated along with the origin of the genital duct, has made a half rotation from right to left around a longitudinal axis, which explains why the genital duct makes a half revolution (180 degrees) round the tube more than in the Limacinidæ.

2. A large number of events in the development prove beyond all possibility of contradiction that the Cavoliniidæ spring from Limacinoid ancestors by the relative displacement of the visceral and cephalic portions of the body.

A. In stating his theory of rotation in the Cavoliniidæ, Boas remarks that the anterior or cephalic portion has performed a rotation of 180 degrees relatively to the posterior part, or *vice versâ*. This manner of expressing the process does

not seem to me quite accurate, although it indicates correctly the practical result
of it. The truth is rather that each part (cephalic or visceral) has performed
a quarter of a rotation around the longitudinal axis, the cephalic portion from
left to right and the visceral portion in the contrary direction. A study of
the retractor muscle shows that such has been the case.

In somewhat advanced larvæ of Cavoliniidæ this muscle may be seen to be
inserted at the right side of the shell. In the adult condition it is always
inserted dorsally close to the middle line, in such a manner that then the muscle
is entirely dorsal and parallel to the axis of the body, whilst in the larvæ it is
very oblique. According to Boas, of the two subdivisions of the retractor
muscle, that which passes on the right side of the œsophagus would be a new
formation.[1] The examination of Fol's figure above referred to shows that
it is nothing of the kind, and that this right branch is the more primitive,
since it passes to the right side of the head and to the two fins, whilst the
left branch, which passes along the other side of the œsophagus and only
supplies the left side of the head, is secondary.

B. The pallial cavity originates on the right side;[2] in the adults it is quite
ventral.

C. The anus is displaced towards the left;[3] in the adult it is situated quite
at the left.

D. The shield (pallial gland), which is quite symmetrical in the adult
Cavoliniidæ, is still asymmetrical and oblique in the older larvæ,[4] its right
side being the more developed, which indicates that it originates on this side
and is displaced towards the left.

E. The embryos of the Cavoliniidæ, on the appearance of the apex of the
shell, curve in order to follow the more rapid development of the right side;
there is then a tendency towards the sinistral coiling of the Limacinidæ,[5] a
coiling which still appears in the development of the Cymbuliidæ, in which
the uncoiling is not brought about so soon as in the Cavoliniidæ.

3. Facts are observed even in the adults which prove the rotation which has brought
about the difference between the coiled and the straight Thecosomata—

A. The dorsal groove of Clio (Styliola) subula. This groove is not parallel
to the axis of the shell, but oblique; it commences at the left and terminates
in the middle line dorsally; it thus describes a quarter of a circle and consequently indicates all the successive positions of the dorsal side during the
quarter of a rotation performed by the visceral portion of the body from left
to right (regarding the animal from the dorsal side).

[1] Spolia atlantica, p. 185, note 3.   [4] Fol, loc. cit., p. 175.   [2] Ibid., p. 146.
[4] Ibid., pl. v. fig. 2, mb.   [3] Ibid., p. 197.

B. The columellar muscle of *Cavolinia longivostris* (Pl. II. fig. 3). This muscle is not inserted in the middle line of the dorsal side of the shell but at the right hand angle of its truncature.

C. The central nervous system of *Limacina* (Pl. I. figs. 7, 8). We have already remarked that in this genus the ganglionic elements of the visceral commissure are united into two asymmetrical masses : the right large and the left small. This asymmetry is easily explained by the fact that the " abdominal " ganglion (the fused posterior visceral ganglia) has united with the "supra-intestinal " ganglion (right anterior visceral) ; the cause of the union is that in the asymmetrical Thecosomata it is the right-hand half of the visceral portion which is the best developed, that side of each set of organs having alone persisted. On examining the central nervous system of the Cavoliniidæ it is seen on the contrary that the left-hand portion of the single ganglionic visceral mass, or the left half, if the two halves are distinguishable, is the larger (*Cuvierina*, Pl. III. fig. 1); this latter mass encloses the abdominal ganglion and the subintestinal (left anterior visceral), and in fact gives origin to the nerves of the "abdominal" ganglion, which arise in *Limacina* from the large right ganglion. Thus the abdominal ganglion has followed the viscera which it innervates (genital gland, kidney, heart, &c.) in their rotation from right to left (regarding the animal from the ventral surface).

It is impossible, then, to deny the existence of this rotation converting the Limacinoid type into straight Thecosomata, or the descent of these latter from the coiled Thecosomata.

In the Cymbuliidæ the rotation has not been so complete as in the Cavoliniidæ. The pallial cavity is not so decidedly ventral, its aperture being less symmetrical, a little oblique and more open towards the right side (Pl. III. fig. 7), showing clearly that it has originated on this side and been displaced towards the left. Besides, the anus has been transported not so far to the left as in the Cavoliniidæ, and is situated only a little to the right of the middle line. The shield (pallial gland), like the orifice of the pallial cavity, is still asymmetrical (Pl. III. fig. 8), as in the Limacinidæ, and not symmetrical, as in the Cavoliniidæ.

Supposing, then, for a moment, that the cephalic portion has remained immovable, the visceral portion of the Cymbuliidæ has made a little less than a half rotation about its longitudinal axis. From this point of view, then, the Cymbuliidæ are a little less specialised than the Cavoliniidæ.

The phylogenetic relations of the different genera of Thecosomata may be expressed graphically by means of the following table :—

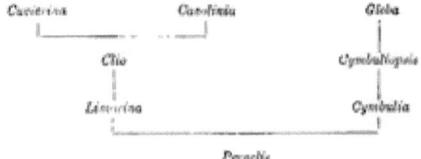

1. We have thus explained the affinities of the Cymbuliidæ and *Peraclis*. We may say, then, that the Cymbuliidæ arise from Limacinidæ resembling *Peraclis* which have lost their calcareous shell towards the end of embryonic development, and the two halves of which (cephalic and visceral) have each performed in opposite directions a little less than a quarter of the rotation about their antero-posterior axis, and, lastly, which have acquired by a subepithelial thickening of the pallial integument a "cartilaginous shell," which makes up for the loss of the calcareous shell.

Gleba is more specialised than *Cymbulia* and *Cymbuliopsis*, and in its development passes through a stage closely resembling *Cymbulia*, with a short proboscis and long appendage to the foot; this appendage shortens and disappears, whilst the proboscis elongates; further, in passing from *Cymbulia* to *Gleba* the cartilaginous shell diminishes in importance.

In the same way *Cymbuliopsis* is more specialised than *Cymbulia*, as shown in its more prominent proboscis and the disappearance of the pedal appendage. The shell has retained more importance than in *Gleba*.

2. *Limacina* is more specialised than *Peraclis*; the head has become less distinct, and the tentacles have lost their symmetry; the nervous system is more concentrated, the abdominal ganglion, which is quite distinct and separate in *Peraclis* (Pl. I. fig. 12, *d*), having fused with the "supra-intestinal" ganglion (Pl. I. fig. 8). The *Limacinæ* have become specialised in two different directions—firstly, by elongating the spire of the shell in such a manner as to attain the extreme form of *Limacina bulimoides*.

This mode of specialisation cannot, however, be very favourable, the most advantageous arrangement for a swimming animal being perfect symmetry, which cannot be realised by a coiled shell. Hence, specialisation in another direction is brought about—the uncoiling of the spire in such a way as to give rise to the straight forms, which, though symmetrical only as regards their external appearance, are thus adapted better for pelagic life. Their symmetry is thus secondary, for their primitive asymmetry remains real, complete, and profoundly impressed upon all their internal organisation.

This uncoiling must have acted like that of the caducous embryonic shell of *Gleba*, a large part of which is straight and separated from the spire.[1] This uncoiling must have

[1] Zool. Chall. Exp., part lxv. pl. ii. fig. 17.

been accompanied by the loss of the operculum; in the large adult *Limacinæ* (in *Limacina helicina*, for example) the tendency is already observed to lose the operculum, and even the partially uncoiled embryonic shell of *Gleba* has none, nor have the embryonic shells of the Cavoliniidæ.

3. The most primitive of the straight Thecosomata (subgenus *Creseis* of *Clio*) are circular in section, and have retained certain traits of the *Limacinæ*; thus *Clio virgula* has the initial part of the shell coiled dorsally, indicating a former coiling. These forms of *Clio* have also on the dorsal margin of each fin the same small tentacular lobe as is found in certain *Limacinæ*. It is easy to see how the forms compressed dorso-ventrally and with lateral keels (*Clio* properly so called) have originated from these species of *Clio* which are circular in section.

4. From these latter the *Cuvierinæ* have arisen by constriction behind the aperture, and by the formation of a diaphragm about the middle of the shell, behind which the initial part of the shell may become lost.

5. Finally, those forms of *Clio* which are compressed dorso-ventrally, in which (as in *Clio cuspidata*, for example) the lateral margins have diverged almost in opposite directions, the aperture being produced into a narrow slit at either side, have given rise to the most primitive *Cavoliniæ*, which, as in the case of *Cavolinia trispinosa* and *Cavolinia quadridentata*, still retain some of the characters of *Clio* or other primitive characters, such as a well-marked embryonic shell, fins distinct from the rather narrow ventral lobe of the foot, ganglionic elements of the visceral commissure still separated into two halves, &c.; and from these forms the passage is easy to all the other *Cavoliniæ*. Embryology confirms the view that the *Cavoliniæ* are the most specialised in this sense; in fact Fol[1] remarks in this connection, ". . . les Hyaléacées sont un extrême."

This account of the phylogeny of the Thecosomata, drawn up from comparative anatomy and based upon embryology, is also found to agree with palæontology, which gives it additional support. We find *Limacina* in the most ancient Tertiary deposits, and also forms resembling *Clio*, with circular transverse section (*Euchilotheca*), as well as nearly related forms which lead on to *Cuvierina* (*Tibiella*). *Clio*, properly so called, however, and *Cavolinia*, do not appear until the Miocene. As for the Cymbuliidæ, it is hardly possible that their "cartilaginous shells" should be preserved.

As regards the fossils considered to be Primary Thecosomata (*Creseis*, *Cleodora*, &c.), and the larval shells of Cymbuliidæ described by Ehrenberg, we shall soon see the slender basis on which rests the systematic position assigned to them.

From what has been stated above, it is easy to see the importance of the position occupied by the Limacinidæ in the morphology of the Thecosomata. By means of the knowledge of *Peraclis* they enable us to understand the relations of the Cymbuliidæ, which were extremely difficult. Wagner[2] even considered them as the most primitive

[1] *Loc. cit.*, p. 206.   [2] Die Wirbellosen des weissen Meeres, Bd. i. p. 119.

of the Pteropods, and as derived from the Heteropods? On the other hand, *Limacina* explains the relations of the Cuvoliniidæ, which if the Limacinidæ no longer existed would never have been understood, in spite of the existence of fossil Limacinidæ; for the morphological results obtained from the study of fossil shells are exceedingly small, and render those who devote themselves exclusively to this study liable to singular misconceptions.

Finally, thanks to the Limacinidæ, it will be possible, as we shall shortly see, to trace out the affinity of the Thecosomata to the other Molluscs, and to determine their phylogenetic origin.

SUMMARY ON THE THECOSOMATA.

The Thecosomata possess only one pair of cephalic tentacles.

The fins embrace the head as far as its dorsal surface.

The mantle presents on the floor of the pallial cavity a large pallial gland.

All the Thecosomata, except *Gleba* and *Cymbuliopsis*, have a radula, the formula of which is 1 : 1 : 1, two jaws placed laterally, and, contrary to the assertions of Gegenbaur, a pair of short salivary glands.

The stomach is a masticatory gizzard with muscular walls, and exhibits four large symmetrical masticatory plates (never two, as stated by Huxley,[1] and copied from him by Woodward and Tryon), a fifth posterior plate, and generally eight small anterior plates. The liver does not pour its secretion into the gizzard, but into the posterior part of the stomach, into which it opens by a very small number of apertures.

At the anus is generally situated an anal gland.

The copulatory organ is situated on the anterior dorsal part of the head near the tentacles.

The cerebral ganglia are situated at the sides of the œsophagus and united by a long supraœsophageal commissure; the pleural ganglia close beside the cerebral, and seem united with them.

II. GYMNOSOMATA.

As may be seen from the systematic Report upon this group,[2] I divide these animals into five families, one of which (Pneumonodermatidæ) includes three genera, whilst the others (Clionopsidæ, Notobranchæidæ, Clionidæ, and Halopsychidæ) include only one each.

Of the family Notobranchæidæ I was not able to obtain a single specimen for anatomical investigation, so that my researches refer only to the other divisions.

[1] On the Morphology of the Cephalous Molluscs, p. 42, *Phil. Trans.*, 1853.
[2] Zool. Chall. Exp., part lviii. p. 11.

Family I. Pneumonodermatidæ.

The three genera which make up this family resemble each other very closely in their general internal organisation, since their principal zoological differential characters are external, taken from the buccal acetabuliferous appendages and the gills.[1] I think, therefore, that the best course will be to examine these three genera simultaneously rather than separately, in order to avoid numerous repetitions; I shall mention in each case, however, the points in which I have observed differences between *Dexiobranchæa*, *Spongiobranchæa*, and *Pneumonoderma*.

The Head in the Pneumonodermatidæ is somewhat elongated. It presents anteriorly the buccal opening, dorso-ventral in direction, and the two anterior or labial tentacles, situated on either side of it and dorsally rather than ventrally. These tentacles are more or less elongated; those of *Spongiobranchæa* are more elongated than in others. They are not the seat of a special sense but of general sensibility; their distal extremity encloses elongated nervous cells.

On the dorsal surface of the cephalic region, near the middle of its length, is a pair of posterior or nuchal tentacles, which are quite symmetrical but only slightly prominent. Each of them receives two cerebral nerves, each of which is swollen at its distal extremity within the tentacle, an arrangement which perhaps led Souleyet to believe that they are bifid.[2]

These tentacles are difficult to discover when retracted in preserved specimens, but are readily found from within owing to the presence of the nerves. We shall shortly see that these are the optic and olfactory nerves, and their distal enlargements are the rudimentary eye and the olfactory ganglion or rhinophore.

The Foot is similarly shaped in all three genera, as has been already described in the systematic portion of this Report. The plicated tubercle at the base of the posterior lobe is glandular in function. All the ventral surface of the foot is ciliated.

The visceral envelope, continuous with that of the head, has several kinds of sparse unicellular glands scattered all over it. The most considerable are aggregated in the middle line on the dorsal surface, where they form a depression known as the dorsal patch. A transverse section through this (Pl. IV. fig. 7) shows the presence of two kinds of glands—(1) the peripheral or lateral glands (*b*), which are very large cells; (2) the median glands (*c*), small in size and whose secretion is of a bright colour.

The Digestive Tract.—The anterior portion from the mouth, as far as the buccal mass, constitutes an evaginable proboscis of the acrembolic type. This has been figured in three genera in the systematic part of this Report; it is least developed in *Dexiobranchæa*.

On the anterior part of the retracted proboscis (posterior part when it is evaginated) are

---

[1] Compare the systematic Report on the Gymnosomata, Zool. Chall. Exp., part lviii. pp. 11–32.
[2] Voyage de la Bonite, Zoologie, t. ii. p. 256.

situated the acetabuliferous appendages, and I wish to lay special stress on the fact that they originate on the proboscis and have no connection with the foot. The form of these appendages varies in different genera, as was shown in the systematic Report on the Gymnosomata. In the different known species of Pneumonodermatidæ these appendages have attained different degrees of development, varying from the condition in which the suckers are directly inserted on the proboscis (*Dexiobranchæa simplex*) to that in which they are carried on two long symmetrical stems (*Spongiobranchæa* and *Pneumonoderma*).

The structure of these suckers has been studied by Niemiec,[1] and by myself; it differs essentially from that of the suckers of Cephalopods, also studied by Colasanti,[2] by Niemiec, and by Paul Girod.[3]

At the posterior end of the proboscis is the buccal mass, in such a manner that it is carried quite forwards, along with the horny pieces which it encloses, when the proboscis is evaginated.

In this buccal mass (Pl. IV. fig. 6) are contained, as we have seen, two jaws united in the middle line (*b*), a powerful radula (*c*), and the organs known under the name of hook-sacs; these last are also seen of all degrees of development in the Pneumonodermatidæ, from *Dexiobranchæa* where they form only two small depressions enclosing short hooks (*a*), to *Pneumonoderma* where they form long evaginable sacs (*a'*) with a wall covered with hooks.[4]

From the fact that the proboscis is evaginable, it follows that when it is expanded it must contain the anterior part of the œsophagus doubled up within it; this latter then must increase in length with the proboscis, always being longer than it. The œsophagus is rather extensible and ciliated throughout its whole length as in other Pteropods. It is rather short and traverses a membranous diaphragm like that which we have seen in the Thecosomata (*Cuvierina*, &c.), and which we shall also find in all the Gymnosomata. This diaphragm divides the general body-cavity into a cephalic portion, enclosing the buccal mass, the central nervous system, the penis, &c., and a posterior visceral portion.

The œsophagus, in its passage through this diaphragm, is accompanied by the salivary glands, which open in the usual position, are much elongated, and do not present a marked separation between the secreting and conducting portions. They have been figured by van Beneden[5] as united by their posterior parts. I have always found, however, both in the various species of *Pneumonoderma* which I have examined, and in other genera, that the two salivary glands are free and distinct throughout their whole extent.

The stomach forms a large pouch, with slightly muscular walls, entirely surrounded by the liver, which pours its secretion into it by numerous apertures; this arrangement is observed in all Gymnosomata.

---

[1] Recherches morphologiques sur les ventouses dans le règne animal, *Recueil Zool. Suisse*, t. ii. 1885.

[2] Ricerche anatomiche e fisiologiche sopra il braccio dei Cefalopodi, *Atti R. Accad. d. Lincei*, ser. 2, t. iii. pt. 2, 1876.

[3] Recherches sur la peau des Céphalopodes, *Arch. de Zool. Expér.*, sér. 2, t. ii, 1884.

[4] Compare the Systematic Report on the Gymnosomata, *Zool. Chall. Exp.*, part lviii. fig. 1, p. 6, I.

[5] Recherches anatomiques sur le Pneumodermon violaceum, d'Orb., *Mém. Acad. Sci. Bruxelles*, t. xi. pl. i. figs. 4, 9.

The intestine arises from the posterior part of the stomach; it is short and passes directly without any flexure to the right side, where the anus is situated. Thus the curvature of the digestive tract is lateral and to the right, and not neural. If it appear a little ventral this is in consequence of the great reduction of the pedal surface. It opens into a cloacal depression, like that of *Clionopsis* (Pl. IV. fig. 10), where is also found the opening of the kidney.

The Respiratory and Excretory Organs.—The situation and structure of the gills have been already described in three genera in the systematic portion of this Report. The primitive gill is the lateral one, which also is nearest to the auricle of the heart, this latter being posterior. For the rest the heart is shaped as in the Thecosomata. The arterial system is more easily followed than in these latter; but it does not present any special or interesting disposition.

The kidney, whose existence was suspected by Gegenbaur,[1] is an organ with thin walls, not very obvious, and difficult to demonstrate by dissection. It is made up, as in *Clionopsis* and *Clione*, of a flattened sac, situated between the visceral mass and the lateral gill, and opening anteriorly into the cloacal depression near the anus.

The Generative Organs.—The genital gland (Pl. IV. fig. 8, a) occupies the posterior part of the visceral cavity. It forms a compact mass, presenting lobes more or less distinctly separated. The genital duct (b) arises from the anterior part of the gland, a little ventrally; it is rather thin at its origin, but dilates as it proceeds as far as the middle of its course.

This duct, somewhat coiled, reaches the accessory genital glands, which are situated ventrally at the anterior end of the visceral mass; among these may be distinguished a coiled muciparous gland (c), and a small albumen gland (d), situated on the back of the other and to some extent embedded in it.

After these two glands the genital duct presents a receptaculum seminis (e) rather long and ovoid in shape; then it opens on the right side of the cervical region behind the posterior margin of the fin of that side. At the genital aperture (f) commences a ciliated spermatic groove, parallel to the fin, and passing forwards in front of the anterior border of the fin to the orifice of the penis, which is situated on the anterior aspect of the right side of the foot. The penis, which is coiled up in a cavity of the head, is rather long, and has the same form as in the other Gymnosomata, such as *Clione.*[2]

The Nervous System.—The only information we possess regarding the nervous system of the Pneumonodermatidæ is derived from the researches of Cuvier,[3] van Beneden,[4] Souleyet,[5] and Gegenbaur,[6] and is based upon the study of the genus *Pneumonoderma* alone.

---

[1] Untersuchungen über Pteropoden und Heteropoden, p. 86.　　　　[2] Zool. Chall. Exp., part lviii. p. 47.
[3] Mémoire sur l'Hyale et la Pneumoderme, *Ann. Mus. Hist. Nat. Paris*, t. iv. p. 225, pl. lix. B, fig. 9.
[4] Recherches anatomiques sur le Pneumodermon violaceum, d'Orb., *Mém. Acad. Sci. Bruxelles*, t. xi. p. 43, pl. i. fig. 2.
[5] Voyage de la Bonite, Zoologie, t. ii. p. 267, pl. xv. figs. 29–35.
[6] Untersuchungen über Pteropoden und Heteropoden, p. 97.

The first two authors have limited themselves to a description of the ganglia, without noticing the various nerves which proceed from them; the last has given no figure. Cuvier recognised the four pairs of ganglia which make up the central nervous system of *Pneumonoderma*; but nothing further is to be learned from his description and figure. Van Beneden has given a better figure of the central nervous system, without, however, distinguishing the cerebro-pleural and cerebro-pedal connectives, which he regards as forming only a single trunk. Gegenbaur confines himself to a very brief description, in the course of which he remarks that the acetabuliferous appendages are innervated by the pedal ganglia! Lastly, the description of Souleyet is much more exact, and my own researches on the nervous system of *Pneumonoderma* have shown that his figures are exceedingly accurate.

On the other hand, the comparative examination which I have made of the genera *Dexiobranchæa*, *Spongiobranchæa*, and *Pneumonoderma* has demonstrated that the central nervous system is essentially similar in composition in these three genera; so much so, indeed, that to describe one of them is to describe all.

The cephalic portion of the Pneumonodermatidæ being somewhat elongated (see Pl. V. fig. 1), as also the anterior part of the digestive tract, the central nervous system is situated relatively farther back than in the other Gymnosomata. As in all these it is composed of eight ganglia (Pl. V. fig. 1) disposed in pairs. For information regarding the form and relative dimensions of these ganglia I may refer to the figures, from which it may be obtained more readily than from even a long description.

Three of the pairs of connectives—cerebro-pleural (Pl. V. fig. 1, *e*), cerebro-pedal (*f*), and pleuro-visceral (*g*) are here rather long, in such a manner that the four pairs of ganglia are less concentrated than in other families. It is in *Dexiobranchæa* that the connectives (especially the cerebro-pleural and cerebro-pedal) are the longest, and that the concentration of the ganglia is least marked; this agrees well with the other archaic characters of this genus.

I. The cerebral ganglia (Pl. V. fig. 1, *a*) are slightly elongated transversely, and almost in apposition. In *Spongiobranchæa* there is a small cerebral commissure, more appreciable than in *Pneumonoderma*.

From each cerebral ganglion issue three connectives—cerebro-pleural (Pl. IV. fig. 9, *f*), cerebro-pedal (*g*), and cerebro-buccal (*i*), the first being the strongest. The last is the most slender, and arises from the œsophageal face of the ganglion (see Pl. IV. fig. 9, *i*, and Pl. V. fig. 3, *j*), whilst the cerebro-pleural and cerebro-pedal connectives issue from the lateral surface, one behind the other, the latter being the anterior.

The anterior part of each cerebral ganglion gives rise to three nerves, or more correctly to two, for the two lateral nerves (Pl. V. fig. 1, *j* and *k*) arise by a common trunk.

1. The median nerve (*l*) passes to the proboscis, the buccal opening, and the lips.

2. The lateral nerve, which is the strongest of those springing from the cerebral ganglion, divides almost immediately into two branches—

(i.) The one nearer the middle line (*j*) innervates the suckers situated on the wall of the proboscis (whether they be disposed as in *Dexiobranchæa* or as in the other genera of the family), and ramifies in the sucker-bearing appendages.

(ii.) The lateral branch (*k*) supplies the anterior or labial tentacle.

3 and 4. Two nerves (Pl. V. fig. 1, *h* and *i*) spring from the dorsal surface of the cerebral ganglion, and proceed to the posterior or nuchal tentacle of each side.

The more anterior and median of these nerves (*h*), which is also the stronger, is the tentacular nerve properly so called, or olfactory nerve (it has been wrongly regarded as the optic nerve by van Beneden). This nerve ends in a ganglionic enlargement, the olfactory ganglion or rhinophore, from which arise many small very ramified nerves, distributed to the terminal surface of the tentacle.

As for the true optic nerve, it is the second dorsal nerve (*i*), which arises more posteriorly and to the side, near the origin of the pedal connective. At the origin of this nerve there is found, as in many Gastropods, a small ganglionic enlargement, which I have seen especially well marked in *Spongiobranchæa*. The rudiment of the eye forms, at the extremity of the optic nerve, an enlargement almost contiguous to the rhinopore.

In a large number of Gastropods the tentacular (olfactory) nerve arises by a common trunk with the optic nerve. In the present case each has its own origin, but they show an anastomosis which recalls the condition seen in some Gastropods (for example, *Truncatella*).[1]

Finally, there arises at the side of the optic nerve, still nearer to the origin of the pleural and pedal connectives, a slender nerve which passes ventrally between the two connectives just mentioned to the otocyst. I have observed this disposition very clearly in *Spongiobranchæa* (Pl. V. fig. 3, *i*),[2] and I cannot doubt that it exists also in other genera.

II. The pedal ganglia (*b*) are united by a strong posterior and by a second anterior commissure (Pl. IV. fig. 9, *l*), more difficult of observation, which I have found in all Gymnosomata, but which has not hitherto been recorded. The homologue of this second commissure is found in a large number of Opisthobranchia (*Aplysia*,[3] for example), where it arises near the nerves of the foot, or even from one of those nerves.

Each pedal ganglion is united to the corresponding cerebral ganglion by a connective (*g*) which arises from its lateral part. The pleuro-pedal connective is invisible, the pleural ganglion being in close juxtaposition to the pedal.

[1] Vayssière, Étude sur l'organisation de la Truncatella truncatula, *Journ. de Conchyl.*, 1885, pl. xiii. fig. 18, *3'*.
[2] I am indebted to Professor Spengel for the specimens of *Spongiobranchæa* which I have dissected.
[3] Compare von Jhering, Vergleichende Anatomie des Nervensystemes und Phylogenie der Mollusken, pl. iv. fig. 14, *ps. pe. co.*

The pedal ganglia are the largest of all, and somewhat triangular in form. A large number of nerves arise from them—seven in *Pneumonoderma* (Pl. IV. fig. 9)—two anterior, two lateral, and three posterior.

1. The more median of the anterior nerves (I) passes forward and innervates the foot.

2. From the ventral surface of the ganglion, near the anterior margin, arises the large nerve (II) which passes to and ramifies in the fin.

3 and 4. The two lateral nerves (III and IV), of which the anterior is the stronger, pass forward to innervate the parts situated between the foot and the integuments of the head.

5, 6, and 7. The three posterior nerves (V, VI, and VII) proceed to the part of the envelop of the body situated dorsally to the foot, behind the head, and in front of the visceral sac. These nerves are also found with the same distribution in the other Gymnosomata, and are incontestably homologous with those which Lacaze Duthiers has described under the name " nerfs cervicaux."[1]

The outermost of these nerves (V) anastomoses with the nerve (j) which springs from the pleural ganglion. Elsewhere I have only observed this anastomosis in *Aplysia* where it was not noticed by Lacaze Duthiers.[2] I have found it in all the typical Gymnosomata, in which it has not hitherto been seen except in *Pneumonoderma* by Souleyet.[3]

The plexus formed by these two nerves contributes to the innervation of the so-called "cervical" region. The details of its composition may vary according to the genus and even according to the species; its general disposition is, however, always the same.

To the posterior border of the pedal ganglion, near the origin of the middle cervical (VI) and near the point where the pedal ganglion is approximated to the pleural ganglion, is situated the otocyst (Pl. V. fig. 3, h), which is just in contact with the pleural ganglion; as has been mentioned above, its nerve (i) is derived from the cerebral ganglion.

III. The pleural ganglion (c) is the smallest of those which make up the central nervous system, and is ovoid in form. It gives origin laterally to the nerve (Pl. IV. fig. 9, j) which unites with the outermost of the cervico-pedal nerves (V) in order to form the cervical plexus above described. The law of Lacaze Duthiers, according to which the pleural ganglion never gives off nerves,[4] must therefore be restricted to the aquatic *Pulmonata*.

[1] Du système nerveux des Gastéropodes pulmonés aquatiques, *Arch. d. Zool. Expér.*, sér. 1, t. i. p. 493, 6°

[2] Système nerveux des Gastéropodes (type Aplysie), *Comptes rendus*, t. cv. pp. 978-982.

[3] Voyage de la Bonite, Zoologie, Mollusques, pl. xv. fig. 37.

[4] Du système nerveux des Gastéropodes pulmonés aquatiques, *loc. cit.*, p. 494, 12°.

From the anterior extremity of the pleural ganglion issues the cerebro-pleural connective, and from its posterior extremity the pleuro-visceral connective (somewhat elongated in *Pneumonoderma*), which leads to the corresponding ganglion of the fourth pair.

IV. This fourth pair is composed of two ganglia (Pl. IV. fig. 9, *d*) in close apposition and almost spherical. Hitherto we have seen in the nervous system of the Pneumonodermatidæ an absolute symmetry in the size of the two ganglia of the same pair (cerebral, pleural, and pedal ganglia), and in the number of nerves which they give off. Now, however, this symmetry ceases.

An attentive examination shows that these two ganglia are slightly unequal, the left being the larger. But the asymmetry becomes more striking when we consider the nerves given off from them. The right ganglion only gives origin to one nerve, while three spring from the left hand one, a lateral nerve and two posterior almost median nerves. This asymmetry is found in all the Gymnosomata, and has only been noticed by Souleyet, who, however, did not attach any importance to it. Spengel[1] is wrong in attempting to modify Souleyet's figure so as to render the visceral nerves symmetrical in their origin.

1. The nerve from the right visceral ganglion (*1*), which is symmetrical with the lateral nerve of the left ganglion, supplies the right half of the visceral sac and the osphradium. This is constituted as in *Clionopsis* (Pl. IV. fig. 10, *a*) by a ganglionic pad occupying the antero-lateral angle of the cloacal depression; a divided branch of the nerve (*1*) passes to it.

2 and 3. The two posterior nerves of the right ganglion (*2* and *3*) innervate the viscera (genital organs, heart, kidney) and the gills.

4. Finally, the lateral nerve of the left ganglion (*4*) arises near the connective, and supplies the left half of the visceral sac.

V. The buccal ganglia, seen for the first time by van Beneden, are situated below the œsophagus, between the two hook-sacs, a little behind the point where the salivary glands open. They are in close juxtaposition, and each of them gives origin anteriorly to a filament on which is situated an accessory ganglion; these threads innervate the salivary glands.

The other nerves which arise from the buccal ganglia are five in number, as is shown in the figures of Souleyet and van Beneden—one azygous anterior nerve arising from the point where the two buccal ganglia are in contact, and innervating the radula; and also a lateral and a posterior nerve from each ganglion. The former supplies the walls of the buccal mass, and the latter the hook-sacs.

[1] Die Geruchsorgane und das Nervensystem der Mollusken, *Zeitschr. f. wiss. Zool.*, Bd. XXXV. pl. xvii. fig. 10.

The proboscis of the Pneumonodermatidæ being rather elongated, the anterior part of the digestive tract is capable of considerable displacement. The cerebro-buccal connectives are also long in this family (Pl. IV. fig. 9, i).

Family II. CLIONOPSIDÆ.

The family includes only the single genus *Clionopsis*.

The Cephalic Region is less elongated in this family than in the preceding. The anterior or labial tentacles are short and shaped as in all the Gymnosomata. The posterior or nuchal tentacles are more conspicuous than in most of these, and are especially well developed in *Clionopsis krohni*. Like those of the Pneumonodermatidæ, they each receive two nerves, each terminating in an enlargement.

The Foot of Clionopsis is characterised by the absence of a posterior lobe ; it presents, however, a plicated tubercle, having the same structure as in other Gymnosomata.

The Visceral Sac exhibits also the glandular dorsal patch, already described in the case of the preceding family.

The Digestive Tract.—As regards these organs, *Clionopsis* only differs from the Pneumonodermatidæ in its anterior portion. Indeed the stomach, liver, and intestine are disposed identically in the two families, and the anus also opens into a cloacal depression near the aperture of the kidney ; this depression is limited anteriorly and to the right by the osphradium (Pl. IV. fig. 10).

The anterior part, however, of the digestive tract of *Clionopsis* is characterised by the great elongation of the proboscis and of the œsophagus (the evaginated proboscis of *Clionopsis* has been figured in the systematic portion of this Report).[1] The elongation of the œsophagus is a necessary consequence of that of the proboscis, since it has to be folded up within the latter when it is everted.

The proboscis is further characterised by the absence of buccal appendages, which is explained by the law of compensation in the organs ; the growth of the proboscis in length renders useless the presence of organs of prehension at its base.

The Respiratory Organs consist, as I have already stated in my systematic Report, of a terminal gill in the adult state, almost analogous to that of *Pneumonoderma*; the lateral gill is absent.

The Excretory and Circulatory Organs.—Of all the Gymnosomata, *Clionopsis* is the one in which the form of the renal apparatus and its relations with the central circulatory organ are the most readily recognisable, owing to the transparency of the integument. Its structure and relations have already been accurately described by Gegenbaur.

The Generative Organs of the Clionopsidæ are quite similar to those of the Pneumonodermatidæ (Pl. IV. fig. 8).

[1] Zool. Chall. Exp., part lviii. pl. iii. fig. 1.

The Nervous System of *Clionopsis* has been described and figured by Troschel[1] and by Gegenbaur,[2] but only in a summary fashion.

Troschel represents the nervous system as formed of three pairs of ganglia, which may be regarded as cerebral, pedal, and visceral. He did not observe the pedal commissure,[3] and only saw nerves issuing from the cerebral ganglia. Among these is to be noted as a curiosity a nerve which, according to Troschel, runs from the posterior or nuchal to the anterior or labial tentacle. Gegenbaur was the first to see the pleural ganglia of *Clionopsis*, but as regards the nerves he only saw some issuing from the pedal ganglia.

According to my own observations[4] the central nervous system of *Clionopsis* is constituted in the same manner as that of *Pneumonoderma*; that is to say, it is composed of four pairs of ganglia, disposed as in this last, the pleuro-pedal connective being quite evanescent as in all Gymnosomata.

The cerebral ganglia are close together, and are shaped like those of the Pneumonodermatidæ. As regards the nerves given off from these ganglia, the chief difference from the preceding forms is dependent upon the absence of the buccal appendages. From the anterior side of each ganglion proceed two large nerves.

1. The lateral, which passes to the anterior tentacle.
2. The median, which soon ramifies freely, and is distributed to the large proboscis, and then to the buccal opening and the lips.
3 and 4. From the dorsal surface of the ganglion arise, as in the preceding genera, two nerves for the posterior or nuchal tentacles. These two nerves were seen and figured by Troschel, but he erroneously represented the left optic nerve as anterior to the olfactory nerve. As for Troschel's nerve from one tentacle to the other, I can positively assert that it does not exist, and suppose that the retractor muscle of the anterior tentacle has been taken by him for a nervous thread.

The description given of the pedal and pleural ganglia of Pneumonodermatidæ is also applicable to the Clionopsidæ. The pedal ganglia also have the second small commissure, and the lateral cervical nerve also anastomoses with the nerve of the pleural ganglion in order to contribute to the innervation of the neck.

The two visceral ganglia are characterised, as in all the typical Gymnosomata, by their asymmetry; that of the right side is smaller than the other, and only

[1] Beiträge zur Kenntniss der Pteropoden, *Archiv f. Naturgesch.*, Jahrg. 11. p. 228, pl. 1. fig. 9, r.

[2] Untersuchungen über Pteropoden und Heteropoden, p. 70, pl. v. fig. 13.

[3] It is strange that the pedal commissure of the Gymnosomata, which are the only true commissures, for the cerebral ganglia as well as those of the visceral commissures are in juxtaposition, have passed unnoticed, even where they are especially strong. Thus Cuvier has not figured the pedal commissures in *Clione*, nor has Souleyet in *Halopsyche*, nor Gegenbaur in *Clionopsis*.

[4] Recherches sur le système nerveux des Ptéropodes, *Arch. de Biol.*, t. vii. pp. 102–104, pl. iv. fig. 5.

gives origin to one, whilst three nerves spring from the left ganglion, which are distributed in a manner precisely similar to the corresponding nerves in the Pneumonodermatidæ. The nerve from the right ganglion innervates the right side of the visceral sac, one of its branches subdivides to supply the osphradium, which has the form of a ciliated nervous band, situated in the antero-lateral angle of the cloacal depression (Pl. IV. fig. 10).

There is no difference between the stomato-gastric nervous system of *Clionopsis* and that of the Pneumonodermatidæ.

Family III. CLIONIDÆ.

The Head of the Clionidæ differs from that of the Pneumonodermatidæ and the Clionopsidæ in its anterior extremity, which is swollen and separated from the body by a "neck." The anterior tentacles are long, and have the same structure as those of the Pneumonodermatidæ. The posterior are situated on the margin of the distended portion of the head towards the neck, and are shaped as in the two preceding families.

The buccal aperture is capable of opening widely, and its margins separate when the anterior portion of the digestive tract is evaginated (Pl. V. fig. 4). When the evaginable parts are retracted, the margins of the buccal opening close upon each other like two half hoods over the buccal cavity.[1]

The Foot is shaped almost exactly as in the Pneumonodermatidæ, but does not exhibit the plicated tubercle at the base of the posterior lobe. The visceral sac has no dorsal glandular patch as in the preceding families.

The Digestive Tract.—The anterior evaginable portion or proboscis is much shorter than in the Gymnosomata already examined (see Pl. V. fig. 4, *a*). At the base of this evaginable proboscis are conical buccal appendages (to the number of two or three pairs, symmetrically disposed on either side), and known as buccal cones or cephaloconi (Pl. V. fig. 4, *c*). I have already[2] described their structure, and now limit myself to mentioning the points which were then demonstrated :—

1. That they do not bear suckers of any kind.

2. That they present special nervous terminations, and enclose in their interior long unicellular glands collected into follicles.

I must add, however, that my sections were made from contracted cones from specimens killed in alcohol, so that the groups of columnar epithelial cells surrounding

---

[1] See Pelseneer, The cephalic appendages of the Gymnosomatous Pteropoda, *Quart. Journ. Micr. Sci.*, 1885, vol. xxv. pl. xxxv. figs. 4, 2.

[2] *Ibid.*, pp. 495-500, pl. xxxv. figs. 11-22.

the nervous terminations are pressed closely against each other, whilst in the living animals these groups are spaced as shown in the following figure :—

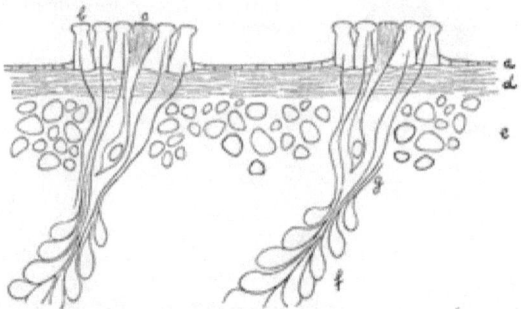

Fig. 1.—Diagrammatic representation of a part of one of the cones of *Clione*. *a*, epithelium ; *b*, elongated epithelial cells surrounding the nervous termination (*c*) ; *d*, longitudinal muscular fibres ; *e*, circular muscular fibres ; *f*, unicellular glands, the secretion of which (*g*) spreads outwards, through the elevated epithelial cells (*b*).

The secretion of the glands contained in the cones serves to attach the prey of *Clione*, as has been observed by Wagner.[1]

At the base of the buccal cones the digestive tract, that is the anterior portion of the retracted proboscis, is contracted by two symmetrical lip-like pads, which I have called false lips ; they close the alimentary canal when the two halves of the cephalic hood are turned back, in order to uncover the buccal cones.

The radula is shaped on the same plan as in the preceding families. There are no jaws. The hook-sacs, which are small in *Clionopsis* as in *Dexiobranchæa*, are here similar to those of *Spongiobranchæa*.[2]

The remainder of the digestive tract (including the accessory glands) is comparable with that of the Pneumonodermatidæ, except that the salivary glands do not exhibit the swelling prior to their termination observed in this latter family. The anus opens in the same place, but not in a cloacal depression common to it and the orifice of the kidney as in the preceding genera.

Several of the visceral openings are very difficult to distinguish from the exterior in *Clione*. Pl. V. fig. 5 shows the various orifices in their relative positions.

In addition to the diaphragm traversed by the œsophagus there is another posterior

---

[1] Die Wirbellosen des weissen Meeres, Bd. i. p. 93.

[2] Compare Pl. V. fig. 4, *a*, with fig. 2 on p. 19 of the systematic Report on the Gymnosomata, Zool. Chall. Exp., part lviii.

to the viscera, separating the visceral cavity from a third cavity, which occupies the caudal region.

Gills are entirely absent in *Clione*. According to Wagner the body-wall presents a hollow space in its thickness, in which the venous blood probably becomes oxygenated, and whence it may return into the auricle by an orifice, which would place this latter in communication with the space in question. I have never seen this orifice, but perhaps it is very difficult to discover it in preserved specimens.

The kidney occupies the same position as in the Pneumonodermatidæ and Clionopsidæ, and its relations with the pericardium are similar. Wagner[1] has been unable to find the reno-pericardial orifice, which may, nevertheless, be discovered by examining serial transverse sections of the kidney. The external opening of this organ is near the anus (Pl. V. fig. 5, *f*), but it does not occupy a common depression with the latter.

The Generative Organs are disposed as in the two preceding families, and do not offer special characters.

The Nervous System of *Clione limacina* has been particularly studied by Eschricht,[2] Souleyet,[3] von Jhering,[4] and Wagner.[5] Cuvier's contribution to this particular subject is almost nothing; his figure shows three pairs of ganglia, of which the median (corresponding to the pedal ganglia) are not united by a commissure, whilst the other two pairs (cerebral and visceral) are said to be both united by *subœsophageal* commissures.

Eschricht's description is equally brief, but more correct. His figure is too small, and in some points inexact.

Souleyet's figures are undoubtedly better; unfortunately they have no explanatory letters, and the accompanying text refers only to the cerebral and buccal ganglia.

As to the drawing given by von Jhering, no less than twenty years after that of Souleyet, it is a complete anachronism, being incomplete, inaccurate, and highly diagrammatic.

Lastly, the illustrations published by Wagner are very detailed, but they indicate several arrangements which my researches[6] seem to me to refute.

The general arrangement of the nervous system of *Clione* resembles that of all the preceding genera, the pleural ganglia being paired, in contradiction to what is stated by von Jhering.

The nerves given off by each cerebral ganglion are five in number; three springing from the anterior and two from the dorsal part.

[1] Die Wirbellosen des weissen Meeres, Bd. i. pl. iv. fig. 2, x.
[2] Anatomische untersuchungen über die Clione borealis, p. 6, pl. iii. fig. 28.
[3] Voyage de la Bonite, Zoologie, t. ii. p. 283, pl. xv. bis figs. 16, 17.
[4] Vergleichende Anatomie des Nervensystemes und Phylogenie der Mollusken, p. 230, pl. v. fig. 20.
[5] Die Wirbellosen des weissen Meeres, Bd. i. pp. 98-105, pl. xi. fig. 4, pl. xii. fig. 1.
[6] Recherches sur le système nerveux des Ptéropodes, Arch. de Biol., t. vii. pp. 96-101, pl. iv. figs. 1-4.

1. Of the three first named the one nearest the middle line is directed forwards and divides into two principal branches which innervate the dorsal and middle cones.

2. The middle nerve as soon as it issues from the ganglion gives origin to a strong thread passing to the anterior tentacle. Farther on a more slender branch springs from this nerve and gives off two branches, which innervate the lateral parts of the head and the retractor muscles of the buccal cones and of the anterior tentacle.

    The main trunk further gives off a branch distributed to the hood covering the head, to the lips, and finally to the ventral cone ; before entering which it exhibits an anastomosis with the nerve to the middle cone.

    Von Jhering describes the nerves of the buccal cones as having each a ganglion united by commissure with the nerves of the two neighbouring cones ; that is to say, they have a disposition identical with that observed in the brachial nerves of the Cephalopoda. This is, however, quite erroneous ; not one of the nerves to the cones presents a ganglion on its course. As for the " commissures " said to exist between these ganglia, I have never been able to observe anything more than the anastomosis indicated above between the ventral and middle cones ; this is oblique and has none of the characters of a regular commissure.

3. The lateral nerve, more slender than the preceding, passes round the buccal mass, and innervates the false lips, a pair of swollen pads situated at the base of the buccal cones.

4 and 5. The two nerves which arise from the dorsal surface of the cerebral ganglion and pass to the posterior tentacle, behave like the corresponding nerves of other Gymnosomata ; that is, they are optic and olfactory nerves, each ending in an enlargement.

    Wagner[1] regards the terminal enlargement of the optic nerve as the olfactory ganglion. Now the constitution of the swelling at the end of the other nerve shows that it is the olfactory ganglion or rhinophore ; in fact it gives rise to a rather large number of small nerves which become lost in the extremity of the nuchal tentacle ; this is well known to be a character of the olfactory ganglion of the Gastropoda. On the other hand, the other swelling is comparable with the corresponding enlargement in the other Gymnosomata, in which, especially in *Pneumonoderma*, may be recognised the component parts of a rudimentary eye.[2]

The pedal ganglia are constituted as in the preceding Gymnosomata. Their second

---

[1] Die Wirbellosen des weissen Meeres, Bd. I. pl. xii. fig. 2, gnr.

[2] Pelseneer, The Cephalic Appendages of the Gymnosomatous Pteropoda, Quart. Journ. Micr. Sci., 1885, pp. 494, 495.

anterior commissure arises at the base of the median nerve of the foot. The cervical plexus formed by the anastomosis of the cervical nerve and the nerve from the pleural ganglion agrees with that of the preceding genera. The pleural ganglia are paired as in all Gymnosomata.

The visceral ganglia resemble those of all the other genera hitherto studied, being characterised by the asymmetry of their nerves.

Eschricht and von Jhering have represented these nerves as symmetrical, and Wagner has figured[1] one of them as taking origin between the two ganglia, which is quite contrary to fact.

As a matter of fact, and as Souleyet alone has accurately depicted, though without description, only one nerve springs from the right ganglion, whilst three nerves issue from the left,—a lateral one, corresponding to the nerve from the right ganglion, and two others almost median.

According to Wagner[2] the lateral nerve of the left ganglion *sometimes arises from the pedal ganglion!* I have never observed such an arrangement in any one of the numerous specimens of *Clione* which I have dissected, and it seems to me almost impossible.

The nerve from the right ganglion behaves like the corresponding nerve in other Gymnosomata. One of its branches supplies the osphradium, situated between the anus and the genital aperture (Pl. V. fig. 9). The osphradium is circular in form and its structure recalls the corresponding organ of the Thecosomata, for it is formed of a mass of ganglionic cells, covered by columnar ciliated epithelium (Pl. V. fig. 7).

The buccal ganglia do not present any characters different from those of other genera; the cerebro-buccal connective always arises from the œsophageal face of the cerebral ganglia, and never, as in von Jhering's figure,[3] from their anterior border by a trunk common to the cerebral nerves.

Family IV. HALOPSYCHIDÆ.

The specimens which I had the opportunity of studying were not in a condition favourable to delicate anatomical investigation. The alcohol had not penetrated well through the thick envelop of the body, so that the viscera were badly preserved.

Hence, as regards a large portion of the visceral anatomy, I have only been able to control and confirm the greater part of the brief description of Souleyet, and to rectify some of his statements which were incorrect.

The Head is cylindrical and very small in proportion to the body of the animal. In

---

[1] Die Wirbellosen des weissen Meeres, Bd. i. pl. xii. figs. 1, 12.
[2] Ibid., p. 100, pl. xi. figs. 4, 11.
[3] Vergleichende Anatomie des Nervensystemes und Phylogenie der Mollusken, pl. v. fig. 20, 1.

my systematic Report on the Gymnosomata, I have stated[1] how in *Halopsyche* the absence of a cephalic hood, shaped like that of *Clione*, is due to the great development of the buccal appendages; and how, in consequence of this, the buccal opening of *Halopsyche* corresponds with the false lips of the latter genus and the anterior tentacles are situated upon a common base with the buccal appendages. As regards the posterior tentacles, I may refer to the same work.

I have also, in that part of my Report, described the form of the foot, which exhibits the same parts as the corresponding organ in other Gymnosomata. Its two antero-lateral symmetrical lobes, situated ventrally to the mouth, were regarded by Souleyet,[2] Owen,[3] and others as tentacles. But since they are innervated by the pedal ganglia, they clearly belong to the foot, as Huxley[4] was the first to point out.

The envelop of the body presents a thickening which has neither the same structure nor the same morphological value as that which is known as the "cartilaginous shell" in the Cymbuliidæ, since it is situated in the visceral sac and not in the mantle, which is entirely wanting in *Halopsyche* as in all the Gymnosomata. From this point of view, therefore, as from any other, there is nothing to justify an approximation of Halopsychidæ to the Cymbuliidæ.

The Digestive Tract.—The absence of the proboscis is explained by the great development of the buccal appendages in the same way as the contrary fact is explained in *Clionopsis*. The mouth opening leads then directly into the buccal mass, which is constructed on the same plan as in other Gymnosomata, except as regards the hook-sacs, whose absence is due to the lack of the proboscis.

The salivary glands, somewhat elongated, appear in transverse sections of the head. The stomach resembles in form that of all the Gymnosomata, and has no masticatory organs whatever, a fact which shows clearly that *Halopsyche* has no relation with the Thecosomata. The intestine is a little longer than in the preceding genera, but ends on the right side[5] in the same position as in them.

The Respiratory and Circulatory Organs.—Souleyet regarded the buccal appendages as two gills, but as a matter of fact, branchiæ are entirely wanting in *Halopsyche* as in *Clione*. I suppose that respiration must be brought as in *Clione* according to Wagner, for the structure of the body wall, as seen in transverse sections, is the same as he represents in the case of *Clione*.[6]

The heart, according to Souleyet,[7] is situated in the middle line, at the base of the cephalic appendages, which he regarded as gills. Nothing of the kind is the case. On

[1] Zool. Chall. Exp., part lxv. p. 53.   [2] Voyage de la Bonite, Zoologie, t. ii. p. 243, pl. xv. fig. 3, 1.
[3] Mollusca, Encyclopædia Britannica, 8th ed., vol. xv. p. 361, fig. 40, d.
[4] On the Morphology of the Cephalous Mollusca, *Phil. Trans.*, 1853, p. 41, pl. iv. fig. 3, aa.
[5] Not on the left side, as said by Huxley, loc. cit., p. 41.
[6] Die Wirbellosen des weissen Meeres, Bd. i. pl. x. fig. 3.
[7] Voyage de la Bonite, Zoologie, t. ii. p. 247.

the right side, a little further forward than in the Pneumonodermatidæ, are certain very delicate organs (which I was not able completely to isolate in the badly preserved specimens examined) which I regard as the heart and kidney.

The Generative Organs.—These resemble those of all the other Gymnosomata, the genital gland and duct being disposed in the same fashion. The hard body situated on the right of the visceral mass, whose relations Souleyet was not able to make out, is nothing else than the muciparous-gland, which, as in some other Mollusca, becomes strongly hardened by alcohol. The receptaculum seminis is like that of other genera.

The genital aperture, as may be demonstrated by transverse sections, is situated in the usual position, behind the base of the right fin, and not as represented by Souleyet,[1] who probably mistook the opening of the penis for it. This latter opens at the base of the right lateral lobe of the foot, and for the rest does not differ from that of other Gymnosomata.

The Nervous System of *Halopsyche* is very difficult to study by dissection. The ganglia are so exceedingly small (the length of the whole animal being scarcely more than 4 mm.), that they are crushed by the points of the finest needles, and can only be properly distinguished by the aid of compound lenses of short focus.

Further, of the three zoologists who have treated of the organisation of *Halopsyche*,[2] two have not mentioned the nervous system. Souleyet is the only one who has described and figured it, and even he does so inaccurately, his representation being defective—

1. In the number of commissures (he shows only the pedal commissure);
2. In the number of ganglia (he records eight, whilst in reality there are only seven).

The arrangement of this nervous system, like the rest of the organisation, supports the view that the genus *Halopsyche* belongs to the Gymnosomata, for it is constructed on a plan very different from that of the Thecosomata, whilst it agrees in its general disposition with that of the Gymnosomata.

The cerebral ganglia, instead of being placed at the sides of the œsophagus and connected by a long supraœsophageal commissure, as in the Thecosomata (Pl. I. fig. 7; Pl. II. fig. 10 ; Pl. III. fig. 11), are approximated to each other and situated above the œsophagus (Pl. V. figs. 9, 10, 11, *a*).

Each of them gives origin to two principal nerves :—

1. A lateral nerve (Pl. V. fig. 10, *f*), soon swelling into an elongated ganglion, which occupies the nuchal tentacle. The optic and olfactory nerves of the preceding Gymnosomata are not then to be distinguished in the present instance, a fact which is due to the atrophy of the eye.

[1] Voyage de la Bonite, Zoologie, Mollusques, pl. xv. fig. 3, *e'*.
[2] Huxley (On the Morphology of the Cephalous Mollusca, *Phil. Trans.*, 1853, p. 40); Macdonald (On the Anatomy of Eurybia gaudichaudi, *Trans. Linn. Soc. Lond.*, vol. xxii. p. 245); Souleyet (Voyage de la Bonite, Zoologie, t. ii. p. 250). Von Jhering (Vergleichende Anatomie des Nervensystemes und Phylogenie der Mollusken, p. 242) only republishes, in a few lines, the data of Souleyet, including the inaccuracies.

2. A median nerve (e) innervating the buccal appendage (which Souleyet regarded as a gill, and to which he attributed a visceral innervation [1]) and the anterior tentacle.[2]

Each cerebral ganglion is connected to two infraœsophageal ganglia. The more anterior of the two is united with it by a rather short connective, which is easily distinguished by its transparence from the opaque white ganglia; the posterior ganglion is almost in contact with the cerebral ganglion.

The anterior subœsophageal ganglion (Pl. V. fig. 10, b) is the pedal ganglion. It is connected with its fellow by a commissure as short as that which connects the cerebral ganglia. In addition to this principal commissure, which does not appear in Souleyet's figure, there is a second very slender one (Pl. V. figs. 8, 9, f) analogous to the second pedal commissure observed in the preceding families.

Each pedal ganglion gives origin to three nerves (Pl. V. fig. 8, l, m), which supply the foot and the fins. On the posterior margin of the pedal ganglia are situated the otocysts (i).

The smaller of the two subœsophageal ganglia (c) which are connected to either cerebral ganglia is connected posteriorly with a large azygous median subœsophageal ganglion. It follows hence that this little ganglion must be either the pleural ganglion or perhaps a ganglion of the visceral commissure.[3]

It cannot, however, be the pleural ganglion, for the pedal ganglion of the same side is not united to it by a connective; on the contrary it is quite separated from it (see Pl. V. figs. 8, 10); it is, therefore, a ganglion of the visceral commissure, as is shown also by the nerves which arise from it and innervate the visceral envelope.

The azygous median ganglion (d) is elongated transversely and is larger than the two lateral ganglia (c and e). The two nerves which spring from it supply the viscera.

The buccal ganglia (Pl. V. fig. 9, c), which were not observed by Souleyet, are situated under the œsophagus. The cerebro-buccal connective (e) is rather strong, and arises from the posterior margin of the cerebral ganglion on its œsophageal surface. The two buccal ganglia are close together, and situated between the œsophagus and the pedal ganglia.

The arrangement of the nervous system of *Halopsyche*, as I have described and figured it, differs in some particulars from Souleyet's account, especially as regards the constitution of the visceral commissure.

In his description Souleyet supplied " par l'analogie " those details which he could

---

[1] Voyage de la Bonite, Zoologie, t. ii. p. 250.

[2] Compare the disposition of the buccal appendage and the anterior tentacle in the systematic Report on the Gymnosomata, Zool. Chall. Exp., part lviii. p. 53, fig. 4.

[3] I differ from Lacaze Duthiers in not regarding the pleural ganglia as a part of the visceral commissure. The distinctive character of the components of this commissure in the asymmetrical Mollusca is that they are devoid of symmetry, that is to say, they are individually unpaired even when the visceral commissure is paired as regards the number of its ganglia, or they are asymmetrical even when they are in pairs. The pleural ganglia, on the other hand, are always in pairs and equal to each other.

not clearly make out;[1] hence he mistook the smallest of the ganglia connected with the cerebral for the homologue of the pleural ganglion of other Gymnosomata, and figured it as connected with the pedal ganglion; in the same way he indicates two large ganglia between these two small ganglia, and at their left side he makes three nerves proceed from them as in *Pneumonoderma* and *Clione*. Nothing of the kind, however, exists in *Halopsyche*.

My drawings were made after the examination of a large number of specimens, and in order to control my dissections I made a series of transverse sections of the central nervous system. The sections, which pass through the visceral ganglia (Pl. V. fig. 11), show beyond all doubt that these are three in number (*b*, *c*, *d*).

SUMMARY ON THE GYMNOSOMATA.

The Gymnosomata possess two pairs of cephalic tentacles—the anterior or labial and the posterior or nuchal, to which the optic and olfactory nerves are distributed.

The fins, or lateral margins of the foot, are separated from its middle portion (ambulatory sole), and do not enclose the cephalic region.

The mantle is entirely wanting, and consequently the shell and pallial cavity.

The anterior part of the digestive tract is evaginable (except in *Halopsyche*) in such a way as to produce a proboscis of the acrembolic type. The outer part (in evagination) is tegumentary in origin; it extends as far as the jaws, radula, and hook-sacs, which mark the commencement of the digestive tract. At the anterior part of this proboscis (except in *Clionopsis*) there are buccal appendages, which are innervated by the cerebral ganglia, and carry suckers or sensory and secretory organs. On the wall of the proboscis two longer or shorter evaginable sacs are developed, the surface of which bears horny hooks. These organs were taken for jaws by Eschricht, and by Lankester for an appendage of the "fore foot." Krohn showed by a study of their development that they are evaginations of the œsophageal wall.[2]

The jaws (except in *Clione*, where they are wanting) are united ventrally in the middle line.

The salivary glands are long, with no distinction between the duct and the gland.

The stomach is an entirely unarmed digestive sac, and is entirely surrounded by the acini of the liver, which open into it by numerous apertures.

The intestine is short, as in all carnivorous animals, and has a straight course from the stomach to the anus; it opens to the right and dorsally with respect to the foot.

The penis is situated anteriorly, and issues at the right side of the foot.

[1] Voyage de la Bonite, Zoologie, t. ii. p. 251.
[2] Beiträge zur Entwickelungsgeschichte der Pteropoden und Heteropoden, p. 7.

The central nervous system is formed of eight ganglia, except in *Halopsyche*, where there are only seven. The cerebral ganglia are closely approximated to each other, and are the only supraœsophageal ones; I lay stress on this point, because so recently as 1877 Garner has stated[1] that *Clione* possesses six ganglia, of which, in contradistinction to the arrangement in *Pneumonoderma*, four are *above* the œsophagus. The pleural ganglia, distinct from the cerebral, are close to the pedal.

III. SUMMARY ON THE PTEROPODA.

In the Pteropoda the lateral portions of the foot are all modified into fins. The jaws are lateral and paired. There are salivary glands. The stomach has "horny" plates in the adult condition, or only during the larval stages (Gymnosomata). The radula has in the same transverse row lateral teeth, which resemble each other in form, differing only in size.

The flexure of the intestine is not neural, but resembles that of the Gastropoda, which is improperly called dorsal, and would be more correctly termed lateral.

The heart is lateral and the excretory organ azygous. The pericardium is isolated from the circulation. This is a statement of importance, because even in 1882 Claus[2] stated that water enters the circulatory system by the kidney and pericardium; and because this same author states that in the Pteropoda the blood goes from the respiratory organs to the heart by way of the pericardial "sinus," even though so long since as 1857 Herman Müller showed the absence of corpuscles in the fluid of the pericardium.

The hermaphrodite genital gland has a single efferent duct and a single common genital aperture, from which a seminal groove leads to the copulatory organ, situated in the cephalic region.

The nervous system is characterised by the asymmetry of the visceral portion. The pedal ganglia have a double commissure.

The Pteropoda are thus essentially characterised by the asymmetry of their internal organisation, combined with the symmetry of their external form.

[1] Malacological Notes, *Ann. and Mag. Nat. Hist.*, ser. 4, vol. xix. pp. 372, 373.
[2] Grundzüge der Zoologie, t. ii. p. 37, 1882.

II. AFFINITIES AND PHYLOGENETIC RELATIONSHIPS OF THE PTEROPODA.

I. HISTORICAL.

Although the Pteropoda have been known for a considerable period,[1] it is only during the present century that their systematic position has been seriously studied.

The opinions on this head may be divided into two principal groups:—

1. The Pteropoda form a distinct class among the Mollusca, of the same value as the Cephalopoda, Gastropoda, Scaphopoda, and Pelecypoda.

2. They may be placed within one of two out of these four classes of Mollusca (Cephalopoda or Gastropoda).

1. Since the time of Cuvier,[2] who established the "classe des Ptéropodes," the former view has always been the more in credit, and it is still the most widely spread at the present day. Indeed, we find it adopted in the general text-books of zoology which now serve for the elementary education of naturalists, thanks to the numerous translations which have been made.[3]

Further, the "class" Pteropoda is generally placed, in the systematic arrangement, beside the Cephalopoda, and stress is generally laid upon the affinity which these two groups bear to each other; and when it happens that the author who emphasises these "affinities" has himself studied the Pteropoda (as in the case of Gegenbaur), the opinion acquires by this means additional weight.

The view, then, that the Pteropods and Cephalopods are intimately related is a very deep-rooted one, and there is scarcely a general zoological text-book or a special treatise on the Mollusca in which it is not stated.

Von Jhering, who was formerly an active supporter of this theory,[4] has since abandoned it,[5] but he still considers the Pteropoda as constituting a distinct class.[6]

---

[1] So early as 1676 Martens described and figured a Pteropod which was no other than *Clione limacina* (Spitzbergische oder grönlandische Reisebeschreibung, p. 169, pl. P, fig. *f*.)

[2] Mémoire sur l'Hyale et le Pneumoderme, *Ann. Mus. Hist. Nat. Paris*, t. iv. p. 232.

[3] Huxley, A Manual of the Anatomy of Invertebrated Animals, 1877, p. 434; Gegenbaur, Grundriss der vergleichenden Anatomie, 2 ed., 1878, p. 333; Claus, Grundzüge der Zoologie, 4 ed., 1882, t. ii. p. 68.

[4] Vergleichende anatomie des Nervensystemes und Phylogenie der Mollusken, p. 272, &c., 1876.

[5] Ueber die Verwandtschaftsbeziehungen der Cephalopoden, *Zeitschr. f. wiss. Zool.*, Bd. xxxv. p. 4, 1880.

[6] Gild es Orthoneuren?, *Zeitschr. f. wiss. Zool.*, Bd. xlv. p. 525, 1887.

2A. But it is in the second group of interpretations of the systematic position of the Pteropoda—that is to say, among those which place them along with some other Molluscan class—that we find the idea of their connection with the Cephalopoda carried to the furthest extreme. This view consists in regarding the Pteropoda as Cephalopoda, and in simply ranking them within this group. It was long since defended by Oken [1] and by Eschscholtz.[2] More recently it has been adopted by Ray Lankester.[3]

2B. We now come to the third hypothesis, according to which the Pteropoda should be placed among the Gastropoda.

In this connection it is interesting to point out that Cuvier, who established the "class" Pteropoda, remarked in his memoir on *Clio borealis*[4] that this animal exhibits "aucun des caractères des Céphalopodes," but that on the contrary it "offre beaucoup de rapports avec les Gastéropodes." In 1800, in his Leçons d'anatomie comparée, he even placed *Clio* (= *Clione*) among the Gastropoda, which, however, did not prevent him four years later from creating a distinct class for the Pteropoda.

It must be noted, however, that certain important points in the morphology of the Pteropoda were incompletely understood by Cuvier; thus he misunderstood the foot (that is the median part of the foot) of the Gymnosomata. This organ was comprehended only by de Blainville, who with remarkable insight affirmed that the relations of the Pteropoda were with the Opisthobranchia ("Bulléens"), at the same time reducing the group Pteropoda to its proper rank, and abstracting from it the foreign forms (Heteropoda, Nudibranchia, Cœlenterata) which had been introduced by Péron and Lesueur, with the exception of *Phylliroë*.[5]

I must admit, however, that the two hypotheses which I have placed in the second main group have not had very favourable receptions. I have already stated that Oken's interpretation, that the Pteropoda are Cephalopoda, is only defended at the present day by Ray Lankester. De Blainville's interpretation, that the Pteropods are Gastropods nearly related to the Bulloidea, which was so ably defended by the lamented Souleyet,[6] who died in 1852, has also fallen into oblivion.

Spengel, however, in his study of the nervous system of the Mollusca, places the Pteropoda among the Euthyneurous Gastropoda, as a group of the same rank as the Opisthobranchia and Pulmonata,[7] though still with a certain amount of reservation.[8]

---

[1] Lehrbuch der Zoologie.
[2] Mollusca, Encyclopædia Britannica, 9th ed., vol. xvi.
[3] It was Souleyet and not Leuckart who first recognised the true affinities of *Phylliroë*. His work dates from 1846 (Comptes rendus, t. xxii. p. 473), whilst that of Leuckart was only published in 1851 (Archiv f. Naturgesch., Jahrg. xvii. p. 130).
[4] Zoologischer Atlas.
[5] Ann. Mus. Hist. Nat. Paris, 1802.
[6] Voyage de la Bonite, Zoologie, t. ii., 1852.
[7] Die Geruchsorgane und das Nervensystem der Mollusken, Zeitschr. f. wiss. Zool., Bd. xxxv. p. 373.
[8] Ibid., p. 381.

Grobben [1] also affirms that the Pteropoda ought to be included in the class Gastropoda, but without deciding to which group they are related.

In 1885 I pointed out, when treating of the cephalic appendages, that the affinities of the Pteropoda are with the Euthyneura (Pulmonata and Opisthobranchia),[2] and since then I have defended their precise affinities with the Opisthobranchia,[3] and especially with the Tectibranchia.[4]

Lastly, Boas, in the morphological introduction to a work systematic in the main,[5] has followed out rigorously the view of de Blainville, and it is to be regretted that this part was not more extensive, and that he did not give at full length a demonstration of the affinities of the Pteropoda with the Tectibranchiate Opisthobranchs, and of the genealogical relations of the two groups.

There are no other instances of avowed adhesion to this view. The "class" Pteropoda still keeps its position everywhere; and its so-called affinities with the Cephalopoda are maintained by the powerful support of timid souls, who not being able to make up their minds to modify the Cuvierian system, and having really no opinion of their own, retain the generally received ideas as a matter of prudence.

From this rapid historical sketch, it appears that there are three different theories regarding the systematic position of the Pteropoda.

1. They form a distinct class.
2. They are Cephalopods.
3. They are Gastropods.

We must therefore attempt to answer the following questions :—

1. Are the Pteropods Cephalopods ?
2. Are the Pteropods Gastropods ?

If we obtain a negative answer to these two questions, then we must clearly retain the Pteropods as a distinct class, but if either of them be answered in the affirmative, the "class" Pteropoda must be abandoned.

In order to answer the two questions we shall compare the Pteropods successively with the Cephalopoda and the Gastropoda, on the basis of those anatomical characters which are common to the Thecosomata and Gymnosomata.

[1] Morphologische Studien uber den Harn- und Geschlechtsapparat sowie die Leibeshöhle der Cephalopoden, Arb. Zool. Inst. Wien, Bd. v. p. 285.
[2] On the Cephalic Appendages of the Gymnosomatous Pteropoda, Quart. Journ. Micr. Sci., vol. xxv., N. S., p. 509.
[3] Recherches sur le système nerveux des Ptéropodes, Arch. de Biol., t. vii. p. 127.
[4] Description d'un nouveau genre de Ptéropode Gymnosome, Bull. Sci. Dép. Nord, 1886, p. 226.
[5] Spolia atlantica, &c., K. dansk. Vidensk. Selsk. Skriv., 6 Raekke, Bd. iv. p. 12.

11. ARE THE PTEROPODA CEPHALOPODA?

In the organisation of the Pteropoda certain points may be seen which indicate a resemblance to the Cephalopoda.

1. The ventral position of the pallial cavity of *certain* Thecosomata (Cavoliniidæ and Cymbuliidæ).

2. The "ventral" flexure of the alimentary canal in the same groups.

3. The presence of acetabuliferous appendages in some Gymnosomata (Pneumonodermatidæ).

It is impossible, however, to show, as Hyatt [1] maintains, that "the general aspect, the arrangement and position of the oral region, and *the disposition of the internal organisation are similar in both*" (Pteropods and Cephalopods). This is, indeed, a heresy, and one must never have dissected a Pteropod to be able to make such an assertion.

It has been said that there are three points in which resemblance may be traced between the Cephalopoda and Pteropoda. We shall soon see how much foundation these resemblances have; but in the meantime it may be remarked that in *not a single point of their organisation* can a true resemblance be found which would justify the assertions which have been made regarding the affinities of the two groups, nor even explain the position which has been assigned to the Pteropods in the neighbourhood of the Cephalopods.

A. *The digestive tract* and its appendages may be first examined :—

    a. Retractile Proboscis.—This organ, so well developed in the Gymnosomata, does not exist in the Cephalopoda.

    b. Radula.—Woodward,[2] speaking of the Cephalopoda, remarks—"The odontophore somewhat resembles that of the Pteropods"—a statement which, though quite incorrect, has been copied into other text-books of Conchology.

        As a matter of fact this radula of the Cephalopoda is characterised by its uniformity; it always has the formula 3-1-3, or more accurately 1-2-1-2-1, that is to say, there is a central tooth, and, on either side, two lateral teeth and a marginal tooth; this last differs from the two lateral teeth by its general form and by its narrower basilar piece. The only exceptions known to this formula, 3-1-3, are *Gonatus* (belonging to the family Onychii) and *Nautilus*. The former has no

[1] On the parallelism between the individual and orders in Tetrabranchiate Cephalopoda, *Mem. Boston Soc. Nat. Hist.*, vol. i. pt. ii. p. 208.

[2] A Manual of the Mollusca, p. 448, 1856.

marginal teeth, and, according to Sars,[1] its formula is 2-1-2; whilst in *Nautilus*, according to Keferstein,[2] there are two marginal teeth on each side, so that the radular formula is 2-2-1-2-2.

In the Pteropoda, on the other hand, the radula varies within wide limits (the extreme formulæ being 1-1-1 and 17-1-17), and besides is characterised by the uniformity of all the lateral teeth, which differ only in their respective dimensions, their form not distinguishing, among them, so-called marginal teeth.

c. *Mandibles.*—In all the Cephalopoda these are dorsal and ventral; in the Pteropoda, on the other hand, they are lateral, sometimes situated ventrally side by side (Gymnosomata).

d. *Salivary Glands.*—In the Cephalopoda there are generally two pairs of these, which consist of two distinct portions, viz., the distended glandular mass and the narrow excretory duct. In the Pteropoda there is never more than one pair of salivary glands, which vary in length and do not exhibit any distinction between duct and gland.

e. *Œsophagus.*—A crop is present in the Cephalopoda but not in the Pteropoda.

f. *Stomach.*—This organ in the Cephalopoda never possesses any masticatory plates, even in the embryonic condition: on the contrary, the Thecosomatous Pteropoda have them always, and according to Krohn[3] the Gymnosomata have them during their larval development. The Cephalopoda have a gastric cæcum into which the ducts of the liver open; upon these latter is situated the gland commonly known as a "pancreas." The Pteropoda have neither such a cæcum nor "pancreas."

g. *Intestine.*—In the Cephalopoda this organ terminates in the middle line, whilst in the coiled Thecosomata (Limacinidæ) and in the Gymnosomata it ends on the right side (in the Gymnosomata it appears to be ventral in consequence of the reduction of the pedal face; in reality it would be quite lateral if this last were of larger size); in the straight Thecosomata (Cavoliniidæ and Cymbuliidæ) it terminates on the left side, in consequence of the rotation which was explained at the end of the first part of this anatomical Report.

B. If we consider the *organs of circulation, respiration*, and *excretion*, we see that in the Pteropoda the heart is asymmetrical, as is also the gill when it exists, whilst in the Cephalopoda these organs (heart and gills) are quite symmetrical. In the same manner

[1] Mollusca regionis arcticæ Norvegiæ, pl. xvii. fig. 2; see also Steenstrup, *Oversigt k. Dansk. Vid. Selsk. Forhandl.*, 1880, p. 10.

[2] Die Klassen und Ordnungen des Thierreichs, Bd. iii. pl. cxv. figs. 2, 3.

[3] Beitrage zur Entwickelungsgeschichte der Pteropoden und Heteropoden, pp. 6, 14.

the kidney of the Pteropoda is azygous and asymmetrical, whilst in the Cephalopoda there are two (four in *Nautilus*) symmetrical kidneys, isolated or in communication.

C. As regards the *genital organs*, we may first remark that the Cephalopods are diœcious, whilst the Pteropods are hermaphrodite.

The genital ducts differ very widely in the two groups—in the Cephalopoda the genital gland is isolated in a kind of cœlomic space, and has no direct continuity with the genital duct, which is only continuous with the wall of the cavity just mentioned. In the Pteropoda, on the contrary, the genital duct is continuous with the envelope of the gland, and, further, these animals have only a single asymmetrical genital duct, whilst in the Cephalopoda there are numerous indications of paired symmetrical ducts—in *Nautilus* in both sexes,[1] in the females of the Octopoda and of *Ommatostrephes*; and finally in *Rossia* and *Spirula*, the oviduct is on the right (as is the functional oviduct in *Nautilus*), whilst in the other Decapoda it is on the left, which proves that originally it was bilaterally symmetrical.

Lastly, the copulatory organ of the Pteropoda is situated on the head, far from the genital aperture, and is not morphologically comparable with the penis of the Cephalopoda.

D. *Nervous System.*—The nervous system of the Pteropoda differs from that of the Cephalopoda mainly in the absence of symmetry in the visceral portion. When there is an apparent symmetry in the disposition of the ganglionic visceral nervous elements, there is real asymmetry in the origin of the nerves. Furthermore, there is in the Cephalopoda a concentration of the central nervous system, so great that the commissures and connectives have almost disappeared; and there exists in all these animals a pair of "brachial" ganglia which are entirely wanting in the Pteropoda. As regards the nervous system, as in other groups there is no indication of direct relation between the Pteropoda and Cephalopods.

The osphradium (Spengel's olfactory organ) is paired in those Cephalopoda which possess it;[2] it is unpaired in the Pteropoda.

The otocysts of the Cephalopoda (except *Nautilus*) enclose a single otolith; in all the Pteropoda there are many otoliths.

E. The Cephalopoda have two symmetrical columellar muscles (formed by the union of the retractor capitis and retractor pedis of either side), whilst the Pteropods have only a single median columellar muscle.

F. *Ontogeny.*—If after examining the adult animal we consider its ontogenetic development comparatively in the two groups, we find constant and clear differences. The segmentation of the ovum, which is complete in the Pteropoda, is only partial in the Cephalopoda. In the original development of the Pteropoda there is observed at the commencement the primitive symmetry of all Mollusca, but during the whole larval

---

[1] Ray Lankester and Bourne, On the Existence of Spengel's Olfactory Organ and of Paired Genital Ducts in the Pearly Nautilus, *Quart. Journ. Micr. Sci.*, vol. xxiii., N. S., p. 345.

[2] *Ibid.*, p. 340; see also Zernoff, Ueber das Geruchsorgan der Cephalopoden, *Bull. Soc. Nat. Moscou*, 1869, p. 71, pls. i., ii.

life the complete asymmetry is very distinct ; and if in the adult we have an apparent external symmetry, there is a real internal asymmetry. And, on the contrary, in the Cephalopoda the complete primordial symmetry never disappears for a moment from the youngest embryonic stage to the perfect adult state.

It is not, however, only in the above facts (anatomical and embryological) that we fail to find traces of affinities between the two groups. Even in the three points already mentioned, as indicating resemblances between them, we shall show that the likenesses are not real but merely superficial.

1 and 2. The flexure of the intestine and the position of the pallial cavity certainly constitute one of the most important and most often quoted arguments in favour of the relation between the Pteropoda and Cephalopoda.[1] It is asserted that the flexure is " neural " in the Cavoliniidæ and in the Cymbuliidæ, and that the anus opens in them, as in the Cephalopoda, into a ventral pallial cavity.

The form of the argument is perfectly fair, but yet the conclusion is entirely false, because of the inaccuracy of the premises. The flexure of the intestines and the position of the pallial cavity in the straight Thecosomata, though apparently similar to those of the Cephalopoda, are really due to quite a different process, and that which is primitive in the Cephalopoda is secondary in the Pteropoda, as Grobben[2] perceived, so that the two are not strictly comparable.

The fact is, that a truly primitive neural flexure of the intestine and a primitive ventral pallial cavity only exist in the three classes—Cephalopoda, Scaphopoda, and Pelecypoda. This flexure is brought about by a displacement (considerable in the Cephalopoda and Scaphopoda) of the posterior part of the body—a displacement resulting, in its turn, from a partial rotation in the neural direction about a transverse axis.

As regards a hæmal flexure, it may be said with truth not to exist. In the Gastropods, where the pallial cavity is dorsal, the flexure of the intestine is always *lateral*, in consequence of a movement of rotation (quite different from that observed in the Cephalopoda) of the posterior part about a short dorso-pedal axis, which has been especially studied by Spengel.[3] Further, the terminal branch of the digestive tract may end either above the œsophagus (as in many Gastropods), which gives the appearance of a hæmal flexure, or on the same level with it (as in a good many Opisthobranchs), or even below the œsophagus, which would bring about almost a neural, but still always lateral, flexure.

As regards the Pteropoda, they have the same lateral flexure of the intestine as the Gastropods, the anus opening on the right, below the œsophagus in the Gymnosomata, in consequence of the reduction of the pedal surface, and about on the same level with it, or

---

[1] Huxley, On the Morphology of the Cephalous Mollusca, *Phil. Trans.*, 1853, p. 44 ; Gegenbaur, Grundriss der vergleichenden Anatomie, p. 378, fig. 190, 1878.

[2] Morphologische studien, &c., *Arb. Zool. Inst. Wien*, Bd. v. p. 241.

[3] Die Geruchsorgane und das Nervensystem der Mollusken, *Zeitschr. f. wiss. Zool.*, Bd. xxxv.

a little above in the Limacinidæ. Even if the flexure appear neural in the straight Thecosomes (the figure of *Creseis* given by Gegenbaur[1] is inaccurate in this particular), it is always in reality lateral, since the anus opens to the left; and we have seen that this difference from the Limacinidæ has been caused by the process of rotation already explained, and that among the Thecosomata the primitive form is the *lateral* flexure found in the Limacinidæ, as also in the Gymnosomata, and differing in both from the true neural median flexure of the Cephalopoda.

In the same way, as regards the pallial cavity of the Thecosomata, it has been shown that the primitive form is the dorsal cavity of the coiled Thecosomata, and that the ventral position of the pallial cavity in the straight forms is due to a process quite different from that which has brought about the analogous situation in the Cephalopoda, and hence that the two arrangements are not at all comparable.

Consequently there is no proof to be found here of any connection between the Cephalopoda and the Pteropoda.

3. The majority of authors have traced a homology between the buccal appendages of the Gymnosomata and the arms of the Cephalopoda. I may specially mention R. Leuckart,[2] Lovén,[3] von Jhering,[4] Gegenbaur,[5] Gronacher,[6] Brooks,[7] Ray Lankester,[8] and Grobben.[9] Huxley alone,[10] even when declaring himself in favour of this interpretation, has maintained a certain reservation regarding the innervation of the appendages of the Gymnosomata.

If, however, these authors agree as to the homology of these two sets of organs, they differ entirely regarding their morphological value.

Huxley[11] and Ray Lankester[12] consider them to belong to the foot, whilst, on the other hand, von Jhering[13] and Grobben,[14] &c., regard them as cephalic organs.

Now, I have shown from their innervation that the appendages of the Gymnosomata are cephalic in their nature.

What, then, is the morphological value of the arms of the Cephalopoda? This question, which has been so often discussed, is of great importance. Indeed, it is upon the pretended homology between the appendages of the Gymnosomata and the arms of

---

[1] Untersuchungen über Pteropoden und Heteropoden, pl. ii. fig. 1, g.
[2] Ueber die Morphologie und die Verwandtschaftsverhältnisse der wirbellosen Thiere.
[3] Bidrag til Kännedom om utveckling af Mollusca Acephala Lamellibranchiata, K. Svensk. Vetensk. Akad. Handl., 1848.   [5] Vergleichende anatomie des Nervensystemes und Phylogenie der Mollusken.
[4] Grundriss der vergleichenden Anatomie.
[5] Zur Entwickelungsgeschichte der Cephalopoden, Zeitschr. f. wiss. Zool., Bd. xxiv.
[7] Development of the Squid, Loligo Pealii, Anais. Mem. Boston Soc. Nat. Hist., 1880.
[8] Mollusca, Encyclopædia Britannica, 9th ed. vol. xvi.
[9] Zur Kenntniss der Morphologie und der Verwandtschaftsverhältnisse der Cephalopoden, Arb. Zool. Inst. Wien, t. vii.   [10] On the Morphology of the Cephalous Mollusca, Phil. Trans., 1853, p. 40.
[11] Loc. cit. pl. v. fig. 5.   [12] Mollusca, Encyclopædia Britannica, 9th ed. vol. xvi. p. 664.
[13] Vergleichende Anatomie des Nervensystemes und Phylogenie der Mollusken, p. 269.
[14] Zur Kenntniss der Morphologie und der Verwandtschaftsverhältnisse der Cephalopoden, Arb. Zool. Inst. Wien, vii. p. 71.

the Cephalopoda that reliance has generally been placed in classing these two groups near together (Claus, Fischer, &c.), or even including them in the same class (Ray Lankester).

This question of the morphological value of the arms of the Cephalopoda has always been the subject of animated discussion. It may be laid down at the outset that there are two hypotheses to be considered :—

1. The arms are pedal in nature ; this is especially the opinion of the English naturalists, Huxley, Ray Lankester, &c.

2. The arms are cephalic in nature ; a view maintained particularly by naturalists of the German school (Grenacher, von Jhering, Grobben).

In investigating this disputed point we may adopt the following methods :—(1) comparative anatomy, (2) embryology.

(1) If the arms of the Cephalopoda are, like the appendages of the Gymnosomata, cephalic in origin, their nerve supply ought at once to make this clear to us.

Topographically there is no difference of opinion regarding the part of the nervous system which gives off nerves to the arms of the Cephalopoda ; viz., the anterior infra-œsophageal or brachial ganglia (" ganglion de la patte d'oie " of Cuvier).

But as regards the morphological value of these ganglia there is the same difference of opinion as regards the arms.

These are pedal ganglia, say the English naturalists.

They are cerebral or cephalic, maintain the Germans.

The solution of the question as to the morphological value of the arms is to be found then by solving this other question :—What is the morphological value of the brachial ganglia of the Cephalopoda ?

A few words are necessary here to explain how such differences of opinion can exist regarding an organ whose topographical anatomy is so well known.

The central nervous system of the Cephalopoda is entirely concentrated in the head, around the œsophagus, and resting in the cephalic cartilage in the Dibranchia ; a little less protected in the Tetrabranchia.

In spite of the great concentration of the component parts the following separate elements may be recognised externally in this central nervous system :—

    1. A supraœsophageal mass.

    2. A subœsophageal mass, including :—

        (i.) An anterior mass.

        (ii.) A middle mass.

        (iii.) A posterior mass.

The supraœsophageal mass gives off the optic and olfactory nerves, and innervates the whole cephalic region ; there is no disagreement regarding its nature, all recognising in it the fused cerebral ganglia.

The anterior suboesophageal mass gives off the nerves to the arms, and hence has been called " brachial."

The middle suboesophageal mass, from which arise the nerves of the siphon, has been universally regarded as constituted by the pedal ganglia.

Lastly, the posterior suboesophageal mass innervates the mantle and the viscera; hence it corresponds with the combined visceral ganglia of other Mollusca.[1]

The supraoesophageal mass (cerebral ganglia) is united to the infraoesophageal masses by two connectives on either side; the anterior is rather thin and passes to the brachial ganglion; the posterior is very large and thick, and joins the cerebral ganglion to the two posterior infraoesophageal masses, that is the pedal and visceral ganglia.

It has already been stated that all observers are agreed as to the interpretation of the supraoesophageal and the two posterior suboesophageal masses. The disagreement relates only to the brachial ganglia, which are regarded by one party as pedal and by the other as cerebral. We shall now proceed to discuss this point.

Those zoologists who maintain that the brachial ganglia are part of the cerebral ganglia explain their position below the oesophagus by saying that on either side a part of the cerebral ganglia has been displaced from the upper to the lower surface of the oesophagus, still remaining united to the cerebral ganglion, and that these two nervous masses have fused below the oesophagus and formed the brachial ganglia. In this manner the brachial ganglia are cerebral in origin, and the arms which they innervate are similarly cephalic.

Against this interpretation the following arguments may be adduced:—

I. It is eminently unlikely that in order to innervate the crown of arms which surrounds the buccal aperture on *all* sides (*lateral* and *dorsal* as well as ventral) a portion of the cerebral ganglia should have descended on either side to the lower aspect of the oesophagus, and that it should be just this particular part of the cerebral ganglia situated entirely below the oesophagus that innervates the arms situated dorsally to and at either side of the latter.

If the arms were really cephalic in origin, the nervous mass which innervates them would not have descended *entirely* to the lower surface of the digestive tract, and those arms, which are situated above the oesophagus, would surely be supplied directly from the supraoesophageal cerebral mass, even if all were not so innervated as in the case of the six cones of *Clione*.

If the muscular mass of the arms had all been displaced from the upper aspect of the head in order to locate itself entirely below the mouth, then it would be reasonable to suppose that a portion of the cerebral ganglia had followed this movement, and descended on either side of the digestive tract. But nothing of the kind is the case. On the

[1] See Paul Pelseneer, Recherches sur le système nerveux des Ptéropodes, *Arch. de Biol.*, t. vii. p. 121.

contrary, the dorsal half of the mass of the arms is sometimes more voluminous than the ventral mass (compare, for example, *Nautilus*), but, nevertheless, the nervous centre which innervates the *whole* brachial mass is situated *exclusively on the lower surface* of the œsophagus. This shows clearly that the brachial mass does not originate from the dorsal, but in the ventral parts of the animal (that is from the foot), and that its two halves have been fused above the head; this view is confirmed, as we shall see in the sequel, by the embryology of these organs.

II. Grobben [1] states that the arms of the Cephalopoda were primitively lateral to the mouth, as are the cones of *Clione*. In the latter, however, all the cones, both ventral and dorsal, are innervated by the supraœsophageal ganglia. If, then, the arms of the Cephalopoda and the cones of *Clione* were morphologically homologous, it would be impossible to understand why, the disposition of these organs being similar, the disposition of their innervating organs should be different. But I have shown that the cones of *Clione* and the buccal appendages of the other Gymnosomata are organs formed on the inner wall of the evaginable proboscis, which is made up of the anterior portion of the digestive tract, and whose cephalic nature is therefore indisputable. The relation of the arms of the Cephalopoda to the anterior part of the digestive tract is entirely different.

Supposing, however, that the arms are really cephalic appendages, primitively situated at the sides of the buccal opening, we might compare them with the absolutely identical arrangement which we see in *Ampullaria*. Here we find on either side of the mouth (not more dorsally than ventrally) a large conical appendage, elongated, voluminous, and relatively as large as several arms of a Cephalopod.

How then are these appendages innervated? By the supraœsophageal or *cerebral* ganglia. [2] These appendages probably correspond with the labial palps of certain Pulmonata (*Helix*, *Glandina*, &c.), whilst the appendage situated in front of the eye corresponds with the nuchal tentacle or rhinophore of the *Euthyneura*, inasmuch as it encloses the highly ramified olfactory nerve. [3]

III. In *Vermetus*, on the other hand, we find between the mouth and the foot two long appendages (buccal tentacles of d'Orbigny; tentacular or antibuccal filaments of Quoy and Gaimard), which stand precisely in the same position as the ventral arms of the Cephalopoda, and as far separated from the pedal disc as these arms are from the funnel, upon the pedal origin of which no doubt has ever been thrown.

How then are these appendages innervated? By the anterior subœsophageal or *pedal* ganglia, as has been shown by Lacaze Duthiers, [4] and as I have been able to convince myself in the case of *Vermetus gigas*.

[1] Zur Kenntnis der Morphologie, &c., *loc. cit.*, pp. 68, 70.
[2] Anatomie von Ampullaria urceus, *Archiv f. Naturgesch.*, Jahrg. xi. p. 200, pl. viii. fig. 3, h.
[3] *Ibid.*, pl. viii. fig. 3, t'.
[4] Mémoire sur l'anatomie et l'embryogénie des Vermets, *Ann. d. Sci. Nat.*, Zoologie, sér. 4, t. xiii. p. 208, pl. vi. fig. 4, t'.

If it be admitted that cephalic appendages may surround the buccal aperture and unite below the alimentary canal (as is demanded by the arguments of von Jhering and of Grobben), then it ought also to be allowed that pedal appendages, such as those of *Vermetus*, may encroach upon the sides of the mouth and unite above the œsophagus, and embryology teaches us that this is what must have taken place in the case of the Cephalopoda.

IV. If, now, these appendages should undergo great development, it is natural that a pair of special ganglia (the brachial ganglia) should be formed for their innervation at the expense of the pedal ganglia. The formation of accessory ganglia in consequence of the great development of certain organs is often observed in the Mollusca, and here we find a case almost identical with that of the Cephalopoda.

In two groups of Gastropoda we find that the head carries a muscular mass as large in proportion as the brachial mass of the Cephalopoda; these are the Bullidæ ("Acères" of Cuvier) and the Naticidæ.

1. In the Bullidæ there is a "cephalic hood," which seems to be analogous to the hood of the *Nautilus* and to the dorsal arms of the Dibranchia; it arises from the fusion of the four tentacles (two labial and two nuchal) of the *Euthyneura*, and assists these animals in digging. The cephalic nature of the hood is thus beyond doubt.

Is then the nervous system of the Bullidæ similar to that of the Cephalopoda, and do we find there in front of the pedal ganglia other suboesophageal ganglia which innervate this cephalic mass? By no means. Here, as in *Ampullaria*, the innervation of this mass has its source in the supraoesophageal or cerebral ganglia.

On other grounds, too, it is impossible to regard the arms of the Cephalopoda as similar in origin to the cephalic tentacles of the Gastropoda. For even if the tentacles do not any longer exist in the adult Dibranchia, I may point out that they are still present in *Nautilus* (which is incontestably more primitive), though their homology has not hitherto been perceived. The structures in question are the ophthalmic tentacles, situated in front of and behind each eye; as a matter of fact these tentacles are innervated by the supraoesophageal ganglia,[1] whilst all the other appendages (whose mass corresponds morphologically to the arms of the Dibranchia) are innervated by the anterior infra-oesophageal ganglia, which also give off the nerves to the funnel.

2. In *Natica* the muscular mass which covers the head can be reflected in front so as to expose the buccal opening. It is the anterior part of the foot, but physiologically is the same part as the cephalic hood of the Bullidæ, and like it aids in burrowing.

[1] Valenciennes, Nouvelles recherches sur le Nautile flambé, *Archives Mus. Hist. Nat. Paris*, t. ii. p. 288, pl. viii. figs. 2, 3, 6 and 7. It is inaccurate to state, as does von Jhering (Vergleichende Anatomie, &c., p. 262), that the anterior ophthalmic tentacle is innervated by the anterior infraoesophageal ganglion, as also the olfactory organ. Its nerve issues from the extreme lateral part of the supraoesophageal ganglion. Compare the figures of Valenciennes above quoted.

We find in *Natica* that the disposition of the anterior suboesophageal ganglia resembles that seen in the Cephalopoda. In front of each pedal ganglion, in the position occupied by the brachial ganglion of the Cephalopoda, there is another corresponding suboesophageal ganglion, and this propedal ganglion innervates the voluminous mass which covers the head. I may here remark that the figures of the nervous system of *Natica* given by Souleyet,[1] which are the only original figures known to me, are inverted, that is to say that the upper (dorsal) surface is indicated as the lower (ventral) surface, and *vice versâ*. It follows from this that the peculiarity of the nervous system of *Natica* in possessing propedal ganglia has not hitherto been observed.

FIG. 2.—The pedal ganglia of *Natica*. *a*, pedal ganglia; *b*, propedal ganglia; *c*, pedal commissure.

The formation of these propedal ganglia and their separation from the pedal ganglia are evidently due to the great development of the anterior part of the foot, which has become transformed into a cephalic shield. Something of the same kind must have taken place in the Cephalopoda, where the formation of the brachial ganglia has been brought about by the great development of that part of the foot which has entirely surrounded the head and produced the arms.

It must not be concluded from what has just been said that I regard the shield of *Natica* and the arms of Cephalopods as exactly homologous; I only wish to draw from these facts the following conclusions:—In *Natica* we observe the formation of a pair of propedal ganglia in consequence of great development of the anterior part of the foot; in Cephalopoda we observe the same propedal ganglia; we may conclude, therefore, that the organs which they innervate are a portion of the foot situated anteriorly, which has taken on considerable development.

In *Natica* this anterior part of the foot covers the head by its anterior border, hence the coalescence with the head could not proceed further, because the mouth could not have remained open. In the Cephalopoda, on the other hand, it is the lateral margins of the foot which have invaded the head, leaving the buccal opening free; the two halves have met on the dorsal aspect of the head, concrescence has taken place, and the head has thus become entirely surrounded by a pedal mass.

Where, then, is the head? asks von Jhering.[2] The postero-lateral portions of it are to be seen in *Nautilus*, with the eye, the olfactory groove, and the two tentacles; and between the pedal appendages is seen the buccal mass. If the head be to a large extent concealed, it is not therefore non-existent.

V. We have already seen how those naturalists who defend the views which regard

[1] Voyage de la Bonite, Zoologie, Mollusques, pl. xxxvi. figs. 13, 14.
[2] Vergleichende Anatomie des Nervensystemes und Phylogenie der Mollusken, p. 268.

the arms of Cephalopods as cephalic structures, interpret the nervous system, and especially the brachial ganglia of the animals. We will now examine the value of this interpretation.

From the point of view of these zoologists, which was briefly stated above, it is evident :—

1. That the union of each brachial ganglion to the corresponding pedal ganglia is a secondary disposition.

2. That the cerebro-brachial connective must be a primitive structure, since it would represent the means by which the brachial ganglion would remain in connection with the cerebral ganglion from which it arose.

We will now consider each of these conclusions separately.

1. If, instead of regarding the nervous system of the Decapod Dibranchiates such as *Sepiola* and *Ommatostrephes*, which, so far as the present question is concerned, form the end of the series, we refer to the nervous system of the Octopoda, we shall find that in *Octopus* the brachial ganglia are only separated from the pedal ganglia by a very slight external constriction ; and in *Cirroteuthis*, which in certain respects (notably in the presence of fins) is a more primitive Octopod than *Octopus*, the brachial ganglia are in such close contact that the nerves to the funnel (which in *Octopus* arise from the pedal ganglia) have their origin quite close to that of the nerves to the ventral arms [1] (which in *Octopus* spring from the brachial ganglia).

And if, in addition to what has been stated above, we do not confine ourselves to a macroscopic examination of the exterior of the nervous system of the Cephalopoda, but study it also, as I have done, by serial microscopic sections, we shall find that in *Octopus* the central substance formed by the prolongations of the cells and giving origin to the nerves is quite continuous between the pedal and brachial ganglia.

If now we pass to the Decapoda and study not only the adults but also the embryos in all stages of development (in *Sepia* for example), we shall see that in the youngest forms the central substance of the pedal and brachial ganglia is in free communication, and that it is only little by little, in the subsequent stages, that they become separated as in the adult, where their central masses only communicate by a very slender bridge.[2]

From this point of view then, the Decapod central nervous system passes in the course of its development through an Octopod stage. These facts show clearly that the brachial ganglion results from the transverse segmentation of the pedal ganglion, and consequently that the union of each brachial ganglion with the corresponding pedal ganglion is not a secondary disposition.[3]

---

[1] Reinhardt og Prosch, Om Sciadephorus Mülleri, K. dansk. Vidensk. Selsk. Afhandl., t. v. p. 19, pl. v. fig. 2.

[2] Süeda, Untersuchungen über den Bau der Cephalopoden, Zeitschr. f. wiss. Zool., Bd. xxiv. pl. xiii. fig. 6.

[3] This subject will be treated at greater length and with illustrations in a paper which I propose to publish in the *Arch. d. Biol.*, t. viii., under the following title,—"Sur la valeur morphologique des bras des Céphalopodes et sur la composition de leur système nerveux central."

2. The cerebro-brachial connective may be either (i.) adventitious or (ii.) primitive.

(i.) It is impossible to deny the tendency of neighbouring ganglia, when they are homonymous or successive, to become united by nervous threads. On considering, for example, a large number of Streptoneura, it will be seen that the left anterior visceral ganglion (subintestinal, left pallial, or parietal ganglion) is united by a connective to the right pleural ganglion, with which it has really nothing to do (e.g., Cassiduria).[1]

In Natica the propedal ganglion is not united to the cerebral ganglion; in the female Nautilus the ganglion which innervates the internal labial tentacles[2] (which does not represent, it is true, the whole brachial ganglion of a Dibranchiate, but nevertheless corresponds to a part of it) has also no cerebral connective. It might possibly be said, then, that the cerebro-brachial connective of the Dibranchia is only an adventitious arrangement.

(ii.) This connective may, however, be a primitive structure, and represent an anterior part of the original cerebro-pedal connective, which the brachial ganglion has carried along with it on its separation from the pedal ganglion.

Grobben[3] regards this connective as a detached part of the primitive cerebro-pedal connective, and I share his opinion; but I may remark that there is a contradiction in Grobben's view, according to which the brachial ganglion should be a detached part of the cerebral ganglion, since then two parts of the cerebral ganglion would be joined by a cerebro-pedal connective.

If, however, I regard the union of the brachial and cerebral ganglia of a Dibranchiate as primitive in the same way as the union of the brachial and pedal ganglia, I must remember that the first union is brought about by a simple connective and the second by the central ganglionic substance, which is a very different matter.

VI. Great importance has been attributed to the supraœsophageal commissure which connects the two brachial ganglia in Eledone,[4] and it has been regarded as a clear proof that the brachial ganglia were primitively supraœsophageal.[5]

This commissure has only been recorded by Dietl, and only in Eledone. I have seen it neither in Sepia, Loligo, nor other Decapods; and I may further remark that the infra-œsophageal commissure between the brachial ganglia existing in all Cephalopods is much

[1] Spengel, Die Geruchsorgane und das Nervensystem der Mollusken, Zeitschr. f. wiss. Zool., Bd. xxxv. pl. xvii. fig. 4, f.   [2] Owen, Memoir on the Pearly Nautilus, pl. vii. fig. 1, 8.

[3] Zur Kenntniss der Morphologie und der Verwandtschaftsverhältnisse der Cephalopoden. Arb. Zool. Inst. Wien, Bd. vii. p. 69.

[4] Dietl, Untersuchungen über die Organisation des Gehirns wirbelloser Thiere, Sitzungsb. d. k. Akad. Wiss. Wien, Bd. lxxvi. pl. v. fig. 23, dir.   [5] Grobben, loc. cit., p. 69.

more important by reason of its volume than the thin supraœsophageal thread mentioned by Dietl in *Eledone* alone.

I will also add that probably in all the Opisthobranchia (Bullidæ,[1] Umbrellidæ,[2] Pleurobranchidæ,[3] Aplysiidæ,[4] many Nudibranchia,[5] &c.), as well as in the Gymnosomatous Pteropoda,[6] there is an infraœsophageal cerebral commissure, which von Jhering has called subcerebral. It is much more slender than the supraœsophageal cerebral commissure, but no one has ventured to suggest in consequence of this, that in the Opisthobranchia the cerebral ganglia were primitively subœsophageal.

So far as I can see, the supraœsophageal brachial commissure of *Eledone* is of no more morphological value than the subœsophageal cerebral commissure of the Gastropoda just mentioned.

Nothing is further from complete demonstration than the hypothesis according to which the brachial ganglia are cerebral in origin. On the other hand, many proofs show that they are only a segmented part of the pedal ganglia.

Such transverse segmentations of ganglia are not rare among the Mollusca. In addition to the instance already quoted of the pedal ganglia of *Natica* and those of the Marseniidæ,[7] we may mention the siphonal ganglia of *Cypræa*,[8] the tentacular ganglion of *Pleurobranchus*,[9] the siphonal ganglion of many Pelecypoda, &c. Even in the Decapod Cephalopoda, too, there is an instance of the division of the cerebral ganglia, quite comparable to that of the pedal ganglia which has led to the formation of the brachial ganglia. Chéron[10] has shown, and his statement has not been disputed, that the ganglion known as the "superior buccal," and still called by that name by Stieda[11] and Bobretzky,[12] is nothing else than the anterior part of the cerebral ganglia. I am able to state further that in the embryos of *Sepia* the formation of these "buccal" ganglia and their separation from the cerebral ganglia takes place in a manner quite parallel to that which has been advanced above as regards the formation of the brachial from the pedal ganglia.

It might be objected that in *Ommatostrephes*, for example,[13] the brachial ganglia are

[1] Vayssière, Recherches anatomiques sur la famille des Bullidés, *Ann. d. Sci. Nat.*, Zoologie, sér. 6, t. ix. pl. vi. fig. 48 (*Gastropteron*), pl. viii. fig. 69 (*Doridium*), pl. ix. fig. 81 (*Philine*), pl. xi. fig. 101 (*Scaphander*), pl. xii. fig. 114 (*Bulla*).

[2] Vayssière, Recherches zoologiques et anatomiques sur les Mollusques Opisthobranches du Golfe de Marseille, i. Tectibranches, *Ann. Mus. Marseille*, t. ii. pl. vi. fig. 149.

[3] Vayssière, *ibid.*, p. 144. [4] Vayssière, *ibid.*, pl. iv. fig. 94.

[5] Von Jhering, Vergleichende Anatomie des Nervensystemes und Phylogenie der Mollusken, p. 263.

[6] Wagner, Die Wirbellosen des weissen Meeres, Bd. i. pl. xii. fig. 1.

[7] Bergh, Die Marseniaden, *Zool. Jahrbücher*, Bd. i. p. 168, fig. 1.

[8] Von Jhering, *loc. cit.*, pl. viii. fig. 35.

[9] Von Jhering, *ibid.*, pl. xi. fig. 8.

[10] Recherches pour servir à l'histoire du système nerveux des Céphalopodes dibranchiaux, *Ann. d. Sci. Nat.*, Zoologie, sér. 5, t. v.

[11] Studien über den Bau der Cephalopoden, *Zeitschr. f. wiss. Zool.*, Bd. xxiv.

[12] Observations on the development of the Cephalopoda, *Proc. Soc. Friends of Nat. Hist. Anthrop. and Ethnogr. Moscow*, 1876 (Russian).

[13] On the Nervous System of Ommastrephes todarus, *Ann. and Mag. Nat. Hist.*, ser. 2, vol. x. pls. i., ii.

very widely separated from the pedal. To this I should reply that in the Dibranchiate Cephalopoda, as has already been said, we may observe, in the degree in which the brachial ganglia are separated from the pedal, a whole series of successive stages (*Ommatostrephes*, *Sepiola*, *Loligo*, *Sepia*, *Octopus*), in which the brachial ganglia are gradually less and less distinctly separated, and in the last-named form a single mass, and are only marked off by a slight constriction.

I may further remark that this gradual separation of the brachial from the pedal ganglia, which is seen in passing from *Octopus* to *Ommatostrephes*, corresponds to an equivalent separation between the "superior buccal" and cerebral ganglia, the former separating from the latter even more than the brachial ganglia separate from the pedal. Whatever be the separation of the brachial and pedal ganglia, the pedo-brachial connective always remains much more important than the cerebro-brachial.

Thus then the great removal of the brachial and pedal ganglia (in *Ommatostrephes*) is not a primitive arrangement. It is adventitious, and due to the cause which separates at the same time all the anterior portion of the main mass of the central nervous system, as well supracesophageal as subcesophageal.

Primitively, the brachial and pedal ganglia of the same side must have been in close apposition, as is shown by the observation of the development of the Decapoda (alluded to above) and as appears still to be the case in *Cirroteuthis*, according to the figures of Reinhardt and Prosch.[1]

In *Nautilus*, which is the most primitive of all, this separation of the brachial from the pedal ganglion has not yet taken place; in the female,[2] however, there is found a small ganglion corresponding to a part of the brachial ganglion, which innervates the internal labial appendages. But all the appendages of the male and the other appendages of the female are innervated directly by the anterior subcesophageal ganglionic ring, and the nerves to the funnel are seen to issue at the side of the last ventral "tentacular" nerves.

Some have desired to see in this anterior subcesophageal ring, which corresponds to the brachial and pedal ganglia of the Dibranchia, an external pedal portion and an internal cerebral portion. But in this case the latter would be only lateral and would not extend below the œsophagus (compare the figure of von Jhering[3]). This part would then innervate the tentaculiferous appendages; in this way it is sought to prove the cephalic nature of these latter.

This division is, however, quite imaginary, and it has remained invisible to those zoologists who have not been prejudiced by attempting to prove the cephalic nature of the appendages (Owen, Valenciennes, &c.). In reality this ring is entirely pedal, and

[1] On Sciadephorus Mülleri, *K. dansk. Vidensk. Selsk. Afhandl.*, p. 19, pl. v. fig. 2.
[2] Owen, Memoir on the Pearly Nautilus, pl. vii. fig. 8.
[3] Vergleichende anatomie de Nervensystemes und Morphologie der Mollusken, p. 262, fig. 14.

(ZOOL. CHALL. EXP.—PART LEVI.—1888.) Uuu 10

exactly corresponds to the pedal and brachial ganglia of the Dibranchia; it innervates the funnel and all the appendages.

It is inaccurate to state, as does Grobben,[1] that there are nerves to the appendages which arise from the cerebral ganglia above the optic nerve. The three nerves figured in this position by von Jhering[2] are the nerves which pass to the cavity situated at the posterior extremity of the cephalic cartilage, and which were regarded by Valenciennes[3] as auditory nerves.

(2) If, on the other hand, we seek in the ontogenetic development for some light on the morphological value of the arms of the Cephalopoda, we see that, the embryo resting with its ventral face on the surface of the vitellus, the arms appear on either side of the mantle against the vitellus, advance successively towards the anterior extremity, and finally meet in front of the mouth (compare the lucid figures of Kölliker[4]).

From what has been said above, we may conclude:—

1. The arms of the Cephalopoda are pedal in origin;

2. The buccal appendages of the Gymnosomata and the arms of the Cephalopoda are not homologous structures.

Ray Lankester[5] has insisted on the fact that in the Pteropoda a part of the foot comes to surround the cephalic region, and it is principally on this that he relies in support of his opinion that the Pteropoda should be classed along with the Cephalopoda.

As regards the Gymnosomata we have already done full justice to this argument by showing that their cephalic appendages have absolutely nothing in common with the foot. But as regards the Thecosomata it is true that a certain portion of the foot (the two fins) comes from either side to surround the head and advances as far as its dorsal aspect, in a manner analogous to that in which the arms of the Cephalopoda (whose pedal nature we have just demonstrated) envelop the head.

Here we have a resemblance which I should not think of disputing, and which Ray Lankester only weakens when he compares the fins of the Pteropods, not to the arms of the Cephalopods, but to their funnel. If, however, we rely upon this solitary resemblance (which is true only of the Thecosomata) to unite the Pteropoda and Cephalopoda, we frame an artificial classification.

A single resemblance, based upon an adaptive modification of a single organ, the foot, which is true only of the Thecosomata among the Pteropoda, cannot invalidate the numerous proofs drawn from all points in the organisation of the entire group, both

---

[1] Zur Kenntniss der Morphologie, &c., Arb. Zool. Inst. Wien, Bd. vii. p. 68.

[2] Loc. cit., fig. 14, p. 262.

[3] Nouveau mémoire sur le Nautile flambé, Archives Mus. Hist. Nat. Paris, t. ii. pl. viii. fig. 2, 3.

[4] Entwickelungsgeschichte der Cephalopoden, pl. ii. figs. 17–27.

[5] Mollusca, Encyclopædia Britannica, 9th ed., p. 664, fig. 75.

of Pteropods and Cephalopods. We might find numerous instances of very dissimilar animals, in which a homologous organ is modified in an analogous manner without proposing to unite them on that account, if the sum total of their organisation showed them to be distinct. In this way we ought to deal with the Cephalopoda and Pteropoda.

On the other hand, a natural classification based upon a comparative examination of the whole organisation of the two groups must show, as we have demonstrated in the preceding pages, that there is no direct relation between the Pteropoda and Cephalopoda, and that they have nothing in common except inasmuch as they belong to the same Molluscan phylum.

The high position which has been accorded to the Pteropoda arises rather from their external form than from their structure, as has already been pointed out by Garner.[1] The adaptation to pelagic life has brought about in these animals a symmetrical exterior[2] in order to insure the perfection of natation. But this symmetry has proceeded no further; and what clearly separates the two groups is the complete asymmetry of the organisation of the Pteropoda as opposed to the perfect symmetry of the Cephalopoda.

III. ARE THE PTEROPODA GASTROPODA?

In the Pteropoda as in the asymmetrical Gastropoda—

1. The jaws are paired and lateral.

2. The flexure of the intestine is lateral, what has been improperly called dorsal or hæmal in the Gastropoda, for the intestine does not bend dorsally in a sagittal median plane in the same way as it curves ventrally in the Cephalopoda.

3. The heart is lateral and has only one auricle; the kidney is unpaired and lateral.

4. The unpaired genital gland has only one asymmetrical unpaired genital duct.

5. The nervous system is asymmetrical as regards the ganglionic masses of the visceral commissure and the nerves which spring from it; the osphradium (olfactory organ of Spengel) is unpaired and lateral.

6. A consideration of the development of the Pteropoda shows that as in the asymmetrical Gastropoda the pallial cavity of the Thecosomata is formed to the right of the anus,[3] and that the Pteropoda like the Gastropoda are asymmetrical even in the larval condition.[4] The first stages of the embryo show the primitive symmetry of all Mollusca; this is soon followed by asymmetry, and in the adult animal, though only as regards the external form, there is an adaptive return to the former symmetry, necessitated by pelagic habits.

[1] Malacological Notes, Ann. and Mag. Nat. Hist., ser. 4, vol. xix. p. 373.
[2] Grobben (Morphologische Studien, &c., Arb. Zool. Inst. Wien, Bd. v. p. 240) also interprets the symmetry of the Pteropoda in the same way.
[3] Fol, Sur le développement des Ptéropodes, Arch. d. Zool. Expér., sér. 1, t. iv. p. 198.
[4] Fol, ibid., p. 197.

In conclusion, as has been said by Fol,[1] the embryonic characters are not sufficient to justify the separation of the Pteropoda from the Gastropoda.

We see then that the Pteropoda possess the principal general characters of the Gastropoda and especially the visceral asymmetry which results from the unilateral development of the visceral organs and characterises the specialised, that is to say the most numerous, Gastropoda.

But if we seek out from among the Gastropoda those forms with which the Pteropoda have the greatest affinity, we find the common characters still more numerous.

1. In the Pteropoda, as in the Tectibranchia,[2] a partition, or species of diaphragm, divides the body-cavity into a posterior visceral and anterior or cephalic portion, this latter enclosing the buccal mass, the central nervous system, and the copulatory organ.

2. The salivary glands of the Pteropoda, like those of the Tectibranchia (e.g., Bulloidea and Aplysioidea) do not exhibit a duct differentiated off from the secretory portion.

3. The stomach in the Thecosomata at all ages and in the larval Gymnosomata has masticatory plates, as in the great majority of the Tectibranchia. The adult Gymnosomata in consequence of their diet have an unarmed stomach like that of the carnivorous Tectibranchia (e.g., Doridium).[3]

4. The liver of the Pteropoda is disposed like that of the Tectibranchia, the Gymnosomata resembling Gastropteron, the Thecosomata the Bullidæ in this respect.

5. The generative gland of the Pteropoda is hermaphrodite like that of the Tectibranchia; as in the Aplysioidea and Bulloidea it possesses a single undivided efferent duct with a single orifice. As in these two the genital aperture is connected by a spermatic groove with the copulatory organ which is situated in the head.

6. The pedal ganglia both of the Thecosomatous and Gymnosomatous Pteropoda have two commissures like those of the above-mentioned Tectibranchia, Aplysioidea, and Bulloidea (the second commissure figured in Cuvierina and also seen in Cavolinia has probably escaped notice in the other genera on account of its small size).

The Pteropoda are thus clearly separated from all the other classes of Mollusca, whilst they present all the characters of the "typical" (asymmetrical but not primitive) Gastropoda.

Further, among the Gastropoda their whole organisation (hermaphroditism and the structure of the nervous system) separates them from the Streptoneura (Prosobranchia

---

[1] Fol, ibid., pp. 197, 198.
[2] Vayssière, Recherches anatomiques sur la famille des Bullidés, Ann. d. Sci. Nat. (Zool.), sér. 6, t. ix. p. 78.
[3] Vayssière, Recherches zoologiques et anatomiques sur les Mollusques Opisthobranches du Golfe de Marseille, i. Tectibranches, Ann. Mus. Marseille, t. ii. p. 44.

and Heteropoda), and unites them closely with the Euthyneura (Opisthobranchia and Pulmonata), which de Blainville had previously designated as the "Paracéphalophores monoïques," including indeed the Pteropoda among them.[1] The Euthyneura differ much more from the Streptoneura than from the Pteropoda. These latter must then be placed in the group Euthyneura as was formerly done by de Blainville and more recently by Spengel.[2]

On the other hand, among the Euthyneura the Pteropoda present such resemblances to the "Opisthobranchia" that they are much more closely related to them (by the respiratory, circulatory, and generative organs) than these latter are to the Pulmonata. The Pteropoda must, therefore, be incorporated among the Opisthobranchia.

Now, as regards the two groups of the Opisthobranchia, Nudibranchs and Tectibranchs, the characters of the digestive tract (gastric armature), of the undivided genital duct, and of the spermatic groove, separate the Pteropoda much less from the Tectibranchs than these differ from the Nudibranchs. Hence the Pteropoda are, as regards their anatomical characters, Tectibranchia.

Among these, too, they have undoubtedly much more affinity for the forms which have been called in recent classifications[3] Cephalaspidea and Anaspidea (that is to say, the Bulloidea and Aplysioidea respectively) than for the group known as Notaspidea (that is the Pleurobranchoidea), and the former of these groups differs in its organisation much less from the Pteropoda than from the Pleurobranchs.

We shall now inquire what are the special affinities which the two subdivisions (Thecosomata and Gymnosomata) have respectively for those Tectibranchia which are their nearest relations among the Gastropoda.

IV. SPECIAL AFFINITIES OF THE THECOSOMATA AND GYMNOSOMATA.

We have just seen (1) that the Pteropoda are Gastropods; (2) that they belong to the group Euthyneura; (3) that they must be classed among the "Opisthobranchia"; (4) that they must be placed with the Tectibranchia, and more particularly in the group formed by the Cephalaspidea and Anaspidea (Bulloidea and Aplysioidea).

These conclusions, however, were reached by reasoning on the basis of those characters which are common to the two groups, Thecosomata and Gymnosomata. If now we

[1] Manuel de Malacologie, pp. 447, 480. H. Milne-Edwards (Note sur la Classification naturelle des Mollusques Gastéropodes, Ann. d. Sci. Nat. (Zool.), sér. 3, t. iv. p. 112) criticises de Blainville's classification of the Gastropoda, because it is based only on the generative organs, whilst the "natural" classification which he proposes is based only on the respiratory organs; besides it unites the Opisthobranchia and the Prosobranchia in a group opposed to the Pulmonata, which is much less natural than de Blainville's classification. As regards the name "Opisthobranchia," von Jhering has already proposed to abandon it because it is inaccurate. It is true that several animals of this group have not the auricle behind the ventricle but on the same level (as for example in Gastropteron); in Actæon the auricle is actually in front of the ventricle, as in Limacina. However, seeing that a new name might in its turn prove to be inaccurate, I preserve the term "Opisthobranchia," the group to which it is applied being quite a natural one.

[2] Die Geruchsorgane und das Nervensystem der Mollusken, Zeitschr. f. wiss. Zool., Bd. xxxv. p. 373.

[3] Fischer Manuel de Conchyliologie, p. 550.

consider each group separately, taking its own special characters into account, and if in this way we inquire with which of the Tectibranchs each group has the greatest affinity, we shall arrive at the conclusion that the two groups are not so closely related to each other as they are to the particular forms of Tectibranchs for which they have each the closest affinity.

This is an impression which must have been produced upon every zoologist who has examined, even in a cursory manner, the organisation of these animals, for the two groups exhibit such clearly marked differences, and each forms such a homogeneous whole, that it is quite impossible to derive one of them from the other, or to find for them an immediate common ancestor.

It is only by limiting oneself to the study of a single form (as Wagner has done in the case of *Clione*,[1] and attempting thence to construct the phylogenetic history of the Pteropoda, that one can regard the Thecosomata as the ancestors of the Gymnosomata.[2] It is true that by following this method one arrives at the strange result that the Pteropoda have been derived from the Heteropoda, and have given origin to the Cephalopoda.[3]

Boas was the first to formulate the opinion of the separate origin of the Thecosomata and Gymnosomata, and to assert that the two groups are " independent of each other."[4]

There is no need to recapitulate here the distinctions between the two divisions; they have been sufficiently expounded in the Report on the Gymnosomata,[5] and in the Summaries on the Thecosomata and on the Gymnosomata (pp. 37 and 55). But I must dwell for a few moments on the statement made by Boas,[6] "that the fins are not homologous in the two groups." This is an opinion which I do not share. The fins, both of the Gymnosomata and Thecosomata, are the modified lateral margins of the foot, and the differences which they present are almost the same as those which exist between the Bulloidea and the Aplysioidea.

In the Bulloidea the pedal surface is continuous with the natatory lobes, *e.g.*, *Acera* and *Gastropteron*), and there is no special creeping surface. In the Aplysioidea, on the other hand, these natatory lobes are distinct from the rather narrow creeping surface, which is clearly marked off (*e.g.*, *Aplysia*, *Notarchus*, *Oxynoë*, &c.).

The Gymnosomata also present an arrangement analogous to that of the Aplysioidea, but carried to an extreme; the natatory lobes are quite separated from the portion of the foot corresponding to the creeping surface.

Embryology shows further that these organs (the fins) are homologous in the Gymnosomata and Thecosomata. Fol[7] has shown that the fins of the Pteropoda cor-

---

[1] Die Wirbellosen des weissen Meeres, Bd. i. p. 119.
[2] Von Jhering, on the other hand, regards the Thecosomata as the descendants of the Gymnosomata (Vergleichende Anatomie des Nervensystemes, &c., p. 273), whilst Grobben holds that the Limacinidæ (Thecosomata) are the most primitive Pteropoda (Morphologische Studien, &c., Arb. Zool. Inst. Wien, Bd. v. p. 240).
[3] Wagner, Die Wirbellosen des weissen Meeres, Bd. i. p. 22.   [4] Spolia atlantica, &c., loc. cit., p. 179.
[5] Zool. Chall. Exp., part lviii. pp. 4-6.   [6] Spolia atlantica, &c., loc. cit., p. 179.
[7] Sur le développement des Ptéropodes, Archives de Zool. Expér., sér. i, t. iv. p. 193.

respond to the lateral parts of the embryonic pedal disc, and are comparable to the whole lateral portion of the foot of the Gastropoda.

De Blainville and Boas have pointed out that it is the Bulloidea among the Tectibranchiata that the Thecosomata approach the most nearly, and we shall see that this view is quite justified. These authors, however, confine themselves to this mere statement without attacking the question whether the Thecosomata are descended from the Bulloidea or vice versâ, and without trying to ascertain by what course the passage has been made.

Further, Boas is unable to point out for which group of the Opisthobranchia the Gymnosomata have the greatest affinity.

We must then enquire what are the special affinities of the Gymnosomata, and whether the Pteropoda are a primitive or a derived group as regards the Tectibranchia ; and, further, according to the answer obtained we must endeavour to show for each group of Pteropods (Thecosomata and Gymnosomata) to which group of Tectibranchs it is most nearly related, and how the passage from the one to the other has been brought about.

A. THECOSOMATA.

If it were necessary to investigate the relationships of the Thecosomata by reference only to the organisation of the Cavoliniidæ, the task would present great difficulties, for, as we have seen, these animals have undergone an anomalous transformation, which quite masks the aspect they would otherwise present, and renders them very different from animals to which they are very closely related.

This is the cause which has led to the affinities of the Pteropoda having been for so long misunderstood :—the Cavoliniidæ have been taken as types of the Pteropoda, and as they could not be classed along with other Mollusca, they have been erected into an independent group.

Fortunately the Limacinidæ still exist in our seas, and we have been able to show that they are the most primitive Thecosomata, whilst the Cavoliniidæ have been derived from them by a process which we have indicated above. It is then upon the Limacinidæ and not upon the Cavoliniidæ that we must rely in endeavouring to trace out the affinities of the Thecosomata.

Considering for a moment the *operculum* of the Limacinidæ, we see that *Actæon*, one of the Bulloidea, is the only operculate Tectibranch, and that its operculum is precisely similar to that of *Limacina*—elongated, semi-lunar, and with few coils. The reversed coiling of its spire arises from the reverse coiling of the animal and of the shell ; *Actæon* is coiled in the direct (right-handed) way, and has an operculum with a sinistral spire ; *Limacina*, which is coiled in a retrograde direction, has an operculum with a dextral spire.

Mantle.—At the place where the " shield " of the Thecosomata is situated, the roof of the pallial cavity of the Bulloidea also exhibits a pallial gland (*Bulla*, Pl. II. fig. 3, *d* ; *Scaphander*, &c.). This pallial gland of the Bulloidea presents different degrees of development ; and in *Actæon* (Pl. I. fig. 6, *a*), where it is rather large, it is quite identical both in form and position with the shield of Limacinidæ (Pl. I. fig. 5, *a*). The situation of this pallial gland in the Bulloidea close to the gill shows that it (and consequently also the "shield" of the Thecosomata) is nothing else than the hypobranchial gland of the Gastropods, which has become asymmetrical in the adult straight Thecosomata in consequence of an adaptive return to the primitive external symmetry.[1]

The margin of the mantle in the Bulloidea is continued on the right side by a large lobe (Pl. II. fig. 3, *f*) which corresponds to the right lobe of the mantle in the Limacinidæ, often called the "balancer" (Pl. I. fig. 1, *g*).

The Digestive Tract. 1. *Radula.*—In the Tectibranchia systematists distinguish marginal and lateral teeth. In reality all the teeth of the same transverse row (except the central tooth) are similar in form, and pass insensibly from the innermost to the outermost by diminishing in size and the gradual loss of the marginal denticulations.

In the Bulloidea, properly so called, there are only a small number of teeth on either side of the central one, for example in *Cylichna* and in some species of *Tornatina* (*Tornatina truncatula* = *Cylichna truncata*[2]) ; Fischer[3] is wrong in denying a radula to the Tornatinidæ ; the outer teeth are here very much reduced in size (these are the so-called "marginal" teeth), whilst the inner ("lateral") tooth on either side of the median one remain well developed, thus exhibiting a formula which, by degeneration and loss of the marginal teeth, comes into agreement with that of the Thecosomata ;[4] this formula (1–1–1) is in fact exhibited by some of the Bulloidea—*Scaphander* (Sars),[5] *Amphisphyra* (Lovén),[6] *Runcina.*[7]

The form of the teeth in the Bulloidea is the same as that in the Thecosomata, especially the most primitive ones, the Limacinidæ.

2. *Salivary Glands.*—In *Scaphander*[8] these have precisely the form and structure of those of the Thecosomata, short, ovoid, and with no differentiated duct.

---

[1] Schiemenz (Ueber die Wasseraufnahme bei Lamellibranchisten und Gastropoden, *Mitth. Zool. Stat. Neapel*, Bd. v. p. 527) has already recognised the relations between the "shield" and the "mucous" (hypobranchial) gland of Gastropoda, but he identifies it also with the ink-bag of the Cephalopoda. This homology does not hold, for the hypobranchial gland exists in the Cephalopoda, and as there are two gills so there are two hypobranchial glands, which have been long known under the name of spleen ("Mila"). Joubin, who has studied these organs (Structure et développement de la branchie de quelques Céphalopodes des Côtes de France, *Arch. d. Zool. Expér.* sér. 2, t. iii. pp. 115–116), has not recognised this homology for want of comparison.

[2] Formula—4–1–1–1–4 ; see Forbes and Hanley, History of the British Mollusca and their Shells, pl. vv. fig. 4c.

[3] Manuel de Conchyliologie, p. 555.

[4] In the genus *Cylichna*, also, the reduction of the number of "marginal" teeth is clearly visible. See Sars, Mollusca regionis arcticæ Norvegiæ, pl. xi. figs. 3 (*Cylichna alba*, Brown, 5–1–1–1–5), 4 (*Cylichna cylindracea*, Penn., 3–1–1–1–3), 5 (*Cylichna propinqua*, M. Sars, 2–1–1–2).

[5] Malacozoologi, *Öfversigt k. Vetensk.-Akad. Förhandl.*, 1847, pl. iii. ; Forbes and Hanley, *loc. cit.*, pl. UU, fig. 2, c.

[6] Gray, Guide to the Systematic Distribution of the Mollusca in the British Museum, part i. (1857), fig. 114, p. 205.

[7] Vayssière, Recherches anatomiques sur la famille des Bullidés, *loc. cit.*, pl. x. fig. 67.

[8] *Loc. cit.*, pl. xi. figs. 13, 14.

3. *Gizzard or Stomach.*—Almost all the Bulloidea have a stomach armed with horny plates, usually three in number, almost symmetrical (one dorsal, and a lateral one on either side). This number is, however, variable, as is also the symmetry of the plates. Thus in *Scaphander* the three plates are irregular, the dorsal being very narrow. In *Acera* there are nine such plates, and in *Runcina* (= *Pelta*) four symmetrically disposed as in the Thecosomata,[1] so that in this respect the Bulloidea differ much more among themselves than *Runcina* differs from the Thecosomata.

Besides this there are in many Bulloidea in front of the three large symmetrical plates twice as many smaller plates, just as in the Thecosomata (*Bulla hydatis*,[1] *Bulla striata*,[2] *Haminea cornea*,[2] &c.).

4. *Liver.*—*Philine* and *Bulla* are said to have two hepatic ducts;[3] the less specialised *Cavoliniæ* (*Cavolinia trispinosa*[3] and *Cavolinia quadridentata*, Pl. III. fig. 4, *h*, *j*) have also two.

5. *Anal Gland.*—The gland which is found in the Cavoliniidæ (*Clio*, *Cavolinia*) to the left of the visceral cavity at the extremity of the rectum, almost symmetrically with respect to the osphradium, exists also in the Bulloidea; I have seen it in *Bulla striata*, *Haminea hydatis* (Pl. II. fig. 3, *h*), and *Haminea cornea*; in *Scaphander* it occupies a prolongation of the mantle which accompanies the visceral sac for several turns of the spire (as Vayssière[7] has already observed); in *Actæon* the arrangement is similar to that of *Scaphander*, but the extension formed by the gland is much longer and reaches as far as the first coils of the spire.

The Generative Organs.—In *Philine*[8] and *Doridium*[9] there is a vesicula seminalis comparable to that of certain species of *Cavolinia* (*e.g.*, *Cavolinia tridentata*).

The Nervous System.—The cerebral ganglia are separated from each other and connected by a long supraœsophageal commissure, both in the Bulloidea and the Thecosomata. The pleural ganglia are fused with the cerebral in the Thecosomata to form a single mass which is usually undivided externally. This is also the case in *Actæon* (Pl. II. fig. 11): in all the other Bulloidea the pleural ganglia are situated near to the cerebral ganglia, so that the cerebro-pleural connectives are either very short or not discernible. We have further seen that in the Thecosomata, *e.g.*, in *Cymbulia* (Pl. IV. fig. 2), the stomato-gastric nervous system has the same arrangement as in the Bulloidea (*Philine*): an anterior and a posterior ring connected by threads passing between the horny stomacal plates.

[1] Vayssière, Recherches anatomiques sur les genres Pelta et Tylodina, Ann. d. Sci. Nat. (Zool.), sér. 6, t. xv. pl. i. fig. 4.   [2] Vayssière, Recherches anatomiques sur la famille des Bullidés, loc. cit., pl. xii. fig. 111.
[3] Vayssière, Recherches zoologiques et anatomiques sur les Mollusques Opistobranches du Golfe de Marseille, i. Tectibranches, loc. cit., pl. i. fig. 4.   [4] Ibid., pl. i. fig. 11.
[5] Vayssière, Recherches anatomiques sur la famille des Bullidés, loc. cit., p. 88.
[6] Souleyet, Voyage de la Bonite, Zoologie, t. ii. pl. ix. fig. 30.
[7] Vayssière, Recherches anatomiques sur la famille des Bullidés, loc. cit., p. 90.
[8] Ibid., pl. x. fig. 83.   [9] Ibid., pl. viii. fig. 68.

Hence it appears that the Thecosomata resemble the Bulloidea more than the Gymnosomata.

We must now inquire what are the special affinities of these latter, that is to say, what are the Tectibranchia to which they are most nearly related?

B. GYMNOSOMATA.

As in the case of the Thecosomata we have based our inquiry on the most primitive of the group, that is, mainly on the Pneumonodermatidæ, and especially on *Dexiobranchæa*. We have already shown in the Report on the Gymnosomata[1] that the Pneumonodermatidæ are the most primitive of the naked Pteropoda, and that *Dexiobranchæa* is the least specialised among them. Wagner[2] is quite wrong in regarding *Clione* as more primitive than *Pneumonoderma*, and the latter as derived from the former.

a. In most Tectibranchs there is a proboscis of the acrembolic type, that is, produced by the evagination of the anterior part of the œsophagus, like the rather short one of *Dexiobranchæa* and *Clione* (Pl. V. fig. 4, a), the somewhat longer one of *Pneumonoderma*[3] and *Spongiobranchæa*,[4] and the very long one of *Clionopsis*.[5] Among the Anaspidea (Aplysioidea) we find a similar rather short proboscis in *Aplysia*, *Notarchus*,[6] &c.

b. Like the Gymnosomata the Aplysioidea have two pairs of cephalic tentacles (*Aplysia*, *Notarchus* (Fig. 4, on p. 83), *Dolabella*, &c.); the anterior pair correspond to the labial pair of the Gymnosomata, and the second pair to the nuchal tentacles of these latter, for the olfactory nerve terminates in their interior and the optic nerve at their base. In the Bulloidea, on the other hand, we know that the cephalic tentacles fuse to form the shield which is of so much importance in connection with the burrowing habits of these animals.

c. The fins of the Gymnosomata are comparable to those of the Aplysioidea.

Von Jhering[7] refuses to admit the homology of the parapodia of *Gastropteron* and the other Tectibranchia with the "pteropodia" of the Pteropoda. If these organs are absolutely homologous with the epipodia of the Prosobranchs which the French school of the Sorbonne (Lacaze Duthiers and his pupils) regard as *pallial* in nature, that is a point which I should not like to affirm; nevertheless, I regard these latter as also pedal in origin.[8] I maintain, however, that the parapodia of the Tectibranchs and the fins of the Pteropods are strictly homologous.

---

[1] Zool. Chall. Exp., part lviii. p. 67.
[2] Zool. Chall. Exp., part lviii. p. 6, fig. 1, 4.
[3] *Ibid.*, pl. iii. fig. 1.
[4] Die Wirbellosen des weissen Meeres, Bd. i. p. 119.
[5] *Ibid.*, p. 19, fig. 2, 1.
[6] Vayssière, Recherches zoologiques et anatomiques sur les Mollusques Opisthobranches du Golfe de Marseille, i. Tectibranches, loc. cit., p. 83.
[7] Vergleichende Anatomie des Nervensystemes und Phylogenie der Mollusken, p. 249.
[8] Paul Pelseneer, Sur la valeur morphologique de l'épipodium des Gastropodes rhipidoglosses, Comptes rendus, t. cv. p. 578.

On dissecting an *Aplysia* and a *Pneumonodermu* it will be seen that the fins of the latter and the parapodia of the former are innervated in exactly the same manner, similar nerves pass to them, issuing from the same points in the pedal ganglia.

In the Bulloidea, the parapodia (specially developed in *Gastropteron*, *Acera*, &c.) are continuous with the plantar or creeping surface of the foot, and form with it an uninterrupted surface. In the Aplysioidea the more ventral portion of the parapodia serves as a part of the visceral wall (Fig. 3, B), so that their origin appears to be separate from the plantar surface; a similar arrangement is found in the Gymnosomatous Pteropods, where, in consequence of the reduction of the plantar surface, the parapodia or fins seem still further separated from the latter.

Fig. 3.—Diagrammatic transverse sections, A, of one of the Bulloidea, B, of one of the Aplysioidea; *a*, creeping surface of the foot; *b*, parapodium or natatory lobe of the foot.

Among the Aplysioidea are found different degrees of freedom of the parapodia relatively to the visceral sac, which lead gradually to the Gymnosomatous type. Thus in *Aplysia leporina* the parapodia are largely united behind; in *Aplysia punctata* they are less so; in *Aplysia fasciata* they are for the most part free.

In all these, however, the plantar surface is fused with the visceral mass, to the posterior extremity of which it extends, and the parapodia reach to the same point as the plantar surface. In *Notarchus*, on the other hand (Fig. 4), the plantar surface has no connection with the visceral sac, and the two parapodia are united dorsally above this latter, being fused throughout their whole length except a small tract anteriorly; they form thus a sac in which floats the visceral mass. In the same manner in the Gymnosomata the foot has no connection with the visceral sac; but here the plantar surface being reduced to the anterior part of the body, the parapodia or fins are also reduced to the same portion.

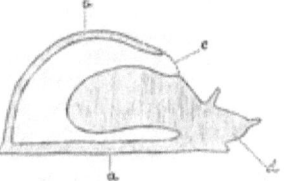

Fig. 4.—Sagittal section of *Notarchus*; *a*, creeping surface of the foot; *b*, parapodia united so as to form a sac around the visceral mass; *c*, aperture of the sac; *d*, head with anterior and posterior tentacles.

If, however, the fins of the Gymnosomata are homologous with the parapodia of the

Aplysioidea, then these must be indisputably so with those of the Bulloidea, for they pass insensibly from one into the other by transitional stages. On the other hand the fins of the Thecosomata correspond with the parapodia of the Bulloidea, and like these latter are continuous with the plantar surface of the foot, and also continuous with the posterior or ventral lobe of the foot. Hence it follows that, contrary to the opinion of Boas,[1] the fins of the Thecosomata and those of the Gymnosomata are strictly homologous.

   d. If we consider the digestive tract :—

     (i.) *Radula.*—The teeth of the Gymnosomata resemble in form those of a large number of Tectibranchs, *e.g.*, *Aplysia*. As in this case it is seen that, in the same transverse row of the radula, all the teeth except the median one are identical in form and only differ by decreasing in size from the innermost to the outermost.

        Furthermore, we have seen that in the Gymnosomata the number of lateral teeth increases with age.[2] In *Aplysia*,[3] and probably in all the other Anaspidea, the state of matters is exactly the same.

     (ii.) *Jaws.*—All the Gymnosomata are provided with paired jaws, which meet in the middle line ventrally. *Clione* alone is without them, as are certain carnivorous Tectibranchs, *e.g.*, *Actæon*, *Doridium*, *Lobiger*.

        But in addition to the jaws united upon the floor of the buccal cavity in front of the radula, the Gymnosomata, except *Halopsyche*, possess hook-sacs, the homologies of which are not clearly explained.

        When Eschricht published the anatomical description of *Clione*[4] the horny buccal organs of other Gymnosomata were not known. Eschricht, finding in this Gymnosome a radula and no jaws, but two hook-sacs, regarded these latter as representing morphologically the jaws of other Molluscs.[5] Since then, however, the study of the Gymnosomata has shown that they possess, in addition to the hook-sacs found in *Clione*, two jaws approximated in the ventral median line which are wanting in this latter.

        The homologies of the hook-sacs are thus still unknown.

        They are not, however, entirely new structures which are not found elsewhere. On the contrary, and in fact in the Aplysioidea (*Notarchus*, *Dolabella*, &c.), there may be observed an arrangement in which it is easy to see the origin of the hook-sacs of the Gymnosomata. This arrangement, to which attention was first called by Vayssière,[6] consists in the presence on

[1] Spolia atlantica, p. 179.
[2] Zool. Chall. Exp., part lviii. pp. 6, 13.
[3] Vayssière, Recherches zoologiques et anatomiques sur les Mollusques Opisthobranches du Golfe de Marseille, i. Tectibranches, loc. cit., p. 61.
[4] Anatomische Untersuchungen über die Clione borealis, 1838.   [5] *Ibid*, p. 10.
[6] Vayssière, Recherches zoologiques et anatomiques sur les Mollusques Opisthobranches du Golfe de Marseille, i. Tectibranches, loc. cit., p. 90.

the roof (superior or dorsal wall) of the buccal cavity of an armature of rather strong and somewhat recurved hooks (Pl. IV. fig. 5).[1] I have satisfied myself of the existence of this armature in *Notarchus punctatus* and *Dolabella neapolitana*.[2]

On comparing this armature, not with the hook-sacs of *Pneumonoderma*, which present the most highly specialised form of these organs, but rather with those of *Dexiobranchæa* (Pl. IV. fig. 6), which actually present the primitive condition, it is easy to understand that it is not a great step from the dorsal buccal wall, covered with hooks, to the small depressions filled with hooks found in *Dexiobranchæa*.

What, however, is the morphological value of this armature of hooks in *Notarchus* and *Dolabella* and of the hook-sacs of the Gymnosomata?

The comparative study of the horny buccal pieces other than the radula is attended with peculiar difficulties, for these pieces have never been the subjects of systematic investigation as has the radula. The knowledge of these organs which we possess is then very fragmentary, and there are scarcely any synthetic documents relating to them.

The only attempt to treat these pieces systematically was made by Mörch more than twenty years ago.[3] But this author, besides including among the extra-radular pieces organs which have no place there (e.g., the pickaxe-like organs of *Conus*, which correspond morphologically to the radula), multiplies the number of different species which, according to him, may be distinguished among these organs, so that he by no means facilitates the systematisation and homologisation of these extra-radular pieces.

These horny extra-radular pieces are wanting in certain Gastropod Mollusca—Toxoglossa (*Conus*, *Pleurotoma*, &c.), Pyramidellidæ, Eulimidæ, many Trochidæ, Heteropoda, *Gadinia*, *Amphibola*, Testacellidæ, many Nudibranchs (*Doridopsis*, *Hervæxa*, *Tethys*), *Phyllidia*, Pelibranchia, certain Tectibranchs (*Actæon*, *Utriculus*, *Scaphander*, *Doridium*, *Lobiger*). But the great majority of the Mollusca called "Odontophora" possess horny buccal pieces other than the radula.

As regards the relative position of these organs, we may state in the first place that the radula is always situated posteriorly to every other horny

---

[1] *Ibid.*, pl. iv. fig. 50.

[2] *Dolabella neapolitana*, delle Chiaje, seems to me to be identical with *Aplysia petalifera*, Rang, *Aplysia webbii*, von Beneden, *Aplysia depressa*, Cantraine, and *Dolabella ernota*, Deshayes; on the other hand, however, it appears to constitute a genus (*Aplysiella*) distinct from *Aplysia* and *Dolabella*. It will probably be necessary therefore to call this species *Aplysiella petalifera* (Rang).

[3] On the Homology of the Buccal Parts of the Mollusca, *Ann. and Mag. Nat. Hist.*, ser. 3, vol. xvi. p. 73.

piece which may be present in the buccal cavity; sometimes these may be near the radula, but they are never behind it.

Furthermore, the radula is always situated in the inferior (ventral or neural) part of the alimentary canal, whilst the extra-radular horny pieces may be at any point whatever of the circumference of the buccal cavity—dorsally, ventrally, or laterally.

To these various situations of the extra-radular horny pieces must certainly be attributed the diversity of the organs which have been distinguished among them, as well as the confusion which reigns among the names which have been applied to them.

The extra-radular horny pieces are inserted directly into the wall of the digestive tract, and can only be removed along with it; the radula, on the contrary, forms an independent mobile ribbon, capable of extensive displacements, and actuated by a muscular and cartilaginous mechanism.

Finally, as to the physiological rôle of the extra-radular horny pieces: by reason of their situation being usually anterior, they have for special duty the retention of the prey, or of such portion of it as they have seized, whilst the radula discharges the function of dividing and comminuting it.

All the extra-radular horny pieces, however diverse their forms and the names by which they have been designated, appear to me on an ultimate analysis to be referable to jaws. The primitive form of these latter organs must have been a horny ring, situated in front of the radula towards the anterior portion of the buccal cavity; the origin of this ring has been the cuticularisation of this latter cavity at the place where it is most exposed.

This annular form may still be seen in a few Molluscs (e.g., in *Umbrella*), where the ring is divided vertically into two lateral halves. By a transverse division into dorsal and ventral portions, the mandibles of the Cephalopoda have taken origin.

The two lateral halves of this ring are also found in the lateral mandibles of nearly all Gastropoda. These horny pieces may have remained as a single united surface, or may have become scaly or covered with spines, which might finally become isolated and independent; lastly, the separate portions may subdivide and reunite in various ways, and give rise to the numerous types of extra-radular horny pieces found among the Gastropoda.

As regards the special case of the Aplysioidea and the Gymnosomata, the scaly jaws (which are approximated in the median ventral line) and the dorsal hooks of *Notarchus* (which have become specialised into the hook-sacs of the Gymnosomata) would represent the modified remains of the primitive horny ring.

(iii.) *Salivary Glands.*—These organs in the Gymnosomata closely resemble the corresponding organs of the Aplysioid Tectibranchia; they are narrow and elongated, and extend, gradually diminishing in diameter, from the distal extremity to their termination in the buccal mass, without any separation into a proper glandular portion and a distinct duct.

(iv.) *Stomach.*—In the adult Gymnosomata this is unarmed. This absence of masticatory plates in the stomach is probably due to the exclusively carnivorous diet of the Gymnosomata. Indeed the most carnivorous of the Bulloides (*e.g.*, *Doridium*) are also without gastric plates.

c. The Respiratory Organs.—The most primitive of the Gymnosomata (Pneumono-dermatidæ) have a lateral gill (on the right side), the position and relations of which leave no doubt as to its homology with the gill of the Aplysioidea and of all the Tectibranchs (the posterior gill of *Pneumonoderma*, *Spongiobranchæa*, *Clionopsis*, and *Notobranchæa* being a new formation). This lateral gill, although simpler than that of the Aplysioidea, is analogous to it in its structure, for in *Pneumonoderma* it is also formed by the folding of a single lamella.

f. The Generative Organs.—The hermaphrodite genital gland of the Gymnosomata is arranged like that of all the Tectibranchs. The conformation of the genital duct in the Aplysioidea is exactly identical with that of the duct in the Gymnosomata, the accessory genital glands (albuminiparous and muciparous glands) and the receptaculum seminis being situated towards its extremity. The structure and position of the copulatory organ also are the same both in the Aplysioidea and the Gymnosomata.

g. The Nervous System.—There is almost absolute identity between the central nervous system of a Gymnosome (*e.g.*, *Spongiobranchæa*, Pl. V. fig. 3) and that of certain Aplysioidea, such as *Notarchus*[1] or *Dolabella* (Pl. V. fig. 2), and the central nervous system of other Aplysioidea only differs from that of the Gymnosomata in the elongation of the pleuro-visceral connectives and the displacement backwards of the visceral ganglia.

In the Gymnosomata and in all the Aplysioidea the cerebral ganglia are closely approximated on the dorsal aspect of the œsophagus; the pleural ganglia are close to the pedal ganglia, so that the cerebro-pleural connectives are almost as long as the cerebro-pedal, and the pleuro-pedal connectives scarcely exist. A long and slender sub-œsophageal cerebral commissure (subcerebral commissure of von Jhering) also exists in both groups.

[1] Vayssière, Recherches zoologiques et anatomiques sur les Mollusques Opisthobranches du Golfe de Marseille, loc. cit., pl. iv. figs. 94, 95.

As regards the visceral ganglia, they are asymmetrical in the Aplysioidea (*Aplysia*, *Notarchus*,[1] *Dolabella rumphii*,[2] *Dolabella neapolitana*, &c.) as in the Gymnosomata ; the right ganglion is larger than the left, and gives origin to three principal nerves (right pallial and two visceral nerves), whilst the left ganglion only gives rise to the left pallial nerve.

In the Aplysioidea (*Aplysia*, &c.) I have observed the same pleuro-pedal anastomoses (cervical plexus) as has been above described in all the Gymnosomata.

The situation of the osphradium is the same both in the Aplysioidea and the Gymnosomata—between the genital opening and the aperture of the kidney, a little ventrally (compare the figure of *Clione*, Pl. V. fig. 5, *j*, with that of *Aplysia* published by my esteemed teacher Professor E. Ray Lankester[3]).

The careful comparison of the Gymnosomata and the Gastropods shows then that the former have very close affinities with the Aplysioidea ; that they differ less from them than from the Thecosomata ; and that, on the other hand, the Aplysioidea differ less from the Bulloidea than from the Gymnosomata.

V. DO THE PTEROPODA CONSTITUTE A PRIMITIVE OR A DERIVED GROUP?

The view has often been expressed that the Pteropoda constitute a primitive group in the phylum Mollusca. Haeckel[4] in his phylogeny of the Mollusca shows that Pteropods are situated at the base of the two groups Cephalopoda and Gastropoda.

In the same way von Jhering[5] considered that Pteropods are the ancestors of the Cephalopods ; but he has since abandoned the idea of the affinity between these two groups. Wagner, on the other hand, points to the Pteropoda as the probable source of the Cephalopods.[6] Lastly, several zoologists still regard the Pteropods as primitive in consequence of the simplicity which is observed in certain parts of their organisation, as for example the circulatory apparatus (Roule,[7] &c.).

To the question at the head of this chapter we have now to reply :—No, the Pteropods are not primitive Molluscs ; on the other hand, they constitute a derived group among the Mollusca.

In support of this view, arguments may be adduced from—(1) comparative anatomy, (2) embryology, (3) palæontology.

1. A. The profound asymmetry of the organisation of the Pteropoda indicates a group

[1] *Ibid.*, pl. iv. figs. 94, 95.
[2] Amaudrut, Le Système nerveux de la Dolabella Rumphii, *Bull. Soc. Philom. Paris, sér.* 7, t. x. p. 70.
[3] Mollusca, in Encyclopædia Britannica, 9th ed., vol. xvi. p. 657, fig. 63, *os*, between *b* and *a*.
[4] Natürliche Schöpfungsgeschichte, ed. 3, p. 475 ; Generelle Morphologie, t. ii. p. cxlii, and pl. vi.
[5] Vergleichende Anatomie des Nervensystemes und Phylogenie der Mollusken, p. 249.
[6] Die Wirbellosen des weissen Meeres, Bd. i. p. 117.
[7] Recherches histologiques sur les Lamellibranches, *Journ. Anat. et Phys.*, 23e année, p. 72.

which has already undergone numerous modifications, and has become widely separated from the primitive symmetrical Archimollusc.

B. The concentration of the nervous centres indicates a very specialised and highly differentiated group.

2. In the course of their development the Pteropods pass through a stage even more asymmetrical than the adult. This fact indicates clearly that they arise from ancestors more asymmetrical than themselves, and that their apparent symmetry has been acquired in the course of time by adaptation to their natatory habits.

Comparative anatomy and embryology indicate then that the Pteropoda are not primitive Mollusca, and furthermore, that they are derived from ancestors which themselves are not primitive, but on the contrary already specialised. Some naturalists entirely misunderstand the degree of specialisation of the Gastropoda ; thus Boutan[1] regards as the most primitive those Gastropods which he calls typical, that is to say those in which the asymmetry is carried to the highest pitch, and he criticises the opinion of Spengel, who regards the Fissurellidæ as primitive Gastropoda. Among the asymmetrical Gastropoda, *Fissurella* and its allies are in fact the most primitive, as is shown by the conformation of some of their organs (*e.g.*, those of circulation and excretion); such is the inaccurate point of view which Boutan has adopted and from which he has been led to confound the judicious conclusions of Spengel with the rash generalisations of von Jhering.

3. The organisms from the Primary formations, which are usually referred to the Pteropoda, have no affinities with these latter, as I shall show further on. In the Secondary rocks there are no traces of Pteropods, the first undoubted remains of this group being found in the lower Tertiaries. They are then of recent origin.

We are consequently justified in saying :—The Pteropoda do not form a primitive group, but on the contrary a recent and specialised one—a terminal group. The greater part of the characters of terminal groups, as formulated by my esteemed teacher, Professor Giard,[2] are entirely applicable to the Pteropoda :—

(1) They are profoundly modified in adaptation to a special mode of existence.

(2) They exhibit very slight variability.

(3) They include only a small number of species.

VI. POLYPHYLETIC ORIGIN OF THE PTEROPODA.

We regard it then as proved that the Pteropoda (both Thecosomata and Gymnosomata) are derived animals and of recent origin, and by no means primitive Mollusca.

[1] Recherches sur l'anatomie et le développement de Fissurella, *Archives de Zool. Expér.*, sér. 2, t. iii. bis, pp. 150, 151.
[2] Observations . . . (sur les mammifères ovipares), *Bull. Scient. Départ. Nord*, 1886, p. 416.

On the other hand, we have seen that each group has different affinities—those of the Theocosomata being with the Bulloidea, those of the Gymnosomata with the Aplysioidea. We must conclude therefore that the Pteropoda are polyphyletic in origin.

We shall now endeavour to show in the case of each group what has been the line of descent.

A. ORIGIN OF THE THECOSOMATA.

Hitherto those authors who have believed that the affinities of the Pteropoda are with the Tectibranchia (de Blainville and Boas) have contented themselves with indicating the proximity of the Thecosomata to the Bulloidea, but without going further and trying to ascertain whether the Thecosomata are phylogenetically derived from these latter, and in what way this descent may have taken place.

It may be most confidently affirmed that the Thecosomata are descended from ancestors resembling the Bulloidea, and that the cause of the modifications which they have undergone is to be found in the increase of natatory habits and the adaptation to pelagic life.

If now we try to ascertain by what process the passage from one group to another has taken place, and by what successive modifications a Bulloid has become a Thecosomatous Pteropod, we are met at first by an apparent difficulty, in the fact that the most primitive Thecosomata, the Limacinidæ, are sinistrorsal, whilst all the existing Bulloidea are dextrorsal. But is this a real difficulty? Is there in fact a great morphological difference between a dextrorsal and a sinistrorsal animal?

Of what importance is the direction of the spiral? It is of scarcely any value, for we see among the species of a single genus (*Neptunea, Pyrula, Vertigo*, &c.), or among the genera of a single family (*Lanistes* and *Ampullaria*), forms coiled in opposite directions.[1] If this be the case with forms so nearly related, there is *a fortiori* no reason for astonishment that the same thing should happen in the case of the Bulloidea and Limacinidæ.

The examples just quoted show that it is very natural and simple that among the Bulloidea there should have arisen in course of time sinistrorsal forms, which, however, have preserved the dextrorsal asymmetry of their internal organisation; that is to say, that in these animals the "sinistrority" has only affected the coiling of the visceral sac and the shell, and these sinistral forms would bear to some of the Bulloidea the same relation that *Lanistes* bears to *Ampullaria*. (Bouvier[2] has shown that *Lanistes* is not sinistral as regards its organisation, and that it differs from *Ampullaria* only by the contrary twisting of its visceral sac.)

These forms, which are still unknown to us, are the extinct ancestry of the Lima-

[1] In the Pyramidellidæ we have a case in which in the same specimen the first cells are sinistral and the subsequent ones dextral.

[2] Sur le système nerveux typique des Prosobranches dextres ou sénestres, *Comptes rendus*, t. ciii. p. 1276.

cinidæ. We know that in these latter also the sinistrorsity has only affected the coiling of the spire.

It is easy to explain the transition from a creeping Bulloid to a swimming Limacinid. Even among the Bulloidea we observe a great tendency to natatory habits; the margins of the foot (parapodia) extend laterally so far that they can be reflected over the shell, and assist by their movements, in a natation at first imperfect then gradually more complete, in the forms which have become more specialised (*Acera*, &c.), and even carried out to a very high degree in *Gastropteron*.

It is quite comprehensible how, among animals having such tendencies, forms should have arisen having the mantle and shell well developed and with sinistral coiling, which by gradual specialisation have become exclusively pelagic animals, the first rough sketch, as it were, of the Limacinidæ.

If we examine the whole series of the Bulloidea (or Cephalaspidea), living and fossil, we shall find that the most ancient are forms resembling *Actæon* (these are probably the most ancient of the Opisthobranchia, and their importance with respect to the phylogeny of the Gastropoda cannot be overrated); the organisation of the recent *Actæon* (especially its nervous system, generative organs, and operculum), and its possible relations with the Pyramidellidæ, show that it may be not very far removed from the common stock of the Streptoneura (Prosobranchs and Heteropods) and the Euthyneura.

The genus *Bulla*, however, properly so called, scarcely appears before the Cretaceous period.

The presence of an operculum in the most primitive Thecosomata (Limacinidæ and the larvæ of the Cymbuliidæ) shows that they are descended from operculate ancestors. *Actæon* still retains this operculum (it is the only Opisthobranch which does not lose it in the adult state), and all the fossil Actæonidæ certainly possessed it. The earliest Bullidæ —*sens. lat.*, i.e., comprising the Scaphandridæ and the Tornatinidæ—(derived from the Actæonidæ) must have possessed it also, and the animals of this family will only have lost it subsequently in the adult condition. It is from some of these operculate forms, intermediate between *Actæon* and *Bulla*, that the first Thecosomatous Pteropods have arisen.

If for example we consider such forms as *Globiconcha* or *Hydatina*; if we allow that some of them have become coiled sinistrally whilst retaining the dextrorsal asymmetry in their organisation (as happens in some Gastropoda, *e.g.*, *Lanistes*); lastly, if in these animals the lateral margins of the foot, already strongly developed, become still more specialised, we shall have the first Limacinidæ.

A sinistral shell from one of the forms above quoted would, in fact, closely resemble a short-spired shell of one of the Limacinidæ, such as the earliest Eocene *Limacina*. On the other hand, owing to more and more exclusive adaptation to pelagic life, the shell of the Bulloidea must have become more delicate, and have acquired a structure very similar to that of *Limacina*, as in the case of the shells of the living *Haminea* and

Acera; and since these Bulloidea probably resembled *Acera*, we may still find a feature of resemblance in the "proboscis" of this latter and that of *Peraclis* and the young Cymbuliidæ.

I have said that the Thecosomatous Pteropods must have arisen towards the end of the Cretaceous or in the early part of the Tertiary epoch. Indeed, in the Secondary period there exists no Pteropod analogous to the Tertiary Thecosomata; and, as I have already said, I cannot admit among the Thecosomata the so-called Primary "Pteropoda."

There exists a considerable number of these fossils (more than a hundred species), which, not being assignable to any other group, have been placed among the Pteropoda on account of certain apparent resemblances.

The absence, which has been already mentioned, of any organic remains in the Secondary rocks which could possibly be attributed to the Pteropoda, and the enormous interval of time which consequently separates these fossils from the true Tertiary Thecosomata, is of itself an argument against the interpretation which has been given by palæontologists of these organisms.

The only so-called "Pteropoda" in the Secondary rocks are two species of *Conularia* analogous to those of the Primary formations—*Conularia* sp , Bittner,[1] from the Trias, and *Conularia cancellata*, Argeliez, from the Lias.

In spite of the distance in time which separates the Primary "Pteropoda" from the true Thecosomata of the Tertiary period, the former have hitherto been always ranged among the latter, although only a small number of them show an external resemblance to certain species of *Clio* of the subgenera *Creseis* and *Hyalocylix*.

The fossils which exhibit this supposed resemblance to the existing Cavoliniidæ are as follows:—

1. The "*Creseis*" and "*Styliola*" of the Silurian and Devonian. These are fossils which are not very well preserved, have no embryonic shell like that of *Clio*, and often exhibiting a longitudinal striation such as is seen in no existing species of *Clio*. No real affinity can be found between these organisms and the genus *Clio* (*Creseis*); on the other hand, the great size of these Primary fossils separates them from all known forms of Pteropoda in the same manner as they are separated by stratigraphical considerations, for from the Devonian to the lower Tertiary there is no fossil which could be referred to an extinct Thecosome of this group.

As to the supposed specimens of *Creseis* of small size described by Ehrenberg,[2] their strong regular curvature, their oblique mouth, their apex without any distinct embryonic shell, separate them entirely from all the known Thecosomata, and render it impossible to unite them with the subgenus *Creseis* of *Clio*.

[1] *Verhandl. k. k. geol. Reichsanst.*, 1878, p. 281.
[2] *Ueber massenhaft jetzt lebende oceanische und die fossile ältesten Pteropoden der Urwelt, Monatsber. d. k. preuss. Akad. d. Wiss. Berlin*, 1861, figs. 19–21.

2. *Tentaculites.*—These are the only Primary " Pteropods" on which one might found arguments in favour of an apparent resemblance to the subgenus *Hyalocylix* of *Clio*. Their external surface, indeed, presents grooves or rather transverse rings. Nevertheless, the comparison of median longitudinal sections of a *Tentaculites* and a *Clio* shows at once that the resemblance is only superficial, and that in reality the two organisms are quite dissimilar in structure.

The Thecosomatous Pteropods such as *Clio* have a shell of almost constant thickness, and distended at the extremity (embryonic shell of Fol). *Tentaculites*, on the other hand, ends in a sharply pointed extremity, and the thickness of the shell gradually increases from the aperture towards the apex.[1]

Fig. 5.—Longitudinal section of the apex, *a*, of *Tentaculites*, *b*, of *Clio*.

In the same way the supposed Devonian *Cleodora* (= *Clio*), described by Ludwig,[2] has the apex like that of *Tentaculites*, and not at all like that of *Clio*.

Among the other Primary " Pteropods" three principal groups may be distinguished— (1) *Conularia*, (2) *Hyolithes*, (3) the Cymbuliidæ described by Ehrenberg, *Ecculiomphalus*, Portlock (= *Phanerotinus*, Sowerby; this was ranged by Bronn[3] among the Pteropods, but is really a Gastropod allied to the Solaridæ).

1. *Conularia.*—These differ from all the Thecosomatous Pteropoda hitherto known in their quadrangular shell and contracted aperture; even the structure of their shell separates them entirely from the Thecosomata. They have been placed along with these by d'Archiac and Verneuil, who, not being zoologists, were unacquainted with the organisation of the Pteropoda; and in consequence merely of this allocation all palæontologists have continued to class *Conularia* among the Pteropods.[4]

2. *Hyolithes.*—These are distinguished from all the Pteropoda by their triangular form, their partitions, and their operculum, which in no respect resembles that of any operculate Mollusc. I must also here allude to the case of *Calceola sandalina*, which was so long referred to the Brachiopoda, and which is only an operculate Polyp. Without committing myself to any opinion regarding *Hyolithes*, which I have not had the opportunity of studying personally, I may ask whether it may not be possible that this also is a species of operculate Polyp.

[1] Ludwig, Pteropoden aus dem Devon und Oligocän in Hessen und Nassau, *Palæontographica*, Bd. xi. pl. l. 58.

[2] *Ibid.* I must mention that the elongated Primary fossils with an initial dilatation resemble Dentaliidæ as much as if not more than Thecosomatous Pteropoda (compare M. Sars, Malakologiske Jagttagelser, *Forhandl. Vid. Selsk.*, 1864, pl. viii. figs. 49-51, and G. O. Sars, On some Remarkable Forms of Animal Life, &c., i. 1872, pl. iii. figs. 14, 15). Some similar Dentaliidæ have been found in the Challenger soundings. This would furnish an argument in favour of the views of Grobben, who regards the Scaphopoda as very primitive forms (Morphologische Studien, &c., *loc. cit.*).

[3] Die Klassen und Ordnungen des Thierreichs, Bd. iii. p. 646.

[4] Lindström (On the Silurian Gasteropoda and Pteropoda of Gothland, *K. Svensk. Vetensk. Akad. Handl.*, Bd. xix. No. 6, p. 40) insists that the septa of *Conularia* furnish a proof of its Pteropod nature, whereas not one of the living Thecosomata has septa of this character.

3. Cymbuliidæ.—The Silurian fossils described by Ehrenberg[1] under the name of *Panderella*, and regarded as larval shells of Cymbuliidæ,[2] are coiled in a plane, and are bilaterally symmetrical like those of *Bellerophon* or *Oxygyrus*.

As to the fossils referred with a "?" to larval shells of *Cymbulia*[3] and *Tiedemannia* (= *Gleba*),[4] they are entirely uncoiled, the turns of the spire not being in contact ; and in most cases they are coiled in one plane, neither spire nor umbilicus being visible. There is thus no connection between these fossils and the larval shells of Cymbuliidæ.

To sum up, we see that in the case of all these Primary so-called "Pteropoda" there is no reason whatever to regard them as Thecosomata. One palæontologist even has recognised the improbability of the organisms being referable to the Pteropoda : Hoernes,[5] in speaking of *Conularia* and *Hyolithes*, says that they "perhaps form a group distinct from the Pteropods and of unknown affinities."

I am strongly inclined to believe that among these Primary "Pteropods" there are organisms belonging to different groups, but I am unable to decide which ; and perhaps, even after a prolonged study, it would be impossible to class them with any known living organisms. What I can definitely assert, however (and Boas, whose authority on this point cannot be doubted, has arrived at the same opinion [6]), is that not one of them has the least affinity of any kind whatever with the Pteropoda, and that these latter are only to be discerned with certainty at the beginning of the Tertiary period.

B. ORIGIN OF THE GYMNOSOMATA.

We have already shown that the Gymnosomata are closely related to the Aplysioidea. Just as we consider that the Thecosomata are descended from the Bulloidea, so we are persuaded that the Gymnosomata have arisen from Aplysiid ancestors, and we have already expressed this opinion several times.[7]

In the present instance we cannot, as with Thecosomata, call palæontology to witness. The shell of the Aplysioidea is quite rudimentary, scarcely calcified, and but little adapted to fossilisation ; and in the Gymnosomata both mantle and shell have entirely disappeared in the adult.

In *Notarchus* among the Aplysioidea, the mantle is already extremely reduced, and the shell has become microscopic, being lodged a little behind the anus.[8] Thus this form

---

[1] Ueber massenhaft jetzt lebende oceanische und die fossile ältesten Pteropoden der Urwelt, *Monatsbr. d. k. preuss. Akad. d. Wiss. Berlin,* 1861, p. 434. Ueber die Obersilurischen und Devonischen microscopischen Pteropoden, Polythalamien und Crinoiden bei Petersburg in Russland, *Ibid.,* 1862, pp. 525, 630.

[2] Ueber massenhaft jetzt lebende, &c., *loc. cit.,* figs. 1–9.   [3] *Ibid.,* figs. 10, 11.

[4] *Ibid.,* figs. 12–18.   [5] Manuel de Paléontologie, p. 573.

[6] Spolia atlantica, pp. 94, 95.

[7] Description d'un nouveau genre de Ptéropode Gymnosome, *Bull. Scient. Dép. Nord,* 1886, p. 226 ; and *Zool. Chall. Exp.,* part lviii. p. 67.

[8] Vayssière, Recherches zoologiques et anatomiques sur les Mollusques Opisthobranches du Golfe de Marseille, i. Tectibranches, *loc. cit.,* p. iii. fig. 81.

leads on to a stage which is found in the Gymnosomata. Furthermore, there are in *Notarchus* many structures in which the whole organisation of the Gymnosomata may be foreseen.

The foot is entirely separated from the visceral sac, as in the Gymnosomata. The parapodia (lateral margins of the foot) have become greatly developed, but owing to a special modification their free borders have fused dorsally, forming around the body a large "epipodial" or parapodial sac, open only in front above the neck, so that swimming is performed in *Notarchus* by the parapodia it is true, but in a manner which recalls the propulsion of the Cephalopoda, the water contained in the parapodial sac being expelled by its contraction.

On the other hand the palatine roof, armed with hooks, of *Notarchus* indicates, as we have seen, the first origin of the hook-sacs of the Gymnosomata, and the lateral gill is homologous with that of the Pneumonodermatidæ. Finally, the conformation of the nervous system is identical in *Notarchus* (and also in the *Dolabella neapolitana*) and the Gymnosomata.

If, then, we assume a form nearly related to *Notarchus*, in which the free margins of the parapodia have not fused ; in which the creeping foot has become shortened by disuse ; in which the small rudiments of mantle and shell seen in *Notarchus* have entirely disappeared ; in which the covering of hooks found on the palatine arch has been divided into symmetrical halves located in two depressions of the wall of the digestive tract (thus becoming transformed into hook-sacs like those of *Dexiobranchæa*) ; in which on the ventral wall of the proboscis there have been formed prehensile organs similar to the primitive suckers of *Dexiobranchæa* ; and lastly, in which the gill has been somewhat simplified in its structure,—we shall have a type very close to the most primitive Pneumonodermatidæ.

In the systematic Report on the Gymnosomata (Relations of the Gymnosomata to each other[1]) I have shown how all the living forms of Gymnosomata may be derived from this primitive type. We are therefore justified in saying that the Gymnosomata are specialised Aplysioiden, adapted to extremely natatory habits, and to an entirely pelagic mode of life.

VII. SUMMARY.

A. The Pteropoda do not constitute among the Mollusca a class of the same value as the Cephalopoda, Gastropoda, Scaphopoda, and Pelecypoda.

B. The Pteropoda are not primitive Mollusca, but are a derived and recent group.

C. They have no affinity with the Cephalopoda.

D. They are Gastropoda in which the adaptation to pelagic life has so modified their external characters as to give them an apparent symmetry.

[1] Zool. Chall. Exp., part lviii. pp. 67–69.

E. Among the Gastropoda they do not constitute a distinct subclass, nor even an order.

F. They belong to the Euthyneura, and among these to the Tectibranchiate Opisthobranchs. They differ less from the Tectibranchs than these differ from the other Opisthobranchs. The different families which make up the Pteropoda must be distributed among the families of the Tectibranchia according to their special affinities.

G. The Pteropoda are polyphyletic in their origin ; in other words, the Thecosomata and Gymnosomata are two independent groups : they have not a common origin and they differ more from each other than each one differs from a group of Tectibranchs to which it is most closely allied.

H. The Thecosomata have descended from the Bulloidea.

I. The Gymnosomata have descended from the Aplysioidea.

VIII. GENERAL CONCLUSIONS.

I have shown that the Pteropoda differ less from the Euthyneurous Gastropoda of the Tectibranchiate Opisthobranch group than these differ from the other Opisthobranchs, and that the different forms which have hitherto been united in one "class" Pteropoda find their natural places besides certain families of Tectibranchs. Furthermore, I have shown that the "Pteropoda" as a whole differ less from those Tectibranchs which are known as Cephalaspidea and Anaspidea (or Bulloidea and Aplysioidea respectively) than these together differ from the third group of Tectibranchs, Notaspidea (or Pleurobranchoidea).

In conclusion then I may say :—The Heteropoda were formerly regarded as a distinct class like the Pteropoda. But for a long time now they have been placed among the Gastropoda, the affinities having been recognised which they bear to the Streptoneura (or Prosobranchia), of which, to use the expression of Spengel, they are forms "modified by adaptation to a pelagic mode of life."[1]

I am strongly in favour of this mode of classifying the Heteropoda according to their natural affinities. Yet the Heteropoda are Gastropoda much more specialised in their organisation than are the Pteropoda ; and they exhibit differences from all the Streptoneura *much greater* than those which separate the Pteropoda from the Euthyneurous Gastropoda of the Tectibranchiate Opisthobranch group.

Henceforth, therefore, we should abstain from making a distinct class of the Pteropoda, but we should rather distribute the animals which have been called by this name among other groups, according to their natural affinities.

The table on the following page shows the manner in which I propose to classify the Pteropoda.

[1] Die Geruchsorgane und das Nervensystem der Mollusken, *Zeitschr. f. wiss. Zool.*, Bd. xxxv. p. 343.

TABLE SHOWING PROPOSED CLASSIFICATION OF PTEROPODA.

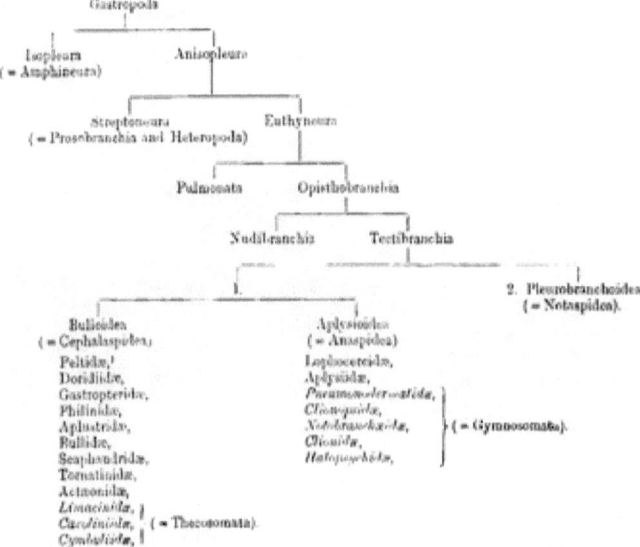

[1] All the authors who allude to this family (Woodward, A Manual of the Mollusca, p. 187 ; Bronn, Die Klassen und Ordnungen des Thierreichs, Bd. iii. p. 795 ; Vayssière, Recherches zoologiques et anatomiques sur les Mollusques Opisthobranches du Golfe de Marseille, loc. cit., p. 104 ; Fischer, Manuel de Conchyliologie, p. 573) have regarded these Mollusca as Pleurobranchoidea. They are, however, true Bulloidea, as is shown by the conformation of the head, of the generative organs, and of the nervous system.

PLATE I.

PLATE I.

Fig. 1. *Limacina helicina.*

Fig. 1. Head seen from the right side; *a*, right tentacle; *b*, fin; *c*, tentaculiform lobe of the fin; *d*, posterior lobe of the foot; *e*, columellar muscle; *f*, mantle; *g*, "balancer," or lateral lobe of the mantle; *h*, genital opening; *i*, seminal groove.

Fig. 2. *Limacina lesueuri.*

Fig. 2. Dorsal view, with the penis (*c*) evaginated; *a*, the head, with two tentacles and the seminal groove; *b*, "balancer"; *c*, penis.

Fig. 3. *Limacina helicina.*

Fig. 3. View from the right side, the mantle, as also the heart and kidney, having been removed from that side; *a*, fin; *b*, posterior lobe of the foot; *c*, buccal mass; *d*, œsophagus; *e*, one of the four large stomachal plates; *f*, the posterior dorsal arygous plate; *g*, intestine; *h*, anus; *i*, gonad or genital gland; *j*, genital duct; *k*, accessory genital glands; *l*, seminal groove; *m*, columellar muscle; *n*, pallial cavity; *o*, central nervous system.

Fig. 4. *Limacina lesueuri.*

Fig. 4. The evaginated penis, seen from the right side.

Fig. 5. *Limacina helicina.*

Fig. 5. Dorsal view; *a*, "shield" or pallial gland; *b*, kidney; *c*, heart, visible owing to the transparency of the mantle.

Fig. 6. *Actæon tornatilis.*

Fig. 6. Dorsal view; *a*, *b*, *c*, as in fig. 5; *d*, cephalic hood.

Figs. 7, 8. *Limacina helicina.*

Fig. 7. Central nervous system, seen from the left side; *a*, buccal mass; *b*, œsophagus; *c*, cerebral ganglion; *d*, cerebral commissure; *e*, pedal ganglion; *f*, right visceral ganglion; *g*, left visceral ganglion; *h*, otocyst; *i*, tentacular nerve; *j*, nerve to the fin; *2, 3,* visceral nerves; *4,* left pallial nerve.

Fig. 8. Central nervous system, seen from the ventral side; *a*, cerebral ganglion; *b*, pedal ganglion; *c*, right visceral ganglion; *d*, left visceral ganglion; *e*, otocyst; *f*, nerve to the fin; *1,* right pallial nerve; *2, 3,* visceral nerves; *4,* left pallial nerve.

Figs. 9–12. *Peraclis reticulata.*

Fig. 9. Dorsal surface of the head; *a*, head with the tentacles; *b*, fin; *c*, posterior lobe of the foot; *d*, operculum.

Fig. 10. Pallial gland seen from within.

Fig. 11. Distal extremity of the genital duct, seen from the right side; *a*, genital aperture; *b*, muciparous gland; *c*, albuminiparous gland; *d*, vesicula seminalis.

Fig. 12. Central nervous system, seen from the ventral surface; the cerebral commissure having been divided and the cerebral ganglia reflected ventrally; *a*, cerebral ganglion; *b*, pedal ganglion; *c*, right visceral ganglion; *d*, arygous median visceral or abdominal ganglion; *e*, left visceral ganglion; *f*, otocyst; *g*, cerebral commissure; *h*, cephalic nerve; *i*, nerve to the fin; *1,* right pallial nerve; *2, 3,* visceral nerves; *4,* left pallial nerve.

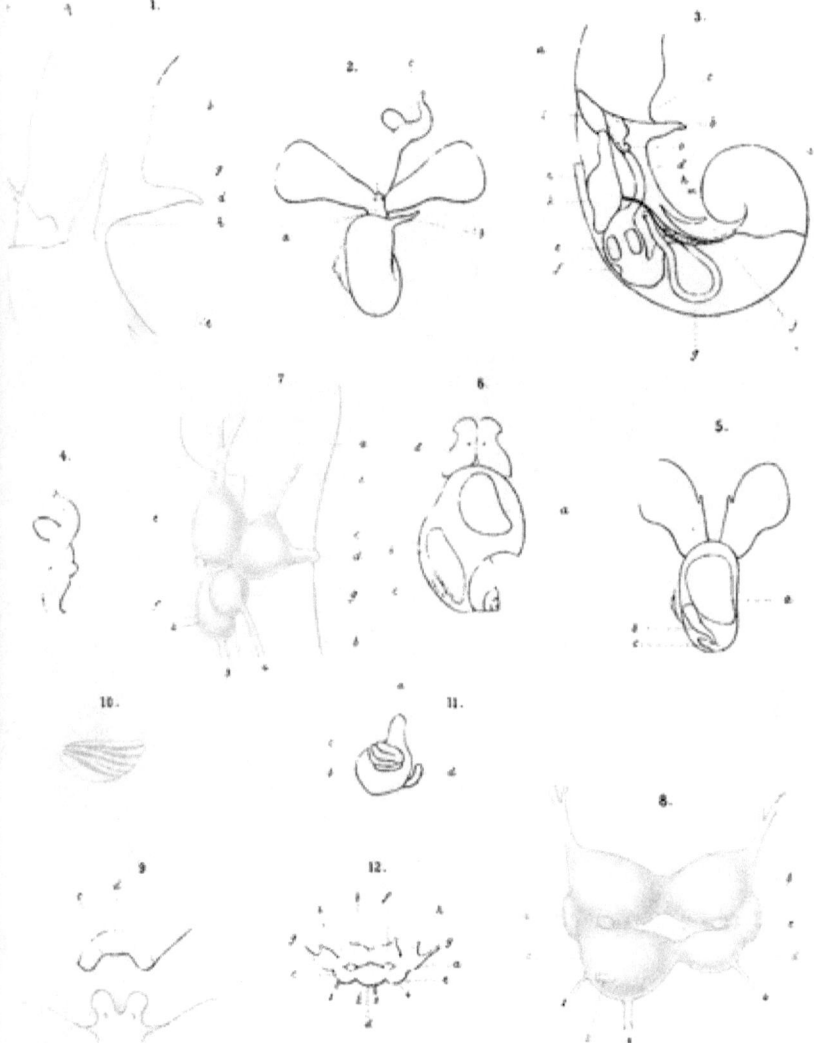

PLATE II.

PLATE II.

Fig. 1. *Clio striata.*

Fig. 1. View from the right side, the mantle, as also the heart and kidney, having been removed from that side; *a*, fin; *b*, posterior lobe of the foot; *c*, right tentacle; *d*, pallial cavity; *e*, buccal mass; *f*, œsophagus; *g*, one of the anterior gastric plates; *h*, posterior azygous gastric plate; *i*, intestine; *j*, bile duct; *k*, genital gland; *l*, genital duct; *m*, accessory genital glands; *n*, distal part of the genital duct; *o*, genital aperture; *p*, penis; *q*, orifice of the penis; *r*, position occupied by the liver.

Fig. 2. *Clio pyramidata.*

Fig. 2. Pallial gland, seen from behind.

Fig. 3. *Bulla (Haminea) hydatis.*

Fig. 3. Dorsal aspect, the mantle having been split and reflected to the left side; *a*, cephalic hood; *b*, parapodium; *c*, point up to which the mantle has been divided along the dotted line; *d*, pallial or hypobranchial gland; *e*, gill; *f*, lateral lobe of the mantle; *g*, anus; *h*, anal gland; *i*, spermatic groove; *j*, genital aperture.

Fig. 4. *Clio striata.*

Fig. 4. Pallial gland, seen from behind.

Fig. 5. *Clio acicula.*

Fig. 5. Stomach opened along the dorsal side; *a*, œsophagus; *b*, the eight small anterior gastric plates; *c*, the four large plates; *d*, the posterior azygous ventral plate; *e*, commencement of the intestine.

Fig. 6. *Cuvierina columnella.*

Fig. 6. The cervical region opened from below; *a*, fin; *b*, posterior lobe of the foot; *c*, buccal mass; *d*, central nervous system; *e*, œsophagus; *f*, diaphragm.

Figs. 7, 8. *Clio pyramidata.*

Fig. 7. Anterior portion, seen from the left side; *a*, fin; *b*, posterior lobe of the foot; *c*, left tentacle; *d*, accessory genital gland; *e*, anus; *f*, anal gland; *g*, intestine; *h*, liver.

Fig. 8. Ventral aspect of the heart and kidney, the latter having been reflected towards the left side; *a*, ventricle; *b*, auricle; *c*, pericardium; *d*, kidney; *e*, opening from the kidney into the pallial cavity; *f*, communication between the kidney and pericardium.

Fig. 9. *Clio.*

Fig. 9. Transverse section through the central nervous system; *a*, cerebral ganglion; *b*, pleural ganglion; *c*, visceral ganglionic mass; *d*, otocyst with otoliths; *f*, œsophagus.

Fig. 10. *Cuvierina columnella.*

Fig. 10. Central nervous system, seen from the left side; *a*, cerebral ganglion; *b*, pedal ganglion; *c*, pleural ganglion; *d*, left visceral ganglion; *e*, otocyst; *f*, cerebral commissure; *g*, tentacular nerve; *2, 3*, visceral nerves; *4*, left pallial nerve.

Fig. 11. *Actæon tornatilis.*

Fig. 11. Central nervous system, seen from the dorsal side; *a*, cerebro-pleural ganglion; *b*, pedal ganglion; *c*, right anterior visceral or supraintestinal ganglion; *d*, abdominal or posterior visceral ganglion; *e*, left anterior visceral or subintestinal ganglion; *f*, genital (accessory) ganglion; *g*, osphradium; *h*, buccal or stomato-gastric ganglion; *i*, cerebral commissure; *j*, cerebro-pedal connective; *k*, cerebro-pleural connective; *l*, pedal commissure; *m*, second pedal commissure; *n*, nerve to the penis.

PLATE III.

(ZOOL. CHALL. EXP.—PART LXVI.—1888.)—Uuu.

PLATE III.

Fig. 1. *Cuvierina columnella.*

Fig. 1. Central nervous system, from the ventral surface; *a*, pedal ganglion; *b*, right visceral ganglion; *c*, left visceral ganglion; *d*, otocyst; *e*, second pedal commissure; *1*, right pallial nerve; *2, 3*, visceral nerves; *4*, left pallial nerve.

Fig. 2. *Cavolinia longirostris.*

Fig. 2. Ventral aspect, the mantle having been removed from this side; *a*, retractor or columellar muscle; *a'*, its left anterior branch; *b*, fin; *c*, œsophagus; *d*, stomach; *e*, intestine; *f*, liver; *g*, genital gland; *h*, vesicula seminalis; *i*, accessory genital glands; *j*, genital duct.

Fig. 3. *Cavolinia quadridentata.*

Fig. 3. Ventral aspect of the digestive tract; *a*, buccal mass; *b*, salivary gland; *c*, œsophagus; *d*, stomach; *e*, cæcum; *f*, intestine; *g*, right lobe of the liver; *h*, its duct; *i*, left lobe of the liver; *j*, its duct.

Fig. 4. *Cavolinia inflexa.*

Fig. 4. Generative organs, seen from the right side; *a*, genital gland; *b*, genital duct; *c*, vesicula seminalis; *d*, accessory genital glands; *e*, genital orifice; *f*, spermatic groove.

Fig. 5. *Cavolinia trispinosa.*

Fig. 5. Horny spicule from the penis.

Fig. 6. Limacinidæ and Cavoliniidæ.

Fig. 6. Comparative diagrams of the organisation of the Limacinidæ and Cavoliniidæ, the animals being seen from the cephalic extremity:—A, Limacinidæ; B, Cavoliniidæ. The following letters have the same significance in the two diagrams; *a*, œsophagus; *b*, stomach; *c*, bile-duct; *d*, posterior azygous gastric plate; *d'*, anus; *e*, origin of the genital duct; *f*, genital orifice; *g*, pallial gland (shield); *h*, pallial cavity.

Fig. 7. *Cymbulia peroni.*

Fig. 7. Anterior aspect, the fin having been cut through ventrally and laterally; *a*, head with the two tentacles; *b*, fin; *c*, "shell"; *d*, pallial cavity; *e*, visceral mass and anus; *f*, pallial gland (shield).

Figs. 8–11. *Cymbulia.*

Fig. 8. *a*, Pallial gland; *b*, outline of the shell.

Fig. 9. Ventral aspect of the generative organs, the accessory glands being reflected to the left side; *a*, genital gland; *b*, genital duct; *c*, receptaculum seminis; *d*, muciparous gland; *e*, albuminiparous gland; *f*, genital orifice.

Fig. 10. Ventral aspect of the central nervous system; *a*, cerebral ganglion; *b*, pedal ganglion; *c*, right visceral ganglion; *d*, posterior visceral or abdominal ganglion; *e*, left visceral ganglion; *f*, otocyst; *g*, nerves to the fin; *1*, right pallial nerve; *2, 3*, visceral nerves; *4*, left pallial nerve.

Fig. 11. Lateral view of the central nervous system; *a*, cerebral ganglion; *b*, pedal ganglion; *c*, right visceral ganglion; *d*, posterior visceral or abdominal ganglion; *e*, cerebral commissure; *f*, otocyst; *g*, nerves to the fin; *h*, œsophagus; *1*, left pallial nerve; *2, 3*, visceral nerves.

Fig. 12. *Gleba cordata.*

Fig. 12. Anterior view of the larva; *a*, buccal aperture; *b*, penis; *c*, posterior lobe of the foot.

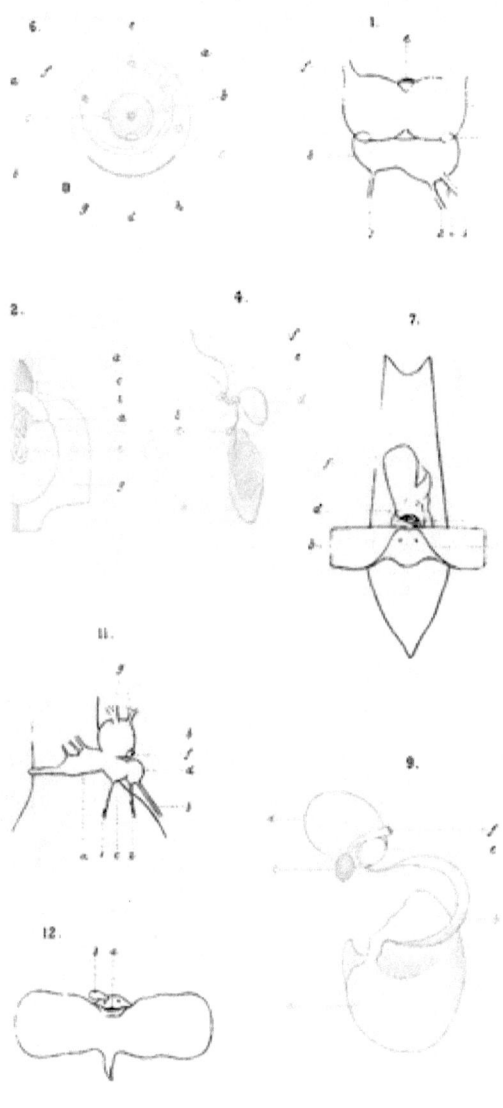

PLATE IV.

PLATE IV.

Figs. 1, 2. *Cymbulia*.

Fig. 1. Central part of the animal, seen from the right side as a transparent object; *a*, "shell"; *b*, truncated fin; *c*, posterior appendage of the fin, cut short; *d*, space between this appendage and the shell; *e*, pallial gland; *f*, entrance of the pallial cavity; *g*, mouth; *h*, visceral mass; *i*, anus; *j*, genital orifice, followed by the spermatic groove leading to the penis; *h*, aperture of the penis; *l*, lumen of the kidney; *m*, aperture leading from the kidney into the pallial cavity; *n*, heart; *o*, central nervous system; *p*, pallial cavity.

Fig. 2. Stomato-gastric nervous system, seen from the left side; *a*, mouth; *b*, buccal mass; *c*, salivary gland; *d*, œsophagus; *e*, stomach; *f*, intestine; *g*, buccal ganglion; *h*, œsophageal nerve leading to *i*, the gastric plexus.

Figs. 3, 4. *Gleba*.

Fig. 3. *a*, Pallial gland; *b*, outline of the shell.

Fig. 4. Central nervous system, seen from the left side; *a*, cerebral ganglion; *b*, pedal ganglion; *c*, left visceral ganglion; *d*, posterior visceral or abdominal ganglion; *e*, cerebral commissure; *f*, otocyst; *g*, nerves to the fin; *h*, nerve to the retractor muscle of the proboscis; *i*, tentacular nerve; *j*, œsophagus; *3*, visceral (genital) nerve; *4*, left pallial nerve.

Fig. 5. *Notarchus*.

Fig. 5. Sagital section of the buccal mass, from a sketch kindly presented by Dr. Vayssière; *a*, palatine teeth; *b*, right jaw; *c*, radula; *d*, mouth; *e*, œsophagus.

Fig. 6. *Dexiobranchæa*.

Fig. 6. Diagramatic sagittal section of the buccal mass; *a*, hook-sac; *a'*, hook-sac as found in *Pneumonoderma*; *b*, jaw; *c*, radula; *d*, mouth; *e*, œsophagus.

Fig. 7. *Pneumonoderma*.

Fig. 7. Transverse section of the dorsal patch; *a*, epithelium; *b*, large glandular cells; *c*, small central glandular cells.

Fig. 8. *Spongiobranchæa*.

Fig. 8. Dorsal view of the generative organs; *a*, genital gland; *b*, genital duct; *c*, muciparous gland; *d*, albuminiparous gland; *e*, receptaculum seminis; *f*, genital orifice.

Fig. 9. *Pneumonoderma*.

Fig. 9. Ventral view of the central nervous system, the cerebral commissure having been divided and the cerebral ganglia reflected ventrally; *a*, cerebral ganglion; *b*, pedal ganglion; *c*, pleural ganglion; *d*, right visceral ganglion; *e*, buccal ganglion; *f*, cerebro-pleural connective; *g*, cerebro-pedal connective; *h*, pleuro-visceral connective; *i*, cerebro-buccal connective; *j*, nerve from the pleural ganglion; *k*, pedal commissure; *l*, second pedal commissure; *i*, nerve to the foot; *ii*, nerve to fin; *iii, iv*, lateral pedal nerves; *v, vi, vii*, cervical nerves; *1*, nerve from the right visceral ganglion; *2, 3*, median nerves from the left visceral ganglion; *4*, lateral nerve from the left visceral ganglion.

Fig. 10. *Clionopsis*.

Fig. 10. Ventral view of the osphradium; *a*, osphradium; *b*, nerve ramifying in the osphradium; *c*, anus; *d*, opening of the kidney; *e*, cloacal depression.

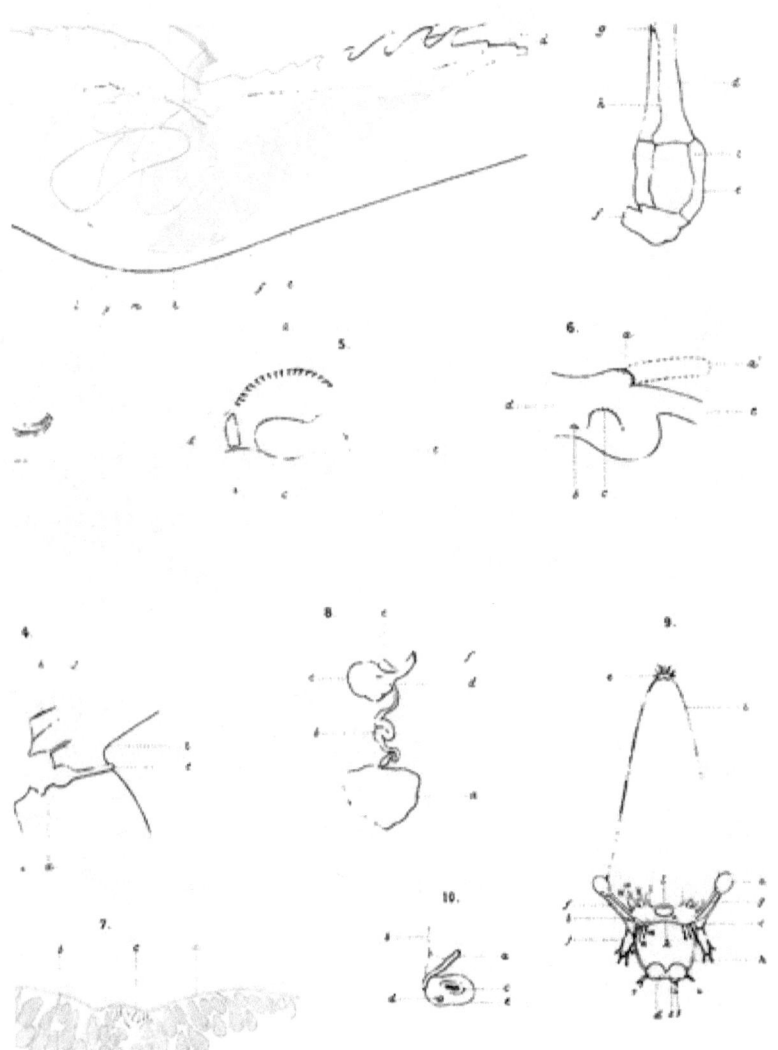

PLATE V.

(ZOOL. CHALL. EXP.—PART LXVI.—1888.)—Uuu.

PLATE V.

Fig. 1. *Pneumonoderma.*

Fig. 1. Dorsal view of the central nervous system; *a*, cerebral ganglion; *b*, pedal ganglion; *c*, pleural ganglion; *d*, visceral ganglion; *e*, cerebro-pedal connective; *f*, cerebro-pleural connective; *g*, pleuro-visceral connective; *h*, olfactory nerve; *i*, optic nerve; *j*, nerve to the acetabuliferous appendage; *k*, nerve to the anterior tentacle; *l*, labial nerve.

Fig. 2. *Dolabella neapolitana.*

Fig. 2. Central nervous system, seen from the right side; *a*, cerebral ganglion; *b*, pedal ganglion; *c*, pleural ganglion; *d*, right visceral ganglion; *e*, cerebro-pedal connective; *f*, cerebro-pleural connective; *g*, pleuro-visceral connective; *h*, œsophagus.

Fig. 3. *Spongiobranchæa.*

Fig. 3. Central nervous system seen from the left side; *a*, cerebral ganglion; *b*, pedal ganglion; *c*, pleural ganglion; *d*, left visceral ganglion; *e*, cerebro-pedal connective; *f*, cerebro-pleural connective; *g*, pleuro-visceral connective; *h*, otocyst; *i*, auditory nerve; *j*, cerebro-buccal connective; *8*, genital nerve; *4*, lateral nerve from the left visceral ganglion.

Fig. 4. *Clione limacina.*

Fig. 4. Ventral aspect of the anterior portion; *a*, evaginated proboscis; *b*, evaginated hook-sacs; *c*, buccal cone; *d*, anterior tentacle; *e*, fin; *f*, lateral lobe of the foot; *g*, posterior lobe of the foot.

Figs. 5–7. *Clione.*

Fig. 5. Anterior region, seen from the right side, in order to show the visceral openings; *a*, anterior tentacle; *b*, head; *c*, foot; *d*, fin cut off at its origin; *e*, anus; *f*, aperture of the kidney; *g*, genital aperture; *h*, spermatic groove; *i*, orifice of the penis; *j*, osphradium.

Fig. 6. Osphradium and its nerve supply, seen from the right side; *a*, cerebral ganglion; *b*, pedal ganglion; *c*, pleural ganglion; *d*, right visceral ganglion; *e*, osphradium; *f*, œsophagus; *g*, anus; *h*, opening of the penis; *i*, lateral lobe of the foot; *j*, posterior lobe of the foot.

Fig. 7. Transverse section of the osphradium; *a*, osphradial nerve; *b*, its sheath, continued by the connective envelope of the osphradium; *c*, ganglionic cells of the osphradium; *d*, sensory epithelium.

Figs. 8–11. *Halopsyche gaudichaudi.*

Fig. 8. Ventral aspect of the central nervous system; *a*, cerebral ganglion; *b*, pedal ganglion; *c*, right visceral ganglion; *d*, posterior visceral or abdominal ganglion; *e*, left visceral ganglion; *f*, second pedal commissure; *g*, cerebral commissure; *h*, cerebro-pedal connective; *i*, otocyst; *j*, nerve to the buccal appendage; *k*, nerve and ganglion of the nuchal tentacle; *l*, nerves to the fin; *m*, nerve to the foot; *1, 2, 3, 4*, visceral nerves.

Fig. 9. Oral view of the central nervous system; *a*, cerebral ganglion; *b*, pedal ganglion; *c*, buccal ganglion; *d*, cerebro-pedal connective; *e*, cerebro-buccal connective; *f*, second pedal commissure; *g*, nerve and ganglion of the nuchal tentacle; *h*, nerve to the buccal appendage; *i*, nerve to the foot; *j*, nerves to the fin.

Fig. 10. Central nervous system, seen from the left side; *a*, cerebral ganglion; *b*, pedal ganglion; *c*, left visceral ganglion; *d*, posterior visceral ganglion; *e*, nerve to the buccal appendage; *f*, nerve and ganglion of the nuchal tentacle; *g*, nerves to the fin; *h*, otocyst; *8, 4*, visceral nerves.

Fig. 11. Transverse section of the central nervous system passing through the visceral ganglia; *a*, cerebral ganglion; *b*, right visceral ganglion; *c*, posterior visceral or abdominal ganglion; *d*, left visceral ganglion; *e*, cerebral commissure; *f*, œsophagus.

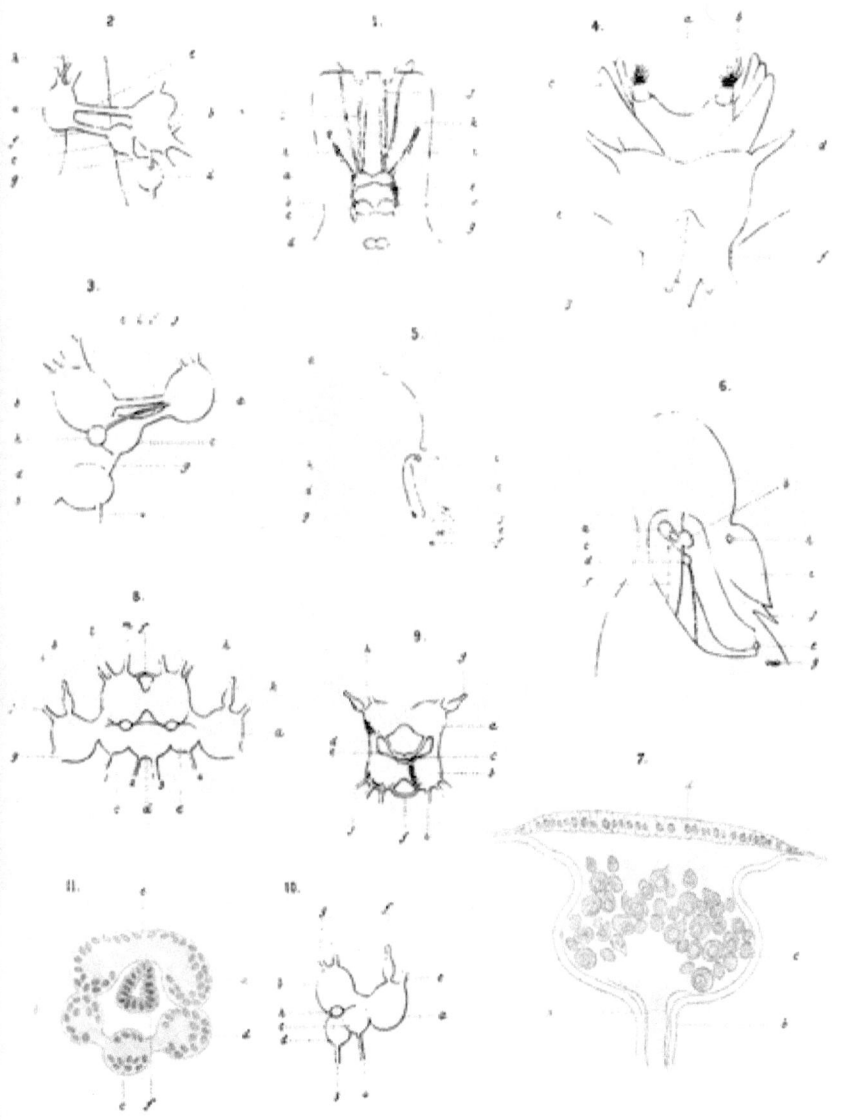

VOYAGE OF H.M.S. CHALLENGER.

ZOOLOGY.

REPORT on the HYDROIDA dredged by H.M.S. Challenger during the Years 1873–76. By Professor G. J. ALLMAN, M.D., LL.D., F.R.C.S.I., F.R.SS. L. & E., M.R.I.A., C.M.Z.S., Mem. Roy. Danish Acad. Sci., &c.

PART II.—THE TUBULARINÆ, CORYMORPHINÆ, CAMPANU- LARINÆ, SERTULARINÆ, AND THALAMOPHORA.

PREFACE

THE collection of Hydroida brought home by the Challenger contains representatives of almost every important group of this order. The Plumularinæ, to which I have devoted a separate examination in that part of the Report which has been already published, are richly represented in the collection, and examples of almost all the leading types of this beautiful group have been found in it. Many of these have afforded the means of working out certain morphological relations which throw light on the architecture of the group and demonstrate a fundamental unity amongst very diverse modifications of structure. The Hydrocorallinæ have been made the subject of a very valuable inde- pendent Report by Professor Moseley,[1] and it is now proposed to consider all the remaining Hydroid groups, examples of which were obtained during the Expedition. In addition to the new species certain previously known ones have been figured, when this seemed desirable.

I have taken advantage of the opportunity afforded by the typical character of the collection to make this the basis of a general exposition of Hydroid morphology, from the

[1] Report on certain Hydroid, Alcyonarian, and Madreporarian Corals, Zool. Chall. Exp., part vii.

standpoint of our present knowledge, in the hope that a higher morphological interest
might be added to a work which would otherwise have contained little more than
descriptive and distributional details.

Two or three species have by an oversight received names which had been already
appropriated. In the Explanation of the Plates, however, and in the Index, legitimate
names have been substituted for those previously used, while the latter have been
retained between brackets, and it is hoped that all danger of confusion will be thus
avoided. The magnified figures contained in the Plates have been all drawn by the
author, and in almost every instance those which represent the natural size of the
species by Miss M. M'Daniel.

To Mr. John Murray, the Director of the Literary Staff of the Expedition, my best
thanks are due for the readiness with which he acceded to everything which might
facilitate my work, for the courtesy which I received from him throughout, and for the
patience with which he met the somewhat tardy appearance of the Report. To Mr.
William E. Hoyle I am also much indebted for valuable assistance in the verification
of localities, and in the general supervision of the proofs.

CONTENTS.

GENERAL INTRODUCTION.

Among the Hydroids to which the present part of the Report is devoted, the Gymno-blastic genera are but sparingly represented, while, on the other hand, a rich and highly interesting collection of Calyptoblastic forms has been obtained. These are for the most part well preserved—so well, indeed, that in many instances the hydranths and other soft parts of the colony have retained their characters in so good a condition as to allow of these parts being drawn with most of the natural features of the living animal.[1]

It is however somewhat disappointing to find that a large proportion of species is represented by the trophosome alone, a fact probably due to the circumstance that many of these species were obtained at seasons when no gonosome is developed by them. Notwithstanding, however, the absence of this important element of the colony, it was seldom that any difficulty was experienced in assigning a specimen to its true place in the system.

No planoblasts or free-swimming sexual buds of Hydroid colonies are contained in the collection placed in my hands. A few deep-sea Craspedote Medusæ, some of which are probably the planoblasts of unknown Hydroid trophosomes, have formed part of a separate Report by Professor Haeckel.[2]

The rare occurrence in the collection of such species as are known to inhabit the European Seas is striking, and points to a definiteness in the geographical distribution of the Hydroida which could scarcely have been expected, and which certainly contrasts with the wide distribution met with among many species of Polyzoa.

Among the new forms described in the present part of the Report are several which render necessary the definition not only of new generic groups, but of new families. Among the groups most richly represented in the collection, and of which compara-

---

[1] Were it not that the Plumularinæ have been dealt with in the former part of this Report (Zool. Chall. Exp., part xx.), they would form the final group in the arrangement of the Hydroids here followed. The group here indicated under the name of Plumularinæ is exactly co-extensive with the Plumularidæ of the former part. The subordination of groups here employed is I believe in accordance with the requirements of Hydroid classification, but had been decided on too late to allow of its adoption in the part of the Report already published.

[2] Report on the Deep-Sea Medusæ, Zool. Chall. Exp., part vii.

tively few examples had hitherto been known, are those to which belong the genera *Cryptolaria* and *Grammaria*, as well as a new and very interesting genus to which I have assigned the name of *Perisiphonia*, and of which the collection contains two species.

An examination of the specimens by which these genera are represented has shown that they possess a remarkable and hitherto unsuspected type of structure, rendering necessary the institution for them of two new families, while to one of these families must also be referred certain other genera with which zoologists have long been familiar, but in which the essential character of the family had been overlooked.

Idia, hitherto known only by the very deficient description and figure of Lamouroux,[1] and of which only a single species, *Idia pristis*, has as yet been discovered, is represented by examples which show that it is constructed on a type quite unique among the Hydroida, and one which demands the allocation of it to a special Hydroid section. To this section I have assigned the name of Thalamophora.

Among other families largely represented is that of the Haleciidæ, with not only many new species, but with one form which must be referred to a new generic type, and which is rendered especially interesting by the fact that the colony is provided with bodies which admit of a close comparison with the sarcostyles and sarcothecæ of the Plumularinæ. Similar bodies are also borne by the two species of *Perisiphonia* already referred to, and by a species referable to the new genus *Hypopyxis*. The presence of these bodies, formerly supposed to be confined to the Plumularinæ, with a very few forms belonging to other groups, has thus been shown to be by no means so limited as had been imagined.

In two species, one of which is referable to *Sertularia* and one to *Thuiaria*, the specimens afford abundant evidence of the fact that the hydranths are incapable of complete retraction within the hydrothecæ. In both of these the body of the hydranth is connected with the wall of the hydrotheca by ectodermal bands quite similar to those which in most Hydroid trophosomes connect the cœnosarc with the walls of the perisarcal tube, or the blastostyle with those of the gonangium. In at least one of these the tentacles of the hydranth are each provided at its base with a prominent cushion loaded with thread-cells, and forming a defensive battery in which we can scarcely avoid seeing a provision, the object of which is to act as a compensation for the comparatively unprotected condition of the hydranth.

The curious genus *Synthecium*, in which the gonangia spring from within the cavity of the hydrotheca, is represented by two new species, both from the Australian seas, thus extending our knowledge of the range of this genus, which had been previously known only through specimens obtained from the region of New Zealand. There also occur fine

---

[1] Mr. Hincks has since sent me a specimen of this Hydroid from the Mergui Archipelago, while I am also indebted to my late lamented friend Mr. Busk for an opportunity of examining singularly fine specimens from the Persian Gulf.

examples of the remarkable genus *Thecocladium*, in which every branch of the colony springs like the gonangium in *Synthecium* from within the cavity of a hydrotheca.

The few Gymnoblastic or Tubularian Hydroids in the collection belong to three genera, *Stylactis*, *Eudendrium*, and *Monocaulus*; the species by which the last is represented being perhaps the most remarkable Hydroid obtained during the Expedition. When we keep in mind that its stem measures half an inch in thickness by seven feet in height, and that its hydranth extends nine inches from tip to tip of its tentacles, we must admit that as regards size every other Hydroid sinks into insignificance when compared with it; while the depth of about four statute miles from which it was brought up adds to the special interest of this marvellous animal. It will further be seen that so far as the specimens admitted of anatomical study certain points of structure which scarcely yield in importance to the other characters have been demonstrated in it. Fortunately a drawing of it was made by Mr. J. J. Wild immediately after its capture, otherwise it would have been impossible to have given a correct delineation of its natural aspect.

The extent of the collection and its representative character render it eminently fitted for the illustration of general Hydroid morphology; for with the exception of the Hydrocorallinæ, which have already formed the subject of a separate Report by Professor Moseley, it contains examples of almost all the leading types of Hydroid form. I believe, therefore, that it will add to the value of the Report, and help to convey a definite conception of the terminology, if, before entering on the purely descriptive zoology of the species, a sketch be given of the morphology and classification of the Hydroida, aided by such illustrations as may be afforded by the various forms included in the Report.

SKETCH OF THE MORPHOLOGY AND LIFE HISTORY OF THE HYDROIDA.

I. FUNDAMENTAL FORM. GENERAL ARCHITECTURE OF THE HYDROIDA.

The fundamental form to which every Hydroid may more or less directly be referred is that of a cylindrical tube closed at one end, and terminating at the opposite end in a conical prolongation, which carries on its apex an orifice through which the cavity of the tube communicates with the exterior. Projecting in a circle which surrounds the base of the cone are certain hollow cylindrical offsets, each of which has its axis occupied by an extension of the central cavity. This cavity is the digestive cavity of the Hydroid, the terminal orifice which opens into it is the mouth, and the cylindrical offsets which encircle the terminal cone or hypostome constitute a system of tentacles which form an apparatus of prehension and defence.

Retaining this fundamental type-form we have the fresh-water *Hydra*, but almost the whole of the remaining representatives of the order present it in a more or less modified condition, while they have in almost every instance become variously complicated by the formation of hollow buds, whose cavity is continuous with that of the primary Hydroid, with which most of them remain in permanent union. Many of these buds become elongated into branches, and thus give rise to complicated colonies, which often present luxuriant tree-like growths, and repeat with wonderful fidelity the most elaborate ramification of the vegetable kingdom (Pls. II., IV., IX., &c.).

Even in *Hydra*, however, this complication by budding, and the consequent formation of dendritic colonies, is foreshadowed by the emission of buds, but here the buds, after attaining maturity, detach themselves, and leave the parent simple as before.

It will be hereafter shown (page xxviii) that even the generative buds which have become detached under the form of Medusæ or "jelly-fish," in order to spend henceforth a free life in the open sea, may be referred to the same fundamental type of form. It must accordingly be borne in mind that not only the polyp-form as shown in *Hydra*, but the Medusa-form as shown in the Craspedotæ or Hydro-Medusæ (see below, page xxv, note), must be included under the common order, Hydroida.

II. DISPOSITION OF THE FUNDAMENTAL LAYERS.

The parts which enter into the composition of the Hydroid body are disposed in two fundamental cellular layers, separated from one another by a thin, structureless, excreted membrane, while the whole is for a greater or less extent, in the great majority of cases, surrounded by another structureless membrane, also the product of excretion.

Of the two cellular layers the more internal one lines the body-cavity and its offsets, and forms the *endoderm;* the more external, which is exactly coextensive with this, is the *ectoderm*, while the thin, structureless membrane which everywhere intervenes between endoderm and ectoderm is the *mesosarc*,[1] and the structureless coat which in almost every case surrounds and protects the soft parts in the stems and branches is the *perisarc*.

A Hydroid colony, then, such as we meet with in the great majority of instances, presents a ramified growth whose stems and branches are elongated, intercommunicating tubes, the common cavity of which forms the nutritive cavity of the colony, and whose walls are composed of endoderm and ectoderm, separated from one another by the mesosarc, and protected externally by the investing perisarc. The living nutritive tube which lies within the perisarc and is the common basis from which all the buds are emitted is known as the *cœnosarc*.

[1] This is the "Stützlamelle" of Reichert, who was the first to call attention to it. It must not be confounded with the "mesoderm" or middle germinal layer of the embryo, a layer which does not occur in the embryonal development of the Hydroida.

III. DIVERSITY OF FORM AND FUNCTION IN THE BUDS.

But it is not simply in the form of elongated branches that the buds become developed. At the extremities of the stem and branches, or on offsets which bud forth from definite points on their sides, the coenosarc frees itself from its close perisarcal coat and undergoes a remarkable and characteristic development, being here transformed into a more or less club-shaped body, which throws out tentacles from its sides and becomes perforated by a terminal mouth. This remarkable body, which thus repeats in all essential features the structure and form of a solitary or primordial Hydroid, is known as the *hydranth* (Pl. II. fig. 2; Pl. VII. fig. 2; Pl. XII. fig. 1c). Within its cavity, which communicates with that of the general cavity of the colony, the most active digestive processes are carried on. It is the element on which the nutrition of the Hydroid specially devolves, and that which gives to the living colony its most characteristic physiognomy, its circlet of tentacles, radiating round a central point, conferring on it that singular resemblance to an expanded flower which had from a remote period arrested the attention of every observer of these animals in their living state.[1]

But, besides these flower-like nutritive buds, there are others which make their appearance at certain seasons, and whose function is not that of procuring and elaborating nutriment for the colony. These are also budded forth from various parts of the colony, and are either in the form of fixed sac-like bodies (Pl. I. figs. 1, 2; Pl. III. fig. 3; Pl. VII. fig. 4, *b*, &c.), in which a suppressed medusoid conformation may in many instances be detected, or in that of completely developed Craspedote Medusæ, which after a time become detached from the colony, and lead henceforth an independent life. The function of these, whether they be fixed sacs or free-swimming Medusæ, is that of protecting the generative elements—ova or spermatozoa—and in some cases giving origin to them. They are known as *gonophores*.

It will be thus seen that a typical Hydroid colony consists of an assemblage of buds, each endowed—whether permanently attached to the colony or free—with a more or less independent life. To these buds different functions have been assigned, and the whole are associated into a community by a common living basis—the coenosarc. Their independent life entitles them to be distinguished from mere organs, and they may be appropriately designated "zooids," as originally proposed by Huxley. They are the "personæ" in the terminology of Haeckel.

[1] Weismann (Die Entstehung der Sexualzellen bei den Hydromedusen) does not confine his conception of the hydranth to this club-shaped body with its mouth and tentacles, and proper stomach cavity, but extends it in the case of the tree-like Tubularian and Campanularian Hydroids to the whole of that portion of the stem which lies between the hydranth as here limited and the first lateral branch. To this portion of the stem he gives the name of hydranth-stalk (Hydranthenstiel), while he designates the proper hydranth as the hydranth-head (Hydranthenkopf), and he justifies this recognition of the stalk as an integral part of the hydranth by the conclusion to which he has been led, that on it, and only on it, in dendritically branched colonies is the "budding zone" or place where a new hydranth bud may be formed.

Now, the whole of the *nutritive* zooids or hydranths with the connecting cœnosarc may be regarded as forming a distinct system, while the *generative* zooids or gonophores, along with such parts as they may be provided with for protection or otherwise, will form another. The former will constitute the *trophosome* of the colony, the latter the *gonosome*.

The zooids, which have just been referred to the trophosome and gonosome, have been found in all Hydroids which have been adequately studied, with the exception of some free Medusæ in which no independent trophosome is present (see below, p. xxviii), of *Hydra* in which the protection of the generative elements is not assigned to distinctly differentiated zooids, and of the somewhat enigmatical *Protohydra* of Greeff, which according to that author is a Hydroid presenting a condition of extreme simplification, being destitute of tentacles and multiplying only by division of its body.[1] In some, however, there occurs an additional set of zooids, whose functions, though scarcely yet ascertained with certainty, would seem to be in some cases chiefly that of the defence of the colony, as may be assumed of the "spiral zooids" of *Hydractinia*, and the "dactylozooids" of the Hydrocorallia; and in other cases that of the prehension of nutriment, as is probably the case with the nematophores or *sarcostyles* of the Plumularinæ and of a few other groups.

It will thus be apparent that the zooids of the Hydroid colony, with their various forms and definite functions, are the expression of a physiological division of labour, while as we advance towards higher groups of the animal kingdom we find the various kinds of physiological work assigned, not to different *zooids*, but to different *organs* which have lost the independence which more or less characterises the zooid.

IV. HISTOLOGY OF THE FUNDAMENTAL LAYERS.

What has now been said will serve to indicate the salient points of the morphology of the Hydroida. For an adequate conception, however, of Hydroid organisation, a more intimate knowledge of structure will be necessary, and this will be best acquired by a detailed examination of each of the fundamental tissue layers.

1. *The Endoderm.*

The endoderm consists generally of a single layer of prismatic cells, whose bases rest externally on the mesosarc, and whose opposite ends bound the common cavity of the colony. Those ends of the endodermal cells, which thus lie free in the nutritive cavity, are each provided with a simple flagelliform cilium, by whose vibrations the contents of the cavity are kept in constant motion.

In *Myriothela* the endoderm of the whole of the main cavity of the body forms a thick layer composed of many cells in depth. The cells, which in *Myriothela* form the

----
[1] R. Greeff, *Zeitschr. f. wiss. Zool.*, Bd. xx., 1869.

greater part of the thickness of this endodermal layer, consist of round nucleated masses of clear protoplasm, while those which lie directly on the walls of the cavity are ciliated, and overlaid by a thin layer of free protoplasm, through which the cilia pass, and which has the faculty of emitting pseudopodia.

In *Tubularia indivisa* also, and in *Corymorpha*, the endoderm of the stem is composed of many layers of round cells. These would form a solid mass, filling the cavity of the stem in these Hydroids, were it not that the endoderm is here traversed by numerous longitudinal canals, which run parallel with the axis, anastomosing with one another here and there, and opening above into the gastral cavity of the hydranth. These canals represent the simple cavity which extends through the axis of the stem in other Hydroids, for there is here no axial cavity in the stem, its place being taken by a large and clear-celled modification of the more peripheral portion of the endoderm.

In *Monocaulus imperator* the endoderm of the stem is traversed as in *Tubularia indivisa* and in *Corymorpha* by longitudinal anastomosing canals (Pl. III. figs. 1, 4); but here a wide, continuous cavity runs through the whole length of the axis.

The nutritive cavity of the Hydroida is generally dilated in the body of the hydranth, so as to form the proper stomach, and then the body of the hydranth with its included cavity contracts towards the mouth into a conical, or in some cases, a trumpet-shaped, proboscis or *hypostome*.

In many species of *Tubularia* and other Hydroids which form the section Gymnoblastea, the endoderm of the hypostome is thrown into longitudinal ridges, mostly four or five, which project into its cavity, and then passing downwards become in the stomach broken up into several branches, which soon lose themselves on the general endodermal lining.

These endodermal ridges, which are also well developed in the nearly allied order of the Siphonophora, were first pointed out by von Koch,[1] and have been since noticed by many observers, but more especially by Hamann,[2] who adopted for them Haeckel's term " tæniola," a term, however, which Haeckel uses in a different sense, applying it to the prominent gastral ridges which are characteristic of the Scyphistoma or polyp form of the Acraspedal Medusæ.[3] Hamann attributes to the endodermal ridges of the Hydroida a high systematic value, and regards their presence as the true grounds on which the Gymnoblastic Hydroids admit of being separated as a natural group from the Calyptoblastic forms.

This, however, is assigning to them an importance greater than they can fairly claim. They are by no means absolutely constant either in their form or their presence in the Tubularians. In *Tubularia indivisa* they are represented by pendulous pyriform lobes

[1] G. v. Koch, Vorläufige Mittheilungen über Coelenteraten, *Jenaische Zeitschr.*, Bd. vii. p. 512, 1873.
[2] O. Hamann, Der Organismus der Hydroidenpolypen, *Jenaische Zeitschr.*, Bd. xv.
[3] Ernst Haeckel, Das System der Medusen, Jena, 1879.

of the gastric cavity of the hydranth, while in *Myriothela* they are replaced by long, nipple-like processes of the endoderm, which project into the gastric cavity throughout its whole extent, except for a short space immediately below the mouth. These processes, like the more external portion of the endoderm, are formed of large, round, nucleated cells, but at their free extremities they are surrounded by numerous smaller cells which are loaded with coloured granules and are probably to be regarded as gland-cells. In the hydranths, indeed, of almost all Hydroids, certain endodermal as well as ectodermal cells would seem to possess the function of gland-cells. These endodermal gland-cells are chiefly developed in the walls of the hypostome.

In almost all Hydroida the endoderm undergoes a remarkable modification in the interior of the tentacles. In *Hydra* and *Myriothela* the tentacles have a hollow tubular axis, which communicates freely with the gastric cavity, and whose endodermal lining is a simple continuation, in a scarcely altered condition, of that of the body cavity.

In *Garveia nutans* also, the tentacle presents a continuous tubular axis, but the endoderm consists here of a regular series of large, clear, flat cells, piled on one another from the base to the apex of the tentacle, having their outer sides turned towards the ectoderm, from which they are separated only by the mesosarc, while their inner sides so encroach on the axial tube as nearly to obliterate it. In every other instance hitherto examined the tentacles of the hydranth are destitute of a cavity and their axis is occupied by a solid core of endoderm. In the great majority of cases this endodermal core is composed of a very remarkable tissue, which consists of large, cylindrical, or disc-shaped cells, which are arranged one over the other in a continuous series like coins in a rouleau. These cells have a distinct membrane and clear contents, with a central nucleus which is embedded in protoplasm, and frequently suspended by protoplasmic filaments to the walls. Kölliker assigns to this structure a place among the connective tissues, and Haeckel, under the name of "chordal tissue," compares it, as it occurs in the tentacles of certain Medusæ, to the tissue of the vertebrate notochord, to which it bears a strong resemblance.

In *Tubularia* and in *Corymorpha* the tentacles are disposed in two circlets, and the axial cells of the tentacles belonging to the proximal circlet become longitudinally divided, so that the axis presents the form of a tissue in which the cells have become multiplied laterally, and which is consequently no longer in the form of regularly superimposed discs. The tentacles of the distal circlet, however, in both these genera possess the ordinary rouleau-like axis.

It would seem that the solid axial tissue of the tentacles is in every instance separated by the mesosarc, not only from the ectodermal layer of the tentacle, but by a duplicature of the mesosarc from the endoderm which lines the body-cavity of the hydranth, as was first pointed out by von Koch[1] in *Tubularia*, where the axial

[1] G. v. Koch, loc. cit.

tissue acquires increased development at the base of the tentacles, and thus forms a circular ridge which, pushing before it the mesosarc and gastral endoderm, projects into the gastral cavity of the hydranth.

Though the axial tissue of the tentacles is thus separated by a layer of mesosarc from the endoderm which lines the gastral cavity, there is no reason why it should not be regarded as a special modification of the general endoderm of the body, and to speak of it, as Jickeli does, under the name of " mesoderm," as a third body layer appears to me to convey an erroneous view of its fundamental nature.

This obliteration of the tentacular cavity, though almost universal in the hydranth, is far from being so in the marginal tentacles of the Medusa. Here, though in many cases (Trachomedusæ and Narcomedusæ, Haeckel) the endoderm presents the rouleau-like condition, with obliteration of the lumen, in many others (Anthomedusæ and Lepto-medusæ, Haeckel) the axis continues pervious, and the endoderm forms a simple lining of the cavity with usually more homogeneous cell contents, but otherwise differing but little from that found in other parts of the body walls.

Though the existence of muscular filaments in the ectoderm of the Hydroida has long been known, it is comparatively lately that evidence has been adduced of their presence in connection with the endoderm. Weismann was the first to point out the existence of these endodermal fibrillæ which he found to occur in *Eudendrium*,[1] while the same have been found by Hamann[2] and by Jickeli[3] in other Hydroids. The fibrillæ of which this musculature consists always run in a circular or transverse direction, thus contrasting with the fibrillæ of the ectoderm which, at least in the trophosome, are always longitudinal. It is in the hypostome that they are most strongly developed, and here only do they occur, according to Hamann, in the Calyptoblastea, while in the Gymno-blastic genera they are found also in the walls of the gastric portion of the hydranth. They have not been detected in the coenosarc. They would seem to be formed as outrunners from certain cells of the endoderm in a way similar to the formation of the longitudinal muscular fibrillæ in the ectoderm, where, as we shall presently see, the fibrillæ form outrunners from the most superficial cells of this layer.

2. *The Ectoderm.*

The ectoderm, like the endoderm, with which it is exactly co-extensive, and from which it is separated by the mesosarc, is also composed of nucleated cells. These cells are sometimes disposed in a single layer as in the ordinary condition of the endodermal cells, sometimes in several, while very frequently the cell-boundaries

---

[1] Weismann, Ueber eigenthümliche Organe, bei Eudendrium, *Mittheil. aus der Zool. Stat. zu Neapel*, Bd. iii.

[2] Hamann, *loc. cit.*

[3] Carl F. Jickeli, Der Bau der Hydroidpolypen, *Morphol. Jahrb.*, Bd. viii.

become obliterated, so that an obvious cellular structure becomes obscured, or entirely effaced.

The muscular fibrillæ of the ectoderm are in most cases well developed. Where they exist in the trophosome they always run longitudinally, and form a continuous fibrillated layer in contact with the external surface of the mesosarc. This ectodermal musculature is well developed in the body and tentacles of the hydranth. In those genera in which the body of the hydranth is much elongated so as to assume the form of a naked stem (Hydractinia, Clava, Clavatella, Gemmelaria, Myriothela), this part of the animal manifests a high degree of contractility, and the fibrillated tissue is here always especially well developed. In the cœnosarc of Tubularia in which this part is closely invested by the perisarc no fibrillæ can be detected, while in the allied genus Corymorpha, whose stem is not as in Tubularia enclosed in a thick perisareal tube, the fibrillated tissue may be traced through the whole length of the stem. It is worthy of remark that though no fibrillæ can be detected in the cœnosarc of the adult Tubularia these are present on the whole body of the Actinula or larval stage of this genus. The fibrillated tissue, however, is not necessarily absent from such cœnosarcs as are enclosed in a firm perisarc. In Plumularia echinulata of Weismann this observer has detected and described the fibrillæ of the cœnosarc.

The tentacles of the hydranth in the various genera have an especially well developed system of ectodermal fibrillæ. In the tentacles of Tubularia indivisa the fibrillæ of the ectoderm may be seen to be true muscle-cells, being greatly elongated fusiform cells, each with a nucleolated nucleus.[1] A similar structure has been shown by Weismann[2] in the fibrillated tissue of the cœnosarc of Plumularia. In Myriothela, however, the fibrillæ would appear to be on a higher grade of development, for here they do not present the condition of nucleated fusiform cells. In this remarkable genus the fibrillæ have a uniform thickness throughout, showing no tendency to thin away into the terminal points of fusiform cells, and are without any visible nucleus.[3]

The ectodermal fibrillæ in the body of Hydra were examined by Kleinenberg[4] and shown by him to be in direct continuation with certain tail-like processes which are given off from the deep side of the most superficial cells of the ectoderm in this genus. Kleinenberg, believing that in this relation we have a low stage of development of a combined muscular and nervous system, designates the whole cell with its caudate process and fibrilliform continuation by the name of "neuro-muscle-cell." This capital discovery of the caudate processes of the ectoderm cells in Hydra, and their connection with the muscular fibrillæ, has been amply confirmed by subsequent observers and extended to many genera besides Hydra, so that it must now be accepted as representing

[1] Gymnoblastic Hydroids, p. 206, pl. xxiii. fig. 6.
[2] August Weismann, Die Entstehung der Sexualzellen bei den Hydromedusen, Jena, 1883.
[3] Allman, On the structure and development of Myriothela, Phil. Trans., vol. clxv. part ii.
[4] Nicolaus Kleinenberg, Hydra, eine anatomisch-entwickelungsgeschichtliche Untersuchung, Leipzig, 1872.

the general structure of the ectoderm in the Hydroida. If, however, Jickeli be correct in assigning a nervous function to certain cells which he finds generally distributed in the ectoderm of the Hydroida, and which he regards as ganglion cells (see below, p. xvii), then the physiological significance which Kleinenberg attributes to his neuro-muscle-cells must be somewhat modified.

While in the Hydroid trophosome the muscular fibrillæ of the ectoderm are thus always longitudinal it is different with the Medusæ. Here a circular musculature is largely and characteristically developed in the ectoderm of the sub-umbrella or concave side of the walls of the bell-cavity, while the velum is itself mainly an offset of the ectoderm in which circularly directed fibrillæ constitute the chief part of its substance. While the muscular fibrillæ of the trophosome, whether in the ectoderm or in the endoderm, show no trace of striæ, the fibrillæ which run in a circular direction in the umbrella of the Medusa are transversely striated.

The ectoderm in most Hydroids is separated from the surrounding perisarcal tube by a wider or narrower space. Across this space, whether it be in the stems or in the gonangia, numerous narrow processes are sent off from the outer surface of the ectoderm to become attached by their ends to the inner surface of the perisarc. In these processes no distinct cell boundaries can be detected, and the same is very frequently the case in the ectoderm from which they proceed. In the living animal a most interesting proto-plasmic movement may be seen in them, the processes constantly changing their form, frequently throwing out branches like the pseudopodia of certain Rhizopods, and ex-tending and withdrawing themselves across the intervening space. When they reach the perisarc their ends flatten themselves out on it and emit radiating filaments of proto-plasm. From these flattened ends the rest of the process frequently breaks away, leaving the extremity with radiating protoplasmic filaments attached to the walls where they have exactly the appearance of typical stellate cells (Pl. XXV. figs. 1a, 2b).

Among the Hydroids of the present Report are species (Pls. XXVII. fig. 1a; Pl. XXXIII. fig. 2a) in which similar ectoderm bands are seen stretching from the body of the hydranth to the walls of the hydrotheca, a condition which I have also observed in some British Sertularians. In the Challenger species in which these bands occur the hydranth would seem to be incapable of complete retraction.

Reichert[1] was the first to call attention to the emission of pseudopodia-like filaments by the ectoderm, and was led by it into the erroneous belief that the Hydroid cœnosarc consists of an undifferentiated protoplasm,—a view which, not obtaining the acceptance of any zoologist who had studied the structure of these animals, resulted in his very interesting and significant observation of protoplasmic movements in the cœnosarcal processes remaining long unrecognised.

Hamann[2] has shown that a similar emission of pseudopodial filaments takes place

[1] Carl B. Reichert, Über die contractile Substanz und ihre Bewegungs-Erscheinungen, Berlin, 1867.
[2] O. Hamann, loc. cit.

in the ectoderm of the foot-disc of *Hydra*. The remarkable development of pseudo-podia by the sarcostyles will be described below when considering the structure of those bodies.

Thread-cells.—Of all the elements of the ectoderm the thread-cells or urticating capsules are the most characteristic. These bodies, however, are by no means confined to the Hydroida, but occur under various forms as a distinguishing and universally present feature in the whole of the Cœlenterata with the exception of the sponges—taking for granted that these have their true place in the Cœlenterate subkingdom.

The thread-cell varies both in form and in size in different species of Hydroids, and even in different parts of the same Hydroid, but it may be described as essentially consisting of a containing capsule and a contained filament which under certain conditions admits of being projected from the capsule.

The thread-cell however possesses a really complicated structure, the exact determination of which is exceedingly difficult, but from what has been satisfactorily established by the most careful observations, it may be regarded as certain that the thread-cell in its typical form, such as is seen in the larger thread-cells which occur in the body of *Hydra* or in the spherical capitula which terminate the tentacles of *Coryne*, consists essentially of an oviform rigid capsule lined by a fine membrane, which at one end of the long diameter of the capsule is invaginated into its cavity in the form of a tube occupying the axis, and there becoming continuous with a very fine and long tubular filament which lies in a congeries of coils within the capsule. The whole is included in an external cell, the *cnidocyst*, within which it has been developed, while the cnidocyst itself sends off from a point close to its summit or discharging pole a minute bristle-like process of its protoplasm, the *cnidocil*, which projects beyond the surface of the ecto-derm into the surrounding water.

This is the condition of the typical thread-cell in its quiescent state, but under the influence of certain stimuli, not yet well understood, and which are probably exerted through the medium of the cnidocil, its characteristic action is brought into play, and a remarkable change takes place in it. The tube, which in the quiescent state lay in the axis of the capsule, is now suddenly projected through the discharging pole, and this act is immediately followed by a similar projection of the fine tubular filament with which at its free end the axile tube is continuous, and the capsule is thus emptied of its contents. The whole of this process consists in an act of evagination by which the wider axile tube and the fine tubular filament into which this is continued are transferred from the inside to the outside of the capsule.

When this sudden act of evagination has been completed it is seen that the portion of the tube which in the inverted state had lain in the axis of the capsule, is provided, in the form of thread-cell here taken as the type, with a verticil of barb-like spines attached to what has now become the outer surface of its walls. It continues to be attached by one end to the summit of the capsule, and thence tapers away to a point where it is continued into the fine filament which is now seen to have uncoiled and extended itself, often to a great length, over the field of the microscope.

F. E. Schulze[1] called attention to the occurrence of a fine process which in *Syncoryne* proceeds from the base of the cnidocyst towards the deeper parts of the ectoderm. Somewhat later[2] I described in *Myriothela* a remarkable modification of the thread-cell, which among other peculiarities is distinguished by the presence of a peduncle in the form of a long slender filament which is attached to the base of the cnidocyst, and thence extends among the cells of the ectoderm towards the deeper parts of this layer. These peduncles are manifestly of the same nature as those described by F. E. Schulze in *Syncoryne*. They may be designated by the name of *cnidopods*.

Similar filaments have since been described by Grobben,[3] Ciamician,[4] and especially by Hamann,[5] who finds them in every Hydroid he has examined, and in all thread-cells, both large and small. He traces them through the thickness of the ectoderm as far as the mesosarc to which he believes them to be attached, and regards them as simply performing the part of mechanical supports of the thread-cells. He finds quite the same condition in the thread-cells of the tentacles of all craspedote Medusae, and in the Siphonophora; also in *Actiniae*, where these filaments had been already described by O. and R. Hertwig.[6]

The cnidopods have also been described by Jickeli,[7] who has subjected them to a careful study in several Hydroids. He regards them as muscular, describes in them a tendency to fibrillation, and believes that he has seen them in various states of extension and contraction. This view of the muscular nature of the cnidopods receives support from an observation by Claus,[8] who in a Medusa, *Charybdea marsupialis*, describes thread-cells from which muscular fibrillae are sent off, and is further supported by an observation which we owe to Chun,[9] who has seen in the Siphonophora thread-cells which are clothed by a plexus of very fine muscular fibrillae which become united below into a stalk. Notwithstanding these facts, however, it does not seem that evidence has yet been adduced which would justify us in accepting as proved the muscular nature of the cnidopods.

As already mentioned, Kleinenberg describes in *Hydra* cells which lie superficially in the ectoderm, and send off from their deep surface tail-like prolongations which become

[1] F. E. Schulze, Ueber den Bau von Syncoryne Sarsii, 1873.
[2] On the Structure and Development of Myriothela, *Phil. Trans.*, vol. clxv.
[3] C. Grobben, Über Polocoryne carnea, *Sitzungsb. d. k. Akad. d. Wiss. Wien*, 1875.
[4] J. Ciamician, Über den feineren Bau und die Entwicklung von Tubularia, *Zeitschr. f. wiss. Zool.*, Bd. xxxii.
[5] O. Hamann, *loc. cit.*
[6] O. und R. Hertwig, Die Actinien, 1879.
[7] Carl F. Jickeli, *loc. cit.*
[8] C. Claus, Untersuchungen über Charybdea marsupialis, *Arb. Zool. Inst. Wien*, Bd. i.
[9] C. Chun, Die Natur und Wirkungsweise der Nesselzellen bei Coelenteraten, *Zool. Anzeiger*, No. 29.[*]

continuous with the longitudinal muscular fibrillæ. Lying between the caudal prolongations of these superficial cells, are other cells destitute of prolongations, and forming a tissue to which Kleinenberg gives the name of interstitial tissue.[1] It is among these interstitial cells of *Hydra*, and among cells which, by their deep position in the ectoderm and freedom from connection with the muscular fibrillæ, correspond to them in other genera, that we find the cnidocysts or cells within which the thread-cells are formed.

The thread-cells are developed out of the protoplasm of the cnidocysts in a way not yet determined, and without the direct participation of the nucleus of the cnidocyst, which after the development of the thread-cell still continues visible in it. Jickeli, from some observations which he has made on the thread-cells of *Hydra*, concludes that the axial tube is at first present as an external extension of the walls of the capsule, and that it subsequently becomes internal by invagination.[2]

Since the thread-cells in order that they may exert their proper function must be among the most superficial cells of the ectoderm, a migration from the deeper to the more superficial parts of this tissue-layer becomes necessary. It will be afterwards shown that the faculty possessed by certain cells, both of the ectoderm and endoderm, of wandering from one part of the Hydroid body to another, is now a well-established fact. No light has yet been thrown on the mode of formation of the cnidopods or filiform processes which are sent off from the bases of the cnidocysts.

That the thread-cells serve as weapons of defence and offence is now generally admitted. Their whole structure, and the phenomena which they present when called into action, are all in favour of the view which would assign to them such an office in the economy of the animal. Their benumbing and even fatal action on the animals with whose surface they come in contact has been too often noticed to allow of any doubt on this point. Semper[3] has described a gigantic Plumularian, a native of the East Indian Archipelago, which attains nearly the height of a man, and which on account of its formidable stinging properties is held in dread by bathers. Kirchenpauer has identified Semper's Plumularian with an *Aglaophenia* to which he assigns the specific name of *philippina*, probably identical with *Aglaophenia macgillivrayi*, examples of which have been obtained by the Challenger, and have been described in the first part of the present Report (Plumularidæ, p. 34, pl. x.). That the stinging property which can thus make itself so severely felt even by the human subject must here reside in the thread-cells will scarcely admit of doubt. Indeed there is no other part of the Hydroid to which it can with any reason be attributed.

The thread-cells of the Hydroida, though almost exclusively confined to the ectoderm, are by no means uniformly distributed in it. They are as a rule most

[1] N. Kleinenberg, *loc. cit.*
[2] Carl F. Jickeli, *loc. cit.*
[3] C. Semper, Reisebericht, *Zeitschr. f. wiss. Zool.*, Bd. xiii.

abundant in the tentacles of both hydranth and Medusa. In such tentacles as possess a terminal enlargement or capitulum (*Coryne*, *Syncoryne*, &c.) they are especially accumulated in this enlargement. In the marginal tentacles of many Hydromedusæ, they form condensed verticillate groups regularly distributed from distance to distance along the length of the tentacle, to which they give a moniliform character. In such cases the tentacle usually terminates in a spherical enlargement which is loaded with thread-cells.

In certain other Medusæ, which are also derived from hydroid trophosomes, we meet with special arrangements of the thread-cells. Thus in the Medusa of *Gemmaria implexa*[1] we find four superficial pyriform chambers extending from the umbrella margin in the outer ectodermal wall of the umbrella, and filled with thread-cells which doubtless originate in the walls of these ectodermal chambers, and thence apparently fall into their cavities. The marginal tentacles of this Medusa give rise along their entire length to filaments endowed with great powers of extension and retraction, each carrying on its summit an oval ciliated sac filled with thread-cells. In the Medusa of *Podocoryne carnea* each of the four lobes into which the mouth of the manubrium is here divided carries a pencil of non-contractile filaments, each of which bears on its extremity a solitary capsule resembling a cnidocyst, with its cnidocil and contained thread-cell. We can scarcely avoid a comparison of these naked pedunculated cnidocyst-like bodies with the cnidocysts as they elsewhere occur embedded in the ectoderm with their basal filiform prolongations.

In *Sertularia exserta* (Pl. XXVII. fig. 1*a*), one of the new forms obtained by the Challenger, small thread-cells are accumulated in a little cushion-like prominence at the base of every tentacle (figs. 1*b*, 1*c*). In this species the hydranth presents the very exceptional character of remaining in a state of habitual extension beyond the protective covering of the hydrotheca, and the batteries of thread-cells thus disposed would seem to have as their object a compensation for the loss of the protection which in most other Calyptoblastic Hydroids is afforded by the hydrotheca.

In certain Hydromedusæ (Trachomedusæ and Narcomedusæ, see below, p. xxix) thread-cells are accumulated on the umbrella margin which they surround in the form of an urticating ring, while in most of these Medusæ accumulations of thread-cells forming narrow urticating patches stretch from the umbrella margin in a meridional direction to the roots of the tentacles, which here spring from the dorsal surface of the umbrella at some distance from the margin.

Ganglion Cells.—Quite recently Jickeli has called attention to certain ectodermal cells which he has found widely distributed in the trophosome of many Hydroids, where they lie scattered between the deeper ends of the other ectodermal cells.[2] He describes

---

[1] Gymnoblastic Hydroids, p. 291, pl. vii.
[2] Carl F. Jickeli, *Morphol. Jahrb.*, Bd. viii.

them under the name of ganglion cells, and regards them as representing a differentiated nervous system. As seen in the tentacles of *Eudendrium ramosum*, they appear as well-defined nucleated masses of protoplasm, which send off outrunning tapering processes, usually three in number, and which under treatment with osmic acid appear thickly filled with black granules. Many of the outrunners, which the ganglion cells send off in the tentacles, unite with one another so as to form a plexus, while others lose themselves between the muscle fibrillæ, but no indubitable connection between nerve fibre and muscles has been found. Others again run to the thread-cells, and probably end close upon the cnidocil.

In other parts of the hydranth the form of these cells is less definite, and here they usually become accumulated in small heaps which lie between the ectoderm and mesosarc, and from which at most a single process is sent off to run between the ectoderm cells. Jickeli has sometimes seen a filament running between the ectoderm cells to a very minute cell with dark granular protoplasm and small elongated nucleus. He regards this as a "sense cell." Besides this mode of peripheral termination he believes that he has also seen one in the form of free nerve endings.

The ganglion cells also occur in great profusion in the cœnosarc. Nothing, however, has anywhere been seen in any Hydroid trophosome which could with any probability be regarded as a specially differentiated nervous centre.

Gland-Cells.—In some places certain cells of the ectoderm appear to act as gland-cells. Such cells have been described by Weismann in some species of *Eudendrium*, where they form a complete ring round the base of the hydranth. They consist of a firm protoplasm which readily takes up colouring matter.

In *Tubularia larynx* and some other species of *Tubularia* a bowl-shaped accumulation of cells, which forms a projecting collar, crowns the stem immediately below the hydranth like the capital of a pillar.[1] The cells composing this collar may also be regarded as gland-cells. A glandular function may also be attributed to peculiar elongated cells with a radial disposition which form the aboral extremity of the Actinula or free larva of *Tubularia* and of *Myriothela*. There can be little doubt that these cells are destined to give origin to an excretion by which the Actinula becomes fixed at the close of its free locomotive existence. Cells of a similar nature would seem to be present in the aboral extremity of *Hydra*.

Sarcostyles.—In connection with the ectoderm, perhaps more appropriately than elsewhere, may be described certain very remarkable zooids which are found throughout the whole of the Plumularinæ, where they occur in the form of minute fleshy outgrowths which are contained in cup-shaped or tubular appendages of the stem, and are in direct communication with the cœnosarc.

To these bodies special attention was called by Busk, who described them under the

[1] Gymnoblastic Hydroids, p. 407, pl. xxi. fig. 5.

name of "nematophores" and insisted with justice on the differences presented by them
as affording characters of primary importance in the systematic distribution of the
Plumularinæ. Since then, however, our knowledge of these zooids has been greatly
extended, and we now know that the character which the term nematophore was intended
to express is one to which they can lay no special claim. I shall, therefore, not only
on this account, but more especially because the term nematophore involves two con-
ceptions which ought to be kept separate, namely that of the fleshy outgrowth and that
of the receptacle in which this is contained, adopt here the terminology proposed by
Hincks, and use the term *sarcostyle* for the fleshy offset from the cœnosarc, and that
of *sarcotheca* for the chitinous receptacle by which this is protected.

The sarcothecæ occur in the Plumularinæ under two principal forms; (1) in that of
fixed cups or tubes which are adnate by the greater part of their sides or by a broad
base to the stem of the Hydroid; and (2) in that of cups which have no adhesion to
the stem except at the very narrow point of origin, on which they are movable. Both
kinds are very constant in their form and position. Under the name of nematophore
they are specially described in the introductory remarks on the Plumularinæ of this
Report.[1]

The contents of the sarcothecæ are very remarkable. Many years ago I drew
attention to the fact that the bodies contained within the sarcothecæ had the faculty of
emitting pseudopodia-like processes, which often extend to a great distance, running
out free into the surrounding water or running straight along the stem or winding
around it, frequently sending off branches which may become fused, one into the other,
and again become separate, while once more the whole might be seen to have withdrawn
itself into the interior of the sarcotheca. The phenomena thus presented so exactly
resemble the emission of pseudopodia by certain Rhizopods that I came to the conclusion that the contents of the sarcothecæ consist chiefly of free protoplasm as in the
body of an *Amœba*, though often with true thread-cells immersed in it.

Subsequent researches have, however, tended to modify this view, and the employ-
ment of the method of staining has led to the belief that the sarcostyles are of a more
complex structure than I had originally supposed. By the use of this method Weismann
believes that he has made it evident that the sarcostyles are composed of cells ; further,
that they are not a mere ectodermal outgrowth, but that besides having an external
ectodermal layer they contain a solid filiform axial process from the endoderm, surrounded
by a closed sac-like extension of the mesosarc.[2]

Since I became acquainted with these views I have had no opportunity of subjecting
to fresh observation the conclusions to which I had been originally led, but any opinion

---

[1] *Kirchenpaueria* is the name of a genus which has been recently defined by Jickeli from some fragments of a
Plumularian trophosome, in which certain sarcostyles are developed without being enclosed in sarcothecæ. The
naked sarcostyles are here protruded through simple orifices in the periarc of the stem (Jickeli, *loc. cit.*, p. 645).

[2] Weismann, Die Entstehung, &c., p. 176, pl. vii. fig. 7.

expressed by so excellent an observer as Weismann must command attention. Whether, however, the protrusible portion of the sarcostyle consists of a simple mass of protoplasm, or shows a differentiation into separate masses in the form of cells, is of little morphological or physiological importance, for such masses must be as destitute of a boundary membrane as the single protoplasmic mass in order to allow of their being the source of the pseudopodial extensions by which the sarcostyle is characterised.

While the views of Weismann have been in most points confirmed by the observations of Jickeli, a view somewhat different is taken by Mereschkowsky,[1] who believes that the sarcotheca contains an extension of the ectoderm, the cells of which do not lie close on one another, but leave between them spaces which are filled by a free protoplasm ; and such a structure would be quite in accordance with the phenomena observed in the living animal.

We have, however, already seen that the ectoderm, in the modified condition which it often presents in the coenosarc, may show an entire obliteration of cell boundaries and may throw out processes having many of the characters of true pseudopodia, and it needs but a further modification of this layer, consisting in a still lower grade of degradation towards the condition of undifferentiated protoplasm, in order that it may possess the faculty of emitting pseudopodia to the extraordinary extent which we meet with in the sarcostyles of the Plumularinæ ; so that even though all the three body layers be present in the sarcostyles, we shall have in these appendages a portion which can scarcely be distinguished from undifferentiated protoplasm. If this portion be not free protoplasm it must be sought for in the ectoderm, for unless we are prepared to admit not only of an amœboid condition of the endoderm but of such a soft gelatinous consistence in the mesosarc as will allow of an indefinite extensibility in this membrane, we cannot believe that the endoderm and the mesosarc follow the pseudopodial outrunners of the sarcostyle.

Bodies in all essential points comparable with the sarcostyles of the Plumularinæ occur also in other Hydroids, and some very remarkable examples of these will be found in species first made known by the explorations of the Challenger. In *Perisiphonia*, one of the new genera of the Challenger collection, the peripheral tubes by which the axial hydrotheca-bearing tube is surrounded carry upon their outer sides multitudes of minute tubular cups whose finely granular contents admit of being protruded, as in the Plumularian sarcostyles, into the surrounding water (Pl. XXI. figs. 2a, 2b; Pl. XXII. fig. 2a) ; while in the singular and beautiful genus, *Diplocyathus*, a form nearly allied to *Halecium*, and also one of the discoveries of the Challenger, every hydrotheca is accompanied at its base by a similar tubular cup with protrusible contents (Pl. VIII. figs. 2, 3).

Whatever be the nature of the sarcostyles we must regard these bodies as true

[1] Mereschkowsky, Structure et Développement des Nematophores chez les Hydroides, *Arch. de Zool. Expér.*, t. x. p. 583.

zooïds, "individuals" or "personæ," having devolving on them as their rôle in the physiological division of labour among the various zooïds some special office which is probably that of aiding the hydranths, by their amœboid prehension of solid matter, in the general nutrition of the colony.

The Ectoderm of Myriothela.—The curious Gymnoblastic genus *Myriothela* has been already more than once referred to as possessing exceptional points of structure. The ectoderm especially presents so many points of interest and significance that no exposition of Hydroid structure would be complete without some special account of it.[1]

The ectoderm of *Myriothela phrygia*, the only known representative of the genus, is composed of two distinct strata—a superficial and a deep. The superficial stratum consists of small round cells, several in depth. These are formed of membraneless protoplasm, and contain throughout the greater part of the body abundance of yellowish corpuscles, while on the summits of the tentacles and in irregular patches on other parts of the body the superficial cells contain granules of a dark brownish-purple colour. In this layer large and small thread-cells may be seen enclosed in their generating cells or cnidocysts, for the most part lying near the surface.

The deep layer of the ectoderm is formed by a very remarkable tissue to which I have elsewhere given the name of "claviform tissue."[2] This is composed of cells consisting of a yellowish granular protoplasm, entirely destitute of membrane, and each drawn out into a long caudal process. An obvious nucleus may frequently be seen in them. By the union of their caudal processes branched groups of claviform cells are produced, and the common stalk of each group runs to the hyaline mesosarc, where it loses itself among the fibrillæ, which here form a well-marked muscle layer. The whole forms a soft, pulpy, and somewhat glandular-looking tissue easily broken down under the compressorium.

If we except the condition of the long transitory arms of the Actinula or free locomotive stage of *Myriothela*, the claviform tissue does not come to the surface of the body. Throughout the whole of the body of the adult it forms a deep zone intervening between the hyaline mesosarc and the superficial layer of the ectoderm.

In *Myriothela* the ectodermal musculature is well developed. It forms a well-marked layer of longitudinal fibrillæ closely applied to the outer side of the mesosarc, from which, after a short maceration in water, it may be separated as a continuous plate composed of fibrillæ which adhere to one another by their sides, forming a stratum of a single fibril in thickness. The fibrillæ are about $\frac{1}{12000}$ of an inch in diameter, soft and compressible, with a very finely granular structure, but otherwise apparently homogeneous. They show no striation, no nucleus can be detected in them, and they admit of being traced to a considerable distance without showing any tendency to taper away in the manner of true muscle cells.

---

[1] For a detailed account of the structure of *Myriothela*, see *Phil. Trans.*, vol. clav. pt. ii.
[2] Structure and development of Myriothela, p. 553, pl. lvi. fig. 6, &c.

It has just been said that the caudal prolongations of the clavate tissue may be traced into the fibrillated layer, but I have not succeeded in satisfying myself that the fibrillæ are directly continuous with these prolongations, as Kleinenberg has shown to be the case with the ectodermal fibrillæ of *Hydra*, in their relations to the caudate ecto-dermal cells of this genus, which, notwithstanding their superficial position, admit of an obvious comparison with the clavate tissue of *Myriothela*.

The general structure of the ectoderm of *Myriothela* is that now described. In the globular capitula, however, which terminate the tentacles, we have a most singular modi-fication of those structures which lie external to the hyaline mesosarc. Here the place of the caudate cells is taken by a remarkable tissue, composed of closely appressed transparent prisms, or, to speak more exactly, of greatly elongated pyramids, which are attached by their apical ends to the mesosarc of the capitulum, and thence radiating outwards, terminate at some distance within the outer boundary of the capitulum in a convex surface, which slightly exceeds that of a hemisphere in extent. The whole body thus formed by this columnar tissue caps the hyaline mesosarc and subjacent endoderm of the summit of the tentacle.

Radiating from its convex surface, a multitude of cnidopods may be seen. These make their way among the cells of the ectoderm, and terminate distally at a short distance within the surface of the capitulum, where each carries on its summit a peculiarly modified large thread-cell with its enclosing cnidocyst. The cnidocyst carries close to its distal end a well-developed cnidocil, and is completely filled by the firm refringent capsule, within which may be seen a transparent cylindrical chord wound in two or three coils. The capsule is easily liberated from its enveloping sac, and under slight pressure the contained chord may sometimes be ejected through its distal end. The whole assemblage of sacs, with their in-cluded capsules, forms a zone parallel to the surface of the capitulum and a little within it.

Notwithstanding the indubitable relationship of the bodies just described to ordinary thread-cells, they differ from these in some important points which would lead us to believe that some function has been assigned to them, which is not that of the defensive or offensive office of the thread-cell.

The difference between them and the thread-cells, as usually seen in the Hydroida, is sufficiently obvious. The included chord does not, like the filament of an ordinary thread-cell, consist of a wider portion continuous with a narrower one, which during ejection becomes evaginated through the wider, but on the contrary possesses a uniform diameter considerably greater than that of the filaments of the typical thread-cell, and instead of presenting, as in the latter, a vast multitude of coils rolled together into a regular spiral or into a complicated mass it has only two or three such coils. Further, when ejected from the capsule—while it still holds on by one end to the point of exit—it does not, like the filament of an ordinary thread-cell, straighten itself, and shoot across the field of the microscope, but immediately on becoming free coils itself again into a

spiral, while it is entirely destitute of the barbs or spines which constitute so characteristic a feature in the typical thread-cell.[1]

It is scarcely possible to avoid suspecting that these capsules with their associated
structures, differing as they do from ordinary thread-cells, are destined for the perform-
ance of some sensory function.

The claviform tissue which is developed in the deeper parts of the ectoderm, and which
is as we have seen in intimate relation with the muscular layer, is obviously comparable
with the caudate cells of Kleinenberg's neuro-muscle layer, and its deep position in the
ectoderm will scarcely detract from the weight of this comparison when we bear in
mind that the necessary stimulus may be carried to it through the cells which form the
thin layer of ectoderm with which it is covered. There can be little doubt that the
rod-like tissue into which the stalks of the capsules may be traced is a special modification of this claviform tissue, while it forcibly recalls the nerve-rods in the sense organs of
higher animals. Though all the necessary connections of the parts have not yet been
demonstrated, we see enough to make us believe that it is at least probable that
the various structures here associated represent an apparatus for the reception and
transmission of impressions received from without.

Another very exceptional condition is seen in the presence of a well-marked layer of
circularly disposed muscular fibrillæ, which are developed in the ectodermal coat which
lies immediately on the generative mass in the gonophore of *Myriothela*, and by contraction of which the contents of the gonophore on attaining maturity are expelled.

3. *The Mesosarc.*

Attention was first called to the existence of this layer in the Hydroid body by
Reichert, who described it under the name of "Stützlamelle."[2] It is in its normal
condition a perfectly hyaline structureless membrane which everywhere intervenes
between the endoderm and the ectoderm, entering the tentacles along with these
layers, and forming a cul-de-sac in the summit of each. It not only separates the
peculiar chorda-like endodermal tissue of the tentacular axis from the surrounding
ectoderm, but sends off at the base of the tentacle a layer which separates the chorda-
like tissue from the proper digestive endoderm. The longitudinal muscular fibrillæ
of the ectoderm lie in close apposition with its outer surface. Its thickness may in
some places be seen to be traversed by very delicate fibrils, which run vertically to its
surfaces and form a connection between the two body layers, ectoderm and endoderm,
which it separates from one another.

In *Monocaulus imperator*, the gigantic Tubularian brought up by the Challenger

[1] Jickeli has described in *Hydra* certain small thread-cells whose filament on ejection remains coiled in a way very
similar to that here seen.

[2] Carl B. Reichert, Über die contractile Substanz und ihre Bewegungs-Erscheinungen, Berlin, 1867.

from a depth of nearly four miles in the North Pacific, the place of the mesosarc appears to be taken by a very remarkable layer, whose most striking character is its extraordinary elasticity (see p. 7). It is comparatively thick, and has a distinctly fibrous structure, the fibres running in a circular direction, and being themselves resolvable into finer fibrillæ (Pl. III. figs. 4, 6). Nothing, however, approaching to a true organisation can be detected in this layer, and we shall be probably justified in regarding not only the mesosarc as it elsewhere occurs, but this remarkable modification of it, as an excreted product of the endoderm, as the perisarc is of the ectoderm.

The clear gelatinous substance which forms the principal part of the umbrella in the Medusa must be regarded as representing the mesosarc. In the Hydromedusæ it takes the place of that portion of the mesosarc which lies on the dorsal or exumbrellar side of the radial canals and "endoderm lamella"; while on the ventral or subumbrellar side the mesosarc retains its character as a thin elastic membrane which lies just within the subumbrellar ectoderm and supports the muscular swimming plate. In such Medusæ as are developed directly from the egg, it can be seen to be deposited as an excretion between the ectoderm and the endoderm of the larva, where it holds exactly the place of the mesosarc. (See below, p. xxxvii).

4. The Perisarc.

The perisarc affords some of the most obvious diagnostic characters of the Hydroida, and being frequently the only part preserved in dead specimens becomes of much practical value in the identification of species, and even of higher groups.

Except in the case of the Hydractininæ and Hydrocorallia it is the most external of all the layers which enter into the formation of the Hydroid body. Like the mesosarc it shows no trace of organised structure; and like that membrane it must be regarded as a simple product of excretion.[1] It is, however, in almost every case much more massive than the mesosarc and often attains a very considerable thickness, showing by its laminated structure indications of its formation by successive deposits from within. As the mesosarc would seem to be an excretion from the outer surface of the endoderm, the perisarc must be regarded as an excretion from the corresponding part of the ectoderm. It shows a remarkable resistance to the action of chemical reagents, which with the exception of the strong acids are usually without any effect on it. In this character as well as in its chemical composition it would seem to be closely allied to chitin, if it be not identical with this substance which forms the principal constituent of the external skeleton of insects and other Arthropoda.

With the exception of Hydra, and possibly some doubtful forms (Nemopsis, Acaulis), there are no Hydroid trophosomes in which the perisarc is not to some extent represented,

---

[1] Jickeli believes that in some cases (Tubularia mesembryanthemum) he has found it to be formed by an induration of the ectoderm.

though in a few its formation takes place on so insignificant a scale as to render its presence liable to be overlooked. In the Hydrocorallia it is replaced by an internal hard calcareous corallum. In by far the greater number of cases it constitutes a firm protective tube by which the cœnosarc is invested, while in the great primary section of the Calyptoblastea, it is continued for a greater or less extent, and in a more or less modified form, over the various zooids of the colony. In these it forms the cup-like receptacles or hydrothecæ into which the hydranths can become retracted, as well as the peculiar receptacles—gonangia—destined for the protection of the generative buds (Pl. X. fig. 2a; Pl. XII. fig. 1a; Pl. XXIV. fig. 1a; &c.). In the Gymnoblastea, on the other hand (Pl. III.), neither of those protective extensions of the perisarc exists. In two very remarkable genera, *Syathecium* and *Thecocladium*, fine examples of which have been brought home by the Challenger, another function besides that of the protection of the hydranth would seem to devolve on certain hydrothecæ. In *Syathecium* some of the hydrothecæ situated on definite parts of the colony contain no hydranths, but on the other hand enclose, each, the peduncle of a gonangium which springs from the bottom of the hydrotheca (Pl. XXXVII. fig. 1a, &c.). In *Thecocladium*, again, every branch of the colony springs from within a hydrotheca, which thus, instead of containing a hydranth, encloses as in a sheath the proximal end of the branch (Pl. XXXVIII. fig. 3). The perisarc varies greatly in thickness, from a strong coat in which numerous layers of deposition may be seen, to a delicate, scarcely recognisable pellicle, and is invariably absent from those zooids which have detached themselves from the colony in order to lead an independent life in the open sea.

While the cœnosarc of the Hydroid colony is, as an almost universal condition, protected by an external perisarcal tube, an exception to this condition is found in *Hydractinia* and *Podocoryne* as well as in the entire section of the Hydrocorallia. In *Hydractinia* and *Podocoryne* the chitinous perisarc forms a continuous thick stratum permeated by a network of anastomosing cœnosarcal tubes, and overlaid by a naked extension of the cœnosarc. In the Hydrocorallia the calcareous corallum, which here forms the hard skeletal tissue of the colony, and is also permeated by anastomosing tubes of cœnosarc, is in a similar way overlaid by a superficial covering of cœnosarc. Indeed the relations between the *Hydrocorallia* and *Hydractinia* are in many respects of the most intimate kind.

V. The Gonosome.

The various zooids and associated structures now described are more or less directly connected with the nutrition of the colony, and may, as has already been said, be collectively designated by the name of *trophosome*. There are, however, other parts of the colony on which a different group of functions—namely, that of sexual reproduction

—specially devolves, and though, as we shall presently see, the formation of the sexual
elements is far from being in all cases dissociated from the trophosome, we may conveniently designate collectively all those parts which have special charge of the protection
and development of these elements, as the *gonosome*.[1]

1. *The Gonophore.*

The most important zooid of the gonosome is the gonophore, as the hydranth is that
of the trophosome. Its office is to give protection to the sexual elements—ova or
spermatozoa—and to bring these to a more or less advanced stage of maturity before
their final liberation.

Throughout the whole of the Calyptoblastic Hydroids, and in many of the Gymnoblastic, the gonophores are produced as buds from the sides of a column-like body which
springs from the cœnosarc. This body is morphologically a hydranth with its tentacles
and mouth suppressed. It is known as the *blastostyle*, and in the Calyptoblastea is
contained within a protective capsule-like chamber, which has its walls lined with
perisarc, and is known as the *gonangium*.

In the Gymnoblastea the gonophores are more usually borne as buds directly by the
cœnosarc without the intervention of a blastostyle, but whether a blastostyle be present
or not, they are in this section never protected under cover of a gonangium.

The gonophores may be divided into two main groups. In one of these, after it
attains a certain degree of maturity, the gonophore becomes detached from the colony,
leads henceforth an independent, locomotive life, and after bringing its sexual products
to maturity discharges these into the open sea. To the gonophores belonging to this
group the name of *planoblasts* (wandering buds) may be given.

In the other group the gonophores never become detached, but discharge their
sexual products while still forming part of the colony. The gonophores belonging to
this group may be distinguished by the name of *hedrioblasts* (sedentary buds).

Form and Structure of the Planoblast.—The planoblasts are all, with a single
known exception,—that presented by *Dicoryne*, in which the planoblast is a ciliated
tentacula-bearing sac [2]—velum-bearing Medusæ (Craspedotæ or Hydromedusæ).[3] In form

---

[1] The sarcostyles do not belong exclusively to either of these systems, and we have both trophosomal and gonosomal sarcostyles.

[2] Gymnoblastic Hydroids, p. 292, pl. viii.

[3] The most obvious character of all Medusæ consists in the presence of a gelatinous umbrella which acts as a swimming organ, and which carries at the centre of its lower or concave surface a more or less prominent gastral tube. The Medusæ are divided into two primary sections—the Craspedotæ (velum-bearing) or Hydromedusæ, and the Acraspedæ (without a velum) or Scyphomedusæ. The Craspedotæ, among which alone we find those Medusæ which admit of being traced in the course of their development to a Hydroid trophosome, differ fundamentally from the Acraspedæ. The most important points of difference by which the Craspedotæ are separated from the Acraspedæ are the following:—1. The possession by the Craspedotæ of a true velum which does not exist in the Acraspedæ. 2. The absence in the Craspedotæ of "gastral filaments" which are always present in the Acraspedæ where they spring from

they are bell-shaped, the walls of the bell or *umbrella* being mainly composed of a transparent substance of gelatinous consistence. From the summit of the bell-cavity hangs a tubular body of variable length,—the *manubrium*—whose distal or free extremity carries the mouth, and on whose cavity devolves the function of digestion. From the basis of the manubrium four (sometimes more) canals pass off and run in equally distant meridian lines in the walls of the umbrella towards its margin, where they open into a circular canal which runs quite round the margin of the umbrella. The opening (*codonostome*) of the bell-cavity is partially closed by a membranous diaphragm, the *velum*, which stretches across it from the margin, and is perforated in the centre by an aperture which allows the surrounding water to enter the bell, and through which it may be again expelled from within, while hollow contractile filaments or *tentacles*, which vary much in number in the different species, hang from the umbrella margin.

The umbrella is eminently contractile, and acts by alternate rhythmical dilatations and contractions (diastole and systole) of its cavity as a powerful organ of locomotion by which the planoblast is propelled through the surrounding water.

The external or convex, and the internal or concave, surfaces of the umbrella are clothed with a cellular epithelium—the representative of the ectoderm. Between these lies the thick elastic gelatinous substance traversed in meridional lines by the radiating canals, and in a circular direction by the marginal or circular canal. Both sets of canals have their walls lined with endoderm.

The researches of the Hertwigs[1] have shown that a thin lamina of endoderm exists in the intervals of the radiating canals, and connects these canals laterally with one another. This "endoderm lamella" represents the obliterated portion of the lumen which existed between the two layers of the double walls of an endodermal cup which was present in the early stages of the developing bud, while the radiating canals represent those portions of the lumen which have continued pervious (see below, p. xxxi).

The great contractility of the umbrella is due to a continuous muscular sheet which lies just under its concave or "subumbrellar" surface. The fibres of this muscular layer are transversely striated and seem to be derived from the epithelial cells. They take a circular course parallel to the umbrella margin. In some cases fascicles of meridionally disposed fibres are also present. A strong muscular layer also exists in the velum, where

the internal surface of the stomach-walls. 3. The absence in the Craspedote of true marginal lobes, into which the margin of the umbrella is divided in the Acraspeda. 4. The fact of the sexual receptacles (genitalia) of the Craspedote discharging their contents externally into the surrounding water instead of internally into the cavity of the gastro-vascular system as in the Acraspeda. 5. The possession by the Craspedote of a double marginal nerve-ring representing a centralised nervous system, while in the Acraspeda where a nerve-ring has been demonstrated this is never double. 6. The fact of the polyp-form which shows itself in the course of the development of a Craspedote Medusa being a Hydropolyp destitute of gastral longitudinal ridges ("tæniola" in the strict sense of the word), while in the Acraspedæ it is a Scyphopolyp or polyp-form with gastral tæniola. 7. The fact of the Craspedote Medusa being formed by lateral budding from its Hydroid trophosome, while the Acraspedote Medusa is formed by terminal budding from its Scyphopolyp.

[1] O. und R. Hertwig, Das Nervensystem und die Sinnesorgane der Medusen, Leipzig, 1878.

it forms the principal thickness of this membrane. Its fibres take a circular course, parallel to the margin of the umbrella.

The manubrium presents the ordinary typical structure of the Hydroid body, its walls being composed of the two cell-layers, ectoderm and endoderm, with an intervening structureless membrane, the mesosarc ; on the ectodermal side of the mesosarc lies a layer of longitudinal muscle fibres.

The nervous system attains in the planoblast a stage of development more highly advanced than that presented by this system in the trophosome. In the planoblast it consists in its principal portion of two chords which run round the margin of the umbrella, one on the upper, and the other on the lower, side of the line of insertion of the velum. They are composed of fibres and ganglion cells, and are overlaid by a sense-epithelium whose cells carry sense-hairs. The organs of sense are situated on the margin of the umbrella and are chiefly of two kinds; of these one consists mainly of accumulations of pigment cells. These are placed each at the base of a marginal tentacle, and are entirely confined to the ectoderm. They occasionally enclose a clear refringent spherule. To this form of sense organ the name of *ocellus* has been given. The other consists of transparent vesicles, within which are one or more cells with calcareous concretions or " otolites." They also enclose so-called " auditory cells," whose hairs surround the otolite cells. They are seated in variable number immediately over the marginal nerve-ring, and on the portions of the margin which lie between the bases of the tentacles.[1] They are known as *otocysts*. The otocysts like the ocelli are entirely ectodermal, and must be regarded as a special differentiation of the epithelium which covers the nerve-ring.

The generative elements are developed either in the walls of the manubrium or along the course of the radiating canals. Those planoblasts in which the generative elements are found in the walls of the manubrium belong to the section Anthomedusæ and have the marginal sense organs, when differentiated, in the form of ocelli, while those in which the genitalia are borne in some part of the course of the radiating canals belong to the section Leptomedusæ, and have the sense organs in the form either of otocysts or of ocelli.[2]

[1] In *Obelia* the otocyst is in contact with the base of the tentacle, but even here it does not lie in the meridional line of this, but is placed laterally, and thus really lies in the inter-tentacular spaces of the umbrella margin. The *Obelia* planoblast is further exceptional in having its umbrella so shallow as to be almost disc-shaped, in the velum being rudimental, and in the marginal tentacles having their roots plunged into the substance of the gelatinous umbrella, being comparatively rigid, and having their axis occupied by a solid endodermal core. In the characters thus presented by the tentacles *Obelia* shows an obvious approach to the Trachomedusæ and Narcomedusæ.

[2] I adopt these names as proposed by Haeckel for the two groups indicated by them, in preference to the names, Ocellatæ (= Anthomedusæ), and Vesiculatæ (= Leptomedusæ), by which these groups have also been designated, the characters expressed by the latter names not being always applicable to the Medusæ to which they are intended to apply. Haeckel divides the Craspedotæ into two primary sections, the Leptolinæ and the Trachylinæ, the former being further divided into the Anthomedusæ and the Leptomedusæ, and the latter into the Trachomedusæ and the Narcomedusæ. The Anthomedusæ among the Leptolinæ, and the Narcomedusæ among the Trachylinæ, are distinguished by having their gonads in the walls of the manubrium ; the Leptomedusæ among the Leptolinæ, and the Trachomedusæ among the Trachylinæ, by having them in the course of the radiating canals.

In every case, with a single recorded exception, when the planoblast referable to the type of the Anthomedusæ has been traced to its trophosome, this is found to belong to the Gymnoblastic section of the Hydroida ; while in every case—also with a single recorded exception—the trophosome to which the planoblast of Leptomedusal type has been traced belongs to the Calyptoblastic section.

The exception in the former case is found in *Leptoscyphus tenuis*, a minute Campanularian Hydroid to which I believed myself justified in referring a little Medusa found free in the jar in which a specimen of *Leptoscyphus* was confined, and which, though it had not yet attained sexual maturity, was an undoubted Anthomedusa referable to the form to which Edward Forbes gave the name of *Lizzia*.[1]

The exception in the second case occurs in a Tubularian Hydroid described by Claus under the name of *Campanopsis*, the planoblasts of which are referred by him to the form known as *Octorchis*, which is a Leptomedusa bearing otocysts on the margin of the umbrella, and having its gonads or sexual pouches formed in the walls of the radiating canals.[2]

While every planoblast—with the exception of that of *Dicoryne*—is thus a true Craspedote Medusa, it is not among all groups of the Craspedotæ that planoblasts—confining this term to the free sexual buds thrown off from a polypoid trophosome—can be found. There are certain Craspedote Medusæ (Trachomedusæ and Narcomedusæ) which, though possessing like all the Craspedotæ a true Hydroid structure, have not yet been known to give rise in the course of their development to a Hydroid trophosome or polyp stage, and are probably all developed directly from the egg of the parent Medusa.[3] They are distinguished by certain well-marked characters from the other Craspedotæ (Anthomedusæ and Leptomedusæ) among which alone we find the planoblasts. The most important of these characters consists in the ectodermal otocysts of the Leptomedusæ being here replaced by peculiarly modified tentacles in the form of short club-shaped appendages which lie either free on the umbrella margin or are each enclosed (part of the Trachomedusæ) in a special vesicle formed by an ectodermal fold sent off from the epithelial covering of the marginal nerve-ring. They have a solid endodermal axis, in certain cells of which calcareous concretions (otolites) are formed, while the ectoderm carries stiff "auditory bristles." To these marginal clubs an auditory function has accordingly been attributed.

Both Trachomedusæ and Narcomedusæ are also characterised by the comparative rigidity of their marginal tentacles, which are originally always provided with a solid chorda-like axis instead of being hollow as is almost always the case with the marginal tentacles of the Anthomedusæ and Leptomedusæ. The margin of the umbrella is further distinguished by being surrounded by an urticating ring formed by an accumulation of thread-cells.

[1] Allman, *Ann. and Mag. Nat. Hist.*, May 1864. [2] Claus, *Arb. Zool. Inst. Wien*, Bd. iv.
[3] Unless the fresh-water Medusa, *Limnocodium*, should prove an exception ; see A. G. Bourne, *Proc. Roy. Soc. Lond.*, vol. xxxviii. p. 9, 1884.

In many Trachomedusæ, and in almost all Narcomedusæ, the marginal tentacles present the remarkable phenomenon of having migrated upwards on the dorsal surface of the umbrella from their original points of attachment close to the margin, so that they finally spring from a zone at some distance from the umbrella margin, with their roots plunged into the substance of the umbrella. In such cases accumulations of thread-cells form meridional urticating streaks ("umbrella clasps" or "peronia" of Haeckel) by which the bases of the tentacles continue to be connected with the marginal urticating ring.

Comparison of the Medusa with the Hydranth.—The Craspedote Medusa as seen in the planoblast, however different its form may appear from that of the Hydropolyp as seen in *Hydra* or in the hydranth of the compound trophosome, may nevertheless be easily reduced to this fundamental type form.

If we suppose the body of *Hydra* to be extended laterally in a plane immediately behind the hypostome, and on a level with the tentacular verticil, carrying between its upper and lower surfaces an extension of the body cavity, a hollow disc will be thus formed, having the tentacles springing from its margin, and with the hypostome which carries the mouth projecting from its centre. If now its upper and lower walls coalesce with one another throughout their entire extent, except along four or more radial lines running from the gastral cavity to the tentacular margin, there will result a disc traversed by radiating canals and margined by tentacles. This disc will manifestly represent the umbrella of a Medusa with its radial canals and marginal tentacles, while the hypostome will correspond to the manubrium; and it only needs the distal ends of the radiating canals to become united to one another by the formation of a circular canal, and the proximal stem-like extension of the *Hydra* with its disc of attachment to be suppressed in order to convert the polyp form in all essential points into the Medusa form. The Medusa is thus nothing but a hydranth whose body-walls are extended in the form of an umbrella with offsets from the gastral cavity, and act as an organ of natation.

Form and Structure of the Hedrioblast.—The hedrioblasts or gonophores, which never become detached from the trophosome as free-swimming zooids, are in the form of fixed sac-like buds. Of these two types must be distinguished. In one the medusoid conformation, however degraded, is yet sufficiently expressed to admit of its being recognised, the essential parts of the umbrella, including the endoderm lamella or "vascular lamella," being always present even though no gastrovascular canals may have been formed in it. In the other neither endoderm lamella nor gastrovascular canals have been formed, and the umbrella is represented solely by its outer ectodermal layer, which here lies directly on the spadix or endodermal *cul de sac* which forms the hollow axis of the gonophore. The first of these varieties of the hedrioblast is known as the *medusoid*, the second as the *sporosac*.

An intermediate form by which the medusoid passes into the fully developed Medusa is seen in *Pennaria*. Here the umbrella has four well-developed radial canals which open into a marginal circular canal, while its codonostome, though never attaining the widely open condition found in the planoblast, and carrying on its margin only the rudiments of tentacles, is sufficiently developed to admit of the free ingress and egress of the surrounding water. Notwithstanding, however, this relatively advanced stage of development, the gonophore remains permanently attached to the trophosome, and thus discharges its generative products without ever becoming free.[1]

Development of the Gonophore.—In the development of the Medusa-bud, the first foundation of the Medusa, like that of every bud in the Hydroid colony, consists of an outbulging of some definite part of the Hydroid body. There is thus formed a sac-like projection whose walls consist of endoderm and ectoderm in direct continuation with the same layers in the colony, and whose cavity is also only an extension of that of the part from which the bud is given off.

The subsequent course of the development has recently been studied more especially by O. and R. Hertwig,[2] and by Weismann.[3] When the hernia-like sac which forms the foundation of the gonophore has attained a certain height the ectoderm of its summit becomes thickened and forms an internal prominence, the "Glockenkern" or *endocodon* of Weismann. This, pressing on the part of the endoderm which lies beneath it, causes an inversion of the endoderm in the form of a cup whose walls, necessarily double as the result of the invagination, rise on all sides round the endocodon. In the meantime a central cavity has been formed in the solid ectodermal endocodon. This is to become the cavity of the umbrella, while by the partial adhesion to one another of the two endodermal layers by which it is surrounded, four (or more) longitudinal channels are produced. These are the radiating canals, while the intervening endoderm, whose lumen has become obliterated by the adhesion, forms the endoderm lamella or vascular lamella of the Hertwigs.

At the same time the bottom of the endodermal cup rises in the form of a hollow cone, pushing before it the ectodermal layer which forms the floor of the cavity of the endocodon. It thus becomes clothed by this layer, and forms the manubrium of the Medusa with its endodermal and ectodermal layer, while the circular canal which in the Medusa runs round the margins of the umbrella is formed by intercommunicating lateral tubular offsets from the distal extremities of the radial canals. Finally, the cavity of the umbrella, still represented by the hollow endocodon, opens externally

---

[1] Another intermediate form between hydroblast and planoblast has been recently described by Clarke (*Mem. Boston Soc. Nat. Hist.*, vol. iii., 1878) in a Gymnoblastic Hydroid from the American coast. In this, which gives origin to medusoids with well-developed radial and circular canals, Clarke has seen some of the medusoids detach themselves before liberation of their generative products, while others discharge these without ever becoming free.

[2] O. und R. Hertwig, Das Nervensystem und die Sinnesorgane der Medusen, Leipzig, 1878.

[3] A. Weismann, Die Entstehung, &c.

and places the interior of the umbrella in free communication with the surrounding water.

This account of the development of the Medusa-bud agrees in almost all points with that previously given by Agassiz, who regarded the radial canals of the umbrella as the result of the non-adhesion of the two layers of the endodermal cup along definite longitudinal lines, while it differs from the view formerly urged by myself, in which I regarded the radial canals as growing out in the form of tubular processes from the basis of the manubrium.

The theory of the formation of the canals by arrested adhesion of the two endodermal layers along the lines of these canals will satisfactorily explain the phenomena, and the truth of this explanation seems to be placed beyond doubt by the discovery of the endoderm lamella shown by the Hertwigs to exist as a persistent structure in the umbrella of the Medusa.

It must not be supposed, however, that radial canals are never formed by an outgrowth of tubes from the base of the manubrium into the walls of the umbrella. Though the primary canals may be always formed as described above, there are instances (*Æquorea*, &c.) in which the canals increase in number after the detachment of the Medusa, and in such cases it is certain that the newly formed canals extend themselves in the umbrella walls from the base of the manubrium in order to open into the circular canal round the margin.[1]

The formation of the medusoid also takes place through the medium of an endocodon, and is similar to that just described for the Medusa, except in the fact that the radiating canals are in most cases entirely suppressed, and that in those rare instances in which they may be seen in a rudimental or even completely developed form the umbrella does not present the wide codonostome of the Medusa, and is not developed so as to be employed as an organ of natation.

In the sporosac, on the other hand, the development does not take place through the formation of an endocodon, and no endoderm lamella being formed, the walls of the sac retain the condition presented in the early stages of the bud, being simply composed of two layers, an internal endodermal layer, and an external ectodermal layer, these two being subsequently separated by the presence between them of the generative products.

Between the medusoids and those gonophores, which as planoblasts have attained the condition of true Craspedote Medusae, there is a close parallelism, the various parts in the one having their representatives in a more or less modified form in the other. In the medusoid, passing from without inwards, we meet with the following layers:— Most externally a layer of ectoderm; then a thin lamina of endoderm in which gastrovascular canals may or may not be developed, and which though present in the early stages of the bud is not always demonstrable in the mature gonophore. To this

[1] *Gymnoblastic Hydroids*, p. 79, fig. 35.

succeed two layers of ectoderm; and lastly, we meet with an endodermal layer surrounding a cavity which occupies the axis of the gonophore, and is in free communication with the general cavity of the colony.[1]

If we now compare this with the structure met with in the Medusa we shall find the external ectodermal layer to be homologous with the outer epithelial layer of the umbrella. The next ectodermal layer will represent the subumbrellar or inner epithelial layer of the umbrella, while the endodermal layer which intervenes between these two layers of ectoderm corresponds to the endoderm lamella in which are formed the radiating canals of the Medusa. The next layer is an ectodermal one and forms the external layer of a *cul de sac* which occupies the axis of the medusoid, and corresponds to the manubrium of the Medusa. This layer represents the ectodermal layer of the manubrium, while the inner or endodermal layer of the *cul de sac* corresponds to the endodermal layer of the manubrium of the Medusa.

When the generative elements make their appearance in the gonophore they are seen in the hedrioblasts to lie between the endoderm and ectoderm of the central *cul de sac* which corresponds to the manubrium of the Medusa; while in the planoblast they lie either between the corresponding layers of the manubrium, or between the endoderm and ectoderm of definite points in the course of the radiating canals.

The intervention of the generative products between the endoderm and ectoderm of the central *cul de sac* in the hedrioblast, necessarily separates these two membranes from one another, and the endodermal portion then extends in the axis as an elongated closed sac surrounded by the generative products, and known as the *spadix*.

2. *Origin of the Generative Elements.*

It had been always believed that the generative elements had their origin in the gonophores in which they constitute so conspicuous and characteristic a feature. It was therefore with no little surprise that during an examination of the common *Sertularia pumila* of our coast I found the walls of the blastostyle of this species loaded with nucleated cells which it was impossible to regard in any other light than as young ova. This condition I described with an accompanying figure, stating my belief "that the true gonophores bud forth from that part of the blastostyle in which the nucleated bodies occur, and that these as young ova pass from the blastostyle into the budding gonophore, where they would then naturally occupy their normal position between the endoderm and ectoderm of an organ representing the manubrium of a Medusa, destined

[1] I do not here include the layer to which in my original description of the gonophore I gave the name of "ectotheca," for though I never regarded this otherwise than as an external capsule-like covering of the true gonophore (see Gymnoblastic Hydroids, pp. 32, 33), I willingly accept the criticism of Weismann, who objects to its enumeration among the layers of the gonophore as misleading. Neither do I include in the account here given of the development and homologies of the gonophore the structureless measure which must be understood as intervening between the ectoderm and endoderm, or the gelatinous excretion by which in the Medusa this is more or less completely represented.

to undergo there a further development before being discharged into the acrocyst," an appendage of the gonophore in the form of an external marsupial chamber which exists in certain species, and receives the ova before their final escape as larvæ into the surrounding water. I described the function of the gonophore in this case as merely that of "a receptacle in which certain intermediate stages of development take place."[1]

The phenomenon, however, thus recorded in *Sertularia pumila*, I believed to be peculiar to this species, with possibly a few others, and I thus overlooked its real significance. The important researches of Edouard van Beneden have since shown that the sexual cells may originate in other parts of the colony at a distance from the gonophore,[2] and Kleinenberg has made it evident that egg-cells which originate in the ectoderm may pass through the mesoarc into the endoderm, and there, surrounded by conditions better suited to their nutrition, may increase in size and make further advance towards maturity;[3] but it was reserved for Weismann by his epoch-making researches into the origin of the sexual elements in the Hydroida,[4] to show that what I had thus regarded as an exception was really the rule, and that the sexual cells originate in most cases in parts of the colony removed from the gonophore, into which they subsequently wander in order to pass through certain later stages of their development.

These remarkable researches of Weismann have shown not only the parts of the colony in which the sexual cells originate, but the special layers—endoderm or ectoderm —which give birth to them, and the unexpected fact has been elicited, that there is no constancy either in the part of the colony or in the particular tissue in which the germ cells, which are to become developed into spermatozoa or into ova, first show themselves.

The observations of Weismann have been made on a very large number of species, and he concludes that the sexual cells arise now here, now there, without rule or connection, and that their origin has no definite relation to the germinal layers of the embryo, that on the contrary, it is now the endoderm, now the ectoderm, now both layers together which give rise to them. Then again it may be the ectoderm which gives origin to the male, the endoderm to the female sexual cells, as is the case in *Campanularia flexuosa*, while in other instances, as in *Eudendrium racemosum*, it is the reverse of this. And not only does the relation of the sexual cells to the two primary layers thus vary, but their relation to the various zooids of the colony is equally without any apparent law; for in some cases the place of origin of these cells may lie in the manubrium of the Medusa, in others in the cœnosarc of the stem or branches, and now again in the buds which are to form sedentary gonophores. It would seem that every

[1] Gymnoblastic Hydroida, p. 150, woodcut fig. 21, p. 50.
[2] E. van Beneden, Sur la distinction originelle du testicule et de l'ovaire, Bull. de l'Acad. Roy. de Belgique, sér. 2, t. xxxvii.
[3] Kleinenberg, Die Entstehung der Eier bei Eudendrium, Zeitschr. f. wiss. Zool., Bd. xxxv., 1881.
[4] August Weismann, Die Entstehung der Sexualzellen bei den Hydromedusen, Jena, 1883.

part of the colony may bring forth sexual cells, and that the elements of the two germinal layers (endoderm and ectoderm) may become transformed in one instance into male, in another into female, sexual cells.

So indefinite and independent of law is all this, that Weismann has been almost led to conclude that in the lowest Metazoa—the bilaminar Cœlenterata—no functional separation of the germinal layers has taken place such as we find in the higher Metazoa ; that in those lowest forms both germinal layers possess the faculty of differentiating sexual cells out of their own elements, while it is in the higher Metazoa that this faculty has for the first time become concentrated on one of their three germinal layers.

At the same time it must be borne in mind that the part of the colony, as well as the special germinal layer in which the sexual cells originate, is fixed for each species.

Weismann has further pointed out that it is never cells already histologically differentiated which are transformed into sexual cells, but only those of young tissue, which are to a certain extent embryonal, or of no determinate external character.

Another fact of great importance, which seems to have been fully established by the researches of Weismann, relates to the manner in which the sexual cells which have originated elsewhere reach the gonophore in which they are to pass through further stages of development. These researches place it beyond doubt, that the sexual cells are carried into the gonophore, not by mere physical pressure, but that they wander from their place of birth by their own proper movements, such as might exist in amœboid protoplasm masses. In this way they move from place to place among the cells of the endoderm and ectoderm, and even pass from one layer into the other by actually perforating the mesosarc which separates these two layers from one another.

Shortly after arrival in the sedentary gonophore, whether this be a medusoid or a simple sporosac, the sexual elements—egg-cells or spermatozoa—are found accumulated round the spadix where they are retained by the *perigonium* or sac formed by the more external parts of the gonophore.[1] It is here that, in at least the great majority of cases, the influence of the male element is exerted on the egg-cells, but by what channel the spermatozoon gain access to them has not yet been satisfactorily determined.[2]

---

[1] The perigonium in the sporosac consists simply of the ectodermal coat which before the intervention of the sexual cells lay close upon the spadix, while in the medusoid it consists not only of this coat but of layers which correspond to those which form the umbrella of a Medusa.

[2] Under the name of *Hydrella oripara*, Goette (*Zool. Anzeiger*, 1880) has noticed a minute Hydroid, of which he obtained a single specimen at Naples, and which would seem to be nearly allied to *Halecium*. In the atrophied and disintegrated coenosarc of the stem were several nucleated cells, which he regards as eggs, and as no gonophores were present in the specimen, he believes that this Hydroid offers an instance of direct sexual reproduction without the formation of special generative zooids.

It is possible that Goette's interpretation may be the right one, and that here as in *Hydra* no true gonophores are developed ; but when we bear in mind the very general presence of eggs in the Hydroid coenosarc, as proved by the researches of Weismann, and the fact that in *Hydrella* the supposed egg-cells are irregularly scattered in the atrophied coenosarc without any tendency to the localisation which we find in *Hydra*, we can scarcely avoid regarding the absence of a gonosome in the specimen as depending on the season of the year, on age, or on abnormal conditions, and cannot but

That form of gonophore which presents the condition of a free Medusa or planoblast, has like the sedentary gonophores the office of bringing to maturity the sexual elements. In almost all these, however, the sexual products arise within the Medusa, and do not therefore need to migrate from a distance into their place of maturation.

In those planoblasts whose generative elements are borne along the course of the radiating canals (Leptomedusæ) that part of the walls of the canal in which these are contained usually projects with the included ova or spermatozoa into the cavity of the umbrella in the form of a pouch or gonad, which has often the appearance of a distinct gonophore budded off as an independent zooid from the canal. I formerly regarded it as such and made this view the grounds for separating the planoblasts into such as give origin to their sexual elements directly in the walls of the manubrium (gonochemes = Anthomedusæ), and such as produce them only through the intervention of a special sexual bud (blastochemes = Leptomedusæ). I now, however, believe it more correct to regard the sexual pouches or gonads which are produced in the course of the radiating canals, not as true buds, but as simple extensions of the canal walls, caused by the presence of the sexual products between their endoderm and ectoderm; and I would accordingly view this second form of planoblast as also giving rise to its sexual elements directly, and therefore, like the first, as the exact locomotive equivalent of the hedrioblast or sedentary gonophore.

3. *Development of the Ovum.*

In by far the greater number of species the development of the ovum results in the formation of a ciliated locomotive larva known as a *planula*. In such cases the ovum, which is mostly destitute of vitellary membrane, after passing through a regular or nearly regular segmentation in accordance with the usual binary law of embryonal development, becomes transformed into a solid spherical mass of cells (blastosphere) from which a peripheral layer soon becomes separated by a process of delamination. The embryo now as a rule becomes more or less elongated, and a central cavity makes its appearance in it.

At this stage the embryo is in the form of a hollow oviform body whose walls are composed of two layers, an external or ectoderm, and an internal or endoderm. It is by delamination, never by invagination, that the two germinal layers, ectoderm and endoderm, are formed. The embryo has now usually escaped from the confinement of the gonophore, and its ectoderm becomes clothed with vibratile cilia, by the aid of which

wish for an opportunity of examining other examples which might supplement the very scanty material at the disposal of Goette.

In some common Hydroids no gonosome has yet been found. Until, however, we know the time of year and other conditions which may be here necessary for the development of the gonosome, an ignorance of this element in certain Hydroids affords no grounds for regarding its absence in these as a constant and permanent occurrence.

it moves about as a free larva in the surrounding water.   It would seem to be about this time that the mesosarc shows itself as a very fine structureless membrane between the endoderm and ectoderm.   To the larva thus formed, Dalyell, by whose observations it was first made known, has given the name of "planula."[1]   The planula is still a completely closed sac.   After enjoying for a time its free locomotive life it loses its cilia and fixes itself by one end—the aboral pole.   A delicate chitinous pellicle, the foundation of the perisarc, is excreted over a greater or less extent of its surface; the free or oral pole becomes perforated by a mouth round which a circle of tentacles has become developed. The larva may now be recognised as the primordial hydranth of the colony, and it only remains for this to become complicated by the budding of other hydranths and of the sexual zooids in order that it may attain the condition of the fully developed dendritic colony.

The mode of formation of the planula now described is in its essential features that which has shown itself in all Gymnoblastic and Calyptoblastic Hydroids in which a planula has been noticed, and subjected to sufficiently careful observation, with the exception of *Eucope polystyla*, one of the Campanularians, in which Kowalevsky has described a somewhat different process.[2]   According to this observer the ovum as the result of segmentation becomes converted into a blastosphere with a large central segmentation cavity, in the walls of which only a single layer is present.   From the inner surface of the walls, cells are now budded off, and these fill the segmentation cavity with a solid cellular mass which represents the endoderm.   The original single layer forms the ectoderm, and becomes clothed with cilia.   In the endodermal mass a slit-like cavity— the primitive gastric cavity—now shows itself, and thus completes the formation of the planula stage of the larva.

We know as yet very little of the development of those Medusæ which pass to their adult state directly from the egg without the intervention of a polypoid trophosome (see above, p. xxix).   The researches of Metchnikoff[3] have shown that in at least two of these, *Polyxenia leucostyla* and *Ægineta flavescens*, the segmentation of the ovum results in the formation of a solid morula, from which a peripheral layer is differentiated by delamination as an ectoderm, which becomes clothed with vibratile cilia.   In the central or endodermal cell-mass of the body thus formed the primitive gastral cavity makes its appearance, and soon opens externally by the formation of a mouth.   On two opposite points the body becomes extended into a solid tentacle, and two other similar tentacles subsequently make their appearance in a median plane at right angles to that of the former, so that the symmetry, at first bilateral, becomes radial.   Between the ectoderm and endoderm a clear gelatinous layer is excreted, and this rapidly increasing in volume while the larva assumes a more lenticular form, becomes the gelatinous umbrella of the

[1] Sir J. Graham Dalyell, Rare and Remarkable Animals of Scotland, London, 1847.

[2] Observations on the Development of Cœlenterata, *Trans. Friends Nat. Hist., Anthrop. and Ethnog. Moscow*, 1873 (Russian).

[3] Studien über die Entwickelung der Medusen und Siphonophoren, *Zeitschr. f. wiss. Zool.*, Bd. xxxiv. p. 1074.

adult. By further changes in the relative lengths of the diameters, an increase in the number of tentacles, and the formation of marginal sense organs and of a velum, the larva assumes the form of the adult.

Metchnikoff[1] and Fol[2] have both, independently of one another, traced the development of the egg in *Geryonia hastata*, another member of the group which never passes through a polypoid trophosome, and have arrived at essentially similar results. In this Medusa the segmentation of the egg gives rise to a blastosphere with a large segmentation cavity, and with walls as yet formed by a single layer of cells. By the transverse division of these cells, the walls of the hollow blastosphere becomes differentiated into an ectodermal and an endodermal layer. Between these a clear homogeneous gelatinous excretion is deposited as the rudiment of a gelatinous umbrella, and by its unequal accumulation renders the segmentation cavity more and more excentric, until its endodermal lining again comes in contact at one point with the ectoderm. At this point a mouth is formed, and the segmentation cavity, now become the gastral cavity of the Medusa, is brought into connection with the exterior. Round the mouth the ectoderm forms a thickened ridge from which the rudiments of the tentacles shoot forth, and from which a perforated diaphragm extends towards the axis as a velum. In none of these cases, however, do the observers give any account of the formation of the gastrovascular canals, and a very important point in the development has thus been left unsolved.

The endoderm and ectoderm of the Hydroida represent, as was first pointed out by Huxley,[3] the inner and outer germinal layers, to the formation of which the early stages of the development of the ovum lead throughout the whole of the Metazoal members of the animal kingdom; but while these become in the higher Metazoa so transformed as to be no longer recognisable as definite layers, they remain as permanent elements in the structure not only of the Hydroida but of all the other members of the Cœlenterata, where they still continue as the endoderm and ectoderm of the adult.

The development of the Hydroid colony through the formation of a planula is characteristic of the great majority of the Hydroida. There are, however, three genera—*Tubularia*, *Myriothela*, and *Hydra*—in which the development of the egg has been proved not to result in the formation of a free planula, while one or two others may possibly come into the same category, though an opportunity of studying them sufficiently to render this point certain has not yet been afforded.

Development of the Egg in Tubularia.—In *Tubularia* and in *Myriothela* there is formed instead of a planula a locomotive actiniform larva which is destitute of a ciliated epithelium and moves about by the aid of long tentacular processes. The development of the embryo in two species of *Tubularia* (*Tubularia indivisa* and *Tubularia laryux*) has been followed by myself, while Ciamician and Weismann have examined it in *Tubularia*

---

[1] Metchnikoff, *loc. cit.*   [2] Fol, *Jenaische Zeitschr.*, Bd. vii.
[3] Huxley, On the Anatomy and Affinities of the Medusæ, *Phil. Trans.*, 1849.

mesembryanthemum. The researches of these last observers have shown that in *Tubularia mesembryanthemum* the sexual cells are derived from that part of the ectoderm which forms the deeper portion of the endocodon in the very young gonophore. It is this portion which ultimately becomes the ectodermal covering of the spadix, and the place of origin of the sexual cells thus coincides with their place of development, so that they do not here require as in other instances to wander from one to the other. Weismann and Ciamician agree in believing that the great majority of the egg-cells serve merely as food-cells, and after attaining a certain size become broken down and dissolved, thus affording nutriment for those egg-cells which are destined for development,—a view which, as we shall presently see, is supported by the phenomena observed in *Myriothela*.

In the very young gonophore—whether male or female—the sexual cells, as may be seen in *Tubularia larynx*,[1] already surround the spadix, and soon quite fill the cavity which is included between the spadix and its now widely separated ectodermal coat, and thus serves in the female as a brood chamber for the developing embryo. In the egg-cells which at this stage fill the brood chamber in *Tubularia larynx* may be seen a large nucleus with nucleolus (germinal vesicle and germinal spot).

With the growth of the gonophore the mass of sexual cells which it contains becomes more and more voluminous, and we soon find that the place of these egg-cells is taken by a plasma-like mass which envelops the spadix, and which still continues to increase in volume with the continued growth of the gonophore. We next see that a portion of the mass has become detached from the rest in order to undergo a special development within the cavity of the gonophore. Whether this detached mass can be regarded as a true ovum may be doubted, but at all events it takes the part of an ovum in passing through various stages of development. It is destitute of external membrane, and it is probable that it is at this stage that the influence of the male element is exerted on it, and that the process of segmentation takes place. This process, however, is here very obscure, and observations have failed in obtaining satisfactory results as to the mode in which it is carried on.

According to Ciamician the segmentation of the ovum in *Tubularia mesembryanthemum* is an irregular one, the embryo being formed by an epibolic extension of some of the segmentation spheres over the remainder, the former giving rise to the ectoderm, and the latter to the endoderm.

This form of segmentation, by which some of the segmentation spheres rapidly multiply and surround the others, closely resembles that of the Ctenophora, and is very different from what takes place in the formation of a planula. I have never seen anything of the kind in the species of *Tubularia* whose development I have studied, and neither Balfour[2] nor Kleinenberg have been able to confirm the conclusions of Ciamician.

---

[1] Gymnoblastic Hydroids, p. 91, pl. xxiii. figs. 19–24.
[2] Balfour's Works, Memorial Edition, vol. ii. p. 154.

The exact significance of the plasma-like mass which surrounds the spadix, as well as the portions which become detached from it, seems open to question. That they contain cell-like elements there can be no doubt, and as these show themselves before any apparent segmentation can be detected, they can scarcely be otherwise regarded than as the remains of the germ-cells, which from an early period filled the gonophore, and are now in process of coalescence with one another so as to form the plasma mass, while others have probably broken down, and served as nutriment for the developing embryo.

Ciamician, however, regards each plasma mass in *Tubularia mesembryanthemum* as an ordinary ovum, and compares the cell-like elements which exist in it to the " pseudo-cells " discovered by Kleinenberg in the ovum of *Hydra*. These cell-like elements are, however, very different in appearance from the hollow thick-walled corpuscles described as pseudo-cells by Kleinenberg, while the phenomena presented by the development of the embryo in *Myriothela* (see below, p. xli) are in favour of regarding the plasma masses of *Tubularia* as formed by the coalescence of the original germ-cells. In whatever light we view them, the further course of development in *Tubularia indivisa* and *Tubularia larynx* is as follows : [1]—

The portion which in the way just mentioned has been detached from the general mass, continues to lie for some time in the cavity of the gonophore, where it becomes further developed into an actiniform larva. During this development, it first acquires a flattened, somewhat disc-shaped form, and in such shape becomes extended over the remaining portion of the sexual mass by which the spadix continues to be surrounded. In the centre of the disc a cavity—the primitive digestive cavity—soon shows itself, while from the circumference short but thick outbulgings of this cavity radiate, and soon become elongated into tentacles. The disc at the same time becomes more gibbous on the side turned away from the spadix, while a mouth makes its appearance in the centre of the opposite side. The embryo now retreats from the residual generative mass, the mouth is seen to be elevated on a conical prominence (hypostome), while the side opposite to the mouth becomes prolonged into the commencement of a stem-like extension which has the digestive cavity of the embryo continued into it. In this state it escapes from the gonosome, a second circle of very short tentacles having in some species (*Tubularia indivisa*) become first developed round the mouth, while in others (*Tubularia larynx*) the oral tentacles do not make their appearance until after the escape of the embryo. The embryo continues free for a period, during which it creeps about by the aid of its circlet of long proximal tentacles, which are now thrown back round the aboral pole. In the meantime the aboral pole has become further elongated into a cylindrical stem which soon clothes itself with a perisarc and fixes the young *Tubularia* to some neighbouring object.

After the escape of the embryo, or even during its development within the gonophore,

---

[1] Gymnoblastic Hydroids, p. 90, pl. xxiii. figs. 11-16 and 19-24.

the remains of the generative mass may still throw off portions giving rise to embryos which become developed in a similar way into free actiniform larvæ. To such larvæ the name of *Actinula* may be given in order to distinguish them from the planula of other Hydroids.

Development of the Egg in Myriothela.—In the development of the egg in *Myriothela* we meet with some remarkable departures from the phenomena usually presented in the embryonic development of the Hydroida.[1]

The eggs of *Myriothela* have their origin in the cells of the endodermal layer which forms the walls of the spadix. Certain cells of this layer in the very young gonophore become transformed into egg-cells which increase in number and in size until the cavity of the gonophore is entirely filled with them. Each egg-cell has now its well-defined germinal vesicle and germinal spot, and its vitelline protoplasm, but without any apparent vitelline membrane.

The egg-cells continue to increase in size with the growth of the gonophore, they remain for some time closely pressed one against the other so as to acquire a polyhedral form, but they gradually become looser, assume an oviform shape, and may now be easily isolated by the needle or by the mere action of the compressorium. Their germinal vesicle is now very large and distinct, and within the large germinal spot a well-defined nucleolus may be detected.

The egg-cells have no sooner thus attained their complete separation from one another, and have acquired their full size in the gonophore, than they begin to present a very remarkable phenomenon. They lose their independent existence, and begin to undergo a fusion into one another; and when the contents of the gonophore are now liberated by rupture of its walls under the microscope, many of these nucleated protoplasm masses may be seen to be united to one another by irregular pseudopodia-like extensions of their substance. By the gradual shortening and thickening of these processes the little masses which they connect are drawn closer to one another, and end by becoming completely fused together into a common protoplasmic mass. In this mass the cell boundaries are completely lost, but numerous nucleolated nuclei may be seen scattered through its substance. These are almost certainly the nuclei with their included nucleoli of the originally independent egg-cells.

Several such masses, eight or more, will thus be formed within the gonophore, from the coalesced ova. They are of an ovoid form, and do not entirely fill the cavity of the gonophore, while the narrow intervals between them, as well as the small space which separates them from the walls of the gonophore, are occupied by a substance which appears to consist chiefly of free nuclei and of dwindled and degraded ova, all apparently undergoing a process of liquefaction, and doubtless an unused residuum of the bodies, by the coalescence of which the compound masses had been formed.

---

[1] See Memoir on the Structure and Development of Myriothela, *Phil. Trans.*, vol. clxv. pt. 2, 1875.

If in this stage the gonophore be laid open, and the protoplasm masses, whose formation we have been tracing, be liberated under the microscope, we shall often succeed in witnessing very minute processes of clear protoplasm, which have become developed over the surface. These, however, are not permanent structures, and they will often, while the object continues under observation, become entirely withdrawn. They are in fact true pseudopodia, and are probably employed in the nutrition of the masses from which they arise.

The contents of the gonophore, however, are destined to undergo further change before the period of their liberation has arrived. The separate protoplasm masses increase in size, the residual matter which had surrounded them has disappeared, having probably afforded material for their nutrition, they begin to coalesce with one another, and there is ultimately formed a single large *plasmodium* which entirely fills the cavity of the gonophore. When this plasmodium is examined under the compressorium, the same nuclei which had hitherto characterised the products of the coalescence of the ova are seen to be scattered in great number through its substance. These nuclei, however, have already begun to suffer a change, for while in some the nucleolus is still distinct, in others it has quite disappeared, and while in some the contents consist of a minutely granular matter, in others they are quite homogeneous.

When the separate protoplasm masses have all united with one another, or a little before they have become so completely fused together as to have their original distinctness entirely lost, the time has arrived when the contents of the gonophore are to be expelled. Its walls, which present the remarkable character of having a strong muscular layer developed in them, now begin to contract on the contained plasmodium, which is thus gradually forced out through the summit of the gonophore. By the continued contraction of the walls of the gonophore, the plasmodium is at last entirely expelled, completely enveloped, however, in a transparent structureless membrane. The empty gonophore may now be seen retracted in the form of a shallow thick-walled cup with everted edges, upon the summit of its short peduncle.

The liberated plasmodium closely enveloped in its structureless capsule is of a nearly spherical form, and now lies upon the retracted gonophore. It does not, however, continue long in this position, for the function of the claspers is soon brought into play. These remarkable bodies, which have no representative in any other known Hydroid, are long, cylindrical, very contractile, tentacle-like organs which spring from the body of the hydranth. Each is slightly enlarged towards its distal extremity where it terminates in a sucker-like disc. One of these claspers (sometimes two or even three) now stretches itself out towards the liberated plasmodium, and as soon as it reaches it, it becomes attached by its sucker-like extremity to the capsule and then by strong contractions pulls the plasmodium still enveloped in its capsule away from the remains of the gonophore on which it had lain.

By this time the coalescence of the separate plasma masses into a single spherical plasmodium has been completed ; but soon after the liberation of the plasmodium and its seizure by the claspers, we find that the whole has become broken up into a multitude of small round or irregularly shaped masses. These all consist of a granular proto-plasmic matter without any distinct boundary membrane, and with numerous nucleus-like bodies immersed in their substance. The common external structureless membrane is distinct, but it is still thin and weak.

Notwithstanding the apparent absence of anything like a definite law of cleavage, it is impossible to avoid comparing this breaking up of the plasmodium with the segmentation of the ovum, and hitherto we have seen nothing which in any way resembles this phenomenon. We must, however, be careful not to push this comparison beyond its legitimate limits, for we are not here dealing with an ovum in the ordinary sense, but with a multitude of egg-cells coalesced into a single *syncytium*.

But subsequent stages no less than that just described recall the phenomena which present themselves in the development of the typical ovum into the planula of other Hydroids. The segmented condition of the plasmodium disappears, and its substance is once more found in the state of an undifferentiated plasma.

Soon, however, a definite histological differentiation begins to show itself. This results in the formation of a single spherical body, within which, probably by a process of liquefaction, a large central cavity has made its appearance. At the same time, the walls of the cavity are seen to possess a distinctly cellular structure, and to have become split, apparently by delamination, into two concentric laminæ, the first indication of the ectoderm and the endoderm.

This is the foundation of the Actinula. The Actinula of *Myriothela*, however, differs from that of *Tubularia* in the possession of long transitory arms which serve for locomotion. These originate in involutions of the walls of the hollow sphere. By this process, which seems to be without parallel among the Hydroida, the transitory arms of the Actinula show themselves first as hollow cæcal projections into the cavity of the sphere. An evagination, however, of these projections soon takes place, so that by their eversion they come to occupy the position of external appendages.

Up to this period the embryo had retained its nearly spherical form, but it now begins to elongate itself and assume an ovoid shape. Then one pole becomes truncated, and a mouth here makes its appearance, while the permanent tentacles begin to shoot out around it in the form of short papilliform processes.

The Actinula is now ready to escape from its enclosing capsule, which since the seizure of the germ by the clasper had all along remained adherent to the extremity of this organ. The capsule now becomes ruptured and allows the larva to enter on a free life in the surrounding water.

The transitory arms like the permanent tentacles are hollow. They terminate each in a well-defined capitulum and are about twenty in number. They form no regular verticil but extend with a scattered disposition over the greater part of the body, Upon the escape of the Actinula they continue to increase in length, and have the faculty of holding on by their clavate extremities to neighbouring surfaces. It is thus by their aid that the larva creeps about on the various objects in its vicinity.

After the Actinula has enjoyed for some days its free locomotive existence, it begins to fix itself by its aboral sucker-like extremity; the permanent tentacles become more numerous and extend further backwards on the body, while the long arms undergo a rapid degradation, become much shortened, and soon entirely disappear. All the essential features of the adult trophosome are thus acquired, and it only remains to complete the development of the Hydroid by the formation of the gonosome, which soon makes its appearance by the budding of the blastostyles and claspers from the hydranth at the proximal side of the tentacles. From the blastostyles the gonophores are subequally budded off, and the animal thus attains its complete maturity.

Myriothela phrygia, the only known species of this remarkable genus, is monœcious, the same hydranth carrying both male and female gonophores, but at what part of the developmental process just described the male influence exerts itself, or what may be the immediate changes which result from this, are points on which the observed facts will not justify a definite conclusion.

It will be seen that the formation of the Actinula in *Myriothela* is connected with certain phenomena which are very remarkable and exceptional. Among the most significant of these is the formation of a plasmodium by the coalescence of numerous primitive egg-cells. Exceptional, however, as this phenomenon is, it is not without a parallel even among the higher animals, and will at once recall the formation of the permanent ovum, as a syncytium, from the coalescence of the "primitive ova" in the early stages of the ovary in certain Elasmobranch fishes.[1]

Development of the Egg in Hydra.—The phenomena presented during the development of *Hydra* are in many respects scarcely less divergent from the ordinary course of Hydroid development than those just described in *Myriothela*.

It is to the researches of Kleinenberg that we are indebted for the first complete account of the development of the sexual structures in *Hydra*.[2] He has shown that both ovaria and testes are derived from certain cells of the ectoderm which lie between

[1] See Balfour's Works, Memorial Edit., vol. i. p. 587; vol. ii. p. 57. Korotneff, who seems to be the only other observer who has studied the structure and development of *Myriothela* (*Zool. Anzeig.*, Bd. i. p. 363, 1878; Bd. ii. p. 182, 1879) takes a different view of the whole process. He supposes that among the multitude of egg-cells which originally fill the cavity of the gonophore, only one becomes a true egg, and that from this alone the Actinula is developed. I cannot, however, accept this view. It is impossible to reconcile it with the facts just described, and a laborious investigation of the animal has, I believe, placed the truth of these facts beyond question.

[2] Nicolaus Kleinenberg, Hydra, eine anatomisch-entwicklungsgeschichtliche Untersuchung, Leipzig, 1872.

the deeper parts of the epithelial muscle-cells, where they form a tissue to which he has given the name of "interstitial tissue."

In a circumscribed portion of this tissue which is to become the testis, a more vigorous growth takes place. The cells composing it enlarge and multiply by division, and form a many-layered, compact, lenticular body. This is the testis; it forms a projection from the body of the *Hydra*, covered by the epithelial muscle-cells.

In the meantime the nucleus of the testicular cells becomes replaced by one or more sharply contoured, strongly refringent corpuscles. The cell is now a perfectly transparent sphere. On one spot of the surface there arises a fine plasma process with active flagellate movements. This is subsequently seen to have become united with one of the corpuscles in the interior of the cell, and by its action the corpuscle to which it had attached itself is finally drawn out from the generating cell, and the mature spermatozoon is thus set free.

The foundation of the ovary agrees essentially with that of the testis. The cells of the interstitial tissue in a zone which in *Hydra viridis* embraces nearly half the circumference of the body multiply and unite with one another into groups, composed each of a single layer of cells. These cells increase in size, and the groups themselves finally unite into a one-layered flattened cell-mass in which a multiplication of cells still goes on.

This cell-mass forms the ovarium, and when it has reached the stage here described a single cell which usually lies exactly in its middle begins to be distinguished by more active growth from the others. This is the young egg. It continues to increase in size, while its surface becomes extended into processes which with the continued growth of the egg pass into broad irregular lobes.

With further growth the egg becomes extended in width without increasing in thickness, and two incisions now show themselves opposite to one another on the edges of the somewhat disc-shaped egg, and extending deep into the interior, cut the egg into two lateral halves connected by a narrow middle isthmus, and having their edges irregularly notched and cleft. The egg continues to increase in width, and the form which it now presents has been compared by Kleinenberg to that of a butterfly with expanded wings, the edges of which are irregularly notched and torn. In the connecting isthmus lies the germinal vesicle with its included nucleolus or germinal spot.

Besides irregularly-shaped granules of apparently albuminous nature chlorophyll grains now show themselves in *Hydra viridis* embedded in the plasma of the egg.

The outgrowths from the plasma increase in size and now form the principal part of the egg. They branch dichotomously, push themselves between the other cells of the ovary, and the egg becomes eminently amœbiform.

At the same time there appear in the plasma sharply contoured corpuscles. These are usually in the form of thick-walled hollow spheres, and in *Hydra viridis* there may be seen in them a conical projection attached by its base to a point on the inner surface of the wall, whence it extends deep into the interior.

These bodies are certainly not cells; they take no direct participation in the development of the embryo, and Kleinenberg, who has traced them from small globular condensations of the plasma, assigns to them the name of "pseudo-cells." They seem to have the significance of reserve matter, and gradually disappear.

The egg still continues to increase in size, but the outrunning extensions of its plasma are gradually withdrawn, and the egg loses its amœboid form, and becomes rounded into a broad ovoid.

About the time when the formation of pseudo-cells has ceased the germinal vesicle and germinal spot begin to undergo a disintegration, and finally disappear long before the commencement of fecundation. The remaining cells of the ovary also become disintegrated and are manifestly used up as nutriment for the ovum.

By the pressure of the subjacent egg the ectoderm which lies over it becomes protruded in the form of a sac, in the summit of which a narrow orifice makes its appearance. Through this the egg is forced out into the surrounding water, though it still continues for some time to hang to the parent *Hydra* by a small part of its surface. It is now that the naked egg is exposed to the influence of the spermatozoa diffused through the water, and becomes fecundated.

The segmentation which now begins in the ovum is in accordance with the common law of binary cleavage, except that when the cleavage advances to a certain stage it loses somewhat of its regularity, some of the segmentation spheres cleaving less rapidly than the others. During this process pseudopodia are developed from the surfaces of cleavage, but these at a later period disappear. When the number of the segmentation spheres has reached thirty-two the surface of the egg has the mammillated condition of the mulberry form. Later on this disappears and the egg becomes quite smooth.

When the segmentation has been completed two kinds of cells may be distinguished in the germ. One of these consists of elongated prismatic cells resembling those of a cylinder epithelium. They form a one-layered stratum on the surface of the germ. The other consists of shorter cells rendered polygonal by mutual pressure. These form the main mass of the germ. All these cells are naked plasma masses, at first destitute of nucleus, but at the end of some hours nuclei make their appearance in the superficial cells, and soon after in the deeper ones. It seems certain that these nuclei arise independently in cells previously destitute of them.

Soon after these occurrences it is seen that the albuminous corpuscles, chlorophyll grains, and pseudo-cells contained in the superficial prismatic cells have retreated into the deeper parts of these cells, while the nucleus remains for some time immediately beneath their free surface, but ultimately disappears.

After these changes in the prismatic cells a continuous membrane can be seen extending over the entire surface of the germ. By maceration it can be separated from the subjacent plasma, and by its resistance to the action of chemical reagents it appears to be of a chitinous nature. The first formed membrane increases in thickness by the formation below it of many successive layers, and the germ instead of being surrounded by a layer of naked prismatic cells has become enclosed in a thick chitinous shell.

After this outer shell has been completed there is formed between it and the germ a second envelope. This is a thin, structureless, transparent, and very elastic pellicle. It is probably formed by the hardening of an excreted liquid.

Kleinenberg regards the outer shell as formed by a total transformation of the entire outer cell stratum. The shell is accordingly an epidermal structure, and the first differentiation of the germ of *Hydra* thus consists in the formation of a peripheral one-layered cellular lamina, the component cells of which die, and have their plasma transformed into chitin so as to form a firm shell which protects the remaining part of the germ from destruction during the long period of its subsequent development. The first organ which proceeds from the *Hydra* germ is thus a transitory one which takes no direct part in the development, and which on the liberation of the definitive body is simply cast off.

As soon as the shell is completed the union of the germ with the maternal body is dissolved, and the germ falls off and sinks to the bottom. A remarkable change now takes place in the structure of the germ. This consists in the fusion of all its cells into an undifferentiated plasmodium. All trace of a cellular structure disappears, and the germ becomes again, like the unsegmented egg, a single large plasma mass, thickly filled with albumen granules, pseudo-cells, and chlorophyll grains.

In this uniform mass there is now formed a small cavity which lies excentrically near the surface. This is the foundation of the body cavity. It enlarges in all directions, and it is clear that it arises by a true liquefaction of a great part of the substance of the germ. The walls, however, of the hollow germ thus formed are as yet uniform and show no trace of differentiation.

In this state the germ remains for many weeks, during which the outer shell becomes softer, and is finally burst and cast off. The germ, however, which it had enclosed continues to be overlaid by the elastic transparent inner shell which lies close upon its surface.

In the hitherto uniform walls of the germ we may now distinguish two layers. This condition is caused by the retreat of the pseudo-cells from the more superficial parts of the wall into its deeper parts, resulting in the appearance of an external clear layer and an internal darker one. This is the first indication of the differentiation of the two germinal layers. Out of the clear layer the ectoderm is formed, out of the darker one the endoderm. By a further differentiation these layers become changed from a continuous plasma into cellular laminae.

The embryo now extends itself and assumes an ellipsoidal form. On one pole the walls grow thinner and soon present a stellate cleft which becomes the mouth. Simultaneously with the formation of the mouth the tentacles show themselves as short, blunt, conical outbulgings of the body walls.

The embryo commonly remains two or three days within the covering of the inner shell. This, however, gradually softens and becomes changed into a tenacious adhesive mucus, which is finally dissolved in the water, and the animal becomes free with all the essential characters of the adult.

It will be thus seen that in *Hydra* no gonophore is formed as an independent zooid, and that the generative elements not only originate in the walls of the body but are retained there up to the period of their liberation in the surrounding water. It will also be apparent that in *Hydra* development takes place without the post-embryonic period of its life presenting anything like a true metamorphosis, and that there is here nothing which can be regarded as a proper larva stage. In this respect *Tubularia* agrees most nearly with *Hydra*, but here the Actinula is a true larva differing from the adult not only in its free mode of life but in its form, though it has no obvious organs which are not also present in a more or less modified shape in the adult. *Myriothela* differs still further in having a more distinctly pronounced larval stage, and in undergoing a well-marked metamorphosis, the Actinula of *Myriothela* being provided in a very characteristic way with transitory organs which entirely disappear during the further course of the development.

PRIMARY MODIFICATIONS OF FORM.—CLASSIFICATION OF THE HYDROIDA.

A complete system of the Hydroida would include not only all Hydroid trophosomes with their associated gonosomes, but all Hydromedusæ, whether traced to polypoid trophosomes or not. There exist, however, many free Hydromedusæ—both Anthomedusæ and Leptomedusæ,—which have not yet been so traced; but so closely do these correspond with Medusæ, which are known to be budded off from fixed trophosomes, that there can scarcely be a doubt that, were we acquainted with their whole life-history, we should find that, like the Medusæ which have been traced to hydriform stocks, these also are planoblasts which had originated as buds from fixed trophosomes. As, however, nothing is known of the trophosomes from which these Medusæ have been derived, it has been generally deemed convenient to treat them independently as members of a general system of the Medusæ, in which the Medusal structure is made the basis of the classification, without necessary reference to the morphological details of the polypoid trophosomes.[1]

There is, however, another group of Craspedotæ or Hydromedusæ, into whose life series a polypoid term does not appear to have been ever intercalated, and which may accordingly be regarded as forming in themselves a separate and well-defined group of the Hydroida.

It is proposed, therefore, in the following sketch of Hydroid classification, to include in the first place those Hydroids with whose trophosomes we are acquainted, making the characters of the trophosome the primary element in the classification; and in the second place, such free Hydromedusæ as there is good reason to believe are never derived from polypoid trophosomes. In the meantime, such free Anthomedusæ and Leptomedusæ as have not yet been traced to their trophosomes must be left to find their proper places among the former group as soon as the discovery of their trophosomes shall afford the necessary data.

The order Hydroida, in the sense in which it is thus proposed to regard it, includes so many well-marked modifications of form, that the zoologist has no difficulty in finding among these such characters as may be legitimately used as the bases of natural systematic groups.

A comparison of the members of the Hydroida with one another shows that—including the extinct Graptolites, whose allocation, however, among the Hydroida, depends on considerations of a more or less hypothetical nature—the order embraces within itself six primary types of form.

[1] See especially Haeckel, Das System der Medusen, Jena, 1879.

In one of these, neither hydrothecæ nor gonangia are developed, so that both hydranths and gonophores are always naked, or if a perisarcal pellicle is excreted over the body of the hydranth, as in *Eudendrium vestitum* (Pl. I. fig. 1), or over the gonophore as in *Cordylophora lacustris*, it is in the former case an adherent coat from which the hydranth is never free as in a true hydrotheca, and in the latter case, it is similarly adherent to the outer surface of the gonophore, and totally different from a gonangium which always includes a blastostyle, from which one or more gonophores are budded off. The gonophores are in some cases hedrioblasts, in others planoblasts, and the planoblasts, with scarcely an exception, belong to the Anthomedusal section of Craspedote Medusæ, and have the generative elements developed in the walls of the manubrium.

To this type the designation of GYMNOBLASTEA has been given.

In another type of Hydroid form the hydranths are protected by hydrothecæ and the gonophores by gonangia; and though in one family (Haleciidæ) the hydrothecæ may be so degraded as to afford scarcely any protection to the hydranth, they are still recognisable under this degraded form. In this type, as in the former, we meet with both hedrioblastic and planoblastic gonophores, and when these are in the form of planoblasts, they belong almost without an exception to the Leptomedusal section of the Craspedote Medusæ, and have their generative elements developed along the course of the radial canals.

The group thus characterised forms the suborder CALYPTOBLASTEA.

Both the Gymnoblastea and the Calyptoblastea, when new hydranth buds are emitted by them, retain these as permanent elements of the colony. There is, however, another small group of Hydroida in which the hydranth buds, after attaining a certain degree of maturity, detach themselves and lead henceforth, like the parent animal, an independent and free life. This group is represented by the fresh-water *Hydra*. No perisarc is here excreted, and the generative elements are not contained in gonophores, but are developed directly in the deeper parts of the ectoderm of the hydranth.

The group thus characterised forms another suborder—that of the ELEUTHERO-BLASTEA.

In a fourth group we have again hydranths united into permanent colonies, but the skeletal structures which when present in the former groups are in the condition of a chitinous perisarc, are here represented by a hard calcareous corallum. This is permeated by a network of inosculating cœnosarcal canals, and is overlaid by an external ectodermal coat. From the cœnosarcal network are developed zooids of two kinds; one (gastrozooids) with a mouth and stomach, and with a circlet of tentacles; the other (dactylozooids) in the form of tentacula-like zooids, and destitute of mouth. The gastrozooids represent the hydranths of the preceding groups. Both kinds of zooids are lodged within chambers excavated in the corallum and lined by reflections of the superficial ectodermal layer.

Our knowledge of the generative system is imperfect; but in one family at least the sexual elements appear to be developed in gonophores lodged in cavities of the corallum.[1]

The Hydroids constructed on the plan thus characterised constitute the fourth sub-order, that of the HYDROCORALLIA.

As already said there are certain free Medusæ (Trachomedusæ and Narcomedusæ) which though they belong to the Craspedotæ are known to be developed directly from the egg without passing through a polypoid stage. Such a phenomenon, showing as it does the omission of a characteristic morphological element in the life-history of the species, renders necessary the association of these directly developed Medusæ into an independent group, which will thus form a fifth suborder of the Hydroida.

To this suborder the name of MONOPSEA has been given. It is exactly equivalent to the Trachylinæ in the system of Haeckel.[2]

If the view which I have elsewhere maintained[3] be correct, that the extinct organisms known as Graptolites were Hydroids in which a longitudinal chitinous rod had become developed in the walls of the coenosarc, and in which the hydranths had been replaced by sarcostyles, which as we know precede the hydranths in the development of certain Plumularidæ, in whose early stages sarcostyles alone are present, then the Graptolites would represent another primary modification of Hydroid structure. I have accordingly, under the name of RHABDOPHORA, considered the Graptolites as representing one of the primary groups of the Hydroida. Having regard, however, to our necessarily very imperfect knowledge of these Palæozoic fossils, I do not desire to assign to this group more than a hypothetical value.

[1] See Moseley, *Phil. Trans.*, vol. clxvii., 1877; and Report on certain Hydroid, Alcyonarian, and Madreporarian Corals, Zool. Chall. Exp., part vii.

[2] In *Limnocodium*, whose relations to the Trachomedusæ are in many respects so close as to justify us in regarding it as an aberrant member of this group, there is some reason for supposing that a Hydroid trophosome shows itself in the course of its development. In the tank where this remarkable Medusa first made its appearance a minute Coelenterate organism, comparable to a fixed Hydroid destitute of tentacles and otherwise in a condition of extreme simplification, was discovered by Mr. A. G. Bourne, and regarded by him as the hydriform trophosome of *Limnocodium*. It is difficult on any other grounds to explain the association of the two organisms in the same tank; but as no genetic connection between them has as yet been discovered, this must for the present be regarded as hypothetical; see A. G. Bourne in *Proc. Roy. Soc.*, 1884, vol. xxxviii. p. 9. A solitary exception to the generally admitted derivation of the Anthomedusæ and Leptomedusæ from polypoid trophosomes has been recorded by Claparède (*Zeitschr. f. wiss. Zool.*, 1863) who believes that he had seen the eggs of an Anthomedusa, referable to the type to which Edward Forbes gave the name of *Lizzia*, directly developed into Medusæ while still lying in the walls of the manubrium of the parent. It is, however, by no means rare for Medusæ to give rise by budding to young Medusæ in a way very similar to that in which planoblasts are budded off from trophosomes; such a formation of Medusa buds is well known to occur in the manubrium of *Lizzia*, and so very easy is it to confound the development of these buds in the Medusa with that of an egg, that even so excellent an observer as Claparède may well have been deceived by it. But even though Claparède's view of the direct development of the egg in *Lizzia* be correct, this solitary fact need not be regarded as constituting a disturbing element in the classification here adopted.

[3] Gymnoblastic Hydroids, p. 379.

TABULAR VIEW OF THE LEADING SYSTEMATIC GROUPS OF THE ORDER HYDROIDA.

SUBORDER	LEGION		FAMILY	EXAMPLES OF GENERA
I. **GYMNOBLASTEA.** No hydrotheca, or gonotheca. Nematophores, which constitute the true family, permanent colonies. Planoblasts in the form of Anthomedusae.	THECLARINA,	Trophosome consisting of a colony of organically united Hydrothecae and with female layer of coenosarc.	Claviidae,	Clava, Rhizogeton, Tubiclava, Merona, &c.
			Coryniidae,	Coryne, Syncoryne, Gemmaria, &c.
			Eudendriidae,	Eudendrium, Pennaria, Eleutheria, Ctenaria, Hydractinia, &c.
			Bougainvilliidae,	Bougainvillia, Garveia, &c.
			Cladoneiidae,	Cladonema, &c.
			Tiaridae,	Tiara, Bythotiara, Sipheria, Stomatoca, Neoturris
			Myriothelidae,	Myriothela
	EUDRACTINA,	Trophosome consisting of a colony of organically united Hydrothecae, which cannot form a colony by a superficial covering of coenosarc.	Eudendriidae,	Eudendrium, Coryngeta.
			Podocorynidae,	
	ORTHOCOCCINA,	Trophosome consisting of a solitary hydranth, perhaps coenosarcal.	Corynopsidae,	Corynopsis, Heterocœla, Acaulia.
			Monocaulidae,	
	HYDROCARINA,	Hydranths unrepresented, with the tentacula one or two in number, springing from one side only of the body.	Lar,	Lar.
			Monobrachiidae,	Monobrachium.
II. **CALYPTOBLASTEA.** Hydranth protected by hydrothecae. Sexual buds protected by gonothecae, forming permanent colonies of Planoblasts in the form of Leptomedusae.	CAMPANULARINA,	Hydrothecae in at least the proximal part of the colony sessile, or attached by their sides to the hydrosome.	Campanulariidae,	Campanularia, Obelia, Thyroscyphus, Hypanthea, Gonothyraa, &c.
			Halecidae,	Halecium, &c.
			Platypodiidae,	Platypodia, Corydendrium, Lafœa, Lictorella.
			Eucopidae,	Eucope, Cophinula, Opleidia
	SERTULARINA,	Hydrothecae developed from more than one side of the hydrocladia, which they do not encircle, but to which for a lesser or less extent they are attached by their sides.	Sertulariidae,	Sertularia, Diphasia, Thuiaria, Desmoscyphus, &c.
			Plumulariidae,	Plumularia, Antennularia, Aglaophenia, Schizotricha, &c.
			Synthecidae,	Synthecium, Thecocladium.
	PLUMULARINA,	Hydrothecae developed from one side of the hydrocladia, which they do not encircle, but to which they are attached by their sides.	Plumulariidae,	Plumularia, Antennularia, Aglaophenia, Schizotricha, &c.
			Eucopidae,	
			Diphasiidae,	Diphasia, Hippurella, Halicornaria, Cladocarpus, &c.
			Halicorniidae,	Halicornaria, Aglaophenia.
	THALAMOPHORA,	Hydrothecae adherent by their sides to the hydrosome. Coenosarcal cavity divided by transverse septa into intercommunicating chambers.	Idiiidae,	Idiia,
				&c.

III **ELEUTHEROBLASTEA.** No hydrosoma, or pseudo-hydrorhiza. Nutritive zooids and forming permanent colonies. No differentiated gonophores.	HYDRIDÆ.	Hydrosoma represented by a free hydrocauli. No present.	Hydrella, Protohydridae,	Hydra, Protohydra.
IV. **HYDROBLASTEA.** A skeleton formed by a coriaceous membrane (ectoderm) surrounded by a system of canals and interfenestrating coenosarcal tubes from which the hydroids (gastrozooids) are developed.	MILLEPORIDÆ.	Hydrosoma helped in every series of the coenosarc which are divided by transverse septa into a series of superimposed chambers.	Milleporidae,	Millepora?
	STYLASTERIDÆ.	Hydrosoma helped in every series of the coenosarc which are destitute of transverse septa.	Stylasteridae,	Spaclangus, Stylaster, Distichopora, &c.
V. **MONOBLASTEA.** Free Hydromedusae, which are developed directly from free stalks, without the intervention of a polyp-trophosome. Corpuscles on the umbrella margin and tiny clubs with ectodermal otoliths.	TRACHOMEDUSÆ.	Gonads in the course of the radial canals.	Petasidae, Trachynemidae, Aglauridae, Geryonidae,	Petasus, Anticongusta, Olindias, &c. Trachynema, Rhopalonema, Persa, &c. Aglaura, Aglantha, Persa, &c. Liriope, Glaucedon, Gorgonia, &c.
	NARCOMEDUSÆ.	Gonads in the walls of the stomach.	Cunninidae, Peganidae, Aeginidae, Solmaridae,	Cunnina, Cunarina, Cunioa, &c. Pegasus, Pegania, Pegantha, &c. Aeginopsis, Aeginura, Solmaris, &c. Solmundella, Solmaridella, Solmaris, &c.
VI. **BLASTOPHORA.** Hydrosoma replaced by necto-stylon. Hydrorrhiza traversed by a continuous longitudinal rod.	GRAPTOLITIDÆ.	Hydrosoma developed from a sclerotised basal gonosome. Gonosomal canals giving origin to a single series of meronidia.	Monograptidae, Diplograptidae,	Monograptus, Rastrites, Didymograptus, &c. Diplograptus, Climacograptus, &c.
	RETIOLITIDÆ.	Scula not present. Coenosarcal canal giving origin to two series of uninidia.	Climacograptidae, Glathograptidae,	Climacograptus, Lasiograptus, &c. Retiolites, Trigonograptus, &c.

DISTRIBUTION.

Though we are still without the data which would enable us to give a complete exposition of the distribution of the Hydroida, our knowledge of this has been very much extended by the explorations of the Challenger, and both in the horizontal distribution of these organisms, and in their bathymetrical range, important accessions have been made to it.

With the view of giving as graphic an expression as possible to the distribution of the species obtained during the voyage, I have divided the whole track of the Challenger into the following sixteen Regions, named either from the adjacent lands or from their position in the great oceans through which the course of the expedition lay. Their boundaries are detailed below and may be seen in the Map at the end of this Report. In order to render them as simple as possible, I have made the Regions to consist of rectangular areas, each limited to the north and south by parallels of latitude, and to the east and west by meridians of longitude. Their size varies much, and they are framed without regard to their occasionally encroaching on the adjacent continents.

Though the species are very unequally distributed among the various Regions, it was only from two of these Regions, the Britanno-Gallic whose Hydroid Fauna has been already well investigated, and the Antarctic, that no Hydroids were brought home.

I. BRITANNO-GALLIC.

Limits—Northern, lat. 51° N.
　　　　Southern, lat. 45° N.
　　　　Eastern, long. 0°
　　　　Western, long. 20° W.
It includes the south-western extremity of England, and the north-western and western coasts of France.

II. THE AZORIC.

Limits—Northern, lat. 45° N.
　　　　Southern, lat. 35° N.
　　　　Eastern, long. 5° W.
　　　　Western, long. 50° W.
It includes the Azores, the western coast of Spain, and Gibraltar.

III. THE NOVA-SCOTIAN.

Limits—Northern, lat. 50° N.
　　　　Southern, lat. 40° N.
　　　　Eastern, long. 50° W.
　　　　Western, long. 75° W.
It includes Nova Scotia and the neighbouring coast of North America.

IV. WEST INDIAN.

Limits—Northern, lat. 40° N.
　　　　Southern, lat. 10° N.
　　　　Eastern, long. 50° W.
　　　　Western, long. 80° W.
It includes Bermuda, the West Indian Islands, and the northern coast of South America.

V. SARGASSIC.

Limits—Northern, lat. 35° N.
  Southern, lat. 0°.
  Eastern, long. 10° W.
  Western, long. 50° W.

It includes the greater part of the Sargasso Sea, Madeira and the Canary Islands, the Cape Verde Islands, Sierra Leone, and the adjacent coast of Africa.

VI. SOUTH ATLANTIC.

Limits—Northern, lat. 0°.
  Southern, lat. 50° S.
  Eastern, long. 10° E.
  Western, long. 60° W.

It includes the eastern coast of South America, and the islands of Ascension and Tristan da Cunha.

VII. CAPE OF GOOD HOPE.

Limits—Northern, lat. 30° S.
  Southern, lat. 50° S.
  Eastern, long. 40° E.
  Western, long. 10° E.

It includes the Cape of Good Hope and Marion Island.

VIII. KERGUELEN.

Limits—Northern, lat. 40° S.
  Southern, lat. 66° S.
  Eastern, long. 90° E.
  Western, long. 40° E.

It includes Kerguelen Island and Heard Island.

IX. ANTARCTIC.

Limits—Northern, lat. 60° S.
  Southern, lat. 67° S.
  Eastern, long. 100° E.
  Western, long. 70° E.

No land is included in this Region. The most southern point attained by the track of the Challenger lies in it.

X. AUSTRALIAN.

Limits—Northern, lat. 20° S.
  Southern, lat. 60° S.
  Eastern, long. 170° W.
  Western, long. 90° E.

It includes Southern Australia, New Zealand, Norfolk Island, Kermadec Islands, Tongatabu, and New Caledonia.

XI. EAST INDIAN.

Limits—Northern, lat. 30° N.
  Southern, lat. 20° S.
  Eastern, long. 170° W.
  Western, long. 90° E.

It includes the northern coast of Australia, the Philippine and other islands of the East Indian Archipelago, the Solomon Islands, Caroline Islands, New Hebrides, and Fiji.

XII. JAPANESE.

Limits—Northern, lat. 50° N.
  Southern, lat. 30° N.
  Eastern, long. 160° E.
  Western, long. 130° E.

It includes Japan and the adjacent coast of Northern Asia.

XIII. North Pacific.

Limits—Northern, lat. 50° N.
       Southern, lat. 30° N.
       Eastern, long. 120° W.
       Western, long. 160° E.

It includes the southern extremity of Vancouver Island, and the Californian coast of North America.

XIV. Mid Pacific.

Limits—Northern, lat. 30° N.
       Southern, lat. 20° S.
       Eastern, long. 80° W.
       Western, long. 170° W.

It includes the Sandwich Islands, the Marquesas Islands, the Low Archipelago, the western coast of Central America, the coasts of Peru.

XV. South Pacific.

Limits—Northern, lat. 20° S.
       Southern, lat. 50° S.
       Eastern, long. 70° W.
       Western, long. 170° W.

It includes the island of Juan Fernandez, with the coast of Chili, and the greater part of the western coast of Patagonia.

XVI. Fuegian.

Limits—Northern, lat. 50° S.
       Southern, lat. 60° S.
       Eastern, long. 50° W.
       Western, long. 80° W.

It includes the coasts of the southern extremity of Patagonia, Cape Horn, Terra del Fuego, and the Falkland Islands.

Among the species obtained are the following ten, which have been already recorded as inhabitants of the shores of Britain:—

Eudendrium rameum.	*Sertularia polyzonias.*
Halecium beanii.	*Sertularia operculata.*
Obelia geniculata.	*Sertularia abietina.*
Lafoëa dumosa.	*Diphasia pinaster.*
Lafoëa fruticosa.	*Thuiaria cupressina.*

Most of these are already known to be widely distributed along both the eastern and the western shores of the North Atlantic, while *Lafoëa fruticosa*, *Sertularia polyzonias*, and *Sertularia operculata* had been identified with species brought from various stations in the Southern Hemisphere. The explorations of the Challenger however have considerably extended our knowledge of the stations in which British species occur, and have shown, as will be seen from the annexed table of distribution, that most of those brought home have a much wider range than had been suspected. It is a fact not destitute of interest that no less than three of these British species, *Obelia geniculata*, *Lafoëa fruticosa*, and *Sertularia polyzonias*, have been brought by the Challenger from the Fuegian Region, and thus indicate a similarity of conditions between the northern and southern regions which shows itself in the appearance of the same species in both.

The Challenger dredgings have yielded two new species of the singular Campanularian genus, *Hypanthea*. One of these comes from the Kerguelen region, where a species of the same genus had already been discovered by the Transit of Venus Expedition. The other is from the Falkland Islands in the Fuegian Region. *Hypanthea* is a comparatively shallow water form, inhabiting a bathymetrical zone which corresponds pretty closely with the Laminarian zone of the British coast. The species from Kerguelen, *Hypanthea aggregata*, came from a depth of from 10 to 60 fathoms, and the Fuegian species, *Hypanthea hemispherica*, from a depth of 12 fathoms. No example of *Hypanthea* has as yet been found outside of these two Regions. In both it covered the fronds of a Laminaria-like seaweed and was associated with *Obelia geniculata*, thus pointing to an interesting parallelism between the Hydroid faunas of Kerguelen and the Falkland Islands, two Regions which, though separated by a wide distance in longitude, lie nearly in the same parallel of latitude.

Our knowledge of the remarkable Perisiphonic genus, *Cryptolaria*, has been enriched by the discovery of eight species, all of which are new. The maximum development of the genus as it appears in the Challenger collection is in the Australian and East Indian Regions, from which three species out of the eight have been obtained. These are *Cryptolaria abyssicola* from a depth of 2600 fathoms, *Cryptolaria geniculata* from a depth of 315 fathoms, and *Cryptolaria gracilis* from a depth of 700 fathoms. The remaining five are more sporadic in their distribution, being dispersed among five Regions, with one species in each, namely, *Cryptolaria humilis*, Azoric, with a depth of 1000 fathoms; *Cryptolaria flabellata*, West Indian, with a depth of 390 fathoms; *Cryptolaria diffusa*, Sargassic, with a depth of 2500 fathoms; *Cryptolaria crassicaulis*, Cape of Good Hope, with a depth of 420 fathoms; and *Cryptolaria pulchella*, North Pacific, with a depth of 20 to 40 fathoms.

The United States exploration of the Gulf Stream, however, has shown that there is a large development of the genus in the West Indian Region, four species having been dredged during that exploration in the Gulf of Mexico. As far as we know at present, therefore, there are two centres of maximum development for *Cryptolaria*, an eastern centre in the East Indian and Australian Seas, and a western centre in the seas around the West Indian Islands, a phenomenon which, as we shall presently see, is also apparent in the distribution of the Plumularinæ.

The bathymetrical range of the various species shows further that *Cryptolaria* is essentially a deep-water genus. Among all the species brought home by the Challenger, only one, *Cryptolaria pulchella*, has been obtained from a depth under 315 fathoms. This comparatively shallow-water species has been dredged from a depth of 20 to 40 fathoms in the North Pacific, while four have been obtained from the great depths of 700, 1000, 2500, and 2600 fathoms respectively. Among those, for the knowledge of which we are indebted to the United States expedition, three have been dredged from depths of 450, 315, and 152 fathoms respectively, while the depth of one, owing to the effacement of the label, has not been recorded.

The genus *Perisiphonia*, also a deep-water form, gives us two species, both obtained in the Australian Region, where *Perisiphonia pectinata* occurred at a depth of 700 fathoms, and *Perisiphonia filicula* at a depth of 150. One of these, however, *Perisiphonia filicula*, was also found in the Azoric Region at a depth of 450 fathoms, and thus affords an instance of the same species occurring in two regions so widely separated as the Azores and Australia, without any intermediate station offering an example of it.

Grammaria, already known as a northern form, is represented in the Challenger collection by three new species, all from a comparatively narrow zone of southern latitude, *Grammaria insignis* having been obtained off Marion Island, near the southern boundary of the Cape of Good Hope Region, and from a depth of from 50 to 100 fathoms, *Grammaria stentor* from Kerguelen with a depth of from 28 to 60 fathoms, and *Grammaria magellanica* from the Fuegian Region, where it was trawled from a depth of 70 fathoms. All the three species thus occur at moderate depths, and their distribution is interesting as affording an example of stations, for the most part widely separated in longitude, and yet lying within a few degrees of the same parallel of latitude.

Sertularia, with the limits assigned to this genus in the present Report, has, as may be expected, yielded to the dredge and trawl of the Challenger a greater number of species than any other genus. Of these—seventeen in all—four have occurred in the Region of the Cape of Good Hope, four in the Kerguelen Region, and three in the Fuegian. Of the remaining species three have been found at the northern side of the equator, where the Azoric, Nova-Scotian, and West Indian Regions have each given one; while on the southern side the Australian, East Indian, and South Pacific Regions have also yielded one each. *Sertularia polyzonias* and *Sertularia filiformis* [*gracilis*], both from the Fuegian Region, are quite littoral, the former occurring at a depth of from 5 to 12 fathoms and the latter at a depth of 9 fathoms, while *Sertularia operculata*, an abundant and characteristic species of the British Laminarian zone, is shown to have a singularly wide area of distribution, having been brought up by the dredge of the Challenger from a depth of 45 fathoms off the western coast of Patagonia.

The genus *Diphasia* is represented in the collection by a single species, *Diphasia penaster*, which was dredged in the Azoric Region from a depth of 450 fathoms.

Thuiaria is represented by six species, two of which come from the seas lying to the north of the equator, and four from the seas lying to the south. They range from the Azoric to the Fuegian Regions, and include only one very deep dwelling species, namely, *Thuiaria hyalina* from the South Atlantic Region, where it inhabited a depth of 770 fathoms. *Thuiaria pharmacopola*, from the Azoric Region, was dredged from a depth of 450 fathoms, while all the others are comparatively shallow water species, their stations varying from 9 to 70 fathoms in depth.

Desmoscyphus has yielded four species which, with the exception of *Desmoscyphus gracilis* from the West Indian Region, have all been found in the South Atlantic. Two of these, however, *Desmoscyphus pectinatus* and *Desmoscyphus obliquus*, afford an instance of unusually wide distribution, *Desmoscyphus pectinatus* having another station in the Australian Region, and *Desmoscyphus obliquus* also another in the East Indian.

Synthecium, hitherto known only as a New Zealand genus, has yielded to the dredge of the Challenger two new species obtained off the south-west coast of Australia.

Idia pristis, the only species as yet known of this remarkable genus, would seem to be widely distributed in the seas lying to the south of the equator. The Challenger obtained it from two stations, one in the South Atlantic Region and the other in the East Indian. In neither of these stations did the depth exceed 20 fathoms.

The Plumularinæ have yielded thirty-one species. As stated in the first part of this Report, it may be generally asserted of the Plumularinæ that they have their greatest development in the warmer seas of both hemispheres, and that in tropical and sub-tropical regions they attain their maximum in multiplicity of forms, in the size of the colonies, and in individual profusion.

Among the species of this group brought home few had been obtained from any considerable depth. *Cladocarpus*, however, which of all the genera of the Plumularinæ would seem to be that which inhabits the greatest depth, is represented in the collection by two species, *Cladocarpus pectiniferus*, which was dredged from a depth of 900 fathoms in the Azoric Region, and *Cladocarpus formosus*, which was obtained by the trawl from a depth of 775 fathoms in the seas lying to the south of Japan. The depth of 900 fathoms from which *Cladocarpus pectiniferus* was dredged is the greatest depth from which any member of the Plumularinæ has as yet been obtained; *Polyplumaria pumila*, *Aglaophenia filicula*, and *Aglaophenia acacia* are also deep-water species, having been all dredged in the Azoric Region from a depth of 450 fathoms. *Plumularia insignis* and *Plumularia abietina* were dredged off Marion Island, in the Region of the Cape of Good Hope, from a depth of from 150 to 310 fathoms; but none of the remaining species of the Plumularinæ came from greater depths than 150 fathoms, most of them from depths under 100 fathoms, while many are quite littoral and came from depths ranging between 8 and 20 fathoms.

The discovery of *Cladocarpus formosus* in the Japanese Region is a fact of considerable interest. This species had previously been obtained by the "Porcupine" from the deep cold area which lies between Shetland and the Færöe Islands, where it was dredged from a depth of 167 fathoms. *Cladocarpus formosus* thus affords an instance of the same species inhabiting two widely separated regions, with its absence, so far as we yet know, from all intervening stations.

The region of maximum development of the Plumularinæ, as far as this group is represented by the species brought home by the Challenger, is that of the East Indian, from which ten species were obtained. It is not, however, only from the number of species, but from the fact that the largest forms and most luxuriant colonies were brought from this region that we are justified in concluding that the conditions most favourable to the development of the Plumularinæ are here found. It is this region which has yielded the large Statoplean forms represented by *Acanthocladium huxleyi*, which attains a height of 15 inches, *Aglaophenia macgillivrayi*, of which a specimen in the collection has also a height of 15 inches, though it has lost the proximal portion of the colony, *Lytocarpus secundus*, which is more than 2½ feet in height, and *Acanthella effusa*, which has a height of 12 inches. One large form, however, *Lytocarpus racemiferus*, was obtained off the coast of Bahia in the South Atlantic Region. It is among these large East Indian Plumularinæ that Semper has described certain species from the Philippine Islands which may probably be identified with *Aglaophenia macgillivrayi*, and *Lytocarpus secundus*, and which in consequence of their formidable stinging properties are held in dread by the natives.[1] Indeed the Philippine Islands appear to afford a habitat specially rich in these fine Hydroids. Off Samboangan, in this group, the trawl and dredge of the Challenger brought up seven species of Hydroids, all belonging to the Plumularinæ, and referable to four genera—*Plumularia*, *Acanthella*, *Aglaophenia*, and *Lytocarpus*.

Our knowledge of the geographical distribution of the Plumularinæ may be supplemented in some important points by the results of the United States exploration of the Gulf Stream. It appears from the dredgings carried on by that expedition that the Plumularinæ are largely represented in the Gulf of Mexico and West Indian seas. The combined results of the explorations made by the Challenger and by the United States expedition thus indicate for the Plumularinæ two centres of maximum development, an eastern centre which lies in the seas which surround the Philippines and other islands of the East Indian Archipelago, and a western centre which lies in the seas of the West Indian Islands, and in the warm waters which bathe the adjacent shores of Central and Equinoctial America. These points in the distribution of the Plumularinæ call to mind two nearly identical centres in which the Cheiroptera have their maximum of development, the Bats of the Old World attaining in the Region of the East Indian Islands that striking development which shows itself in the gigantic species which are so characteristic of the lands lying in that part of the globe, while these Old World Bats are represented by other groups of gigantic Bats which belong to the New World, and have their metropolis in the West Indian Islands and in the neighbouring lands of Central and Equinoctial America.

In comparing, however, the Challenger explorations with those carried on by the

[1] Semper, *loc. cit.*

United States in the Gulf Stream, we must not lose sight of the fact that the more limited area investigated by the latter allowed of a greater concentration of work and of more exhaustive examination than it seems possible for the Challenger to have bestowed on most of the stations comprehended in the vast area over which its explorations extended.

The detailed distribution of the Hydroids brought home by the Challenger will be seen from the following list of Stations and from the appended table, giving the Region which each species inhabited, and the depth from which it was taken.

STATION LIST.

The following is a list of the localities at which Hydroida were collected by the Expedition, with the physical conditions at each. In it are included the Plumularinæ described in the first part of this Report.[1]

STATION 23. Off Sombrero Island, March 15, 1873; lat. 18° 24′ N., long. 63° 28′ W.; depth, 450 fathoms; bottom, Pteropod ooze. Dredged.

Lafoëa dumosa.

STATION 24. Off Culebra Island, March 25, 1873; lat. 18° 38′ 30″ N., long. 65° 5′ 30″ W.; depth, 390 fathoms; bottom, Pteropod ooze. Dredged.

Cryptolaria flabellum. | *Sertularia catena.*

STATION 36. Off Bermuda, April 22, 1873; lat. 32° 7′ 25″ N., 65° 4′ 0″ W.; depth, 30 fathoms; bottom, coral. Dredged.

Campanularia insignis. | *Desmoscyphus gracilis.*

STATION 48. Off Halifax, Nova Scotia, May 8, 1873; lat. 43° 4′ N., long. 64° 5′ W.; depth, 51 fathoms; bottom, rock. Dredged.

Sertularia abietina. | *Thuiaria cupressina.*

STATION 73. Near the Azores, June 30, 1873; lat. 38° 30′ N., long. 31° 14′ W.; depth, 1000 fathoms; bottom, Pteropod ooze; bottom temperature, 39°·4. Dredged.

Cryptolaria humilis.

STATION 75. Near the Azores, July 2, 1873; lat. 38° 38′ 0″ N., long. 28° 28′ 30″ W.; depth, 450 fathoms; bottom, volcanic mud. Dredged.

Polyplumaria pumila.	*Perisiphonia filicula.*
Aglaophenia filicula.	*Sertularia laxa* [*exigua*].
Aglaophenia acacia.	*Diphasia pinaster.*
Halecium beanii.	*Thuiaria pharmacopola.*

STATION 76. Off the Azores, July 3, 1873; lat. 38° 11′ N., long. 27° 9′ W.; depth, 900 fathoms; bottom, Pteropod ooze; bottom temperature, 40°. Dredged.

Cladocarpus pectiniferus.

[1] Zool. Chall. Exp., part xx.

Porto Praya, St. Iago ; depth, 100 fathoms.

Streptocaulus pulcherrimus.

STATION 101.   Atlantic, south-west of Sierra Leone, August 19, 1873 ; lat. 4° 48′ N.,
long. 14° 20′ W.; depth, 2500 fathoms ; bottom, blue mud ; bottom temperature,
36°·4.   Trawled.

Cryptolaria diffusa.

STATION 122B.   Off Barra Grande, Brazil, September 10, 1873 ; lat. 9° 9′ S., long.
34° 53′ W.; depth, 32 fathoms ; bottom, red mud.   Trawled.

Halicornaria plumosa.

STATION 126.   Off the Rio San Francisco, Brazil, September 12, 1873 ; lat. 10° 46′ S.,
long. 36° 8′ W.; depth, 770 fathoms ; bottom, red mud.

Thuiaria hyalina.

Off Bahia ; depth, probably 10 to 20 fathoms.

Aglaophenia calamus.   *Sertularia integritheca.*
Lytocarpus racemiferus.   *Desmoscyphus pectinatus.*
Campanularia ptychocyathus.   *Desmoscyphus obliquus.*
Thyroscyphus ramosus.   *Desmoscyphus acanthocarpus.*
Sertularia cylindritheca.   *Idia pristis.*

STATION 135C.   Off Nightingale Island, Tristan da Cunha, October 17, 1873 ; lat.
37° 25′ 30″ S., long. 12° 28′ 30″ W.; depth, 110 fathoms.   Dredged.

Plumularia stylifera.   *Antennularia fascicularis.*
Halecium fastigiatum.   *Sertularia leiocarpa.*

Simon's Bay, Cape of Good Hope ; depth, 10 to 20 fathoms.

Aglaophenia attenuata.   *Thuiaria pectinata.*
Halecium dichotomum.   *Thecocladium flabellum.*

STATION 144A.   Off Marion Island, December 26, 1873 ; lat. 46° 48′ 0″ S., long.
37° 49′ 30″ E.; depth, 69 fathoms ; bottom, volcanic sand.   Dredged.

Plumularia flabellum.

STATION 145.   Off Marion Island, December 27, 1873 ; lat. 46° 43′ 0″ S., long.
38° 4′ 30″ E.; depth, 50 to 100 fathoms ; bottom, volcanic sand.   Dredged.

Halecium flexile.   *Grammaria insignis.*

STATION 145A.   Off Marion Island, December 27, 1873 ; lat. 46° 41′ S., long. 38° 10′
    E.; depth, 310 and 150 fathoms ; bottom, volcanic sand.   Dredged.

Plumularia insignis. | *Plumularia abietina.*
                          Staurotheca dichotoma.

STATION 149.   Off Accessible Bay, Kerguelen, January 9, 1874 ; depth, 20 fathoms.
                          Sertularia secunda [unilateralis].

STATION 149D.   Royal Sound, Kerguelen, January 20, 1874 ; lat. 49° 28′ S., long.
    70° 13′ E.; depth, 28 to 60 fathoms ; bottom, volcanic mud.   Dredged.

Grammaria stentor. | *Sertularia echinocarpa.*
                          Sertularia articulata.

STATION 149J.   Off Cumberland Bay, Kerguelen Island, January 29, 1874 ; lat. 48° 43′
    S., long. 69° 15′ E.; depth, 105 fathoms ; bottom, volcanic mud.   Dredged.

Schizotricha unifurcata. | *Eudendrium rameum.*
                          Halecium arboreum [robustum].

Off Kerguelen Island ; depth, 10 to 60 fathoms.

Schizotricha unifurcata. | *Obelia geniculata.*
                          Hypanthea aggregata.

STATION 150.   Off Heard Island, February 2, 1874 ; lat. 52° 4′ S., long. 71° 22′ E.;
    depth, 150 fathoms ; bottom, coarse gravel ; bottom temperature, 35°·2.   Dredged.
                          Campanularia tulipifera.

STATION 151.   Off Heard Island, February 7, 1874 ; lat. 52° 59′ 30″ S., long.
    73° 33′ 30″ E.; depth, 75 fathoms ; bottom, volcanic mud.   Dredged.

Schizotricha multifurcata. | *Eudendrium vestitum.*
                          Sertularia exserta.

STATION 160.   South of Australia, March 13, 1874 ; lat. 42° 42′ S., long. 134° 10′ E.;
    depth, 2600 fathoms ; bottom, red clay ; bottom temperature, 33°·9.   Trawled.

Halisiphonia megalotheca. | *Cryptolaria abyssicola.*

STATION 161.   Off Melbourne, April 1, 1874 ; lat. 38° 22′ 30″ S., long. 144° 36′ 30″ E.;
    depth, 33 fathoms ; bottom, sand.   Trawled.
                          Azygoplon rostratum.

STATION 162. Off East Moncœur Island, Bass Strait, April 2, 1874 ; lat. 39° 10′ 30″ S., long. 146° 37′ 0″ E.; depth, 38 fathoms ; bottom, sand and shells. Dredged.

Heteroplon pluma.	*Calamphora parvula.*
Diplocheilus mirabilis.	*Desmoscyphus pectinatus.*

Dictyocladium dichotomum.

STATION 163A. Off Twofold Bay, Australia, April 4, 1874 ; lat. 36° 59′ S., long. 150° 20′ E.; depth, 150 fathoms ; bottom, green mud. Trawled.

Plumularia laxa.	*Halecium beanii.*
Perisiphonia filicula.	*Hypopyxis labrosa.*

STATION 163B. Off Port Jackson, June 3, 1874; lat. 33° 51′ 15″ S., long. 151° 22′ 15″ E.; depth, 35 fathoms ; bottom, hard ground ; bottom temperature, 63°. Dredged.

Plumularia armata.	*Sertularia annulata.*
Halecium telescopicum.	*Synthecium campylocarpum.*

Synthecium alternans.

STATION 169. Near New Zealand, July 10, 1874 ; lat. 37° 34′ S., long. 179° 22′ E.; depth, 700 fathoms ; bottom, blue mud ; bottom temperature, 40°. Trawled.

Cryptolaria gracilis.	*Perisiphonia pectinata.*

STATION 173. Off Matuku, Fiji Islands, July 24, 1874 ; lat. 19° 9′ 35″ S., long. 179° 41′ 50″ E.; depth, 315 fathoms ; bottom, coral mud. Dredged.

Cryptolaria geniculata.

STATION 177. Off the New Hebrides, August 18, 1874 ; lat. 16° 45′ S., long. 168° 7′ E.; depth, 63 to 130 fathoms ; bottom, volcanic sand ; surface temperature, 78°·7.

Lictorella cyathifera.

Off Somerset, Cape York ; depth, 8 to 2 fathoms. Dredged.

Sciurella indivisa.	*Thyroscyphus simplex.*
Acanthella effusa.	*Lictorella halecioides.*
Diplocyathus dichotomus.	*Desmoscyphus obliquus.*

STATION 186. Flinders Passage, Torres Strait, September 8, 1874 ; lat. 10° 30′ S., long. 142° 18′ E.; depth, 8 fathoms ; bottom, coral mud. Dredged.

Lytocarpus spectabilis.	*Thuiaria vincta.*

STATION 188.   Arafura Sea, September 10, 1874 ; lat. 9° 59′ S., long. 139° 42′ E.;
    depth, 28 fathoms ; bottom, green mud.   Trawl and dredge both used.

Acanthocladium huxleyi.

STATION 190.   Arafura Sea, September 12, 1874 ; lat. 8° 56′ S., long. 136° 5′ E.;
    depth, 49 fathoms ; bottom, green mud.   Trawled.

Acanthocladium huxleyi.

STATION 203.   Off Panay, Philippine Islands, October 31, 1874 ; lat. 11° 6′ N., long.
    123° 9′ E.; depth, 20 fathoms ; bottom, mud.

Idia pristis.

STATION 212.   Off Samboangan, Philippine Islands, January 30, 1875 ; lat. 6° 54′ N.,
    long. 122° 18′ E.; depth, 10 fathoms ; bottom, sand.   Trawl and dredge both
    used.

Plumularia dolichotheca.	*Aglaophenia coarctata.*
Acanthella effusa.	*Lytocarpus secundus.*
Aglaophenia macgillivrayi.	*Lytocarpus spectabilis.*

Lytocarpus longicornis.

STATION 214.   South of the Philippine Islands, February 10, 1875 ; lat. 4° 33′ N.,
    long. 127° 6′ E.; depth, 500 fathoms ; bottom, blue mud ; bottom temperature,
    41°·8.   Trawled.

Sertularia producta [geniculata].

STATION 236.   South of Japan, June 5, 1875 ; lat. 34° 58′ N., long. 139° 29′ E.; depth,
    775 fathoms ; bottom, green mud ; bottom temperature, 37°·6.   Trawled.

Cladocarpus formosus.

STATION 237.   Near Yokohama, June 17, 1875 ; lat. 34° 37′ N., long. 140° 32′ E.;
    depth, 1875 fathoms ; bottom, blue mud ; bottom temperature, 35°·3.   Trawled.

Monocaulus imperator.

STATION 244.   North Pacific, June 28, 1875 ; lat. 35° 22′ N., long. 169° 53′ E.; depth,
    2900 fathoms ; bottom, red clay ; bottom temperature, 35°·3.   Trawled.

Stylactis vermicola.

STATION 248. North Pacific, July 5, 1875; lat. 37° 41′ N., long. 177° 4′ W.; depth, 2900 fathoms; bottom, red clay; bottom temperature, 35°·1. Trawled.

Monocaulus imperator.

Honolulu; depth, 20 to 40 fathoms.

Campanularia retroflexa. | *Cryptolaria pulchella.*

STATION 304. Port Otway, Patagonia, December 31, 1875; lat. 46° 53′ 15″ S., long. 75° 12′ 0″ W.; depth, 45 fathoms; bottom, green sand; surface temperature, 57°·2. Dredged.

Sertularia operculata.

STATION 312. Off Port Famine, Patagonia, January 13, 1876; lat. 53° 37′ 30″ S., long. 70° 56′ 0″ W.; depth, 9 fathoms; bottom, blue mud. Dredged.

Halecium flexile. *Hebella striata.*
Halecium cymiforme. | *Lafoëa fruticosa.*
Sertularia filiformis [gracilis].

STATION 314. Near the Falkland Islands, January 21, 1876; lat. 51° 35′ S., long. 65° 39′ W.; depth, 70 fathoms; bottom, sand; bottom temperature, 46°. Trawled.

Grammaria magellanica. | *Sertularia implexa.*
Thuiaria quadridens.

STATION 315. Port William, Falkland Islands, January 26, 1876; lat. 51° 40′ S., long. 57° 50′ W.; depth, 12 fathoms; bottom, sand, gravel. Dredged.

Obelia geniculata. | *Hypanthea hemispherica.*
Sertularia polyzonias.

STATION 320. Off Monte Video, February 14, 1876; lat. 37° 12′ S., long. 53° 52′ W.; depth, 600 fathoms; bottom, green sand; bottom temperature, 37°·2. Trawled.

Sertularia clausa.

STATION 344. Off Ascension Island, April 3, 1876; lat. 7° 54′ 20″ N., long. 14° 28′ 20″ W.; depth, 420 fathoms; bottom, volcanic sand. Dredged.

Cryptolaria crassicaulis.

GEOGRAPHICAL AND BATHYMETRICAL DISTRIBUTION OF THE SPECIES.

(The Numbers in the columns corresponding to the Geographical Regions refer to the Depths.)

* Probable Depth.

DESCRIPTION OF GENERA AND SPECIES.

GYMNOBLASTEA.

Family BOUGAINVILLIDÆ.

Character of the Family. *Trophosome.*—Hydranths with conical hypostome, tentacles filiform in a single verticil.

Gonosome.—Gonophores, planoblasts or hedrioblasts.

Stylactis, Allman.

Stylactis, Allman, Ann. and Mag. Nat. Hist., May 1864

Generic Character. *Trophosome.*—Hydrocaulus rudimental, being reduced to short tubular processes which spring at intervals from a creeping stolon-like hydrorhiza and support the hydranths on their summit; hydrorhiza destitute of external cœnosarcal investment. Hydranths clavate, with a single circlet of filiform tentacles which surround the base of a conical hypostome.

Gonosome.—Gonophores adelocodonic, borne by the hydranth at the proximal side of the tentacles, or by the creeping stolon.

The genus *Stylactis* was founded for two Hydroids originally described by Sars,[1] who referred them to the genus *Podocoryne.* If, however, we accept the validity of the principles which have more recently guided the limitation and systematic position of Hydroid groups, these two species of Sars have really no claim to admission into the genus *Podocoryne.* The gonophores are adelocodonic and sedentary, while those of *Podocoryne* are medusiform planoplasts; and while the creeping stolon of the two species described by Sars is destitute of a cœnosarcal covering, that of *Podocoryne* agrees with *Hydractinia* in being overlaid by a naked fleshy extension of the cœnosarc.

To the two species made known by Sars I was enabled to add another from the Mediterranean,[2] and a fourth species has now been contributed by the dredgings of the Challenger.

[1] Faun. lit. Norv., p. 7, 1846, and Middelhavets lit. Fauna, p. 40.   [2] Gymnoblastic Hydroids, p. 305, 1871.

Stylactis vermicola,[1] n. sp. (Pl. I. figs. 2, 2a).

Trophosome.—Hydranths clavate, with a circlet of about eight tentacles, and with their rudimentary stems springing at short intervals from a creeping, loosely branched, stolon-like hydrorhiza which is destitute of spine-like appendages.

Gonosome.—Gonophores oviform, shortly pedunculate, springing from the hydranth close to its proximal end, or from the hydrorhiza.

Locality.—Station 244, North Pacific; lat. 35° 22′ N., long. 169° 53′ E.; depth, 2900 fathoms.

Stylactis vermicola derives special interest from its singular habitat as well as from the great depth at which it was found living. Professor M'Intosh, while engaged with his Report on the Annelids collected by the Challenger, found that a colony of Hydroids had attached itself to the back of a specimen of *Lætmonice producta*, an *Aphrodita*-like Annelid obtained by the trawl in the North Pacific, from a depth of 2900 fathoms. The Hydroid lay entirely under cover of the scales, which are disposed in two imbricated series over the back of this Annelid, and an examination of a specimen sent to me by Professor M'Intosh has shown it to be an undescribed species of *Stylactis*.

The hydrorhizal stolon crept over the back of the Annelid and was crowded with thick, club-shaped hydranths of various sizes and in various stages of contraction. From the creeping stolon numerous very short tubular offsets were emitted. These formed so many rudimental stems which were invested like the hydrorhiza with a perisarc, while each supported on its summit a claviform hydranth, with about eight filiform tentacles disposed in a single circlet round the base of a thick conical hypostome.

Some of the hydranths gave support to gonophores which were carried on very short peduncles close to the proximal end of the hydranth, while similar short-peduncled gonophores were also borne by the hydrorhiza close to the base of a hydranth. No difference either in form or size could be seen between those hydranths which carried gonophores and those which were without them.

Family EUDENDRIDÆ.

Character of the Family.   Trophosome.—Hydranths with trumpet-shaped hypostome, tentacles filiform in a single verticil.

Gonosome.—Gonophores hedrioblastic.

[1] It is to this species that allusion has been made in the **Narrative of the** Cruise (vol. i. part ii. p. 753), where it is spoken of as referable to a new Calyptoblastic genus. More mature consideration has led me to believe that it has no characters which would justify its separation from *Stylactis*, the generic group in which it is here included.

Eudendrium, Ehrenberg (in part).

Eudendrium, Ehrenberg, Corall. Rothen Meeres, p. 72

Generic Character. *Trophosome.*—Colony dendritic; hydrocaulus invested with a well-developed perisarc. Hydranths with a trumpet-shaped hypostome, which is surrounded by a single verticil of filiform tentacles.

Gonosome.—Gonophores adelocodonic, developed from the body of the hydranth at the proximal side of the tentacles, or from the sides of the hydrocaulus, monothalamic in the female colony, polythalamic in the male.

The genus *Eudendrium* was separated by Ehrenberg from *Tubularia*, with which it had been previously confounded. Its foundation as an independent genus is quite in accordance with its structural characters, though the grounds on which Ehrenberg believed himself justified in insisting on it are derived from characters comparatively trivial and destitute of generic value. The genus as defined by Ehrenberg accordingly contains forms which cannot be generically associated in a natural system. It was reserved for subsequent systematists, especially van Beneden and Strethill Wright, to indicate the true grounds of the revision, the most important of which, so far as concerns the trophosome, are found in the trumpet-shaped hypostome with its single verticil of tentacles.

Among the comparatively small number of Gymnoblastic Hydroids admitting of determination in the collection of the Challenger, are two species of *Eudendrium*— one a well-known European species, the other an undescribed species presenting some remarkable and distinctive characters.

Eudendrium vestitum, n. sp. (Pl. I. figs. 1, 1a).

Trophosome.—Hydrocaulus slender, monosiphonic, much branched, branches alternate, dilated at the summit and with the perisarc extended over the base of the hydranths. Hydranths partially retractile within the dilated summit of the branches.

Gonosome.—Gonophores (female?) oviform, pedunculate, springing from the sides of the branches.

Locality.—Station 151, off Heard Island; depth, 75 fathoms.

The specimen of *Eudendrium vestitum* contained in the collection forms a dense tuft of slender profusely branched stems fixed to the detached spine of an Echinus, and attaining a height of about three-fourths of an inch. The branches are given off at a high angle and are remarkable for the way in which their chitinous perisarc is continued over the base of the hydranths, so that these when contracted have the appearance of being partly enclosed in a chitinous cup which recalls in some respects the hydrotheca of the Calyptoblastea. Here, however—a condition which has its parallel in certain species of *Perigonimus* and in some allied forms—the perisarc is adherent for a greater or less extent to the body of the hydranth, and does not form as in a true hydrotheca a detached receptacle from the walls of which the hydranth is entirely free.

The gonophores are borne singly on rather long peduncles which spring from the sides of the branches, at variable distances below the hydranth. Though the opacity of the perisarcal clothing of the gonophores rendered it impossible to determine the nature of their contents with sufficient certainty to remove all doubt as to their sex, we may safely assume that like similar bodies in other species of *Eudendrium* they enclose ova, the male gonophores in *Eudendrium*, so far as has been hitherto observed, differing from these in form and arrangement.

The perisarc, not only in the trophosome but in its extension over the gonophores, is of a dull brown colour, and is so opaque that a view of the included parts cannot be obtained through it. In these respects, as well as in the long-peduncled oviform gonophores distributed along the ultimate ramuli, *Eudendrium vestitum* forcibly recalls the general facies of *Bimeria vestita*; from which, however, it is separated by the form of its hypostome, which presents the condition of a distinctly differentiated trumpet-shaped appendage characteristic of *Eudendrium*, instead of being a simple fusiform extension of the hydranth as in the Bimeridæ.

Eudendrium rameum (Pallas) (Pl. II. figs. 1, 2).

Tubularia ramea, Pallas, Elenchus, p. 83.
Eudendrium rameum, Johnston, Brit. Zooph., p. 43, 1847.

Trophosome.—Hydrocaulus profusely and for the greater part of its extent very irregularly branched, main stem and principal branches strongly fascicled, but becoming monosiphonic distally where the irregular ramification gives place to an alternate disposition of the ramuli; monosiphonic ramuli with several distinct annulations at their origin, and often with one or more groups of annulations at variable distances along their length. Hydranths with about sixteen tentacles.

Gonosome not present.[1]

Locality.—Station 149*i*, off Cumberland Bay, Kerguelen Island; depth, 105 fathoms.

I can find no character which would justify the separation of the Hydroid which has afforded the subject of the description here given from the *Tubularia ramea* of Pallas = *Eudendrium rameum* of Johnston, a species by no means rare on the British coast. It is true that no gonosome is present in the Kerguelen specimen, and the want of this essential part of the colony renders the identification of the species less certain than it would otherwise be. In the absence, however, of any character inconsistent with the determina-

---

[1] In the gonosome, as observed in British specimens, the male gonophores are two-chambered, borne on the body of the hydranth in a verticil immediately below the tentacles; the female are oviform, scattered on the hydrocaulus for some distance below the hydranth.

tion here adopted, we may safely regard the Kerguelen Hydroid as specifically identical with the European.

Eudendrium rameum is eminently dendritic in its habit, and the tree-like disposition of its zooids, in an assemblage which so forcibly recalls the physiognomy of some of the most characteristic forms of the vegetable kingdom, may well justify the appellation of "zoophyte" by which the Hydroida have been designated in the writings not only of the earlier observers but in those of many zoologists of our own day.

The Kerguelen specimen has a height of between 5 and 6 inches, and the fascicled stem has a diameter of nearly a quarter of an inch at its base.

Family MONOCAULIDÆ.

Character of the Family. *Trophosome.*—Tentacles filiform, in two sets, a proximal and a distal. Hydrocaulus solitary, naked.

Gonosome.—Gonophores hedrioblastic.

Monocaulus, Allman.

Monocaulus, Allman, Ann. and Mag. Nat. Hist., May 1864.

Generic Character. Trophosome.—Hydrocaulus solitary, naked. Hydranths abruptly distinct from the hydrocaulus, with a proximal and a distal set of filiform tentacles; proximal set longer than the distal, and disposed in a single verticil near the base of the hydranth, the distal set scattered over a zone close to the summit of the hydranth.

Gonosome.—Gonophores in the form of simple sacs borne upon peduncles which spring from the body of the hydranth between the proximal and distal sets of tentacles.

The genus *Monocaulus* was constituted for the *Corymorpha glacialis* of Sars, a form which, though its trophosome is that of a *Corymorpha*, is distinguished from that genus by the condition of its gonophores, which are adelocodonic, or in the form of simple closed sacs, instead of being as in every true *Corymorpha* phanerocodonic or medusiform.

Monocaulus imperator, Allman (Pl. III. figs. 1-7).

Monocaulus imperator, Allman, Narr. Chall. Exp., vol. i. p. 753, fig. 265, 1885.

Trophosome.—Hydranth about an inch and a half in height, separated by a deep constriction from the hydrocaulus; proximal tentacles about 4 inches in length, scarcely retractile, pendulous, about one hundred in number; distal tentacles about half an inch in length, contractile, forming a dense fringe round the mouth, forty-eight or fifty in number. Hydrocaulus about half an inch in diameter, very extensile, and when fully extended many feet in height, marked by undulating longitudinal striæ, nearly cylindrical, but enlarging at its proximal end into a bulbous expansion which gives off from its base a dense plexus of capilliform tubes.

Gonosome.—Gonophores ovate, borne in clusters on short, closely crowded, branching peduncles, which spring from a zone just above the base of the proximal circlet of tentacles.

Localities.—Station 237, off Yokohama, Japan; lat. 34° 37′ N., long. 140° 32′ E.; depth, 1875 fathoms.

Station 248, North Pacific; lat. 37° 41′ N., long. 177° 4′ W.; depth, 2900 fathoms.

The magnificent species of *Monocaulus* to which the name of *imperator* has been here assigned was obtained in the North Pacific Ocean, from the enormous depths of 1875 and 2900 fathoms. It far exceeds in size all known Hydroids. One of the specimens captured had its dimensions noted by Sir Wyville Thomson and Mr. Moseley immediately after being brought on board, and was found to measure 9 inches from tip to tip of the tentacles which form the proximal circlet, while its stem rose from its point of attachment to a height of 7 feet 4 inches. As Sir Wyville Thomson remarked, however, in a letter to myself describing the capture, the animal was measured as it lay extended over the surface of the trawl net, and though, of course, capable in life of becoming extended to the length then measured, this may not have represented the height habitually assumed by it. When in the state of extension which would seem to be normal to it the stem had a diameter of about half an inch.

Immediately after the capture a drawing of one of the specimens was made by Mr. Wild, the artist of the expedition, and it is fortunate that this precaution had been taken, for though the specimens were at once put into spirits they have lost almost every character of importance. Indeed, Sir Wyville Thomson, writing to me from on board the Challenger soon after the capture of the great Hydroid, says "these delicate things, drawn up rapidly through the water from a depth of nearly four statute miles, and transported into such totally different conditions of temperature, pressure, &c., suffer greatly from this violent change. They are, in fact, almost knocked to pieces, and their fine tissues are in a nearly deliquescent state, so that our great anxiety is to put them at once into some reagent which may tend to harden them. It is wretched to see them melting away absolutely under our eyes. When put into any of our fluids they at once contract out of all form. But this cannot be helped, and I thought it best that you should have them as well preserved as we could manage, so I only gave them a cursory glance and sent them on."

Notwithstanding the impossibility of preserving the animal in anything like a satisfactory state, some points by no means without interest have been made out in its structure. One of the most important of these is the fact that the stem, instead of having its axis occupied by a pith-like core as in *Corymorpha*, contains a wide cavity which extends through its entire length, and enlarges into a bladder-like receptacle at the base. Sir Wyville Thomson informed me that, when living, liquid was seen to gravitate down the stem, and collect in the basal expansion.

The cavity which thus occupies the axis of the stem is lined by the endoderm (fig. 4, c), of which, however, only traces remained in the specimens. The cells of which this is composed seem to have contained coloured granules, and it must have been traversed by the longitudinal canals (d) which, as in *Corymorpha*, represent the proper body cavity. Such at least may be inferred from the presence in *Monocaulus imperator* of the longitudinal striæ which in *Corymorpha* are the external expression of the internal canals. These striæ, as Sir Wyville Thomson informed me, were very well marked in the living animal, and they are so represented in Mr. Wild's drawing. In the specimens as they reached me, however, rather faint indications of the canals were all that could be obtained.

Immediately external to the endoderm lies a very remarkable tissue (figs. 4, b, 5, a, and 6). Indeed the presence of this tissue is probably the most striking feature in the histology of the Hydroid. It shows itself in the form of a fibrillated membrane whose most marked property is its extraordinary elasticity. The fibres of which it is composed take a circular course and are comparatively thick, about $\frac{1}{500}$th of an inch in diameter, and are resolvable into finer fibrillæ, but are otherwise homogeneous (fig. 6).

Besides this fibrillated structure no other histological elements can be detected in the elastic tissue, which forms a transparent, colourless, and comparatively thick layer extending through the whole length of the stem. It is of a firm, even cartilaginous consistence, and its elasticity is such that separated portions of the stem-wall curl up forcibly on themselves. Sir Wyville Thomson describes the stem in the living animal as "enormously extensile." This extensibility is to a great extent retained in the dead specimen, in which the longitudinal extension of the stem is permitted by the elastic layer, which, when the extending force is withdrawn, brings back the stem to its previous length. Though the course of the fibres of the elastic layer is transverse, its elasticity would thus appear to exert itself in antagonising longitudinal as well as transverse extension of the stem. The elasticity, however, is more strongly marked transversely, or in the direction of the component fibres by which the stem in the dead animal is thrown into irregular longitudinal flutings (fig. 7). Though it is pretty certain that in the living animal the elastic layer must be associated with a proper contractile tissue, which it antagonises and controls, the state of the specimens did not allow any trace of this to be detected.

Resting on the outer side of the elastic layer is the ectoderm (figs. 4, a, 5, b), consisting of a single layer of loosely aggregated cells, irregular in form and size, and with granular contents which in the preserved specimens were opaque and of a brown colour. This layer would seem to be in direct contact with the surrounding water, for nothing like a perisarc, even in the condition of the thin pellicle which occurs in *Corymorpha*, could be detected.

I regard the elastic tissue of *Monocaulus imperator* as the homologue of the mesosarc, or supporting lamella, differing, however, from this layer as it shows itself in every other known instance by its massive development, its more decidedly fibrillated structure, and its great elasticity.

I could find no trace of the papilliform processes which in *Corymorpha*, and in at least one species of *Monocaulus*, are developed near the base of the stem. In *Monocaulus imperator*, however, the stem sent off from its proximal end a multitude of fine capillary tubes which, unlike the stem, were each invested by a very delicate chitinous pellicle, and were aggregated into a dense terminal plexus.

The tentacles composing the proximal circlet as noted by Sir Wyville Thomson were in life about 4 inches long, almost transparent, and in most instances of a pale pink colour, while the mass of gonophores which lay just above their base was of a maroon colour. The colour of the stem in the recent animal was in most of the specimens a pale pink, becoming darker towards the base.

The specimens when brought up were for the most part found to have the proximal extremity coated with mud, a fact which renders it pretty certain that in its natural attitude this gigantic *Monocaulus* lives with its proximal end plunged into the muddy sea bottom.

With regard to the associates of *Monocaulus imperator*, the editor gives the following list from the same dredging. Actiniaria :—*Paractis tubulifera*, *Lipomema multiporum*, *Cereus spinosus*, and *Porponia robusta*; Asteroidea:—*Porcellanaster tuberosus* and *Hyphalaster inermis*; Echinoidea :—*Phormosoma tenue*; Ophiuroidea :—*Ophioglypha orbiculata*, *Ophioglypha sculptilis*, and *Ophiomusium granosum*; Holothurioidea:—*Holothuria thomsoni*; Brachiopoda :—*Terebratula dalli* and *Discina atlantica*; Mollusca :—*Malletia dunkeri*, *Glomus japonicus*, *Arca (Barbatia) pteroessa*, *Pleurotoma* sp., and *Octopus januarii*; Fish :—*Neobythites grandis*, *Macrurus asper*, *Macrurus altipinnis*, *Macrurus liocephalus*, *Gonostoma microdon*, and *Bathysaurus mollis*; in addition to *Phoxichilidium mollissimum*, *Scalpellum vitreum*, and a number of other Crustacea which perhaps may not have come from the bottom. All the above were new species, with the exception of the *Discina*.

CALYPTOBLASTEA.

Family HALECIIDÆ.

Character of the Family. *Trophosome.*—Hydrothecæ replaced by shallow saucer-shaped pedunculate appendages (hydrophores). Hydranths with conical hypostome. *Gonosome.*—Gonophores hedrioblastic.

Halecium, Oken.

Halecium, Oken, Lehrbuch d. Naturgesch., 1815.

Generic Character. *Trophosome.*—Colony dendritic, with fascicled or monosiphonic stem. Hydrothecæ replaced by shallow pedunculated cups (hydrophores), too small to receive the hydranths in retraction. Sarcothecæ not present.

Gonosome.—Gonophores adelocodonic. Gonangia with terminal or lateral orifice.

There is no more natural and definitely marked genus among the Calyptoblastic Hydroids than that of *Halecium*, with two or three others which must be united with it in one and the same family. The hydrotheca so well developed in other Calyptoblastea is in these genera rudimental, being reduced to the condition of a peduncle, with its distal-end expanded so as to form a very shallow membranous cup, quite incapable of receiving the hydranth, even in its state of extreme retraction. The term hydrotheca is thus inapplicable to it, and that of "hydrophore" may be conveniently used to designate the peduncle with its terminal expansion or "limbus."

The primary hydrophore is always immovably fixed by its base to the hydrocaulus, but in most cases it becomes, with the growth of the colony, prolonged by the successive formation of new hydrophores which originate within the limbus of the preceding one, and the primary hydrophore is thus extended by a succession of similar segments piled one on the other in a single continuous series, which is strongly suggestive of a telescope with its tubes drawn out.

The limbus of the hydrophore is in almost every instance ornamented by minute refringent puncta which run round its walls in the form of a circular wreath. What may be their meaning is unknown, but that they are not without significance may be assumed from the constancy of their occurrence. They are found in the most widely separated species, in species in which the limbus is least developed as well as in those in which this part is most obvious, and occur not only in *Halecium* proper but in forms which, though belonging to the same family, must be placed in different genera. Among the various species which I have had an opportunity of examining, there is only one (*Halecium cymiforme*, Pl. VII.) in which I have failed to detect them.

The gonangia of *Halecium* spring in some cases from the proximal or primary segment of a hydrophore, sometimes from the side of a branch, and sometimes as a continuation of its distal end. The orifice is sometimes terminal, sometimes lateral, and there is probably always a difference of form between the gonangia of male and female colonies. In some cases the blastostyle develops from its expanded summit on the outer side of the gonangium a pair of well-formed hydranths with tentacles and mouth, a remarkable phenomenon of which we have no other example in any Hydroid.

In the family of the Haleciidæ must be included a beautiful Hydroid obtained by the Challenger, and forming the type of a new genus, *Diplocyathus* (Pl. VIII.). In the same family the remarkable genus *Ophiodes* of Hincks will also find a place, while I am strongly of opinion—though I have had no opportunity of examining a specimen—that we ought to bring into the same association the singular genus, *Hydranthea*, Hincks, which Mr. Hincks places among the Gymnoblastic Hydroids.

Halecium robustum, n. sp. (Pl. IV. figs. 1–3).

Trophosome.—Colony attaining a height of upwards of eight inches; stem profusely and irregularly branched, with the branches extending for the most part, but not exclusively, in a single plane; main stem and principal branches very thick, fascicled; ultimate branches monosiphonic, disposed in alternate pinnæ, each springing from the side of the basal segment of a hydrophore; pinnæ divided into short internodes by obliquely transverse joints, each internode supporting on alternate sides a hydrophore with a very narrow non-everted limbus; basal segment of hydrophore adnate by its side to the hydrocaulus. Hydranths very large, with about eighteen tentacles.

Gonosome not present.

Locality.—Station 149J, off Cumberland Bay, Kerguelen Island; depth, 105 fathoms.

This is a large and very robust form, the stem towards the root measuring a quarter of an inch in diameter, and the principal branches two-tenths of an inch. The primary segment of the hydrophore is adnate to the internode, and is frequently prolonged by two or three supplementary tubuli. The limbus of the hydrophore is exceedingly narrow, and is marked by a girdle of minute brilliant points.

The presence of a zone of refringent puncta on the almost evanescent limbus of the hydrophore of *Halecium robustum* points to the all but universal presence of this apparently insignificant character throughout *Halecium* and its immediate allies. In only one instance among the various species of *Halecium* which I have examined have I failed to detect these puncta, though the specimens had been obtained from very various and widely distant localities.

The soft parts are in this fine species, as in almost all the Haleciidæ contained in the collection, sufficiently well preserved to admit of the form of the hydranth being observed in most of its important features.

Halecium telescopicum, n. sp. (Pl. V. figs. 1, 1a).

Trophosome.—Hydrocaulus irregularly branched, with the branches given off nearly in one plane. Hydrophores with the limbus narrow and slightly everted, and with the first of the accessory segments provided with two oblique annuli at its base.

Gonosome not present.

Locality.—Station 163B, off Port Jackson; depth, 30 to 35 fathoms.

The branches of this species are very slender and flaccid, and the internodes of moderate length. The hydrophores are often very much extended by the superposition of consecutive segments, as many as nine such segments being occasionally present. The basal or primary segment is not adnate by its side to the hydrocaulus. The first of the accessory segments, or that which immediately succeeds the primary segment, is usually the longest, and is always provided with two oblique annuli at its base. The branches spring from the sides of the primary segments of the hydrophores. The fasciculation of the stem and larger branches would seem to cease soon, leaving an extensive portion of the colony to be continued in a monosiphonic condition for the remainder of its course.

The specimen consists of a portion of a colony about two inches in height, and it is probable that the height attained by the entire colony does not much exceed that of the specimen.

Halecium flexile, n. sp. (Pl. V. figs. 2, 2*a*).

Trophosome.—Hydrocaulus attaining a height of about four inches; main stem and principal branches fascicled, becoming monosiphonic towards the distal portion of the colony, slender and flexile; ramification pinnate and alternate, every branch springing from the base of a hydrophore, divided by oblique joints into moderately long internodes, each internode with a shallow annular constriction at its proximal end. Hydrophores cylindrical, usually prolonged by several consecutive similar segments.

Gonosome.—Gonangia (male ?) obuviform capsules springing by a short peduncle from the side of the basal segment of the hydrophore, and provided with a terminal orifice.

Locality.—Station 145, off Marion Island; depth, 50 fathoms.

Station 312, Port Famine, Patagonia; lat. 53° 37' 30" S., long. 70° 65' 0" W.; depth, 9 fathoms.

This is a flexile and graceful species, thus contrasting in its habit with the rigidity which is characteristic of many species of *Halecium*. The hydrophores have their basal segment standing out free from the internode, while they are in almost every instance prolonged by the superposition of several similar segments.

The soft parts were sufficiently well preserved in the specimens to allow of their more important details of form being observed. The hydranths, which are very large, have, as in other species of *Halecium*, a well-defined, thick, fusiform dilatation of the body just behind the tentacles. These spring from the margin of an expanded disc, which on its upper side carries the conical hypostome, and are about twelve in number.

Two very different localities, Marion Island and the region off Tierra del Fuego, have yielded specimens of *Halecium flexile*; at least I do not hesitate in referring the specimens from both of these localities to the same species, for though no gonosome is present in the examples coming from the region of Tierra del Fuego, the trophosome of these is specifically indistinguishable from that of the others.

Halecium beanii, Johnston (Pl. XII. figs. 3, 3*a*).

Halecium beanii, Johnston, Brit. Zooph., ed. 2, p. 59, pl. ix.
   „   „   Hincks, Brit. Hydroid Zooph., p. 224, pl. xliii. fig. 2.

Trophosome.—Hydrocaulus attaining a height of three inches; main stem and principal branches fascicled, becoming monosiphonic distally; main stem irregularly branched, the smaller ramuli pinnately disposed, and for the most part carrying secondary and tertiary pinnæ, ultimate ramuli very slender. Hydrophores commencing with a short basal offset from the distal end of each internode, and almost always continued by a consecutive series of short superimposed tubes, each slightly widening upwards and ending in a narrow everted limbus.

Gonosome.—Gonangia springing each by a very narrow base from the side of an internode close to the origin of a hydrophore; female slipper-shaped, with tubular lateral orifice; male elongate, ovoid, with terminal orifice.[1]

Locality.—Station 75, off the Azores; lat. 38° 38′ 0″ N., long. 28° 28′ 30″ W.; depth, 450 fathoms.

Station 163A, off Twofold Bay; lat. 36° 59′ S., long. 150° 20′ E.; depth, 150 fathoms.

The slenderness of the ramuli in the monosiphonic portion of the colony and the slipper-shape form of the female gonangia afford distinguishing characteristics of the present species. The general ramification of the colony is in a single plane, and the ramuli spring each from a point on the side of an internode close to the base of a hydrophore. The number of superimposed segments in the hydrophore is usually very considerable and may amount to as many as seven or eight. The limbus of the hydrophore, though narrow, possesses the wreath of brilliant puncta characteristic of the genus and its allies.

The slipper-shaped form of the female gonangia, though this condition is not confined to the present species, is remarkable and characteristic. The quadrate orifice, instead of being as in most cases terminal, is here placed near the middle of the side which faces the branch, and is raised upon the summit of a short tube. The point from which the gonangium springs is situated close to the origin of a hydrophore, and corresponds exactly to the origin of a branch whose place is thus taken by the gonangium.

Halecium beanii is one of the few British Hydroids brought home by the Challenger. It was obtained during the voyage from two localities; one of these was in the neighbourhood of the Azores, where it occurred at a depth of 450 fathoms, the other off the southeast coast of Australia at a depth of 150 fathoms.

[1] As seen in European specimens. No male gonosome occurs among the specimens of *Halecium beanii* brought home by the Challenger.

Halecium fastigiatum, n. sp. (Pl. XV. figs. 2, 2a).

Trophosome.—Hydrocaulus with the main stem and principal branches fascicled, becoming monosiphonic and slender towards their distal extremities; ramification profuse and irregular, with the branches given off in different planes and at a high angle.

Gonosome.—Gonangia (male) springing from the side of the basal segment of the hydrophores, sessile, compressed goblet-shaped, deep.

Locality.—Station 135c, off Nightingale Island, Tristan da Cunha; depth, 110 fathoms.

This is a slender and flexile species. The specimens are but fragmentary and destitute of hydrorhizal extremity, and the largest has a height of upwards of two inches. The branches, which like the gonangia spring from the fixed basal segment of the hydrophore, are given off at an acute angle and become directed in various planes. The internodes are of moderate length.

The hydrophores usually present two or three superimposed segments, but are often formed alone by the fixed lateral process of the stem, which then carries the hydranth directly. The segments are of variable length and the limbus is well developed. The wreath of brilliant points just within the margin is distinct. The hydranths are large and were well preserved in the specimen, where they might be observed in various states of extension.

The gonangia are large, their height being nearly twice that of an internode. They spring, as is usual in the genus, from the basal segment of the hydrophore. When viewed in the plane of the hydrophores they present the outline of a deep wide-mouthed goblet, slightly everted towards the rim, and narrowed at their point of attachment without forming a distinct peduncle. When viewed in a plane at right angles to this they are seen to be much compressed.

The gonangia present in the specimen were those of a male colony. The blastostyle carried a single sporosac, which projected for some distance through the orifice of the gonangium.

Halecium dichotomum, n. sp. (Pl. VI. figs. 1–4).

Trophosome.—Hydrocaulus consisting of jointed stems which branch dichotomously and are continuous at their proximal ends with a plexus of branching and inter-communicating tubes; internodes of stem long and cylindrical, branches given off close to the distal ends of the internodes. Hydrophores either direct continuations of the internodes, or springing from the sides of the tubes which form the basal plexus, nearly cylindrical, with a few annular rugæ at the base, and with very narrow, scarcely everted limbus.

Gonosome.—Gonangia (female) springing each by a short peduncle from the sides of the hydrophores, pyriform, with a lateral tubular orifice and rounded summit, or with the summit broadly truncate, regularly and distinctly annulated throughout.

Locality.—Simon's Bay, Cape of Good Hope; shallow water.

Halecium dichotomum is a very distinct and remarkable species. The beautifully annulated condition of the gonangia presents a character not elsewhere met with in *Halecium.* In the general architecture of the hydrocaulus, and in the plexus of tubes with which the proximal ends of the stems are continuous, *Halecium dichotomum* closely approximates to *Halecium cymiforme* (Pl. VII.), but presents a combination of characters which separate it by a wide interval from every other known species of *Halecium.*

The stems, which rise free from the basal plexus to a height of from about half an inch to an inch, consist of a series of cylindrical tubes, each tube springing from a point close to the distal end of that which precedes it. These tubes represent the internodes of the stem, but instead of being as in other cases directly continuous with one another, they have their distal ends free. Each of these ends either directly supports a hydranth —the entire internode thus representing the basal segment of a hydrophore—or is continued by one or more superimposed segments. The stem may thus be regarded as a series of long, nearly straight, cylindrical hydrophores, either simple or extended by the superposition of accessory segments, each hydrophore springing, one from the other, so close to the distal end of that which precedes it, and at so high an angle, as to form a geniculate linear series. The long cylindrical internodes which in this way make up the stem are often prolonged by two instead of a single internode, both springing opposite to one another from points close to the distal end. Two branches which exactly repeat that from which they spring are thus formed, and give the dichotomous character to the ramification of the colony.

The basal plexus consists of an entangled mass of tubes whose branches unite freely with one another. These tubes, though their diameter is scarcely less than that of the stem, do not present the regular succession of internodes met with in the latter. Their walls are marked by rather irregular annular rugæ. They give off hydrophores which spring here and there from their sides, and some of these as in the hydrophores of the stem support laterally situated gonangia.

The fascicled condition of the stem found in most species of *Halecium* is usually but slightly marked in *Halecium dichotomum*, though some of the old stems may become very much branched and fascicled. The fasciculation, however, is in most cases chiefly confined to the basal plexus, where two or three tubes may here and there be seen united by their sides to one another.

The gonangia present a slight difference in form. While the greater number have the summit rounded and arched over the lateral orifice, this part is in others broadly truncate. The difference is probably dependent on different degrees of maturity; at all events it does not, as might be supposed, indicate a difference of sex, ova being present in both forms.

Like most of the examples of *Halecium* contained in the collection, the present species had its soft parts fairly well preserved, so that the general form of the hydranths could be delineated while the germinal vesicle and spot were quite distinct in the ova.

The collection contained no example of a colony with male gonosome.

Halecium cymiforme, n. sp. (Pl. VII. figs. 1–5).

Trophosome.—Hydrocaulus a very slender sub-dichotomously branched stem, which springs from a bundle of creeping tubular filaments. Hydrophores borne on the summits of the branches, and with a moderately wide, reflexed limbus.

Gonosome.—Gonangia (male?) pyriform, compressed, borne like the hydrophores on the summits of the branches, and having their contents crowned with a cap which disappears as the gonophore advances towards maturity.

Locality.—Station 312, Port Famine, Patagonia; lat. 53° 37′ 30″ S., long. 70° 56′ 0″ W.; depth, 9 fathoms.

Halecium cymiforme presents a multitude of very slender branches of uniform thickness, each springing from a point near the distal end of its predecessor, the whole forming a combination not unlike what may be seen in certain forms of the definite inflorescence known to botanists as a cyme. Usually two small branches are given off close to one another near to the distal end of the preceding one, thus giving a dichotomous character to the ramification.

The hydrorhizal portion of the specimen examined consisted of numerous tubular filaments, which ran in close apposition to one another along the stems and branches of another Hydroid, giving off from distance to distance their slender stems, which soon began to multiply by ramification, and which scarcely differed in diameter from the hydrorhizal filaments from which they sprang. The branches are provided with a few annulations at their origin, and occasionally a few in the course of their length; but they present no true joints, and we must regard the entire hydrocaulus as composed of a succession of internodes, each springing laterally from its predecessor, instead of being in direct continuation with it. The ramification of *Halecium cymiforme* is thus very similar to that which occurs in *Halecium dichotomum*. The distal extremity of every internode or segment of the ramification is free, and becomes in some cases continued into a hydrophore, while in others it carries a gonangium.

The hydrophores are represented by the free ends of the segments crowned by a limbus whose extreme rim is usually reflexed, and are frequently continued by one or two accessory hydrophores. The wreath of brilliant points, by which the limbus of the hydrophore is in the genus *Halecium* almost universally ornamented, cannot here be detected.

The mode in which the hydrophores form direct continuations of the segments of the stem is quite similar to the condition met with in *Halecium dichotomum*.

The gonangia are for the most part borne in an entirely similar way on the free summits of the segments of the ramifications, thus taking the places which in other parts of the colony are occupied by the hydrophores. Gonangia are also occasionally borne on the summits of short lateral branches given off close to the free end of the segment.

The gonangia present in the specimen appeared to be male, and their contents exhibited some curious and interesting features. Through the axis of the compressed pyriform gonangium the blastostyle (figs. 4 and 5, *a*) extends as a continuation of the cœnosarc of the stem, and soon emits from its side a single gonophore (figs. 4 and 5, *b*) which continues to be surrounded by an ectodermal envelope (figs. 4 and 5, *c*) from the sides of the blastostyle. The distal half of the cavity of the gonangium is occupied by a remarkable structure which lies like a cap over the summit of the gonophore, and consists of two concentric but laterally compressed hollow thick-walled hemispheres, the inner entirely embraced by the outer. The outer (fig. 4, *e*), which is in contact with the inner surface of the gonangium walls, is composed of radiating filaments, each of which under a sufficiently high power of the microscope may be resolved into a linear series of spherical corpuscles. The structure of the inner hemisphere (*d*) which lies in contact with the membranous envelope of the gonophore is more obscure, but would seem to consist of a plasmatic mass containing irregularly disposed nucleus-like corpuscles. The double cap which thus lies upon the summit of the gonophore in the young gonangium gradually atrophies as the gonophore advances towards maturity, and ultimately disappears (fig. 5) or leaves behind only a few radiating irregular threads as evidence of its former existence.

Diplocyathus, n. gen.

Name from διπλόος, double, and κύαθος, a cup, in allusion to the accessory cup at the base of the hydrotheca.

Generic Character. Trophosome.—Hydrocaulus a branching stem on which the hydrothecæ are replaced by hydrophores, each having a small cup of a different form at its base. *Gonosome* not known.

This remarkable genus has strong affinities with *Halecium*, from which it differs in the presence of a second cup-like receptacle at the base of every hydrophore. This receptacle is probably a true sarcotheca, and *Diplocyathus* would thus afford an additional instance of the presence of such bodies in Hydroids not belonging to the Plumularinæ.

It is impossible, however, to avoid a comparison of the accessory cup and its contents with the "tentaculoid organs" described by Hincks in *Ophioides*,[1] another genus having close affinities with *Halecium*. An examination of living specimens can alone afford

[1] *Ann. and Mag. Nat. Hist.*, ser. 3, vol. xviii. p. 421, pl. xiv., 1866; British Hydroid Zoophytes, p. 230, pl. xiv.

the means of determining with certainty the nature of the soft parts which fill the little accessory cups of *Diplocyathus*; and the most that could be made out from an examination of the preserved specimens was the presence within the cups of simple granular contents, which might occasionally be seen to extend beyond the margin, thus suggesting the commencement of a pseudopodial protrusion of the sarcode contents. In other respects the agreement between *Ophioides* and *Diplocyathus* is so decided that the close affinity of the two genera can hardly be questioned.

The hydrophore in *Diplocyathus dichotomus*, the only known representative of the genus, is funnel-shaped, with a well-developed limbus, a form which closely resembles that of the hydrophore in *Ophioides mirabilis*. In *Ophioides* as figured by Hincks the hydrophores terminate the branches, while in *Diplocyathus* they are disposed alternately from distance to distance along their sides.

Diplocyathus dichotomus, n. sp. (Pl. VIII. figs. 1, 2, 3).

Trophosome.—Hydrocaulus monosiphonic, dichotomously and profusely branched; branches given off in various planes and frequently reuniting with one another so as to form a bulky reticulated mass. Hydrophores widely funnel-shaped, rather closely set, alternate, supported through the medium of a very short annular segment on a lateral process of the stem. Accessory cups cylindrical, sessile, each seated in the axil of the lateral process.

Gonosome not present.

Locality.—Off Somerset, Cape York, Torres Strait; depth, 8 to 12 fathoms.

In its general physiognomy *Diplocyathus dichotomus* is so distinct as to be easily recognised at a glance. It is of remarkably rigid habit, and by the profusion of its branches, which extend in all directions, and their frequent union with one another, it forms a bulky reticulated mass which forcibly recalls the skeletons of some of the horny sponges.

The ramification is regularly dichotomous, and the branches are here and there—but not at exactly regular intervals—intersected by transverse joints. The hydrophores with their accessory cups are borne along the sides of the branches in two very regular alternate series. Their limbus is well developed, but though the cup it forms is deeper than in any of the species of *Halecium*, the hydranth even in its condition of extreme retraction is quite incapable of being included within it, as the soft parts still well preserved in the specimens plainly show. In no instance were the hydrophores in the specimen continued by the superposition of accessory tubes.

The accessory cups, which are situated on the distal side of each of the lateral processes and in the re-entrant angle between this process and the stem, are cylindrical in shape.

Their height is about half that of the hydrophore and their width is about one-third of their height. The orifice is quite even. They are attached to the stem by a narrow continuation of the base, which however is never so elongated as to form a true peduncle.

The Challenger specimen has a height of about four inches. The ramuli which are given off from the main stem are sometimes simple, sometimes once or twice branched.

Among the characters which indicate the close affinity of *Diplocyathus* with *Halecium* must further be mentioned the wreath of minute brilliant points which surrounds the limbus of the hydrophore. Judging from Hincks' figure of *Ophioides* a similar feature would seem to be present in that genus, and indeed is scarcely ever wanting in any species of *Halecium* or of the allied genera.

The hydranth is large and furnished with about twenty-six tentacles.

Family CAMPANULARIDÆ.

Character of the Family. *Trophosome.*—Hydrothecæ borne by peduncles, campanulate or tubular; hydrocaulus not enveloped by peripheral tubes.

Gonosome.—Gonophores planoblasts or hedrioblasts.

Campanularia, Lamarck (*in part*).

Campanularia, Lamarck, Hist. Anim. sans Vert., ed. 2, vol. ii.

Generic Character. *Trophosome.*—Hydrothecæ pedunculate, campaniform, with serrate or entire margin destitute of operculum, and with the cavity distinctly differentiated by a perforated diaphragm from that of the peduncle, peduncle springing from the sides of a simple or ramified, free or adherent hydrocaulus. Hydranths with a trumpet-shaped hypostome.

Gonosome.—Gonophores adelocodonic, never issuing from beneath the cover of the gonangium.

The genus *Campanularia*, as originally defined by Lamarck, included several forms which the closer examination to which they have been since subjected has shown to be more correctly distributed under separate generic groups. Even among those species in which the hydrothecæ present the true campanulate form, there are some in which the gonophores are sedentary sacs without any obvious medusiform conformation, and others in which the gonophores are true medusiform planoblasts.

A difference of this kind is of sufficient importance to justify its being made the grounds of a generic separation, and I believe with Mr. Hincks that it will be better to limit the genus *Campanularia* so as to make it include only those species in which, with the trophosome presenting the characters here enumerated, the gonophores are destitute of obvious medusiform structure. So limited, it will include the greater number of the species with true campanulate and pedunculate hydrothecæ, and will leave the remainder of those which would have come under Lamarck's definition to find their places in other genera.

It is unfortunate, however, that the trophosome seldom presents any character which would enable us to assert that its gonophores are hedrioblasts rather than planoblasts, and since in many of the species obtained by the Challenger the gonosome is entirely absent, we are forced to regard the allocation of these species to definite genera as possessing only a provisional validity, liable to be set aside on the discovery of the gonosome.

Campanularia insignis, n. sp. (Pl. IX. figs. 1, 2).

Trophosome.—Colony attaining a height of six inches; stem monosiphonic, clustered, springing from a creeping tubular fibre, regularly set with pinnately disposed alternate ramuli, but otherwise simple or very sparingly branched, both stem and ramuli divided into internodes by equidistant transverse joints. Hydrothecæ borne both by stem and ramuli in two alternate series, every internode supporting a hydrotheca on a point close to its distal end; hydrothecæ deep, cylindrical for some distance from the orifice, and then gradually narrowing into a short peduncle which is borne through the medium of a very short annular segment on the summit of a lateral process of the internode; margin perfectly entire and surrounded by a narrow band.

Gonosome not present.

Locality.—Off Bermudas; depth, 30 fathoms.

Campanularia insignis is a large and handsome species. The long, almost always undivided stems spring from the hydrorhizal plexus in clusters of five or six, and carry along nearly their entire length alternately disposed pinnæ. Every pinna carries two opposite series of alternate hydrothecæ, and two exactly similar series are carried by the stem.

The walls of the hydrotheca are towards the base slightly more convex on the side which is turned away from the internode than on that which faces it, and the perforated diaphragm which forms the floor of the hydrotheca and separates its true cavity from that of the peduncle is oblique. The peduncle joins the supporting process of the internode through the medium of a very short annular segment.

Campanularia insignis comes very near to one of the Gulf Stream Hydroida which, under the name of *Obelia marginata*, was in the absence of the gonosome referred provisionally to the genus *Obelia*. It differs, however, from that species in the shape of the hydrothecæ, which in the Gulf Stream species have rather the form of an inverted cone caused by the gradual diminution of the diameter towards the base; while a further difference is found in the interposition in *Campanularia insignis* of a short annular segment between the peduncle of the hydrotheca and its supporting internode.

No trace of gonosome was present in any of the specimens of *Campanularia insignis*, and our ignorance of this part of the colony gives a purely provisional value to our generic allocation of the species.

Campanularia tulipifera, n. sp. (Pl. X. figs. 1, 1a, 1b).

Trophosome.—Hydrocaulus attaining a height of about one inch, monosiphonic, sparingly branched. Hydrothecæ supported on peduncles which spring from the sides of the branches with, for the most part, a pinnate and alternate disposition, large, deep, slightly narrowed behind the orifice, and again widening towards the base; margin with wide and shallow crenations, walls with very regular longitudinal plicæ which extend from the orifice to the base, and correspond in number with the marginal crenations.

Gonosome not known.

Locality.—Station 150, off Heard Island; lat. 52° 4′ S., long. 71° 22′ E.; depth, 150 fathoms.

Campanularia tulipifera is a beautiful little Hydroid, remarkable for the large size and graceful form of its hydrothecæ. These are three-twentieths of an inch long, and nearly one-twentieth of an inch wide at a point a little above the base. The margin of the orifice is slightly everted, and is indented with eight shallow crenations, from each of which a narrow longitudinal fold of the delicate, perfectly transparent walls passes backwards to the base, thus giving to the hydrothecæ an aspect of extreme elegance which bears a resemblance not very remote to that of the flower of a tulip. The peduncles vary in height but have usually about half that of the hydrothecæ, and are for the most part provided with a distinct joint which is situated near the middle point of their length. The stem though thick is monosiphonic and springs from a creeping tubular filament.

The walls of the hydrothecæ are extremely thin and absolutely transparent, and the plicæ with which they are ornamented are most obvious when the specimen has been just removed from the preserving liquid, and before it is allowed to become dry.

Campanularia ptychocyathus, n. sp. (Pl. X. figs. 2, 2a).

Trophosome.—Hydrocaulus a creeping stolon sending off at short intervals the peduncles of the hydrothecæ. Hydrothecæ obconical, deep, with the margin deeply dentate and with the walls for some distance below the orifice very thin and collapsible; peduncles long, annulated at intervals.

Gonosome.—Gonangia borne by the creeping stolon, destitute of annulation, deep, cylindrical, but narrowing towards the base where they are supported on a short annulated peduncle, and with a constriction just below the wide truncated summit; orifice wide, circular, occupying the summit of the gonangium.

Locality.—Bahia.

Campanularia ptychocyathus is a minute creeping form and is rendered specially remarkable by the difference of texture in the walls of the hydrothecæ. These for about the distal third of their height become so thin and collapsible that during the retracted state of the hydranth they are generally seen to have fallen towards one another and become thrown into irregular plicæ which obscure the true form of the hydrotheca, withdrawing from view its regularly dentate margin, a condition, however, which must not be confounded with that of the opercular segments which crown the hydrothecæ in *Campanulina* and some allied forms. The proximal two-thirds of the hydrothecæ possess on the contrary the usual firmness of these parts, and the hydrotheca here retains at all times its true form. The peduncle presents two or three annulations just below the hydrotheca, and several at its origin from the stolon, while a group of rings near the middle of its length is also generally present.

The gonangia are developed from the creeping stolon between the peduncles of the hydrothecæ. They are rendered striking by their nearly cylindrical form, and the constriction which exists immediately below the broad truncated summit. On one or two occasions gonangia were found springing from the peduncle of the hydrotheca.

The gonangia in the specimen are those of a female colony.

Campanularia retroflexa, n. sp. (Pl. XI. figs. 1, 1*a*).

Trophosome.—Hydrocaulus a creeping, filiform, reticulated stolon from which the peduncles of the hydrothecæ are sent off at short intervals. Hydrothecæ deep, cylindrical, with the margin divided into about fourteen blunt teeth and abruptly everted. Peduncles either quite continuous or divided by transverse joints into long clavate internodes.

Gonosome not known.

Locality.—Honolulu ; depth, 20 to 40 fathoms.

The abruptly everted margin of the deep cylindrical hydrothecæ gives to this little *Campanularian*, which attains a height of about two-tenths of an inch, a well-marked character. The margin is everted in a plane at right angles to the axis of the hydrotheca, and the teeth into which the rim is divided stand up from it parallel to the axis, thus suggesting the form of the escapement-wheel of a watch.

The peduncles of the hydrothecæ are in most instances intersected by rather distant constrictions, and thus divided into a series of segments. Each of these has a somewhat clavate form, being slightly thicker at its distal than at its proximal end. This condition, however, notwithstanding its rather striking character, is not universally present, some of the peduncles being of uniform thickness and destitute throughout of constrictions.

The specimen occurs growing over the surface of a Millepore.

Campanularia cheloniæ, n. sp. (Pl. XI. figs. 2, 2a).

Trophosome.—Hydrocaulus minute ; main stems springing at short intervals from a creeping stolon, and sending off from opposite sides alternate, rather distant ramuli, some of which send off secondary ramuli ; ramuli distinctly and regularly annulated either in their entire length or at their proximal and distal ends ; main stem similarly annulated just above the origin of every ramulus. Hydrothecæ terminating the ramuli obconical, with even margin.

Gonosome not present.

Locality.—Found attached to the back of a Turtle, locality not recorded.

This very minute, delicate, and graceful little species attains a height of about two-tenths of an inch, and is rendered remarkable by the deep, regular, and elegant annulation which occurs in its perfectly transparent chitinous perisarc at definite parts of the stem and ramuli. This annulation sometimes extends from the hydrotheca along the whole length of the supporting ramulus, while sometimes it occurs only at the distal and proximal ends of the ramuli, leaving a space free from annulation towards the middle. The main stem presents a group of similar annulations just above the points from which the ramuli are emitted. Many of the hydranths were well preserved in the specimen.

Obelia, Péron and Lesueur.

Obelia, Péron and Lesueur (the planoblast only), Char. gen. et sp. de Méduses, Ann. du Museum, t. xiv. p. 355, 1809.

Generic Character. Trophosome.—Hydrocaulus simple or branched, fascicled or monosiphonic. Hydrothecæ campanuliform, destitute of operculum, pedunculate, with the cavity distinctly differentiated from that of the peduncle.

Gonosome.—Gonophores medusiform vesiculate planoblasts with shallow umbrella, four radial canals on which the gonads are developed, short manubrium with four-lobed mouth, numerous rather rigid marginal tentacles whose roots are plunged into the substance of the umbrella, otocysts carried each close to the base of a tentacle, velum rudimental.

The most important diagnostic characters of *Obelia* are found in its gonosome. The trophosome agrees in its essential features with that of other Campanularian Hydroids,—whether their gonophores be planoblasts or hedrioblasts—but the planoblasts of *Obelia* present characters so well marked as to render it impossible to confound these with the planoblasts of any other genus.

Among these characters must be specially noted the shallow, almost discoid umbrella, the rudimental velum, the prolongation of the basal portion of the rather rigid marginal tentacles into the substance of the umbrella, and the close approximation of every otocyst with the base of a tentacle.

Among the Hydroids of the Challenger one species of *Obelia* (*Obelia geniculata*), a very common European form, has been identified.

Obelia geniculata, Linnæus, sp. (Pl. XII. figs. 1, 1*a*).

Sertularia geniculata, Linn., Syst. Nat., 1312.
Leaversia geniculata, Lamx., Cor. flex., 205.
Europa diaphana, Agassiz, Nat. Hist. of U.S., vol. iv. p. 322, pl. xxxiv. figs. 1–9.
Obelia geniculata, Allman, Ann. and Mag. Nat. Hist., May 1864.
„ „ Hincks, Brit. Hydroid Zooph., p. 149, pl. xxv.

Trophosome.—Hydrocaulus consisting of simple or sparingly branched stems, which arise from a network of creeping fibres, and attain a height of about an inch. Hydrothecæ obconical, with entire margin, alternate, supported each on a strongly annulated peduncle, which springs from a projecting hook-shaped process of the stem situated immediately below the salient angle of every geniculation, and supported by a bracket-like thickening of the chitinous perisarc.

Gonosome.—Gonangia borne on short annulated peduncles which spring from the angles between the hydrotheca and the stem, urn-shaped, gradually widening from below upwards and terminating distally in a short conical neck, which carries the orifice on its summit.

Locality.—Kerguelen Island ; depth, 20 to 26 fathoms.

Station 315, Port William, Falkland Islands; lat. 51° 40′ S., long. 57° 50′ W.; depth, 5 to 12 fathoms.

Among the whole of the Campanularian Hydroids there is perhaps not one in which the characters of the trophosome are so definite and so easily recognisable as in *Obelia geniculata*. The remarkable development of the chitinous perisarc which occurs on one side of every internode, and supports the alternately disposed hydrothecæ in the manner of a bracket, has not been found in any other species.

Obelia geniculata is one of the few British Hydroids obtained by the Challenger. In the British and European seas it is one of the commonest and most widely distributed species, while it has also been obtained on the eastern and western shores of the United States, and on the coast of Labrador (Hincks), as well as in the seas round the North Cape.

The Challenger dredged it from two localities, one in the region of Kerguelen Island, and the other in that of the Falkland Islands. Both therefore in nearly the same southern latitudes, though separated by about 130° of longitude. The distance between these extreme southern localities and the Arctic Ocean in which it has been found by Sars, affords one of the most striking examples known of the wide geographical distribution of a single species.

The internodes of the stem in the southern form are perhaps slightly longer and more slender than those of the northern, but no difference can be found which would justify the specific separation of the two forms.

The soft parts of the trophosome were well preserved in the specimens.

Thyroscyphus, Allman.

Thyroscyphus, Allman, Hydroids of the Gulf Stream, p. 10.

Generic Character.   Trophosome.—Hydrocaulus composed of consecutive internodes, each supporting a pedunculate hydrotheca. Hydrothecæ with the cavity divided from that of the peduncle by a perforated diaphragm, and having the orifice surmounted by a roof which is composed of four triangular membranous valves.

Gonosome not known.

The genus *Thyroscyphus* was formed for a Hydroid dredged off Sand Key, from a depth of 10 fathoms, during the United States' exploration of the Gulf Stream. The species which compose it differ from the other operculate forms of the Campanularinæ in the operculum of its campanuliform hydrothecæ consisting of exactly four valves well differentiated from the walls of the hydrotheca, instead of the much greater and indeed indefinite number of segments which in others crown the hydrotheca, or into which the margin of the hydrotheca in these is cleft; and in the fact of the hydrocaulus being composed of a succession of distinct internodes, each with its pedunculate hydrotheca.

Thyroscyphus ramosus, Allman (Pl. XII. figs. 2, 2a).

Thyroscyphus ramosus, Allman, Hydroids of the Gulf Stream, p. 11, pl. vi. figs. 5, 6.

Trophosome.—Hydrocaulus monosiphonic, consisting of a main stem set with pinnately disposed, alternate, simple or branched ramuli. Hydrothecæ borne both by main stem and ramuli, distichous and alternate, large and deep, cylindrical towards the summit, but gibbous below on the side which faces the internode; peduncle short, composed of two oblique, annular segments.

Gonosome not known.

Locality.—Bahia.

Though the present Hydroid differs to some extent in habit from *Thyroscyphus ramosus* of the collections obtained by the United States' exploration of the Gulf Stream, I have no hesitation in regarding it as specifically identical with that form.

The Challenger specimen has a height of about four inches. The ramuli which are given off from the main stem are sometimes simple, sometimes once or twice branched. The peduncles of the hydrothecæ always spring from a point close to the distal end of an internode, where they are supported on the summit of a short, thick, lateral process of the internode, and the extreme rim of the hydrotheca is surrounded by a narrow band of a colour somewhat lighter than that of the rest of the walls. The main stem has a thickness which is about twice that of the ramuli, and is divided into internodes, each carrying a hydrotheca on alternate sides exactly as in the ramuli.

The ramuli are given off from the main stem, each close to the point from which the peduncle of a hydrotheca springs. In the more proximal portion of the stem they all lie in one and the same plane with the hydrothecæ, but towards the distal parts they frequently, immediately after their origin, take different directions, and have thus, though all simply distichous at their origin, the appearance of being irregularly scattered.

Thyroscyphus simplex, n. sp. (Pl. XIII. figs. 1, 2).

Trophosome.—Colony attaining a height of nearly six inches; stems monosiphonic, clustered unbranched, and carrying along nearly their entire height pinnately disposed alternate ramuli. Hydrothecæ borne both by main stem and ramuli, deep, cylindrical, terminating below in a short unjointed peduncle, which is supported directly on the summit of a stout lateral process of the internode.

Gonosome not known.

Locality.—Off Somerset, Cape York, Torres Strait; depth, 8 to 12 fathoms.

Thyroscyphus simplex occurs in clusters of three or four erect simple stems which spring from a common creeping tubular fibre, and are regularly set throughout with alternate pinnæ, which towards the middle of the stems attain a length of nearly an inch. Every internode of stem and pinnæ carries close to its distal end, and on alternate sides, a short lateral process which directly supports the short peduncle of the hydrotheca. The hydrotheca at its base loses its exactly symmetrical outline and becomes slightly gibbous on the side which is turned towards the internode, and here an oblique diaphragm forms the boundary between its cavity and that of the peduncle. The four valves with which the hydrotheca is crowned are very thin and membranous, and form when in apposition a beautiful pyramidal roof. There is no marginal band.

In habit and general physiognomy *Thyroscyphus simplex* so closely resembles *Campanularia insignis* that a careful examination is needed in order to distinguish the two forms.

Hypanthea, Allman.

Hypanthea, Allman, Report on the Collections made by the Transit of Venus Expedition to Kerguelen Island, Phil. Trans., 1879, vol. clxviii. p. 281.

Generic Character. Trophosome.—Hydrothecæ borne each on the summit of a cylindrical peduncle, which springs from a creeping stolon, inoperculate, with the cavity so reduced by the great thickness of its chitinous walls as to be incapable of receiving the hydranth in retraction.

Gonosome.—Gonophores in the form of simple sporosacs developed within chitinous gonangia, which spring, aggregated or scattered, from the creeping stolon.

The genus *Hypanthea* was founded for a Calyptoblastic Hydroid brought home from Kerguelen Island by the section of the Transit of Venus Expedition whose observations were carried on in that island.

The species obtained by the Transit Expedition is distinct from that dredged by the Challenger off the same island, and differs still more widely from another species of the same genus obtained by the Challenger off the Falkland Islands.

The genus is very remarkable, the place of the hydrothecæ being taken by bodies which differ from proper hydrothecæ in having the cavity so reduced by the great thickness of the chitinous walls, that they may be said to support rather than contain the hydranths, which are thus nearly as much unprotected as the hydranths in *Halecium*, where the hydrothecæ remain in a condition quite rudimental.

Hypanthea aggregata, n. sp. (Pl. XIV. figs. 1, 1a).

Trophosome.—Hyrocaulus a creeping and reticulated stolon, from which are emitted scattered simple peduncles ; peduncles about a quarter of an inch in height, cylindrical, smooth, with a swollen summit which, through the intervention of a single globular segment, supports the hydrotheca. Hydrothecæ obconical, compressed, with oblique entire margin.

Gonosome.—Gonangia (female) springing like the peduncles of the hydrothecæ from the creeping stolon, densely crowded, fusiform, each tapering below to its point of attachment without forming a definite peduncle, and terminating distally in a laterally compressed orifice.

Locality.—Kerguelen Island ; depth, 20 to 26 fathoms.

The present species differs from *Hypanthea repens* of the Transit of Venus Expedition in its densely aggregated instead of scattered gonangia. These form in *Hypanthea aggregata* a densely crowded mass, and the hydrostyles, instead of arising in the intervals of the gonangia, spring separately from the stolon. The gonangia in the Challenger specimen are exclusively such as contain female sporosacs, thus again differing from those of *Hypanthea repens*, in which it would appear that the colony may be monœcious, male and female gonangia being there associated on the same stolon.

The cavity of the hydrotheca is represented by a comparatively shallow saucer-like depression, prolonged by a narrow canal which extends downwards nearly in the axis of the hydrotheca to its base, where it is slightly dilated and then becomes continuous with the canal of the peduncle.

The chitinous walls of the hydrotheca are enormously thickened, and in their thickness so far encroach on the cavity as to reduce this to the condition of the saucer-like depression with its tubular prolongation. Towards the free margin of this depression the walls thin away, and here terminate in a comparatively thin edge.

The hydrotheca is remarkable for its want of symmetry; for not only is its summit truncated obliquely, but the walls on one side are much thicker than on the other, and the cavity is thus thrown out of the axis. The hydrotheca is laterally compressed, and it is when viewed from its broad side that the departure from symmetry is apparent. When the narrower side is turned towards the observer the hydrotheca appears quite symmetrical. Between the hydrotheca and the summit of the peduncle there exists a short, nearly globular segment, and this, with the hydrotheca which it carries, may be depressed laterally on the peduncle.

The body of the hydranth rests in the saucer-like depression on the summit of the hydrotheca, and is extended through the canal as a cylindrical tube, in order to become continuous with the cœnosarc of the peduncle. Though the hydranths were imperfectly preserved in the specimen it was evident that for some distance from their oral end they lay permanently outside of the hydrotheca, and that the oral disc with its circlet of tentacles was, even in the state of extreme retraction, entirely exposed.

The gonangia are fusiform capsules attaining a height equal to about half that of the peduncles of the hydrotheca, and contain each a single sporosac which forms an elongated oval sac springing from the side of the blastostyle near its base, and containing numerous ova. Immediately above the point from which the sporosac arises the blastostyle breaks up into a network of tubes by which the sporosac is surrounded, and which unite in the plug-like operculum which occupies the summit of the gonangium.

The excessive development of the chitinous perisarc is not confined to the hydrotheca, but shows itself in the peduncles, in the gonangia, and in the reticulated stolon, all which parts are remarkable for the great thickness of their walls. The perisarc is further remarkable for its density and transparency.

Hypanthea aggregata was found spreading over the fronds of a Laminaria-like sea-weed.

Hypanthea hemispherica, n. sp. (Pl. XIV. figs. 2, 2a).

Trophosome.—Hydrocaulus a creeping, sparingly branched stolon, which gives off both peduncles and gonangia at intervals along its length; peduncles varying in length from one-twentieth to one-tenth of an inch, cylindrical and smooth, with the distal end slightly swollen, and carrying the hydrotheca through the medium of a small globular segment. Hydrothecæ hemispherical with oblique margin.

Gonosome.—Gonangia elongate ovate, with slightly expanded and truncated summit, smooth, supported on very short but definite peduncles which spring from the creeping stolon in the intervals of the hydrothecal peduncles never clustered.

Locality.—Station 315, Port William, Falkland Islands; lat. 51° 40′ S., long. 57° 50′ W.; depth, 5 to 12 fathoms.

The present species is very distinct from both *Hypanthea repens* and *Hypanthea aggregata.* It is a much smaller form than either of these, while the hydrothecæ are much shorter and relatively wider than those of either of the Kerguelen species. The gonangia, moreover, instead of being fusiform as in these, widen at the summit, and instead of forming dense groups as in *Hypanthea aggregata*, are distributed along with the hydrothecæ singly over the length of the stolon. Where the gonangia are present there is usually one between every two hydrothecæ.

Hypanthea hemispherica, like the other two described species, spreads over the fronds of a Laminaria-like seaweed. While both the former are inhabitants of the seas off Kerguelen Island, the present species was dredged off the Falkland Islands. Though the two localities agree pretty closely in latitude they differ widely in longitude, and the fact of so remarkable a genus being represented—though by different species— in both, points to an interesting parallelism between the faunæ of the two regions. A still further feature of parallelism is seen in the occurrence of *Obelia geniculata* both in the region of Kerguelen and in that of the Falkland Islands.

Calamphora, n. gen.

Name from καλὸς, beautiful, and ἀμφορεὺς, a pitcher, in allusion to the form of the hydrotheca.

Generic Character. Trophosome.—Hydrocaulus a creeping stolon. Hydrothecæ lageniform, inoperculate, almost sessile on the stolon.

Gonosome.—Gonangia oviform, subsessile on the stolon.

The genus *Calamphora* differs from all the other Campanularians in the form of its hydrothecæ, which are neither campanulate as in *Campanularia* and its more immediate allies, nor tubiform as in *Callicella, Lafoëa,* &c. They are on the contrary wide and ventricose towards the middle and contracted at both distal and proximal ends.

The hydrotheca is provided at its proximal end with a diaphragm or floor perforated for the transmission of the cœnosarc which is to become developed into a hydranth in the cavity of the hydrotheca. In this respect the present genus agrees with *Campanularia* but differs from most of the species in which the hydrotheca departs from the campanulate type of form, for in these the cavity of the hydrotheca is directly continuous with that of the peduncle or with that of the common stem.

Calamphora parvula, n. sp. (Pl. X. figs. 3, 3a).

Trophosome.—Hydrocaulus a narrow, creeping, adherent tube, to which the hydrothecæ are attached at short intervals by very short, almost evanescent, peduncles. Hydrothecæ with very regular closely set annular ridges, and contracted distally into a short neck which terminates in a tetragonal orifice, and is directed towards one side so as to form an obtuse angle with the axis of the hydrotheca.

Gonosome.—Gonangia oviform, considerably larger than the hydrothecæ, regularly and distinctly annulated throughout, subsessile on the creeping tube from which each springs close to the origin of a hydrotheca, and opening on the summit by a circular four-toothed orifice.

Locality.—Station 162, off East Moncœur Island, Bass Strait; depth, 38 fathoms.

This beautiful little species, which scarcely attains a height of one-fortieth of an inch, occurred in abundance creeping over specimens of *Dictyocladium dichotomum*. The hydrothecæ are rendered bilateral by the direction of the neck towards one side, while the tetragonal orifice and regular annulation of their walls contribute still further to the singularity and elegance of their form. This distinct annulation of the walls of the hydrothecæ, as distinguished from mere striæ indicative of successive elongations in growth, is indeed a character in the highest degree exceptional among the Campanularians. An instance of it occurs in *Hebella striata*, one of the species dredged by the Challenger, and in *Lafoëa* (*Hebella*) *venusta*, a species obtained during the United States' exploration of the Gulf Stream. In *Hebella striata*, however, the annulation is very much more delicate than in *Calamphora parvula*. The gonangium in *Calamphora parvula* is also annulated in a manner quite similar to that of the hydrothecæ. The annulation of the gonangium, however, is of frequent occurrence among the Campanularian and Sertularian Hydroids.

Hebella, n. gen.

Name from Hebe, the cup-bearer of classical mythology.

Generic Character. Trophosome.—Hydrocaulus a creeping monosiphonic stolon. Hydrothecæ cylindrical, with entire margin, destitute of operculum, and with the cavity distinctly differentiated from that of the peduncle.

Gonosome not known.

The genus *Hebella* includes a number of minute Hydroids with cylindrical cup-shaped hydrothecæ. Most of these have been arranged by Hincks under the genus *Lafoëa*. From this genus, however, as here limited, they differ in their monosiphonic hydrocaulus, and in the distinct differentiation of the hydrothecal cavity from the cavity of the peduncle. From *Campanularia* and its immediate allies *Hebella* is distinguished by the cylindrical form of its hydrothecæ. Our knowledge of the group, however, is still imperfect, for not only are we entirely ignorant of the gonosome, but even the true form of the hydranth is imperfectly known to us. It is probable, however, that this, like the hydranth of *Lafoëa* and the allied genera, is provided with a conical hypostome, instead of having the hypostome, as in *Campanularia* and its allies, trumpet-shaped.

The Challenger collection contains one beautiful representative of the genus *Hebella*.

Hebella striata, n. sp. (Pl. XV. figs. 3, 3*a*).

Trophosome.—Hydrocaulus a creeping monosiphonic stolon giving off the hydrothecæ from distance to distance along its length. Hydrothecæ large, cylindrical, marked by very delicate, closely set, annular striæ, contracted below into a peduncle of variable length.

Gonosome not known.

Locality.—Station 312, Port Famine, Magellan Strait; lat. 53° 38′ S., long. 70° 56′ W.; depth, 10 to 15 fathoms.

Hebella striata is a beautiful little Hydroid. Its relatively large hydrothecæ are borne at intervals along a creeping stolon. They are cylindrical through nearly their entire height, and then gradually taper into a peduncle which varies much in length. They are deep and relatively wide, and with the margin for the most part very slightly everted. Occasionally they present a decided curvature of the axis. Their walls are perfectly transparent, and marked by an exceedingly delicate sculpture of fine, closely set, annular striæ, rendering them, when viewed with a good illumination under a moderate power of the microscope, objects of extreme beauty. Though the hydranth was fairly well preserved in the specimen the form of the hypostome could not be determined.

The specimens occur creeping over the fascicled stems of *Lafoëa fruticosa*.

Halisiphonia, n. gen.

Name from ἅλς, *sea, and* σίφων, *a tube, in allusion to the tubular form of the hydrothecæ.*

Generic Character. *Trophosome.*—Hydrocaulus a monosiphonic stolon. Hydrothecæ tubiform, with entire margin, destitute of operculum, with the cavity directly continuous with that of the peduncle or stolon, and with the hydrothecal walls never adnate to the hydrocaulus. Hydranth with conical hypostome.

Gonosome.—Gonangial capsules borne by the hydrocaulus.

The genus *Halisiphonia* is constituted for certain Campanularian Hydroids which would find their place in *Lafoëa* as defined by Mr. Hincks. Since the publication, however, of Mr. Hincks's classical work on the British Hydroid Zoophytes, our knowledge of the species which he would bring together under that genus has been increased to such an extent as to render necessary a revision of the group by a more stringent limitation of *Lafoëa*. See below, p. 32.

The genus *Halisiphonia* is represented in the Challenger collection by a single species, which presents many points of special interest.

Halisiphonia megalotheca, n. sp. (Pl. XVI. figs. 1, 1*a*).

Trophosome.—Hydrocaulus a creeping and adherent tube which supports at irregular intervals pedunculated hydrothecæ. Hydrothecæ very large, cylindrical, gradually passing below into the long, smooth, cylindrical peduncle.

Gonosome.—Gonangia spatuliform, borne on short peduncles and with the summit opening by a long, narrow, transverse slit.

Locality.—Station 160, south of Australia; lat. 42° 42′ S., long. 134° 10′ E.; depth, 2600 fathoms.

The very long tubular hydrothecæ gradually passing into their long peduncles confer on this remarkable species an aspect as striking as it is distinctive. The hydrothecæ measure about one-tenth of an inch in length, and are borne on peduncles whose length is for the most part nearly the same. The creeping stolon from which they spring twines in irregular contortions round the body to which it has attached itself. The deep cylindrical hydrotheca begins, at about three-fourths of its height from the margin, to taper into the peduncle, with the cavity of which its own is uninterruptedly continuous, so that it is not easy to say where the one ends and the other begins.

The gonangia are, like the hydrothecæ, borne by the creeping stolon-like hydrocaulus. Their form is remarkable. They are much compressed, so as to present a spatuliform shape, widening upwards, and gradually narrowing into a short peduncle below. They are widest at the summit, where they terminate in a sharp edge. Along this edge the walls of the gonangium admit of being separated from one another so as to bring into view a narrow slit through which the contents of the gonangium may be liberated. The appearance, indeed, of the gonangium with its slit-like opening is such as to suggest rather forcibly that of a flat bivalve shell, or the ovarian nidus of certain Gasteropodous Mollusca. Nothing can be asserted of its contents, which had in every case disappeared.

The collection contains but a single and somewhat fragmentary specimen, which twined round a portion of a fascicled stem, probably that of *Cryptolaria abyssicola*, a species with which it was associated.

The enormous depth of 2600 fathoms from which both *Halisiphonia megalotheca* and *Cryptolaria abyssicola* were obtained has much significance, in connection with the fact that in both species the gonangia are present, *Halisiphonia megalotheca* affording the only known instance, and *Cryptolaria abyssicola* one of the very few, in which any part of the gonosome has been observed in these genera.

Family PERISIPHONIDÆ.

Character of the Family. *Trophosome* formed of two essential constituents—an axial and a peripheral, the axial consisting of a single tube which carries the hydrothecæ and the peripheral, formed of numerous tubes destitute of hydrothecæ, and united into a fascicle which surrounds the axial to a greater or less extent, and allows the hydrothecæ to project through intervals between its component tubes. Hydrothecæ never adnate by their sides to the axial tube where this is covered · by the peripheral. Peripheral and axial tubes not inseparably coalesced.

There is among the Calyptoblastic Hydroids no more natural and distinctly defined family than that of the Perisiphonidæ. The remarkable structure of the trophosome with its axial hydrotheca-bearing tube enveloped by the peripheral fascicle is, except in *Grammaria*, quite unknown in any other group; for this condition must not be confounded with the fasciculation of the stem which occurs in many Plumularinæ and is common in *Halecium*, *Sertularia*, *Thuiaria*, and other genera (see Part I. p. 4), in which the component tubes are not divisible into an axial tube which carries the hydrothecæ and peripheral tubes which are destitute of hydrothecæ. Except in *Cryptolaria* the gonosome of the Perisiphonidæ is entirely unknown.

Four genera, all of which occur among the dredgings of the Challenger, must be assigned to the family Perisiphonidæ. The essential points of difference between these are given in the following scheme :—

PERISIPHONIDÆ	{ Axial tube not wholly enveloped by the peripheral. Hydrothecæ sessile or pedunculate, never adnate to the axial tube, and with the cavity directly continuous with that of the stem or peduncle. No sarcothecæ present. }	*Lafoëa.*
	{ Axial tube not wholly enveloped by the peripheral. Hydrothecæ pedunculate, never adnate to the axial tube, and with the cavity distinctly differentiated from that of the peduncle. No sarcothecæ present. }	*Lictorella.*
	{ Axial tube wholly enveloped by the peripheral. Hydrothecæ pedunculate, distichous. Sarcothecæ developed on the stem. }	*Perisiphonia.*
	{ Axial tube not wholly enveloped by the peripheral. Hydrothecæ sessile on the axial tube, to the free portion of which they are more or less adnate; distichous or scattered. No sarcothecæ present. }	*Cryptolaria.*

Lafoëa, Lamouroux.

Lafoëa, Lamouroux, Expos. Méthod., 1821.

Generic Character. *Trophosome.*—Hydrocaulus in its main stem and principal branches consisting of a single axial tube, enveloped by numerous peripheral tubes, but ceasing to be covered by the peripheral tubes towards the distal parts of the colony. Hydrothecæ tubiform, with entire margin, destitute of operculum, sessile or pedunculate, with their walls never adnate to the hydrocaulus, and with the cavity uninterruptedly continued into that of the peduncles or of the parts of the stem from which they directly spring. Hydranths with a conical hypostome.

Gonosome not known.

The genus *Lafoëa* was founded by Lamouroux in 1821, and since then has been more exactly defined by Sars, and further limited by Hincks. Our increased knowledge of the species, however, and the detection of the perisiphonic nature of the fascicled stem, render necessary a still further amendment of the definition, and the diagnosis here given will, I believe, mark out the true limits of the genus.

The most important characters of this diagnosis will be found in the perisiphonic fasciculation of the stem, the complete freedom of the hydrotheca walls from the hydrocaulus, and the uninterrupted continuity of the cavity of the hydrotheca with that of the peduncle, or, where no peduncle is present, with that of the axial tube from which it springs. By this last character among others it is distinguished from such forms as *Campanularia*, in which the cavity of the hydrotheca is differentiated from that of the supporting peduncle by a basal constriction, forming a more or less pronounced perforated diaphragm.

The distal parts of the colony are always free from the peripheral tubes, a character which *Lafoëa* possesses in common with *Cryptolaria*. In *Lafoëa* the hydrothecæ are never adnate to the axial tubes in any part of the colony; in *Cryptolaria* they are so adnate where the axial tube ceases to be covered by the peripheral.

It is a remarkable fact that, notwithstanding the great abundance of some of the species, no trace of the gonosome has as yet been detected in any true *Lafoëa*.

Hincks has united under *Lafoëa* a number of minute Campanularian Hydroids which the definition here given will exclude, not only on account of their non-fascicled stem, but of the distinct differentiation of the cavities of their pedunculated hydrothecæ. Though we know nothing of their gonosome, while our knowledge of them is in other respects also imperfect, we shall I believe be justified in uniting these little cup-bearing species under a separate genus, to which I have assigned the name of *Hebella*. Their separation from *Campanularia* (as limited above, p. 18) may possibly appear arbitrary, but the more cylindrical cup-shaped form of their hydrothecæ contrasts with the campanulate form of *Campanularia*, and in our very imperfect knowledge of the species will justify the provisional allocation here suggested.

A form with tubiform hydrothecæ but with creeping non-fascicled stem is regarded by Hincks as a variety of *Lafoëa dumosa*, Fleming. I am unable to accept this view, for I regard the perisiphonic stem as an essential character of every true *Lafoëa*. I have accordingly united in a separate genus the monosiphonic Campanularians with tubiform hydrothecæ and non-differentiated hydrotheca-cavity. To this I have assigned the name of *Halisiphonia*. A remarkable example of it is contained in the collection of the Challenger.

The collection contains two species of the genus *Lafoëa* as limited by the diagnosis here given. Notwithstanding some differences of habit, I cannot find grounds for separating them from the *Lafoëa dumosa* and *Lafoëa fruticosa* of the European seas.

Lafoëa dumosa, Fleming, sp. (Pl. XV. figs. 1, 1a).

Sertularia dumosa, Fleming, Edin. Phil. Journ., vol. ii. p. 83.
Lafoëa dumosa, Hincks, Brit. Hydroid Zooph., p. 200, pl. xli. fig. 1.

Trophosome.—Hydrocaulus free, slender, irregularly branched, main stem and principal branches becoming monosiphonic distally. Hydrothecæ springing from all sides of the stem and branches, tubular, with the axis curved away from the stem, gradually narrowed towards the base into a short ill-defined peduncle of attachment.

Gonosome not known.

Locality.—Station 23, off Sombrero Island, West Indies ; depth, 450 fathoms.

This is a very slender form, of delicate habit, and quite destitute of the vigorous growth by which some of the other species of *Lafoëa* are characterised. The specimen has a height of about two inches. The hydrothecæ are deep and rather wide, but towards the base become gradually narrowed into a short peduncle, which is so imperfectly defined that the hydrothecæ may almost be regarded as sessile. The branches in their monosiphonic portion present here and there a shallow, scarcely recognisable, constriction, but there are no true joints dividing them into internodes.

Apart from its more slender form and delicate habit, the present Hydroid possesses no character which would afford grounds for its separation from *Lafoëa dumosa ;* and as these differences seem to lie within the limits of variation of a species, I believe we must regard it as specifically identical with the European form.

Lafoëa fruticosa, Sars (Pl. XVI. figs. 2, 2a).

Lafoëa fruticosa, Sars, Bemærk. over flere norske Hydroider, Vidensk. Forhandl., 1862.
Lafoëa fruticosa, Hincks, Brit. Hydroid Zooph., p. 202, pl. xli. fig. 2.

Trophosome.—Stem free, attaining a height of upwards of three inches, profusely branched, branches mostly in one and the same plane, primary branches irregular, closely set with pinnately disposed alternate ramuli, which are themselves for the most part set with secondary pinnæ. Hydrothecæ springing irregularly from all sides of the hydrocaulus, deep and narrow, with the axis gently curved away from the supporting stem, gradually narrowing into a loosely twisted peduncle.

Gonosome not present.

Locality.—Station 312, Port Famine, Magellan Strait; lat. 53° 37′ S., long. 70° 56′ W.; depth, 9 to 15 fathoms.

I cannot find any character which would justify the separation of this beautiful Hydroid from the *Lafoëa fruticosa* of Sars. Its pinnate ramification, lying nearly in one and the same plane, and stretching laterally to an extent which nearly equals that of the height of the colony, gives to the entire assemblage a somewhat flabelliform shape. The stem and principal branches are fascicled on the perisiphonic type, but towards the distal extremities become monosiphonic. The long and narrow hydrothecæ gradually taper towards the base into peduncles which are but slightly narrower than the body of the hydrotheca, from which they are not separated by any definite line of demarcation. The peduncles are not annulated, but present about two turns of a very open spiral.

The soft parts were well preserved in the specimen, and the hydranths could in many instances be seen in sufficient detail to render most of their external characters easily recognisable.

Lictorella, n. gen.

Name suggested by the resemblance of the perisiphonic stem to the bundle of rods carried by the Roman lictor.

Generic Character. Trophosome.—Hydrocaulus consisting of a single axial tube enveloped to a greater or less extent by numerous peripheral tubes but free in its more distal parts. Hydrothecæ cylindrical, pedunculate, with entire margin, destitute of operculum, and with the cavity distinctly differentiated from that of the peduncle, their walls never adnate to the hydrocaulus.

Gonosome not known.

The genus *Lictorella* includes certain Campanularian Hydroids with branching perisiphonic hydrocaulus. Though it approaches *Lafoëa* in its perisiphonic hydrocaulus and in its deep and somewhat tubiform hydrothecæ, the presence of a limiting floor by which the cavity of the hydrotheca is distinctly differentiated from that of the peduncle renders it necessary to keep it generically distinct. Though the hydranth has not yet been observed, the analogy of allied forms renders it probable that the hypostome is conical.

The collection contains two species referable to the genus *Lictorella*.

Lictorella halecioides, Allman (Pl. XVII. figs. 1, 2).

Lafoëa halecioides, Allman, Report on the Hydroida collected during the Expedition of H.M.S. "Porcupine," Trans. Zool. Soc. Lond., vol. viii.

Trophosome.—Hydrocaulus attaining a height of about four inches; perisiphonic stem irregularly branched, stem and branches sending off very regular, pinnately disposed, alternate monosiphonic ramuli, which carry along their entire length two series of alternate shortly peduncled hydrothecæ. Hydrothecæ borne both by the perisiphonic stem and the monosiphonic ramuli, deep and narrow, with the axis slightly curved away from the supporting ramulus or stem; margin scarcely everted, peduncle formed of two short annular segments.

Gonosome not present.

Locality.—Off Somerset, Cape York, Torres Strait; depth, 8 to 12 fathoms.

The deep narrow hydrothecæ of the present species resemble in form those of a *Lafoëa*, from which, however, they differ in the presence of the limiting diaphragm or floor at the basal end. The ramuli which carry the hydrothecæ in two alternate series are here and there divided into internodes by transverse joints. These occur chiefly towards the distal extremity of the ramulus, where two hydrothecæ usually intervene between two joints. The ramuli are very regularly disposed, forming a series of equidistant alternate pinnæ on each side of the fascicled stem. Those of one side, however, are not placed exactly opposite to the middle points between the pinnæ of the opposite side.

I have little hesitation in regarding the present Hydroid, notwithstanding its more robust habit and somewhat more irregular ramification, as specifically identical with *Lafoëa hatecioides* of the "Porcupine" collection, a species which, in accordance with the limitation of *Lafoëa* here insisted on, must be removed from that genus and placed in the genus *Lictorella*, keeping in mind, however, that so long as the gonosome is unknown, no generic allocation can be regarded as otherwise than provisional. The removal from *Lafoëa* is justified by the fact of the hydrothecæ being provided with a definite floor instead of having their cavity, as in the true *Lafoëa*, directly continuous with that of the hydrothecæ.

The specific identification of the Challenger Hydroid with that of the "Porcupine" is not without significance, when we bear in mind the widely separated localities and very different conditions under which the two were found. The specimens brought home by the "Porcupine" were dredged from the cold area which lies between Shetland and the Færöe Islands, and from depths of 640 and 345 fathoms; while those of the Challenger were dredged off Cape York, Torres Strait, from a depth of about 8 fathoms.

Lictorella cyathifera, n. sp. (Pl. XI. figs. 3, 3*a*).

Trophosome.—Hydrocaulus pinnately branched; stem and principal branches perisiphonic, becoming monosiphonic towards their extremities, and sending off very regular, pinnately disposed, alternate monosiphonic ramuli, which are destitute of distinct joints, and carry the pinnately disposed alternate hydrothecæ. Hydrothecæ deeply cyathiform, with an entire and very slightly everted rim, and supported on a very short unjointed peduncle which springs from a short fixed process of the hydrocaulus.

Gonosome not known.

Locality.—Station 177, off the New Hebrides; lat. 16° 43′ S., long. 168° 7′ E.; depth, 63 to 130 fathoms.

Lictorella cyathifera attains a height of about two inches. The main stem is stout and strongly perisiphonic towards the base, the principal branches are similarly peri-siphonic, and the whole colony is characterised by a peculiarly rigid habit.

The hydrothecæ, while pinnately disposed and exactly alternate, have their axes slightly directed towards one side of the ramulus. The rim is perfectly circular, even, and very slightly everted.

Most of the hydrothecæ exhibit just behind the rim one or two delicate annular striæ, indicative of successive periods of growth. The hydrothecæ-bearing ramuli present no distinct joints, and thus show no division into internodes.

Lictorella cyathifera comes very near to *Lictorella halecioides* of the present Report, which I have identified with *Lafoëa halecioides* of the "Porcupine" collection.

Lictorella halecioides, however, is altogether a larger and stronger species, while its ultimate ramuli are intersected by distinct though not exactly equidistant joints, and the hydrothecæ are narrower in proportion to their height, and have their peduncles jointed.

The two species, however, undoubtedly come very near to one another, and the wide distribution of a type of form, the variation of which is so slight as to be almost within the limits of mere varietal distinction, is exceedingly interesting. *Lictorella halecioides*, as represented by the examples dredged by the "Porcupine," was obtained from the cold area which lies between Shetland and the Færöe Islands, from depths of 640 and 345 fathoms, with a bottom temperature of 36° F.; the Challenger examples of the same species were dredged off Cape York, Torres Strait, from a depth of from 8 to 12 fathoms ; while the station of *Lictorella cyathifera* lies off the New Hebrides, where it was dredged from depths of from 63 to 130 fathoms.

Cryptolaria, Busk.

Cryptolaria, Busk, Quart. Journ. Micr. Sci., ser. 1, vol. v. p. 173, 1857.

Generic Character. Trophosome.—Hydrocaulus consisting of two parts, an axial and a peripheral, the peripheral consisting of a fascicle of simple tubes, the axial of a single tube, simple or branched, whose proximal portion lies under cover of the peripheral, and whose distal portion is free. Hydrothecæ borne both by the covered and the free portions of the axial tube, tubiform, destitute of peduncles, with the cavity directly con-tinuous with that of the axial tube, and with their walls never adnate to the axile tube, where this is covered by the peripheral fascicle, but more or less adnate to the tube in the free portion of its course.

Gonosome.—Gonangia consisting of sac-like receptacles, which spring at intervals from the axial tube and protrude externally through interstices between the tubes of the peripheral fascicle.

The genus *Cryptolaria* was founded by Busk for a group of Calyptoblastic Hydroids, whose fascicled stems and sessile tubular hydrothecæ, destitute of limiting floor, and adnate to the axial tube on its free portion, afford easily recognisable characters.

The specimens obtained by the Challenger have furnished the means of working out in further detail the structure of this curious group, and not only of satisfactorily determining the essential constitution of its trophosome, but of rendering us to some extent acquainted with its gonosome, which had not previously been detected.[1]

The existence of two distinct elements, a peripheral and an axial, in the hydrocaulus of *Cryptolaria* is an important and unexpected character, and with the exception of four other genera, *Lafoëa*, *Lictorella*, *Perisiphonia*, and *Grammaria*, for a knowledge of whose essential structure we are also indebted to the dredgings of the Challenger, *Cryptolaria* is the only genus, so far as is yet known, in which this condition is present.

In all the known species of *Cryptolaria* the peripheral tubes cease to envelop the axial at some distance from the distal extremities of the branches, and the axial tube thus becoming free and naked shows here, without further preparation, the relation between it and the hydrothecæ. The structure of that part of the colony where the axial tube is still covered by the peripheral can be best demonstrated by careful maceration in caustic potash, which diminishes the adhesion between the constituent tubes and facilitates their separation under the microscope.

The gonosome has as yet been found only in three species of *Cryptolaria*. Two of these, *Cryptolaria abyssicola* and *Cryptolaria diffusa*, have been dredged from the vast depths of 2600 and 2500 fathoms respectively, while the third, *Cryptolaria geniculata*, has been brought up from a depth of 315 fathoms. In all these the relation of the gonangia to the axial tube is very similar to that of the hydrothecæ, and like the hydrothecæ, they protrude at intervals from between the component tubes of the peripheral fascicle. They suggest indeed an obvious comparison with the hydrothecæ, from which they differ chiefly in their greater size and more sac-like form. No other element of the gonosome beyond the gonangia has been detected.

The collection of the Challenger is very rich in the species of *Cryptolaria*. These have been obtained from widely separated localities and from various depths, ranging from 20 fathoms to nearly the greatest which have yielded any living forms to the dredge. No species of *Cryptolaria* have as yet been recorded from European seas.

In distinguishing the species for purposes of systematic description the zoologist

---

[1] In the Report on the Hydroids of the Gulf Stream I described a remarkable structure which was found attached to the stems of a species of *Cryptolaria*, and which I regarded as exhibiting undoubted affinities with the Hydroid genus *Coppinia*, suggesting at the same time the possibility of its turning out to be the gonosome of the *Cryptolaria*, nothing having been at that time known of the gonosome of this genus. It is now evident that the structure in question is an independent growth, having nothing to do with the gonosome of the Hydroid on which it had taken up its abode.

has comparatively little to rely on. Parts which in other Hydroids afford convenient specific characters here present little or no variation. The instances in which the gonosome is known are so few that the use of this for diagnosis is necessarily very limited, while the form of the hydrothecæ is in all the known examples of *Cryptolaria* so much alike, that we can seldom find in it a character of undoubted diagnostic value. In the disposition of the hydrothecæ some sufficiently convenient characters may be found, while beyond this scarcely anything is left for the determination of specific difference but the form of the ramification, and even this varies within very narrow limits.

The species of *Cryptolaria* defined in the present Report have been founded on the characters just indicated, and notwithstanding the paucity of the material available for diagnosis, I believe that they may be accepted as legitimate groups.

Cryptolaria humilis, n. sp. (Pl. XVIII. figs. 1, 1a, 1b).

Trophosome.—Colony attaining a height of somewhat more than an inch, rooted by a plexus of fine branching filaments; stem sparingly and irregularly branched. Hydrothecæ alternate and distichous.

Gonosome not known.

Locality.—Station 73, near the Azores; lat. 38° 30′ N., long. 31° 14′ W.; depth, 1000 fathoms.

It was from the examination of this little species that I first obtained evidence of the true structure of *Cryptolaria*. By boiling the stem in caustic potash the adhesion of the component tubes with one another can be so weakened that it becomes easy to separate them by means of the dissecting needle. The axial tube with its hydrothecæ will then be brought into view, and its relation to the peripheral tubes will be at once made apparent.

Where the axial tube lies under cover of the peripheral it will be seen that the hydrothecæ spring from it at equal intervals, and that they are alternate and distichous. They are long and tubular, gently curving outwards, cylindrical towards the orifice, and thence tapering gradually to their point of origin from the axial tube, into which they directly open instead of being, as in the allied genus *Perisiphonia*, connected with this tube by the intervention of a definite peduncle.

At a short distance from the distal extremities of the branches the peripheral tubes cease to envelop the axial, which thus becomes naked for the remainder of its course. This condition, so far as is yet known, is universal among the *Cryptolariæ*. In the continuation of the axial tube beyond the peripheral fasciculus, the epicauline wall of the hydrothecæ is to a greater or less extent adherent to the opposed wall of the tube, while in the more proximal parts of the colony where the axial tube lies under cover of the peripheral no adhesion of this kind exists, the walls of hydrothecæ being here quite free from the supporting tube.

The locality from which the present species was obtained is in the neighbourhood of the Azores, where it was dredged from a depth of 1000 fathoms.

Cryptolaria abyssicola, n. sp. (Pl. XVIII. figs. 2, 2a).

Trophosome.—Hydrocaulus much and very irregularly branched, branches rather slender, flaccid. Hydrothecæ disposed on all sides of the stem.

Gonosome.—Gonangia springing at intervals along the stem, and forming long, tubular receptacles, ventricose towards the base, and then tapering to their point of attachment, and terminating distally in a truncated summit which is occupied by the wide circular orifice.

Locality.—Station 160, south of Australia; lat. 42° 42′ S., long. 134° 10′ E.; depth, 2600 fathoms.

The vast depth from which *Cryptolaria abyssicola* has been dredged gives it a special interest, which is greatly enhanced by the fact that it affords one of the very few instances as yet known in which the gonosome of *Cryptolaria* has been detected. It was associated with *Halisiphonia megalotheca* (p. 31) brought up in the same haul.

The scattered instead of distichous disposition of the hydrothecæ is a peculiar and exceptional character.

The specimen is only fragmentary, and no exact assertion can be made as to the size which the species may naturally attain. The largest fragments preserved measure about two inches in height.

Cryptolaria flabellum, n. sp. (Pl. XIX. figs. 1, 1a).

Trophosome.—Colony attaining a height of about one inch; hydrocaulus rigid, rooted by a thick disc-like expansion, ramification in a single plane, and irregular. Hydrothecæ alternate, distichous, very long and slender.

Gonosome not known.

Locality.—Station 24, off Culebra Island, West Indies; depth, 390 fathoms.

Cryptolaria flabellum is an unusually well-marked form. Its long curved hydrothecæ resemble slender lateral branches, while its rigid habit, and the fact of the ramification being all in one and the same plane, call to mind the general aspect of certain Gorgonian Corals.

Cryptolaria pulchella, n. sp. (Pl. XIX. figs. 2, 2a).

Trophosome.—Colony attaining a height of nearly three inches, main stem irregularly branched, branches carrying regular, pinnately disposed, alternate ramuli. Hydrothecæ alternate, very regularly distichous.

Gonosome not known.

Locality.—Honolulu; depth, 20 to 40 fathoms.

The very regularly pinnate disposition of the ramuli, and the absolutely distichous and regular disposition of the hydrothecæ, give to this species an aspect of considerable elegance. It is a strong growing form with rather close-set, stout, and short hydrothecæ.

It is an inhabitant of rather shallow water, having been obtained from a depth of between 20 and 40 fathoms; one of the specimens had adherent to it a species of the Rhizopodous genus *Myriotrema*—a characteristic littoral form.

Cryptolaria crassicaulis, n. sp. (Pl. XIX. figs. 3, 3*a*).

Trophosome.—Colony attaining a height of four inches, profusely and very irregularly branched main stem, and primary branches very thick. Hydrothecæ alternate and distichous.

Gonosome not known.

Locality.—Station 344, off Ascension Island; depth, 420 fathoms.

The present species is remarkable for the profuseness and irregularity of its ramification, and for the great thickness of its stem and principal branches. The ultimate branches on the other hand are slender and flaccid. The hydrothecæ are stout, and the exserted portion rather long. Here and there, and at uncertain intervals, slight constrictions may be noticed in the branches.

Cryptolaria geniculata, n. sp. (Pl. XX. figs. 1, 1*a*, 1*b*).

Trophosome.—Colony attaining a height of three inches or more, irregularly branched, stem and branches rather rigid, very regularly geniculate. Hydrothecæ alternate, distichous, springing from the salient angle of every geniculation; orifice with two membranous valves.

Gonosome.—Gonangia somewhat flask-shaped, each occupying the entire interval between two successive geniculations of the stem, to which it is adnate by nearly the whole of its epicauline side.

Locality.—Station 173, off Matuku, Fiji Islands; depth, 315 fathoms.

Cryptolaria geniculata is, of all the species of *Cryptolaria*, the most strongly defined,—so distinct is it indeed that one might almost be justified in assigning it to a new generic group. The valvular orifice of the hydrothecæ affords in itself a striking character, while the singularly geniculate form of the stem is a condition not met with in any other known species of *Cryptolaria*.

The hydrothecæ when traced to their origin from the axial tube are seen to be funnel-shaped, gradually tapering away from the orifice to the point of origin, and curving gently and with great elegance away from the supporting tube. The orifice is capable of being closed by the two membranous valves, which meet so as to form a ridge like that of the roof of a house, and which are composed of numerous, easily separated, very thin laminæ.

Cryptolaria geniculata is one of the three species in which the gonosome has been detected. While the two others—*Cryptolaria abyssicola* and *Cryptolaria diffusa*—have been dredged from the great depths of 2600 and 2500 fathoms respectively, the present species has been brought up from the comparatively moderate, though still very considerable, depth of 315 fathoms.

Cryptolaria gracilis, n. sp. (Pl. XX. figs. 2, 2a).

Trophosome.—Colony attaining a height of about two inches; stem slender, flaccid, much and irregularly branched, and with the distal portion for a great extent destitute of the peripheral tubes. Hydrothecæ alternate and distichous.

Gonosome not known.

Locality.—Station 169, near New Zealand; lat. 37° 34′ S., long. 179° 22′ E.; depth, 700 fathoms.

Cryptolaria gracilis is an unusually well marked species. It forms small, tree-like, much-branched colonies, and while the slender flexile branches have their distal portions formed as in the other species by the free extension of the axial tube, this tube is here destitute of the peripheral investment for a greater extent than is the case in any other with which I am acquainted. It is apparently on this condition that the slenderness and flaccidity of the branches mainly depends.

Cryptolaria diffusa, n. sp. (Pl. XXI. figs. 1, 1a).

Trophosome.—Stem slender, loosely and irregularly branched. Hydrothecæ narrow, rather widely set, and with a nearly dichotomous arrangement.

Gonosome.—Gonangia springing from distance to distance along the stem, flask shaped, about twice the width of the hydrothecæ, curving away from the stem, solitary or geminate.

Locality.—Station 101, off Sierra Leone; depth, 2500 fathoms.

This is a very loosely branched slender form, with a straggling unattractive habit, and is of special interest from the great depth at which it has been found, and from the fact that it is one of the only three species of *Cryptolaria* in which the gonosome has been detected.

As in the other species of *Cryptolaria* in which the gonangia have been found, these receptacles spring from the axial tube where this is covered by the peripheral, and have their distal ends curving away from the stem. In *Cryptolaria diffusa*, however, they present the singular feature of being sometimes geminate, while this condition is found on the same branch which carries the ordinary solitary form of gonangium. The geminate gonangia spring from a very short common peduncle, and immediately become adherent, back to back, for about three-fourths of their height, the distal fourth being free and divergent. It is impossible with our present knowledge to assign with confidence any reason why there should be this difference in the gonangia of one and the same colony. If it be not an abnormal occurrence of merely individual significance, it may possibly point to a monœcious condition of the colony, involving a sexual difference between the solitary and geminate gonangia.

Perisiphonia, n. gen.

Name from περί, around, and σίφων, a tube, in allusion to the way in which the axial tube is surrounded by the peripheral ones.

Generic Character. Trophosome.—Hydrocaulus composed of two constituents, an axial and a peripheral; the axial formed by a continuous tube which carries at intervals along its length pedunculated hydrothecæ; the peripheral formed by numerous tubes which completely surround the axial in its entire length, are destitute of hydrothecæ, but allow the hydrothecæ of the axial tube to project through interstices between them into the surrounding water; the superficial tubes of the peripheral fascicle set with tubular sarcothecæ.

This remarkable genus has very obvious affinities with *Cryptolaria*, from which, however, it essentially differs in its hydrothecæ being provided with well-defined peduncles, instead of having their cavities directly continuous with that of the tube from which they spring, in the axial tube never becoming free from the cover of the peripheral, and in the presence of a well-developed system of sarcode-bearing receptacles.

In *Perisiphonia filicula* and in *Perisiphonia pectinata*, the only two species as yet known, the hydrothecæ are flask-shaped and are disposed alternately in regular sequence along the entire length of the axial tube. The peripheral tubes completely envelop the axial, are continuous throughout the entire length of the branch, and although separable as in the other Perisiphonidæ, are adherent to one another except at the places through which the ends of the hydrothecæ protrude. Hence no part of the axial tube becomes exposed as in *Cryptolaria*, the peripheral tubes continuing to invest it to the extreme ends of the branches.

Another very remarkable feature in *Perisiphonia* consists in the presence of minute tubular receptacles which are borne by the superficial tubes of the peripheral fascicle. In both species these are carried all along the length of the tubes, and under a low magnifying power they give a hirsute appearance to the surface of the colony. They are in the form of very slender cylindrical tubes, open at the summit, and contain a granular matter which is directly continuous with the contents of the peripheral tube from which they spring. In *Perisiphonia filicula* similar receptacles occur in connection with the axial system, one being here fixed on the peduncle of every hydrotheca, while the lateral offsets of the axial tube in this species carry each a pair of such bodies near their origin.

These little receptacles must certainly be regarded in the same light as the sarcothecæ or nematophores so characteristic of the Plumularinæ, which in some rare cases are also present in a modified form among other groups of the Hydroida.

That their contents, like those of the nematophores of the Plumularinæ, consist essentially of sarcode—whether in connection with a true cell-tissue or not—there can be very little doubt, and, judging from the analogy of the Plumularinæ, it is also nearly certain that, like the sarcothecæ of these, their contents have the power of emitting pseudopodial extensions of the enclosed sarcode.

A living specimen of a *Perisiphonia* must thus when seen under the microscope present an appearance as singular as it must be beautiful; for besides the flower-like hydranths which expand over the surface of the colony, countless fine contractile filaments of sarcode will be seen like the pseudopodia of the Foraminifera extending in all directions into the surrounding water.

Perisiphonia filicula, n. sp. (Pl. XXII. figs. 1–4).

Trophosome.—Colony attaining a height of between two and three inches, stem simple or sparingly branched, and very regularly set with pinnately disposed opposite or subopposite ramuli. Hydrothecæ flask-shaped, curving away from the axial tube, and with the neck short and stout.

Gonosome not known.

Locality.—Station 75, near the Azores; lat. 38° 38′ 0″ N., long. 28° 28′ 30″ W.; depth, 450 fathoms.

Station 163A, off Twofold Bay, Australia; depth, 150 fathoms.

Perisiphonia filicula is a rather strong, rigid species, and in common with *Perisiphonia pectinata*, presents in its nearly opposite ramuli a distinct and easily recognised physiognomy. The somewhat robust stem springs from a complex plexus of tubular filaments, and soon begins to send off from each side its pinnately disposed ramuli. These are considerably more slender than the stem, and are either opposite or so nearly opposite that close inspection is necessary in order to discover any deviation from an exactly opposite arrangement. This deviation, however, becomes sufficiently obvious when the pinnæ are traced to their origin from the axial tube of the stem. It is only at the points where they leave the peripheral fascicle that they show any decided approximation to an opposite disposition.

Under a low power the whole surface may be seen to be thickly studded with the little tubular sarcothecæ, which constitute so remarkable a character of the genus. The hydrothecæ project but slightly from the surface and are regularly alternate and distichous, with entire circular orifice. When the axial tube of the stem is carefully exposed by the removal of the investing peripheral tubes, it will be seen that close to the base of several of the hydrothecal peduncles a branch is sent out at nearly a right angle from the main tube, from which it scarcely differs in thickness. Some of these branches soon terminate abruptly, while others are continued beyond the peripheral fascicle, bear pedunculated hydrothecæ, and constitute the axial portion of a lateral ramulus or pinna. This becomes surrounded by a fascicle of peripheral tubes, which are given off from the peripheral tubes of the stem. The peduncle of every hydrotheca carries a sarcotheca similar to those of the peripheral tubes, while two or three similar bodies are also frequently borne by the lateral offset near its base. The peripheral tubes terminate at the distal end of the ramuli in truncated but apparently closed extremities, and no part of the axial tube is here exposed, as is always the case in *Cryptolaria*.

The walls of the peripheral tubes are much thinner than those of the axial, and under the action of certain reagents, as caustic potash, shrivel and collapse, while the axial tube retains almost completely its original form. About ten tubes usually enter into the composition of the peripheral fascicle of a pinna.

Perisiphonia pectinata, n. sp. (Pl. XXI. figs. 2, 2a, 2b).

Trophosome.—Colony with the main stem sparingly branched, attaining a height of about five inches, stem and branches thick, carrying pinnately disposed, equidistant, nearly opposite, slender ramuli. Hydrothecæ flask-shaped, curved away from the axial tube, and with the neck rather long and slender.

Gonosome not known.

Locality.—Station 169, off New Zealand; lat. 37° 34′ S., long. 179° 22′ E.; depth, 700 fathoms.

The very regular, nearly opposite, disposition of the ramuli in this species is accompanied by a somewhat rigid habit, which gives a pectinate aspect to the branches. The more elongated and more slender neck of the flask-shaped hydrothecæ, and its greater extension beyond the surface of the peripheral fascicle, are among the characters which distinguish *Perisiphonia pectinata* from *Perisiphonia filicula*. Another point in which the present species differs from *Perisiphonia filicula* will be found in the greater slenderness of the pinnately disposed ramuli, which have here not more than half the diameter of these ramuli in *Perisiphonia filicula*. The slenderness of the pinnæ in

Perisiphonia pectinata is the result not only of the small number of peripheral tubes which enter into their composition, but of the fact that both peripheral and axial tubes are themselves more slender in this species than in the other. While the number of peripheral tubes in the pinnæ of *Perisiphonia filicula* is as many as ten or possibly more, I have always found the number of these tubes in the peripheral fascicle of *Perisiphonia pectinata* to be limited to six.

The superficial sarcothecal system is particularly well developed in *Perisiphonia pectinata*, in which the sarcothecæ are considerably longer than in *Perisiphonia filicula*. They spring from the peripheral tubes by a slightly dilated base.

Family GRAMMARIDÆ.

Character of the Family. Trophosome.—Hydrocaulus consisting of an axial tube which carries the hydrothecæ, and is entirely surrounded by a definite number of peripheral tubes which are destitute of hydrothecæ. Axial and peripheral tubes inseparably coalesced. All the hydrothecæ adnate by their sides to the axial tube. Hydranths with conical hypostome.

Gonosome not known.

Grammaria, Stimpson.

Grammaria, Stimpson, Marine Invertebrata of Grand Manan.

Generic Character.[1] *Trophosome.*—Colony, a ramified hydrocaulus composed of a fascicle of longitudinal tubes definite in number and inseparably adnate to one another, of which one is axial and the others peripheral, the axial tube entirely covered by the peripheral, and sending off, from distance to distance along its length, tubular, non-pedunculated hydrothecæ, which are at first adnate to it by their sides, and then, passing between the peripheral tubes, reach the surface of the fascicle, where they form definite longitudinal series directed on all sides round its circumference.

Gonosome not known.

The tubes which are combined into the fascicle which forms the stem and branches of the colony in *Grammaria* are very definite in number and arrangement, though their close adhesion to one another renders it difficult to determine their exact relation to the hydrothecæ. One of these tubes always occupies the axis of the fascicle and gives off from distance to distance the hydrothecæ, which are at first inseparably adnate to the tube from which they spring, and then, becoming free, bend outwards between the peripheral tubes so as to reach the surface of the fascicle, and thence project into the surrounding water.

[1] The facts brought to light by a study of the specimens of *Grammaria* obtained by the Challenger have rendered necessary a fundamental revision of the characters hitherto regarded as diagnostic of this genus.

In a transverse section of a branch of *Grammaria magellanica*, three hydrothecæ (Pl. XXIII. fig. 2ᵇ, *b*) may be seen nearly in the same plane projecting from the circumference of the branch, and at equal distances from one another, while alternating with these may be seen in section three others (*a*), whose bases lie in a plane above that of the former and whose distal ends have been removed by the section. Again alternating with the last may be seen the sections of three others (*a*) which spring from the axial tube in a plane still nearer to the observer, and have consequently a greater portion cut off by the section. These last, from the fact of the section passing nearer to their origin, are filled with the basal portion of the hydranth. The hydrothecæ of *Grammaria magellanica* are thus arranged in six longitudinal series, so disposed that the hydrothecæ of the six series lie in a succession of transverse planes, each plane containing three hydrothecæ, which exactly alternate with those of the plane on each side of it.

A similar disposition exists in *Grammaria stentor*, while in *Grammaria insignis* the number of longitudinal series is four, each transverse plane containing two nearly opposite hydrothecæ (fig. 3ᵇ, *b*) which alternate with those immediately above and below them. The arrangement as seen in all these instances in transverse sections of a branch is thus very regular and symmetrical.

Lying external to the axial tube and its hydrothecæ are the peripheral tubes of the fascicle. These were always six in number in the species which I examined. They run quite superficially, and here and there separate in order to give exit to the free portion of the hydrothecæ. They accompany the axial tube to its distal extremity, resembling in this respect the peripheral tubes of *Perisiphonia*, and differing from those of *Cryptolaria*, in which the axial tube for a greater or less extent towards its distal end ceases to be covered by the peripheral.

All the tubes entering into the composition of the fascicle, not excepting even the included portion of the hydrothecæ, are in such close approximation as to assume a prismatic form, and are inseparably adherent to one another. So intimate is this adhesion that I have found no treatment, even prolonged boiling in caustic potash, capable of in any way overcoming it. *Grammaria* in this respect presents a striking contrast to *Cryptolaria* and *Perisiphonia*, as well as to the other genera of the Perisiphonidæ, in all of which maceration in a solution of caustic potash so weakens the adhesion of the tubes to one another that these may then be easily separated by the dissecting needle.

As in *Cryptolaria* so also in *Grammaria* it is difficult to find characters available for the systematic diagnosis of the species. Throughout the genus the hydrothecæ present but little variation, while the gonosome from which differential characters might be expected has not yet been found in any species. A really good character is afforded by the number of longitudinal series in which the hydrothecæ are disposed upon the stem and branches, but even here the variation takes place within very narrow limits, six and four having been as yet the only numbers in which the longitudinal series of hydrothecæ are known to be present. Beyond these variations the ramification and general habit of the colony afford almost the only grounds for the systematic differentiation of the species.[1]

Grammaria stentor, n. sp. (Pl. XXIII. figs. 1, 1a).

Trophosome.—Colony attaining a height of between three and four inches, set with pinnately disposed ramuli which are alternate, subopposite or opposite, thinner than the stem, and often carrying secondary ramuli similar in disposition to the primary ones. Hydrothecæ rather long and wide and abruptly though slightly dilated at the orifice, and disposed in six longitudinal series.

Gonosome not known.

Locality.—Station 149D, Royal Sound, Kerguelen; depth, 28 to 60 fathoms.

This is a strong-growing species with the main stem thick towards the base and becoming gradually thinner towards the distal end. From either side the stem sends off pinnately disposed ramuli, which are sometimes opposite, but more frequently alternate or subopposite. The pinnæ, except at their origin, where, as in all the known species they are greatly constricted, are of uniform thickness. They are thinner than the stem from which they spring, and are sometimes simple, sometimes pinnately branched.

The graceful curve of the rather wide tubular hydrothecæ, and the slight trumpet-like dilatation of the orifice, confer on a magnified view of this fine species an aspect of great elegance.

Grammaria magellanica, n. sp. (Pl. XXIII. figs. 2, 2a, 2b).

Trophosome.—Hydrocaulus set with pinnately disposed alternate ramuli which are given off at rather wide intervals, and very much contracted at their origin. Hydrothecæ cylindrical, with even, circular, non-everted orifice, and disposed in six longitudinal series.

Gonosome not known.

Locality.—Station 314, near the Falkland Islands; lat. 51° 5′ S., long. 65° 39′ W.; depth, 70 fathoms.

The specimens of this species are fragmentary, the hydrorhizal extremity has in no instance been preserved, and the size and general habit of the Hydroid cannot be

---

[1] Mr. Hincks regards Lamouroux's genus *Salacia* (Exposition Méthodique, p. 15) as identical with the *Grammaria* of Stimpson, whose name he accordingly suppresses in favour of the earlier one. If, however, Lamouroux had really a *Grammaria* before him, his figure of it is altogether so bad, and his description so inadequate, that it is impossible to feel satisfied in the identification with *Grammaria* of the zoophyte to which the French zoologist assigned the name *Salacia*; so that even though Mr. Hincks be right in his reference of the *Grammaria* of Stimpson to the *Salacia* of Lamouroux, the uncertainty which must always hang over the nature of Lamouroux's animal will fully justify us in accepting Stimpson's name for a genus which this zoologist has described so fully as to leave no doubt as to the form intended by him.

ascertained with accuracy. The largest fragments measured about one inch and a half in height, and the pinnately disposed branches attained a length of from one-half to three-fourths of an inch. Hydrothecæ in all respects like those of the branches are carried by the stem along its entire length. The branches, as in all the known species of *Grammaria*, are greatly contracted at their origin. This contracted portion is occupied by a simple cavity into which the tubes of the compound branch open.

Grammaria insignis, n. sp. (Pl. XXIII. figs. 3, 3*a*, 3*b*).

Trophosome.—Colony attaining a height of six inches, set with pinnately disposed alternate ramuli, which often carry secondary ramuli with a similar disposition. Hydrothecæ cylindrical, not dilated at the orifice, disposed in four longitudinal series.

Gonosome not known.

Locality.—Station 145, off Marion Island ; depth, 50 to 75 fathoms.

This is a large and handsome species. The main stem is towards its base much thicker than the ultimate ramuli, but gradually tapers towards the distal end of the colony. The hydrothecæ, as in all the known species of *Grammaria*, are borne both along the stem and the branches, and the ultimate ramuli are here, as in every other known species, very much constricted at the origin. *Grammaria insignis* is the only species of *Grammaria* in the collection which has its hydrothecæ disposed in four longitudinal series. In all the others six such series are present.

Family SERTULARIDÆ.

Character of the Family. Trophosome.—Hydrothecæ in two or more series, with the cavity differentiated by a more or less complete floor from that of the hydrocaulus, to which their sides are for a greater or less extent adnate. Hydrocaulus not formed by inseparably coalesced tubes, of which one is axial and carries the hydrothecæ, and the others peripheral, definite in number, and destitute of hydrothecæ. Hydranths with conical hypostome.

Gonosome.—Gonophores hedrioblastic.

Sertularia, Linnæus (in part).

Sertularia, Linnæus, Syst. Nat. (Gmel.), p. 3844.

Generic Character. Trophosome.—Hydrocaulus simple or branched, divided by equidistant joints into internodes, each carrying a pair of opposite hydrothecæ, or two alternate hydrothecæ, or a single one. Hydrothecæ sessile, in two series, flask-shaped, or barrel-shaped, or cylindrical, with the margin entire or variously cleft or dentate, and with the sides to a greater or less extent adnate to the hydrocaulus, orifice with or without an operculum. Hydranth with conical hypostome.

Gonosome.—Gonophores adelocodonic, gonangia springing from one side of the hydrocaulus, each from a point near the base of a hydrotheca, and without a chitinous marsupium in either sex.

The old Linnæan genus *Sertularia* included, as may well be expected, many forms which subsequent systematists have placed in distinct generic groups. Even after the *Sertularia* of Linnæus had undergone the revision to which it had been subjected by Lamouroux and by Lamarck, there still remained species which later authors believed themselves justified in removing from it.

J. E. Gray broke up the genus *Sertularia* as left by Lamarck into two genera, *Sertularia* and *Sertularella*, the former including such species as had their hydrothecæ opposite, and the latter such as had them alternate. The insufficiency of the grounds on which this dismemberment was based soon became apparent, and Hincks, while accepting Gray's genus *Sertularella*, attempted to give it a greater systematic value by connecting with it characters of more importance than those derived merely from the alternate disposition of the hydrothecæ. The characters especially insisted on by Hincks as affording legitimate grounds for the dismemberment proposed by Gray are found in the condition of the margin of hydrotheca, which in *Sertularella* carries three or four denticles or cusps, and gives support to an operculum formed of three or four triangular membranous valves; while in *Sertularia* proper the margin is either even or with a simple cleft, and according to Hincks is destitute of an operculum.

Since the time when Hincks published his history of British Hydroid Zoophytes, many species from various parts of the world have come under examination, and show that the distinctions relied on in that valuable work have by no means the systematic importance which had been attributed to them. Some species which by their even or merely cleft hydrothecal margin would come under *Sertularia* proper have their hydrothecæ as truly alternate as in the most typical representatives of *Sertularella*, and even the characters derived from the presence of an operculum in *Sertularella*, and its supposed absence in *Sertularia*, are found to be by no means of universal application. Some species whose hydrothecæ in no essential point differ from those of the typical *Sertularia pumila*, either in the condition of the rim or in their absolutely opposite disposition (*e.g.*, *Sertularia distans* and others, see Hydroids of the Gulf Stream), are provided with opercular membranous valves, and yet few systematists would think of separating these generically from the closely allied species in which no valves are present.

What has been called the operculum consists in most cases of three or of four very thin membranous triangular valves, composed, like the general perisarc, of chitin, and forming when in apposition a four-sided or three-sided pyramidal roof for the hydrotheca. In some cases (e.g., *Sertularia distans*) there are but two valves, and these when in apposition form a wedge-shaped roof over the orifice of the hydrotheca.

The valves in all these cases are so thin and perishable that it is only in recent or exceptionally well preserved specimens we can hope to meet with them, a fact which in itself deprives the distinctions derived from them of that practical value which ought if possible to be found in all well-selected systematic characters.

On the grounds here adduced, then, I must regard the removal from *Sertularia* of the species for which Gray founded his genus *Sertularella* as a step not borne out by fundamental differences in the species; and although Gray's revision has been adopted by so high an authority as Hincks, and though I had followed it myself in former publications, I shall in the present Report suppress the genus *Sertularella* and refer to *Sertularia* all species which agree with the diagnosis of this genus as given above.

A revision much more in accordance with natural affinities was proposed by Agassiz, who, under the name of *Diphasia* separated from *Sertularia* those species in which the female gonangium differs from the male in possessing an external chamber with chitinous walls, into which the ova are expelled from the main cavity of the gonangium in order to pass through certain stages of their development before escaping into the surrounding water.

Sertularia gracilis, n. sp. (Pl. XXIV. figs. 1, 1a).

Trophosome.—Stem monosiphonic, slender, profusely branched; primary ramification pinnate or subpinnate, many of the primary and secondary branches presenting a similarly pinnate or subpinnate ramification. Hydrothecæ alternate, distant, one borne on every internode, nearly cylindrical, adnate to the internode for about two-thirds of their height, then bending outwards; orifice with a broad cusp on each side.

Gonosome.—Gonangia springing each from a point just below the base of a hydrotheca, urniform, with very prominent annular ridges, distal end continued as a narrow cylindrical tube, which carries the even, circular orifice on its summit.

Locality.—Station 312, Port Famine, Patagonia; lat. 53° 37′ 30″ S., long. 70° 56′ 0″ W.; depth, 9 fathoms.

This slender and very elegant species was brought up in luxuriant masses about five inches in height, and richly laden with gonangia. The ramification, which is very profuse, commences with pinnately disposed branches, many of which soon branch in a similar way, and the primary ramification is further repeated in ramuli of a secondary, tertiary, and even higher order. The branches are given off each close to the base of a hydrotheca.

The gonangia are very beautiful. The regularity and prominence of the annular ridges constitute a feature in the highest degree attractive. The distal end is prolonged into a short, wide neck, which terminates in a saucer-shaped summit, from the centre of which rises a narrow, cylindrical tube, which carries the relatively small orifice of the gonangium.

The annular ridges, which are very prominent on the apocauline or outer side of the gonangium, are nearly obsolete on the inner or epicauline side, a condition which is obviously connected with the close proximity of this side to the opposed surface of the stem.

Sertularia gracilis has considerable resemblance to *Sertularia tricuspidata*, Alder. It differs from it in the absence of annulation at the distal side of every hydrotheca, in the hydrothecæ having only two marginal cusps, and in the more elongated gonangia.

Sertularia annulata, n. sp. (Pl. XXIV. figs. 2, 2a).

Trophosome.—Stem fascicled towards the base, becoming monosiphonic distally, irregularly or subpinnately branched, set with pinnately disposed, alternate ramuli, stem and ramuli divided into short internodes, every internode carrying a hydrotheca. Hydrothecæ alternate, nearly cylindrical, adnate to the internode for somewhat more than half their height, then becoming free and divergent, distinctly annulated for some distance from the orifice, margin of orifice with four short, broad cusps.

Gonosome not present.

Locality.—Station 163B, off Port Jackson, Australia; depth, 35 fathoms.

Sertularia annulata is a strong-growing form. The main stem and its principal branches are stout, and fascicled towards the proximal ends, but become monosiphonic distally, and are regularly set with rather long, alternate, equidistant, monosiphonic pinnæ. The annulation of the hydrothecæ is well marked, and extends from the orifice about halfway towards the base.

Sertularia leiocarpa, n. sp. (Pl. XXV. figs. 1, 1a).

Trophosome.—Hydrocaulus monosiphonic, irregularly branched, geniculated, every internode increasing in thickness from its proximal to its distal end. Hydrothecæ alternate, springing from the salient angles of the geniculations, distant, deep, tubular, narrowing towards the summit, adnate to the internode for about one-third of their height, then diverging at a wide angle, and terminating in a subquadrate orifice with four minute cusps.

Gonosome.—Gonangia large, oviform, perfectly smooth, narrowing below into a short peduncle which springs from a point just below a hydrotheca, and terminates in a short and wide tubular prolongation which carries the circular entire orifice.

Locality.—Station 135c, Nightingale Island; depth, 100 to 150 fathoms.

Sertularia leiocarpa is a rather strong-growing form with large distant hydrothecae, each borne close to the distal end of an internode, where the hydrocaulus forms a well-marked geniculation. The joints separating the internodes are often obscure. The specimen has a height of about three inches, and springs from a small plexus of hydro-rhizal filaments, while the proximal end of the stem is for some distance destitute of hydrothecae.

The gonangium is large, its height exceeding twice that of an internode. It is perfectly smooth, showing no trace of annulation or rugae.

The perisarc is transparent and allows of a good view of the included soft parts, which are well preserved in the specimen. The hydranths have about fifteen tentacles, and in extreme retraction present a condition hitherto unnoticed among Hydroids, the gastric cavity emitting then a lateral, long, hernia-like protrusion which extends from the base of the hydranth to a point beyond the origin of the tentacular crown (fig. 1a). This remarkable condition gives to the body of the hydranth the appearance of being doubled on itself, and forcibly recalls the formation of the alimentary canal in a Polyzoon.

The fleshy bands which extend from the sides of the gonophore to the walls of the gonangium were well preserved, and at their points of attachment to the gonangium were flattened out in a stellate fashion. The bands had often become broken away from their points of attachment, leaving these behind in the form of stellate cells (fig. 1a).

Sertularia unilateralis, n. sp. (Pl. XXV. figs. 2, 2a, 2b).

Trophosome.—Hydrocaulus many times pinnately branched, forming a dense tuft in which the ramuli are all directed towards one side of the colony. Hydrothecae alternate, borne close to the distal end of each internode, those of opposite sides lying in two different planes, adnate to the internode for about one-third of their height, epicauline side ventricose towards the base, margin divided into four strong teeth, and with a thickened rim.

Gonosome.—Gonangia oviform, equalling in height about three internodes of the stem, attached by a short peduncle to the internode just below a hydrotheca, annulated for the greater part of their height, and opening by a tridentate terminal orifice.

Locality.—Station 149, off Accessible Bay, Kerguelen Island; depth, 20 fathoms.

Sertularia unilateralis by the profusion of its branches forms a dense tuft which is upwards of an inch in height, and in which the ramification is rendered remarkable by having the ramuli all directed towards one and the same side, so as to give to the colony a front and a back aspect. In the hydrothecæ also a similar unilateral direction is apparent, for those of opposite sides, instead of lying as usual in a single plane, are directed obliquely towards one side of the stem, and thus lie in two planes which converge towards its axis.

Sertularia clausa, n. sp. (Pl. XXV. figs. 3, 3a).

Trophosome.—Stem slender, transparent, irregularly branched, internodes carrying each a single hydrotheca. Hydrothecæ alternate, distant, conical, slightly tumid below, adnate to the internode for about half their height, then diverging; orifice subquadrate, covered by a pyramidal lid which is composed of four triangular valves.

Gonosome not present.

Locality.—Station 320, off Monte Video; lat. 37° 17′ S., long. 53° 52′ W.; depth, 600 fathoms; bottom, green sand; bottom temperature, 37°·2.

Sertularia clausa is a small, much-branched, slender form, with a thin very transparent perisarc. The branches are given off at a wide angle, each from a point just below the base of a hydrotheca, and are irregular in their disposition and direction. The hydrothecæ are separated from one another by rather wide intervals. From a somewhat wide base they become gradually narrower towards the orifice, which is obscurely quadrate. As in many other species, the orifice is provided with a membranous four-valved operculum, but instead of this being filmy and perishable as in most of the species which possess it, it has here considerable firmness and forms a well-developed, permanent, pyramidal lid. This is composed of four triangular valves, which when in apposition form the four sides of a pyramid.

The delicacy and transparency of the periderm is probably connected with the very considerable depth of 600 fathoms from which the species was dredged.

Sertularia implexa, n. sp. (Pl. XXVI. figs. 1, 1a).

Trophosome.—Stem profusely and irregularly branched; branches slender, given off in all directions, and forming loosely entangled masses. Hydrothecæ alternate, rather distant, deep, adnate to the internode for somewhat less than half their height, apocauline side nearly plane, epicauline side ventricose, orifice with the margin divided into four teeth and provided with four delicate membranous valves.

Gonosome not present.

Locality.—Station 314, between Cape Virgins and the Falkland Islands; lat. 51° 35′ S., long. 65° 39′ W.; depth, 70 fathoms.

Sertularia implexa grows in complex entangled tufts which attain a height of nearly three inches. The hydrothecæ are borne close to the distal ends of the rather long internodes, and their margin is divided into four triangular equidistant teeth, whose intervals support four very delicate, membranous, triangular valves, which, when in apposition, form a pyramidal roof over the orifice of the hydrotheca. The branches spring each from a point close to the base of a hydrotheca.

Sertularia exigua, n. sp. (Pl. XXVI. figs. 2, 2a).

Trophosome.—Stem monosiphonic, slender, much and irregularly branched, divided by well-marked joints into equal internodes, which are slightly inclined at an angle to one another, each internode carrying a single hydrotheca near its distal end. Hydrothecæ alternate, distant, adnate to the internode for about half their height, then diverging at a rather wide angle, tumid below, much narrower and cylindrical towards the four-toothed orifice.

Gonosome.—Gonangia borne by the internodes near the bases of the hydrothecæ, oviform, annulated, tapering below to a narrow point of attachment; orifice tridentate, borne on a short tubular extension of the summit.

Locality.—Station 75, near the Azores; lat. 38° 38′ 0″ N., long. 28° 28′ 30″ W.; depth, 450 fathoms.

Sertularia exigua is a very slender profusely branched species. The internodes are inclined to one another at a slight angle, so that the stem presents a somewhat zigzag or geniculate form. The hydrothecæ are distant, and present a sufficiently obvious character in their narrow cylindrical distal end with its four-toothed margin.

The gonangia are in most cases distinctly annulated. Sometimes, however, the annulation is nearly obliterated.

The species comes very near to *Sertularia polyzonias*, from which it differs chiefly in its much more slender habit and in the narrower and more elongated free portion of the hydrothecæ.

Sertularia polyzonias, Linnæus (Pl. XXVI. figs. 3, 3a).

> *Sertularia polyzonias*, Linn., Syst. Nat. (Gmel.), p. 3856.
> „ „ Lamk., Anim. sans Vert. (Ed. 2), t. ii. p. 142.
> *Sertularella polyzonias*, Hincks, Brit. Hydroid Zooph., p. 235, pl. xlvi. fig. 1.

Trophosome.—Stem monosiphonic, irregularly branched. Hydrothecæ alternate, distant, adnate to the internode for about one-third of their height, then divergent, tumid below, contracted and cylindrical towards the quadrate, four-toothed orifice.

Gonosome.—Gonangia each springing from a point just below a hydrotheca, elongated ovate, tapering below into an ill-defined peduncle, strongly annulated, with a terminal obscurely four-toothed orifice.

Locality.—Station 315, Port William, Falkland Islands; lat. 51° 40′ S., long. 57° 50′ W.; depth, 5 to 12 fathoms.

There do not appear to be any legitimate grounds for separating the form here described from the widely distributed *Sertularia polyzonias*. Though the specimen is scarcely more than an inch in height it has probably attained nearly its full size, as the presence of a well-developed gonosome would seem to indicate. It is thus of much humbler habit than the typical *Sertularia polyzonias*, from which it further differs in the more elongated and more deeply annulated gonangia. These differences, however, I regard as merely local variations to which we should not be justified in assigning a specific value. The membranous valves of the hydrotheca had not been preserved so as to be recognisable in the specimen.

The specimen here described was dredged in the region of the Falkland Islands. The collection also contains specimens obtained at Port William, which I do not hesitate to refer to the same species.

Sertularia exserta, n. sp. (Pl. XXVII. figs. 1, 1a, 1b, 1c).

Trophosome.—Hydrocaulus monosiphonic, slender, subdichotomously and profusely branched, divided by distinct joints into internodes, each of which carries a hydrotheca. Hydrothecæ exactly alternate, each borne at the distal end of an internode, adnate to the internode for about one-third of their height, deep, nearly cylindrical, margin of orifice with two strong cusps at its apocauline side, and one at its epicauline side. Hydranths incapable of complete retraction within the hydrothecæ.

Gonosome.—Gonangia springing each from a point just below the base of a hydrotheca, oviform, encircled by very prominent transverse annular ridges, and terminating distally in a short neck with a saucer-like terminal expansion which carries the orifice.

Locality.—Station 151, off Heard Island; depth, 75 fathoms.

Sertularia exserta is a very beautiful and interesting species. Its hydranths, like those of *Thuiaria hyalina* (Pl. XXXIII. figs. 2, 2a), are incapable of complete retraction, the tentacular crown being never withdrawn into the hydrotheca; and here also as in that Hydroid the body of the hydranth sends off in all directions fleshy bands (fig. 1a) by which it becomes tied to the hydrotheca-walls, and is thus rendered incapable of that complete retraction by which in ordinary cases the hydranth is enabled to retire within the cavity of the hydrotheca.

In this imperfect retraction of the hydranth we have a condition which may be compared with that of the various species of *Halecium*. While in these, however, the hydrothecæ are evanescent, and not only the tentacular crown but the body of the hydranth always remains uncovered, in *Sertularia exserta* and in *Thuiaria hyalina* the hydrothecæ are especially well developed, and though the tentacular crown in these two Hydroids always remains exposed, the body of the hydranth remains under cover of the hydrotheca.

Another feature of great interest and significance is found in the fact that in the present species every tentacle is provided at its base with a remarkable organ in the form of a little cushion-like prominence loaded with slightly curved, rod-shaped thread-cells (figs. 1b, 1c). It is scarcely possible not to recognise in these little batteries of thread-cells defensive organs compensating for the loss of the protection which in other cases is afforded by the hydrothecæ. Whether, however, similar organs occur in the equally exposed hydranths of *Thuiaria hyalina* the state of the specimen did not allow me to determine; while we cannot overlook the fact that in the still more exposed hydranths of *Halecium* no such organs have been detected.

The gonangia of *Sertularia exserta* are exceedingly beautiful. The thin but very prominent annular ridges with which they are encircled give to them the appearance of a symmetrical pile of discs, while the profusion in which the gonangia are developed gives to the entire colony an aspect no less pleasing than striking.

The specimens in the collection have a height of between one and two inches, while the comparatively good state of preservation in which the soft parts are retained allowed of a satisfactory determination of the points here described.

Sertularia echinocarpa, n. sp. (Pl. XXVIII. figs. 1, 1a).

Trophosome.—Stem fascicled towards the root, becoming monosiphonic distally, pinnately branched, branches alternate. Hydrothecæ alternate, large, tubular, cylindrical, slightly tumid towards the base on the aposauline side, free for about two-thirds of their height, orifice quite even and circular.

Gonosome.—Gonangia springing each by a short peduncle from a point close to the base of a hydrotheca, pyriform, thickly set with hollow, blunt, spine-like outgrowths of their chitinous perisarc.

Locality.—Station 149D, Royal Sound, Kerguelen Island; depth, 28 to 60 fathoms.

Sertularia echinocarpa is a large and strong form, attaining a height of upwards of six inches. The main stem is slightly wavy and set with hydrothecæ along its entire length. It sends off at nearly equal intervals shorter pinnately disposed alternate branches, which are set with hydrothecæ and differ in no respect except in length from the main stem.

The long tubular hydrothecæ, free for the greater part of their height, afford a very obvious character. They are strictly alternate; their orifice is perfectly circular and destitute of serration, and it thus presents a character which is exceptional among the *Sertulariæ* with alternate hydrothecæ. Here and there a well-marked transverse joint occurs just above the base of a hydrotheca, but this is found at distant and uncertain intervals, and elsewhere the joints are nearly or quite obliterated.

Immediately below the base of every hydrotheca are two oval spaces in which the chitinous periderm is very thin and transparent. They occur one on each side of the hydrotheca, and have the appearance of apertures in the perisarc. It is from these spaces that the gonangia take their origin. The greater number, however, are found with no gonangia attached to them; and as they are quite constant and occur on both sides of the hydrothecæ, we cannot regard them as indications of the points from which gonangia had already fallen. Similar transparent aperture-like spaces are by no means unusual among the Sertularian Hydroids. I am not able to assign to them their real significance.

The gonangia constitute a very striking character in the species. They are pyriform vesicles, thickly covered with long blunt spine-like outgrowths of their walls, these are hollow and open into the cavity of the gonangium.

Sertularia catena, n. sp. (Pl. XXVIII. figs. 2, 2a).

Trophosome.—Hydrocaulus fascicled, becoming monosiphonic distally; internodes inclined to one another at a very decided angle, gradually widening from their proximal towards their distal ends, where each carries a hydrotheca. Hydrothecæ alternate, large, deep, cylindrical, with four low marginal cusps, every hydrotheca springing by its base from a point near the distal end of an internode, and free for somewhat more than two-thirds of its course.

Gonosome.—Gonangia springing each from an internode at a short distance below the base of a hydrotheca, elongate ovate, destitute of annulation, with a small terminal, bicuspate orifice.

Locality.—Station 24, off Culebra Island, West Indies; depth, 390 fathoms.

Sertularia catena, though a rather strong-growing form, does not appear to attain a large size, the specimen in the collection measuring about two inches in height. Its large, cylindrical hydrothecæ, except at the base where they rest on the supporting internode, and for a short extent of the epicauline side, are entirely free from the hydrocaulus. The internodes are clavate in form, and each springs by its narrow end from the wide end of the internode which precedes it, and to which it is inclined by a well-pronounced angle, thus giving to the hydrocaulus a decidedly geniculate habit, which is rendered still more obvious by the direction of the hydrothecæ, whose axis is always in direct continuation with that of the supporting internode.

Sertularia geniculata, n. sp. (Pl. XXVIII. figs. 3, 3*a*, 3*b*).

Trophosome.—Stem monosiphonic, very slender and hyaline, irregularly branched, internodes very long, inclined to one another at a wide angle so as to give a geniculate form to the stem. Hydrothecæ alternate, borne close to the distal ends of the internodes, to which they are adnate by about one-third of their epicauline side, very deep, tumid towards the base, and thence gradually narrowing and becoming cylindrical towards the summit, which is occupied by the quadrilateral orifice.

Gonosome.—Gonangia obovate, with truncated summit, springing by a narrow proximal end from a point on the internode just below the base of a hydrotheca.

Locality.—Station 214, south of the Philippines; lat. 4° 33′ N., long. 127° 6′ E.; depth, 500 fathoms.

Sertularia geniculata is a very slender, perfectly hyaline form. The collection contains but a single example, which is less than an inch in height, but as the specimen is fragmentary and has lost its hydrorhizal extremity, no assertion can be made as to the height which the species may naturally attain. It is probable, however, that the perfect colony does not much exceed in size the portion which has been preserved.

The internodes, which are nearly twice as long as the very deep, narrow hydrothecæ, become wider towards their distal ends, thus adding to the knee-like form of the joints.

The hydrothecæ, for some distance below the orifice, are marked by parallel, transverse striæ, and the orifice itself is crowned by an exceedingly delicate, four-valved, membranous operculum, so delicate indeed that it was only in a few of the hydrothecæ that it was sufficiently well preserved to allow of demonstration.

Just within the orifice may be seen in optical section two broad, conical projections of the chitinous walls, one on the epicauline, and the other on the aporauline side of the hydrotheca. It is not improbable that in the living animal they give attachment to contractile bands employed in the closing of the operculum.

Sertularia cylindritheca, n. sp. (Pl. XXIX. figs. 1, 1*a*).

Trophosome.—Main stem monosiphonic, not divided into branches, but set with pinnately disposed, alternate ramuli. Hydrothecæ borne both by stem and pinnæ, one only on every internode, alternate, cylindrical, adnate by the base to the hydrocaulus, and free for nearly the whole of their epicauline side, margin with four low cusps.

Gonosome not present.

Locality.—Off Bahia.

Sertularia cylindritheca, though destitute of fasciculation, is a strong-growing, rather rigid form. The specimen in the collection is fragmentary, and though broken away from its hydrorhizal end has a height of four inches. From the main stem, which is simple, are emitted alternate pinnæ, which are themselves occasionally branched. The hydrothecæ are absolutely cylindrical, and arise close to the distal ends of the internodes. They have but a very small portion of their epicauline side adnate to the internode, and from the fact of this portion being nearly in the same plane with the true base the hydrothecæ have the appearance of being entirely free from the base to the summit. That the attached portion, however, must be regarded as consisting not only of the true base but of a portion of the epicauline side, will be apparent from a comparison with such species as *Sertularia echinocarpa* and *Sertularia geniculata* (Pl. XXVIII.), and it will thus be seen that the present species offers no real exception to the general character of the family. The four-cusped margin of the hydrotheca distinguishes this species from *Sertularia integritheca*, which it closely resembles in almost every other respect, and with which it was associated in the contents of the dredge.

Sertularia integritheca, n. sp. (Pl. XXIX. figs. 2, 2a).

Trophosome.—Hydrocaulus consisting of unbranched, monosiphonic stems, set with pinnately disposed alternate ramuli. Hydrothecæ borne both by stems and ramuli, one on every internode, alternate, exactly cylindrical, each springing from the hydrocaulus by its base, and then free for nearly its entire height, orifice circular and entire.

Gonosome not present.
Locality.—Off Bahia.

Sertularia integra is a large and strong-growing species, chiefly characterised by its absolutely cylindrical hydrothecæ, whose perfectly circular and entire orifice occupies the whole summit of the hydrotheca.

The stems spring at intervals from a creeping, tubular filament, and attain a height of about four inches. They are rather thick, monosiphonic throughout, not dividing into branches, but set along nearly their entire length with alternate pinnæ.

The hydrothecæ are each attached to the hydrocaulus by its base and by a very small extent of the epicauline side. In this character they entirely agree with the preceding species (*Sertularia cylindritheca*). The joints which separate the internodes occur just above the hydrothecæ. They are sufficiently distinct towards the distal ends of the ramuli, but in the more proximal or older parts they frequently become indistinct or even obliterated.

The species is a member of the rich Hydroid fauna of Bahia, but though the specimens obtained were finely developed they were quite destitute of gonosome.

Sertularia articulata, n. sp. (Pl. XXIX. figs. 3, 3*a*).

Trophosome.—Hydrocaulus irregularly branched, slender, divided into equal internodes by strongly marked transverse joints, every internode carrying a hydrotheca close to its distal end. Hydrothecæ alternate, adnate to the internodes for somewhat more than half their height, the free portion diverging at a high angle and very slightly tapering towards the orifice, which at its apocauline margin has a deep sinus bounded by two strong lateral cusps.

Gonosome not present.

Locality.—Station 149D, Royal Sound, Kerguelen Island; depth, 28 to 60 fathoms.

The most striking character in this delicate species is found in the depth and distinctness of the joints, a peculiarity which gives to the hydrocaulus a decidedly articulated appearance, the distal end of each internode being slightly wider than the proximal end of the internode which rests upon it. The specimen contained in the collection is a mere fragment, destitute not only of gonosome but of hydrorhizal extremity.

In some respects the present species approaches *Sertularia johnstoni*, Gray. From this, however, which is a New Zealand species, it differs in the form of its hydrothecæ, which in *Sertularia johnstoni* are slightly tumid below, as well as in their position, which in *Sertularia johnstoni* is near the middle of the internode instead of being as in the present species close to the distal end.[1] The jointing of the hydrocaulus, though very distinct in *Sertularia johnstoni*, does not in that species present the well-defined character which we meet with here as the result of the difference of diameter in the extremities of the two internodes where they unite to form the joint.

Sertularia operculata, Linnæus (Pl. XXX. figs. 1, 1*a*).

Sertularia operculata, Linn., Syst. Nat. (Gmel.), p. 3844.
      ,,   ,,   Lamk., Anim. sans Vert. (ed. 2), t. ii. p. 144.
      ,,   ,,   Hincks, Brit. Hydroid Zooph., p. 263, pl. liv.

Trophosome.—Hydrocaulus monosiphonic, slender, profusely branched, ramification dichotomous or subdichotomous. Hydrothecæ exactly opposite, adnate to the hydrocaulus by somewhat more than half their height, gently curving outwards, opening by a very oblique orifice which occupies the greater part of the epicauline side of the free portion of the hydrotheca, apocauline side of orifice with a deep sinus, each of whose sides is produced into a strong, sharp tooth.

Gonosome.—Gonangia elongate, oviform, tapering below to a short and narrow

[1] *Journ. Linn. Soc. Lond.* (Zool.), vol. xii. p. 261.

peduncle, summit truncated and occupied by the circular, entire orifice, which is closed by a chitinous lid.

Locality.—Station 304, Port Otway, Patagonia ; lat. 46° 53′ 15″ S., long. 75° 12′ W.; depth, 45 fathoms.

I do not hesitate to refer the Hydroid here described to the *Sertularia operculata*, Linn., an abundant species of the European seas.

The orifice of the hydrotheca extends from the apocauline wall of the divergent distal end almost to the point where the hydrotheca ceases to be adnate to the hydrocaulus. The apocauline margin of the orifice presents a deep notch or sinus, each side of which is produced into a sharp tooth-like lobe. This account of the hydrothecal margin differs somewhat from the descriptions hitherto given of this part, as seen in European specimens, descriptions which seem to be based on incorrect interpretation of the perspective under which the object usually presents itself when viewed beneath the microscope.

The Challenger specimens have a height of about four inches. They were dredged off Patagonia from a floor of green sand, with a depth of 45 fathoms. Another station is thus added to the already determined wide geographical distribution of the species.

Sertularia abietina, Linnæus (Pl. XXVII. figs. 2, 2a).

   Sertularia abietina, Linn., Syst. Nat. (Gmel.), p. 3845.
   „   „   Lamk., Anim. sans Vert. (ed. 2), t. ii. p. 131.
   „   „   Hincks, Brit. Hydroid Zooph., p. 266, pl. lv.

Trophosome.—Main stem monosiphonic, set for nearly its entire length with pinnately disposed, rather close set, alternate ramuli, and often emitting branches which are similarly set with pinnæ so as to repeat in all respects the habit of the stem from which they spring. Hydrothecæ subalternate, two borne on each internode, adnate to the hydrocaulus for about one-third of their height, flask-shaped, ventricose below, then narrowing into a tubular neck which diverges strongly from the internode, and terminates in an entire circular orifice with slightly everted margin.

Gonosome.—Gonangia subsessile, springing from the front of the pinnæ, each from a point close to the base of a hydrotheca, ovate, with a slightly elevated, circular and entire orifice.[1]

Locality.—Station 48, off Halifax, Nova Scotia ; lat. 43° 4′ N., long. 64° 5′ W.; depth, 51 fathoms.

The specimens of this Hydroid obtained by the Challenger were dredged off the Atlantic shores of North America. They differ in no essential point from the form as it

---

[1] No gonangia were present in the Challenger specimens.

occurs on the British coast, where it is perhaps the most abundant of all the large Hydroids there found, while it is also one of the most widely distributed throughout the North Atlantic region. It is of rather robust habit, and is at once distinguished from every other species by its flask-shaped hydrothecæ, with their attenuated diverging necks.

Diphasia, Agassiz.

Sertularia, Linn. (in part).
Diphasia, Agassiz, Nat. Hist. U.S., vol. iv. p. 355.

Generic Character. *Trophosome.*—Colony dendritic; hydrocaulus divided by equidistant joints into internodes, each of which carries a pair of hydrothecæ. Hydrothecæ sessile, more or less adnate by their walls to the hydrocaulus, distichous, opposite or subopposite, with entire or emarginate rim, and with a lid-like operculum formed by a single valve.

Gonosome.—Gonophores adelocodonic. Gonangia in female colonies crowned by a marsupial chamber enclosed within chitinous walls, gonangia in male destitute of marsupium.

The genus *Diphasia* was founded by Agassiz for the purpose of including species hitherto placed in *Sertularia*, but which differ from the true *Sertulariæ* in the gonangia of the female colony carrying on their summit a special chamber enclosed within lobe-like extensions of the chitinous walls of the proper gonangium. Into this chamber the ova are at an early stage expelled from the gonangium in order to undergo further development before the escape of the embryo into the surrounding water. No marsupium is present in the male.[1]

The hydrothecæ are provided with a peculiar membranous lid, which springs by a hinge-like joint from one point of the rim, and forms when depressed a transverse septum just within the margin.

Diphasia pinaster (Ellis and Solander) (Pl. XXX. figs. 2, 2a, 2b, 2c).

Sertularia pinaster, Ellis and Solander, Zooph., p. 55, pl. vi.
Diphasia pinaster, Agassiz, Nat. Hist. United States, vol. iv. p. 355.
        „   „   Hincks, Brit. Hydroid Zooph., vol. i. p. 252, pl. l. fig. 1.

Trophosome.—Stem monosiphonic, unbranched, set with alternate pinnæ. Hydrothecæ borne both by stem and pinnæ, subopposite, cylindrical, adnate to the hydrocaulus for about two-thirds of their height, then diverging at a wide angle; orifice oblique, crowned by a membranous valve-like lid.

---

[1] The "acrocyst" which in certain species of *Sertularia* (e.g. *Sertularia pumila*) is formed on the summit of the female gonangium, differs from the marsupium of *Diphasia* in the fact of its being never included within an external chamber bounded by chitinous walls.

Gonosome.—Gonangia shortly pedunculate, borne by the pinnæ, each from a point just below a hydrotheca; male gonangia urn-shaped, crowned by a conical projection which carries the orifice on its summit, and is surrounded by four symmetrically disposed flattened spines; female gonangia obovate, crowned by four spinous valves which enclose the marsupial chamber.

Locality.—Station 75, near the Azores; lat. 38° 38′ 0″ N., long. 28° 28′ 30″ W.; depth, 450 fathoms.

Though the specimens obtained by the Challenger differ somewhat from the *Diphasia pinaster* of the European seas, especially in their shorter and rather more rigid pinnæ, and in the more elongated form of their female gonangia, I have little hesitation in referring them to this species.

Diphasia pinaster is a well-marked species, and when the pinnæ are laden with their large and elegantly formed gonangia constitutes a striking and beautiful object. The specimens obtained by the Challenger have a height of four or five inches. The hydrothecæ are decidedly subopposite in the pinnæ, but more nearly opposite in the stem. The orifice is oblique, having a wide sinus at its epicauline side and is provided with a thin membranous lid which is hinged on to the bottom of the marginal sinus. When depressed this lid lies within the orifice, and then stretches transversely across the cavity of the hydrotheca. No distinct joints are present in any part of the stem or pinnæ.

The male gonangium has the small circular orifice raised on the summit of a conical projection of the roof, and this is surrounded by four symmetrically placed strong spines, which are laterally compressed, and have their bases extended downwards as four keel-shaped ridges along the walls of the gonangium.

The female gonangia with the marsupium are nearly twice the length of the male. The marsupial chamber is of about the same height as that of the gonangium proper. The four valves by which the marsupium is enclosed have a row of two or three strong spines extending along the mesial line of each.

The specimens obtained by the Challenger were dredged from a depth of 450 fathoms, and form part of the rich Hydroid fauna which the region of the Azores has yielded to the dredge.

Thuiaria, Fleming.

Thuiaria, Fleming, British Animals, p. 545.

Generic Character. *Trophosome.*—Colony dendritic; hydrocaulus divided by well-marked joints at regular or irregular intervals into internodes, each of which carries many hydrothecæ. Hydrothecæ distichous, opposite or alternate, sessile, adnate by a greater or less extent of their walls to the hydrocaulus, margin of orifice entire or variously cleft or dentate. Hydranth with conical hypostome.

Gonosome.—Gonophores adelocodonic; gonangia springing from one side of the hydrocaulus, no marsupium present in either sex.

The genus *Thuiaria* was separated by Fleming from *Sertularia* on grounds derived from the supposed immersion of the hydrothecæ in the hydrocaulus, instead of their being as in *Sertularia* merely adnate to its surface.

The character, however, thus relied on has really no existence. The hydrothecæ of the species separated on this ground from *Sertularia* are not more deeply immersed in the hydrocaulus than are the hydrothecæ of most species of *Sertularia*, and the appearance of immersion is given by the greater extent in which the walls of the hydrothecæ are in some species adnate to the hydrocaulus, while even this is never greater than what occurs in many species which are allowed to remain in *Sertularia*.

There can, however, be no doubt that the general aspect of *Thuiaria* contrasts strongly with that of the species with which it had been previously associated, but the true source of this is to be found in a character very different from that of the supposed immersion of the hydrothecæ in the hydrocaulus.

In the species of *Sertularia* with opposite hydrothecæ every pair of hydrothecæ has an internode of the stem to itself, being separated on each side from the adjacent pair by a joint. In those species in which the hydrothecæ are alternate the internodes carry each, sometimes two alternate hydrothecæ, but most frequently a single one. In these various cases the intervals between the joints are constant, every internode in the same colony carrying the same number of hydrothecæ.

In *Thuiaria* it is different. The internodes here always carry many hydrothecæ, whether in pairs or alternate. The joints moreover are in most cases so decided as to form well-marked constrictions in the stem, a character which in combination with the length of the internodes confers upon *Thuiaria* an aspect very striking and distinctive. Moreover, the internodes are often of variable length, the number of hydrothecæ carried by each frequently varying in different parts of the same colony.

It is true that in *Sertularia* we may sometimes meet with examples in which for a considerable length of the stem no joints are apparent. This, however, is a secondary condition resulting from the effacement in the older parts of the hydrocaulus of the joints which had been present in an earlier period;[1] while in *Thuiaria* the very well marked joints are at all times separated from one another by intervening series of many hydrothecæ.

If the diagnostic characters of *Thuiaria* be such as are here contended for, some species which had been hitherto referred to *Sertularia* must be removed to *Thuiaria*. *Sertularia cupressina*, Linn., and *Sertularia argentea*, Ellis and Solander, will thus find their places in *Thuiaria*. Indeed there is not a single character which would justify the inclusion of these Hydroids in *Sertularia* rather than in *Thuiaria*.

[1] I believe that the *Thuiaria articuloides* of The Hydroids of the Gulf Stream is a case of this kind, and that the species is truly a *Sertularia* which, on account of the effacement of the joints, I have erroneously referred to *Thuiaria*.

Thuiaria quadridens, n. sp. (Pl. XXXI. figs. 2, 2a).

Trophosome.—Stem monosiphonic, pinnately branched, joints at irregular intervals. Hydrothecæ alternate, deep, subcylindrical, adnate to the internode for somewhat more than half their height, and then diverging at a rather high angle; margin divided into four teeth, two of which are narrow and situated at the epicauline side, and two broader at the apocauline.

Gonosome not present.

Locality.—Station 314, between Cape Virgins and the Falkland Islands; lat. 51° 35′ S., long. 65° 39′ W.; depth, 70 fathoms.

Thuiaria quadridens was dredged from the same ground with *Sertularia implexa*. It is a rather slender form of much elegance, and attains a height of nearly two inches.

Thuiaria pharmacopola, n. sp. (Pl. XXXI. figs. 1, 1a, 1b, 1c, 1d).

Trophosome.—Stem strongly fascicled below, becoming monosiphonic distally, sparingly branched, set with alternately disposed pinnæ. Hydrothecæ opposite, adnate to the hydrocaulus for nearly their entire height, cylindrical, deep, terminating in an oblique orifice whose apocauline margin forms an acute tooth.

Gonosome.—Gonangia borne upon the front of the pinnæ, each springing from a point in the interval between two pairs of hydrothecæ, urniform, with the roof raised as a conical projection which carries the circular even orifice on its apex, and is surrounded by about six compressed spines.

Locality.—Station 75, off the Azores; lat. 38° 38′ 0″ N., long. 28° 28′ 30″ W.; depth, 450 fathoms.

Thuiaria pharmacopola is a large and beautiful species. It grows to a height of upwards of six inches, while the pinnæ, which are rather closely set, may attain a length of more than one inch. The stem towards its base is thick and densely fascicled, but becomes monosiphonic towards its summit. The hydrothecæ composing each pair in the pinnæ are approximate, but not connate. The intervals which separate the pairs from one another are short, and joints occur here and there in the pinnæ, but at long and very uncertain intervals.

A transverse section of the stem near its base (fig. 1c) presents an areolar structure resulting from its fascicled composition, the component tubes being very thick-walled and inseparably adnate to one another. Such a section affords a good illustration of the difference between the more common forms of fasciculation and the true perisiphonic fasciculation of the Perisiphonidæ.

Hydrothecæ are also borne by the stem, but these are smaller than the hydrothecæ of the pinnæ, and those of each pair are separated from one another by a much wider interval than in the pinnæ.

The gonangia (fig. 1b) have the form of certain antique jars. They are perfectly symmetrical, and the circle of compressed spines with which they are ornamented round the base of the neck gives further force to this comparison and adds much to the attractiveness and singularity of their form. They occur in a closely set row along the front of each pinna, and by the quaintness of their shape and the regularity of their arrangement they recall the rows of jars which may be still occasionally seen in old continental towns on the shelves of apothecaries' shops. The name which I have assigned to the species has been suggested by this comparison.

Thuiaria cupressina, Linnæus, sp. (Pl. XXXII. figs. 1, 1a, 1b, 1c).

Sertularia cupressina, Linn., Syst. Nat. (Gmel.), p. 3847.
,,   ,,   Lamk., Anim. sans Vert., ed. 2, vol. ii. p. 144.
,,   ,,   Hincks, Brit. Hydroid Zooph., p. 270, pl. lvii.

Trophosome.—Main stem unbranched, monosiphonic, jointed at uncertain intervals, set with alternate, dichotomously divided pinnæ, which are provided with well-marked joints, one of which always occurs just below every bifurcation, and another just above it on one of its two branches, while others occur at distant intervals on the branches. Hydrothecæ subalternate, deep, conical, adnate to the hydrocaulus for about half their height, then divergent from the axis, and terminating in a narrow, two-lipped orifice.

Gonosome.—Gonangia springing each from a point just below the base of a hydrotheca, obconical, terminating distally in a short, conical process, which carries the even, circular orifice, and is flanked by two short spines.[1]

Locality.—Station 48, off Halifax, Nova Scotia; lat. 43° 4′ N., long. 64° 5′ W.; depth, 51 fathoms; bottom, rock.

Though the Hydroid here described differs in some minor points from the forms occurring on the European coasts, I have no hesitation in referring it to the "Sea-Cypress" of Ellis, the *Sertularia cupressina* of Linnæus and of subsequent authors, a species common on many parts of the British coast.

I have already insisted on the necessity of removing this species, as well as the nearly allied *Sertularia argentea* of authors, from *Sertularia*, and allocating them to *Thuiaria*, with which in all the essential points of this genus they entirely agree.

Thuiaria cupressina is an interesting and beautiful species. The specimen in the

[1] No gonosome was present in the specimen. The description is from the condition of this part in European examples.

collection has a height of about seven inches, and consists of a smooth, cylindrical, monosiphonic stem, set for the greater part of its length with delicate, alternate, pinnately disposed ramuli, each springing by a distinct joint from the summit of a well-developed cladophore, and usually presenting two, sometimes three or four bifurcations. Every bifurcation is immediately preceded by a very distinct joint, while a similar joint occurs, in one of the two branches of the bifurcation, close to the origin of the branch. Joints also occur at distant intervals on the branches. The stem carries a hydrotheca in the axil of every pinna, and is provided with very well marked joints at distant but uncertain intervals.

The margin of the hydrothecal orifice is deeply cleft, and the orifice thus becomes bounded by two triangular lips, which give to the summit of the hydrotheca the form of a mitre. The perisarc of the stem is thick and of a dark-brown colour, that of the pinnæ is very thin and transparent, and nearly colourless. In many of the ramuli the soft parts were well preserved and allowed of a good view of the cœnosarc and hydranths.

Thuiaria vincta, n. sp. (Pl. XXXII. figs. 2, 2a).

Trophosome.—Stem monosiphonic, simple, set with pinnately disposed, equidistant, alternate ramuli, which are divided into internodes by constrictions at uncertain intervals. Hydrothecæ borne both by stem and pinnæ, closely set on the pinnæ, alternate, nearly cylindrical, wide, adnate to the hydrocaulus for nearly their entire height, those of opposite sides bound to one another by strong chitinous bands formed by thickenings of the intervening perisarc, orifice circular and entire.

Gonosome not present.

Locality.—Station 186, Flinders Passage; lat. 10° 30′ S., long. 142° 18′ E.; depth, 8 fathoms.

The only specimen of this curious form contained in the collection is a fragment about an inch and a half in height, which scarcely allows of a satisfactory estimate of the size and habit of the colony. It is very regularly pinnate, and both stem and pinnæ carry alternate hydrothecæ which in the pinnæ are closely set.

Its most remarkable feature consists in thickenings of the perisarc of the hydrocaulus, which in the form of strong bands stretch from the proximal angle of the epicauline side of every hydrotheca to the opposed wall of a hydrotheca of the opposite side, thus giving to the hydrothecæ the appearance of being bound together by strong chitinous bands. The angle to which one end of each band is attached presents a knob-like thickening of its chitinous walls.

Thuiaria pectinata, n. sp. (Pl. XXXIII. figs. 1, 1*a*).

Trophosome.—Stem unbranched, monosiphonic, set with equidistant, opposite pinnæ, pinnæ usually with a joint occurring at no definite distance from the base. Hydrothecæ borne both by stem and pinnæ, opposite on stem, subopposite on pinnæ, conical, deep, adnate to the hydrocaulus for their entire height, and thence prolonged for a short distance by a free, thin, membranous extension of their walls.

Gonosome not present.

Locality.—Simon's Bay, Cape of Good Hope.

Thuiaria pectinata is a very elegant little species, attaining a height of between two and three inches. It is of a rather rigid habit, and in its exactly opposite pinnæ it presents a feature which is as unusual as it is striking.

The pairs of pinnæ are situated at equal distances, being separated from one another by three pairs of opposite hydrothecæ.

The hydrothecæ proper are entirely adnate to the hydrocaulus, but their walls are continued for a short distance in the form of a free, very thin, membranous tube, which, however, is not always preserved in the specimen.

The hydrothecæ are exactly distichous, and follow one another at very short intervals.

Thuiaria hyalina, n. sp. (Pl. XXXIII. figs. 2, 2*a*).

Trophosome.—Stem fascicled, sending off pinnately disposed, alternate ramuli, whose perisarc is colourless and transparent. Hydrothecæ borne both by stem and pinnæ, cylindrical, slightly tumid below, adnate to the hydrocaulus for their entire height, and gently curving away from the axis; orifice with four indistinct cusps.

Gonosome not present.

Locality.—Station 126, south of Pernambuco; lat. 10° 46′ S., long. 36° 2′ W.; depth, 770 fathoms.

The specimen of *Thuiaria hyalina* contained in the collection is but fragmentary, and has a height of upwards of three inches. The stem is strongly fascicled below, but becomes monosiphonic towards its distal end. It carries along its length short, simple ramuli, with a regularly pinnate disposition.

The ramuli and the monosiphonic portions of the stem are perfectly transparent and colourless, and allow a good view to be obtained of their contents. These, in some parts of the specimen, have been well preserved, and afford evidence of the remarkable fact that in this species the hydranths are but imperfectly retractile. The greater part of the body of the hydranth is fixed within the hydrotheca by bands which stretch from it to the walls of the hydrotheca, and it is only the distal end of the hydranth which admits of retraction and extension. The tentacular crown, even in its state of extreme contraction, is incapable of being withdrawn into the cavity of the hydrotheca, and, notwithstanding the complete development of the hydrotheca, the hydranths derive almost as little protection from them as those of *Halecium* do from the hydrothecæ in that genus, where these receptacles are rudimental. However extensile may be the bands which stretch from the body of the hydranth to the walls of the hydrotheca, it would seem that they operate in fixing the body of the hydranth and thus preventing the complete retraction of the hydranth within the hydrotheca. A condition entirely similar to this occurs in *Sertularia exserta*. See above, p. 56.

The depth of 770 fathoms from which *Thuiaria hyalina* was dredged adds to the interest of the species, and the transparency and absence of colour in its perisarc has probably some relation with the great depth of its habitat.

Desmoscyphus, Allman.

Desmoscyphus, Allman, Journ. Linn. Soc. Lond. (Zool.), vol. xii.

Generic Character. Trophosome.—Colony dendritic; hydrocaulus divided by joints into internodes, each internode corresponding to one or more pairs of hydrothecæ. Hydrothecæ of the ramuli all brought to one side of the ramulus and adnate to it by their epicauline walls, adnate also or in close apposition to one another by their opposed sides.

Gonosome.—Gonophores adelocodonic, gonangia destitute of marsupium.

The genus *Desmoscyphus* was originally constituted for a Hydroid from New Zealand. In the extent to which the hydrothecæ are adnate to the hydrocaulus it agrees with many species of *Thuiaria*, while another point of agreement with that genus will be found in the fact that in some parts of the colony a single internode may carry many hydrothecæ. From *Thuiaria*, however, it is obviously separated by the hydrothecæ on the ramuli being all brought to one side of the ramulus, where they become in almost every instance adnate to one another in pairs along their opposed sides. In *Desmoscyphus pectinatus*, one of the species obtained by the Challenger, while the hydrothecæ are closely approximate, their walls have not actually coalesced with one another, though the hydrothecæ present the essential character of the genus in being all brought to one side of the branch, instead of being distichous as in *Thuiaria* and *Sertularia*.

It is only in the branches that the characteristic condition of the hydrothecæ is constant. In the main stem, especially towards its proximal end, the hydrothecæ may recede from one another and ultimately become disposed in two opposite series, separated as in *Thuiaria* and *Sertularia* by the entire width of the stem.

Desmoscyphus pectinatus, n. sp. (Pl. XXXIV. figs. 1, 1a, 1b).

Trophosome.—Main stem monosiphonic, simple, carrying alternate pinnately disposed ramuli along nearly its entire length. Hydrothecæ of pinnæ exactly opposite, those of each pair closely approximate but not connate, adnate to the internode for somewhat more than half their height, and diverging towards their summits at a low angle; those of the stem alternate, distichous, adnate to the internode for nearly their entire height; all the hydrothecæ tapering towards the summit, where they terminate in a two-lipped orifice.

Gonosome not present.

Locality.—Station 162, off East Moncœur Island, Bass Strait; depth, 38 to 40 fathoms.

Also off Bahia.

This is a small but elegant species. The largest of the examples contained in the collection had a height of about two inches. The hydrothecæ are carried both by the stem and pinnæ. While those of the pinnæ are opposite and closely approximate by their opposed sides, those of the stem are alternate and widely separate. The orifice is cloven so as to present two lips, an anterior smaller and a posterior larger. The interval between the lips would seem capable of being closed in the living state by two valve-like membranes of extreme tenuity, some shreds of which were occasionally retained in the specimens.

The joints of the pinnæ are usually distinct between each pair of hydrothecæ. In some specimens, however, they were here and there nearly or quite obliterated.

The stem is divided by well-marked equidistant joints into regular internodes, each internode carrying one, or in some cases two, pinnæ. Three hydrothecæ occupy the interval between every two pinnæ on each side.

The hydrothecæ of the pinnæ, though all brought to one side of their supporting internodes and closely approximate, are not exactly connate. This slight departure, however, from absolute coalescence affords no grounds for regarding the species as other than a true *Desmoscyphus*. The close approximation of the hydrothecæ, and the fact of their being all brought to one side of the internode, are decisive in favour of its allocation in the genus *Desmoscyphus*.

Desmoscyphus pectinatus was obtained from two widely separated localities, Bass Strait and the region off Bahia.

Desmoscyphus gracilis, n. sp. (Pl. XXXIV. figs. 2, 2a, 2b, 2c).

Trophosome.—Stem monosiphonic, not divided into branches, springing at intervals from a creeping, filiform stolon, gently undulated, sending off regular, pinnately disposed, alternate ramuli, every ramulus supported by a rather long cladophore, and having its proximal internode united to the next by a very oblique, splice-like joint. Hydrothecæ borne both by main stem and pinnæ; those of the pinnæ in distant pairs, exactly opposite, adnate to one another along their opposed sides, then strongly divergent, and terminating in an orifice with a broad cusp on each side; apocauline wall with a strong, inflected fold at somewhat more than half its height from the base; hydrothecæ of main stem subopposite in distant pairs, with a solitary hydrotheca in the axil of every pinna; those of each pair not adnate to one another by their opposed sides.

Gonosome not present.

Locality.—Station 36, off Bermuda; depth, 30 fathoms.

Desmoscyphus gracilis is a small and elegant species. It attains a height of about two inches, and its slender, undivided stems, with their regular, pinnately disposed ramuli, give to it a symmetrical and graceful habit. The pinnæ are divided by distinct joints into well-defined, rather long internodes, each of which carries close to its distal end a pair of connate hydrothecæ. The deep inflexion of the apocauline wall of the hydrotheca forms in the interior of its cavity a prominent, transverse ridge. The pinnæ are supported on rather long cladophores, and the proximal internode, which is cylindrical and destitute of hydrothecæ, is united to the next by a very oblique, overlapping, splice-like joint, the opposed sides of these two internodes being here cut away to an acute point. The union between the internodes is weaker at this joint than at any other, and the pinna here becomes easily separated from the proximal internode, which remains still attached to the cladophore, its sharp, distal end giving it the appearance of a rigid spine. Many of the pinnæ, towards the hydrorhizal end of the stem, have in the greater number of the specimens become detached at this joint, and the stem has then the appearance of being, for some distance from its base, armed on each side with a series of sharp spines.

The main stem is also divided into distinct internodes by joints which are situated one just below every pinna. The hydrothecæ of the stem are not as in the pinnæ exactly opposite. They are subopposite, and those of each pair, instead of being adnate to one another as in the pinnæ, are separated by a considerable interval.

Desmoscyphus obliquus, n. sp. (Pl. XXXIV. figs. 3, 3a).

Trophosome.—Stem monosiphonic, unbranched, divided into short internodes, each of which sends off a pinna from alternate sides; pinnæ composed of well-defined internodes, each carrying a pair of obliquely opposite hydrothecæ. Hydrothecæ of pinnæ wide, adnate to internode for nearly their entire height, and with their free ends slightly divergent; margin with a broad cusp on each side.

Gonosome not present.

Localities.—Off Somerset, Cape York, Torres Strait; depth, 8 to 12 fathoms. Bahia; depth, 10 to 20 fathoms.

This is a graceful plumose form, attaining a height of about three inches, and exceptional among the species of *Desmoscyphus* in having the hydrothecæ which compose each pair in the pinnæ not strictly opposite, but so disposed that a line joining the centres of both will be oblique to the axis of the pinna.

While the hydrothecæ of the pinnæ, notwithstanding this obliquity, are adnate to one another by their opposed sides, those of the stem are widely separate. Here they are alternate and smaller than those of the pinnæ, while every internode carries two on one side and one on the other; one which is somewhat smaller than the others being always borne in the axil of a pinna.

Desmoscyphus obliqua was dredged from widely separated localities—Torres Strait, where it occurred at a depth of from 8 to 12 fathoms, and off Bahia, where specimens were brought up from depths of 10 to 20 fathoms.

Desmoscyphus acanthocarpus, n. sp. (Pl. XXXV. figs. 2, 2a, 2b, 2c).

Trophosome.—Stem monosiphonic, unbranched, carrying alternate pinnæ; stem and pinnæ composed of well-defined internodes, every internode carrying a pair of opposite hydrothecæ which are connate in the pinnæ but disjunct towards the proximal end of the stem. Hydrothecæ deep, tubular, adnate to the front of the internode for nearly their entire height; margin of orifice having at its epicauline side a wide sinus, the edge of which supports a thin, membranous, hood-shaped operculum which arches over the orifice.

Gonosome.—Gonangia elongated pyriform, with the axis slightly curved, springing with an alternate disposition each by a very short peduncle from an internode of the main stem just below the base of a hydrotheca, terminating distally in an even circular orifice, and thickly set with minute spines.

Locality.—Off Bahia; depth, 10 to 20 fathoms.

Desmoscyphus acanthocarpus is a curious and interesting species. The hydrothecæ along the entire length of the pinnately disposed ramuli are all brought to one side of the ramulus, and are here connate to one another for nearly their entire height. Those which are borne by the stem are similarly connate towards the distal end of the stem, but towards the proximal end they become disjunct and more and more widely separated from one another, until ultimately they lie in two exactly opposite marginal series. The stem for some distance from its hydrorhizal end is destitute of hydrothecæ, and here forms a cylindrical peduncle to which the hydrotheca-bearing portion is attached by a very oblique splint-like joint (fig. 2c).

The hood-like roof which arches over the orifice of the hydrotheca is present in all the hydrothecæ, whether of the pinnæ or of the stem, and consists of a very thin, transparent, chitinous membrane. So delicate is it that it is easily torn away, and it was only in some cases that it was sufficiently perfect to enable its form to be satisfactorily determined.

The gonangia are beautiful objects and constitute a striking feature of the species. They are relatively narrow, but have a length which is equal to about twice that of an internode of the stem. With their axis gently curved they gradually taper from a rounded base towards the terminal circular orifice. They are thickly set from base to summit with minute spines, whose points are directed towards the summit of the gonangium. When the stem is viewed in profile the gonangia, though strictly distichous in their origin, are seen to be for the most part directed with a secund disposition towards one side of the stem.

The largest example of *Desmoscyphus acanthocarpus* in the collection measured about two inches in height. The species is a member of the rich Hydroid fauna occurring off the coast of Bahia.

Hypopyxis, n. gen.

Name from 'υπό, under, and πυξίς, a box, in allusion to the cup-like appendages which lie below the hydrothecæ.

Generic Character. Trophosome.—Hydrocaulus divided by well-marked joints into internodes, each carrying numerous pairs of hydrothecæ. Hydrothecæ opposite, adnate to one another by their opposed sides, each having attached to its base two minute cup-shaped appendages.

Gonosome.—Gonangia destitute of marsupium, springing from the hydrocaulus in the intervals of the pairs of hydrothecæ.

The genus *Hypopyxis* has in its opposite and connate hydrothecæ close relations with *Desmoscyphus*. From *Desmoscyphus*, however, it is distinguished by the presence of the cup-like appendages at the base of the hydrothecæ.

That these appendages must be regarded as sarcothecæ can scarcely be doubted, and *Hypopyxis* will thus afford an additional example of the very exceptional occurrence of these bodies in genera not referable to the Plumularinæ.

Hypopyxis labrosa, n. sp. (Pl. XXXV. figs. 1, 1a).

Trophosome.—Stem simple or very sparingly branched, monosiphonic, and set with pinnately disposed, alternate ramuli, which are divided by very oblique joints into internodes of various lengths. Hydrothecæ borne both by stem and pinnæ, deep, tumid below, slightly narrowing upwards, those of each pair adnate to one another for nearly two-thirds of the height of their opposed sides, then diverging and terminating in a circular orifice which is directed laterally, and is surrounded by a thin, membranous, expanded lip.

Gonosome.—Gonangia fusiform, contracting below into a very short, narrow peduncle, and terminating distally in an even circular orifice.

Locality.—Station 163A, off Twofold Bay, Australia; depth, 150 fathoms.

Hypopyxis labrosa attains a height of about four inches. The pinnæ are given off at a moderate distance from one another along nearly the whole length of the stem. Each is supported on a short cladophore which springs from the side of the stem between two pairs of hydrothecæ. Every pinna commences with a short proximal segment which is destitute of hydrothecæ, and is united to the remainder of the pinna by a very oblique splice-like joint. The orifice of the hydrotheca is surrounded by a membranous expanded lip. This is very thin, and would seem to be easily lacerated and destroyed, for it was only occasionally preserved in a sufficiently perfect state in the specimens examined. The joints which separate the internodes of the pinnæ from one another are very oblique and splice-like, and the number of pairs of hydrothecæ borne by each internode varies from five to seven, or perhaps more. The hydrothecæ are all brought to one side (the front) of the internode, the opposite side remaining uncovered.

The cup-like appendages of the base of the hydrothecæ have, when viewed in front, the form of a wide bell, but when viewed laterally are seen to be compressed. They measure about one-sixth of the height of the hydrotheca. Each hydrotheca carries two, one on the front of its base near its junction with the opposite hydrotheca, the other on a point of its base which lies diametrically opposite to this.

The gonangia spring from the front of the pinna in the intervals between the pairs of hydrothecæ, and correspond in height to about three pairs of hydrothecæ.

Staurotheca, n. gen.

Name from σταυρός, a cross, and θήκη, a receptacle, in allusion to the decussation of the hydrothecæ.

Generic Character. Trophosome.—Hydrocaulus carrying opposite hydrothecæ, which are arranged in decussating pairs.

Gonosome.—Gonangia simple capsules springing from the hydrocaulus, and destitute of marsupium.

The genus *Staurotheca* has close affinities with *Sertularia*, from which, however, it is distinguished by its decussating hydrothecæ. These are so disposed that the plane passing through any one pair of hydrothecæ is at right angles with the planes which pass through the pairs at each side of it.

Staurotheca dichotoma, n. sp. (Pl. XXXVI. figs. 1, 1a).

Trophosome.—Stem strongly fascicled towards its proximal end, becoming mono-siphonic distally, dichotomously branched in a single plane, the branches mostly extended at their distal ends by a tendril-like prolongation, which when it reaches a neighbouring branch becomes attached to it by its extremity. Hydrothecæ deep, nearly cylindrical, slightly tumid below, orifice circular, entire.

Gonosome.—Gonangia elongated ovoid, narrowing below into a short peduncle which springs from a point just below a hydrotheca, and narrowing above into a short tubular prolongation, which is terminated by the small circular orifice.

Locality.—Station 145a, off Marion Island ; depth, 85 to 150 fathoms.

This is a well-marked form, with a somewhat flabelliform habit, caused by its dichotomous ramification in a single plane, with the frequent inosculations of its strong and rather rigid branches. It attains a height of about three inches. The pairs in which the hydrothecæ are grouped are not regularly separated from one another by distinct constrictions, these occurring only at distant and uncertain intervals.

The tendril-like prolongations of the branches usually terminate in a little sucker-like disc, which attaches itself to some neighbouring branch. The point of its attach-ment may be the walls of a hydrotheca or some part of the surface of the hydrocaulus ; while in some cases the tendril was seen to have entered the orifice of a hydrotheca.

A condition closely resembling this may be seen in certain other Hydroida, as in *Dictyocladium dichotomum* of the present Report (p. 77), and in *Thuiaria persocialis*, in which the branches of the colony are frequently connected to one another by similar bonds of union.[1]

Dictyocladium, n. gen.

Name from δίκτυον, a net, and κλάδος, a branch, in allusion to the net-like disposition of the branches.

Generic Character. Trophosome.—Hydrocaulus consisting of a ramified monosi-phonic tube, the branches given off in a single plane, united to one another in such a way as to form a network, and with joints at distant and unequal intervals. Hydro-thecæ more or less adnate to the branches, on all sides of which they are disposed.

Gonosome.—Gonangia situated in the axils of the ramification.

[1] *Journ. Linn. Soc. Lond.* (Zool.), vol. xii. p. 271, pl. xvii. figs. 4–6.

The remarkable network formed by the branches of *Dictyocladium dichotomum*—the only known representative of the genus—confers on this Hydroid a physiognomy, one of the most distinct and striking to be found among the Calyptoblastic genera. The extent to which the hydrothecæ are adnate to the hydrocaulus, and the occurrence of joints at distant and irregular intervals, indicate an affinity with *Thuiaria*, from which, however, it differs not only in its reticulate ramification, but in the disposition of the hydrothecæ on all sides of the branches.

Dictyocladium dichotomum, n. sp. (Pl. XXXVI. figs. 2, 2a).

Trophosome.—Hydrocaulus profusely and dichotomously branched, with the branches united so as to form a broad, fan-shaped, angular-meshed net, a joint occurring usually at the base of one, and sometimes of both arms of the bifurcation, and also here and there on the branches at distant and indefinite intervals. Hydrothecæ tetrastichous, alternate flask-shaped, adnate for more than half their height to the branch, and with the distal end continued into a long free tubular neck, which terminates in the small, circular, even orifice.

Gonosome.—Gonangia sessile in the angles of the bifurcations, ellipsoidal, encircled by very prominent and regular annular ridges, and having the summit continued into a short conical process which carries the small circular orifice on its apex.

Locality.—Station 162, off East Moncœur Island, Bass Strait; depth, 38 to 40 fathoms.

Dictyocladium dichotomum is a very remarkable and beautiful species. The mode in which the branches become united with one another so as to form the meshes of the net is very singular. When a branch is destined to form a union of this kind its distal extremity becomes elongated into a tendril-like continuation destitute of hydrothecæ. When this meets a neighbouring branch, the end of the tendril unites with the branch, not however with any part of the surface of the branch indifferently, but, directing itself towards the orifice of a hydrotheca, it here attaches itself, its axis becoming directly continuous with that of the hydrotheca. The branches are all in the same plane, and the collection contains specimens which have a height and width of more than five inches.

Synthecium, Allman.

Synthecium, Allman, Journ. Linn. Soc. Lond. (Zool.), vol. xii. p. 265.

Generic Character. Trophosome.—Hydrocaulus divided into definite internodes, each internode carrying a pair of opposite hydrothecæ, or a single hydrotheca which alternates with those of the internodes on each side of it. Hydrothecæ adnate for a greater or less extent to the internode.

Gonosome.—Gonangia borne on peduncles which spring from within the cavity of certain hydrothecæ, where they take the place of the hydranths.

The genus *Synthecium* was originally characterised by me from a New Zealand Hydroid in the collection of Mr. Busk. It forms one of the most definitely marked generic groups among the Calyptoblastic Hydroids, and in the singular relation of the gonosome to the hydrothecæ is absolutely unique. This relation is found in the fact that the peduncles of the gonangia are enclosed each within the cavity of a hydrotheca. The cavity is completely filled by the peduncle, which thus takes the place occupied in other hydrothecæ by the hydranth, and has its cœnosarc directly continuous through the base of the hydrotheca with the cœnosarc of the stem; the hydrothecæ which thus carry gonangia differ in no respect, either in form or in position, from those which continue to exercise their normal function of giving protection to the hydranth.

To this condition we have a very interesting parallelism in the genus *Thecocladium* (p. 80), in which, as in *Synthecium*, the usual function of certain hydrothecæ becomes changed into another. Here, however, the place of the hydranth is taken, not by any part of the gonosome, but by the origin of a branch which in *Thecocladium* occupies the cavity of the hydrotheca exactly as the peduncle of the gonangium does in *Synthecium*. In *Thecocladium* the gonangia spring as usual from the side of an internode.

Since the first determined example of the genus was described under the name of *Synthecium elegans*,[1] another closely allied to this and possibly only a variety of it has been characterised as *Synthecium ramosum*.[2] To these the Challenger collection now contributes two very distinct and well-marked species, one of which differs from all the others described in the fact of its having its hydrothecæ alternate instead of opposite.

Synthecium campylocarpum, n. sp. (Pl. XXXVII. figs. 1, 1a, 1b, 1c).

Trophosome.—Stem simple, monosiphonic, set with pinnately disposed opposite ramuli; pinnæ divided into equal internodes by well-marked joints, every internode carrying a pair of hydrothecæ. Hydrothecæ strictly opposite, tubular, cylindrical, with circular even orifice.

Gonosome.—Gonangia (female?) pod-shaped, compressed, slightly curved towards the supporting pinna, the two wider sides carrying closely set, prominent, transverse ridges, which thin away towards the edges of the gonangium where they finally disappear. Male (?) gonangia oviform, destitute of the transverse ridges, and with the axis straight.

Locality.—Off Port Jackson; depth, 30 to 35 fathoms.

Synthecium campylocarpum presents in its trophosome little to distinguish it from *Synthecium elegans*, the first described species of this remarkable genus. The elongated,

[1] *Journ. Linn. Soc. Lond.* (Zool.), vol. xii. p. 266, pl. iv.   [2] *Ibid.*, vol. xix. p. 137, pl. xii.

somewhat curved, compressed, and pod-shaped form of the gonangia will, however, at once distinguish it. The specimens in the collection have a height of more than two inches. The main stems arise from a prostrate, branched, tubular filament, and while they are themselves unbranched are set from end to end with exactly opposite pinnæ. A joint more or less distinct exists on the stem at the distal side of every pair of pinnæ. With the exception of an occasional pair of hydrothecæ in the interval between two pinnæ, no hydrothecæ are borne by the stem. The pinnæ are given off at a very wide angle, being nearly at right angles with the stem. They are divided by deep constrictions into short equal internodes, each internode carrying a pair of exactly opposite hydrothecæ. The hydrothecæ are deep, tubular, adnate to the internode for about two-thirds of their height, and then abruptly divergent at a high angle. The orifice is perfectly circular, and its margin entirely destitute of serration.

The gonangia are usually, but not exclusively, carried by those hydrothecæ which lie near the base of the pinna. They have the appearance of being absolutely sessile on the summit of the hydrotheca. In reality they have a long peduncle which passes down through the hydrotheca and completely fills its cavity. They would seem to differ in the two sexes. Those which I regard as female (fig. 1a) are compressed, so as to be elliptical in transverse section, are slightly curved towards the axis of the pinna, and are very elegantly ornamented on the two broad faces by prominent, transverse, parallel ridges, which gradually thin away towards the edges, where they become finally effaced. Gonangia which differ from these in form were present in one specimen (fig. 1b). I regard them as those of a male colony. They are oviform, with the axes straight, and are destitute of the ridges which form a characteristic feature in the others. Both forms of gonangia open on the summit by a small, scarcely elevated, even orifice.

In one of the specimens of *Synthecium campylocarpum* in the collection no gonangia were present; but the place of a gonangium was taken by a branch which thus had its origin within the hydrotheca, from the orifice of which it protruded (fig. 1c). This branch carried pairs of opposite hydrothecæ, and differed in no respect from an ordinary pinna.

Though I regard this as an entirely abnormal condition, it is by no means destitute of morphological interest as repeating in *Synthecium* a feature which constitutes the essential character of *Thecocladium*; while the substitution of a typical nutritive element of the colony for a typical reproductive one is not without significance.

Synthecium has been hitherto known only as a New Zealand genus, *Synthecium elegans* being apparently an abundant and characteristic species of the New Zealand coast. The same haul of the dredge, however, which brought up *Synthecium campylocarpum* from a depth of between 30 and 35 fathoms off Port Jackson, yielded also *Synthecium alternans*, another very distinct and interesting member of the genus.

Synthecium alternans, n. sp. (Pl. XXXVII. figs. 2, 2a).

Trophosome.—Stem unbranched, fascicled towards the base, set with pinnately disposed, equidistant, alternate ramuli ; ramuli divided into equal internodes, each of which carries a hydrotheca near its distal end.   Hydrothecæ alternate, tubular, deep, adnate to the internode for about half their height, then diverging at a high angle and terminating in a circular and entire orifice.

Gonosome.—Gonangia oval, compressed, destitute of annulation, and with a terminal, scarcely elevated orifice.

Locality.—Off Port Jackson ; depth, 30 to 35 fathoms.

The present species is of great interest as affording an instance of the characteristic synthecial structure, with an alternate disposition, of the hydrothecæ.   It is a strong, rather rigid form, with the stem fascicled towards the base, but becoming monosiphonic distally, and attaining a height of between two and three inches.

The gonangia are compressed so as to present a lenticular form, more convex on one side than on the other, the more convex side being that which is turned towards the supporting pinna.   They are entirely destitute of all trace of annulation and have their walls perfectly smooth.   The male gonangium is smaller than the female, but otherwise differs but little from it in shape.

This highly interesting species was obtained along with *Synthecium campylo-carpum*, from a depth of between 30 and 35 fathoms, off Port Jackson.

Thecocladium, Allman.

Thecocladium, Allman, Journ. Linn. Soc. Lond. (Zool.), vol. xix. p. 149, pl. xix. figs. 4, 5.

Generic Character.   Trophosome.—Branching stems set with disjunct hydrothecæ and jointed at distant and uncertain intervals.   Branches having their origin within the hydrothecæ.

Gonosome.—Gonangia ovate vesicles borne along the stems and branches and destitute of marsupium.

The genus *Thecocladium* agrees with *Thuiaria* in the absence of internodes of definite length.   It differs from it, however, in the very remarkable origin of the branches, which invariably spring from within the hydrothecæ, passing out through the orifice, and then extending themselves externally.

The proximal end of the branch in *Thecocladium* can be traced through the axis of a hydrotheca whose cavity it completely fills, while its cœnosarc is continuous through the floor of the hydrotheca with the cœnosarc of the stem or branch from which it springs.

We are here reminded of the genus *Synthecium*, in which the gonangia have an origin exactly similar to that of the branches in *Thecocladium*, the peduncle of the gonangium occupying in *Synthecium* the cavity of the hydrotheca, at the orifice of which it becomes free in order to bear the gonangium on its summit.

Thecocladium flabellum, n. sp. (Pl. XXXVIII. figs. 1–4).

Trophosome.—Stems springing from one side of a rooted but otherwise free stolon-like tube, monosiphonic, much branched, branches alternate, all in one plane ; stems and branches closely set with hydrothecæ. Hydrothecæ alternate, tubular, tumid below, adnate to the hydrocaulus for nearly their entire height ; orifice circular and entire, with the margin continued for a short distance as a free, thin, membranous prolongation.

Gonosome.—Gonangia springing each from a point just below the base of a hydrotheca, oboviform, annulated, terminating distally in a sessile, even orifice, and with a longitudinal furrow running along the epicauline side.

Locality.—Simon's Bay, Cape of Good Hope ; depth, 10 to 20 fathoms.

Thecocladium flabellum is the only representative as yet known of the remarkable genus to which it belongs. The stolon-like tube from which the stems arise sends off from distance to distance a cluster of root-fibres, but is free in the intervening spaces instead of being as in other Hydroids creeping and adherent throughout. It usually assumes an arched form, and from the convexity of the arch the stems arise at nearly equal intervals. The stolon is destitute of hydrothecæ, but the stems carry them along their entire length.

Soon after their origin the stems begin to give off pinnately disposed branches, which differ in no respect from the main stems except in being shorter. The branches as well as the stems all lie in the same plane, and this gives to the colony a somewhat flabelli-form habit, which, however, is not strictly maintained in the older specimens. The branches are sometimes prolonged by tendril-like, coarsely annulated extensions of the axis, which, uniting with neighbouring branches, contribute still further to the flabelli-form habit of the colony. These prolongations of the branches usually direct themselves towards the orifice of a hydrotheca, where they become attached, and are probably here in direct communication with the contents of the hydrotheca.

The hydrothecæ are very regularly alternate, and with their tumid bases give a slightly wavy outline to the stems and branches. Their distal ends are continued for a short distance by a delicate and easily torn membranous extension of their margin.

The disposition of the branches is alternate and pinnate in accordance with that of the hydrothecæ, out of whose orifices they extend themselves. They occur, however, at no regular distances, and there is nothing in the position or form of the hydrothecæ from which they are emitted to give any indication that these are destined for branches and not for hydranths.

The gonangia are borne along the stems and branches. They spring each from a point just below a hydrotheca, and extend over a space corresponding in height to that of about three consecutive hydrothecæ. They are oboviform and strongly annulated, but are closely pressed to the hydrocaulus, and in consequence present at their epicauline side a deep, longitudinal furrow, whose sides overlap the hydrocaulus, and into which the annulation does not extend. Their summit carries the sessile, elliptical orifice.

The specimens have a height of between two and three inches, and were dredged in Simon's Bay, from a depth of 10 to 20 fathoms.

In a collection of Hydroids belonging to Miss H. Gatty is a small dry specimen of a Hydroid from an unknown locality, which, notwithstanding some slight differences, must be referred to the species here described.[1] It differs from the Challenger specimen in having the orifice of the hydrotheca surrounded by a slightly thickened rim. The hydrotheca was probably prolonged beyond this rim by a membranous extension of its margin, but in the dried specimen nothing but a faint indication of this could be detected.

Another feature, probably transitory, in Miss Gatty's specimen, consists in the presence of a delicate diaphragm, apparently chitinous, which intersects the hydrotheca obliquely, passing from a point near the middle of the apocauline wall downwards to a point on the epicauline wall a little above the base of the hydrotheca. No trace of these diaphragms was present in the specimens collected by the Challenger. The diaphragm is apparently complete and strongly recalls the so-called epiphragm excreted by certain snails as a defence against the injurious action of climate and other unfavourable surroundings.

I am not disposed to regard either of these differences as affording grounds for specific separation. It is by no means improbable that the diaphragm seen in the hydrotheca is a temporary structure excreted over the retracted hydranth for protection during a resting or inactive period of its existence; and the differences between the two forms ought probably to be regarded as pointing to different states of one and the same species.

No gonosome was present in the specimen contained in Miss Gatty's collection.

Family IDIIDÆ.

Character of the Family.   Trophosome.—Hydrothecæ adnate to the hydrocaulus. Cœnosarc divided into segments which form two longitudinal series of intercommunicating chambers, each of which corresponds to a hydranth, with the gastral cavity of which it is continuous.

[1] See *Journ. Linn. Soc. Lond.* (Zool.), vol. ix., March 1885.

Gonosome.—Gonangia simple capsules destitute of marsupial chamber.

The character here assigned to the family of the Idiidæ includes certain points of structure which must be regarded as of high systematic value, rendering necessary the allocation of the family to a separate section or legion of the Calyptoblastea. To this section the name of Thalamophora may be assigned (see Introduction, Scheme of Hydroid Classification).

The facts which appear to justify this view will be obvious from the anatomical details given below under the description of the genus.

Idia, Lamouroux.

Idia, Lamouroux, Polyp. Coral. flex., p. 199.

Generic Character. Trophosome.—Hydrocaulus consisting of a main stem with pinnately disposed ramuli which support numerous alternate hydrothecæ adnate to one another along the mesial line of the ramulus.

Gonosome.—Gonangia (in the only known species) urn-shaped capsules springing from the main stem.

The characters given above are all that are needed for the generic diagnosis of *Idia*, and will prevent its being confounded with any other genus hitherto described. From *Desmoscyphus*, whose hydrothecæ are, as in *Idia*, connate to one another along the mesial line of the ramulus, it may at first sight appear not easily distinguishable. But we must bear in mind that while in *Desmoscyphus* the hydrothecæ are opposite, they are in *Idia* strictly alternate, though notwithstanding this alternate disposition, the close approximation in a longitudinal line of the hydrothecæ composing each linear series allows of the two series laterally coalescing with one another in the median line of the pinna.

It is, however, when we come to examine its anatomical structure that we meet with features in *Idia* so peculiar and so distinct from those of any other known Hydroid, that we are compelled to regard this remarkable form as the representative of an entirely new family.

The specimens of *Idia pristis* obtained by the Challenger have the soft parts of the trophosome fairly well preserved, and though the oral extremities of the hydranths with the tentacles have entirely disappeared, the cœnosarc is sufficiently perfect to allow of a satisfactory determination of some of its more important features.

Perisarc.—The skeleton or chitinous perisarc of *Idia pristis* is very remarkable. In every ramulus or pinna we must distinguish two aspects:—A front aspect along which the hydrothecæ are adnate to one another by their opposed sides, and a posterior aspect on which they do not show themselves.

On the anterior side (Pl. XXXIX. fig. 2) the union of the adnate hydrothecæ-walls may be seen to form on the surface of the ramulus a continuous zigzag line lying in the general direction of its axis. The posterior side, on the contrary, is destitute of markings of any kind, but when focused at a little distance below the surface (fig. 3) there will be brought into view two longitudinal series of irregularly polygonal areolæ, those of each series alternating with those of the other, and being throughout in close contact with them. They are bounded by chitinous laminæ which pass off from the anterior walls of the common perisarcal tube, and penetrating into the interior of this, give rise to two longitudinal series of chambers which are lined by the cœnosarc in the way about to be seen.

Between the posterior walls of the ramulus and this double series of chambers is a space occupying the entire width of the ramulus, and forming a posterior longitudinal chamber which extends continuously through the entire ramulus (fig. 5; fig. 8, c).

The hydrothecæ terminate each in a very oblique orifice, which is directed posteriorly and is provided with a delicate membranous valve (figs. 3, 4, 9).

Cœnosarc.—All the areolæ or anterior chambers just mentioned are lined by the cœnosarc, which instead of forming as in other Hydroids a continuous uninterrupted tube, is broken up into two longitudinal series of segments (figs. 4, 5; fig. 8, b). There can be little doubt that the segments of one and the same series freely communicate with one another through the chitinous walls of the chambers.

The cœnosarc by which these segmental chambers are lined consists of a thick endodermal layer overlaid by a thin ectoderm, and enclosing that portion of the common somatic cavity which lies in each segment. With each of these segments a hydranth is directly continuous (fig. 5), and every hydranth thus corresponds to one of the transverse segments into which the common cœnosarc of the ramulus is divided, and has its gastral cavity opening directly into the cavity of the segment.

The great longitudinal posterior chamber (fig. 5; fig. 8, c) is also lined by a layer of cœnosarc. This, however, is thinner than that of the anterior transverse chambers, and was but imperfectly preserved in the specimen.

The pinnately disposed ramuli of *Idia pristis* thus present a structure which, so far as is known, does not occur elsewhere among the Hydroida. The division of the common chitinous perisarcal tube into distinct chambers, and the consequent division and segmentation of the cœnosarc, constitute a combination of characters which, however far we may be from assigning to it its true significance, is of sufficient systematic value to necessitate the relegation of *Idia* to a separate section among the Calyptoblastic Hydroids.

While the structure of the pinnæ is thus so very exceptional, that of the common stem (fig. 6) differs but little from the usual condition of this part in the Sertularian Hydroids. The hydrothecæ are as in the pinnæ alternate, but those of opposite sides show no tendency to coalesce, being on the contrary separated from one another by a wide interval of the stem, into the cavity of which that of the hydrotheca opens through the medium of a short tubular continuation of its proximal end.

The perisarcal tube of the stem is simply continuous and monothalamic, and its contained cœnosarc is consequently quite destitute of the peculiar segmentation which is so striking in the pinnæ. The cœnosarc of the stem lines the perisarc with a rather thin layer, whose endoderm is thrown into an irregular network of tubular ridges, a condition which prevails also in *Antennularia*, and is elsewhere not without its parallel among the Hydroida.

Idia pristis, Lamouroux (Pl. XXXIX. figs. 1–10).

Idia pristis, Lamouroux, Polyp. Coral. flex., p. 200, pl. v. fig. 5.

Trophosome.—Stem monosiphonic, simple,[1] springing from a plexus of tubular filaments, and sending off along nearly its entire length moderately long, rather close-set, alternate pinnæ, which are for the most part intersected by transverse joints at distant and variable intervals. Hydrothecæ of pinnæ alternate, with their opposed sides adnate to one another, and with the free distal end diverging at a wide angle from the hydrocaulus, tapering to a point and opening by a very oblique orifice which is directed backwards, and closed by a membranous valve; hydrothecæ of stem not adnate by their opposed sides.

Gonosome.—Gonangia borne exclusively by the main stem, each springing from a point just below the base of a hydrotheca, urniform, longitudinally fluted, attached to the stem by a short but definite peduncle; summit abruptly narrowed into a conical roof, which bears on its apex the wide, circular orifice.[2]

Locality.—Station 203, off Panay, Philippine Islands; lat. 11° 61′ N., long. 123° 9′ E.; depth, 20 fathoms.

Off Bahia; depth, probably 10 to 20 fathoms.

Idia pristis is the only known representative of the genus; and the only description of it hitherto published consists in the short and inadequate diagnosis given by Lamouroux.

It occurs in the form of groups of undivided stems which send off along nearly their

[1] The apparently branched condition of the main stem is due to a cause different from that of a true ramification. See below, p. 86.

[2] Lamouroux, to whom we owe the original definition of the genus *Idia*, knew nothing of the gonosome, and, except in a short notice by Mr. Hincks (*Journ. Linn. Soc. Lond.* (Zool.), vol. xxi., 1887), this important part of the colony has hitherto remained undescribed. Mr. Busk, however, had many years ago examined it in specimens from the Persian Gulf, and I am indebted to him for an opportunity of inspecting the excellent figures which he then made of the gonangia. He has also placed his specimens in my hands, and I have thus been enabled to compare these with the examples brought home by the Challenger. One of the examples of *Idia pristis*, dredged by the Challenger off Bahia, is furnished with gonangia. No gonosome is present in any of the other specimens.

entire course short pinnæ which differ but little in length. The wide angle at which the distal ends of the hydrothecæ diverge from the pinnæ, and the narrow point in which they terminate, give to the pinnæ with its two rows of hydrothecæ a not very distant resemblance to the saw of a sawfish,—a resemblance which suggested to Lamouroux the specific name of *pristis*.

The pinnæ spring by a narrow base, each from a short cladophore. Some of them present one or two well-marked constrictions, which are not situated at any regular distance from one another, and by which the pinna becomes divided into two or more internodes of variable length. Some of the pinnæ, however, show no constriction in any part of their course, and no trace of division into distinct internodes.

The distal extremities of the hydrothecæ in both pinnæ and main stem, after diverging at a wide angle end in a point which forms the apocauline boundary of a wide orifice. The plane of this orifice in the pinnæ is directed backwards, while in the stem it looks more towards the distal end of the colony. In both the orifice is completely covered by a thin membrane, the distal half of which is free and capable of being raised from the orifice in the form of a valve-like lid.

The structure of the stem differs widely from that of the pinnæ, and in most respects resembles the usual structure of this part in the Sertularian Hydroids. It is divided by well-marked joints into a series of equal internodes, each of which sends off a pinna from alternate sides near its proximal end. The hydrothecæ, which are deep and nearly cylindrical, are alternately disposed and are confined to one aspect of the stem, which thus presents as in the pinnæ an anterior and a posterior aspect, but the hydrothecæ of the stem show no tendency as in the pinnæ to coalesce with one another along the mesial line.

The hydrothecæ of the stem do not open directly into the common tube, but each communicates with it through the medium of a small chamber, which forms an appendage to the base of the hydrothecæ and opens by a well-defined circular orifice into the cavity of the stem. These little chambers are probably the representatives of the much larger adnate chambers into which the hydrothecæ open in the pinnæ.

The gonangia arise each from a point close to the base of a hydrotheca, and care must be taken not to mistake the optical expression of the orifice of the accessory chambers just mentioned for the spot from which a gonangium had become detached. The short neck, which carries on its summit the orifice of the gonangium, is encircled by a wreath of minute puncta, which recalls a very similar condition in the limbus of the hydrophore of *Halecium*.

A very interesting feature in the economy of *Idia pristis* consists in the apparent ramification of the stem. In all the specimens which I have examined, whether those brought home by the Challenger or those in the possession of Mr. Busk, the main stems, besides sending off the pinnæ, have the appearance of dividing into a greater or smaller number of branches, which repeat in all respects the primary stems with their pinnæ. In a magnificent specimen belonging to Mr. Busk, which was obtained in the Persian Gulf and attains a height of nearly a foot, the trophosome consists of numerous stems which spring in a close cluster from a plexus of tubular fibres. Soon after their origin almost all these stems appear to give off a great number of branches, and the specimen, instead of consisting essentially of a cluster of undivided stems with pinnately disposed ramuli, appears to form a profusely branched colony. The apparent branches, however, are in reality so many separate colonies which had attached themselves to the primary stems, which they grasp by their hydrorhizal tubules (Pl. XXXIX. fig. 10).

An entirely similar condition occurs in the Challenger specimens, both in those from the Philippine Islands and in those dredged off Bahia, none of which, however, possess a height of more than five inches, and in which the associated stems are but few. Among the Hydroids collected by the "Rattlesnake" is also a specimen of *Idia pristis* from the Australian Seas. Like the Challenger specimens it is of small size, and the separate colonies associated with it in the form of branches are but few.

Mr. Hincks lately sent me a specimen of *Idia pristis* which he had identified in a collection of Hydroids brought home from the Mergui Archipelago. The specimen, which is abundantly supplied with gonangia, presents a pseudo-ramification similar in all respects to that of the other examples here noticed.

INDEX.

This Index includes the Genera and Species of Hydroida described both in this Report and in the former Report on the Plumularidæ (Zool. Chall. Exp., vol. vii. part xx., 1883).

Aaaa 12

PLATE I.

(ZOOL. CHALL. EXP.—PART LXX.—1888.)—Aaaa.

PLATE II.

PLATE II.

Figs. 1, 2.—*Eudendrium rameum* (p. 4).

Fig. 1.—An entire colony; natural size.

Fig. 2.—A portion of a colony; magnified about 15 diameters.

EUDENDRIUM RAMEUM

PLATE III.

(ZOOL. CHALL. EXP.—PART XX.—1888.)—Aaaa.

PLATE III.

Figs. 1–7.—*Monocaulus imperator* (p. 5).

Fig. 1.—The hydranth and gonophores, with the distal portion of the stem; natural size.

Fig. 2.—The proximal end of the stem; natural size.

Fig. 3.—One of the branching peduncles of the gonosome with its clusters of gonophores; magnified about 15 diameters.

Fig. 4.—A portion of a transverse section of the wall of the stem; magnified about 12 diameters, and slightly diagrammatic.

    a. Ectoderm.
    b. Elastic tissue of the stem.
    c. Endoderm.
    d. Longitudinal canals of the endoderm.

Fig. 5.—Portion of stem seen from the outer surface after maceration; magnified 50 diameters.

    a. Elastic tissue partly denuded of the ectoderm.
    b. Some of the ectoderm cells still adhering to the outer surface of the elastic tissue.

Fig. 6.—Some of the fibres of the elastic coat breaking up into finer fibrillæ; magnified 100 diameters.

Fig. 7.—Outline of a transverse section of the stem, showing the manner in which the walls are thrown into folds by the action of the elastic coat; slightly enlarged.

MONOCAULUS IMPERATOR.

PLATE IV.

PLATE IV.

Figs. 1–3.—*Halecium arboreum* [*robustum*][1] (p. 10).

Fig. 1.—An entire colony ; natural size.

Fig. 2.—Portion of a colony ; magnified 15 diameters.

Fig. 3.—A hydrophore, showing its basal segment adnate by its epicauline side to the
supporting internode, and its very narrow limbus ; magnified 20 diameters.

[1] It has been found necessary to change the name since the plate was printed off.

HALECIUM ROBUSTUM

PLATE V.

(ZOOL. CHALL. EXP.—PART LXX.—1888.)—Mmm.

PLATE V.

Figs. 1, 1a.—*Halecium telescopicum* (p. 10).

Fig. 1.—Portion of a colony; natural size.

Fig. 1a.—Portion of the same colony; magnified 15 diameters.

Figs. 2, 2a.—*Halecium flexile* (p. 11).

Fig. 2.—An entire colony; natural size.

Fig. 2a.—A portion; magnified 15 diameters.

1. 1ᵃ HALECIUM TELESCOPICUM.   2. 2ᵃ HALECIUM FLEXILE.

PLATE VI.

PLATE VI.

Figs. 1–4. *Halecium dichotomum* (p. 13).

Fig. 1.—A colony; natural size.

Fig. 2.—A portion of a colony; magnified 15 diameters.

Fig. 3.—Two consecutive hydrophores; magnified about 20 diameters.

Fig. 4.—Ovum with germinal vesicle and spot; magnified 30 diameters.

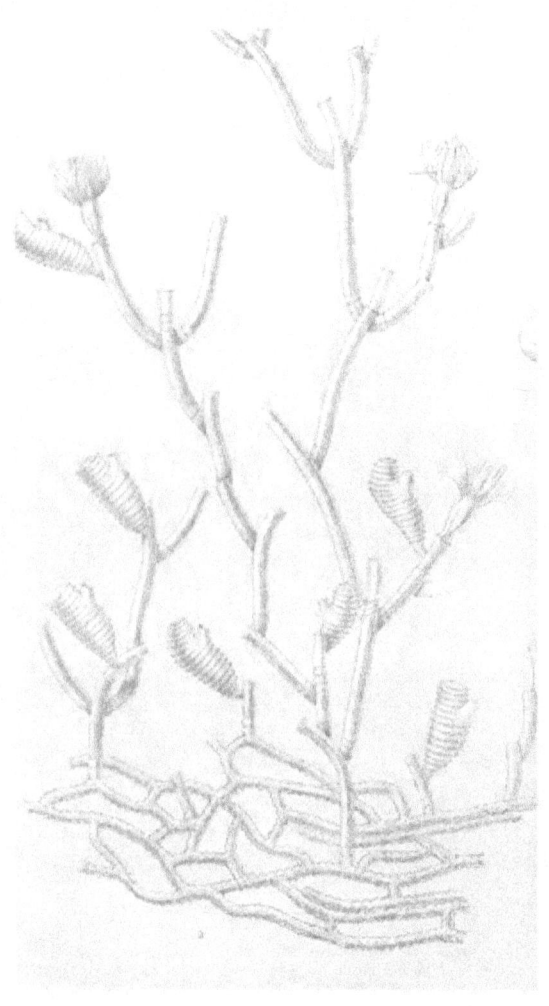

HALECIUM   DICHOTOMUM

PLATE VII.

(ZOOL. CHALL. EXP.—PART LXX.—1888.)—Abaa.

PLATE VII.

Figs. 1–5.—*Halecium cymiforme* (p. 15).

Fig. 1.—A colony growing over the stems and branches of some other dendritic Hydroid ; natural size.

Fig. 2.—Portion of a colony ; magnified 20 diameters.

Fig. 3.—Outline of portion of a colony near its base, showing the fascicled basal tubes and the origin of the free portion of the colony ; magnified about 15 diameters.

Fig. 4.—Young gonangium (male ?) with its contents ; magnified about 60 diameters.

    a. Blastostyle.
    b. Sporosac.
    c. Ectodermal investment of the sporosac, sent off from the walls of the blastostyle.
    d. Inner layer of the cap-like covering of the sporosac.
    e. Outer layer of same.

Fig. 5.—More mature gonangium (male ?) with its contents ; magnified about 40 diameters.

    a. Blastostyle.
    b. Sporosac.
    c. Ectodermal investment of the sporosac, sent off from the walls of the blastostyle. The structures forming the cap of the sporosac have here disappeared.

PLATE VIII.

PLATE VIII.

Figs. 1–3.—*Diplocyathus dichotomus* (p. 17).

Fig. 1.—A colony; natural size.

Fig. 2.—Portion of a colony; magnified 20 diameters.

Fig. 3.—A hydrophore with hydranth and sarcotheca. The sarcostyle is seen to be partly protruded from the sarcotheca; magnified 25 diameters.

DIPLOGYATHUS DICHOTOMUS.

PLATE IX.

(ZOOL. CHALL. EXP.—PART LXX.—1888.)—Aaaa.

PLATE IX.

Figs. 1, 2.—*Campanularia insignis* (p. 19).

Fig. 1.—A colony; natural size.

Fig. 2.—Portion of a colony; magnified about 10 diameters.

CAMPANULARIA INSIGNIS.

PLATE X.

PLATE X.

Figs. 1, 1a, 1b.—*Campanularia tulipifera* (p. 20).

Fig. 1.—A colony; natural size.

Fig. 1a.—The same; magnified 5 diameters.

Fig. 1b.—A hydrotheca, still further magnified.

Figs. 2, 2a.—*Campanularia ptychocyathus* (p. 20).

Fig. 2.—A colony; natural size.

Fig. 2a.—Portion of a colony; magnified 10 diameters.

Figs. 3, 3a.—*Calamphora parvula* (p. 29).

Fig. 3.—A colony; natural size.

Fig. 3a.—Portion of a colony; magnified 25 diameters. The large gonangium is seen springing from the creeping stolon close to the base of a hydrotheca.

PLATE **XI.**

(ZOOL. CHALL. EXP.—PART LXX.—1888.)—Aaaa.

PLATE XI.

Figs. 1, 1a.—*Campanularia retroflexa* (p. 21).

Fig. 1.—A colony; natural size.

Fig. 1a.—Portion of a colony; magnified 15 diameters.

Figs. 2, 2a.—*Campanularia cheloniæ* (p. 22).

Fig. 2.—A colony; natural size.

Fig. 2a.—Portion of a colony; magnified 25 diameters.

Figs. 3, 3a.—*Lictorella cyathifera* (p. 36).

Fig. 3.—A colony; natural size.

Fig. 3a.—Portion of a colony; magnified 15 diameters.

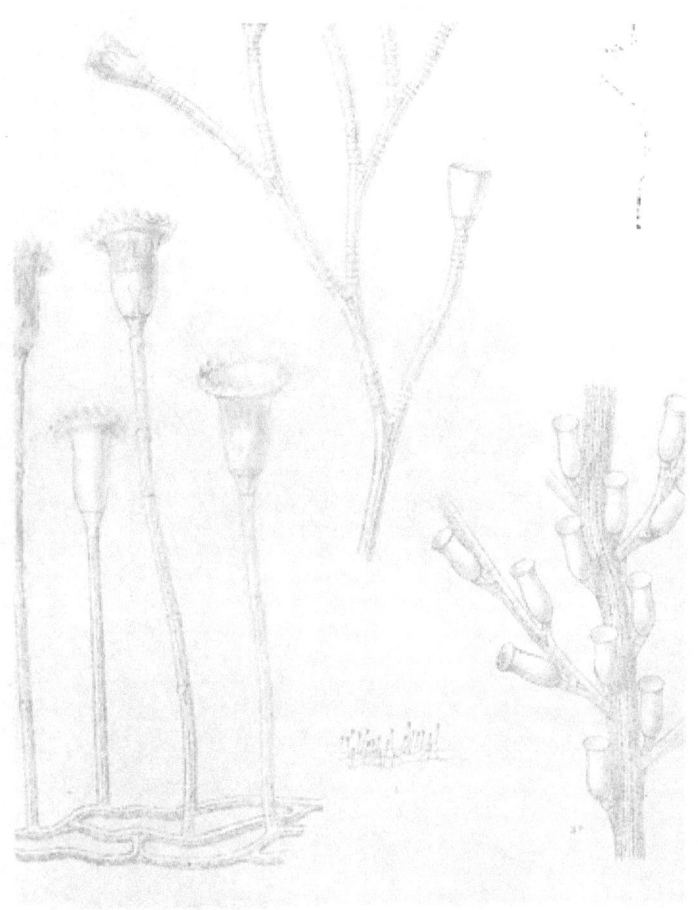

1. 1ª CAMPANULARIA RETROFLEXA. 2. 2ª CAMPANULARIA CHELONIA.
3. 3ª LICTORELLA CYATHIFERA.

PLATE XII.

PLATE XII.

Figs. 1, 1a.—*Obelia geniculata* (p. 23).

Fig. 1.—A colony ; natural size.

Fig. 1a.—Portion of a colony ; magnified 15 diameters.

Figs. 2, 2a.—*Thyroscyphus ramosus* (p. 24).

Fig. 2.—Portion of colony ; natural size.

Fig. 2a.—Portion of the same ; magnified 15 diameters.

Figs. 3, 3a.—*Halecium beanii* (p. 12).

Fig. 3.—A colony ; natural size.

Fig. 3a.—Portion of a colony with female gonangia ; magnified 15 diameters.

1. 1ᵃ OBELIA GENICULATA   2. 2ᵃ THYROSCYPHUS RAMOSUS
3. 3ᵃ HALECIUM BEANII.

PLATE XIII.

PLATE XIII.

Figs. 1, 2.—*Thyroscyphus simplex* (p. 25).

Fig. 1.—A colony; natural size.

Fig. 2.—Portion of a colony; magnified 15 diameters.

PLATE XIV.

PLATE XIV.

Figs. 1, 1a.—*Hypanthea aggregata* (p. 26).

Fig. 1.—A colony ; natural size.

Fig. 1a.—Portion of a colony ; magnified 15 diameters.

     a. Gonangia occupied by the solitary sporosac surrounded by a network of tubes into which the blastostyle has become broken up.
     b. Empty gonangia.

Figs. 2, 2a.—*Hypanthea hemispherica* (p. 27).

Fig. 2.—A colony ; natural size.

Fig. 2a.—Portion of a colony ; magnified 15 diameters.

1 1ª HYPANTHEA AGGREGATA.   2. 2ª HYPANTHEA HEMISPHERICA.

PLATE XV.

(ZOOL. CHALL. EXP.—PART LXX.—1888.)—Aaaa.

PLATE XV.

Figs. 1, 1a.—*Lafoëa dumosa* (p. 34).

Fig. 1.—A colony; natural size.

Fig. 1a.—Portion of a colony; magnified 15 diameters.

Figs. 2, 2a.—*Halecium fastigiatum* (p. 13).

Fig. 2.—A colony; natural size.

Fig. 2a.—Portion of a colony; magnified 15 diameters.

Figs. 3, 3a.—*Hebella striata* (p. 30).

Fig. 3.—Portion of a colony; natural size.

Fig. 3a.—Portion of same; magnified 25 diameters.

1. 1ª LAFOÉA DUMOSA.   2, 2ª HALECIUM FASTIGIATUM
3, 3ª HEBELLA STRIATA.

PLATE XVI.

PLATE XVI.

Figs. 1, 1a.—*Halisiphonia megalotheca* (p. 31).

Fig. 1.—Portion of a colony growing on the stem of another Hydroid.

Fig. 1a.—Portion of the same ; magnified 10 diameters.

Figs. 2, 2a.—*Lafoëa fruticosa* (p. 34).

Fig. 2.—A colony ; natural size.

Fig. 2a.—Portion of a colony ; magnified 15 diameters.

1. 1ᵃ HALISIPHONIA MEGALOTHECA.   2. 2ᵃ LAFOËA FRUTICOSA.

PLATE XVII.

(ZOOL. CHALL. EXP.—PART LXX.—1888.)—Asia.

PLATE XVII.

Figs. 1, 2.—*Lictorella halecioides* (p. 35).

Fig. 1.—A colony ; natural size.

Fig. 2.—Portion of a colony ; magnified 15 diameters. The lower end shows the axial tube exposed by the removal of the peripheral tubes.

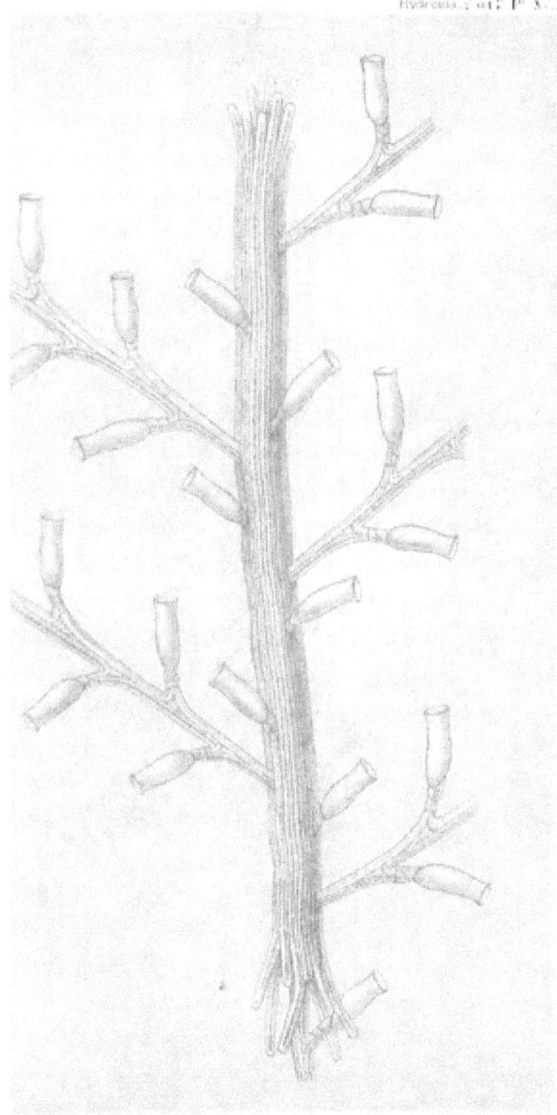

LICTORELLA HALECIOIDES.

PLATE XVIII.

PTOLARIA HUMILIS   2 2ª CRYPTOLARIA ABYSSICOLA

PLATE XIX.

(ZOOL. CHALL. EXP.—PART LXX.—1888.)—Xxxx.

PLATE XIX.

Figs. 1, 1a.—*Cryptolaria flabellum* (p. 40).

Fig. 1.—A colony; natural size.

Fig. 1a.—Portion of a colony; magnified 10 diameters.

Figs. 2, 2a.—*Cryptolaria pulchella* (p. 40).

Fig. 2.—Portion of a colony; natural size.

Fig. 2a.—Portion of same; magnified 10 diameters.

Figs. 3, 3a.—*Cryptolaria crassicaulis* (p. 41).

Fig. 3.—A colony; natural size.

Fig. 3a.—Portion of a colony; magnified 10 diameters.

1, 1ª CRYPTOLARIA FLABELLUM.   2, 2ª CRYPTOLARIA PULCHELLA
           3, 3ª CRYPTOLARIA CRASSICAULIS.

PLATE XX.

PLATE XX.

Figs. 1, 1a, 1b.—*Cryptolaria geniculata* (p. 41).

Fig. 1.—Portion of a colony; natural size.

Fig. 1a.—Portion of same, with two gonangia; magnified 10 diameters.

Fig. 1b.—Same after maceration in caustic potash. The axial and peripheral tubes separated from one another; magnified 10 diameters.

Figs. 2, 2a.—*Cryptolaria gracilis* (p. 42).

Fig. 2.—A colony; natural size.

Fig. 2a.—Portion of a colony; magnified 10 diameters.

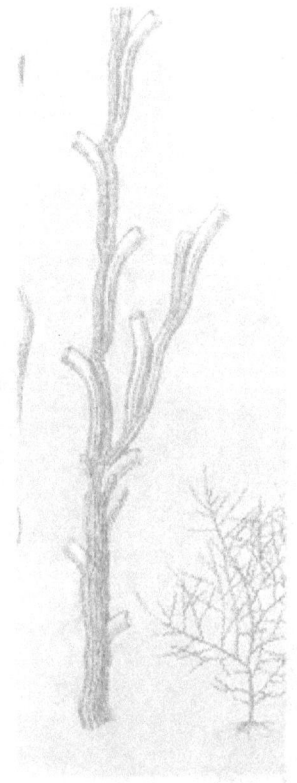

2ᵃ CRYPTOLARIA GRACILIS

PLATE XXI.

(ZOOL. CHALL. EXP.—PART LXX.—1888.)—Aaaa.

PLATE XXI.

Figs. 1, 1a.—*Cryptolaria diffusa* (p. 42).

Fig. 1.—Portion of a colony ; natural size.

Fig. 1a.—Portion of same, with gonangia ; magnified 10 diameters.

Figs. 2, 2a, 2b.—*Perisiphonia pectinata* (p. 45).

Fig. 2.—A colony ; natural size.

Fig. 2a.—Distal end of a pinna, showing the extremities of the hydrothecæ projecting from between the peripheral tubes which carry the sarcothecæ ; magnified 25 diameters.

Fig. 2b.—Portion of a pinna after maceration in caustic potash ; the peripheral tubes detached from the axial tubes and carrying sarcothecæ ; magnified 25 diameters.

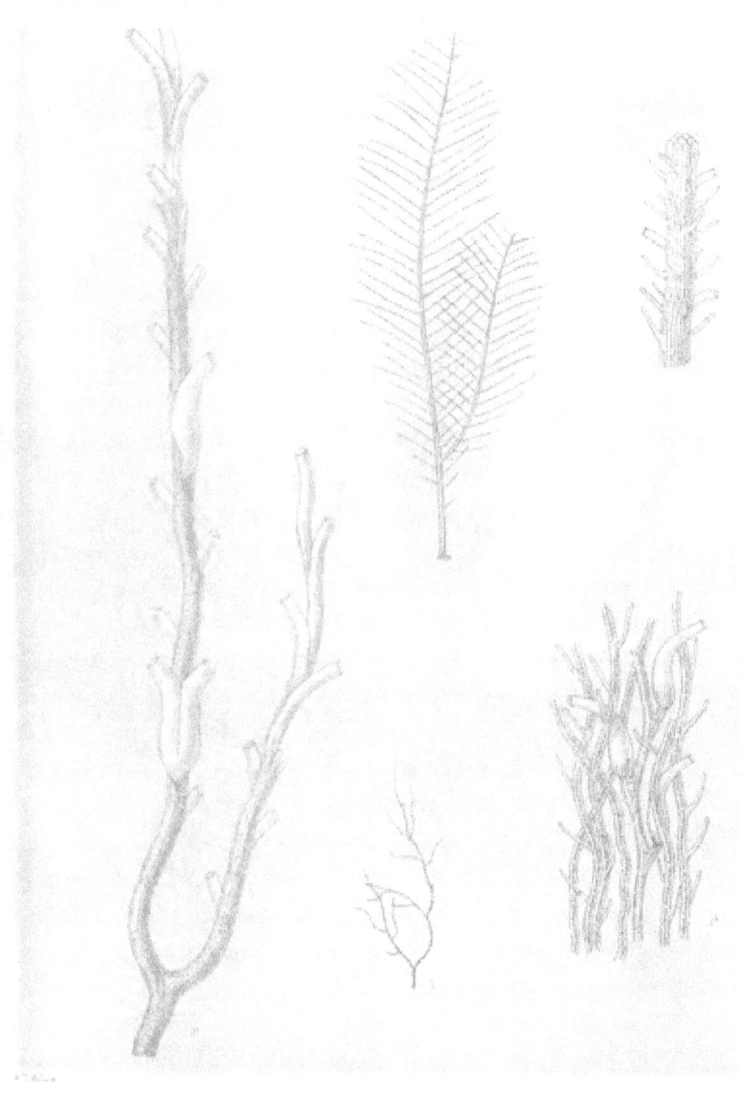

1. 1ᵃ CRYPTOLARIA DIFFUSA   2. 2ᵃ. 2ᵇ PERISIPHONIA PECTINATA

PLATE XXII.

Figs. 1–4.—*Perisiphonia filicula* (p. 44).

Fig. 1.—A colony; natural size.

Fig. 2.—Distal end of a pinna; magnified 25 diameters. The axial and peripheral tubes are partly separated from one another after maceration in caustic potash. Where the peripheral tubes still remain in their natural position, the distal extremities of the hydrothecæ are seen projecting from between them. Sarcothecæ are seen to be carried by the outer peripheral tubes.

Fig. 3.—Portion of the stem after maceration in caustic potash; magnified 25 diameters. The axial tube has been nearly freed from the surrounding peripheral tubes. The origins of the pinnæ from the main stem are seen.

Fig. 4.—Outline of hydrotheca, showing a sarcotheca springing from its peduncle.

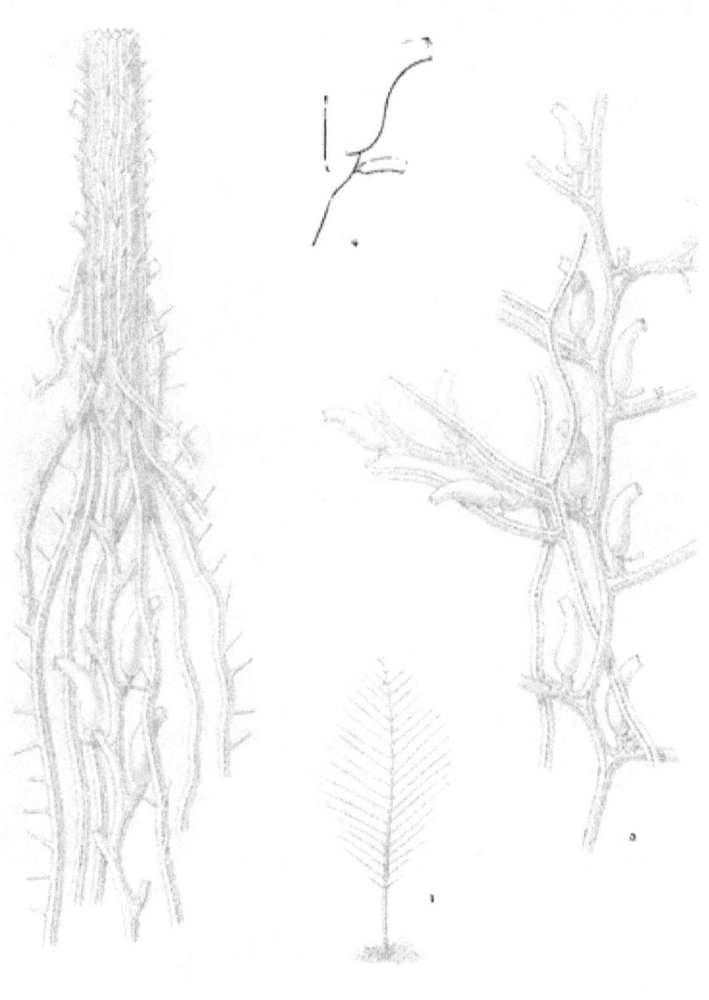

PLATE XXIII.

1. 1ª GRAMMARIA STENTOR.   2. 2ª 2ª GRAMMARIA MAGELLANICA
3. 3ª 3ª GRAMMARIA INSIGNIS.

PLATE XXIV.

PLATE XXIV.

Figs. 1, 1a.—*Sertularia filiformis* [*gracilis*][1] (p. 51).

Fig. 1.—A colony; natural size.

Fig. 1a.—Portion of a colony; magnified 15 diameters.

Figs. 2, 2a.—*Sertularia annulata* (p. 52).

Fig. 2.—A colony; natural size.

Fig. 2a.—Portion of a colony; magnified 15 diameters.

[1] It has been found necessary to change the name since the plate was printed off.

1. 1ª SERTULARIA GRACILIS   2. 2ª SERTULARIA ANNULATA.

PLATE XXV.

(ZOOL. CHALL. EXP.—PART LXX.—1888.)—Aaaa.

Figs. 1, 1a.—*Sertularia leiocarpa* (p. 52).

Fig. 1.—A colony ; natural size.

Fig. 1a.—Portion of a colony; magnified 15 diameters. In the retracted hydranth (*a*) near the distal end of the figure the gastral cavity is seen to be doubled on itself. In the gonangium the peripheral points of attachment of the transverse ectodermal bands which extend from the central structures to the gonangium walls, are seen in the form of stellate cells adherent to the inner surface of the walls.

Figs. 2, 2a, 2b.—*Sertularia secunda* [1] [*unilateralis*] (p. 53).

Fig. 2.—A colony, front view; natural size.

Fig. 2a.—The same, dorsal view.

Fig. 2b.—Portion of a colony; magnified 15 diameters.

Figs. 3, 3a.—*Sertularia clausa* (p. 54).

Fig. 3.—A colony ; natural size.

Fig. 3a.—Portion of a colony ; magnified 15 diameters.

[1] It has been found necessary to change the name since the Plate was printed off.

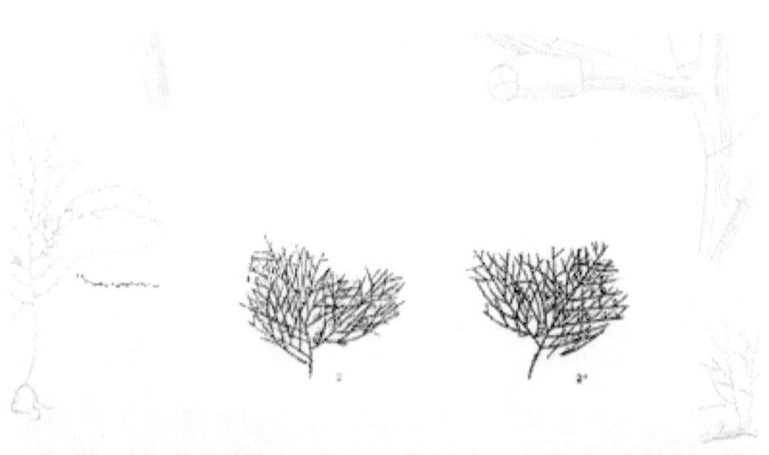

1. 1ᵃ SERTULARIA LEIOCARPA   2 2ᵃ 2ᵇ SERTULARIA UNILATERALIS
3. 3ᵃ SERTULARIA CLAUSA.

PLATE XXVI.

PLATE XXVI.

Figs. 1, 1a.—*Sertularia implexa* (p. 54).

Fig. 1.—Portion of a colony; natural size.

Fig. 1a.—Portion of the same; magnified 15 diameters.

Figs. 2, 2a.—*Sertularia laxa* [1] [*exigua*] (p. 55).

Fig. 2.—A colony; natural size.

Fig. 2a.—Portion of a colony; magnified 15 diameters.

Figs. 3, 3a.—*Sertularia polyzonias* (p. 55).

Fig. 3.—A colony; natural size.

Fig. 3a.—Portion of a colony; magnified 15 diameters.

[1] It has been found necessary to change the name since the Plate was printed off.

SERTULARIA IMPLEXA   2. 2ª SERTULARIA EXIGUA
3. 3ª SERTULARIA POLYZONIAS.

PLATE XXVII.

PLATE XXVII.

Figs. 1, 1a, 1b, 1c.—*Sertularia exserta* (p. 56).

Fig. 1.—A colony ; natural size.

Fig. 1a.—Portion of a colony ; magnified 25 diameters. The hydranths are here shown in their permanently exserted condition, and ectodermal bands are seen to extend from the body of the hydranth to the walls of the hydrotheca.

Fig. 1b.—Base of a tentacle showing the cushion with its battery of thread-cells ; magnified 100 diameters.

Fig. 1c.—Thread-cells detached from the cushion ; magnified 150 diameters.

Figs. 2, 2a.—*Sertularia abietina* (p. 62).

Fig. 2.—Portion of a colony ; natural size.

Fig. 2a.—Portion of the same ; magnified 15 diameters.

PLATE XXVIII.

Figs. 1, 1a.—*Sertularia echinocarpa* (p. 57).

Fig. 1.—Portion of a colony; natural size.

Fig. 1a.—Portion of same; magnified 10 diameters.

Figs. 2, 2a.—*Sertularia catena* (p. 58).

Fig. 2.—A colony; natural size.

Fig. 2a.—Portion of a colony; magnified 10 diameters.

Figs. 3, 3a, 3b.—*Sertularia producta* [1] [*geniculata*] (p. 59).

Fig. 3.—Portion of a colony; natural size.

Fig. 3a.—Portion of same; magnified 15 diameters.

Fig. 3b.—A hydrotheca, further magnified; showing the striation of its summit, the operculum, and the internal projecting ridges.

[1] It has been found necessary to change the name since the Plate was printed off.

Pac. 11.

ECHINOCARPA.   2. 2ᵗ SERTULARIA CATENA.
3.3ᵗ 3ᵗ SERTULARIA GENICULATA.

PLATE XXIX.

PLATE XXIX.

Figs. 1, 1a.—*Sertularia cylindritheca* (p. 59).

Fig. 1.—Portion of a colony; natural size.

Fig. 1a.—Portion of same; magnified 10 diameters.

Figs. 2, 2a.—*Sertularia integritheca* (p. 60).

Fig. 2.—A colony; natural size.

Fig. 2a.—Portion of a colony; magnified 10 diameters.

Figs. 3, 3a.—*Sertularia articulata* (p. 61).

Fig. 3.—Portion of a colony; natural size.

Fig. 3a.—Portion of same; magnified 20 diameters.

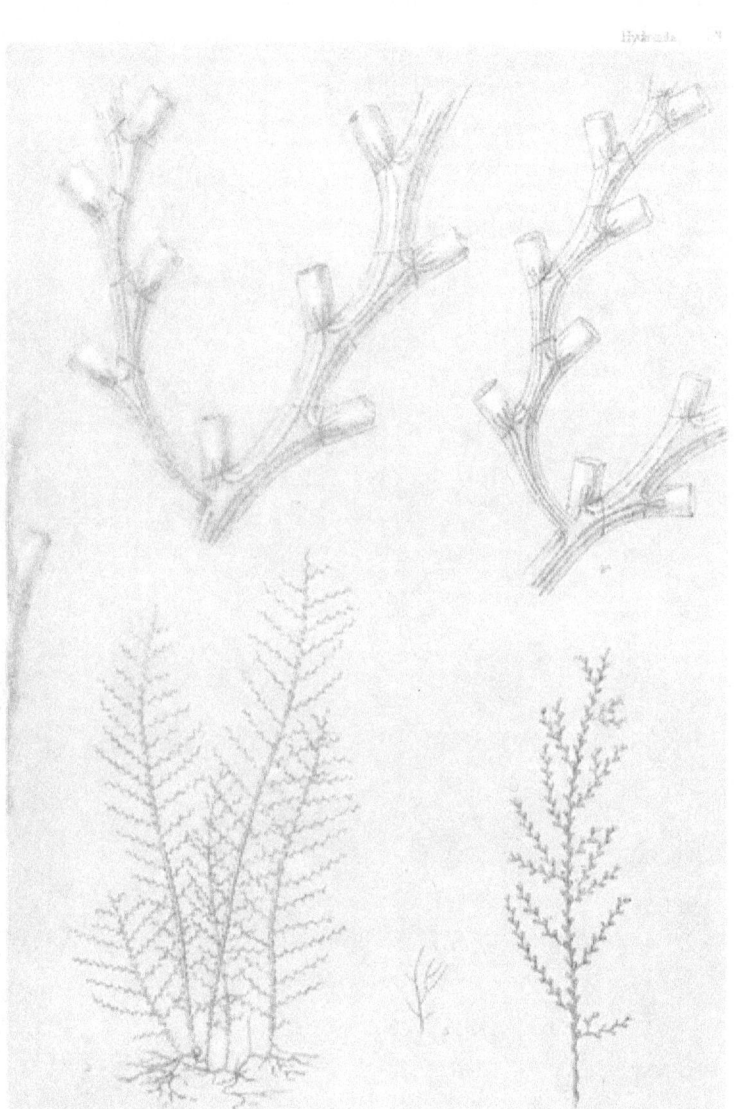

1 1ª SERTULARIA CYLINDRITHECA.   2 2ª SERTULARIA INTEGRITHECA
3.3ª SERTULARIA ARTICULATA.

PLATE XXX.

PLATE XXX.

Figs. 1, 1a.—*Sertularia operculata* (p. 61).

Fig. 1.—Portion of a colony ; natural size.

Fig. 1a.—Portion of same ; magnified 20 diameters.

Figs. 2, 2a, 2b, 2c.—*Diphasia pinaster* (p. 63).

Fig. 2.—A male colony ; natural size.

Fig. 2a.—Part of a female colony with its gonangium ; magnified about 20 diameters.

Fig. 2b.—Part of a male colony with its gonangium ; magnified about 20 diameters.

Fig. 2c.—Part of a female colony ; natural size.

1. 1ª SERTULARIA OPERCULATA 2. 2ª 2ᵇ 2ᶜ DIPHASIA PINASTER.

PLATE XXXI.

(ZOOL. CHALL. EXP.—PART LXX.—1888.)—Aam.

Figs. 1, 1a, 1b, 1c, 1d.—*Thuiaria pharmacopola* (p. 66).

Fig. 1.—A colony; natural size.

Fig. 1a.—A portion of main stem, near its distal end, with a pinna; magnified 15 diameters. One gonangium is present on the pinna and the points from which others have fallen are seen between some of the pairs of hydrothecæ; front view.

Fig. 1b.—Portion of a pinna with three gonangia; lateral view; magnified 15 diameters.

Fig. 1c.—Transverse section of the stem towards the base with the cœnosarc removed by maceration in caustic potash, showing its cavity consisting of numerous longitudinal chambers formed by the coalescence of the thick chitinous walls of the tubes which compose the fascicled stem; magnified about 10 diameters.

Fig. 1d.—Transverse section of the stem near the distal end, similarly treated, showing a single cavity enclosed within the thick chitinous walls of the stem, here become monosiphonic; magnified about 20 diameters.

Figs. 2, 2a.—*Thuiaria quadridens* (p. 66).

Fig. 2.—A colony; natural size.

Fig. 2a.—Portion of a colony; magnified 20 diameters.

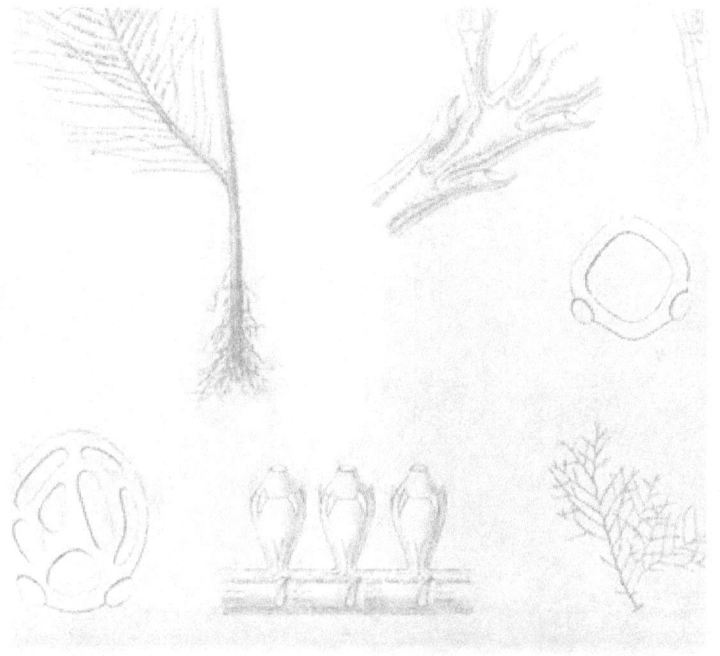

1 1ᵃ 1ᵇ 1ᶜ 1ᵈ THUIARIA   PHARMACOPOLA   2 2ᵃ THUIARIA   QUADRIDENS

PLATE XXXII.

PLATE XXXII.

Figs. 1, 1a, 1b, 1c.—*Thuiaria cupressina* (p. 67).

Fig. 1.—A colony ; natural size.

Fig. 1a.—A portion of a pinna ; magnified 30 diameters.

Fig. 1b.—Part of the main stem with the origin of a pinna ; magnified 15 diameters.

Fig. 1c.—Outline of part of a pinna near its origin, showing its mode of bifurcation ; magnified 15 diameters.

Figs. 2, 2a.—*Thuiaria vincta* (p. 68).

Fig. 2.—Part of a colony ; natural size.

Fig. 2a.—Part of a colony deprived of its cœnosarc by maceration in caustic potash, showing the chitinous bands by which the hydrothecæ of opposite sides are connected to one another ; magnified 15 diameters.

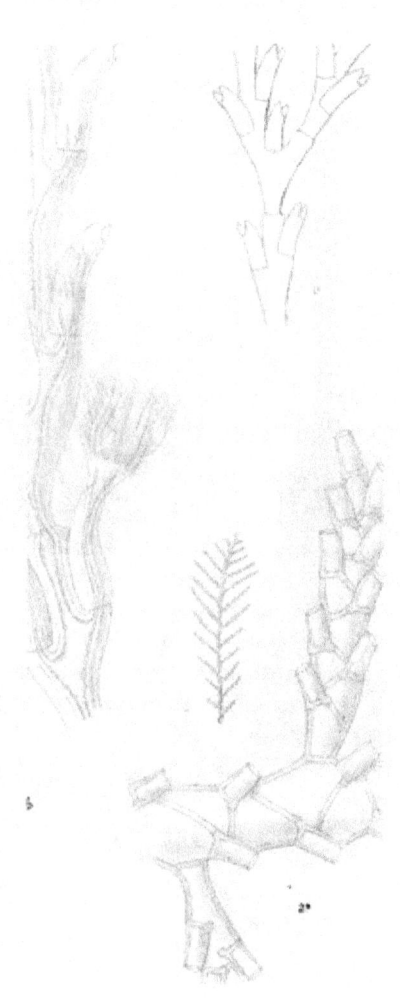

PLATE XXXIII.

(ZOOL. CHALL. EXP.—PART LXX.—1888.)—Asss.

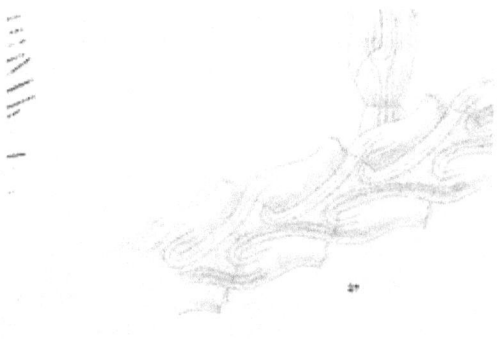

THUIARIA PECTINATA   2. 2ª THUIARIA HYALINA

PLATE XXXIV.

Figs. 1, 1a, 1b.—*Desmoscyphus pectinatus* (p. 71).

Fig. 1.—A colony; natural size.

Fig. 1a.—Part of a colony; magnified 15 diameters.

Fig. 1b.—Outline of part of a pinna, viewed in profile, showing the hydrothecæ all brought to one side of the internodes; magnified 15 diameters.

Figs. 2, 2a, 2b, 2c.—*Desmoscyphus gracilis* (p. 71).

Fig. 2.—A colony; natural size.

Fig. 2a.—Part of a colony; magnified 15 diameters. Towards the basal end of the stem the proximal part of a pinna (*a*) is seen with the spine-like termination from which the more distal part had become detached.

Fig. 2b.—A pair of connate hydrothecæ; magnified about 30 diameters. Front view.

Fig. 2c.—The same, dorsal view.

Figs. 3, 3a.—*Desmoscyphus obliquus* (p. 72).

Fig. 3.—A colony; natural size.

Fig. 3a.—Part of the same; magnified 15 diameters.

1ª 1ᵇ DESMOSCYPHUS PECTINATUS.   2, 2ª 2ᵇ 2ᶜ DESMOSCYPHUS GRACILIS
3. 3ª DESMOSCYPHUS OBLIQUUS

PLATE XXXV.

(ZOOL. CHALL. EXP.—PART LXV.—1888.)—Axxx

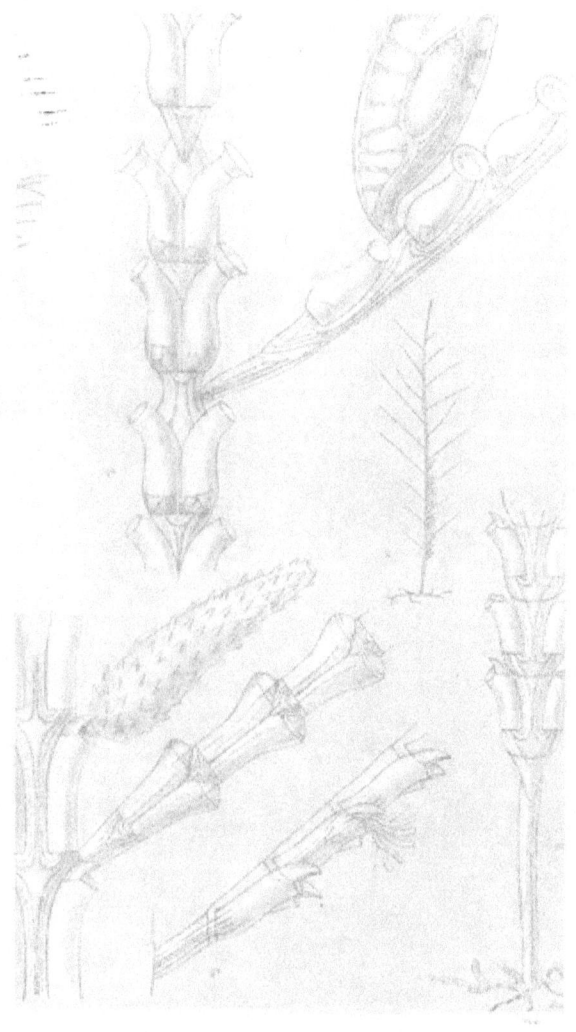

LABROSA   2 ?' 2' 2' DESMOSCYPHUS ACANTHOCARPUS

PLATE XXXVI.

PLATE XXXVI.

Figs. 1, 1a.—*Staurotheca dichotoma* (p. 76).

Fig. 1.—A colony; natural size.

Fig. 1a.—Part of a colony; magnified 10 diameters. The extremity of a neighbouring branch is seen with its tendril-like continuation, which has become attached by its extremity to the hydrocaulus near the base of a hydrotheca.

Figs. 2, 2a.—*Dictyocladium dichotomum* (p. 77).

Fig. 2.—A colony; natural size.

Fig. 2a.—Part of a colony; magnified 15 diameters. The tendril-like continuation of one of the branches is seen to have attached itself by its extremity to the orifice of a hydrotheca on a neighbouring branch.

1. 1ᵃ STAUROTHECA DICHOTOMA   2. 2ᵃ DICTYOCLADIUM DICHOTOMUM

PLATE XXXVII.

(ZOOL. CHALL. EXP.—PART LXX.—1888.)—Aaaa.

PLATE XXXVII.

Figs. 1, 1a, 1b, 1c.—*Synthecium campylocarpum* (p. 78).

Fig. 1.—A colony ; natural size.

Fig. 1a.—Part of a colony ; magnified 15 diameters.

Fig. 1b.—A pair of hydrothecæ with a gonangium from what is probably a male colony of the same species ; magnified 15 diameters.

Fig. 1c.—Basal portion of a pinna in which the gonangia are replaced by hydrotheca-bearing ramuli ; magnified about 8 diameters.

Figs. 2, 2a.—*Synthecium alternans* (p. 80).

Fig. 2.—A colony ; natural size.

Fig. 2a.—Part of a colony ; magnified 15 diameters.

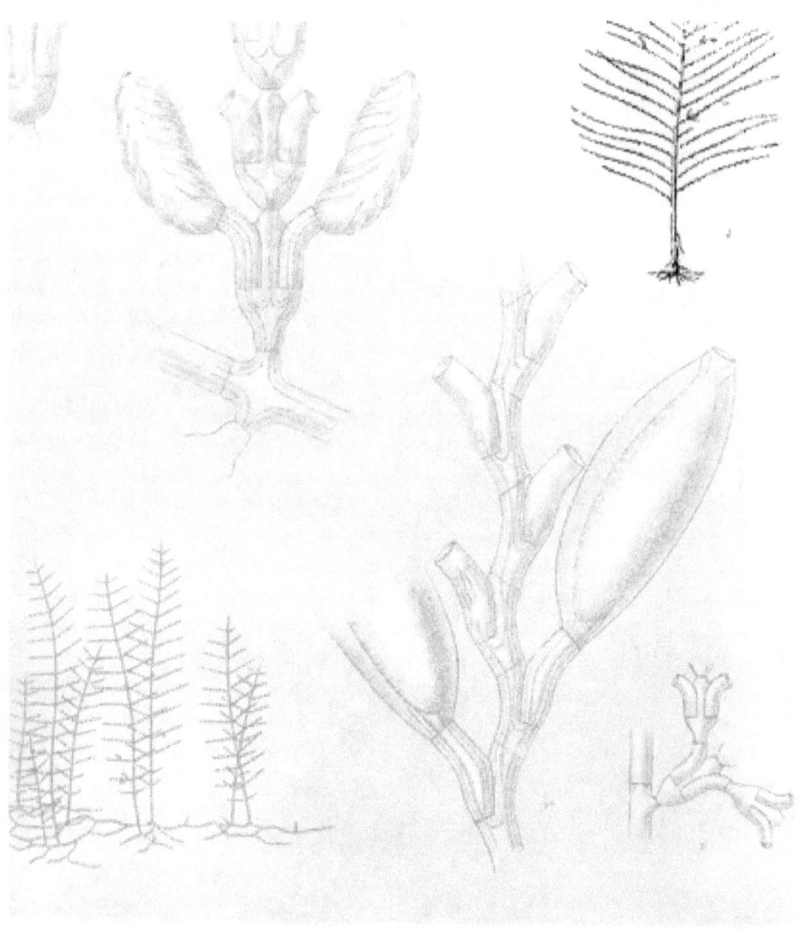

1. 1^a 1^b 1^c SYNTHECIUM CAMPYLOCARPUM.
2. 2^a SYNTHECIUM ALTERNANS.

PLATE XXXVIII.

Figs. 1–4.—*Thecocladium flabellum* (p. 81).

Fig. 1.—A colony ; natural size.

Fig. 2.—Outline of proximal part of a colony, showing the mode in which the stolon is rooted, with the origins of some of the stems ; magnified about 8 diameters.

Fig. 3.—Portion of a colony, magnified 15 diameters ; showing the origin of the branches, each from within the cavity of a hydrotheca. One of the branches is seen to terminate in a tendril-like continuation.

Fig. 4.—Outline of part of a branch, viewed laterally, showing the deep furrow in one side of the gonangium ; magnified about 10 diameters.

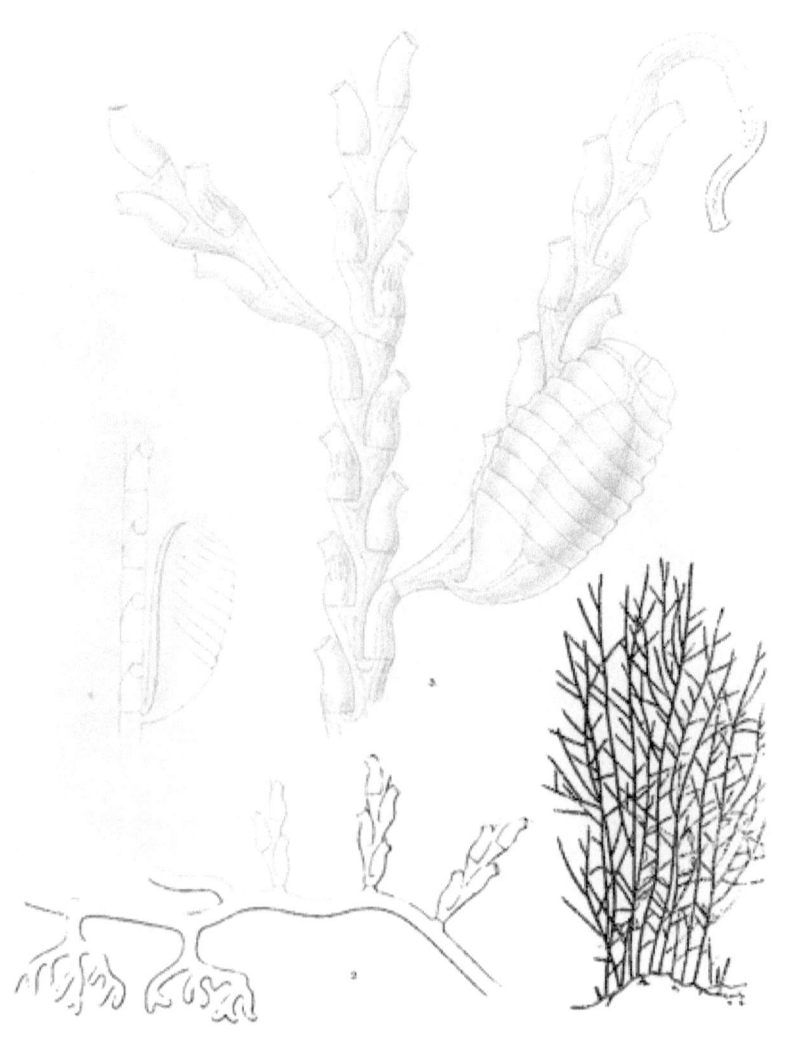

PLATE XXXIX.

Figs. 1–10.—*Idia pristis* (p. 85).

Fig. 1.—A colony ; natural size.

Fig. 2.—Part of a pinna, superficial view from the front ; magnified 15 diameters.

Fig. 3.—The same, posterior aspect, focussed at some distance from the surface, showing the polygonal areas into which the common cavity is divided by offsets of the perisarc ; magnified 15 diameters.

Fig. 4.—The same ; optical longitudinal section, deeper than that of fig. 3, showing the anterior chambers with their coenosarcal lining ; magnified 15 diameters.

Fig. 5.—Lateral view ; longitudinal section showing the common posterior chamber and two of the anterior chambers with their corresponding hydrothecæ, in which the bases of the hydranths are still preserved ; magnified 25 diameters.

Fig. 6.—One of the internodes of the main stem, showing the reticulated condition of its coenosarcal lining ; magnified about 15 diameters.

Fig. 7.—Portion of main stem with gonangia ; magnified about 12 diameters.

Fig. 8.—Transverse section through a pinna ; magnified 25 diameters.
  a. Basal part of hydrotheca.
  b. Anterior chamber.
  c. Common posterior chamber.

Fig. 9.—Outline of distal extremity of hydrotheca, showing its valvular orifice.

Fig. 10.—Origin of a pseudo-branch ; slightly magnified.

IDIA PRISTIS.

Foldouts/Maps

VOYAGE OF H.M.S. CHALLENGER.

ZOOLOGY.

REPORT on the Entozoa collected by H.M.S. Challenger during the Years 1873-76. By Dr. O. von Linstow of Göttingen.

INTRODUCTION.

The number of Entozoa included in the spoils of the Challenger Expedition is remarkably small in comparison with the large collection of Vertebrates. This is mainly due to the fact that the exploration was for the most part marine, and not terrestrial, and that it concerned not only the regions near the coast, but also to a very large extent the deep sea. For it follows from the nature of the life-history of Helminths, that these forms must occur more and more sparsely in proportion to the distance from the shore. In the Nematoda, Gordiacea, Acanthocephala, Trematoda, and Cestoda, with few exceptions (among Nematodes and Trematodes), the sexually mature forms are parasitic in some organ, such as the stomach, which communicates with the outer world, and from which the numerous eggs pass out with the excrement. On the soil or in the water the ova find their way into another organism, within which they develop into larvæ, and are usually encapsuled until they pass along with their intermediate host into the original victim, where they become sexually mature. Not a few Helminths, such as many digenetic Trematodes and the Gordiaceæ, have in their developmental cycle to pass through two intermediate hosts. That the Vertebrata which inhabit the high seas are remarkably free from Helminths is without doubt due to the fact that the ova are too widely scattered in the infinite mass of water to have much chance of reaching their proper intermediate hosts; and, further, that even when they do so, there is again in the wide ocean but a slight chance that infected intermediate hosts become the prey of the final victims.

The Acanthocephala, Gordiacea, and Trematoda are altogether unrepresented in the Challenger collection. The absence of the first is perhaps only accidental; while the Gordiacea are entirely fresh-water forms, and the Trematodes are, as free-swimming larvæ, too delicate to withstand the pressure of a deep-sea life, and are restricted either to quiet fresh-water basins or to sheltered littoral regions.[1]

A. NEMATODA.

1. *Ascaris simplex*, Rudolphi (*non* Dujardin) (Pl. I. figs. 1–4).

Specimen labelled : "Ascaris from stomach of *Otaria jubata*, January 27, 1874. Kerguelen Island."

The vessel contained thirteen specimens, of which the largest was 79 mm. long and 2·2 mm. broad. The upper lip is semicircular, with an anterior protrusion; the pulp sends two cylindrical protrusions into the latter, and these are rounded off anteriorly; the anterior end bears a dentigerous ridge with pointed teeth; there are no accessory lips; the upper lip (0·12 mm. across) is much smaller than the two under lips (0·30 mm.). The cuticle exhibits transverse wrinkles (0·023 mm. in breadth), between which there are again finer markings about eight times as narrow. The lateral areas are 0·23 mm. in breadth, the dorsal and ventral regions measure 0·035 mm. The male is 37 mm. in length, and 0·9 mm. in breadth; the tail bears on each side of the very extremity four conical papillæ; two or three others of a round form occur just in front of the cloaca; at each side of these six others shortly stalked, and again in front an inconstant row of fifty or more. Krabbe has given a good representation of the posterior end of the male, in which the long cirri (1·68 mm. in length) are seen to exhibit a sabre-shaped curvature. In the female, which measures 79 mm. in length, and 2·2 mm. in breadth, the anus is situated at a distance of 0·48 mm. from the tail end; the latter is rounded, and bears embedded in the cuticle a small styliform process. The vulva lies somewhat in front of the middle of the body, and the anterior region thus defined bears to the posterior the proportion of three to four. The ova are spherical. The hyaline sheath, separated by a considerable interspace from the large yolk (0·036 mm.) which it surrounds, bears small roundish elevations, and measures 0·052 mm.

Ascaris simplex was first described in a few words by Rudolphi,[2] who discovered it in *Delphinus phocæna* and *Delphinus gangeticus*.

---

[1] Notices of one Acanthocephalan, two Trematodes (one of which comes from deep water), and some *Gordii* will however, be found in the Appendix.

[2] Entoz. Hist. Nat., Amstelodami, 1808–1810, ii. p. 170 ; Synopsis, Berolini, 1819, pp. 49, 54, 296.

The opportunity of studying this parasite must indeed be a rare one, since the next naturalist who investigated and described "*Ascaris simplex*" was Dujardin.[1] He described the spicules as unequal, measuring 15 and 27 mm. in length in a specimen 79 mm. long ; the ventral surface bore eight to ten papillæ ; the female was 100 mm. in length ; the ova measured 0·041–0·043 mm. ; the vulva was situated far forward, so that the anterior and posterior regions exhibited a proportion of 5 to 12 or 2 to 5. The specimens were found in a Dolphin captured near the Maldives. The enormous length and marked inequality of the cirri, the position of the vulva, the size of the ova, the number of papillæ, all go to prove that the species was not the same as that which we have described above. From the size and inequality of the cirri it may indeed be inferred that the form studied by Dujardin was not an *Ascaris* at all.

Krabbe[2] was the first to distinguish *Ascaris simplex* from the other Ascarids found in Seals and Dolphins ; that is to say, from (1) *Ascaris osculata*, Rudolphi, from *Phoca grœnlandica* and *Phoca barbata*, *Halichœrus grypus*, *Cystophora cristata*, and *Trichechus rosmarus*; (2) *Ascaris decipiens*, Krabbe, from *Phoca grœnlandica*, *Phoca barbata*, *Phoca hispida*, *Phoca vitulina*, *Cystophora cristata*, and *Trichechus rosmarus*; (3) *Ascaris lobulata*, Schneider, from *Platanista gangetica*; (4) *Ascaris conocephala*, Krabbe, from *Delphinus delphis* and *Clymenia*. He described *Ascaris simplex* from *Lagenorhys albirostris*, *Beluga leucas*, *Hyperoodon rostratus*, and *Monodon monoceros*, and figures the upper lip and the posterior extremity of the male.

The *Ascaris patagonica*, which I have described[3] from an *Otaria jubata* captured off Patagonia by Professor Behn on his voyage round the world, is entirely different from *Ascaris simplex*, as a glance at the figure will at once show.

That this parasite, hitherto found only in Dolphins, should occur in *Otaria jubata*, Forster, is somewhat remarkable, as no other case is known of a species infesting both Seals and Cetacea.

2. *Ascaris spiculigera*, Rud. (Pl. I. figs. 5–7).

Specimen labelled : "*Ascaris* from the stomach of *Phalacrocorax verrucosus*,[4] January 1874, Kerguelen Island (Shag.)."

The vessel contained thirty-eight Nematodes, of which thirty-six belonged to the above species.

The body is short and thick ; the smallest specimens, still sexually immature, were 5·44 mm. in length by 0·27 mm. in breadth. The cuticle exhibits regular transverse wrinkles, 0·003 mm. in breadth. The œsophagus measures $\frac{1}{7}$, and the tail $\frac{1}{5}$ of the total

[1] Histoire des Helminthes, Paris, 1845, pp. 220, 221.
[2] Kong. dansk. Vidensk. Forh., 1878, pp. 47–49, fig. 2, tab. i. fig. 4.
[3] Archiv f. Naturgesch., Jahrg. xlvi. Bd. i., 1880, pp. 41, 42, pl. iii. fig. 1.
[4] Zool. Chall. Exp., vol. ii. pt. viii., Phalacrocorax verrucosus, Cab., p. 122.

length of the worm. The intestine leads anteriorly into a diverticulum, which has a distinct lumen, measures 0·78 mm. in length and 0·036 mm. in breadth, and lies anteriorly on the dorsal side of the œsophagus. The œsophagus, lying in the ventral side of the animal, is also continued backwards into a cæcum lying below the intestine, and measuring 1·86 mm. in length by 0·072 mm. in breadth. The lips bear dentigerous ridges, and between them there are accessory lips. The upper lip is quadrangular with rounded anterior angles, it is 0·043 mm. in length and 0·066 mm. broad; the outer surface is flat, the inner gives off two rounded processes, which extend outwards and forwards, and protrude terminally on either side below the outer surface. The accessory lips are hook-shaped and bent inwards; they are but slightly smaller than the principal lips, from which they are markedly distant. The tail end is conical and pointed. The two uniform sabre-shaped cirri of the male are 7·2 mm. long, and are protruded for about 6 mm. They can be recognised with the naked eye, and to this the specific title obviously refers. Of postanal papillæ there are four median, and somewhat towards the ventral surface three lateral, while in front of the anus there is a variable row of thirty-eight to forty or so.

The largest female was 24 mm. long and 1·1 mm. broad. The vulva is situated about the boundary between the first and second quarter of the body, dividing the latter in the proportion of 5 to 13. The ova are spherical, the shell measures 0·0049 mm. in thickness, and is considerably distant from the yolk. It exhibits a very beautiful marking, due to regular, uniformly distributed, minute, shining elevations. The diameter measures 0·072 mm., while that of the yolk is 0·042 mm.

Ascaris spiculigera was first described by Rudolphi,[1] and has been subsequently observed by a great number of naturalists. The hosts are very numerous[2]—*Mergus merganser* and *Mergus serrator*, *Pelecanus americanus*, *Pelecanus onocrotalus*, *Pelecanus tetrarhynchus*, and *Pelecanus fuscus*, *Carbo brasiliensis*, *Carbo cormoranus*, *Carbo cristatus*, *Carbo dilophus*, *Carbo graculus*, and *Carbo pygmæus*, *Plotus anhinga*, *Lestris pomarinus*, *Larus tridactylus*, *Colymbus arcticus*, *Colymbus rufogularis*, and *Colymbus septentrionalis*, *Podiceps auritus*, *Podiceps dominicensis*, and *Podiceps minor*, *Uria troile*, *Alca torda*. The stomach and œsophagus are infested. The best descriptions are those of Dujardin[3] and Schneider.[4] The geographical distribution is remarkably extensive, for the species occurs in Europe (Germany, Scandinavia, Austria, Sardinia, France), in Asia (Turkestan[5]), in Africa, in America (Brazil), and in the Antarctic region.

[1] Entoz. Hist. Nat., Amstelædami, t. ii., 1808–1810, p. 168.
[2] Von Linstow, Compendium der Helminthologie, Hannover, 1878, pp. 162–178.
[3] Loc. cit., pp. 206–208.
[4] Monographie der Nematoden, Berlin, 1866, p. 45, pl. i. fig. 14.
[5] Von Linstow, Fedtschenko's Journey in Turkestan, Soc. Nat. Hist. Moscow, sec. 18, vol. ii. pp. 3, 4, 1886 (in Russian).

3. *Ascaris biloba*, n. sp. (Pl. I. figs. 8, 9).

Specimen labelled : "January 1876 ; Straits of Magellan."

The host is not noted ; the vessel contained five specimens, which were immature females, with the ovaries and uteri well developed, but without ova.

The maximum length was 48 mm., the breadth 2·2 mm. The body is rounded off at both ends, and the posterior extremity is the thicker. The cuticle is thick and transversely wrinkled at intervals of 0·14 mm., while between these main markings there is a finer transverse wrinkling, with intervals of 0·006 mm. The musculature is divided by the usual four longitudinal ridges into four longitudinal bands ; the dorsal and ventral ridges measure 0·13 mm. in breadth, the two laterals 0·24 mm. The head bears three lips, with dentigerous plates and accessory lips ; the upper lip is pentagonal with rounded corners, and is about as long as broad, measuring 0·25 mm. in length and 0·26 mm. in breadth ; the base is 0·098 mm. broad. The anterior margin bears a dentigerous plate, and the pulp broadens from the base forwards for the first third of the length, at this point there are two large papillæ, thence onwards it narrows markedly, and forms two anteriorly rounded terminal lappets. The conical accessory lips are 0·15 mm. in length ; the œsophagus has a length of 4 mm. ; the vulva lies in the ventral line a little in front of the middle of the body, and the anterior region thus marked off bears to the posterior portion the proportion of 23 to 25. The anus lies 0·3 mm. from the tail end ; the extreme point of the tail is produced into a minute finger-shaped point, 0·048 mm. in length.

There can be no doubt that this species is indeed parasitic, for there are no known free-living Ascarids in which the structural features entirely correspond to those of parasitic forms.

Schneider[1] describes the following Ascarids, in which the lips bear tooth plates and accessory lips are developed :—*Ascaris depressa* from *Vultur fulvus*, and *Ascaris ensicaudata* from singing birds (with upper lips, and with a mouth aperture exhibiting anterior processes quite different from the above), *Ascaris rubicunda* from *Python molurus*, and *Ascaris radiosa* from *Echidna rhinocerotis* (with the anterior processes quadrangular), *Ascaris quadrangularis* from *Crotalus*, *Ascaris holoptera* from *Testudo græca*, and *Ascaris sulcata* from *Chelone midas* (with the upper lip forming a quadrangular aperture).

I have previously described[2] the following related species :—The above-mentioned *Ascaris ensicaudata*, Zed. (= *Ascaris cornicis*, Gmel., *Ascaris crenata*, Zed., *Ascaris heteromera*, Crepl., *Ascaris semiteres*, Zed.), from *Turdus*, *Sturnus*, *Corvus*, *Salicaria*, *Vanellus*, *Himantopus*, *Œdicnemus*, *Charadrius* (with an upper lip, with the maximum

[1] *Loc. cit.*, pp. 40-44, tab. i. figs. 6, 7, 8, 9, 10, 11, 12.
[2] *Archiv f. Naturgesch.*, Jahrg. l. Bd. i., 1884, pp. 125-127, pl. vii. figs. 1-3.

breadth in the anterior third, and with two lobes with large pointed processes on the anterior part of the pulp: *Ascaris gallinulæ* and *Ascaris philomelæ* from *Gallinula chloropus* and *Luscinia philomela*[1] (probably to be united with *Ascaris ensicaudata*); *Ascaris spiralis*, Zed.,[2] from *Bubo maximus* and other Owls (with an upper lip, with the finger-shaped, anterior, terminal lobes of the pulp converging inwards, and not expanding outwards). In *Ascaris microcephala*, Rud.,[3] from *Ardea comata*, the accessory lips are as long as the principal lips, the upper lip and its aperture are quadrangular.

It would thus appear that the Challenger form described above is a new species, and it is to be regretted that the host—doubtless some marine Vertebrate—is unknown.

4. *Ascaris diomedeæ*, n. sp. (Pl. I. figs. 12, 13).

Specimen labelled : "From the stomach of *Diomedea brachyura*, No. 344, June 1875." The vessel contained two specimens. The length measured 35, the breadth 0·78 mm. ; the wrinkling of the cuticle is 0·013 mm. broad ; the contour of the body is saw-like. The lips bear tooth-plates, and there are no accessory lips. The upper lip is broad and inconspicuous, and rounded off laterally. It exhibits anteriorly a small round protrusion, and to the inside of the latter a projection with tooth-plates. At a distance of 0·49 mm. from the end of the body, to right and left in the lateral lines are two large, semiconical nuchal papillæ, measuring 0·046 mm. The œsophagus lies rather towards the dorsal side, and at its passage into the intestine bends round at right angles, extending backwards along the ventral side. At the point of union with the intestine a cæcum is given off, 0·12 mm. in breadth. This extends forwards on the ventral side of the œsophagus for 1·8 mm., while a second and broader, 0·24 mm. in diameter anteriorly, runs backwards for 2·7 mm. along the dorsal surface of the intestine. The œsophagus occupies $\frac{1}{15}$, the rounded tail $\frac{1}{142}$ of the total length. The specimens are not sexually mature.

Ascaris arctica, von Linstow,[4] from the Kiel Zoological Museum, discovered in *Diomedea leucops*, in the North Pacific, bears no resemblance to the form described above from *Diomedea brachyura*, Temm.[5] The upper lip is semicircular with an anterior point, the œsophagus is proportionately much larger, for it occupies $\frac{1}{4}$ of the entire length. The upper lip of *Ascaris diomedeæ* most resembles that of *Ascaris tiara*, von Linstow,[6] from *Varanus ornatus*, in which the œsophagus occupies $\frac{1}{13}$ of the entire length. The differences in the structure of the head make a union of the two forms impossible, and the two hosts also certainly hint at two distinct species.

[1] *Würtemb. naturw. Jahresh.*, xxv., 1879, pp. 321, 325, pl. v. figs. 4, 5.
[2] *Archiv f. Naturgesch.*, Jahrg. xli. Bd. i., 1875, pp. 203, 204, pl. iv. figs. 30, 31, A.
[3] Von Linstow, *op. cit.*, Jahrg. xlix. Bd. i., 1883, pp. 276, 277, pl. iv. figs. 1, 2.
[4] *Archiv f. Naturgesch.*, Jahrg. xlvi. Bd. i., 1880, p. 42, pl. iii. figs. 2, 3.
[5] Report on the Birds, Zool. Chall. Exp., part viii. pp. 147, 148.
[6] *Würtemb. naturw. Jahresh.*, 1879, p. 330, pl. v. fig. 1.

5. *Ascaris macruri*, n. sp. (Pl. I. figs. 10, 11).

Specimen labelled : " Ascarides of large *Macrurus rudis*, 15 July 1874. Depth, 600 fathoms. Station 171.

" When the specimen of Macrurus was placed in a tub of water, the two Ascarides came from it."

The glass contained two specimens, 140 and 94 mm. in length, and 2 mm. in breadth. The body is straight and stretched. There was no noticeable elastic tension of the cuticle, such as was observed (see below) in a species of Nematode from the great depths. The animal is, of course, protected from a greater pressure of water by the body of the host in which it lives. Both specimens were females. The cuticle is transversely wrinkled at intervals of 0·04 mm. The lips are without tooth-plates, but with accessory pieces, and exhibit on their outer margins indentations or "spoons." The upper lip is quadrangular, with anteriorly rounded corners ; the anterior third is expanded, and measures 0·25 mm. in breadth by 0·23 mm. in length. The spoon-like indentations are found posteriorly on the two posterior thirds. The blunt, anteriorly rounded accessory pieces measure four-sevenths of the length of the main lips. The œsophagus measures $\frac{1}{9}$ of the entire length. The tail end becomes suddenly narrower about 2 mm. from the point, so that the end has a general styliform shape, with a sharp needle-like point. The thicker portion stands at a right angle to the thinner part. The anus opens on the projecting portion. The ova are spherical, the shell is separated by a marked interval from the yolk, and measures 0·0049 mm. in breadth. The ovum has a diameter of 0·085, and the yolk of 0·062 mm.

Helminths have never before been observed in *Macrurus*, and it is to be regretted that of this remarkable species of *Ascaris* only two female specimens were obtained, as the characters of the male would have been of much interest.

6. *Ascaris macruroidei*, n. sp.

This Nematode was contained in a tube labelled " From the stomach of large Macrurid. Station 147. Date 30 Dec. 1873. Lat. 46° 16′ S., Long. 48° 27′ E. Depth 1600 fms." There were three fragments, one anterior and two posterior extremities; of 27, 34, and 55 mm. length, and 0·66 to 1·06 mm. breadth. Since one anterior and one posterior part have exactly the same breadth, they probably belong to the same specimen, which would thus have a total length of 82 mm. Transverse wrinkles of the cuticle could not be perceived. The lateral ridges have a breadth of 0·18 mm. and are marked at the right and left side by two longitudinal rows of large cells with a diameter of 0·036 mm., containing a bright, round nucleus, which is 0·012 mm. in diameter. There are three lips with accessory lips without dentigerous ridges; the accessory lips have two-thirds of the dimensions of the principal lips. The upper lip is oval with truncated base; it has a breadth of 0·26 mm. and a length of 0·29 mm., the base of 0·18 mm., the pulp has on the outside two rounded processes, to the outer sides of which are placed two large papillæ; the inside of the lip shows two reniform protrusions, surmounting the lip anteriorly. Two slightly prominent nuchal papillæ are situated 1·5 mm. from the

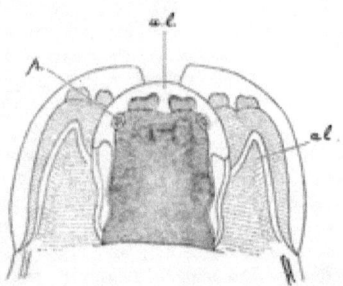

Fig. 1.—Cephalic end of *Ascaris macruroides*, n. sp., from the dorsal surface; *u.l.*, upper lip; *p.*, papilla; *a.l.*, accessory lip.

anterior end, their stalks piercing the cuticle. The œsophagus has a length of 5·5 mm., and the tail has a length of 0·68 mm. and is conically pointed.

The specimens are females, not yet sexually mature.

The species is without any doubt different from *Ascaris macruri*, as is shown by a comparison with this form.

7. *Filaria (Spiroptera) cirrohamata*, n. sp. (Pl. I. figs. 14–16).

Specimen labelled : "*Ascaris* from the stomach of *Phalacrocorax verrucosus*, &c.; along with *Ascaris spiculigera.*"

Two specimens were obtained, a male and a female.

The wrinkling of the skin is 0·006 mm. broad; the head end exhibits two conical lips, and short, rudimentary neck frills. The first quarter of the œsophagus is somewhat narrower than the remaining portion, which is exceptional in being without any glandular coating. At a distance of 0·14 mm. from the head, the lateral line exhibits a three-pointed nuchal papilla.

The male is 7·58 mm. in length, and 0·25 mm. in breadth, the very long œsophagus measures somewhat less than half the entire length, while the tail occupies $\frac{1}{10}$ of the same.

The tail end is rounded off and exhibits a broad bursa. On the ventral surface on each side there are 4 pre- and 5 post-anal, long-stalked papillæ, and between the third and fourth post-anals there is a large interspace. The cirri are very unequal; the smaller and thicker is 0·14 mm. in length; the larger and narrower measures 0·6 mm., and bears a terminal process projecting at right angles.

The female measures 9·72 mm. in length, and 0·35 mm. in breadth; the œsophagus occupies $\frac{1}{12}$ of the total length; the conical-pointed tail $\frac{1}{31}$. The vulva lies far forward just in front of the passage of the œsophagus into the intestine. The very thick-shelled ova are 0·039 mm. in length, and 0·019 mm. in breadth. Similarly three-pointed nuchal papillæ are exhibited by the following forms:—*Filaria squamata*, von Linstow,[1] from the intestines of *Phalacrocorax carbo* (with conspicuous neck fringes, and very short ($\frac{1}{212}$) tail, *Filaria involuta*, von Linstow,[2] from the skin of the stomach of *Strix flammea*, also with marked neck fringes, *Filaria (Dispharagus) laticeps*, Rud.,[3] from *Falco, Strix, Ægolius* (also with neck fringes), *Filaria tridentata*, von Linstow,[4] from *Colymbus arcticus* (with nuchal papillæ of a different form, and with the œsophagus occupying only $\frac{1}{4}$ of the total length), *Filaria triænucha*, Wright,[5] from *Ardea minor* (only known as a female with ova, 0·027 mm. in length, and 0·018 mm. in breadth). In these five species the fish-hook like process of the longer cirrus is absent.

The latter is exhibited by *Filaria hamata*, von Linstow,[6] from *Astur nisus*, a species with strongly developed neck fringes, and by *Filaria penihamata*, Molin,[7] from *Strix albomarginata, Strix atricapilla, Strix flammea*, and *Strix griseata*, which has only two post-anal papillæ on either side.

8. *Filaria flabellata*, n. sp. (Pl. II. figs. 1–5).

Specimen labelled: "*Filaria sub cute et in cav. abdom.* of *Paradisea apoda*, from Aru Islands."

The specimens were all burst, and in part torn. The body is short and compressed; the two ends of the body are rounded off, and not narrowed. The breadth averages 1·08 mm., and bears a ratio of 1 : 14–15 to the length. The mouth cavity is supported on each side by tripartite, fern-shaped, chitinous plates, measuring 0·21 mm., and rounded off at the corners. The œsophagus measures $\frac{1}{17}$ of the total length.

[1] *Archiv f. Naturgesch.*, Jahrg. xlix. Bd. i., 1883, pp. 287, 288, pl. vii. figs. 18, 19.
[2] *Wiirttemb. naturw. Jahresh.*, xxxv., 1879, pp. 323, 324, pl. ii. fig. 7.
[3] Schneider, *Monographie der Nematoden*, pp. 93, 94, pl. vi. fig. 3 ; von Drasche, *Verhandl. d. k. k. zool.-bot. Gesellsch. Wien*, 1883, p. 200, pl. xiv. fig. 2.
[4] *Archiv f. Naturgesch.*, Jahrg. xliii. Bd. i., 1877, pp. 10, 11, pl. i. fig. 17.
[5] Contributions to American Helminthology, Toronto, 1879, pp. 21, 22, pl. i. fig. 16.
[6] *Archiv f. Naturgesch.*, Jahrg. xliii. Bd. i., 1877, pp. 11, 12, pl. i. fig. 19; Jahrg. xlv. Bd. i., 1879, p. 172, pl. xi. fig. 17.
[7] Von Drasche, *Verhandl. d. k. k. zool.-bot. Gesellsch. Wien*, 1883, Bd. xxxiii. pp. 198, 199, pl. xiii. fig. 6.

The male is 13 to 16 mm. in length; the tail end occupies $\frac{1}{36}$ of the total length; the two cirri are of equal breadth, and measure 0·72 and 0·86 mm. in length; the shorter has a bow-shaped curvature in the middle, and the longer is sabre-shaped; in front of the cloaca there are on each side four very small, scarcely perceptible papillæ. The female measures 29 to 31 mm.; the tail end occupies only $\frac{1}{121}$ of the total length; the vulva lies very far forward, only 0·6 mm. distant from the head end. The ova are elliptical and very thick shelled; the shell is 0·0066 mm. in thickness; the ova are 0·049 mm. in length and 0·031 mm. in breadth.

This *Filaria* was found by R. von Willemoes Suhm, who died on the Challenger Expedition. He has referred to it in the following lines:[1]—" Under the skin and on several positions in the abdominal cavity I found free *Filariæ*, such as not unfrequently occur in our crow-like birds. There were no other Helminths in the intestine. This is probably the first time that any one has examined fresh Birds of Paradise in search for Helminths, and the case is on that account worth noting, since the beautiful creature is always mentioned in the first rank of birds, although it is in reality nothing more than ' a crow developed by sexual selection.' "

Five species of *Filaria* are known in which the mouth exhibits a chitinous armature similar to that of the above form.

Filaria tricuspis, Fedtschenko,[2] from *Corvus cornix*, which is very similar to the above species, but has larger cirri, which measure 1·6 and 1·2 mm. in length, while the chitinous plates on the head are smaller, attaining a length of only 0·12 mm. The total length is, however, much greater, for the female is 150 mm. in length. *Filaria ecaudata*, Oerley,[3] from *Lamprotornis aeneus*, is very probably identical with *Filaria tricuspis*. *Filaria obtusa*, Rudolphi[4] (*non* Schneider), from *Hirundo rustica*, *Hirundo urbica*, and *Hirundo riparia* has its breadth and length in the proportion of 1 : 80, and the shorter spicule is twice as broad as the longer.

Filaria pungens, Schneider,[5] has numerous large papillæ on the tail end of the male, and was found in *Turdus cyaneus*.

The unnamed *Filaria* found by Parona[6] in *Buceros nasutus* was a female, so that comparison is impossible.

It is remarkable that these species, which resemble one another so closely, were all found in Birds.

[1] Challenger Briefe von R. v. Willemoes Suhm, Leipzig, 1877, pp. 127, 128; Zeitschr. f. wiss. Zool., Bd. xxvi. p. lxii., 1875.
[2] Soc. Nat. Hist. Moscow, x. pp. 10-11. Von Linstow, Archiv f. Naturgesch., Jahrg. xlix. Bd. i., 1883, p. 285, pl. vii. fig. 16.
[3] Oerley, Report on the Nematodes in the possession of the British Museum, Ann. and Mag. Nat. Hist., ser. 5, vol. ix. pp. 312, 313, pl. x. figs 1 a–d, 1882.
[4] Dujardin, Hist. Nat. des Helminthes, pp. 53-54, pl. iii. fig. J, 1-2.
[5] Monographie der Nematoden, pp. 92, 93, pl. vi. fig. 2.
[6] Di alcuni elminti raccolti nel Sudan orientale, Genova, 1885, pp. 433, 434, pl. vii. fig. 14.

9. *Filaria paradiseæ*, n. sp. (Pl. II. figs. 6, 7).

From *Paradisea apoda*, Aru Islands, in the same tube as *Filaria flabellata*.

There is only one specimen—a male, which measures 19·2 mm. in length and 0·38 mm. in breadth, the proportion of breadth and length being thus 1 : 52. The body is decidedly elongated, narrowing rapidly after the head. The latter bears two small round lips. The œsophagus occupies $\frac{1}{20}$ of the entire length, and is 0·036 mm. in breadth ; the tail portion measures only $\frac{1}{112}$ of the whole. The cuticle is distantly wrinkled. The tail end is rolled up in a spiral, and is on that account very difficult to study. One cylindrical spicule (0·098 mm. long by 0·049 mm. broad) was visible ; a second was not to be found. The very end is conically rounded. I was not able to study exactly the nature of the papillæ on the tail, since it was impossible to unroll the coil, or to place the object with the ventral surface directed upwards. Only this could be certainly demonstrated, that the above form is not identical with *Filaria flabellata*. An exact diagnosis was impossible with such scanty material.

10. *Prothelmins profundissima*, n. gen., n. sp. (Pl. II. figs. 8–10).

Specimen labelled : " 3 March 1874. Depth 1950 fathoms."

The vessel contained two Nematodes, 58 and 65 mm. in length, 0·9 and 0·96 mm. in breadth respectively. The colour is yellowish, but the alimentary canal shines through as a blackish tract on the dorsal surface. Both extremities of the body are rounded, the posterior somewhat broader. The anus is situated 0·35 or 0·43 mm. from the tail end ; the latter occupies $\frac{1}{15}$ of the entire length. The œsophagus measures in one specimen 1·42 mm., the other 1·62 mm., and thus occupies about $\frac{1}{40}$ of the total length. Both head and tail ends are entirely devoid of papillæ, or other normal characteristics.

The cuticle is very firm and thick, measuring 0·084 mm. in transverse section, and consists of two systems of fibres crossing at an angle of 55°. The individual fibres are 0·0025 mm. in breadth. The cuticle is covered externally by a hyaline epidermis, 0·0033 mm. in thickness.

Below the cuticle is a muscular layer, 0·02 mm. in breadth. It belongs to the Holomyarian type as defined by Schneider, and consists of longitudinal fibres, with an average breadth of 0·013 mm. Each fibre exhibits a row of vacuoles and a system of transverse striæ. In transverse sections the fibres lie with the long diameter of their spindle-shaped cross section disposed obliquely to the surface of the cuticle, and the vacuoles appear as dark median points. No interruption of the muscular sheath by lateral, dorsal, or ventral ridges was to be observed.

The body-cavity is filled by the alimentary canal, which is attached to the dorsal surface of the body-wall. It is coloured black by pigment balls, 0·002 mm. in size. The cavity also contains a colourless, partly granular, partly hyaline, protoplasmic mass.

No reproductive organs were developed.

The internal wall of the musculature bears a simple layer of non-nucleated cells.

The slightest injury to the animal causes the epidermis to roll up, and the same happens to a less extent with the cuticular fibres, and still less with the muscles. This is not to be wondered at when we remember the enormous pressure to which the animal is subjected at a depth of 11,000 to 12,000 feet. All elastic membranes and fibres roll up when suddenly relieved from a great pressure or strain to which they have been subjected. The very firm and hard cuticle can obviously bear a great pressure. The species appears to spend its entire life free, for the head end exhibits no boring apparatus by which the worm might penetrate the organs of other animals. The specimens are all without reproductive organs, and may be described as larval. They are the largest free-living Nematode larvæ as yet known, and the adult form must be one of the largest free-living Nematodes.

It is unfortunate that no sexually mature specimens were found, as they could not but have exhibited peculiarities, probably more marked than those which make even the larvæ interesting.

The most closely related genera are *Gordius* and *Mermis*, which are, however, destitute of an anus, and parasitic in their larval life. The musculature of the above-described genus is markedly peculiar, and quite different from that observed in other Nematodes.

B. CESTODA.

11. *Tænia clavulus*, n. sp. (Pl. II. figs. 11, 12).

Specimen labelled : " *Tænia* from intestine of *Ptilorhis alberti*, Cape York."

The vessel contains numerous fragments of *Tæniæ*, which probably belong to two specimens, and also the anterior portion of a proglottis chain with the attached scolex. The latter is oval, 0·84 mm. long by 0·6 mm. broad, the suckers are elongated (0·3 mm.), situated on the anterior third of the scolex, and exhibit firm, prominent, almost contiguous margins. The apical surface of the scolex bears a smaller fifth sucker, 0·084 mm. in diameter, armed with a double row of nail-shaped rods. These have not the usual form of *Tænia* hooks, are very small (only 0·011 mm.), and number about sixty. The first proglottides measure 0·29 mm. in breadth and 0·048 mm. in length ; the last are 1·1 mm. broad and 0·72 mm. long. The segmentation begins about 0·9 mm. behind the scolex.

Helminths have not been previously observed in *Ptilorhis alberti*, Elliot.[1]

[1] Report on the Birds, Zool. Chall. Exp., part viii. p. 67.

The nail or thorn-shaped armature of the fifth sucker recalls that of *Tænia australis*, Krabbe,[1] but in the latter they form the apparatus of attachment of the four large suckers. The suckers are also armed with spines in *Tænia friedbergeri*, von Linstow, from *Phasianus colchicus; Tænia frontina*, Dujardin, from *Picus viridis;* and *Tænia infundibuliformis*, Goeze, from *Gallus domesticus.*

12. *Tænia increscens*, n. sp. (Pl. II. figs. 13, 14).

Specimen labelled: "*Tænia* from *Hæmatopus unicolor*,[2] from Hardy Bay, New Zealand."

Of this form there is only one specimen, which measured 54 mm. in length. The scolex is pear-shaped, 0·6 mm. long and 0·4 mm. broad. The apex bears a small pear-shaped rostellum, not armed with hooks. The suckers which lie in the anterior third of the scolex are spherical, and have a small aperture directed forwards. The so-called neck is in comparison very thin and delicate, and measures 0·11 mm. in breadth. At a distance of 6 mm. from the scolex the body suddenly expands, increasing both in breadth and thickness. Directly behind the scolex the limy bodies in the proglottides begin to appear. The first proglottides are 0·06 mm. long and 0·3 mm. broad; the last are 0·54 mm. long, 2·5 mm. broad, and 1·5 mm. thick. In the last proglottides the formation of ova has begun, but no mature ova are yet developed. The ova are apparently spherical, and have two envelopes, of which the outer measures 0·066 mm., and the inner 0·046 mm., while the oncosphere measures 0·033 mm.

13. *Tænia diomedeæ*, n. sp. (?).

Specimen labelled: "Tæniodes from Stomach of *Diomedea brachyura*,[3] No. 244, 28th June 1873, Pacific."

The vessel contains seven specimens and several fragments. In none, however, was the scolex present. The same vessel contained a specimen of *Tetrabothrium torulosum*, mentioned below.

No final designation is possible, since the absence of scolex implies the absence of diagnostic characteristics. The maximum length was 250 mm.; the anterior proglottides are 0·58 mm. in breadth, and 0·12 mm. in length; while those furthest back measure 1·9 by 0·78 mm. The development of the male reproductive organs begins about 120 mm. from the anterior end. The cirri occur on one side. The ova are not yet developed.

This form is, perhaps, identical with *Tænia sulciceps*, Baird,[4] which is found in *Diomedea exulans*, but the absence of the scolex leaves this undecided.

[1] Bidrag til Kundskab om Fuglenes Bændelorme, K. dansk. Vidensk. Selsk. Skriv, 5 R. B4. viii. pp. 95, 96, pl. i. figs. 296-299.
[2] *Hæmatopus unicolor, jr.* (f), Report on the Birds, Zool. Chall. Exp., part viii. p. 115.
[3] *Diomedea brachyura*, Tenim., op. cit., pp. 147, 148.
[4] Proc. Zool. Soc. Lond., 1859, p. 111; Ann. and Mag. Nat. Hist., ser. 3, vol. iv. p. 240, 1859.

14. *Tænia trichoglossi*, n. sp. (?) (Pl. II. fig. 15).

Specimen labelled : " *Tænia* from intestine of *Trichoglossus swainsoni*,[1] from Cape York, Australia."

The vessel contained nine fragments of a *Tænia*, but without a scolex. The most anterior proglottides are 0·18 mm. in length, and 0·84 mm. in breadth, while those furthest back are 1·1 mm. long by 2·1 mm. broad. The largest fragment measures 80 mm., and the chain of proglottides has a wreath-like form. The specimens possibly belong to *Tænia leptosoma*, Diesing, found in various Parrots. The ova are spherical, and have two transparent sheaths, of which the outer measures 0·036 mm., and the inner 0·026. The oncosphere has an elliptical contour, and measures 0·023 mm. in length by 0·018 mm. in breadth.

15. *Tetrabothrium torulosum*, n. sp. (Pl. II. figs. 16, 17).

This form was in the same tube as *Tænia diomedeæ*; its locality of occurrence was therefore the stomach of *Diomedea brachyura*, Temm. The vessel contained three specimens and four fragments. The length of the largest animal was 175 mm., the breadth 0·84 mm., increasing to 5 mm. posteriorly, with a thickness in the same region of 2 mm. The scolex is 1 mm. in breadth, and 0·96 mm. in length. No proglottides are recognisable, but the body exhibits close folds about 0·12 mm. in length. The body is very compact. The intact adult must be very long, for even in the posterior portion of the not inconsiderable length, no mature ova are to be seen. One only finds spherical balls, 0·023 mm. in diameter, from which the ova probably develop. The large scolex exhibits on both ventral and dorsal surface a pair of three-cornered suckers surrounded by strongly developed coiled pads. The lateral lines also exhibit strong protrusions, and further back there is a second pair. The folding of the body is characteristic of *Tetrabothrium*, and so is the form of the scolex and suckers.

16. *Tetrabothrium auriculatum*, n. sp. (Pl. II. figs. 18–20).

Specimen labelled : " *Tænia* from the intestines of *Thalassæca glacialoides*,[2] February 22, 1874, Antarctic Ocean ;" and also specimen labelled : " *Tetrabothrium* from *Daption capensis*,[3] October 10, 1873, South Atlantic."

The animal attained a length of 112 mm. The scolex is 0·48 mm. in breadth, and 0·34 mm. in length. The four powerful suckers occupy almost the whole of the scolex, and each exhibits anteriorly and externally a round, ear-shaped protrusion. The apex bears a round protrusion, while the ventral and dorsal surfaces show on either side three

[1] *Trichoglossus swainsoni*, Gould, Report on the Birds, Zool. Chall. Exp., part viii. p. 90.
[2] *Thalassæca glacialoides*, Smith, op. cit., p. 142.   [3] *Daption capensis*, Linn., op. cit., p. 144.

small apertures, which appear to be the openings of the water vascular system. At a distance of 0·6 mm. behind the scolex the segmentation begins. The first proglottides are 0·012 mm. long and 0·41 mm. broad, those in the middle are 0·29 mm. by 1·64 mm., while those furthest back measure 0·42 mm. in length by 2·5 mm. in breadth. Immediately behind the scolex calcareous bodies begin to appear. They are found even in that part of the former which is in direct connection with the proglottis. The generative apertures occur on one side, not however quite marginally, as in the *Tæniæ*, nor yet in the median line of the joint surface as in *Bothriocephali*, but in the anterior third of the proglottis at a distance of 0·066 mm. from the margin. The cylindrical cirrus is protruded to a length of 0·082 mm., and is 0·016 mm. in breadth. In *Thalassœca* and *Daption* no Helminths have been previously observed, and in the related genera, such as *Diomedea* and *Procellaria*, no *Tetrabothria*.

Survey of Helminths in Relation to their Hosts.

	Host.	Name of Helminth.	Organ of Occurrence.
Mammal.	*Otaria jubata*,	*Ascaris simplex*,	stomach.
Bird.	*Trichoglossus swainsoni*,	*Tænia trichoglossi*.	
,,	*Ptilorhis alberti*,	*Tænia clavata*,	stomach.
,,	*Paradisea apoda*,	*Filaria paradisea*.	
,,	*Paradisea apoda*,	*Filaria flabellata*,	below skin and in abdominal cavity.
,,	*Hæmatopus unicolor*,	*Tænia increscens*.	
,,	*Phalacrocorax verrucosus*,	*Filaria cirrohamata*,	stomach.
,,	*Phalacrocorax verrucosus*,	*Ascaris spiculigera*,	stomach.
,,	*Thalassœca glacialis*,	*Tetrabothrium auriculatum*,	stomach.
,,	*Daption capensis*,	*Tetrabothrium auriculatum*.	
,,	*Diomedea brachyura*,	*Ascaris diomedeæ*,	stomach.
,,	*Diomedea brachyura*,	*Tænia diomedeæ*,	stomach.
Fish.	*Macrurus rudis*,	*Ascaris macruri*.	
,,	*Macrurus sp.* (?)	*Ascaris macruroidei*,	stomach.
	Unknown,	*Ascaris biloba*.	
	Free in deep sea,	*Prothelmins profundissima*.	

APPENDIX.

Representatives of the Acanthocephala, Trematoda, and Gordiacea are not totally wanting in the Challenger collection, but there were none among the specimens sent to me, because only a few very delicate larval forms were discovered, and these had already been described by the authors who treated of their hosts. In the Reports already published the following species are mentioned, for the knowledge of which I have to thank Mr. John Murray.

C. ACANTHOCEPHALA.

Echinorhynchus corrugatus, Sars.

> *Echinorhynchus corrugatus*, G. O. Sars, Report on the Schizopoda, Zool. Chall. Exp., vol. xiii. part xxxvii. pp. 221, 222, pl. xxxviii. figs. 15–18.

A large larval form, that occurs in the cavity of the abdomen of *Euphausia pellucida*, Dana.

D. TREMATODA.

Distomum filiferum, Sars.

> *Distomum filiferum*, G. O. Sars, op. cit., p. 222, pl. xxxviii. figs. 19–23.

Larva from the abdominal cavity of *Nematoscelis megalops*, Sars, and *Thysanoëssa gregaria*, Sars.

Distomum glauci, Bergh.

> *Distomum glauci*, Bgh., Report on the Nudibranchiata, Zool. Chall. Exp., vol. x. part xxvi. p. 18, pl. x. figs. 5–17.
>
> *Distomum glauci*, Bgh., K. dansk. Vidensk. Selsk. Skrift., R. 5, Bd. vii., 1864, pp. 282–283.

This species was found in *Glaucus glacialis*, Bergh, and *Glaucus longicirrus*, Rhdt., and in the Challenger expedition it was discovered by the same author in *Glaucus atlanticus*, Forster, and described and figured. It also is a larval form, and destined to attain its definitive sexual development in some other animal.

E. GORDIACEA.

Dr. R. v. Willemoes Suhm mentions in his letters from the Challenger[1] a *Gordius* found in a Crab dredged near New Zealand and another in an Orthopteron without wings from the same island, where species of *Gordius* are also said to be very common in water.

[1] Challenger Briefe, pp. 103, 107.

CONTENTS.

PLATE I.

(ZOOL. CHALL. EXP.—PART LXXI.—1888.)—Bbbb.

PLATE I.

Fig. 1. Animal; natural size.
Fig. 2. Upper lip, from dorsal aspect.
Fig. 3. Lips, viewed from the anterior aspect. *a,* Upper lip; *b,* mouth aperture; *c,* lower lip.
Fig. 4. Ovum.

Fig. 5. Animal; natural size.
Fig. 6. Head end, with upper lip and accessory lips (*a*).
Fig. 7. Tail end of male.

Fig. 8. Animal; natural size.
Fig. 9. Head end, from dorsal surface.

Fig. 10. Animal; natural size.
Fig. 11. Head end, from dorsal surface.

Fig. 12. Animal; natural size.
Fig. 13. Head end, from dorsal surface. *a,* Neck papillæ.

Fig. 14. Animal; natural size.
Fig. 15. Head end. *a,* Neck papillæ.
Fig. 16. Tail end of the male, from the ventral surface.

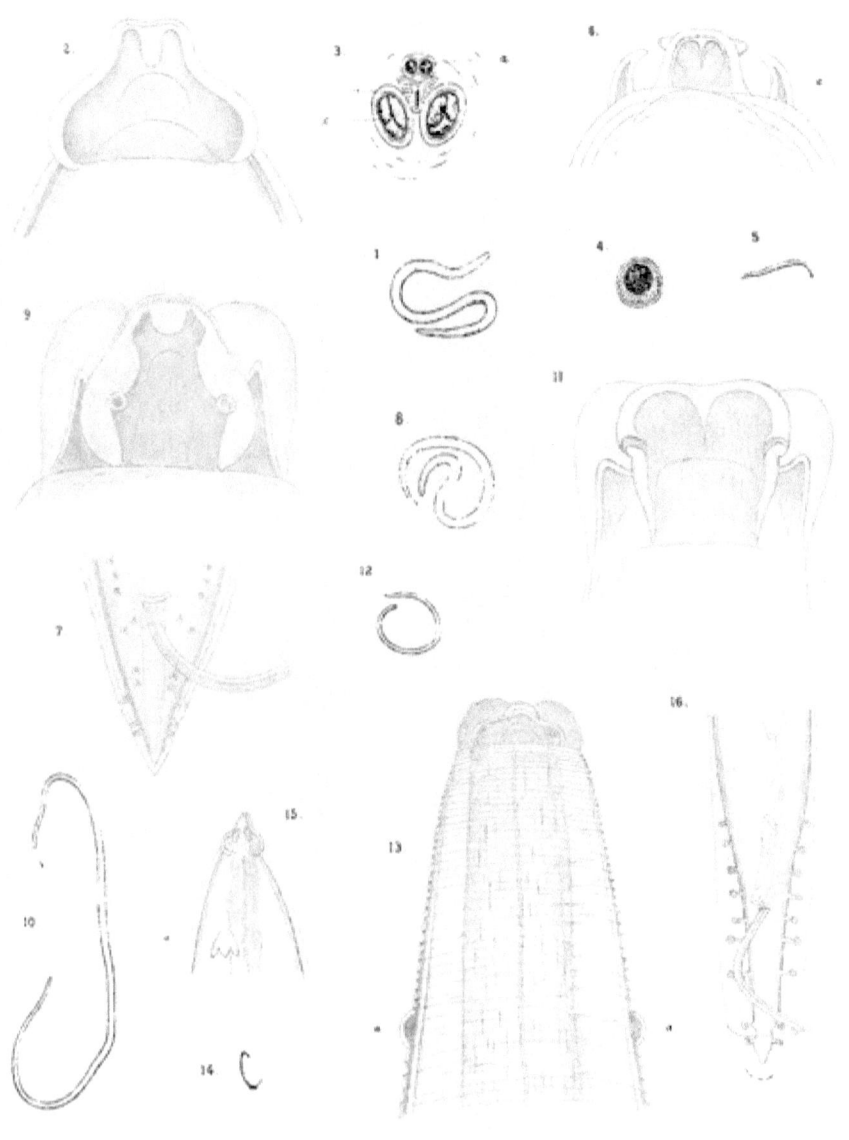

1-4. ASCARIS SIMPLEX, Rud.   5-7. ASCARIS SPICULIGERA, Rud.   8, 9. ASCARIS BILOBA, n sp
10, 11. ASCARIS MACRURI, n sp   12, 13. ASCARIS DIOMEDEA, n sp   14-16. FILARIA CIRROHAMATA, n sp

PLATE II.

PLATE II.

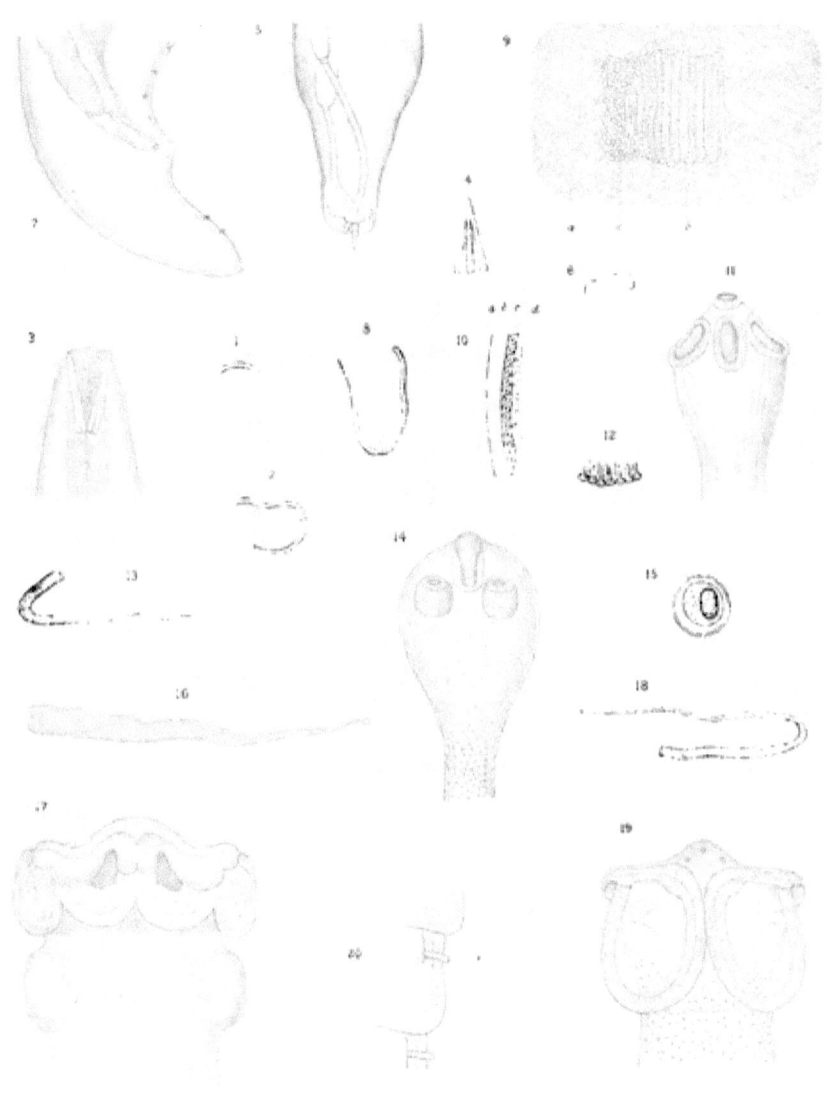

1-5. FILARIA FLABELLATA, n. sp.   6,7 FILARIA PARADISEÆ, n. sp.   8-10 PROTHELMINS PROFUNDISSIMA n. gen., n. sp.
11,12. TÆNIA CLAVULUS, n. sp.   13,14. TÆNIA INCRESCENS, n. sp.   15. TÆNIA TRICHOGLOSSI, n. sp.
16,17. TETRABOTHRIUM TORULOSUM, n. sp.   18-20. TETRABOTHRIUM AURICULATUM, n. sp.

VOYAGE OF H.M.S. CHALLENGER.

ZOOLOGY.

REPORT on the HETEROPODA collected by H.M.S. Challenger during the Years 1873-76. By EDGAR A. SMITH, F.Z.S., Assistant in the Zoological Department of the British Museum.

INTRODUCTION.

THE collection of Heteropoda submitted to me for examination and description consists of a number of dead shells of Atlantidæ, which were dredged at various stations in the Atlantic and Pacific Oceans, and of a few specimens of the same family and others belonging to the Pterotracheidæ which were obtained occasionally by surface dredging. Most of the latter specimens are not in very good condition, the majority being more or less mutilated, so that their identification has been all the more difficult and in some cases impossible.

As no list of the species of this group of Mollusca has been attempted for many years, it was suggested by Mr. John Murray that I should compile a synonymic catalogue of the various families, genera, and species, which might prove of service to those who may have occasion to study the Heteropoda.

Such a catalogue I have prepared, and have endeavoured to make the references as complete as the leisure time[1] at my disposal would allow. The chronological sequence has been adopted in order that the priority of names can be seen at a glance and the progressive knowledge of each species the more readily traced.

[1] The collection was placed in my hands on October 1, 1887.

CONTENTS.

LITERATURE OF THE SUBJECT.

Besides the accounts relating to the Heteropoda which are given in the various manuals on Mollusca by Rang, Woodward, Philippi, H. and A. Adams, Chenu, Tryon, Fischer, and others, several more detailed narratives are to be found in the works of d'Orbigny, Souleyet, Huxley, Krohn, Leuckart, Gegenbaur, Macdonald, &c.

A very excellent work upon this group of animals by Keferstein, which was published in Bronn's Thierreich,[2] gives a detailed account of the knowledge of this subclass of Mollusca up to the year 1866.

The work commences with an introductory chapter (pp. 809–813), containing (1) a historical account of the study of this group of animals; (2) some observations upon the various names which have been applied to it; and (3) a list of the principal works which treat upon the subject.

The second chapter (pp. 814–835) enters very fully into the external structure and the internal anatomy; the third (pp. 835–838) is devoted to the history of the development of these animals; the fourth (pp. 838–843) gives an account of the economy, their pelagic mode of life, the positions in which they swim and the food they subsist on. The fifth chapter (pp. 843–850) discusses the classification of the Heteropods, their natural position in the systematic arrangement of the Mollusca, gives succinctly the characters which distinguish the group, and concludes with diagnoses of the families and genera. The sixth and last chapter (pp. 851–852) treats upon the distribution of the species, both recent and fossil.

Such being the scope of this work, it may in the main be consulted as a sound text-book upon this branch of Mollusca. It would therefore be of little use to reproduce in this Report a detailed account of the Heteropoda (as at one time I thought of doing) such as that set forth in Keferstein's treatise; but several very important memoirs have been published since the production of that work which give further information respecting

[2] Die Klassen und Ordnungen des Thierreichs, vol. iii. pt. ii. pp. 809–852, pls. 68–70.

the anatomy, histology, and development of certain groups, and of these the following
are the principal :—

1869. BOLL, Beiträge zur vergleichenden Histiologie des Molluskentypus, pp. 1–112, pls. i.–iv., 1869.

1871. BATTRAY, On the Anatomy, Physiology, and Distribution of the Firolida. Trans. Linn. Soc. Lond.,
      vol. xxvii. p. 255, pls. xliii., xliv.

1875. RANKE, Der Gehörvoegang und das Gehörorgan bei Pterotrachea. Zeitschr. f. wiss. Zool., 1875,
      Suppl. vol. xxv. pp. 77–102, pl. v.

1876. RANKE, Das acustische Organ im Ohre der Pterotrachea. Archiv f. mikrosk. Anat., 1876, vol. xii.
      pp. 565–569.

1876. FOL, Sur le développement embryonnaire et larvaire des Hétéropodes. Arch. d. Zool. Expér., 1876,
      vol. v. pp. 105–158, pls. i.–iv.

1876. CLAUS, Das Gehörorgan der Heteropoden. Archiv f. mikrosk. Anat., 1876, vol. xii. pp. 103–117, pl. x.

1877. EDINGER, Die Endigung der Hautnerven bei Pterotrachea. Archiv f. mikrosk. Anat., 1877, vol. xiv.
      pp. 171–176, pl. xi.

1878. CLAUS, Ueber den acustischen Apparat im Gehörorgan der Heteropoden. Archiv f. mikrosk. Anat.,
      1878, vol. xv. pp. 341–348.

1880. KRUKENBERG, Die pendelartigen Bewegungen des Fusses von Carinaria mediterranea. Vergleich.
      Physiol. Studien, 1880, pp. 177–180.

1885. PANETH, Beiträge zur Histiologie der Pteropoden und Heteropoden. Archiv f. mikrosk. Anat., 1885,
      vol. xxiv. pp. 230–288, pls. xiv.–xvi.

1886. WARLOMONT, Étude de quelques points de la structure des Firoles. Journ. Anatomie et Physiol.,
      1886, vol. xxii. pp. 331–350, pl. xii.

1886. GRENACHER, Abhandlungen zur vergleichenden Anatomie des Auges. II. Das Auge der Hetero-
      poden. 2 plates, 65 pages, Abhandl. naturf. Gesellsch. Halle, vol. xvii.

Family PTEROTRACHEIDÆ.

Pterotrachea, n. sp. (?)	Off Banda, September 29, 1874.
,, (?)	North Atlantic, January 28, 1873.
,, (?)	Off Boston, U.S.
Firoloida desmaresti,	South Atlantic, March 2 and 3, 1876.
Cardiopoda placenta,	Off Arrou Island, September 23, 1874.
,, sp. jun.,	North Pacific, July 4, 1875.
Carinaria cristata,	Near Papua, September 15, 1875. Also Station 218, North of Papua, at bottom.
,, ,, (?) jun.,	North of the Admiralty Islands, March 16, 1875.
,, *lamarcki* (?) jun.,	Station 84, at bottom.
Carinaria, n. sp. (?),	North Atlantic, January 28, 1873.
,, sp. fry,	Station 24, at bottom.
,, sp. jun.,	Station 185, at bottom.

Family ATLANTIDÆ.

Atlanta peronii,	Stations[1] 23, 24, 33, 75, 78, 85, 120, 122, at bottom. Also at surface, near Cape York, August 25, 26, 1874; North of New Guinea, February 1875; Pacific, July 12, 21, 1875; Mid-Pacific Ocean, September 6, 1875.
Atlanta inflata,	Stations 33, 85, 104, at bottom.
Atlanta lesueurii,	Stations 23, 33, at bottom.
Atlanta gaudichaudi,	Station 185, bottom. Also at surface, West Pacific, February 1875.
Atlanta souleyeti,	Stations 23, 24, 33, 75, 78, 85, 120, 122, at bottom.

---

[1] Stations 23, 24, 33, 75, 78, 84, and 85, are North Atlantic; 120 and 122, South Atlantic; Station 185, Torres Strait, North Australia.

Atlanta fusca, . Stations 23, 24, 33, 75, 85, 120, 122, 185, at bottom. Also at surface, off Kandavu, Fiji, August 11, 12, 1874 ; near Cape York, August 25, 26, 1874 ; North Pacific, July 21, 1875.

Atlanta inclinata, . Stations 23, 24, 33, 120, 122, 185, at bottom. Also at surface, North Pacific, July 21, 1875.

Oxygyrus keraudrenii, At surface, South Atlantic, March 2, 3, and April 28, 1876.

SYNONYMY OF THE HETEROPODA.

MOLLUSCA.

Class GASTROPODA.

Subclass HETEROPODA.

1812. *Hétéropodes*, Lamarck, Extrait du cours de Zool., p. 124.
1821. *Gasteropterophora*, Gray, London Medical Repository, vol. xv. p. 235.
1822. *Hétéropodes*, Lamarck, Anim. sans Vert., vol. vii. p. 669; ed. 2, vol. xi. p. 373.
1822.   „   Férussac, Tabl. syst., p. xxxvii.
1824. *Nucleobranchiata*, Blainville, Dict. d. Sci. Nat., vol. xxxii. p. 282.
1824. *Heteropoda*, Children, Quart. Journ. Sci. Lit. and Arts, vol. xvi. p. 256.
1825. *Urobranchia (partim)*, Latreille, Fam. nat. Règne anim., p. 173.
1825. *Heteropodes*, Eschscholtz, Oken's Isis, p. 735.
1825. *Nucleobranchiata*, Blainville, Dict. d. Sci. Nat., vol. xxxv. p. 212.
1825.   „   *id.*, Man. de Malacol., p. 491.
1827. *Nucléobranches*, Rang, Mem. Soc. Hist. Nat., vol. iii. p. 372.
1828. *Caryobranchiata*, Menke, Synopsis Moll., p. 5 ; ed. 2 (1830), p. 9.
1829. *Nucléobranches*, Rang, Man. Moll., p. 119.
1830. *Hétéropodes*, Cuvier, Règne Anim., ed. 2, vol. iii. pp. viii, 66.
1830.   „   Deshayes, Encycl. Méthod., vol. ii. p. 270.
1832. *Nucléobranches*, *id.*, loc. cit., vol. iii. p. 632.
1832. *Heteropoda*, Wiegmann and Ruthe, Handbuch d. Zool., p. 517.
1833. *Heteropoden*, Oken, Naturgesch., p. 553.
1834. *Heteropoda*, Gray, Griffith's Anim. Kingd., vol. xii. p. 49.
1836.   „   d'Orbigny, Voy. Amér. Mérid., vol. v. p. 139.
1838. *Nucléobranches*, Potiez and Michaud, Galerie Moll., vol. i. p. 47.
1839. *Heteropoda*, d'Orbigny, Hist. Nat. Canaries Moll., p. 34.
1839. *Heteropoden*, Krohn, Müller's Archiv f. Anat. u. Physiol., p. 333 (On the Eyes).
1839. *Heteropoda*, Anton, Verzeich. Conch., p. 27.

1841. *Nucleobranchiata*, d'Orbigny, Sagra's Hist. Cuba, Moll., vol. i. p. 93.

1841. *Heteropoda*, Cantraine, Malacol. Médit., p. 35.

1841. *Nucleobranchiata*, Reeve, Proc. Zool. Soc. Lond., p. 74.

1842.   „   *id.*, Conch. Syst., vol. ii. p. 55.

1842.   „   d'Orbigny, Pal. franç. Terr. Crét., vol. ii. p. 16.

1843.   „   Forbes, Report Brit. Assoc., p. 132.

1843. *Heteropoda*, Gravenhorst, Vergleich. Zool., p. 65.

1843. *Heteropoden*, Oken, Lehrbuch Naturphil., ed. 3, p. 459.

1845. *Nucleobranchiata*, Geinitz, Grundriss der Verstein., p. 317.

1845.   „   Catlow, Conch. Nomencl., p. 116.

1845. *Heteropoda*, Gravenhorst, Das Thierr. nach d. Verwandt., p. 33.

1847.   „   Lovèn, Öfversigt k. Vetensk.-Akad. Förhandl., p. 191 (Dentition).

1850. *Heteropods*, Johnston, Introd. Conch., pp. 106, 118, 119.

1850. *Nucleobranchiata*, Jay, Cat. Shells, ed. 4, p. 114.

1852. *Heteropoda*, Huxley, Ann. and Mag. Nat. Hist., vol. x. p. 455 (Anatomy).

1852. *Hétéropodes*, Souleyet, Voy. "Bonite" Zool., vol. ii. p. 289.

1853.   „   Verany, Journ. de Conchyl., vol. iv. p. 381.

1853. *Heteropoden*, Gegenbaur, Zeitschr. f. wiss. Zool., Bd. iv. p. 335 (Anatomy).

1853. *Heteropoda*, Philippi, Handbuch Conch., p. 281.

1854. *Heteropoden*, Leuckart, Zool. Untersuch., Heft iii. pp. 3–68.

1854. *Nucleobranchiata*, Woodward, Man. Moll., pp. 197, 451.

1854. *Heteropoden*, Gegenbaur, Zeitschr. f. wiss. Zool., Bd. v. p. 113 (On the Excretory
          Organ).

1855.   „   *id.*, Untersuch. Pteropoden und Heteropoden, pp. 101–185, 213.

1856.   „   Krohn, Archiv f. Anat. u. Physiol., pp. 515–522 (Development).

1856. *Heteropoda*, Troschel, Gebiss d. Schneck., vol. i. pp. 39–46.

1857.   „   Gray, System. Arrang. Moll., p. 131.

1857. *Heteropoden*, Krohn, Müller's Archiv f. Anat. u. Physiol., p. 466 (Development).

1858. *Heteropoda*, Owen, Encycl. Brit., vol. xv. p. 375.

1860. *Nucleobranchiata*, Reeve, Elements Conch., vol. ii. p. 42.

1860. *Heteropoden*, Krohn, Beiträge Entwick. Pterop. und Heterop., p. 4.

1866. *Heteropoda*, Keferstein, Bronn's Thierreich, vol. iii. pt. 2, pp. 809–852.

1869. *Heteropoda*, Boll, Beiträge vergl. Histiol. Moll., pp. 6, 57, 75, 97.

1873.   „   Weinkauff, Cat. Europ. Meer. Conch., p. xiii.

1876. *Hétéropodes*, Fol, Arch. d. Zool. Expér., vol. v. p. 105, pl. 1–4 (Development).

1876. *Heteropoden*, Claus, Archiv f. mikrosk. Anat., vol. xii. p. 103, pl. x. (On the
          Organ of Hearing).

1878.   „   *id.*, *op. cit.*, vol. xv. p. 341, pl. xxi. (On the Acoustic Apparatus
          in the Organ of Hearing).

1878. *Heteropoda*, Kobelt, Illust. Conchylienbuch, p. 25.

1880. „ Hutton, Man. New Zeal. Moll., p. 118.

1883. „ Fewkes, Amer. Natur., vol. xvii. p. 206 (The Sucker on the Fin not a Sexual Characteristic).

1883. *Azygobranchia*, section *Natantia*, Lankester, Ency. Brit., vol. xvi. p. 653.

1883. *Nucleobranchiates*, Amer. Cyclopæd., vol. xii. p. 530.

1883. *Nucleobranchiata*, Tryon, Struct. Syst. Conch., vol. ii. p. 347.

1883. „ Fischer, Man. Conch., p. 573.

1884. „ Grasset, Index Test. vivent., p. 146.

1885. *Heteropoden*, Paneth, Archiv f. mikrosk. Anat., vol. xxiv. pp. 230-288, pls. xiv.-xvi. (Histology).

1886. „ Grenacher, Abhandl. d. naturf. Gesellsch. zu Halle, vol. xvii., two plates (On the Eyes).

Family I. PTEROTRACHEIDÆ.

1810. *Pterapoda* (*partim*), Péron et Lesueur, Ann. Mus. Hist. Nat., vol. xv. pp. 58, 64.

1814. *Ptenchidia*, Rafinesque-Schmaltz, Précis des découv., p. 29.

1822. *Pterotrachiæ*, Ferussac, Tab. Syst., p. xxvii.

1824. *Nectopoda*, Blainville, Dict. d. Sci. Nat., vol. xxxii. p. 282.

1825. „ *id.*, Man. Moll., p. 491.

1829. *Firolides*, Rang, Man. Moll., p. 120.

1830. „ Deshayes, Ency. Méth., vol. ii. p. 130.

1830. *Pterotrachies*, *id.*, Ency. Méth., vol. iii. p. 860.

1832. *Firolida*, Wiegmann and Ruthe, Handb. d. Zool., p. 518.

1833. *Pterotrachean*, Oken, Naturgesch., vol. iv. p. 553.

1836. *Nucleobranchiotes*, d'Orbigny, Voy. Amér. mérid., vol. v. p. 130.

1838. *Firolidæ*, Potiez and Michaud, Gal. Moll., vol. i. p. 47.

1840. *Pterotracheidæ*, Gray, Synop. Brit. Mus., p. 148.

1841. „ *id.*, *loc. cit.*, p. 126.

1841. *Carinariana*, Reeve, Proc. Zool. Soc. Lond., p. 74.

1842. *Firolidæ*, d'Orbigny, Paléont. Franç., Terr. crét., vol. ii. p. 18.

1843. *Pterotracheidæ*, Gray, Dieffenbach's New Zeal., p. 244.

1843. *Pterotrachean*, Oken, Lehrbuch Naturphil., ed. 3, p. 459.

1844. *Pterotracheidæ*, Gray, Rev. Zool., p. 358.

1846. *Firolina*, Agassiz, Nomen. Zool. Univ., p. 155.

1846. *Pterotracheoidæ*, *id.*, *op. cit.*, p. 315.

1850. *Pterotracheidæ*, Gray, Fig. Moll. Anim., vol. iv. p. 99.

1852. *Firoles*, Milne-Edwards, Ann. d. Sci. Nat., vol. xvii. p. 146 (On the Auditory Organ)

1854. *Firolidæ*, Woodward, Man. Moll., p. 199.

1854. *Pterotracheidæ*, H. and A. Adams, Gen. Moll., vol. ii. p. 92.

1855. { *Firolida*, Carinariæta, } Gegenbaur, Untersuch. Pterop. und Heterop., p. 214.

1856. *Firolidæm*, Krohn, Müller's Archiv f. Anat. Physiol., p. 520 (Development).

1856. $\left\{ \begin{array}{l} Carinariacea, \\ Firolacea, \end{array} \right\}$ Troschel, Gebiss d. Schneck., vol. i. p. 43.

1857. *Pterotracheidæ*, Gray, Syst. Arrang. Moll., p. 131.

1859. *Firolidæ*, Chenu, Man. Conch., vol. i. p. 122.

1866. *Pterotracheacea*, Keferstein, Bronn's Thierreich, vol. iii. pt. 2, p. 850.

1868. *Firolidæ*, Weinkauff, Conch. Mittelm., vol. ii. p. 431.

1871. „ Rattray, Trans. Linn. Soc. Lond., vol. xxvii. p. 255, pls. xliii., xliv. (Anatomy, Physiology, Distribution).

1880. „ Hutton, Man. New Zeal. Moll., p. 118.

1883. „ Tryon, Struct. Syst. Conch., vol. ii. p. 348.

1883. $\left\{ \begin{array}{l} Pterotracheacea, \\ Carinariacea, \end{array} \right\}$ Lankester, Ency. Brit., vol. xvi. p. 654.

1883. $\left\{ \begin{array}{l} Pterotracheidæ, \\ Carinariidæ, \end{array} \right\}$ Fischer, Man. Conch., p. 578.

1884. *Carinariidæ*, Gramet, Index Test. vivent., p. 146.

Genus *Pterotrachea*, Forskål.

1775. *Pterotrachea*, Forskål, Descrip. Anim., p. 112.

1789. „ Gmelin, Syst. Nat., vol. vi. p. 3137.

1791. *Firola*, Bruguière, Tab. Ency. et méth., vol. i. pl. lxxxviii.

1801. *Pterotrachea*, Lamarck, Syst. des Anim., p. 61.

1803. *Pterotrachée*, Bosc, Nouv. dict. Hist. Nat., vol. viii. p. 483.

1805. *Pterotrachea*, Roissy, Hist. Nat. (Suite à Buffon), vol. v. p. 78.

1810. *Firola*, Péron et Lesueur, Ann. du Mus., vol. xv. pp. 64, 70–6.

1812. *Firola*, Lamarck, Extrait du cours de Zool., p. 125.

1814. *Hypterus*, Rafinesque-Schmaltz, Précis des decouv., p. 29.

1816. *Firole*, Blainville, Bull. Soc. Philom. Paris, p. 30.

1817. „ Lesueur, Bull. Soc. Philom. Paris, p. 157.

1817. *Firola*, *id.*, Journ. Acad. Nat. Sci. Philad., vol. i. p. 3.

1817. *Pterotrachea*, Bosc, Nouv. dict. Hist. Nat., vol. xii. p. 530.

1818. *Firola*, Oken, Isis, p. 1557.

1820. *Pterotrachea*, Blainville, Dict. d. Sci. Nat., vol. xvii. p. 62.

1821. „ Chamisso, Nova Acta Acad. Leop. Carol., vol. x. pt. 2, p. 346.

1821. „ Gray, London Medical Repository, 1821, vol. xv. p. 235.

1822. „ Lamarck, Anim. sans Vert., vol. vii. p. 675 ; ed. 2, vol. xi. p. 381.

1822. *Firola*, Férussac, Tab. Syst., p. xxxvii.

1824. *Pterotrachea*, Blainville, Dict. d. Sci. Nat., vol. xxxii. p. 282.

1825. „ *id.*, Man. Mal., p. 491.

1825. „ Chiaje, Mem. Stor. Anim. senza Vert., vol. ii. p. 193.

1825. „ Eschscholtz, Oken's Isis, p. 736.

1826. *Pterotrachea*, Risso, Hist. nat. Europ., vol. iv. p. 28.

1828. „ Heusinger, Zeitschr. f. Organ. Phys., vol. ii. p. 194–6.

1829. „ Chiaje, Mem. Stor. Anim. senza Vert., vol. iv. p. 197.

1829. *Firola*, Rang, Man. Moll., p. 120.

1830. „ Cuvier, Règne Anim., ed. 2, vol. iii. p. 69.

1830. *Pterotrachea*, Bosc, Hist. nat., vers, ed. 2, vol. i. p. 63.

1830. „ Deshayes, Ency. Méth., vol. ii. p. 127 ; 1832, vol. iii. p. 859.

1830. *Hiptère*, *id.*, loc. cit., vol. ii. p. 284.

1832. *Pterotrachea*, Wiegmann and Ruthe, Handb. d. Zool., p. 518.
1834. *Firola*, Gray, Griffith's Anim. King., vol. xii. p. 51.
1835. *Pterotrachea*, Oken, Naturgesch., vol. v. p. 513.
1836. *Firola*, d'Orbigny, Voy. Amér. mérid., vol. v. pp. 145, 150.
1836. *Anops*, *id.*, *op. cit.*, p. 140.
1838. *Firola*, Potiez and Michaud, Galer. Moll., vol. i. p. 47.
1838.   „   Eydoux and Souleyet, L'Institut, vol. vi. p. 376 (Auditory Organ).
1841.   „   Cantraine, Mal. Medit., p. 42.
1841. *Pterotrachea*, Chiaje, Descriz. e notom. anim. invert. Sicil., vol. ii. p. 93.
1842.   „   Gray, Synopsis Brit. Mus., pp. 65, 90.
1842. *Firola*, d'Orbigny, Paléont. franç., Terr. crét., vol. ii. p. 18.
1842. *Anops*, d'Orbigny, *loc. cit.*, p. 18.
1843. *Firola*, Forbes, Rep. Brit. Assoc., p. 132.
1843. *Pterotrachea*, Chiaje, Rendiconti Accad. Sci. Soc. Borbon. Napoli, vol. ii. p. 106.
1850. *Firole*, Huxley, Ann. d. Sci. Nat., vol. xiv. p. 193.
1850. *Pterotrachea*, Gray, Fig. Moll. Anim., vol. iv. p. 100.
1850. *Anops*, *ibid.*, *loc. cit.*, p. 100.
1852. *Firola*, Souleyet, Voy. "Bonite," Zool., vol. ii. p. 345.
1853.   „   Leuckart, Wiegmann's Archiv f. Naturgesch., p. 253.
1853. *Pterotrachea*, Philippi, Handbuch Conch., p. 284.
1853. *Anops*, *id.*, *op. cit.*, p. 284.
1854. *Firola*, Woodward, Man. Moll., p. 199.
1854.   „   Leuckart, Zool. Untersuch., Theil iii. pp. 3–68.
1855. *Pterotrachea*, Untersuch. Pterop. und Heterop., pp. 153, 214.
1855.   „   H. and A. Adams, Gen. Moll., vol. ii. p. 94.
1856.   „   Troschel. Gebiss d. Schneck., vol. i. p. 44.
1856.   „   Krohn, Müller's Archiv f. Anat. Physiol., p. 520.
1857.   „   Gray, Syst. Arrang. Moll., p. 131.
1857. *Anops*, *id.*, *op. cit.*, p. 131.
1859. *Firola*, Chenu, Man. Conch., vol. i. p. 123.
1859. *Anops*, *id.*, *op. cit.*, p. 123.
1860. *Pterotrachea*, Krohn, Beiträge Entwick. Pterop. und Heterop., p. 26.
1863. *Firola*, Macdonald, Trans. Roy. Soc. Edin., vol. xxiii. p. 189, pl. ix. fig. 4 (Anatomy).
1866. *Pterotrachea*, Keferstein, Bronn's Thierreich, vol. iii. pt. 2, p. 850.
1869.   „   Boll, Beiträge vergleich. Histiol. Moll., p. 11.
1871. *Firola*, Macdonald, Quart. Journ. Micr. Sci. (series 2), vol. xi. p. 274, woodcut (buccal teeth).
1873. *Pterotrachea*, Weinkauff, Cat. Europ. Meer. Conch., p. 44.
1875.   „   Hanke, Zeitschr. f. wiss. Zool., Suppl. Bd. xxv. p. 77, pl. v. (On the Auditory Organ).
1876.   „   *id.*, Archiv f. mikrosk. Anat., vol. xii. p. 564 (On the Acoustic Organ of the Ear).
1876.   „   Fol, Arch. d. Zool. Expér., vol. v. pp. 105–158 (Development).
1877.   „   Edinger, Archiv f. mikrosk. Anat., vol. xiv. p. 171, pl. xi. (Anatomy).
1883. *Firola*, Tryon, Struct. Syst. Conch., vol. ii. p. 349.
1883. *Pterotrachea*, Fischer, Man. Conch., p. 579.
1886.   „   Warlomont, Journ. Anat. et Physiol., vol. xxii. pp. 331–343 (Anatomy).

The determination of the species of the shell-less Heteropods is extremely difficult.
Many of the forms of *Pterotrachea* are most unsatisfactorily determined; some are past

recognition, either through the inadequacy of the descriptions or the rough inaccurate character of the figures which are supposed to represent them. Of the first four species described, *Pterotrachea coronata*, *Pterotrachea pulmonata*, *Pterotrachea aculeata*, and *Pterotrachea hyalina* of Forskål, only the first has since been recognised. Even the figure of that species is extremely crude and fanciful. Nothing is known of the three others beyond the information given by Forskål, and since this is so incomplete and the figures so bad, I think it would certainly be advisable to reject these so-called species as beyond recognition.

The next to describe some species belonging to this genus was Lesueur, who in 1817 published short diagnoses and figures of six so-called new species, which he separated on account of the presence or absence of a fin-sucker, the want or possession of the caudal appendage, and the number of "gelatinous points" or denticles in front of the eyes. The stability of these species has been doubted by d'Orbigny and others, and it seems to me probable that in three or four instances only varieties or different sexes of the same species are depicted. Quoy and Gaimard and Risso have also described and figured species which probably will never be recognised, and of several other forms nothing is known except the original figures and descriptions, some of which evidently are inaccurate and incomplete. Still, as it is impossible to relegate them with absolute certainty as synonyms of well-recognised forms, I think it best to let them stand as separate species until it can be shown beyond a doubt what their true position is. It is dangerous to deny or doubt the existence or value of a species because we do not happen to have had the opportunity of examining or possessing an example. Although we may feel most confident that a certain so-called new species is either identical or merely a variety of some well-established form, still we are not warranted in "sinking" an author's species (as is often done by certain writers) upon mere suspicion. It is an injustice, and creates endless confusion in the nomenclature.

In the following list the species are not arranged in the order of their apparent affinity, but merely according to priority of date of publication :—

Pterotrachea coronata, Forskål.

1775.	*Pterotrachea coronata*, Forskål, Descript. Anim., p. 117.
1776.	" " id., Icones, p. 10, pl. xxxiv. fig. A.
1789.	" " Gmelin, Syst. Nat., p. 3137.
1791.	" " Bruguière, Ency. Méth., pl. lxxxviii. fig. 1 (copy of Forskål).
1801.	" " Lamarck, Syst. Anim., p. 61.
1805.	" " Roissy, Hist. Nat. (Suite à Buffon), vol. v. p. 79.
1822.	" " Lamarck, Anim. sans Vert., vol. vii. p. 676; ed. 2, vol. xi. p. 383.
1826.	" " Risso, Hist. nat. Europ., vol. iv. p. 28.
1829.	" " Chiaje, Mem. Stor. Anim. senza Vert., vol. iv. pp. 182, 197.
1830.	" " Bosc, Hist. nat., vers, ed. 2, vol. i. p. 64.

1830. *Pterotrachea coronata*, Deshayes, Ency. Méth., vol. ii. p. 129.
1830. *Firola coronata*, Cuvier, Règne anim., ed. 2, vol. iii. p. 69.
1835. *Pterotrachea coronata*, Oken, Naturgesch., vol. v. p. 514.
1841. „ „ Chiaje, Descriz. e Notom. Anim. Invert. Sicil., vol. ii. p. 93, pl. lxv.
1841. *Firola coronata*, Cantraine, Mal. Médit., p. 43.
1843. *Pterotrachea coronata*, Chiaje, Rendiconto Accad. Sci. Soc. Borbon. Napoli, vol. ii. p. 106.
1844. „ „ Philippi, Enum. Moll. Sicil., vol. ii. p. 204, pl. xxviii. fig. 15.
1850. „ „ Gray, Fig. Moll. Anim., pl. clix. fig. 1 (copy of Philippi).
1850. „ „ *id., loc. cit.*, pl. clvii. fig. 1 (copy of Chiaje).
1850. „ „ *id., loc. cit.*, pl. clviii. fig. 3 (copy of Forskål).
1851. *Firola coronata*, Leydig, Zeitschr. f. wiss. Zool., Bd. iii. p. 328 (Anatomy).
1853. „ „ Vérany, Journ. de Conch., vol. iv. p. 381.
1854. „ „ Leuckart, Zool. Untersuch., Heft iii. pp. 3–68, pl. i.
1855. *Pterotrachea coronata*, Gegenbaur, Untersuch. Pterop. und Heterop., p. 215, pl. vii. fig. 6.
1855. „ „ H. and A. Adams, Gen. Moll., vol. ii. p. 94.
1856. „ „ Troschel, Gebiss d. Schneck., vol. i. p. 44, pl. ii. fig. 12.
1866. „ „ Keferstein, in Bronn's Thierreich, vol. iii. pt. 2, pl. lxviii. fig. 15 (Odontophore); pl. lxx. figs. 2, 10–14.
1876. „ „ Fol, Arch. d. Zool. Expér., vol. v. p. 107, pl. iv. figs. 9–15 (Development).

Habitat.—Mediterranean.

Pterotrachea cuvieri (Péron et Lesueur).

1810. *Firola cuvieri*, Péron et Lesueur, Ann. Mus. Hist. Nat., vol. xv. p. 69, pl. ii. fig. 8.
1817. *Firola cuvieri*, Lesueur, Journ. Acad. Nat. Sci. Philad., vol. i. p. 7, pl. i. fig. 4.
1817. „ „ *id.*, Bull. Soc. Philom. Paris, p. 159.
1818. „ „ Oken, Isis, p. 1550.
1820. *Pterotrachea cuvieri*, Blainville, Dict. d. Sci. Nat., vol. xvii. p. 67.
1821. „ *cuvieri*, Chamisso, Nova Acta Acad. Leop. Carol., vol. x. pt. 2, p. 346.
1825. „ „ Eschscholtz, Isis, p. 736.
1827. „ *peronii*, Ency. Méth., pl. ccclxi. fig. 1 (copy of Lesueur).
1830. „ *coronata (partim)*, Gray, Fig. Moll. Anim., vol. iv. p. 100, pl. clx. fig. 1 (copy of Lesueur).

Habitat.—Mediterranean (Lesueur).

Pterotrachea peronia (Lesueur).

1817. *Firola peronia*, Lesueur, Journ. Acad. Nat. Sci. Philad., vol. i. p. 7, pl. i. fig. 6.
1817. „ *peronigna, id.*, Bull. Soc. Philom. Paris, p. 159.
1818. „ „ Oken, Isis, p. 1559.
1820. *Pterotrachea peronia*, Blainville, Dict. d. Sci. Nat., vol. xvii. p. 67.
1830. „ *coronata (partim)*, Gray, Fig. Moll. Anim., vol. iv. p. 100, pl. clx. fig. 6 (copy of Lesueur).

Habitat.—Mediterranean.

Pterotrachea gibbosa (Lesueur).

1817. *Firola gibbosa*, Lesueur, Journ. Acad. Nat. Sci. Philad., vol. i. p. 6, pl. i. fig. 2.
1817.   „   „   *id.*, Bull. Soc. Philom. Paris, p. 159.
1818.   „   „   Oken, Isis, p. 1559.
1820. *Pterotrachea gibbosa*, Blainville, Dict. d. Sci. Nat., vol. xvii. p. 66.
1850.   „   *coronata* (partim), Gray, Fig. Moll. Anim., vol. iv. p. 100, pl. clx. fig. 4
                        (copy of Lesueur).

Habitat.—Mediterranean (Lesueur).

Pterotrachea frederica (Lesueur).

1817. *Firola frederica*, Lesueur, Journ. Acad. Nat. Sci. Philad., vol. i. p. 7, pl. i. fig. 5.
1817.   „   „   *id.*, Bull. Soc. Philom. Paris, p. 159.
1818.   „   „   Oken, Isis, p. 1559.
1820. *Pterotrachea frederica*, Blainville, Dict. d. Sci. Nat., vol. xvii. p. 67.
1825.   „   (*Firola*) *frederici*, Blainville, Man. Malacol., p. 492, pl. xlvii. fig. 4.
1826.   „   *peronii* (*non* Lesueur), Ency. Méth., pl. cccclxiv. fig. 1.
1830. *Firola frederica*, Cuvier, Règne anim., ed. 2, vol. iii. p. 69, note.
1841.   „   „   Cantraine, Mal. Médit., p. 43.
1843.   „   „   Forbes, Report Brit. Assoc., p. 132.
1844. *Pterotrachea fredericia*, Philippi, Enum. Moll. Sicil., vol. ii. p. 204.
1850.   „   *frederica*, Gray, Fig. Moll. Anim., vol. iv. p. 100, pl. clx. fig. 3 (copy of
                        Lesueur).
1850.   „   „   *id.*, op. cit., p. 100, pl. clvii. fig. 2 (copy of Chiaje).
1850.   „   *coronata* (partim), *id.*, loc. cit., p. 100, pl. clv. fig. 7 (copy of Blainville).
1853. *Firola fredericiana*, Vérany, Journ. de Conchyl., vol. iv. p. 381.
1854.   „   „   Leuckart, Zool. Untersuch., Heft iii. pp. 3–68, pls. i., ii.
1855. *Pterotrachea friderici*, Gegenbaur, Untersuch. Pterop. und Heterop., p. 215, pl. vii.
1855.   „   *frederica*, H. and A. Adams, Gen. Moll., vol. ii. p. 94.
1856.   „   *fridericiana*, Troschel, Gebiss d. Schneck., vol. i. p. 44, pl. ii. fig. 11.
1866.   „   *fredericiana*, Keferstein, Bronn's Thierreich, vol. iii. pt. 2, pl. lxix.
                        figs. 9, 10.
1876.   „   *frederici*, Fol, Arch. d. Zool. Expér., vol. v. p. 107, pl. iv. fig. 3 (Develop-
                        ment).
1886. *Firola frederici*, Warlomont, Journ. Anat. et Physiol., vol. xxii. p. 349, pl. xii. figs. 1–4
                        (Anatomy).

Habitat.—Mediterranean.

Pterotrachea forskalia (Lesueur).

1817. *Firola forskalia*, Lesueur, Journ. Acad. Nat. Sci. Philad., vol. i. p. 7, pl. i. fig. 3.
1817.   „   *forskalea*, *id.*, Bull. Soc. Philom. Paris, p. 159.
1818.   „   „   Oken, Isis, p. 1559.
1820. *Pterotrachea forskalia*, Blainville, Dict. d. Sci. Nat., vol. xvii. p. 66, pl. xlvii. fig. 4.
1850.   „   *coronata*, Forskål, Gray, Fig. Moll. Anim., vol. iv. p. 100, pl. clx. fig. 5
                        (copy of Lesueur).

Habitat.—Mediterranean (Lesueur).

Pterotrachea mutica (Lesueur).

1817. *Firola mutica*, Lesueur, Journ. Acad. Nat. Sci. Philad., vol. i. p. 6, pl. i. fig. 1.
1817. „ „ *id.*, Bull. Soc. Philom. Paris, p. 159.
1818. „ „ Oken, Isis, p. 1559.
1820. *Pterotrachea mutica*, Blainville, Dict. d. Sci. Nat., vol. xvii. p. 66.
1841. *Firola mutica*, Cantraine, Mal. Médit., p. 44.
1844. *Pterotrachea mutica*, Philippi, Enum. Moll. Sicil., vol. ii. p. 204.
1853. *Firola mutica*, Vérany, Journ. de Conchyl., vol. iv. p. 381.
1854. „ „ Leuckart, Zool. Untersuch., Heft. iii. pp. 3–68, pl. i.
1855. *Pterotrachea mutica*, H. and A. Adams, Gen. Moll., vol. ii. p. 94.
1855. „ „ Gegenbaur, Untersuch. Pterop. und Heterop., p. 215.
1856. „ „ Troschel, Gebiss d. Schneck., vol. i. p. 45, pl. ii. figs. 13, 13a.
1866. „ „ Keferstein, in Bronn's Thierreich, vol. iii. pl. 2, p. 69, fig. 1: pl. lxx. fig. 1.
1876. „ „ Fol, Arch. d. Zool. Expér., vol. v. p. 107, pl. iv. figs. 4–8 (Development).
1883. „ „ Lankester, Ency. Brit., vol. xvi. p. 654, fig. 51 (copy of Keferstein reversed).

Habitat.—Mediterranean (Lesueur).

Pterotrachea rufa, Quoy and Gaimard.

1824. *Pterotrachea rufa*, Quoy and Gaimard, Voy. "Uranie" et la "Physicienne," Zool., p. 491, pl. lxxxvii. figs. 2, 3.
1827. „ „ Oken, Isis, p. 1016.
1833. „ „ Oken, Isis, p. 187, pl. vi. figs. 2, 3 (reversed copy of Quoy and Gaimard).
1855. „ „ H. and A. Adams, Gen. Moll., vol. ii. p. 94.

Habitat.—Indian Ocean (Quoy and Gaimard).

Pterotrachea lesueuri, Risso.

1826. *Pterotrachea lesueuri*, Risso, Hist. nat. Europ., vol. iv. p. 29, pl. ii. fig. 14.
1850. „ „ Gray, Fig. Moll. Anim., pl. clix. fig. 4 (copy of Risso).
1855. „ „ H. and A. Adams, Gen. Moll., vol. ii. p. 94.

Habitat.—Mediterranean.

Pterotrachea adamastor, Lesson.

1830. *Pterotrachea adamastor*, Lesson, Voy. "Coquille," Zool., vol. ii. p. 249, pl. iii. fig. 1, g.a.
1850. „ *coronata*, Gray, Fig. Moll. Anim., vol. iv. p. 100, pl. clvi. fig. 1 (copy of Lesson, reduced).
1855. „ *adamastor*, Küster, Conch. Cab., Heteropoda, pl. i. fig. 3 (copy of Lesson).

Habitat.—Near the Cape of Good Hope (Lesson).

Pterotrachea hippocampus, Philippi.

    1829. *Pterotrachea hyalina*, Chiaje, Mem. Stor. Anim. senza Vert., vol. iv. pp. 183, 198, pl. xlvii.
              fig. 13.
    1829.   ,, *frederici*, Chiaje, *loc. cit.*, pp. 184, 198, pl. lxix. fig. 2.
    1836.   ,, *hippocampus*, Philippi, Moll. Sicil., vol. i. p. 242; vol. ii. p. 204, pl. xxviii.
              fig. 16.
    1841.   ,, *fredericiana*, Chiaje, Descriz. e Notom. Anim. Invert. Sicil., vol. ii. p. 93.
    1843.   ,, *frederici*, *id.*, Rendicont. Accad. Sci. Soc. Borbon. Napoli, vol. ii. p. 106.
    1850.   ,, *frederica* (*part.*), Gray, Fig. Moll. Anim., vol. iv. p. 100, pl. clvii. fig. 2 (copy
              of Chiaje).
    1850.   ,, *hyalina*, Gray, *loc. cit.*, pl. clvii. fig. 3.
    1850.   ,, *hippocampus*, Gray, *loc. cit.*, pl. clv. fig. 5 (copy of Philippi).
    1855.   ,,   ,, H. and A. Adams, Gen. Moll., vol. ii. p. 94, pl. lxix. fig. 7
              (copy of Philippi).
    1855.   ,, *hyalina*, H. and A. Adams, *loc. cit.*, p. 94.
    1855.   ,,   ,, Gegenbaur, Untersuch. Pterop. und Heterop., p. 215.

Habitat.—Mediterranean.

In placing with this species *Pterotrachea frederici* and *Pterotrachea hyalina* of Chiaje, which are evidently distinct from the species described under those names by Lesueur and Forskål respectively, I have followed Philippi.

Pterotrachea quoyana (d'Orbigny).

    1836. *Firola quoyana*, d'Orbigny, Voy. Amér. mérid., vol. v. p. 150, pl. xi. figs. 1, 2.
    1850. *Pterotrachea quoyana*, Gray, Fig. Moll. Anim., vol. iv. p. 100, pl. lxii. figs. 1, 1a (copy of
              d'Orbigny).
    1855.   ,,   ,, H. and A. Adams, Gen. Moll., vol. ii. p. 94.
    1859.   ,,   ,, Chenu, Man. Conch., vol. i. p. 123, fig. 536 (after d'Orbigny
              reversed).
    1883. *Firola quoyana*, Tryon, Struct. Syst. Conch., vol. ii. pl. lxxxvi. fig. 97 (copy of d'Orbigny
              reversed and reduced).

Habitat.—South Atlantic (d'Orbigny).

Pterotrachea edwardsii (Deshayes).

    1836–1846. *Firola edwardsii*, Deshayes, Cuvier's Règne Anim. Moll., pl. xxxix. fig. 1.
    1850. *Pterotrachea edwardsii*, Gray, Fig. Moll. Anim., pl. clix. fig. 2 (copy of Deshayes).
    1855.   ,,   ,, H. and A. Adams, Gen. Moll., vol. ii. p. 94.

Habitat.—Mediterranean (Deshayes).

Pterotrachea umbilicata, Chiaje.

    1841. *Pterotrachea umbilicata*, Chiaje, Descriz. e Notom. Anim. Invert. Sicil., vol. ii. p. 94,
              pl. lxiv. figs. 12–14.
    1843.   ,,   ,, *id.*, Rendicont. Accad. Sci. Soc. Borbon. Napoli, vol. ii. p. 107.

Habitat.—Mediterranean.

Pterotrachea kerandrenii (Eydoux and Souleyet).

1841. *Firole de kerandren*, Eydoux and Souleyet, Voy. " Bonite," Atlas, pl. xvi. figs. 8–10.
1847. *Firola kerandrenii*, Chenu, Leçons élém. Hist. nat., p. 130, fig. 417 (reduced copy of Eydoux and Souleyet).
1850? „ „ Deshayes, Traité Conch., pl. cii. fig. 6 (copy of Eydoux and Souleyet).
1850. *Pterotrachea kerandrenii*, Gray, Fig. Moll. Anim., pl. cexxxviii. fig. 3 (copy of Eydoux and Souleyet).
1852. *Firola kerandrenii*, Souleyet, Voy. " Bonite," Zool., vol. ii. p. 349.
1855. *Pterotrachea kerandrenii*, H. and A. Adams, Gen. Moll., vol. ii. p. 94.

Habitat.—Mid Atlantic (Eydoux and Souleyet).

Pterotrachea scutata, Gegenbaur.

1855. *Pterotrachea scutata*, Gegenbaur, Untersuch. Pterop. und Heterop., pp. 185, 215, pl. viii. figs. 19, 20.

Habitat.—Messina (Gegenbaur).

SPECIES BEYOND RECOGNITION.

Pterotrachea hyalina, Forskål.

1775. *Pterotrachea hyalina*, Forskål, Descrip. Anim., p. 118.
1776. „ „ *Id.*, Icones, p. 10, pl. xxxiv. fig. B.
1789. „ „ Gmelin, Syst. Nat., vol. vi. p. 3137.
1791. „ „ Bruguière, Ency. Méth., pl. lxxxviii. fig. 2 (copy of Forskål).
1805. „ „ Roisey, Hist. Nat. (Suite à Buffon), vol. v. p. 79.
1817. *Firole trans-parente*, Bosc, Nouv. Dict. Hist. Nat., vol. xi. pl. D.xx. fig. 11 (reversed copy of Forskål).
1822. *Pterotrachea hyalina*, Lamarck, Anim. sans Vert., vol. vii. p. 676; ed. 2, vol. xi. p. 384.
1825. „ „ Eschscholtz, Isis von Oken, p. 736.
1830. „ „ Deshayes, Ency. Méth., vol. ii. p. 130.
1830. „ „ Bosc, Hist. nat., vers, ed. 2, vol. i. p. 64, pl. ii. fig. 1 (reversed copy of Forskål).
1841. „ „ Chiaje, Descriz. e Notom. Anim. Invert. Sicil., vol. ii. p. 93.
1843. „ „ *id.*, Rendicont. Accad. Sci. Soc. Borbon. Napoli, vol. ii. p. 106.
1843. *Firola hyalina*, Forbes, Report Brit. Assoc., p. 132.

Habitat.—Not stated by Forskål. Probably Mediterranean.

This species I am inclined to think must be a small *Firoloïda*.

Pterotrachea pulmonata, Forskål.

1775. *Pterotrachea pulmonata,* Forskål, Descrip. Anim., p. 118.
1776.   „   „   *id.,* Icones, p. 14, pl. xliii. fig. A.
1789.   „   „   Gmelin, Syst. Nat., vol. vi. p. 3137.
1791.   „   „   Bruguière, Ency. Méth., pl. lxxxviii. fig. 3 (copy of Forskål).
1805.   „   „   Roissy, Hist. Nat. (Suite à Buffon), vol v. p. 80.
1822.   „   „   Lamarck, Anim. sans Vert., vol. vii. p. 676 ; ed. 2, vol. xi. p. 384.
1830.   „   „   Deshayes, Ency. Méth., vol. ii. p. 130.
1830.   „   „   Bosc, Hist. nat., vers, ed. 2, vol. i. p. 65.
1850.   „   „   Gray, Fig. Moll. Anim., pl. clviii. fig. 4 (copy of Forskål).
1855.   „   „   H. and A. Adams, Gen. Moll., vol. ii. p. 94.

Habitat.—(?) (Forskål).

Pterotrachea aculeata, Forskål.

1775. *Pterotrachea aculeata,* Forskål, Descrip. Anim., p. 118.
1776.   „   „   *id.,* Icones, p. 10, pl. xxxiv. fig. C.c.
1789.   „   „   Gmelin, Syst. Nat., vol. vi. p. 3137.
1791.   „   „   Bruguière, Ency. Méth., pl. lxxxviii. fig. 4 (copy of Forskål).
1805.   „   „   Roissy, Hist. Nat. (Suite à Buffon), vol. v. p. 80.
1822.   „   „   Lamarck, Anim. sans Vert., vol. vii. p. 677 ; ed. 2, vol. xi. p. 384.
1830.   „   „   Bosc, Hist. nat., vers, ed. 2, vol. i. p. 65.
1850.   „   „   Gray, Fig. Moll. Anim., pl. clviii. figs. 1, 2, 5 (copy of Forskål).

Habitat.—Mediterranean (Forskål).

Pterotrachea (?).

1814. *Hypterus appendiculatus,*[1] Rafinesque-Schmaltz, Précis des decouv., p. 29.

Habitat.—Mediterranean.

Pterotrachea (?).

1814. *Hypterus erythrogaster,*[2] Rafinesque-Schmaltz, loc. cit., p. 29.

Habitat.—Mediterranean.

Pterotrachea (?).

1836. *Firola (Anops) peronii,* d'Orbigny, Voy. Amér. mérid., vol. v. p. 149, pl. x. figs. 8–10.

Habitat.—South Pacific Ocean.

Under this name d'Orbigny appears to have described a mutilated specimen of *Pterotrachea.*

[1] Considered by Chiaje synonymous with *Pterotrachea friderici, vide* Mem. Stor. Anim. senza Vert., vol. iv. p. 196.
[2] Placed by Chiaje with *Pterotrachea coronata.*

The following is a description of the only species of *Pterotrachea* in the Challenger collection :—

Pterotrachea sp.

Body rather long and slender, smooth, with the exception of a few flat circular spine-bearing scales which are most numerous on each side of the fin. They vary somewhat in size, the largest being about a millimetre in diameter. They are more or less regularly circular, sometimes feebly tinted with red towards the middle and pale at the margin, and the soft spine or tentacle is colourless. The margin is free all round and only the central part is attached to the integument. The proboscis is rather slender, and is marked with a thread-like line or groove, which, starting from a point a short distance from the mouth, passes between two small conical denticles in front of the eyes and terminates a little beyond. The muscular skin on the ventral side of the proboscis is clearly defined, appearing thicker and more opaque than the sides. This construction of the proboscis is the same as in other species which I have examined. The fin is situated a little nearer the nucleus than to the eyes, and has a small opaque sucker at the vertex. The caudal portion of the body, which terminates in two small transverse fins, is rather short, and is strengthened along the sides by two narrow muscular bands,

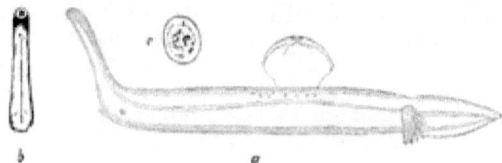

Fig. 1.—*a, Pterotrachea* sp.; *b*, front of rostrum ; *c*, dorsal scale (magnified).

of which the upper is the largest. The nucleus is elongate, pyriform, and supports a branchial plume of about a dozen branchlets.

Habitat.—Off Banda Island, September 29, 1874.

Besides the specimen from Banda there are three other examples in the collection, all from different parts of the Atlantic, which apparently belong to this or some closely allied species. They are, however, so mutilated that it is impossible to pronounce them the same with absolute certainty.

I have hesitated to name this species, as it presents so great a resemblance to several others which are only known to me by their figures and descriptions. It is peculiar in having only two denticles in front of the eyes, but what the specific value of this character may be I have no means of testing.

Genus *Firoloida*, Lesueur.

1817. *Firoloida*, Lesueur, Journ. Acad. Nat. Sci. Philad., vol. i. p. 38.
1817.   „   *id.*, Bull. Soc. Philom. Paris, p. 159.
1818. *Firoloides*, Oken, Isis, p. 1557.
1820. *Firoloida*, Blainville, Dict. d. Sci. Nat., vol. xvii. p. 67.
1824. *Firoloida*, *id.*, op. cit., vol. xxxii. p. 283.
1830. *Firoloides*, Deshayes, Ency. Méth., vol. ii. p. 130.
1830. *Cerophora*, d'Orbigny, Voy. Amér. mérid., vol. v. p. 151.
1841.   „   *id.*, in Sagra's Hist. Cuba, Moll., vol. i. p. 97.
1842.   „   *id.*, Paléont. franç., Terr. crét., vol. ii. p. 18.
1850.   „   Gray, Fig. Moll. Anim., vol. iv. p. 100.
1852. *Firoloida*, Souleyet, Voy. "Bonite," Zool., vol. ii. p. 339.
1853. *Firoloides*, Leuckart, Wiegmann's Archiv f. Naturgesch., p. 253.
1853. *Ceratophora*, Philippi, Handbuch Conch., p. 283.
1854. *Firoloides*, Leuckart, Zool. Untersuch., Heft. iii. pp. 3–68.
1854.   „   Woodward, Man. Moll., p. 199.
1855. *Firolella*, Troschel, Wiegmann's Archiv f. Naturgesch., p. 301.
1855. *Firoloides*, Gegenbaur, Untersuch. Pterop. und Heterop., p. 215.
1855. *Firoloides*, H. and A. Adams, Gen. Moll., vol. ii. p. 95.
1856. *Firoloides*, Troschel, Gebiss d. Schneck., vol. i. p. 45.
1856. *Firolella*, *id.*, loc. cit., p. 46.
1856. *Firoloides*, Krohn, Müller's Archiv f. Anat. Physiol., p. 520.
1857. *Firoloida*, Gray, Syst. Arrang. Moll., p. 132.
1857. *Cerophora*, *id.*, loc. cit., p. 132.
1859.   „   Chenu, Man. Conch., vol. i. p. 124.
1860. *Firoloides*, Krohn, Beiträge Entwick. Pterop. und Heterop., p. 27.
1862.   „   Macdonald, Trans. Roy. Soc. Edin., vol. xxiii. p. 5.
1866. *Firoloida*, Keferstein, Bronn's Thierreich, vol. iii. pt. 2, p. 850.
1876. *Firoloides*, Fol, Arch. d. Zool. Expér., vol. v. p. 103.
1883.   „   Tryon, Struct. Syst. Conch., p. 349.
1883. { *Firoloida,* } Fischer, Man. Conch., p. 580.
       { *Cerophora,* }

There seems to be considerable diversity of opinion with regard to the value of the three so-called genera which I have united under *Firoloida* of Lesueur.

This genus was founded for a group of Heteropods which differed from *Pterotrachea*, to which they evidently were closely related, in having the visceral nucleus situated at the posterior end of the body, and scarcely any caudal prolongation beyond the nucleus. Lesueur also thought that the absence of a fin-sucker and of tentacles were essential features of his genus, but this has since been proved not to be the case.

Two of the specimens figured by Lesueur were females, as is shown by the egg-tube being represented in both of his illustrations. Neither of these has tentacles in front of the eyes. His third figure represents an animal (*Firoloida aculeata*) with two "elongate gelatinous points" in front and no egg-tube posteriorly. This I am inclined to think was a mutilated male in which the genital organ has been broken away, and the two "elongate gelatinous points" were in reality tentacles. This opinion is strengthened by the fact that the presence of denticles in front of the eyes, which are so usual in species of *Pterotrachea*, have not since been observed in any form of *Firoloida*.

D'Orbigny was the next to describe two animals belonging to this genus, which he named *Firola (Cerophora) gaimardii* and *Firola (Cerophora) lesueurii*. The figures of these two so-called species, which were considered (probably correctly) identical by Souleyet, appear to be rather fanciful, judging by the more accurate illustrations of Eydoux and Souleyet and Macdonald, and an examination of the Challenger and other specimens, both *Firoloida gaimardii* and *Firoloida lesueurii* exhibit tentacles and doubtless were males.

Souleyet in the Voyage of the "Bonite" next described an animal which he identified with the *Firoloida desmarestii* of Lesueur. This also was a female without tentacles. He also described and figured a second example under the name *Firoloida lesueurii*, which was a male and provided with tentacles.

In 1855 Troschel characterised two new species which he believed to represent a new genus, and which he styled *Firolella*, considering it distinct from *Firoloida* in having no tentacles. It seems to me certain that he never consulted Lesueur's account of that genus, but must have based his opinion upon the writings of d'Orbigny and Souleyet. Lesueur distinctly mentions the absence of tentacles in his diagnosis of the genus.

The first of Troschel's species, *Firolella gracilis*, was a female, the second, *Firolella vigilans*, he supposed to be a male. In the latter I should have expected the presence of tentacles, but according to Troschel none existed. Their absence, I think, might possibly be due to the very young state of the animal, which was less than a quarter of an inch in length. They might not have been developed in an animal apparently so young,[1] or even have escaped observation on account of their minuteness.

The next representation of a species of *Firoloida* is that given by Macdonald, who describes and figures a male with tentacles and *a sucker on the ventral fin*, a feature not previously noted. Fewkes has since recorded the presence of a fin-sucker in females of *Firoloida lesueurii*. In the Challenger specimens and others which I have examined belonging to this genus, the males only have this organ, and also possess tentacles, the females on the contrary being destitute of both.

From these remarks it will be observed that *the presence or absence of tentacles is presumed to be a sexual and not a specific or generic character*.

Formerly the possession or want of a sucker on the fin was regarded as indicative of sex in the species of *Pterotrachea*, and a similar result might have been expected with regard to *Firoloida*. In both instances, however, it has been demonstrated by Paneth and Fewkes that the presence or absence of this character is not constant in either

---

[1] Krohn also regards this as a very young, recently metamorphosed, example of a *Firoloida* or *Pterotrachea*.

males or females; but it has been noticed by the former that the sucker was usually smaller in female specimens than in males.

After studying the various figures and descriptions of *Firoloida* which have been published, I have not been able to arrive at any satisfactory or definite opinion with regard to the value of the species. Whether they will eventually all resolve themselves into one or two variable forms, or how many distinct species they constitute, is uncertain. In order to arrive at a definite decision it would be necessary to have a much larger series of specimens from various localities for examination than I have had the opportunity of studying. I think then it will be the safest course to leave this question unsettled, and also not to attempt to decide which of the figured males and females should be associated together.

I might, however, point out that Macdonald has erroneously stated that *Firoloida desmarestia* is the female of *Pterotrachea keraudrenii*. The latter has a rather unusual form for a *Pterotrachea*, but still I believe it belongs to that genus, as it has a caudal prolongation, the nucleus being far from terminal, and no tentacles, the latter, if my surmise be correct, being an essential characteristic of the males of *Firoloida*, their absence, therefore, clearly showing that the animal in question was not the male of *Firoloida desmarestia*.

Firoloida desmaresti, Lesueur.

1817. *Firoloida desmarestia*, Lesueur, Journ. Acad. Nat. Sci. Philad., vol. i. p. 39, pl. ii. figs. 1, 1b,
1817.   „   „   id., Bull. Soc. Philom. Paris, p. 160.
1818. *Firloides desmarestia*, Oken, Isis, p. 1559.
1820. *Firoloida desmarestia*, Blainville, Dict. d. Sci. Nat., vol. xvii. p. 68.
1825. *Pterotrachea (Firoloida) desmarestiana*, id., Blainville, Man. Malacol., p. 492.
1850.   „   „   *desmarestia*, Gray, Fig. Moll. Anim., pl. clv. fig. 5 (copy of Lesueur).
1850.   „   „   „   id., op. cit., pl. cxxxviii. fig. 1 (copy of Eydoux and Souleyet).
1850 ? *Firoloides desmaresti*, Deshayes, Traité Conch., pl. cii. fig. 4 (copy of Eydoux and Souleyet).
1852. *Firoloida desmarestia*, Eydoux et Souleyet, Voy. "Bonite," Zool., vol. ii. p. 342, pl. xvi. figs. 1–4.
1853. *Firloides desmaresti*, Huxley, Phil. Trans., vol. cxliii. pp. 30–36, pl. ii. figs. 1–8, (Anatomy).
1855. *Firoloides desmaresti*, Gegenbaur, Untersuch. Pterop. and Heterop., p. 215.
1855. *Pterotrachea desmarestina*, H. and A. Adams, Gen. Moll., vol. ii. p. 94.
1856. *Firoloides desmaresti*, Troschel, Gebiss d. Schneck., vol. i. p. 45.
1876.   „   *desmaresti*, Fol, Arch. d. Zool. Expér., vol. v. p. 105, pls. i., ii., iii. (Development).

Habitat.—Atlantic, near Martinique (Lesueur); Atlantic and Pacific Oceans (Eydoux and Souleyet).

Of this species there are two males and two females in the Challenger collection, obtained on the 3rd of March 1876, at the surface, in the South Atlantic Ocean. One of the females is remarkable for the length of the filiform appendage,[1] at the end of the short caudal prolongation being considerably longer and more thread-like than that figured by Eydoux and Souleyet (Voy. "Bonite," pl. xvi. fig. 1). In the other specimen it is altogether wanting, its absence doubtless being due to accident. The male examples have much the general aspect of the females, but are at once recognised by the presence of tentacles and the genital organs behind the nucleus. This portion of the animal is fairly like the representation of that of *Firoloida lesueuri* (op. cit., pl. xvi. figs. 5, 6, 7), but the narrow prolongation or caudal extremity is not so distinctly jointed as depicted in the figures. Neither of the females have a sucker on the fin, but it is present in both males. The egg-tube of one of the specimens is 10 mm. in length, and of precisely the same construction as that figured by Troschel (*Firoloida gracilis*). It contains between four hundred and four hundred and fifty ova packed together apparently without any definite arrangement.

Firoloida lesueurii (d'Orbigny).

1836. *Firola (Cerophora) lesueurii*, d'Orbigny, Voy. Amér. mérid., vol. v. p. 151, pl. x. figs. 11, 12.

1841. *Firole de Lesueur*, Eydoux and Souleyet, Voy. "Bonite," Atlas, pl. xvi. figs. 5–7.

1850. *Pterotrachea (Firoloida) eydouxii*, Gray, Fig. Moll. Anim., vol. iv. p. 100, pl. ccxxxviii. fig. 2 (copy of Eydoux and Souleyet).

1850. *Cerophora lesueurii*, Gray, op. cit., pl. lxii. fig. 4 (copy of d'Orbigny).

1852. *Firoloida lesueurii*, Souleyet, Voy. "Bonite," Zool., vol. ii. p. 343.

1853. „ „ Vérany, Journ. de Conchyl., vol. iv. p. 381.

1854. *Firoloides lesueurii*, Leuckart, Zool. Untersuch., Heft. iii. pp. 3–68, pls. i., ii.

1855. *Firoloides eydouxii*, H. and A. Adams, Gen. Moll., vol. ii. p. 95.

1855. „ *lesueurii*, id., loc. cit., p. 95, pl. lxix. fig. 8 (copy of d'Orbigny).

1858. *Firoloides lesueurii*, Owen, Ency. Brit., vol. xv. p. 378, fig. 71.

1866. *Firoloides lesueurii*, Keferstein, Bronn's Thierreich, vol. iii. pt. 2, pl. lxix. fig. 8 (reduced copy of Eydoux and Souleyet).

Habitat.—Indian and Atlantic Oceans (Eydoux and Souleyet).

A comparison of d'Orbigny's figures and description with those of Souleyet will show considerable differences in several points. This I presume induced Gray and the Messrs. Adams to believe that two distinct forms were indicated. However, as most likely d'Orbigny's figures and his account of this animal are more or less defective, it seems probable, or at all events possible, that Souleyet was right in associating his specimens with this species.

---

[1] Fol (Arch. d. Zool. Expér., 1876, vol. v. p. 107) erroneously states that *Firoloida* has no filiform appendage. It was described and figured by Souleyet in 1852, and again by Macdonald in 1862.

Firoloida blainvilliana, Lesueur.

> 1817. *Firoloida blainvilliana*, Lesueur, Journ. Acad. Nat. Sci. Philad., vol. i. p. 39, pl. ii. figs. 2, 2b.
> 1817.   ,,   ,,   *id.*, Bull. Soc. Philom. Paris, p. 160.
> 1818. *Firoloida blainvilliana*, Oken, Isis, p. 1559.
> 1820. *Firoloida blainvilliana*, Blainville, Dict. d. Sci. Nat., vol. xvii. p. 68.
> 1850. *Pterotrachea (Firoloida) blainvilliana*, Gray, Fig. Moll. Anim., vol. iv. p. 100, pl. clv. fig. 1 (copy of Lesueur's figure).
> 1855. *Pterotrachea blainvilliana*, H. and A. Adams, Gen. Moll., vol. ii. p. 94.

Habitat.—Atlantic, near Martinique (Lesueur).

Lesueur's brief description and figure is all that is known respecting this species.

Firoloida gracilis (Troschel).

> 1855. *Firolella gracilis*, Troschel, Archiv f. Naturgesch., p. 301, pl. xi. fig. 1.
> 1856.   ,,   ,,   *id.*, Gebiss d. Schneck., vol. i. p. 46, pl. ii. figs. 14, 14a.

Habitat.—Messina (Troschel).

Firoloida gaimardii (d'Orbigny).

> 1836. *Firola (Cerophora) gaimardii*, d'Orbigny, Voy. Amér. mérid., vol. v. p. 153, pl. x. figs. 13, 14.
> 1850. *Cerophora gaimardii*, Gray, Fig. Moll. Anim., vol. iv. p. 100, pl. lxii. fig. 3 (copy of d'Orbigny).
> 1855. *Firoloides gaimardii*, H. and A. Adams, Gen. Moll., vol. ii. p. 95.
> 1859. *Cerophora gaimardii*, Chenu, Man. Conch., vol. i. p. 123, fig. 537 (copy of d'Orbigny reversed).

Habitat.—North Atlantic (d'Orbigny).

Firoloida aculeata, Lesueur.

> 1817. *Firoloida aculeata*, Lesueur, Journ. Acad. Nat. Sci. Philad., vol. i. p. 40, pl. ii. fig. 3.
> 1817. *Firoloida aculeata*, Lesueur, Bull. Soc. Philom. Paris, p. 160.
> 1818. *Firoloides aculeata*, Oken, Isis, p. 1559.
> 1820. *Firoloida aculeata*, Blainville, Dict. d. Sci. Nat., vol. xvii. p. 68.
> 1850.   ,,   ,,   Gray, Fig. Moll. Anim., pl. clv. fig. 9 (copy of Lesueur).
> 1855. *Firoloides aculeata*, H. and A. Adams, Gen. Moll., vol. ii. p. 95.

Habitat.—Atlantic (Lesueur).

Firoloida vigilans (Troschel).

> 1855. *Firolella vigilans*, Troschel, Archiv f. Naturgesch., p. 305, pl. xi. fig. 3.
> 1856.   ,,   ,,   *id.*, Gebiss d. Schneck., vol. i. p. 46, pl. i. fig. 4.
> 1859.   ,,   ,,   Chenu, Man. Conch., vol. i. p. 123, fig. 538 (copy of Troschel reduced).

Habitat.—Messina (Troschel).

Firoloida sp.

1862. *Firoloida* sp., Macdonald, Trans. Roy. Soc. Edin., vol. xxiii. p. 5, pl. i. figs. 1-4.

Habitat.—Bass Straits.

Firoloida sp.

1832. *Firola* sp., jun., Quoy and Gaimard, Voy. "Astrolabe," pl. xxix. fig. 17.

The specimen figured by Quoy and Gaimard appears to be a species of *Firoloida*.

Firoloida sp.

1850. *Pterotrachea* (*Firoloida*) sp., Gray, Fig. Moll. Anim., vol. iv. p. 100, pl. clv. figs. 3, 3a.

Nothing is known respecting this species beyond the above rough figure.

Genus *Cardiopoda*, d'Orbigny.

1836.	*Cardiopoda*, d'Orbigny, Voy. Amér. mérid., vol. v. p. 154.
1840.	„	Eydoux and Souleyet, Rev. Zool., p. 233 (On the Shell).
1841.	„	d'Orbigny, in Sagra's Hist. Cuba, Moll., vol. i. p. 97.
1842.	*Cardiopus*, d'Orbigny, Pal'ont. franç., Terr. crét., vol. ii. p. 19.
1846.	*Cardiopoda*, Agassiz, Index Zool. Univer., p. 66.
1850.	*Cardiopoda*, Gray, Fig. Moll. Anim., vol. iv. p. 100.
1852.	*Cardiopoda*, Eydoux and Souleyet, Voy. "Bonite," Zool., vol. ii. p. 351.
1853.	*Cardiopoda*, Philippi, Handbuch Conch., p. 283.
1854.	„	Woodward, Man. Moll., p. 200.
1855.	„	H. and A. Adams, Gen. Moll., vol. ii. p. 96.
1857.	„	Gray, Syst. Arrang. Moll., p. 132.
1859.	„	Chenu, Man. Conch., vol. i. p. 126.
1862.	„	Macdonald, Trans. Roy. Soc. Edin., vol. xxiii. pl. i. fig. 11, pl. ii. fig. 5. (Dentition).
1866.	„	Keferstein, Bronn's Thierreich, vol. iii. pt. 2, p. 850.
1883.	„	Fischer, Man. Conch., p. 580.
1883.	„	Tryon, Struct. Syst. Conch., vol. ii. p. 350.
1883.	*Cardiopoda*, Lankester, Ency. Brit., vol. xvi. p. 654.

The species of *Cardiopoda* are at present very unsatisfactorily determined. Macdonald has expressed the opinion that all the described forms belong to one and the same species, and it seems to me that this may really be the case, considering that it is very probable that the different sexes have been described as separate species. After carefully studying the various accounts by Souleyet, d'Orbigny, Macdonald, Rang, and Lesson, I believe that *the sexes are indicated by the branchiæ alone*. Eydoux and Souleyet[1] figure an animal which they consider the female of *Cardiopoda placenta*,

[1] Voy. "Bonite," pl. xvii. fig. 1.

Lesson. In this it will be observed that the branchial plume extends right round the posterior side of the nucleus just as depicted in Lesson's original figure,[1] in d'Orbigny's representation of *Cardiopoda pedunculata*,[2] and also as in the only specimen in the Challenger collection. These four I am inclined to regard as females of the same species. Undoubted male *Cardiopodæ* have been figured by Eydoux and Souleyet,[3] by d'Orbigny,[4] and by Macdonald.[5] The figure of *Cardiopoda caudina* given by Rang[6] also I believe represents a male. In each instance it will be noticed that the branchiæ are on the anterior side of the nucleus, and as in the case of the females I think it very probable that only one species exists. If this opinion be correct the species known as *Cardiopoda caudina* and *Cardiopoda carinata* are the male, and those named *Cardiopoda placenta* and *Cardiopoda pedunculata* the females, of one and the same species.

The specimen obtained by the Challenger was captured off Arrou Island on

FIG. 2.—*Cardiopoda placenta*, ♀.

September 23, 1874. It is about 77 mm. in length, and has at the slender caudal extremity a small dentate sucker not nearly so large as that represented by Eydoux and Souleyet in their figure of *Cardiopoda placenta*. The tail is strengthened by muscular bands on each side as in the species of *Carinaria*, and the sucker on the ventral fin is very minute and somewhat behind the centre. It is very likely that the suckers in females will be found to be smaller than in the males, as has been shown to be the case in the species of the genus *Pterotrachea*. Besides this apparently adult example, six very small specimens representing the early stages of growth of *Cardiopoda* were obtained in the North Pacific on July 4, 1875. These are not all alike, but exhibit certain variations which may be due to difference of age or sex, but not any of them are precisely like the figures of the young as represented by Macdonald and Souleyet.

[1] Voy. "Coquille," pl. iii. fig. 2.
[2] Voy. Amér. mérid., pl. xi. fig. 5.
[3] See *Cardiopoda caudina*, Voy. "Bonite," pl. xvii. fig. 11.
[4] *Cardiopoda carinata*, Voy. Amér. mérid., pl. xi. fig. 4.
[5] Trans. Roy. Soc. Edin., 1862, vol. xxiii. pl. i. fig. 10.
[6] Mag. Zool., 1832, pl. v.

Cardiopoda placenta (Lesson).

1830. *Pterotrachea placenta*, Lesson, Voy. "Coquille," Zool., vol. ii. p. 253, pl. iii. fig. 2, *q.v.*
1841. *Carinaroia placenta*, Eydoux and Souleyet, Voy. "Bonite," Atlas Zool., pl. xvii. figs. 1–10.
1850. *Cardiopoda placenta*, Gray, Fig. Moll. Anim., vol. iv. p. 100, pl. ccxxxix. fig. 1 (copy of Eyd. and Soul.).
1850 ? *Carinaroides placenta*, Deshayes, Traité Conch., pl. cii. fig. 5 (copy of Eyd. and Soul.).
1852. *Carinaroia placenta*, Souleyet, Voy. "Bonite," Zool., vol. ii. p. 353.
1854. *Cardiopoda placenta*, Woodward, Man. Moll., pl. xiv. fig. 20, Shell (copy of Eyd. and Soul.).
1853.   „   H. and A. Adams, Gen. Moll., vol. ii. pp. 96, 97; vol. iii. pl. lxx. figs. 2–2b (copy of Eyd. and Soul.).
1855.   „   „   Owen, Ency. Brit., vol. xv. p. 377, fig. 70, Shell (copy of Eyd. and Soul.).
1859.   „   „   Chenu, Man. Conch., vol. i. p. 127, figs. 546–548 (copy of Eyd. and Soul.).
1866.   „   „   Keferstein, in Bronn's Thierreich, vol. iii. pt. 2, pl. lxviii. figs. 12–14.
1883.   „   „   Tryon, Struct. Syst. Conch., vol. ii. pl. lxxxvi. figs. 1–3 (reduced copy of Eyd. and Soul.).
1883. *Cardiopoda placenta*, Lankester, Ency. Brit., vol. xvi. p. 654, figs. 50, c., D. (same as Owen).

Habitat.—Near New Guinea (Lesson); Pacific Ocean near the Sandwich Islands, and Mid Atlantic (Eydoux and Souleyet).

Cardiopoda pedunculata, d'Orbigny.

1836. *Cardiopoda pedunculata*, d'Orbigny, Voy. Amér. mérid., vol. v. p. 156, pl. xi. fig. 5.
1850.   „   „   Gray, Fig. Moll. Anim., pl. lxii. fig. 5 (copy of d'Orbigny).
1855.   „   „   H. and A. Adams, Gen. Moll., vol. ii. p. 97.
1859.   „   „   Chenu, Man. Conch., vol. i. fig. 549 (copy of d'Orbigny reversed and slightly altered).

Habitat.—North Atlantic (d'Orbigny).

Cardiopoda caudina (Rang).

1832. *Firola caudina*, Rang, Mag. d. Zool., Classe v. pl. iii.
1833–44. „   „   Guérin, Icon. Règne Anim., pl. xi. fig. 3.
1850.   „   „   Gray, Fig. Moll. Anim., pl. clv. fig. 6 (copy of Rang).
1850.   „   „   *id., loc. cit.*, pl. ccxxxix. fig. 3 (copy of Eydoux and Souleyet).
1852. *Carinaroia caudina*, Eydoux and Souleyet, Voy. "Bonite," Zool., vol. ii. p. 355, pl. xvii. figs. 11–18.
1855. *Cardiopoda caudina*, H. and A. Adams, Gen. Moll., vol. ii. p. 97.

Habitat.—Atlantic, near the equator (Rang); a young variety from the Pacific Ocean (Eydoux and Souleyet).

Cardiopoda carinata, d'Orbigny.

    1836. *Cardiapoda carinata,* d'Orbigny, Voy. Amér. mérid., vol. v. p. 157, pl. xi. figs. 3, 4.
    1850.   „   „   Gray, Fig. Moll. Anim., pl. lxii. figs. 7, 7a (copy of d'Orbigny).
    1855.   „   „   H. and A. Adams, Gen. Moll., vol. ii. p. 97.

Habitat.—Atlantic (d'Orbigny).

Cardiopoda sp., jun.

    1852. *Cardiapoda* sp., jun., Macdonald, Trans. Roy. Soc. Edin., vol. xxiii. p. 17, pl. i. fig. 10.

Habitat.—South-west Pacific (Macdonald).

Cardiopoda sp.

    1850. *Cardiapoda* sp., Gray, Fig. Moll. Anim., vol. iv. pp. 32, 100, pl. clv. figs. 4, 4a.

Habitat.—(?).

Genus *Carinaria,* Lamarck.

    1766. *Patella,* Linné, Syst. Nat., ed. 12, p. 1260.
    1769. *Nautilus,* Martini, Conch. Cab., vol. i. pp. 227, 239.
    1783. *Argonauta,* Schröter, Einleit., vol. i. p. 6.
    1784. *Patella, ibid.,* op. cit., vol. ii. p. 421.
    1789.   „ Gmelin, Syst. Nat., vol. vi. p. 3710.
    1789. *Argonauta,* Gmelin, op. cit., p. 3368.
    1801. *Carinaria,* Lamarck, Syst. des Anim., p. 98.
    1803.   „   Bosc, Nouv. Dict. Hist. Nat., vol. iv. p. 355.
    1809. *Carinaire,* Lamarck, Philosoph. Zool., vol. i. p. 323.
    1810. *Carinaria,* Péron and Lesueur, Ann. Mus. Hist. Nat., vol. xv. pp. 59, 67.
    1810. *Carinarius,* Montfort, Conch. Syst., vol. ii. p. 3.
    1811. *Argonauta,* Perry, Conchol., pl. xlii.
    1812. *Carinaria,* Lamarck, Extr. du cours de Zool., p. 125.
    1815.   „   Cranch, Introd. Conchol., p. 89.
    1816.   „   Bosc, Nouv. Dict. Hist. Nat., vol. v. p. 292.
    1817. *Argonauta,* Dillwyn, Cat. Rec. Shells, p. 338.
    1817. *Carinaria,* Blainville, Dict. d. Sci. Nat., vol. vii. p. 105.
    1817. *Pterotrachea,* Cuvier, Mém. Hist. Anat. Moll., p. 28.
    1820. *Carinaria,* Schweigger, Handb. Naturgesch., p. 720.
    1821.   „   Gray, London Medical Repos., vol. xv. p. 235.
    1822.   „   Férussac, Tab. Syst., p. xxxvii.
    1822.   „   Lamarck, Anim. sans Vert., vol. vii. p. 671.
    1822.   „   Bowdich, Elem. Conch., pp. 23, 72, pl. xiv. fig. 17.
    1824.   „   Blainville, Dict. d. Sci. Nat., vol. xxxii. p. 283.
    1825. *Argonauta,* Wood, Index Test., pl. xiii.
    1825. *Carinaria,* Blainville, Man. Malacol., p. 492.
    1835. *Pterophora,* Caulini, teste Chiaje, Mem. Stor. Anim. senza Vert., vol. ii. p. 197.

1825. *Carinaire*, Latreille, Fam. Nat., p. 173.
1825. *Carinaria*, Eschscholtz, Oken's Isis, p. 736.
1826. *Pterotrachea*, Poli, Test. utrius. Sicil., vol. iii. p. 29.
1826. *Carinaria*, Risso, Hist. nat. Europ., vol. iv. p. 27.
1826. *Argonauta*, Poli, Test. utrius. Sicil., vol. iii. p. 26.
1827. *Carinaire*, Quoy and Gaimard, Ann. d. Sci. Nat., vol. x. p. 227.
1827. *Carinaria*, Rang, Bull. Sci. Nat., vol. xii. p. 339–342.
1829.   „   Rang, Man. Moll., p. 121, pl. iii. figs. 1, 2. ♀♂
1830. *Carinaires*, Cuvier, Règne Anim., ed. 2, vol. iii. p. 68.
1830. *Carinaria*, Deshayes, Ency. Méth., vol. ii. p. 202.
1831.   „   Vérany, Zool. Journ., vol. v. p. 325.
1832.   „   Wiegmann and Ruthe, Handbuch Zool., p. 518.
1834.   „   Gray, Griffith's Anim. Kingd., vol. xii. p. 50.
1835.   „   Oken, Naturgesch., vol. v. p. 514.
1836.   „   d'Orbigny, Voy. Amér. mérid., vol. v. p. 158.
1838.   „   Potiez and Michaud, Gal. Moll., vol. i. p. 47.
1838.   „   Eydoux and Souleyet, L'Institut, vol. vi. p. 376 (Auditory Organ).
1839.   „   Sowerby, Conch. Man., p. 19.
1840. *Carinaires*, Milne-Edwards, Ann. d. Sci. Nat., vol. xiii. p. 195.
1840.   „   id., L'Institut, p. 175.
1840. *Carinaria*, Milne-Edwards and Peters, Edin. New Phil. Journ., vol. xxix. p. 162.
1841.   „   Chiaje, Descriz. e Notom. Anim. Invert. Sicil., vol. ii. p. 94.
1841.   „   Gray, Ann. and Mag. Nat. Hist., vol. vi. p. 232.
1841.   „   Cantraine, Mal. Médit., p. 40.
1842.   „   Reeve, Conch. Syst., vol. ii. p. 56.
1842.   „   d'Orbigny, Paléont. franç., Terr. crét., vol. ii. p. 10.
1842. *Carinaires*, Milne-Edwards, Ann. d. Sci. Nat., vol. xviii. p. 323.
1843. *Carinaria*, Chiaje, Rendiconti. Accad. Sci. Soc. Borbon. Napoli, vol. ii. p. 107.
1843.   „   Forbes, Report Brit. Assoc., p. 132.
1843.   „   Gravenhorst, Vergleich. Zool., p. 65.
1845.   „   Lamarck, Anim. sans Vert., ed. 2, vol. xi. p. 376.
1845.   „   Catlow, Conchol. Nomencl., p. 116.
1845.   „   Geinitz, Grundriss der Verstein., p. 317.
1845.   „   Macgillivray, Conchol. Textbook, pp. 66, 199.
1847.   „   Lovén, Öfversigt k. Vetensk.-Akad. Förhandl., p. 191.
1850.   „   Gray, Fig. Moll. Anim., vol. iv. p. 100.
1852.   „   Eydoux and Souleyet, Voy. "Bonite," Zool., vol. ii. p. 357.
1853.   „   Philippi, Handbuch Conch., p. 283.
1854.   „   Woodward, Man. Moll., p. 200.
1854.   „   Leuckart, Zool. Untersuch., Heft. iii. pp. 3–68.
1855.   „   H. and A. Adams, Gen. Moll., vol. ii. p. 95.
1855.   „   Gegenbaur, Untersuch. Pterop. und Heterop., pp. 130–153, pl. vii.
1857.   „   Krohn, Müller's Archiv f. Anat. Physiol., p. 407.
1857.   „   Gray, Guide Syst. Arrang. Moll., p. 132.
1859.   „   Chenu, Man. Conch., vol. i. p. 125.
1860.   „   Reeve, Elem. Conch., vol. ii. p. 42.
1860.   „   Krohn, Beiträge Entwick. Pterop. und Heterop., pp. 36, 38.
1865.   „   Reeve, Conch. Icon., vol. xv.
1866.   „   Keferstein, Bronn's Thierreich, vol. iii. pt. 2, pp. 809–852.
1868.   „   Hogg, Quart. Journ. Micr. Sci., vol. viii. N.S., pl. ix. fig. 25.

1868. *Carinaria*, Knocker, Proc. Zool. Soc. Lond., p. 616.
1869.   „   Boll, Beiträge vergleich. Histiol. Moll., pp. 10, 59.
1873.   „   Weinkauff, Cat. Europ. Meer. Conch., p. 44.
1876.   „   Fol, Arch. d. Zool. Expér., vol. v. p. 105.
1880.   „   Hutton, Man. New Zeal. Moll., p. 118.
1880.   „   Krukenberg, Vergl. physiol. Studien, p. 177.
1883.   „   Tryon, Struct. Syst. Conch., vol. ii. p. 349.
1883.   „   Fischer, Man. Conch., p. 580.
1886.   „   Warlemont, Journ. Anat. et Physiol., vol. xxii. p. 343, pl. xii. fig. 5 (? Larval Form).

Carinaria cristata (Linné).

1756. *Nautile vitré*, Argenville, Hist. nat. éclair. Conchyl., nouv. édit., p. 383, pl. i. fig. B.
1766. *Patella cristata*, Linné, Syst. nat., ed. xii., p. 1260.
1769. *Nautilus exiguus, vitreus dictus*, Martini, Conch. Cab., vol. i. pp. 227, 239, pl. xviii. fig. 163.
1780. *Le grand Nautile vitré*, Favanne Conchyl., vol. i. p. 719, pl. vii. fig. C2.
1783. *Argonauta No. 1*, Schræter, Einleit., vol. i. p. 6.
1784. *Patella cristata*, Schræter, op. cit., vol. ii. p. 421.
1789.   „   „   Gmelin, Syst. Nat., vol. vi. p. 3710.
1789. *Argonauta vitreus*, Gmelin, op. cit., p. 3368.
1798. *Le nautile vitré*, Cubières, Hist. Abrégée Coquill., p. 197, pl. iv. fig. 8.
1801. *Carinaria vitrea*, Lamarck, Syst. des Anim., p. 99.
1810. *Carinarius vitreus*, Montfort, Conch. Syst., vol. ii. p. 3, pl. on p. 2.
1811. *Argonauta vitrea*, Perry, Conchol., pl. xlii. fig. 2.
1816. *Carinaire vitrée*, Bosc, Nouv. Dict. Hist. Nat., vol. v. pl. B 15, fig. 6.
1817. *Carinaria vitrea*, Blainville, Dict. d. Sci. Nat., vol. vii. p. 106.
1817. *Argonauta vitrea*, Dillwyn, Cat. rec. shells, p. 336.
1820. *Carinaria vitrea*, Schweigger, Handb. Naturgesch., p. 721.
1820. *Argonauta vitrea*, Rees's Cyclopæd. Nat. Hist., vol. v. pl. iv.
1822. *Carinaria vitrea*, Lamarck, Anim. sans Vert., vol. vii. p. 674, ed. 2, vol. xi. p. 380.
1822.   „   „   Bowdich, Elem. Conch., pt. i. pl. v. fig. 16.
1823.   „   „   Bory de Saint Vincent, Dict. Classique Hist. Nat., vol. iii. p. 216.
1825.   „   *cristata*, Dubois, Epit. Lamarck's Test., p. 310.
1825. *Argonauta vitrea*, Wood, Index Test., pl. xiii. fig. 6.
1830. *Carinaria vitrea*, Deshayes, Ency. Méth., vol. ii. p. 205.
1840.   „   „   Pfeiffer, Register Konch. Kab., p. 6.
1841.   „   „   Gray, Ann. and Mag. Nat. Hist., vol. vi. p. 239.
1842.   „   *gracilis*, Reeve, Ann. and Mag. Nat. Hist., vol. ix. p. 140, pl. ii. figs. 3–5.
1842.   „   „   Reeve, Conch. Syst., vol. ii. pl. clviii. figs. 3–5.
1845.   „   „   Catlow, Conchol. Nomen., p. 116.
1855.   „   „   H. and A. Adams, Gen. Moll., vol. ii. p. 96.
1855.   „   *cristata*, H. and A. Adams, loc. cit., p. 96, pl. lxx. fig. 1a.
1859.   „   *vitrea*, Chenu, Man. Conch., vol. i. p. 125, fig. 543.
1865.   „   „   Reeve, Conch. Icon., vol. xv. pl. i. fig. 2a–2b.
1866.   „   „   Sowerby, Thesaur. Con., vol. iii. p. 303, pl. cexciii. fig. 4.
1878.   „   „   Kobelt, Illust. Conchylienbuch., pl. i. fig. 14.
1883.   „   „   Tryon, Struct. Syst. Conch., vol. ii. pl. lxxxvi. fig. 100.

Habitat.—Indian Ocean (Reeve); Probably near the Molucca Islands (Reeve for var. *gracilis*); Amboina (Favanne).

A specimen obtained by the Challenger near Papua, and of which the anterior portion is wanting. probably belongs to this species, as the small shell agrees very well in form with the upper part of adult specimens with which I have compared it. The skin is minutely tuberculated, and the crest of the caudal extremity is rather broad and commences quite close up to the nucleus. The figure (fig. 4) represents the natural size. Three very young specimens of *Carinaria*, which probably belong to this species, were

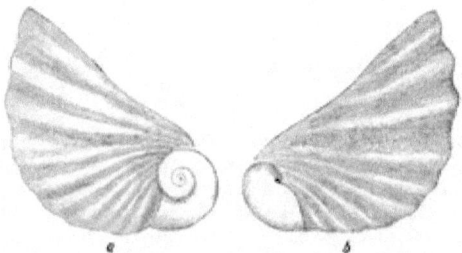

Fig. 3.—*Carinaria cristata* (young); *a*, left side; *b*, right side (magnified about seventeen diameters).

captured between the Admiralty Islands and Japan. One of these has the minute shell attached, and is represented in the accompanying woodcut. The embryonic helicoid shell is very peculiar, and it is remarkable that it has never been described as a genus of itself, as has been the case with the embryonic shells of other Gastropods.

The name most frequently applied to this species is that of *Carinaria vitrea*. This is owing to the fact that Lamarck employed it in preference to that of *cristata*, which he placed in the synonymy. There can be no question that the *Patella cristata* of Linné is

Fig. 4.—*a*, *Carinaria cristata*; *b*, shell.

undoubtedly this species, and therefore that name should be retained. The form described by Reeve as *Carinaria gracilis*, which he subsequently regarded as a variety of this species, is distinguished by the straightness of the keeled edge, which is much less curved than the typical form as represented by the figures of Argenville and others. The adult animal of *Carinaria cristata* must be of considerable dimensions, and it is remarkable that it has never been discovered.

Carinaria fragilis, Bory de Saint Vincent.

1804. *Carinaria fragilis*, Bory de Saint Vincent, Voy. dans les quatres princip. Iles d'Afrique, vol. i. p. 142; Atlas, pl. vi. fig. 4.
1817.   ,,   ,,   Blainville, Dict. d. Sci. Nat., vol. vii. p. 107.
1822.   ,,   ,,   (*partim*), Lamarck, Anim. sans Vert., vol. vii. p. 674 ; ed. 2, vol. xi. p. 380.
1823.   ,,   ,,   Bory de Saint Vincent, Dict. Classiques Hist. Nat., vol. iii. p. 216.
1825.   ,,   ,,   (*partim*), Dubois, Epit. Lamarck's Test., p. 311.
1830.   ,,   ,,   Cuvier, Règne Anim., ed. 2, vol. iii. p. 68.
1838.   ,,   ,,   (*partim*), Potiez and Michaud, Gal. Moll., vol. i. p. 47.

Habitat.—Off South Africa (Bory de Saint Vincent).

The only account of this species is that given by Bory de Saint Vincent. It has been considered by some authors identical with the Mediterranean species commonly called *Carinaria mediterranea*. If only the animal had been figured and described there would have been no hesitation in pronouncing the identity of the two species ; but in the description of the shell Bory de Saint Vincent points out certain features which clearly separate his species. He describes it as being "sans carène, et avec de légères stries qui, au lieu d'être circulaires, partent du sommet et arrivent au limbe en divergeant."

No other known species of *Carinaria* has radiating sculpture of that kind, but on the contrary they all exhibit similar circular or concentric plications. Still the account given by the author is so explicit that one can scarcely suppose that the radiating striæ were imaginary. The absence of a keel might be accounted for, supposing the shell to be damaged.

Carinaria lamarckii, Péron et Lesueur.

1554. *Species secunda Holothuriorum*, Rondelet, De Test., p. 126.
1558.   ,,   ,,   Boussuet, De Nat. aquat. Carmen, p. 68, lower fig.
1810. *Carinaire Lamarck*, Péron and Lesueur, Ann. du. Mus., vol. xv. p. 69, pl. iii. fig. 15.
1817. *Carinaria lamarkii* (Péron et Lesueur), Blainville, Dict. d. Sci. Nat., vol. vii. p. 107.
1817. *Pterotrachée* sp., Cuvier, Mém. Moll., pl. iii. figs. 15–17.
1820–5. *Carinaria mediterranea*, Sowerby, Rec. and Foss. Shells, pl. cclxxix.
1823.   ,,   *lamarckii*, Bory de Saint Vincent, Dict. Classique Hist. Nat., vol. iii. p. 217.
1824.   ,,   *vitrea*, Children, Quart. Journ. Sci. Lit. and Arts, vol. xvi. p. 257, pl. vi. fig. 239 (Shell only, copy of Ency. Méth.).
1825.   ,,   *mediterranea*, Blainville, Man. Mal., p. 493, pl. xlvii. fig. 3.
1825. *Pterotrachea lophyra*, Chiaje, Mem. Anim. sans Vert., vol. ii. p. 199, pls. xiv., xv.
1825. " *Pterotrachea navigera*, Macri, Act. Soc. Borb., vol. iii.," *teste* Chiaje, Mem., vol. ii. p. 198.
1825. " *Pterophora conchacea*, Caulini, Moll. Cent. Neap., pl. i. figs. 1–4," *teste* Chiaje, Mem., vol. ii. p. 197.
1826. *Pterotrachea lophyra*, Poli. Test. utrius. Sicil., vol. iii. p. 29, pl. xliv. figs. 1, 3.

1826. *Carinaria mediterranea*, Risso, Hist. nat. Europ., vol. iv. p. 27.

1826. *Argonauta vitrea*, Poli. Test. utrius. Sicil., vol. iii. p. 26, pl. xliv. fig. 2.

1826. *Carinaria fragilis*, Crouch, Introduct. Lamarck's Conch., p. 43, pl. xx. fig. 19 (Shell, copy of Ency. Méth.).

1827. ,, ,, Bory de Saint Vincent, Ency. Méth., pl. ccclxiv. fig. 3 (copy of Péron and Lesueur).

1828. *Pterotrachea lophira*, Chiaje, Mem. Stor. Anim. senza Vert., vol. iii. p. 161, pl. xli. fig. 1.

1829. *Carinaire vitrie*, Costa, Ann. d. Sci. Nat., vol. xvi. p. 107, pl. i.

1829. *Pterotrachea lophyra*, Poli, Férussac's Bull. Sci. Nat., vol. xviii. p. 293.

1829. *Carinaire mediterranie*, Quoy and Gaimard, Ann. d. Sci. Nat., vol. xvi. p. 134, pl. ii. figs. 1–12.

1829–44. *Carinaria cymbium*, Guérin, Icon. Règne Anim., pl. xi. fig. 1.

1830. ,, *mediterranea*, Deshayes, Ency. Méth., vol. ii. p. 206.

1830. ,, *cymbium*, Cuvier, Règne Anim., ed. 2, vol. iii. p. 68.

1833. ,, *vitrea*, Oken's Isis, p. 185, pl. vi. figs. 1–12 (copy of Quoy and Gaimard).

1836. ,, *mediterranea*, Philippi, Enum. Moll. Sicil., vol. i. p. 242; vol. ii. p. 204.

1836–46. ,, *cymbium*, Deshayes, Cuvier's Règne Anim. Moll., pl. xxxviii. fig. 1.

1838. ,, ,, Potiez and Michaud, Gal. Moll., vol. i. p. 47.

1839. ,, *mediterranea*, Anton, Verzeich. Conch., p. 27.

1839. ,, ,, Brown, Conch. Text-Book, p. 57, pl. x. fig. 1.

1839. ,, ,, Sowerby, Conch. Man., fig. 488.

1839. ,, ,, Bosset, Mém. Soc. Sci. Nat. Neuchatel, vol. ii. p. 2, pl. i. fig. 1.

1841. " *Pterophora convexa*, Carolini," Chiaje, Descriz. e Notomia Anim. Invert. Sicilia, vol. ii. p. 104, pl. clxxiii. figs. 1–5.

1841. *Carinaria mediterranea*, Chiaje, op. cit., p. 94, pl. li. figs. 1, 2; pl. lxii. figs. 1–11.

1841. ,, ,, Cantraine, Mal. Médit., p. 42.

1842. ,, ,, Reeve, Ann. and Mag. Nat. Hist., vol. ix. pl. ii. figs. 1, 2.

1842. ,, ,, Reeve, Conch. Syst., vol. ii. pl. clviii. figs. 1, 2.

1843. ,, ,, Chiaje, Rendicont. Accad. Sci. Soc. Borbon. Napoli, vol. ii. p. 107.

1843. ,, ,, Forbes, Report Brit. Assoc., p. 132.

1844. ,, ,, Chiaje, Rendicont. Accad. Sci. Soc. Borbon. Napoli, vol. iii. p. 45 and plate.

1845. ,, *fragilis*, Macgillivray, Conch. Text-Book, p. 66, pl. x. fig. 1.

1846. ,, ,, Reeve, Init. Conch., pl. k. (Animal).

1847. *Carinaire gondole*, Chenu, Leçons élém. Hist. Nat., p. 131, fig. 418 (reduced copy from Deshayes' Traité).

1847. *Carinaria vitrea*, Lovén, Öfversigt k. Vetensk.-Akad. Förhandl., p. 191, pl. iv. (Dentition).

1848. ,, *mediterranea*, Requien, Moll. de Corse, p. 88.

1850. ,, ,, Gray, Fig. Moll. Anim., vol. iv. p. 100, pl. clxi. fig. 1 (copy of Deshayes).

1850. ,, ,, Gray, loc. cit., pl. lxiii. fig. 4 (copy of Blainville).

1850. ,, ,, Gray, loc. cit., pl. clix. fig. 3 (copy from Cuvier's Mem. Moll.).

1850. ,, ,, Gray, loc. cit., pl. clxi. fig. 2 (copy of Chiaje).

1850? ,, ,, Deshayes, Traité élém. Conch., pl. ci. fig. 5.

1851. ,, ,, Leydig, Zeitschr. f. wiss. Zool., Bd. iii. p. 325, pl. ix. (Anatomy).

1853. ,, ,, Vérany, Journ. de Conchyl., vol. iv. p. 381.

1854. ,, *cymbium*, Woodward, Man. Moll., p. 200, fig. 105 (copy of Blainville), and pl. xiv. fig. 19.

1855. ,, *mediterranea*, Gegenbaur, Untersuch. Pterop. und Heterop., p. 214,

1855. *Carinaria mediterranea*, Küster, Conch. Cab. Heteropods, pl. i. fig. 1 (enlarged copy of Blainville).
1856.   „   „   Troschel, Gebiss d. Schneck., vol. i. p. 43, pl. ii. figs. 6–9.
1856.   „   „   Jeffreys, Ann. and Mag. Nat. Hist., vol. xvii. p. 180.
1858.   „   „   Owen, Ency. Brit., vol. xv. p. 377, fig. 70 (copy of Eydoux and Souleyet, reduced).
1859.   „   *cymbium*, Chenu, Man. Conch., vol. i. p. 125, figs. 544, 545.
1860.   „   *fragilis*, Reeve, Init. Conch., ed. 2, vol. ii. p. 43, pl. k. (Animal).
1860.   „   *mediterranea*, Krohn, Beiträge Entwick. Pterop. und Heterop., p. 36, pl. ii.
1865.   „   *fragilis*, Reeve, Conch. Icon., vol. xv. pl. i. figs. 1a–b.
1865.   „   *cristata*, Sowerby, Thes. Conch., vol. iii. p. 303, pl. cclxxix. figs. 2, 3.
1866.   „   *cymbium*, Keferstein, in Bronn's Thierreich, vol. iii. pl. 2, p. 809, fig. 56 ; pl. lxviii. figs. 9–11; pl. lxix. figs. 5–7.
1868.   „   *mediterranea*, Weinkauff, Conch. Mittelm., vol. ii. p. 431.
1876.   „   „   Fol, Arch. d. Zool. Expér., vol. v. p. 107, pl. iv. figs. 1–3 (Development).
1878.   „   „   Kobelt, Illust. Conch., pl. i. fig. 15.
1880.   „   „   Krukenberg, Vergleich. Physiol. Studien, p. 177 (Movement of the Foot).
1883.   „   „   Fischer, Man. Conch. p. 577, fig. 342 (reduced copy of Eydoux and Souleyet).
1883.   „   „   (*partim*), Lankester, Ency. Brit., vol. xvi. p. 654, fig. 50a (from Owen).
1883.   „   „   Martens, Weich- und Schaltiere, p. 157 (woodcut).
1883.   „   *fragilis*, Tryon, Struct. Syst. Conch., vol. ii. pl. lxxxviii. fig. 99 (copy of Blainville).

Habitat.—Mediterranean.

This, the commonest of the *Carinariæ*, has been generally known as *Carinaria mediterranea*. It has also been called *Carinaria vitrea*, *Carinaria fragilis*, *Carinaria cymbium*, and by two or three other appellations. Who was the first to impose upon it the name of *Carinaria mediterranea* is somewhat uncertain, but as far as I can judge the credit rests either with Sowerby or de Blainville. The name *Carinaria vitrea* certainly was not applied to this species by Gmelin, but to the rarer eastern form which I call *Carinaria cristata*. The term *Carinaria fragilis* was assigned by authors to this species under the supposition that the *Carinaria fragilis* of Bory de Saint Vincent and the Mediterranean species were the same. I have in connection with that species made some observations which tend to show that these forms are different. Should, however, it be possible to prove them to be identical, the name *fragilis* should be used, as it has priority over any other which has been given to this species.

Argonauta cymbium of Linné was considered a *Carinaria* by Lamarck and Cuvier, and others mistook it for this species.

The shell described by Linné[1] under this name has been considered by von Martens[2]

<hr/>

[1] Syst. Nat., ed. 12, p. 1161.   [2] Ann. and Mag. Nat. Hist., 1867, vol. xx. p. 103.

(and probably correctly I think) "a foraminiferous shell (*Peneroplis planatus*, Montfort)." Whether it be this or not it is certain that it has nothing to do with the present species of *Carinaria*.

In 1850 Péron and Lesueur figured this species in the Annales du Museum, and imposed upon it the name of "Carinaire Lamarck," which seven years later was rendered into Latin (*Carinaria lamarkii*) by de Blainville.

This name, which has been overlooked by all subsequent writers, has some years' priority over that of *Carinaria mediterranea*, and should therefore be employed. It is remarkable that Deshayes should not have been acquainted with this fact, and that de Blainville subsequently designated this species with the name *Carinaria mediterranea*.

In the Dictionaire classique d'histoire naturelle Bory de Saint Vincent pointed out that the shell figured in the Encyclopédie Méthodique as *Carinaria fragilis* is different from that species, and imposed upon it the name of *Carinaria lamarckii*. This is now always regarded the same as the well-known Mediterranean species, and it is a curious coincidence that Bory de Saint Vincent should have given to it the same name as that proposed by Péron and Lesueur.

Carinaria depressa, Rang.

    1827. *Carinaria depressa*, Rang, Bull. Sci. Nat., vol. xii. p. 343.
    1829.   „   „   Rang, Ann. d. Sci. Nat. p. 140.
    1830.   „   „   Rang, Férussac's Bull. Sci. Nat., vol. xxi. p. 331.
    1830.   „   „   Cuvier, Règne Anim., ed. 2, vol. iii. p. 68.
    1833.   „   „   Oken, Isis, p. 186.
    1853.   „   „   H. and A. Adams, Gen. Moll., vol. ii. p. 96.

Habitat.—Near Madagascar (Rang).

Carinaria australis, Quoy and Gaimard.

    1832. *Carinaria australis*, Quoy and Gaimard, Voy. "Astrolabe," Zool., vol. ii. p. 394, pl. xxix. figs. 9-16.
    1843.   „   „   Gray, Dieffenbach's New Zeal., p. 244.
    1844.   „   „   id., Rev. Zool., p. 356 (from Dieffenbach).
    1850.   „   „   Gray, Fig. Moll. Anim., pl. lxiii. fig. 2 (copy of Quoy's figure).
    1855.   „   „   H. and A. Adams, Gen. Moll., vol. ii. p. 96.
    1880.   „   „   Hutton, Man. New Zeal. Moll., p. 119.

Habitat.—South Pacific, between Australia and New Zealand (Quoy and Gaimard).

Carinaria galea, Benson.

    1835. *Carinaria galea*, Benson, Journ. Asiat. Soc. Bengal, vol. iv. p. 216.

Habitat.—Indian Ocean (Benson).

Carinaria cithara, Benson.

> 1835. *Carinaria cithara*, Benson, Journ. Asiat. Soc. Bengal, 1835, vol. iv. p. 215.

Habitat.—Indian Ocean (Benson).

Carinaria punctata, d'Orbigny.

> 1836. *Carinaria punctata*, d'Orbigny, Voy. Amér. mérid., vol. v. p. 160, pl. xi. figs. 6-15.
> 1845.   „   -   „   Catlow, Conchol. Nomencl., p. 116.
> 1855.   „   „   H. and A. Adams, Gen. Moll., vol. ii. p. 96.

Habitat.—South Pacific, near the island of Juan Fernandez (d'Orbigny).

Carinaria gaudichaudii, Eydoux and Souleyet.

> 1841. *Carinaire de Gaudichaud*, Eydoux and Souleyet, Voy. "Bonite," Atlas, pl. xvii.
>   figs. 19-22.
> 1850. *Carinaria gaudichaudii*, Gray, Fig. Moll. Anim., vol. iv. p. 100, pl. ccxxxix. fig. 4 (copy
>   of Eydoux and Souleyet).
> 1852.   „   „   Souleyet, Voy. "Bonite," Zool., vol. ii. p. 359.
> 1855.   „   „   H. and A. Adams, Gen. Moll., vol. ii. p. 96.
> 1858.   „   „   Owen, Ency. Brit., vol. xv. p. 377, fig. 70 (Shell, copy of Eydoux
>   and Souleyet).
> 1862.   „   „   Macdonald, Trans. Roy. Soc. Edin., vol. xxiii., pl. ii. figs. 4, 4', 5d.
> 1883.   „   *mediterranea* (partim), Lankester, Ency. Brit., vol. xvi. p. 654, fig. 50v (same
>   as Owen).

Habitat.—China Seas (Eydoux and Souleyet).
Atlantic and Pacific Oceans (Macdonald).

Carinaria atlantica, Adams and Reeve.

> 1848. *Carinaria atlantica*, Adams and Reeve, Voy. "Samarang," Moll., p. 63, pl. xiii. fig. 12.
> 1850.   „   sp. n., Gray, Fig. Moll. Anim., vol. iv. p. 100, pl. ccxxxix. fig. 2.
> 1855.   „   *atlantica*, H. and A. Adams, Gen. Moll., vol. ii. p. 96, pl. lxx. fig. 1.
> 1865.   „   „   Reeve, Conch. Icon., vol. xv. pl. i. fig. 3.
> 1866.   „   „   Sowerby, Thesaur. Conch., vol. iii. p. 303, pl. cclxxix. fig. 1.

Habitat.—North Atlantic Ocean (A. Adams).

Carinaria cornucopia, Gould.

> 1861. *Carinaria cornucopia*, Gould, Proc. Boston Soc. Nat. Hist., vol. vii. p. 408.
> 1861.   „   „   id., Otia, Conch., p. 152.

Habitat.—South of the Caroline Islands (Gould).

Carinaria sp.

Habitat.—Atlantic ; June 28, 1873 ; lat. 35° 47' N., long. 8° 23' W.

Of this species there are two specimens in the Challenger collection, both deprived of their shells. I have been unable to identify them satisfactorily with any of the described forms, but it seems distinct from the common Mediterranean species. It is peculiar in having the entire surface minutely dotted with white, besides numerous tubercles which are also very generally distributed. It is possible it may be the same as *Carinaria*

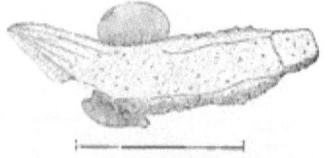

Fig. 5.—*Carinaria* sp.

punctata of d'Orbigny, but it does not quite answer his description as regards colour, and the form of the fin and the tail do not correspond with his figure.

I have not ventured to give a name to this species, as I think it would be more advisable to wait until living specimens and the shell can be examined, for, as is the case with all Mollusks when placed in spirit, the colours change or vanish, and through shrinkage a very poor notion of the living form is to be obtained.

Family II. ATLANTIDÆ.

1825. *Pterocephala (partim)*, Latreille, Fam. Règne Anim., p. 109.

1829. *Atlantidæ*, Rang, Man. Moll., p. 123.

1832. *Atlantidæ*, Wiegmann and Ruthe, Handbuch d. Zool., p. 516.

1836. *Atlantidæa*, d'Orbigny, Voy. Amér. mérid., vol. v. p. 162.

1838. *Atlantidæ*, Potiez and Michaud, Gal. Moll., vol. i. p. 46.

1839. *Atlantidæa*, d'Orbigny, Hist. Nat. Canaries, Moll., p. 35.

1840. *Atlantidæ*, Gray, Synopsis Brit. Mus., p. 147.

1841.   ,,   *id.*, *op. cit.*, p. 125.

1841. *Atlantides*, Cantraine, Mal. Médit., p. 36.

1841. *Atlantidæ*, d'Orbigny, Hist. Nat. Cuba Moll., vol. i. p. 98.

1843.   ,,   d'Orbigny, Paléont. franç., Tert. crét., vol. ii. p. 19.

1850.   ,,   Gray, Fig. Moll. Anim., vol. iv. p. 101.

1853. *Atlantacea*, Philippi, Handbuch Conch., pp. 283, 284.

1854. *Atlantidæ*, H. and A. Adams, Gen. Moll., vol. ii. p. 90.

1854.   ,,   Woodward, Man. Moll., p. 200.

1855. *Atlantida*, Gegenbaur, Untersuch. Pterop. und Heterop., p. 214.
1856. *Atlantacea*, Troschel, Gebiss d. Schneck., vol. i. p. 41.
1856. *Atlanta*, Krohn, Müller's Archiv f. Anat. Physiol., p. 519 (Development).
1857. *Atlantidæ*, Gray, System. Arrang. Moll., p. 133.
1859.   „   Chenu, Man. Conch., vol. i. p. 121.
1866. *Atlantacea*, Keferstein, Bronn's Thierreich, vol. iii. pt. 2, p. 850.
1868. *Atlantidæ*, Weinkauff, Conch. Mittelm., vol. ii. p. 430.
1883.   „   Tryon, Struct. and Syst. Conch., vol. ii. p. 350.
1883.   „   Fischer, Man. Conch., p. 581.
1883. *Atlantacea*, Lankester, Ency. Brit., vol. xvi. p. 653 (as a suborder).
1884. *Atlantidæ*, Grasset, Index Test. Viv., p. 146.

Genus *Atlanta*, Lesueur.

1797. *Corne d'Ammon*, Lamanon, Voy. de La Perouse, vol. iv. pp. 134–139, pl. lxiii. figs. 1–4
        at bottom.
1817. *Atlanta*, Lesueur, Journ. de Physique, vol. lxxxv. p. 390, pl. ii.
1819. *Atlantis*, Oken's Isis, p. 41.
1822. *Atlanta*, Férussac, Tab. Syst., p. xxv.
1824.   „   Blainville, Dict. d. Sci. Nat., vol. xxxii. p. 284.
1825.   „   Latreille, Fam. Nat. Règne Anim., p. 169.
1825. *Steira*, Eschscholtz, Isis von Oken, p. 735.
1825. *Atlanta*, Blainville, Man. Malacol., p. 493.
1827.   „   Rang, Mém. Soc. Hist. Nat. Paris, vol. iii. p. 372, pl. ix.
1829.   „   Rang, Man. Moll., p. 123.
1830.   „   Cuvier, Règne Anim., ed. 2, vol. iii. p. 68.
1830.   „   Deshayes, Ency. Méth., vol. ii. p. 80.
1830. *Steira*, Menke, Synopsis Moll., ed. 2, p. 9.
1832. *Atlanta*, Wiegmann and Ruthe, Handbuch d. Zool., p. 518.
1834.   „   Gray, Griffith's Cuvier Anim. King., vol. xii. p. 51.
1835.   „   Oken, Naturgesch., vol. v. p. 515.
1835. *Steira*, Oken, Naturgesch., vol. v. p. 515.
1836. *Atlanta*, d'Orbigny, Voy. Amér. mérid., vol. v. p. 162.
1838.   „   Potiez and Michaud, Gal. Moll., vol. i. p. 48.
1839.   „   Sowerby, Couch. Man., p. 10.
1839.   „   d'Orbigny, in Webb and Berthelot's Hist. Nat. Canaries, Moll., pp. 35, 36.
1841.   „   Cantraine, Mal. Médit., p. 39.
1841.   „   d'Orbigny, in Sagra's Hist. Cuba, Moll., vol. i. p. 101.
1842.   „   *id.*, Paléont. franç., Terr. crét., vol. ii. p. 19.
1843.   „   Gravenhorst, Vergleich. Zool., p. 65.
1843.   „   Forbes, Report Brit. Assoc., 1843, p. 132.
1844.   „   Philippi, Enum. Moll. Sicil., vol. ii. p. 205.
1847.   „   Lovén, Öfversigt k. Vetensk.-Akad. Forhandl., p. 191 (Dentition).
1850.   „   Gray, Fig. Moll. Anim., vol. iv. p. 101.
1850.   „   Huxley, Ann. d. Sci. Nat., vol. xiv. p. 193 (Circulation).
1852.   „   Souleyet, Voy. "Bonite," Zool., vol. ii. p. 361.
1852.   „   Costa, Fauna Reg. Napoli Moll., Eteropodi, p. 1.
1853.   „   Philippi, Handbuch Conch., p. 284.
1854.   „   Woodward, Man. Moll., p. 200.

1854. *Atlanta*, H. and A. Adams, Gen. Moll., vol. ii. p. 91.
1855. „ Gegenbaur, Untersuch. Pterop. und Heterop., pp. 105–130, 214.
1856. „ Troschel, Gebiss d. Schneck., vol. i. p. 42.
1857. „ Gray, Syst. Arrang. Moll. Brit. Mus., p. 134.
1859. „ Chenu, Man. Conch., vol. i. pp. 121, 122.
1860. „ Keohn, Beiträge Entwick. Pterop. und Heterop., p. 33.
1862. „ Macdonald, Trans. Roy. Soc. Edin., vol. xxiii. pl. ii. figs. 1, 1', 5g.
1865. „ Keferstein, Bronn's Thierreich, vol. iii. pt. 2, p. 850, pl. lxviii. figs. 1, 2, 3, 4.
1868. *Atalanta*, Knocker, Proc. Zool. Soc. Lond., p. 616.
1873. *Atlanta*, Weinkauff, Cat. Europ. Meer. Conch., p. 44.
1883. „ Tryon, Syst. Struct. Conch., vol. ii. p. 390.
1883. „ Fischer, Man. Conch., p. 581.

There is a very great similarity in the general construction and form of the species of this genus, but on careful comparison certain features are recognisable which will distinguish them. They are to be separated chiefly on account of differences in the shells, as few observers have had the opportunity of seeing living specimens in their native element. The number, form, size, and position of the apical whorls constitute good distinguishing characters, but very careful observation and study are requisite. In determining the Challenger specimens I have had the very great advantage of comparing them with Eydoux and Souleyet's collection in the British Museum.

Atlanta peronii, Lesueur.

1817. *Atlanta peronii*, Lesueur, Journ. de Physique, vol. lxxxv. p. 390, pl. ii. figs. 1, 2.
1824. „ „ Blainville, Dict. d. Sci. Nat., vol. xxxii. p. 284, pl. lxviii. figs. 9, 9a (copy of Lesueur, reversed).
1825. „ „ *id.*, Man. Malacol., pl. xlviii. *bis*, figs. 9, 9a (same fig.).
1827. „ „ Rang, Mém. Soc. Hist. Nat. Paris, vol. iii. p. 360, pl. ix. figs. 1, 2, 3, 7.
1830. „ „ Deshayes, Ency. Méth., vol. ii. p. 83.
1830. „ „ Cuvier, Règne Anim., ed. 2. vol. iii. p. 68.
1832. „ *kerandreni* (non Lesueur), Quoy and Gaimard, Voy. "Astrolabe," Zool., vol. ii. p. 599, pl. xxix. figs. 18–23.
1836. „ *peronii*, d'Orbigny, Voy. Amér. mérid., vol. v. p. 171, pl. xii. figs. 1–15.
1836–46. „ „ Deshayes, Cuvier's Règne Anim., Moll., pl. xxxviii. fig. 2 (copy of Rang).
1838. „ „ Potiez and Michaud, Gal. Moll., vol. i. p. 48.
1839. „ „ d'Orbigny, Hist. Nat. Canaries, Moll., p. 36.
1840. „ *costæ*, Pirajno, Elem. Sci. Sicil., vol. xxviii. p. 149, figs. 1a, cn.
1841. *Atlanta de Péron*, Eydoux and Souleyet, Voy. "Bonite," Atlas Zool., pl. xix. figs. 1–8.
1841. *Atlanta peronii*, Cantraine, Mal. Médit. p. 39, pl. i. fig. 1.
1841. „ „ d'Orbigny, Sagra's Hist. Cuba, Moll., vol. i. p. 102.
1843. „ „ Forbes, Report Brit. Assoc., p. 132.
1844. „ „ Philippi, Enum. Moll. Sicil., vol. ii. p. 205.
1850. „ „ Gray, Fig. Moll. Anim., pl. cxvii.*b*, fig. 5 (copy of Rang).
1850. „ „ *id.*, *op. cit.*, pl. cxvii.*b*, fig. 4 (copy of Quoy and Gaimard).
1850. „ „ *id.*, *op. cit.*, pl. cxxi. fig. 6 (copy of Eydoux and Souleyet).
1850. „ „ *id.*, *op. cit.*, pl. cxvii.*b*, figs. 2–2b (copy of d'Orbigny).

1850. *Atlanta peronii*, Gray, *op. cit.*, pl. cxviii.c, fig. 1 (copy of Blainville).
1852.   „   „   Souleyet, Voy. "Bonite," Zool., vol. ii. p. 373.
1852.   „   „   Costa, Fauna Reg. Napoli, Eteropodi, p. 3, pl. i. fig. 2 (copy of Pirajno).
1853.   „   „   Vérany, Journ. de Conchyl., vol. iv. p. 382.
1854.   „   „   Woodward, Man. Moll., pl. xiv. figs. 21–23.
1854.   „   „   H. and A. Adams, Gen. Moll., vol. ii. p. 91; vol. iii. pl. lxix. figs. 5–5b.
1855.   „   „   Gegenbaur, Untersuch. Pterop. und Heterop., p. 214, pl. vi.
1856.   „   „   Troschel, Gebiss d. Schneck., vol. i. p. 42, pl. ii. fig. 4.
1858.   „   „   Owen, Ency. Brit., vol. xv. p. 375, fig. 66; p. 376, fig. 67.
1866.   „   „   Keferstein, Bronn's Thierreich, vol. iii. p4. 2, pl. lxviii. figs. 1–4; pl. lxix. fig. 2.
1868.   „   „   Weinkauff, Conch. Mittelm., vol. ii. p. 430.
1878.   „   „   Sowerby, Conch. Icon., Pteropoda, pl. iii. fig. 20a–b.
1883.   „   „   Fischer, Man. Moll., pl. xiv. figs. 21–23 (same as Woodward).
1884.   „   „   Sowerby, Thes. Conch., vol. v. p. 148, pl. ccclxxiv. figs. 63, 64.

Habitat.—Atlantic, Pacific, and Indian Oceans.

Atlanta turriculata, d'Orbigny.

1836. *Atlanta turriculata*, d'Orbigny, Voy. Amér. mérid., vol. v. p. 173, pl. xx. figs. 5–11.
1852.   „   „   Eydoux and Souleyet, Voy. "Bonite," Zool., vol. ii. p. 391; Atlas (1841), pl. xxi. figs. 30–35.
1850.   „   „   Gray, Fig. Moll. Anim., pl. ccxlii. fig. 6 (copy of Eydoux and Souleyet).
1859.   „   „   Chenu, Man. Conch., vol. i. p. 122, figs. 533, 534.
1883.   „   „   Tryon, Struct. Syst. Conch., vol. ii. pl. lxxxvi. figs. 4, 5 (copy of Eydoux and Souleyet, reduced).

Habitat.—South Pacific (d'Orbigny); Pacific and Indian Oceans (Eydoux and Souleyet).

Atlanta lesueurii, Eydoux and Souleyet.

1852. *Atlanta lesueurii*, Eydoux and Souleyet, Voy. "Bonite," Zool., vol. ii. p. 380; Atlas (1841), pl. xx. figs. 1–8.
1850.   „   „   Gray, Fig. Moll. Anim., pl. ccxli. fig. 5 (copy of Eydoux and Souleyet).
1853.   „   *lesueurii*, Huxley, Phil. Trans., vol. cxliii. pp. 36–39, pl. iii. figs. 1–6 (Anatomy).

Habitat.—Atlantic Ocean.

The figure of the dentition given by Lovén[1] as that of *Atlanta lesueurii* apparently is that of *Oxygyrus keraudrenii*.

[1] *Öfversigt k. Vetensk.-Akad. Förhandl.*, 1847, pl. iv.

Atlanta involuta, Eydoux and Souleyet.

1852. *Atlanta involuta*, Eydoux and Souleyet, Voy. "Bonite," Zool., vol. ii. p. 388 ; Atlas (1841), pl. xxi. figs. 9-14.

1850.   ,,   ,,   Gray, Fig. Moll. Anim., pl. ccxlii. fig. 3 (copy of Eydoux and Souleyet).

Habitat.—Pacific Ocean (Eydoux and Souleyet).

Atlanta inflata, Eydoux and Souleyet.

1852. *Atlanta inflata*, Eydoux and Souleyet, Voy. "Bonite," Zool., vol. ii. p. 376 ; Atlas (1841), pl. xix. figs. 8-21.

1850.   ,,   ,,   Gray, Fig. Moll. Anim., pl. ccxlii. fig. 3 (copy of Eydoux and Souleyet).

Habitat.—China Sea.

The shell figured by Sowerby[1] under the name of *Atlanta inflata* appears to be *Spirialis rostralis* of Eydoux and Souleyet.

Atlanta inclinata, Eydoux and Souleyet.

1852. *Atlanta inclinata*, Eydoux and Souleyet, Voy. "Bonite," Zool. ii. p. 375; Atlas (1841). pl. xix. figs. 9-15.

1850.   ,,   ,,   Gray, Fig. Moll. Anim., pl. ccxlii. fig. 1 (copy of Eydoux and Souleyet).

Habitat.—Pacific and Atlantic Oceans (Eydoux and Souleyet).

Atlanta helicinoides, Eydoux and Souleyet.

1852. *Atlanta helicinoides*, Eydoux and Souleyet, Voy. "Bonite," Zool, vol. ii. p. 384 ; Atlas (1841), pl. xx. figs. 23-30.

1850.   ,,   ,,   Gray, Fig. Moll. Anim., pl. ccxlii. fig. 2 (copy of Eydoux and Souleyet).

Habitat.—Pacific Ocean (Eydoux and Souleyet).

Atlanta gibbosa, Eydoux and Souleyet.

1852. *Atlanta gibbosa*, Eydoux and Souleyet, Voy. "Bonite," Zool., vol. ii. p. 386 ; Atlas (1841), pl. xxi. figs. 1-8.

1850.   ,,   ,,   Gray, Fig. Moll. Anim., pl. ccxl. fig. 5 (copy of Eydoux and Souleyet).

1850.   ,,   *spirata*, Souleyet, Deshayes Traité Conch., pl. ci. figs. 6-8 (copy of Eydoux and Souleyet, figs. 2-4).

1858.   ,,   *gibbosa*, Owen, Ency. Brit., vol. xv. p. 376, fig. 69 (copy of Eydoux and Souleyet).

1859.   ,,   *gibba*, Chenu, Man. Conch., vol. i. figs. 531-2 (copy of Eydoux and Souleyet).

Habitat.—Atlantic Ocean (Eydoux and Souleyet).

---

[1] Conch. Icon., Pteropoda, pl. vi. fig. 48, and Thes. Conch., vol. v. pl. ccclxxiv. fig. 65.

Atlanta gaudichaudii, Eydoux and Souleyet.

    1852. *Atlanta gaudichaudii*, Eydoux and Souleyet, Voy. "Bonite," Zool., vol. ii. p. 397; Atlas
             (1841), pl. xix. figs. 29–34.
    1850.   „   „   Gray, Fig. Moll. Anim., pl. ccxli. fig. 4 (copy of Eydoux and
             Souleyet).
    1859.   „   „   Chenu, Man. Conch., vol. i. p. 121, fig. 525 (also apparently after
             Eydoux and Souleyet).

Habitat.—Pacific Ocean (Gaudichaud *fide* Eydoux and Souleyet).

Atlanta fusca, Eydoux and Souleyet.

    1852. *Atlanta fusca*, Eydoux and Souleyet, Voy. "Bonite," Zool., vol. ii. p. 389; Atlas (1841),
             pl. xxi. figs. 15–29.
    1850.   „   *brunnea*, Gray, Fig. Moll. Anim., vol. iv. p. 101, pl. ccxlii. fig. 5 (copy of Eydoux
             and Souleyet).

Habitat.—All seas (Eydoux and Souleyet).

Gray named this species *Atlanta brunnea* through a false rendering into Latin of
"Atlante brune" of the French authors. An excellent distinctive feature of this species,
overlooked by the authors, are the fine spiral raised lines which are visible on both sides
of the spire but not upon the last whorl. This character will assist in distinguishing it
from *Atlanta turriculata*, d'Orbigny, an allied form.

Atlanta depressa, Eydoux and Souleyet.

    1852. *Atlanta depressa*, Eydoux and Souleyet, Voy. "Bonite," Zool., vol. ii. p. 385; Atlas (1841),
             pl. xx. figs. 31–37.
    1850.   „   „   Gray, Fig. Moll. Anim., pl. ccxli. fig. 4 (copy of Eydoux and Souleyet).

Habitat.—Pacific Ocean (Eydoux and Souleyet).

Atlanta rosea, Eydoux and Souleyet.

    1852. *Atlanta rosea*, Eydoux and Souleyet, Voy. "Bonite," Zool., vol. ii. p. 377; Atlas (1841),
             pl. xix. figs. 16–29.
    1850.   „   „   Gray, Fig. Moll. Anim., pl. ccxli. fig. 2 (copy of Eydoux and Souleyet).

Habitat.—Atlantic Ocean (Eydoux and Souleyet).

Atlanta quoyana, Eydoux and Souleyet.

    1852. *Atlanta quoyana*, Eydoux and Souleyet, Voy. "Bonite," Zool., vol. ii. p. 383; Atlas,
             (1841), pl. xx. figs. 16–22.
    1850.   „   *quoyii*, Gray, Fig. Moll. Anim., vol. iv. p. 101, pl. ccxlii. fig. 1 (copy of Eydoux
             and Souleyet).

Habitat.—Pacific Ocean (Eydoux and Souleyet).

Atlanta mediterranea, Costa.

1852. *Atlanta mediterranea,* Costa, Fauna Reg. Napoli, Eteropoda, p. 4, pl. i. figs. 1a, a.b.c.

Habitat.—Bay of Naples.

This appears to be a large species, supposing that Costa's figure (1a) represents the natural size. The shell is peculiar on account of the keel extending to the aperture as in *Oxygyrus keraudrenii,* and not embracing the whorls of the spire as is the case in *Atlanta peronii.*

Atlanta violacea, Gould.

1852. *Atlanta violacea,* Gould, U.S. Explor. Exped., vol. xii. p. 493; Atlas, figs. 599–599b.
1862.   ,,   ,,   id., Otia, Conch., p. 236.

Habitat.—Mid Atlantic (Gould).

Atlanta tessellata, Gould.

1852. *Atlanta tessellata,* Gould, U.S. Explor. Exped., vol. xii. p. 494; Atlas, figs. 600–600b.
1862.   ,,   ,,   id., Otia, Conch., p. 236.

Habitat.—Mid Atlantic (Gould).

Atlanta primitia, Gould.

1852. *Atlanta primitia,* Gould, U.S. Explor. Exped., vol. xii. p. 491; Atlas, fig. 597.
1862.   ,,   ,,   id., Otia, Conch., p. 235.

Habitat.—Equatorial Atlantic (Gould).

Atlanta cunicula, Gould.

1852. *Atlanta cunicula,* Gould, U.S. Explor. Exped., vol. xii. p. 492; Atlas, figs. 598–598c.
1852.   ,,   ,,   id., Otia, Conch., p. 236.

Habitat.—Pacific Ocean, west of the Sandwich Islands (Gould).

Atlanta souleyeti, Smith.

1852. *Atlanta lamanonii,* Eydoux and Souleyet, Voy. "Bonite," Zool., vol. ii. p. 371; Atlas (1841), pl. xviii. figs. 30–37.
1850.   ,,   ,,   Gray, Fig. Moll. Anim., pl. ccxl. fig. 3 (copy of Eydoux and Souleyet).

Habitat.—Atlantic Ocean.

Eschscholtz employed the specific name *lamanonii* in 1825, and although I am inclined to consider that species beyond recognition, still I think that to prevent confusion another name should be given to the present species. I therefore propose to designate it *Atlanta souleyeti*.

In 1852 Costa named a fossil species *Atlanta lamanoni*. This should also receive a fresh name.

The membranous keel which is one of the distinguishing features of this species is not present in any of the dead shells dredged by the Challenger, and probably decays rapidly after death. The absence of the carina imparts a peculiar roundness to the last whorl, producing a very unusual appearance for a species of *Atlanta*.

This species has been considered by Macdonald to belong to the genus *Oxygyrus*. Although the keel upon the last whorl is described as cartilaginous as in *Oxygyrus rangii* and *Oxygyrus keraudrenii*, the shell itself is of the same vitreous character and the operculum the same as that of *Atlanta*. I think therefore this species must belong to that genus, and especially as Souleyet associates it with the recognised species of that group.

Undefined Species.

1. *Steira lamanoni*.

> 1825. *Steira lamanoni*, Eschscholtz, Oken's Isis, p. 735, pl. v. fig. 3.
> 1850.   „   „   Gray, Fig. Moll. Anim., vol. iv. p. 101.

Habitat.—South Sea (Eschscholtz).

The figure given by Eschscholtz is apparently not at all reliable, and although beyond doubt representing an *Atlanta*, the particular species intended cannot be determined with certainty.

2. *Atlanta helicialis*.

> 1839. *Atlanta helicialis*, Sowerby, Conch. Man., fig. 220.

The shell figured by Sowerby under the above name appears to resemble *Atlanta lesueurii*, Eydoux and Souleyet, more closely than any other. The drawing, however, is of so coarse a character that the certain identification of it is quite impossible.

3. and 4. *Atlanta* sp. (?).

Two species are roughly figured by Gray [1] from drawings by Dr. Hooker. This being all that is known respecting them, they are quite beyond certain recognition. The species represented by figure 7 may be *Oxygyrus keraudrenii*.

> [1] Fig. Moll. Anim., pl. cxviii. figs. 2, 7.

5. *Ladas planorboides*, Forbes.

    1843. *Ladas planorboides*, Forbes, Report Brit. Assoc., p. 186.

Habitat.—Ægean Sea.

"L. testa pellucida, alba, lævi, compressa, carinata, exalata, aufractibus 4. Diam. 0,¼."

This is all the information respecting this species which is given by Forbes. It is impossible to identify it from this description, and therefore it seems advisable to reject it entirely.

6. *Helicophlegma candei*, d'Orbigny.

    1841. *Helicophlegma candei*, d'Orbigny, Sagra's Hist. Cuba, Moll., vol. i. p. 100, pl. xi.
        figs. 15, 17.
    1858.   „   „   Chenu, Man. Conch., vol. i. p. 122, figs. 529, 530 (reduced copy
        of d'Orbigny).

Habitat.—Antilles (d'Orbigny).

This form is probably the embryonic stage of a Gastropod such as *Lamellaria*, &c. D'Orbigny (*loc. cit.*), conjecturing its distinctness from *Helicophlegma* (= *Oxygyrus*), proposed the genus *Brownia* for its reception.

Genus *Oxygyrus*, Benson.

    1835. *Oxygyrus*, Benson, Journ. Asiat. Soc. Bengal, vol. iv. p. 174.
    1836. *Helicophlegma*, d'Orbigny, Voy. Amér. mérid., vol. v. p. 168 (as subgen.).
    1837. *Oxygyrus*, Benson, op. cit., vol. vi. p. 316.
    1839. *Helicophlegma*, d'Orbigny, Hist. Nat. Canaries, Moll., p. 35.
    1841.   „   id., Sagra's Hist. Cuba, Moll., vol. i. p. 98.
    1841. *Ladas*, Cantraine, Mém. Acad. Sci. Bruxelles, vol. xiii. p. 37.
    1842. *Helicophlegma*, d'Orbigny, Paléont. franç., Terr. crét., vol. ii. p. 19.
    1843. *Ladas*, Forbes, Report Brit. Assoc., pp. 132, 186.
    1844.   „   Philippi, Enum. Moll. Sicil., vol. ii. p. 205.
    1850. *Oxygyrus*, Gray, Fig. Moll. Anim., vol. iv. p. 101.
    1853.   „   Philippi, Handbuch, p. 285.
    1854.   „   H. and A. Adams, Gen. Moll., vol. ii. p. 92.
    1854.   „   Woodward, Man. Moll. p. 201.
    1856.   „   Troschel, Gebiss d. Schneck., vol. i. p. 41.
    1857. *Oxygyrus*, Gray, Syst. Arrang. Moll., p. 133.
    1859. *Helicophlegma*, Chenu, Man. Conch., vol. i. p. 122.
    1862. *Oxygyrus*, Macdonald, Trans. Roy. Soc. Edin., vol. xxiii. pl. ii. figs. 2, 2', 3, 5e, 5f.
    1866.   „   Keferstein, Bronn's Thierreich, vol. iii. pt. 2, p. 850.
    1868. *Ladas*, Weinkauff, Conch. Mittel., vol. ii. p. 430.
    1873.   „   id., Cat. Europ. Meer. Conch., p. 44.
    1883. *Oxygyrus*, Tryon, Struct. Syst. Conch., vol. ii. p. 351.
    1883.   „   Fischer, Man. Conch., p. 582.

Macdonald places in this genus *Atlanta rangii*, *Atlanta keraudrenii*, and *Atlanta lesueuronii*, which he states are "characterised by having an involute instead of a spiral nucleus to the shell, greater fullness in the whorls, and a comparatively small amount of calcareous matter as a component, particularly near the mouth and in the keel."

These observations are applicable to the two first-named species but not to the last. This, which I have previously referred to as *Atlanta souleyeti*, resembles the other species of *Oxygyrus* in having a membranous and not a hardened glossy keel to the shell as in the rest of the species of *Atlanta*, but it has not an involute spire, and the operculum according to Eydoux and Souleyet's figure is quite of the normal type of *Atlanta* and not like that of *Oxygyrus*. I think, therefore, it should be retained in the former genus.

Oxygyrus keraudrenii (Lesueur).

1817. *Atlanta keraudrenii*, Lesueur, Journ. de Physique, vol. lxxxv. p. 391, pl. ii.
1827. „ „ Rang, Mém. Soc. Hist. Nat. Paris, vol. iii. p. 380, pl. ix. figs. 4, 5, 6, 8.
1830. „ „ Deshayes, Ency. Méth., vol. ii. p. 83.
1830. „ „ Cuvier, Règne Anim., ed. 2, vol. iii. p. 69.
1832. „ „ Rang, Mag. de Zool., classe v. pl. iv. figs. 1–7.
1832–44. „ „ Guérin, Icon. Règne Anim., pl. xi. fig. 2 (copy of Rang, 1832).
1836. „ „ Deshayes, Cuvier's Règne Anim. Moll., pl. xxxviii. fig. 3 (copy of Rang, Mem. Soc. Hist. Nat.).
1836. „ (*Helicophlegma*) *keraudrenii*, d'Orbigny, Voy. Amér. mérid., vol. v. p. 169, pl. xi. figs. 16–23, pl. xx. figs. 3, 4.
1839. „ „ id., Hist. Nat. Canaries, Moll., p. 35.
1840. „ *bivona*, Pirajno Elém. Sci. Sicil., vol. xxviii. p. 14ff, figs. 2a, b, &c.
1841. *Helicophlegma keraudrenii*, d'Orbigny, Sagra's Hist. Cuba, Moll., vol. i. p. 99.
1841. *Atlante de keraudren*, Eydoux and Souleyet, Voy. "Bonite," Atlas Zool., pl. xviii. figs. 1–17.
1841. *Ladas keraudrenii*, Cantraine, Mal. Médit., p. 38, pl. i. fig. 2.
1844. „ „ Philippi, Enum. Moll. Sicil., vol. ii. p. 205.
1847. *Atlanta keraudrenii*, Chenu, Leçons Elém. Hist. Nat., p. 132, fig. 419.
1847. „ *lesueurii* (?), Lovén, Öfversigt k. Vetensk-Akad. Förhandl., pl. iv.
1848. *Ladas keraudrenii*, Requien, Cat. Coq. de Corse, p. 88.
1850. *Oxygyrus keraudrenii*, Gray, Fig. Moll. Anim., pl. ccxl. figs. 2, 2a (copy of Lesueur).
1850. „ „ id., op. cit., pl. cxvii.e, fig. 3 (copy of Rang, 1832).
1850. „ „ id., op. cit., pl. cxvii.e, figs. 3–3c (copy of Rang, 1827).
1850. „ „ id., op. cit., pl. cxvii.e, fig. 6 (copy of Cantraine).
1850. „ „ id., op. cit., pl. ccxxxviii. fig. 3 (copy of Eydoux and Souleyet).
1850. „ „ id., op. cit., pl. cxvii.b, fig. 1 (copy of d'Orbigny).
1850? *Atlanta keraudrenii*, Deshayes, Traité de Conch., pl. ci. figs. 1–4 (copy of Eydoux and Souleyet).
1851. „ „ Souleyet, Voy. "Bonite," Zool., vol. ii. p. 364.
1852. „ „ Costa, Fauna Reg. Napoli, Eteropodi, p. 5, pl. i. fig. 3 (copy of Pirajno).
1853. „ „ Vérany, Journ. de Conchyl., vol. iv. p. 381.
1854. *Oxygyrus keraudrenii*, H. and A. Adams, Gen. Moll., vol. ii. p. 92; vol. iii. pl. lxix. figs. 6–6b.

1834. *Oxygyrus keraudrenii*, Woodward, Man. Moll., pl. xiv. figs. 24, 25.

1855. *Atlanta keraudrenii*, Gegenbaur, Untersuch. Pterop. und Heterop., p. 214.

1856. *Oxygyrus keraudrenii*, Troschel, Gebiss d. Schneck., vol. i. p. 41, pl. ii. fig. 2.

1858. *Atlanta keraudrenii*, Owen, Ency. Brit., vol. xv. p. 375, fig. 65; p. 376, fig. 68.

1859. „ „ Chenu, Man. Conch., vol. i. p. 121, figs. 526–528 (copy of Eydoux and Souleyet).

1866. *Oxygyrus keraudrenii*, Keferstein, Bronn's Thierreich, vol. iii. pt. 2, pl. lxviii. figs. 5–8.

1868. „ „ Knocker, Proc. Zool. Soc. Lond., 1868, p. 616.

1868. *Ladas keraudrenii*, Weinkauff, Conch. Mittel, vol. ii. p. 450.

1878. *Atlanta (Oxygyrus) keraudrenii*, Sowerby, Conch. Icon., Pteropoda, pl. iii. fig. 21a–b.

1883. *Atlanta (Oxygyrus) keraudrenii*, Lankester, Ency. Brit., vol. xvi. p. 654, fig. 49 (same as Owen).

1883. *Oxygyrus keraudrenii*, Tryon, Struct. Syst. Conch., vol. ii. pl. lxxxvi. figs. 6, 7 (copy of Eydoux and Souleyet, reduced).

1883. „ „ Fischer, Man. Moll., pl. xiv. figs. 24–25 (same as Woodward); p. 582, fig. 347 (copy of d'Orbigny).

1884. *Atlanta keraudrenii*, Sowerby, Thes. Conch., vol. v. p. 148, pl. ccclxxiv. figs. 61, 62.

Habitat.—Atlantic and Indian Oceans

Oxygyrus rangii, Eydoux and Souleyet.

1832. *Atlanta rangii*, Eydoux and Souleyet, Voy. "Bonite," Zool., vol. ii. p. 369; Atlas (1841), pl. xviii. figs. 18–24.

1847. „ „ Lovén, Översigt k. Vetensk.-Akad. Förhandl., p. 191, pl. iv. (Dentition)

1850. „ „ Gray, Fig. Moll. Anim., pl. ccxl. fig. 1 (copy of Eydoux and Souleyet).

Habitat.—Pacific Ocean (Eydoux and Souleyet) ; var., Indian Ocean.

INDEX.